THE SAND PEBBLES

CLASSICS OF NAVAL LITERATURE

JACK SWEETMAN, SERIES EDITOR

The Sand Pebbles

By Richard McKenna
With an introduction by Robert Shenk

40144

NAVAL INSTITUTE PRESS
Annapolis, Maryland

This book was originally published
in 1962 by Harper & Row.

Copyright © 1962
by Richard McKenna

Second printing, 1987

Library of Congress Cataloging in Publication Data
McKenna, Richard.
    The sand pebbles.

    (Classics of naval literature)
    Reprint. Originally published: New York: Harper & Row, c1962.
    1. United States—History, Naval—20th century—
Fiction.   2. China—History—1912–1937—Fiction.
1. Title.   II. Series.
PS3563.A3155S26   1984   813'.54   83-27007
ISBN 0-87021-592-2

Printed in the United States of America

ACKNOWLEDGMENTS

I wish especially to thank Eva Grice McKenna for her great assistance in my study of her husband's works. Without her help, first during my visit to her home in Chapel Hill, and ever since in our correspondence and in her other efforts in my behalf, my work would not have been possible. I also appreciate the help of Mr. William E. Lind of the National Archives. Finally, as always, my thanks to my parents for their support, and to my wife, Paula, for her constant love and understanding.

INTRODUCTION

That Richard McKenna's novel *The Sand Pebbles* is readable and entertaining is a contention not open to dispute. Its appearance on the bestseller lists and its incarnation in a highly popular motion picture testify to the novel's appeal to the public. However, according to the inflated language of some of the original billing, the book consists of nothing more than a string of sensational episodes. "It carries no pot of message: its purpose is simply to excite and entertain"—so one version of the paperback cover exclaimed, while another screamed what was supposedly James Michener's judgment: "A torrent of incident, adventure, outrage, and sex. . . ."[1] No doubt many people picked up the novel and read it for these very qualities, though those who did must have experienced a flicker of disappointment in at least one respect: even by the standards of 1962, the year the novel was published, its "sex" is awfully tame. Certainly the book delivers a good dose of incident and adventure, outrage and humor, but every other bestseller can be awarded the same cries of praise. Such laurels, needless to say, are of dubious value, and to

---

1. In his review, published in the *New York Herald Tribune* of 7 April 1963, Michener has much concrete praise to give. He takes the "vivid and rewarding" novel seriously, analyzes the various plot lines, and pronounces what is, on the whole, a very favorable judgment. Among other things, he comments that "the degeneration of the *San Pablo* is excellently handled and as real in its impact as any similar account I have ever read."

give *The Sand Pebbles* its due one must turn to the book between the covers. Does it have in addition to its touted worth any pith, any substance?

The answer to this question is affirmative, but to explain why this is so we must backtrack and take a look at the author's life, which was unique. For unlike some novelists who serve single tours of duty in the service and then use their superficial knowledge as padding for novels and stories, McKenna had a career in the navy and habitually accompanied his intense endeavors to make that career worthwhile with wide reading and reflection. His novel grew out of a unique combination of significant personal experience and a lifelong ambition to educate himself.

Richard Milton McKenna was born into a poor family in the small town of Mountain Home, Idaho, on 9 May 1913. His father hauled freight for the mines, and the family struggled to make ends meet. The boy's delights were reading and going to movies, but without money for the latter and with only a few books at home, he was reduced to reading scraps of material now and then. When he discovered the small local library and looked for the first time at the book covers on the shelves over his head, a new world was opened up to him. He imagined the books all contained movies, movies that were playing any time he wanted to drop in. Reading took on a fascination for McKenna from that moment on, and over the years that particular library saw almost all its fiction and most of its nonfiction pass through the hands and into the heart of the boy. However, his passion had to be pursued in the face of opposition from his mother, who thought excessive reading was bad and who often forbade him to bring books home.[2]

Although McKenna was a good student, those early years were difficult for him. His father left home when the boy was still young, and the family was so poor that at one point they were evicted from their home. Such a cloud of financial difficulty overshadowed McKenna's boyhood that he did not feel regret later on for missing college as a young man. As he put it, the problem was "much more starkly elemental: How to escape the iron pinch of enforced idleness and poverty and the terrible

2. The author recounts this experience in "Adventures with Libraries," *New Eyes for Old: Nonfiction Writings by Richard McKenna*, ed. Eva Grice McKenna and Shirley Graves Cochrane (Winston-Salem, 1972), pp. 22–23. I am indebted to this volume for much of the biographical information mentioned in this introduction.

sense of personal unworth they generated."[3] He had been out of work a year by the time he was able to enlist in the navy in 1931, and even then he had to send most of his salary home.

Once on active duty, he spent some time as an apprentice hospital corpsman on the West Coast before being shipped to Guam on a transport, the USS *Chaumont*, famous for ferrying troops to the Far East. On this vessel and throughout his career, McKenna continued his reading, even though ships' libraries at this time were not very amply stocked. One that McKenna looked into held a grand total of three books, these housed in a cabinet the key to which someone had lost. Many years later a shipmate of his recounted that such was the scarcity of books on ships and such was McKenna's love of reading that he would even peruse from cover to cover the pages of a railroad timetable if nothing better was available. The young sailor eventually learned to stuff volumes of English poetry in the nooks and crannies of the enginerooms he worked in, and even in the *Chaumont* he knew enough to provide himself with a bundle of old magazines, which he spread evenly under his mattress, the only place in transient quarters where reading material could be kept.[4] Thus there were limits to his quest for books, chief among them being the time he had to spend immersed in an educational experience of a much different kind—learning the mysteries of shipboard engineering.

He began this enterprise as a fireman in the USS *Gold Star*, station ship at Guam, which he was with from 1933 to 1937. There he worked in the firerooms, in the enginerooms, and in the ship's large refrigeration plant, eventually mastering his rate of machinist's mate in the traditional naval system of apprenticeship. The young sailor learned a great deal in the slow, step-by-step method then customary, and perhaps he wakened more deeply to the wonders of engineering in the *Gold Star* than he would have had his knowledge come from lectures or a book. It was at this point in his life that McKenna learned to see the grace of simple physical work. So important was his practical experience that in all the author's serious fiction sooner or later he sings a song of praise to a machinist or to an engine or even to energy itself.

After his tour of duty in the *Gold Star* he received orders to the

---

3. "The Wreck of Uncle Josephus," *New Eyes for Old*, pp. 40. McKenna did spend a year at the College of Idaho before enlisting in the service.

4. "Adventures with Libraries," pp. 28–29.

gunboat USS *Asheville*, which he boarded in Shanghai in October 1937 after a few months back in the United States. He remained attached to this ship through 1938. In that year he also reported aboard the destroyer USS *Edsall* (DD 219) for a short tour. Whereas the *Gold Star* had been stationed in Guam and occasionally cruised to China, the Philippines, and more often Japan, the other two ships operated out of Shanghai primarily along the Chinese coast. But it was in his two years in the USS *Luzon*, which he joined on 10 June 1939, that McKenna received his deepest impressions of China and became a "river rat." This gunboat, with a comparatively shallow 6.5-ft draft, had been built in the late twenties, specifically for service on the Yangtze.[5] The *Luzon* steamed frequently between Shanghai and Hankow when McKenna was with her, a time of growing confrontation with Japan. The Japanese had occupied eastern China in 1937 and 1938 and put the local cities under their administration. Indeed, when Japan took over the eastern Yangtze, American vessels had to request permission (which they often did not receive) to get under way, and sometimes they were forced to steam from port to port under Japanese escort.

McKenna would later write a short story about this period, "King's Horsemen," and if that story is at all representative of the author's personal preferences, it can be said that he remained more interested in the engines than in political events and spent most of his working life below decks. It was the drama of the engineroom that fascinated the sailor, and moreover, he was intent on making rate. He became a machinist's mate second class in 1937 and was advanced to first class in 1939.

McKenna didn't stay long in any of these gunboats; when the war came the vessels were either scuttled within six months of Pearl Harbor or sunk by the Japanese as they literally annihilated the U.S. Asiatic Fleet.[6] Instead he returned to the United States in 1941. The sailor spent

5. After the *Luzon* was built, even this draft was judged to be too small, especially for operations "upriver" (the stretch of rapids upriver from Ichang to Chunking) and for steaming in other low-water areas often visited by the gunboats. Interestingly, one of these low-water areas was Changsha, which was off the Yangtze up the Chien River. The *Luzon* was much better off than the U.S. ship that was historically stationed at Changsha and after which the USS *San Pablo* was modeled—the USS *Villalobos*. Her draft was 9 feet. See Rear Admiral Kemp Tolley's *Yangtze Patrol: The U.S. Navy in China* (Annapolis, 1971), pp. 220–21, 297–302.

6. The *Asheville* and the *Edsall* were sunk by the Japanese off Java in early March 1942. The *Luzon* was scuttled in Manila Bay on 6 May to prevent her capture by the Japanese; however, they soon salvaged and used the ship for fighting.

most of World War II as a machinist's mate on the transport USS *Mount Vernon*, which ferried troops from San Francisco to Australia, New Zealand, and Hawaii. The ship later steamed through the Panama Canal to cities on the East Coast and made several trips to the Mediterranean and back.

In 1942 McKenna was promoted to the rank of chief petty officer, a rank he retained after the war. Throughout his career he remained dutiful, supportive of his country, and committed to the naval service, but he did have complaints. For example, dissatisfied with the postwar employment of chief petty officers, he wrote an essay, "Post-War Chief Petty Officer: A Closer Look," which was published in 1948.[7] For this article—his first published work—he won a $500 prize and was assigned a tour of duty in 1948 as a writer at Great Lakes. But although he liked the work, he did not take up this opportunity to shift his rating to navy journalist: he resented having to put the navy's "message" into everything he wrote. The result of this decision was an obligation to return to the enginerooms of a destroyer at the outbreak of the Korean War, when his service was involuntarily extended for two years.

In 1953 he was finally able to retire. With the support of the GI Bill, he attended the University of North Carolina to quench his thirst for a formal education. The ex-sailor found college a magnificently enriching experience, largely because of the background and reading he brought to it. In class after class he found his great store of miscellaneous knowledge, facts, and impressions organized and given coherence, and his was a continuous sense of wonder at the grand schemes of education. Moreover, he contributed not a little to those classes himself. He looked back to his naval career for subjects for term papers and discussed his recollections of the Far East with professors in history, anthropology, and geology classes. His engineering background gave him an especially strong appetite and aptitude for science, and in literature and philosophy courses he could test much that he was taught against his naval background. Not surprisingly, professors discovered him to be a superior student, one who without prompting would read all of their reserve books cover to cover. He graduated in 1956 with high academic honors.

In the months after college he began to teach himself how to write. He had long planned to launch his career with science fiction, believing this would provide him a good apprenticeship. He used scientific matter

7. It appeared in the U.S. Naval Institute *Proceedings* (December 1948): pp. 1481–85.

for subjects and motifs in most of his early literary work and published a number of science fiction stories, among them "The Night of Hoggy Darn" and "Mine Own Ways." But he was not very happy with his work. Although critics would later call McKenna an innovator in science fiction, he soon discovered that fans of this genre didn't share his thirst for hard science.

It is perhaps significant that the characters in his first published science fiction story, "Casey Agonistes," are naval enlisted men.[8] McKenna learned early to base his writing on subjects he knew from his own experience. As he later recounted, "My material is everything I know, . . . all new knowledge I take into myself must become somehow assimilated to my lived experience before I can make effective use of it in putting words on paper."[9] He eventually turned from science fiction to purely naval subjects and wrote stories that had familiar settings—predictably, the enginerooms of naval vessels stationed in China, Guam, or Japan. Many crucial episodes of *The Sand Pebbles* were based on the tales his navy shipmates had told years before about the Chinese Revolution. He worked hard to master the history of that period, insisting on the seemingly impossible task of uncovering the historical origins of the sailor folk-legends he remembered before he would use any of them in his work.[10] And so he kept reading and reflecting, until he found his memory merge with his reading so closely that he could hardly tell which was which. Until his death in November 1964, his own experience as understood through reading and education came more and more to form the basis of his literary endeavor. In the end it was this combination that allowed him to produce work of high quality.

How did McKenna's background contribute to *The Sand Pebbles?* It first enabled him to render believably and accurately the novel's setting.

The story takes place in 1925–27. During this period, indeed off and on since 1854, vessels of the U.S. Asiatic Fleet patrolled the Yangtze on missions to protect American property, American political interests, and the businessmen, missionaries, and diplomats who were U.S. citizens. Vessels belonging to other foreign countries, among them Italy, France, Japan, and Britain, also patrolled these waters. Of the foreigners the most prominent were the British, who ran the major clubs

8. In *Casey Agonistes and Other Science Fiction and Fantasy Stories* (New York, 1973), pp. 1–12.

9. "The Writer's Materials," *New Eyes for Old*, pp. 123–24.

10. He even discovered the source of his story of the martyrdom of the coolie Po-han. See "The Fiction of History," *New Eyes for Old*, pp. 110–11.

and provided most of the social accommodations ashore, but each of these countries had widespread trading and business interests in China, the pursuit of which had been legalized by the so-called unequal treaties forced on the Chinese in the nineteenth century under the Open Door policy. In the "treaty cities" along the Yangtze, many foreign powers owned concessions, that is, large sections of the cities where they set up their warehouses, general business operations, and diplomatic headquarters, and which they administered without allowing the Chinese any say. Maritime customs, some mail, and many other domestic operations in China were also under the administrative or financial control of the Western nations, whose citizens could travel virtually anywhere they wanted in the country without Chinese permission and outside of Chinese jurisdiction. Given this freedom of movement, not only businessmen but large numbers of Christian missionaries overran China in successive waves. The missionaries not only took full advantage of the special privileges accorded Westerners but also secured the additional right to own mission properties in the countryside. Meanwhile, what little governmental power Chinese officials were allowed to exercise was often ineffective, and the Chinese countryside was a patchwork quilt of local warlords and ever-contending Chinese political factions.

Except for a few earlier port visits to the major coastal cities, McKenna saw the Yangtze a decade after the revolution, indeed after the Japanese had conquered the eastern third of the nation. However, during his tour the basic political and social structure of foreign domination and Chinese impotence remained intact, so that riverine commerce and life in the gunboats carried on much the same way in McKenna's time as in the revolutionary era. As the author wrote, "It was not too hard for me to recreate those times from a Naval viewpoint. . . . I had only to extrapolate the attitudes and behavior of the men I knew a few years backward into a scene which had not changed much physically."[11] And as we have seen, what he didn't know personally, for example about Chinese history or American missionary opinion, he was able to understand through extensive study and research.

As a result, McKenna's setting is studiously accurate.[12] Whether he is picturing the legendary battles between crews of small upriver gunboats and sailors from big seagoing ships or describing the mysterious walled

11. "Our Own Houses," *New Eyes for Old*, pp. 114.
12. This is certainly borne out by Rear Admiral Kemp Tolley's sketches of Asiatic Fleet life of the 1920's in *Yangtze Patrol*.

cities or the navigational hazards of the Yangtze at Changsha, the author is speaking in large part from lived experience. The same is true of the novelist's dramatization of larger historical movements, though of course there were limits to his presentation that were dictated by the laws of fiction. McKenna cautioned that because of "technical considerations, such as viewpoint limitation, and more literary considerations, such as the classical unities," he had to shift about specific dates and times of historical events.[13] Nevertheless, his account of the fundamental waves of Chinese history during this period provoked one historian to ask, "If someone unaccustomed to detailed historical works were interested in understanding the enormous struggles that have transformed the Chinese people since 1911, what better beginning could he make than to read *The Sand Pebbles*, that magnificent first and last novel written by . . . the late Richard McKenna?"[14] Accurate in both the small details and the larger phenomena of the cultural milieu with which it deals, *The Sand Pebbles* gives the reader a feel for the very texture of the times, for what it was like to be a crewman on the eve of the Chinese Revolution in a gunboat of the U.S. Asiatic Fleet.

The author's experience also enabled him to paint sympathetically and convincingly the background of his main character, the machinist Jake Holman. McKenna pictured Holman as having been raised in circumstances very much like those he had suffered himself. Jake is born into a poor family from a western town. As a boy his classmates tease him unmercifully because he wears his friends' cast-off clothing. After troubles with his school superintendent, Jake enlists in the navy as an alternative to reform school. While the author himself joined the navy eagerly, he knew well the troubles of poverty and how they could help lead a young man like Jake into violent conflicts which might be punished with a sentence of service in the navy. And McKenna knew intimately the difficulties a man would have to confront upon enlisting.

The troubles Jake has after joining the navy become a kind of outcry on the part of McKenna for the humane treatment of enlisted personnel. If we believe the picture offered by the novel, the life of a bluejacket in the early twentieth century could be rather demeaning. That judges could sentence young offenders to the navy as an alternative to reform school is a familiar fact. But other less widely known policies and official

13. "The Fiction of History," p. 110.
14. George V. Taylor, "History, Literature, and the Public at Large," *North Carolina Historical Review* 42 (1965): p. 181.

attitudes seem surprisingly stark and oppressive when presented bluntly in the text: "The navy would not let an enlisted man marry until he was a second-class petty officer, and by then he was supposed to be seasoned enough to know better. If he didn't, he had better not expect any official favors just because he had a wife. Good sailors were supposed to make do with whores" (p. 263). If there is bitterness here, it seems justified by today's standards. A similar cynicism is heard in the narrator's opinion of the corrective facilities in the navy of the day: "Forty-eight was the naval prison at Cavite. If a man went in there with a scrap of spirit, the marines would beat it out of him or they would beat him to death" (p. 437). Jake Holman does not go to the naval prison at Cavite, but he does find contact with authority figures difficult: he gets embarrassed and flustered during military drills or in the presence of officers, and he characteristically flings himself into the engineering spaces when the situation topside is too much for him to handle.

Jake Holman's conflict with his superiors is what leads him into engineering. Overcome by "military fear" in the presence of anyone who has authority over him, Jake is listless, friendless, and despondent. But then he discovers "the secret." It "was simple. They could not get along without the machinery. If it did not run, the ship would be a cold, dark, dead hulk in the water. And it did not work with engines to order them to run and to send down the marines to shoot them if they did not run. No admiral could court-martial an engine" (pp. 46–47). Eventually the sailor learns to develop his technical skills and becomes indispensable in the enginerooms so that he can evade topside military duties and the contact with authorities that upsets him so. Still, though, on the USS *San Pablo* everyone has to stand topside watches, and the problems Jake has with this duty generate the major plot conflict of the first half of the novel between the frustrated Holman and his unrelenting officer, between the peace-loving engineering gang and the war-minded ship.

But engineering is not only a source of conflict for the characters; McKenna translated his love of machinery into a dominant and memorable theme of the book. First using his expertise with machinery as a defense, Jake begins to discover the possibilities of mutual respect between a machine and a person; he finds that there is a living relationship at the heart of the engineering profession. The embattled sailor Jake begins to emerge from his shell of bitter confusion through love of his work with engines, a love that is best expressed by sharing his knowledge with the lowly coolie Po-han.

Originally Jake doubts Po-han's ability to learn: "Po-han could not get the idea of breaking down the great mass of piping into separate systems. He could not say what was moving in what direction through any of the pipes that Holman pointed out. He did not even have the idea of stuff moving through pipes" (pp. 40–41). But Jake determines to teach the Chinaman anyway, a task that requires him to tap the deepest reservoir of his imagination. Consider his attempt to teach Po-han about pressure. At first it seems impossible to get the notion across: "Po-han could not understand the difference between live steam going in and exhaust steam coming out. He just did not have the basic words. . ." (p. 41). But after a few futile explanations and a moment of hesitation,

> . . . Holman acted it out. He was live steam, coming along the line snorting and bulging his muscles, and the live steam did work in the feed pump, Holman reaching in to the crosshead with both arms, grunting heavily, pretending to lift the piston rod up and down as it stroked, and then the steam came out the exhaust valve wheezing, drooping, muscles slack, staggered over to the condenser and went to sleep, Holman's folded hands beside his head. (p. 41)

The sailor continues his ingenious performance until Po-han suddenly starts a joyous imitation of the white man's antics. He grasps the concept of pressure and immediately wants to learn more.

Jake eventually teaches his companion virtually everything he knows of the steam cycle until Po-han can do each job as well as he and understand it too. Finally Po-han evinces a sense of wonder at what he sees as the "wild white horses" of the sun—the energy involved in steam engineering:

> There were tricks with tools that Holman could still teach Po-han, but otherwise he had taken Po-han as far as he could go himself. Once he saw Po-han with a lump of coal in his hand, staring at it. Po-han had the strained, aching look on his face. He was trying to understand how wild white horses could be locked up so cool and safely in a black stone. Jake Holman could not tell him. He had often looked at a lump of coal like that himself. (p. 284)

Jake's friendship with Po-han and the tumult this generates sets up yet one more conflict that runs through the novel, between two different races and cultures. But perhaps more important to us is the author's account of the experience of the *San Pablo*'s enlisted crew, the so-called Sand Pebbles. The milieu in which they move is made up of bars, whorehouses, enginerooms and mess decks, and it is far removed from the clubs and tennis courts officers frequent while ashore—which are most conspicuous in *The Sand Pebbles* by their absence. Again, McKenna believed enlisted men in the twenties and thirties were the subject of oppression of a sort. But the physical circumstances, close quarters, sudden personnel transfers, and overbearing authority—these were not what ultimately demoralized the sailor. According to the author, the final humiliation for a sailor of this era came with the realization that despite his rough life, despite a career spent in the service of his country, he was regarded with contempt by many if not most of his fellow countrymen.

The American missionaries in the novel won't marry the Chinese girl Maily and the American sailor Frenchy Burgoyne because the couple are scum in the missionaries' eyes, nor will an American journalist whom the crew runs across write a story lamenting the lovers' tragedy, for he knows the papers back home would never print it. As the journalist explains to the sailors, "They have to sell papers to stay in business. . . . Everybody knows our gallant boys in blue go to bed with native women—what the hell, I have myself, and maybe I will tonight—but the kind hearts and gentle people don't like to be reminded of it in print" (p. 441). McKenna explained in an essay what he understood to be the result of this attitude: "It was of no interest to tradition-bound civilian minds what sort of human being might be inside the uniform. So, very humanly, many of the American citizens inside the uniform became indeed persons of relative moral unworth. . ."[15] But *The Sand Pebbles* not only vividly portrays unfairness and inequality; it also depicts the potentially disastrous consequences of institutionalized oppression.

The novel traces the moral degeneration of the crew through a series of "identity crises" forced upon them by the unjust social order to which they are bound. At first the Sand Pebbles are led by their situation and self-doubt to identify themselves as superior Americans with the natural right to lord it over the lowly Chinese. The crewmembers tend to compensate for their lack of genuine self-respect by maltreating the Chinese both on board ship and off. They shack up with the local girls, get fat on Chinese cooking, kick coolies around on the beach, and take advantage of Chinese obsequiousness.

But suddenly, behind the banner of Chiang Kai-shek, the cringing Chinese begin to fight back. The crew of the USS *San Pablo* is pictured as the first American group to encounter the Kuomintang. With no warning, and in the same mission school courtyard where the sailors had

15. "The Wreck of Uncle Josephus," p. 48.

previously disdained slovenly warlord soldiers, crack Kuomintang troops face down the Sand Pebbles. As the Americans are escorted back to their ship a gleeful crowd pelts them with filth. This event stuns the crewmembers and shakes their sense of identity. It is shattered later when a stash of opium is found in the coolie quarters of the *San Pablo* and American journalists interrogate the Sand Pebbles themselves about the drugs. These troubles and others like them begin to drive the men to drink.

But if the Sand Pebbles are confused about their social status, both in relation to the Chinese and to the people back home, they are even more perplexed about their role as fighting men. Through certain specifics of the *San Pablo*'s history and Lieutenant Collins' peculiar style of leadership, the men have come to regard themselves primarily as soldiers or marines rather than as a navy crew. On this ship the coolies do all the real work, and no naval enlisted man except for a gunner's mate and the maverick Holman actually works in his rate. The men are exempted from standard naval vocations for their supposedly more important "military" duties. When the American authorities forbid the gunboats to fight back if fired at or confronted by the revolutionaries, and when the coolies desert the ship fearing reprisals for serving on a foreign boat, the Sand Pebbles are caught in the paradoxical situation of having to refrain from the fighting for which they are trained and take up naval rates to which they are completely unaccustomed.

Thus, in the midst of the great moral challenges, social pressures, and physical hardships of the Chinese Revolution, the Sand Pebbles are deprived of any psychological support on which they may have previously depended. The Chinese turn out to be at least as good at fighting as they, so the sailors can't take refuge in an imagined racial or social superiority; at the same time, the crewmen are forced to face the realities not only of Chinese hatred but of their fellow Americans' contempt as well. If Frenchy's Chinese wife Maily, who because of her relationship with an American finds that her own people have turned on her, can ask, "'If I'm not Chinese, what am I?'" (p. 333) then the Sand Pebbles themselves could with as much justification ask: If as Americans we're treated as dirt, and are not superior as we have been taught; if we're not sailors with a love of our work nor even marines who can fight, and moreover, if our treatment in China suggests that we're not even human beings meriting love and respect, then just *who are we?* And on what basis and for what reason are we to summon up the "moral heroism" which has been asked of us? Under the enormous pressure of their circumstances the crewmembers degenerate rapidly in a series of episodes that is as penetrating an account of the underlying causes of mutiny as any in nautical literature.

What is it about McKenna the man that has him pose in his novel existential questions? What, in a larger context, is the source of McKenna's intensity, his deep intellectual curiosity, and the strong thematic currents running through *The Sand Pebbles*? Partly it was his habit of reading that kept him intellectually and spiritually alive all through the service; partly it was the illumination provided by his college education. However, a catalyst was needed to bring a sharp personal interest to bear on his reflections, and it came in the form of an agonizing personal crisis that the author experienced when he returned home in March 1942 for the first time since the war had begun.

> The turning point came for me with World War II, when I was twenty-eight years old. I had long intended to serve out my twenty years and retire in the Orient, as many men did in those old days. When I had to return to the States, with the uneasy conviction that those old days were gone forever, it was not pleasant. My future was suddenly all uncertain. I had let myself become too deeply aware of the common humanity I shared with Chinese and Japanese to force myself easily into the mental and emotional state proper to wartime. My ship came into San Francisco in March of 1942 at the time when Americans of Japanese ancestry were being dispossessed and imprisoned. The mood of the people, as I sampled it in the places where I went ashore, seemed to me almost that of a lynch mob. A few unpleasant experiences quickly taught me that it was dangerous to speak my thoughts and possibly a sin even to think them. I had to relieve my feelings with drunken mutterings to which no one listened. I ached with self-contempt and a shattering sense of opposed loyalties which I could not reconcile. I was undergoing a genuine crisis of faith. . . .
>
> I went through all the war in that state. . . . For the first time I began to read books in clear, conscious pursuit of the thought in them. I was no longer seeking entertainment only, but information and the hope of a way out of pain.[16]

Eventually, after a period of years, he did find a way out of pain, and instrumental in leading him there was Thoreau's *Walden*, which consoled him, confirmed him in his humanity, and committed him anew to the value of education. But education now meant for him the quest for an answer to the larger questions of existence—the nature of man and the

16. "New Eyes for Old: The Quest for Education," *New Eyes for Old*, pp. 8–9.

significance of human life. And not only during his subsequent college career but in the eight years he spent painstakingly teaching himself how to write, this goal underlay everything that he took up.

Above all, it is the fictional expression of this quest, this far-reaching educational experience, this discovery of the nature of the world and of man's place within it, that makes *The Sand Pebbles* an exceptional book. Jake Holman's own crisis comes to a head two-thirds of the way through the novel. Most of the early part of the story, as we have seen, has to do with Jake's struggles to create a place for himself on the ship, to fit in with the crew, and to service the great engine. Eventually these conflicts recede and the sailor finds a measure of peace. But then Po-han is killed, the revolution begins, and larger questions suddenly arise.

After the revolution heats up, Jake is unexpectedly offered the opportunity to desert his ship and join a group of missionaries planning to teach with the Kuomintang at the "China Light" mission. There his work would be operating machinery and teaching. Partly prompted by Po-han's death, partly by his relationship with the missionary girl Shirley Eckert, Jake finds the proposal highly attractive. But he is afraid to make this kind of absolute commitment—the navy could find him and court-martial him for deserting. Nevertheless, with this choice being offered to him, Holman begins to realize for the very first time that there's more to life than engineering: "You need a reason for being alive. Machinery ain't—isn't enough" (p. 402). This questioning precipitates Holman's crisis and the end of the book.

Some readers find the ending unacceptable: it's not Hollywood enough. It is interesting to note that McKenna himself had trouble with the conclusion. He also wanted his book to end "happily," that is, with a simple and optimistic message of hope. But when he wrote his first draft of the ending this way and sent it to New York, both his agent and his editor rejected it, saying, simply, that it didn't ring true. What he had to do with the plot and the characters in order to finish the novel did not please McKenna as a person, yet as a writer and artist he acknowledged its rightness and necessity: "At once all the pieces fell into place for me, and I could see the ending in all of its inescapable truth."[17] It was not until McKenna had put the final touches on his book that its central concern, the link between personal destiny and inescapable historical causality, emerged in its fullness.

17. "The Fiction of History," p. 112.

That is, under pressures caused by the revolution, and with the illumination that results from a new approach to life, Jake Holman begins to consider seriously a course he had decided against only a few weeks earlier—deserting to the mission. What happens when in an unexpected way he actually gets there effectually solves his "crisis of faith." Could the novel end as McKenna had first wanted it to, with the missionary's ideals "triumph[ing] and surviv[ing] at one remote, imaginary place in China"?[18] Such an ending would have been unfaithful to reality: the great rush of events that surged through China eventually thrust out all the foreigners—Japanese, French, Italians, British, Americans—and committed Christianity and democracy to the trashcan along with them. It only makes sense that the novel not end like a shallow romance. Nevertheless, some form of contentment is demanded by the reader of almost any story—and the demand is just if it is true that a novel should give a reader some higher sense of understanding, insight, or fulfillment. In this connection, the key question to raise about *The Sand Pebbles* is whether the hero's experience, his personal destiny, is coherent and insightful. This writer believes it is—events bring Jake Holman to a crucial moment when he must make a fundamental "life choice" which he has been incapable of making before, a choice he has been, as it were, in training for all his life. One thing is certain, however: on such grounds as these McKenna would have wanted his book to be judged, that is, on the basis of whether it imputes meaning to the life of one specific human being. And the fact that the character in question is an enlisted man, not at all a highly cultured or intellectually accomplished individual—well, if McKenna succeeded in showing this kind of life as having the potential for great dignity and meaning, so much the better.

Despite its exciting plot and its readability, then, *The Sand Pebbles* is a weighty book, befitting such a serious fellow and exceptional student as Richard McKenna seems to have been. As we have seen, the author worked a wide range of material into his novel, which gives expression to such a variety of topics as the beauties of physical labor, the importance of the humane treatment of enlisted men, and the profound satisfaction to be won from cross-cultural and cross-racial friendship. There is also a marvelous portrait of a group of American missionaries discovering the meaning of love, and a magnificent vista of the Chinese Revolution. But

18. Ibid., p. 111.

The Sand Pebbles is more than the sum of all these parts. It is, above all else, the story of a philosophical quest, a metaphorical journey up a river. The journey is that of a young man coming of age, his reaching the point of maturity, his awakening spiritually into a world that is neither inimical nor universally beneficent—a world, in other words, not very different from our own.

ROBERT SHENK

THE SAND PEBBLES

1

"Hello, ship," Jake Holman said under his breath.

The ship was asleep and did not hear him. He lowered his big canvas thirty-year bag to the ground and stood there in the moon shadow of a brick wall and had his long first look at her. She looked stubby and blocky and topheavy down there at the edge of the black, rolling river, and she was all moon-white except for her slender black smokestack that rose very high, high as her two masts. Four guy wires slanted down from the stack like streamers from a maypole. She had a stubby, shielded gun on her open bow and a doubled, man-high hand steering wheel on her open fantail aft, but in between she looked more like a house than a ship. Her square, curtained windows and screened doors opened on a galleried main deck like a long, narrow veranda and on a pipe-railed boat deck under taut white awnings. It was after midnight and they were asleep down there, all but the watch. In a few minutes he'd go aboard and find a bunk and wake up with them in the morning like a strange bird in their nest.

Jake Holman knew he was a strange bird and he was used to going aboard new ships. By the time they realized they were in a struggle Jake Holman would already have made for himself the place he wanted on their ship and they could never dislodge him. Or wish to. It was going to be the same on the U.S.S. *San Pablo*. He did not know why he was reluctant to go right aboard. This one might be a pretty strange nest, too, he thought.

Since he had gotten his orders a month ago in Manila he had not been able to find anyone who had ever seen the ship or who had even been shipmates with an ex-*San Pablo* sailor. Nobody knew any more about her than Holman already knew himself, after six years on the China Station, and that was more legend than fact. She was one of the ancient gunboats captured from Spain and sent to form the Yangtze Patrol during the Boxer Rebellion, in the year Jake Holman was born. They were all relics now, in June of 1925, and a flotilla of modern gunboats was building in Shanghai to replace them. The others sometimes appeared in Shanghai, but the *San Pablo* never came further downriver than Hankow. They said she was least and ugliest of Comyang's gunboats and he was ashamed to show the flag on the likes of her down around the glitter of Shanghai. She did not even operate on the Yangtze, but on some nameless tributaries from the south, and on a big lake that was said to expand and contract mysteriously and to have mermaids in it. From the legends, the *San Pablo* spent half her time high and dry on sand bars in the nameless rivers with the crew ashore cultivating gardens and slaughtering their own beef and mining their own coal, while the natives took pot shots at them.

Holman did not believe the legends, but he thought she was still a funny-looking ship. A lighted quarterdeck was inset amidships on the main deck with a short gangplank leading up from the pontoon through a gap in the solid steel bulwark. Two men stood on watch there beside a pulpitlike log desk, one in regulation undress whites and the other in the white shorts and short-sleeved sport shirt that was summer uniform for Yangtze Patrol sailors. At least two more in shorts were patrolling with rifles on the shadowy boat deck. That was a lot of men for the topside watch on a quiet midnight, Holman thought.

He was a sandy-haired, squarely built, powerful man in dress whites and he stood there in the moon shadow thinking and nuzzling his chin with a fat brown envelope. The envelope held his records and pay accounts and it was wound with red tape sealed in four places with blobs of red wax so that Jake Holman could not examine or tamper with the Navy's little paper image of himself. Paper Jake Holman, he sometimes called it in his thoughts. When he turned Paper Jake in down on that quarterdeck, he would be aboard officially on paper. He would be in the thick of it again.

Well, *go on down,* he told himself, but he did not go. He sniffed the cool, damp breeze off the river and listened to the lapping, rustling murmur of the moving water and he heard the steady plashing sound of a cooling water overboard discharge. He could not see it along the ship's steel side. Must be on the port side, he thought. It's late, he thought, and the first few days are always rough ones. *Go aboard,* you stupid bastard, and get some sleep. He picked up the thirty-year bag and started down the plank walkway to the flat steel pontoon.

"Here I come, ship," he said softly.

The man in regulation whites ran out on the pontoon to take Holman's seabag. He was Chinese. Holman stepped aboard and saluted aft, according to regulation. The man in shorts returned the salute, which was not regulation, because he was an enlisted man in a white hat.

"Reckon you're Holman," he said. "Was wondering when you'd get here, all the trouble they're having downriver."

The man was tall and skinny and heavily tattooed on arms and legs and he had a drooping brown mustache. He wore a holstered pistol. Holman nodded and handed him the brown envelope. The man glanced at the seals and lifted the hinged top of the log desk, like a gaping mouth, dropped in the envelope and let the top fall with a thud.

"Now you're a Sand Pebble," he told Holman. "That's what we call this ship, the U.S.S. *Sand Pebble.*" He had a slow, lazy voice. "Welcome aboard. I'm Frenchy Burgoyne, first-class watertender." He held out his hand.

"Call me Jake." They shook hands. "How come an engineer on

watch up here?" Holman asked. "You standing by for somebody?"

"All hands stand topside watches," Burgoyne said.

That was the first bad thing, but Holman did not let his face show it. The Chinese was standing beside the seabag.

"Might as well unlock your bag and they'll stow your locker for you," Burgoyne said. "Won't need your navy mattress on here. Your bunk's already made up with ship's gear."

The Chinese, whose name was Fang, went away with the seabag. Burgoyne was copying Holman's orders into the log book. He held the pencil awkwardly and squinted and wrote from the shoulders down. The quarterdeck was a triangle with the inner point opening into a passageway that led through to the port side. Sounds and smells from a lighted doorway in the passage told Holman it led to the engine room, and machinery sounds came up through the teak planking under his feet. Pumps clanked and groaned down there, and something throbbed lightly and quickly.

" 'Spect you're about ready to flake out, ain't you?" Burgoyne asked. "How'd you get here? How was the trip?"

"Commercial from Shanghai. Steamer named *Loong Wo,*" Holman said. "I had hell's own time finding out where you was and getting a taxicab to come all the way down here."

It was a dockyard about five miles downriver from Hankow.

"We just finished overhaul. Every two years we come here for overhaul," Burgoyne said.

"Ought to be in good shape down below, then," Holman said. "How's the chief engineer?"

"Ain't got one, less'n you figure it's Lynch, the chief machinist's mate. We only got two commissioned officers, skipper and exec." He smoothed his mustache with a knuckle. "Lynch is all right. Drinks right much, but he's maskee. Right now he's all fouled up with a Russky he found in Mumm's." Burgoyne chuckled. "No sir, won't see much of that old boy till we go south again."

"When's that?"

"Week or so. We start summer cruising."

Fang came back and spoke in pidgin to Burgoyne.

"Your gear's stowed and your bunk's ready, if you want to turn in now," Burgoyne told Holman.

"Not right now. That's service, though. I always heard you guys had it good on the river gunboats."

"You don't know the half of it yet. We got them main river boats beat hollow." Burgoyne stood up straight. He was proud of his ship. "If you ain't sleepy, we got coffee in the galley. I can have Fang fetch us a cup."

"If you don't mind, I'll go down and have a cup in the engine room and shoot the breeze with the watch a minute," Holman said. "I want to look around, see what I'm getting into."

"Ain't no coffee down there. I got the engine room watch."

Holman looked at him, shocked, and Burgoyne grinned.

"Oh, I got a bilge coolie helper down there handling the routine," he said. "He'll call me if something's wrong. I'll go down at four o'clock and write up the log."

Holman thought that was very bad. He did not let his face show what he thought.

"How many black gang on here, all told?"

"Five. Eight, you count Lynch and Waxer and Harris."

"That all? You can steam with only that many?"

"We got a dozen bilge coolies. They stoke, help out on watch, clean up and all. Hell, we got it good."

Holman shook his head. Burgoyne took a can of Copenhagen out of the log desk and packed his lower lip. His bulging lip made his gaunt cheeks look even more hollow.

"Who pays the coolies?" Holman asked.

"Welfare fund, what's in it. Mostly, they squeeze."

"Do they do repair work?"

"No-count jobs, packing rods and stuff, they do. We supervise 'em on the big jobs."

"So that's howcome the black gang has time to stand topside watches?" Holman was trying not to show his dismay. "I don't know anything about this topside military crap," he said. "I started forgetting that crap the minute I left boot camp."

"I never used to favor it my own self, till I come on here," Burgoyne said. "It's different on here. The old *Sand Pebble*'s a home, boy!" He worked his lip and walked to the side and spat. "It sure God beats sweat and dirt and heaving around down on them floor plates!"

"I guess," Holman said. "I'm going below and look around, anyway."

Four things were important on a ship: bunk, locker, place at the mess table and the engine room. The engine room was most important, because it was always Jake Holman's sanctuary from the saluting and standing at attention and saying *sir* that went with life on the topside. Monkey-on-a-stick life, he called that in his thoughts.

"Go right ahead. Help yourself, boy," Burgoyne said. He was a bit angry.

Holman stepped through the door onto the gratings and into the smell and noise. All live engine rooms had the same smell of burnt rubber and hot oil and steam and sometimes coffee and a whiff of bilge. This one smelled clean. The engine cylinder block rose waist high above the gratings like a black flatiron twenty feet long. Beyond its tapered nose a door led into the fireroom uptakes, and insulated steam piping came through the white bulkhead like fat white snakes to branch and loop down to the machinery on the lower level. Above the engine a skylight opened to the boat deck and cool air came down. He was already beginning to sweat. A grating walkway with polished steel handrails ran all around the engine and at the forward end ladders on either side led down to the floorplates. Through the gratings he could not see anyone on watch down there, but the lower level was wider and extended further aft than the narrow grating space, and he could not see it all from above.

He went down to the floorplates and walked slowly around the engine room, taking it all in. It was very clean, painted white, bare metal polished and oiled, and the corrugations on the old, old floorplates were worn almost smooth, but the floorplates were clean and shiny and oiled. The pumps, erect like men, and the hot well and feed heater and auxiliary condenser stood along the sides, with a clear space between them and the big central engine, and the skin of the ship behind the pumps was bulged in oddly here and there, like dents in a tin can. The pumps were all old Davidsons and Camerons and Worthingtons. The running ones clanked and ran jerkily. When Holman shook the valve gear on the idle pumps, he found too much play in all the bushings. But the pumps were clean and shined and oiled. He bit his lip and nodded. There was a lot of looksee pidgin in this engine room.

He heard a shovel scrape out in the fireroom. The engine coolie was probably doping off out there, talking to the stroker coolie. Holman frowned.

The light, quick throbbing came from one of a pair of old reciprocating generators aft on the port side, with a small railed-off switchboard behind them. The black brushes sparked smoothly over the clean copper bars of the commutator; both commutators looked as if they had just had a cut taken on them in the dockyard. An eccentric drive for an oil pump jigged and winked on the end of the armature shaft, and above the steam cylinder a belt-driven flyball governor spun like a little man with his hands on his hips. None of the bearings were hot. Holman got a spot of oil on his dress white jumper sleeve, in finding that out.

Damn it, he thought, where's that watch coolie? He had no faith in Chinamen looking after machinery. And damned little in some Americans, as far as that goes, he thought.

He made another slow circuit of the engine room, looking at the engine this time. It was triple expansion with the familiar double bar link gear, but very old, dating back to the days when they could not make fine steel and cast iron and made up for it by size. It was a big, heavy engine and it filled the center of the engine room, with the cylinder block rising above the gratings and the crank pits going deep below the floorplates, a three-level engine, but it was probably not very powerful. It was just heavy and old-fashioned and it likely took most of its power just to move itself, Holman thought.

It was massive and it was well and truly made, he saw. The three pairs of cast-iron columns measured about two feet on a side and the great clumsy shaft couplings were six inches thick. The bearing shells were all heavy, smooth brass and he could not span round the connecting rods with both his hands. All the ordered maze of working parts were cleanly oiled and softly shining under the lights, and that was looksee pidgin, which told nothing about how well it would run, but a warm feeling went out from Holman to the engine and his hands lingered on the sculptured metal.

"Hello, engine," he said softly.

The main condenser was a large white cylinder that lay aft of the engine like the crossbar of a T. The drain well was displaced to port to make room for the shaft to run beneath the condenser and the squat, long thrust bearing rose aft of the condenser. The main circulator and the main air pump snugged into the angles of the T on either side and it made a queer arrangement, but a very neatly balanced one. Forward on the starboard side was the throttle station and a log desk with a metal gauge board up behind it. The clock read two-fifteen. Holman stood for a moment with one hand on the throttle wheel overhead and one on the reversing lever.

"Hey, engine," he said softly. "Hey, engine!"

He went to the long steel workbench on the starboard side abreast the engine. It had two old vises and at one end a rag barrel and at the other a trash bucket. Up behind it was a tool board with big wrenches on brass clips. The wrenches were scarred and splayed and sprung-jawed and the workbench was marked with a thousand chisel cuts and half-round gasket punch scars, but everything was clean and oiled. Holman sat on the workbench, careless of oil on his dress whites. The spell of the engine was on him.

It was a fine, handsome old engine, much older than Jake Holman himself. He looked at it, massive, dully gleaming brass and steel in columns and rods and links arching above drive rods from twinned eccentrics, great crossheads hung midway, and above them valve spindles and piston rods disappearing into the cylinder block. He knew them all, each part and its place in the whole, and his eye followed the pattern, three times repeated from forward to aft, each one-third of the circle out of phase, and it was all poised and balanced there like three chunks of frozen music. Under his controlling hands, when they steamed, it was going to become living, speaking music. Under his tending hands, with oil can and grease swab. Under his healing hands, with hammer and wrench and scraper.

"Hello, engine. I'm Jake Holman," he said under his breath.

Jake Holman loved machinery in the way some other men loved God, women and their country. He loved main engines most of all, because they were the deep heart and power center of any ship and all the rest was trimming, much of it useless. He sat and looked at the engine without thinking, until a wild, yelling argument in the fireroom snapped him out of it.

It was the whang, yang, high, wailing screech of angry Chinese. Holman went over to the head of the engine, where two steps led down to the narrow passageway between the boilers, and then stopped. They wouldn't know him. Burgoyne must hear it up there; he'd come and break it up. The noise got worse and Burgoyne did not come down. The circular sterns of the two boilers stuck through the light bulkhead into the engine room like huge pop eyes, one on either side of the engine. The feed checks and water columns were in the engine room. The glass tube on the steaming boiler was so dirty-brown inside from scale that Holman had to move his finger slantwise behind it to be sure where the water level was. It was all right. The screeching in the fireroom was becoming frantic. Sometimes scale lodged in a valve and the glass showed a false level. You might think you were riding along easy with plenty of water and all the time your crown sheets were melting and when they let go it could blow the ship apart like a busted cigar. You had to blow the glass down every hour and let the column reform, to be sure.

"God damn it!" Holman said.

He opened the blowdown cock. The glass emptied with a roar and steam billowed under the floorplates. One of the ball checks stuck and it kept on blowing, so he closed the cock. A half-naked Chinese came running from the fireroom and Burgoyne clattered down the ladder behind Holman.

"What the Willy Jesus?" Burgoyne said, frowning.

"I blew the glass," Holman said. "One of your checks leaks."

"It don't leak bad. We only blow down once a watch on this ship," Burgoyne said. "I blew the glass when I came on watch."

"I blow 'em once an hour," Holman said.

"Maskee. You blow 'em every half hour if you want, when you got the watch. Right now I got it."

He was angry. He had a right to be. You did not interfere with another man's watch. But if he turned it over to a coolie, and the coolie was not standing it but out fighting . . .

"I'm sorry," Holman said slowly. "I been down here twenty minutes, maybe more, and your coolie ain't been in the engine room once to check the plant. Hellfire, you must've heard 'em fighting out there—"

He broke off at Burgoyne's sudden grin. The good-humor crinkles at the corners of his eyes replaced the frown between them.

"They ain't but one coolie down here for both places," he said. "What you heard was Po-han singing." He looked at the coolie at Holman's left. "You sing song, Po-han, he tinkee you, othah man, makee fight fight." Burgoyne chuckled and milled his fists and grinned at the coolie.

"My no sabby any man stop this side," the coolie said. He was grinning, but embarrassed.

"The laugh's on me," Holman said. "I sure thought two of 'em was about to take the shovels to each other."

"Po-han'll sure enough get into the Chinee opera yet," Burgoyne said. "He's all the time singing down here by himself." He looked hard at Holman. "Po-han's a good man. Anything ain't right, he'll find it and tell you. You can trust Po-han."

"Sure. I feel like a jackass," Holman said. "I'm sorry. I blew that glass, Frenchy."

"It's all right, Jake. Well, I better go back up." Burgoyne started up the ladder. "Ain't supposed to leave the quarterdeck except for emergencies," he said from the gratings.

A white hat on a swab handle could stand that quarterdeck watch this time of night, Holman thought. There was no day or night in the engine room. The coolie was standing by and Holman did not know what to say to him or how to treat him. He saw that the water column had reformed in the same place. It had been all right, but now he knew. The way to get killed around machinery was to take things for granted.

"All thing plopah," the coolie said. "You makee looksee, Mastah. Any side plopah."

He was grinning and looking Holman right in the eye and Holman had to recognize him. The coolie had short black hair above his head rag and a smooth, squarish face with very Chinese eyes and a strong chin. Except for the eyes and low nose, it was the same-model face as Jake Holman's, and that added to Holman's unease. Holman had gray eyes and bushy eyebrows and short, sandy hair.

"My takee looksee, Joe," he said, to break the encounter.

He walked around the engine, glancing at things, and sat again on the workbench. This business of coolies, he thought. He was used to them hired by the hour to muck out bilges or clean firesides. He knew the gunboats stationed permanently in China kept coolies living aboard to do all the hard and dirty work, bilges, passing coal, garbage detail, that stuff. But coolies tending machinery: he could not see that. He just could not see that, and it was going to make things unexpectedly complicated for Jake Holman aboard the U.S.S. *San Pablo*.

Through the engine, Holman watched the coolie tending the pumps on the port side. He took up neatly on a blowing gland, then swabbed the rod, then wiped up the spattered grease and water. He took a little make-up feed into the hot well. He moved quickly and surely and he seemed to know what he was doing. He wore old leather steaming shoes and the kind of thin black coolie pants that were tight at the ankle and so loose at the waist that the extra material had to be folded and lapped, and they were held up by a white sash that went around two or three times. The seats always sagged slaunchwise and the sailors laughed and called them "droopy drawers."

Suddenly, Holman saw the sense of it. Air went through the thin cloth and they did not bind in the crotch or even touch, and the cloth in the sash soaked up the sweat that rolled down. It beat hell out of skintight dungarees and leather belts. But no sailor would ever wear coolie pants. They would rather go on doctoring the spick itch in their crotches and the prickly heat across their hip bones. Besides, coolie pants would be nonregulation.

What about that, Holman thought.

The coolie was adjusting the boiler feed. He was shorter and lighter than Holman but built to the same plan, stocky and well padded with muscles that held their shape like a washboard down his stomach and worked together rounded and smoothly on his arms and across his chest. He did not look like a coolie. Coolies were scrawny and corded, ribs showing, and they had ugly purple calluses the size of cantaloupes on their humped shoulders. Squeeze merchants ashore were fat as Buddha. This coolie was what a Chinaman could look like when he had enough to eat and still had to work.

What the hell, Holman thought. That coolie's all right. Machinery only cared about what a man knew and what he could do with his hands, whether he was a coolie or an admiral, and that was the secret, very good thing about machinery. The coolie was an engineer; well then, he was not a coolie, he was another engineer like Jake Holman. Po-han turned and caught Holman's gaze and came over grinning.

"All thing plopah, Mastah?" he asked. He knew it was, and he was proud.

"Ding hao!" Holman made the double thumbs-up sign and grinned back. "You no moh speakee my name *Mastah,"* he said. "You speakee me *Jake . . . Holman."* He pronounced it very distinctly.

"Jeh-ki," Po-han said. "Ho-mang."

"Jehk."

"Jehk. Jehk."

Holman slid off the workbench. There was no more strain in the encounter. "I'm going up and turn in," he said, dropping the pidgin. "I'm glad to be shipmates with you, Po-han." He held out his hand.

Po-han was embarrassed, because shaking hands was not old custom in China, but he shook hands. Both men had hard, square hands and a powerful grip.

"Keep her steaming, Po-han," Holman said, and headed for the
ladder. He had seen the engine room and he could go to sleep now.

He did not go right to bed. He needed time to appreciate his new
bunk. It was against the port side forward, just aft of the door, and
it was half again as wide and much softer than the thin horsehair
mattress he was used to. The crew's compartment was big enough
for a hundred bunks, by navy standards, and there were only about
twenty in it, as far as he could judge by the dim blue night lights.
Holman was used to sleeping on narrow pipe-and-wire shelves stacked
four high on either side of pipe stanchions. You were practically
in a double bed with the guy across from you. Somebody's rump
sagged in your face and someone else's feet were next to your pillow.
The air was always thick with bad smells and strangled snoring. Bunk-
ing like that was supposed to work you out of any private and personal notions you had about yourself. When you learned to like living that way, you were a good bluejacket and Uncle Sam loved you.

He undressed and sat on his bunk. A huge upright locker at either
end made a little alcove of it. Above it a fresh breeze off the river
fluttered curtains in the two square windows. *Curtains!* The place
smelled airy and clean, of wax and soap and metal polish. Suddenly
he stretched out his legs and waved them and raised his arms and
waved them and no matter where he stretched and reached, he was
still in his own space. It was his body catching up, starting to believe
it, taking possession.

He sprawled luxuriously on the edge of sleep, believing and enjoying it. A sailor without his own ship was like a hermit crab without
a shell. It was good to have a shell again. This bunk was no better
than the one he had had on the commercial steamer up from Shanghai.
But a paid-for bunk was like a whore. Your own bunk on your own
ship was what a wife was probably like. You could really rest, in your
own bunk.

His mind moved to the missionary girl on the commercial steamer.
She was new in China, going to her first mission job. She did not
know the score and she did not know the rules. That first morning

in the lower Yangtze she had even thought he was part of the steamer crew. She had stopped where he was standing by the saloon deck rail.

"Are we really in a river?" she asked him.

"Yeah. It's a river," he said.

The starboard shore was a green horizon. The port shore was out of sight across choppy brown water. You couldn't see it as a river. You could just know it was there.

"It's so huge," she said. She was blonde, fresh and clean-looking in a sleeveless brown dress, but not very pretty. "I've just come to China," she said. "There's so much. So different." She looked down at the Chinese passengers crowding the main deck and back out across the water. "It's just so enormous," she repeated.

"I guess it gets smaller as you go up," he said. "I guess if you went far enough, you could straddle it and scoop it all up in a bucket."

That was a secret thought he always had about rivers. He had never told it to anyone before. She thought about it.

"I'm from Minnesota. I've seen where the Mississippi starts," she said. "It just rises up out of the land all around. You couldn't scoop it up in a bucket."

They talked for half an hour. She found out he was a navy sailor and a passenger like herself. She did not know it hurt a missionary girl's reputation to be friendly with a sailor. She told him her brother Charley had been a reserve lieutenant on the *Delaware* during the war. Holman didn't tell her he hated battleships and had very little use for lieutenants. Her name was Miss Eckert and she called him Mr. Holman. It was a strange, pleasant little talk.

"I've so much to learn," she said. "It's so confusing, so far."

It was indeed. Holman was confused also with the talk he heard at meals in the saloon. Things were set up in China so that sailors were never around nice people, and he had not heard such talk before. The other passengers were three businessmen and two buck missionaries and they wrangled about China. Holman knew his place and kept it and said nothing. Riots were going on in Shanghai because some students had been shot, and a naval landing force was ashore to back up the police. They wrangled about that.

"Chinese think we're demoralized!" the bulky old Englishman, Mr. Outscout, said. "Think so myself, by George! Gone soft, rotten, since the war!"

He had stiff gray hair that he tossed for emphasis. His main target was the oldest missionary, Miss Eckert's new boss, a tall, bearded man named Craddock. Craddock would stick out his beard for emphasis. He and Outscout were a good match.

"No, sir!" Craddock said once. "I say you shall not extend your unequal treaties yet further over this unhappy nation!"

"Our unequal treaties! *Ours,* I say!"

Outscout banged the table. The crystal chandelier tinkled. The businessmen ganged up on Craddock. They asked him if he owned title to his mission lands, what taxes and import duties he paid, how often he interfered in Chinese courts on behalf of converts and how often he had fled to a gunboat.

"Twice, to my shame," he said, glaring at them. "I will not flee again."

The saloon was paneled in dark wood and had a brown rug. White-coated Chinese stewards served neatly and silently. There were silver and white linen and wine glasses and they all had very good eating manners. Miss Eckert often asked questions. Both sides were trying to win her over. Her questions helped Holman to understand.

He learned that the missionaries wanted a lot more than just pulling the gunboats out of China. They wanted to turn customs and salt tax and postal system control back to the Chinese. They wanted all the palefaces to be under Chinese law and need Chinese permission to be in the country. It was complicated and it was all mixed up in Holman's mind with Miss Eckert asking questions.

Sailors did not know about any treaties. They thought navy ships operated in Chinese waters the same way they did on the high seas. The sailors knew the missionaries despised them and wanted to run them out of China. They knew that, all right. But they thought it was only because sailors were so sinful. You would never hear a good word for missionaries from any China sailor. The businessmen said it would be time enough to think about giving China equal treaties when China was able to form a stable and civilized government. It was Craddock's turn to thump the table.

"Your unequal treaties create a situation that compels their use! You know they are cancerously self-extending!" he said fiercely. "You know, and well you know, that China will remain helpless to put her house in order unless you first put away your enslaving treaties!"

"*Our* enslaving treaties! You'll *not* come that on me, sir!"

Outscout looked ready to reach across and throttle Craddock. Miss Eckert slipped away, looking distressed.

"Your kind came in with the treaties, forcibly as opium!" Outscout said. "Suspend them and we all go! Chaff in a typhoon!" He flailed his arm. "Your kind, too. Chinese hate and despise you, sir! Dare you know that?"

"I dare love them in return!" The beard stuck out like a rammer bow. "I dare trust God rather than guns! Dare you, sir? Dare you?"

"I dare no less than yourself. You know well enough you're not permitted to renounce your personal treaty rights." Outscout's voice turned scornful. "Cheap talk, sir, when you know you'll not have to make it good."

Respectable people really had control, Holman thought. Sailors could not get half that angry and nasty with each other without having to stand up and fist it out.

Near Chinkiang the river narrowed and low green hills humped along the south bank. A pagoda stood on a wooded point. The *Paul Jones* passed them making thirty knots, with signals fluttering, deck guns manned and boats swung out. She hailed, saying there was rioting in Chinkiang. The steamer people made a great fuss slamming and locking the steel gratings that shut the Chinese deck passengers away from topside. All male passengers were called to the pilot house. Holman went. The two missionaries were not there. Outscout seemed to have charge. He was digging in an arms chest.

"Ingram! Where d'ye keep your ammo?" he barked. The captain said someone was bringing it. Outscout thrust a rifle at Holman. "Pop down and do sentry-go on the cabin deck, lad," he ordered. "Keep the deck passengers in hand." Holman hefted the empty rifle doubtfully. "Just show yourself through the bars forward and aft," Outscout said. "The sight of your uniform and rifle is all they'll want to keep them in order."

"Aye aye, sir," Holman said.

The deck passengers did not look at Holman and his uniform and his empty rifle. They crowded the port rail to look at black smoke rising above trees as the steamer rounded the point. Holman felt very foolish. He did not even know how to work his empty British rifle. What am I doing here? he thought. Only three Chinese children stared solemnly up at him through the bars. They knew something was wrong. The littlest one was about to cry. Holman grinned and pointed his finger down at them.

"Bang, bang. You're dead," he told them.

They considered that seriously. Then the two older ones smiled. The smallest one laughed and pointed his finger at Holman and said, "Cah cah cah!" Holman felt better about things. He grinned more widely. Then he felt eyes on the back of his neck. Someone behind him was watching. He stiffened and turned, cheeks burning.

It was Miss Eckert. She was smiling, understanding and sharing the little play instead of mocking it. Holman really saw her then, for the first time, and after that he could always really see her. She had a fresh, soft, sweet look to her face, and a curving build. Her straw-colored hair was bobbed and shingled. Her forehead was smooth and wide and her clear blue eyes looked right at everybody. Her rather wide mouth always showed her feelings, drooping in sympathy when someone was hurt. Now she was smiling very tenderly. He tried to smile back at her.

They could not say much. Craddock came and insisted that she take shelter. But for the rest of the trip to Hankow it was different between them. She was more than just a pleasing appearance. She was always real and there. It was clear that Craddock did not like her to be with Holman and also clear that she was ignoring Craddock's advice. Holman knew Craddock was right, for the long run. He knew it was a good thing that he would never see Miss Eckert again, after they reached Hankow.

Holman began to think Craddock also had the right of it in the running argument at meals. At dinner on the last day he spoke up for the first time, in support of something Craddock said. It was embarrassing. There was a pause. Even Craddock did not look pleased. Then Mr. Johnson, the gaunt American with glasses, said something vague. The talk went on. Johnson began telling Miss Eckert about the gunboats.

"Until we get our new gunboats built, you will have to depend largely on Mr. Outscout's flag for your protection," he told Miss Eckert. "American gunboats in Central China now are a painful local joke."

He talked about the old Spanish relics, how they broke down and lacked power to get up the rapids.

"The most ludicrous one of all is named the *San Pablo*," he said. "Mercifully, the admiral keeps it hidden away down in Hunan."

Miss Eckert knew he was needling Holman. She joined Holman on deck after dinner. It was dark already. They would reach Hankow in a few hours.

"China Light is hidden away down in Hunan, too," she said. That was the name of her mission, where she was going to teach English. She was trying to make up for what Johnson had said. "It doesn't matter what the ships are like," she went on. "They're all manned by brave American boys. That's what really counts."

Somehow it angered Holman more than anything Johnson had said. She was just too dumb about some things.

"China sailors ain't exactly clean-cut American boys," he told her. "The clean-cut boys don't stay in China."

He tried to explain. Sailors came to China on a thirty-month tour of duty. If they liked it, if they fitted the pattern of things, they could extend and stay on and in time retire and die of old age in China, if they wanted to. If not, they went back to the States. She saw where he was going with it and tried to change the subject. It hurt her to hear him downgrade himself, even in that roundabout way. But he had to do it. For her sake. She had to learn about the pattern of things and how it did a missionary girl no good at all to be associated with a China sailor.

Holman shifted comfortably in his new bunk and sighed. He was almost asleep.

So a few hours ago he had hurried ashore from the commercial steamer with his seabag on his shoulder and without saying any good-byes. He would never see her again. And if by some wild chance he did, she would have had time to learn the rules. It would be almost the same as not seeing her.

2

He woke to reveille on a bugle. They were all putting on the white shorts, so he put on undress whites. The head and washroom opened off the rear of the bunkroom and also out onto the fantail. They were clean, airy places with plenty of room and of course no fresh-water rationing. When Holman came back a Chinese messcook was putting gray enamel pitchers of hot coffee on the mess tables and another Chinese was making up Holman's bunk. He poured himself a cup of coffee at the mess table nearest his bunk.

"You'll sit here, across from me, old Pitocki's place," a red-bearded man said. A white lanyard came from under his beard to a bosun's pipe in his shirt pocket.

"Thanks," Holman said.

He sat down. In a chair. A solid wooden chair. The table was solid wood, with a bare, scrubbed top. Only three men to a side. Another table like it stood on the starboard side and there was a larger table aft, where the bunks were two high. The after table was for nonrated men, Holman thought, and even they had chairs. He saw the boatswain's mate watching him and grinned.

"I'm just taking it all in," he said. "It's all right."

"She's a home, all right."

That was the best thing a man could say for a ship, and it was not said of many. The worst thing you could say was "She's a madhouse." Holman was not ready to say anything yet. He felt the chair with his body. It was solid, separate, a chair. A regulation navy mess had rickety ten-man folding tables and narrow folding benches that sagged so that all the rumps kept sliding together and often the benches collapsed. Holman's place was at the head of this table and he could lean back and touch his bunk and locker and just outside the door and around the corner was the engine-room hatch. He knew he was going to like being all gathered together like that. On the other ships he had always been scattered around. The compartment was clean and attractive with white enamel paint and green curtains and varnished wood and bright brass fittings. The deck was polished red linoleum. Forward of the mess tables the sides slanted in to leave a trapezoidal open space set off by two white stanchions. The open space held a wooden barber chair and some gear lockers. It was a fine place.

The other men on his mess, his new messmates, came up and poured coffee and sat down. One was Burgoyne.

"Morning, Jake," he said. "What you think of the old *Sand Pebble* by now?"

"I'm still taking it in," Holman said. "They made up my bunk for me. Do they always do that?"

"Every blessed morning." Burgoyne grinned.

"They pick up your dirty clothes and wash and iron 'em and stow 'em clean back in your locker," the red-bearded one said. The others called him Farren.

"They mend your clothes," the round-faced machinist's mate said. "When something wears out, they survey it and make you a new one. You always got a locker full of clean, new clothes." His name was Wilsey.

They all began telling Holman things. Just about everything a sailor had to do for himself on other ships was done for him on this one. They all watched Holman, wanting to see surprise and pleasure in his face, the same delight they had felt when they first came aboard this ship. Holman felt it, but he would not show it. He did not like being pushed to feel, or pretend to feel, anything, and he thought there must be a hidden catch in all of this.

"It's a pretty good deal," he said. "How in hell do you pay for all that service?"

Farren shrugged. "They squeeze. They squeeze the bejesus out of everything," he said. "And they collect from us on payday."

"It ain't never very much," the craggy, white-haired electrician said.

"We call it our club dues," Restorff said.

He was a stubby, brown, blunt-faced gunner's mate, and he sat on Holman's right. Farren sat across from Holman. On other ships the engineers always lived and messed separately. It was going to be strange eating with topside sailors. They had a Chinese messcook named Wong to wait tables in the crew's mess, Farren said. Another one named Lemon took care of the CPO mess. The ship's cook and master of the galley was named Big Chew, and he was the best cook in China. All the sailors nodded agreement to that. Wong was bringing in rations on separate plates to the other tables. Burgoyne stopped him and asked for bacon and hot cakes.

"Jake, we run a short-order breakfast on here," he said. "Wong'll fetch you anything you want."

"Ham, bacon, hot cakes and eggs," Farren said. "Any combination."

"And all you want," Harris, the electrician, said. He clicked his teeth. They were big and white and looked false.

"I love fried eggs," Holman said.

On Fleet ships you always got eggs scrambled and padded with cornstarch, except for the hard-boiled eggs that went with corned beef hash. Only now and then on a Sunday you might get a couple of cold, burnt, leathery fried eggs, and you never got more than two. When Wong brought Holman's order, on a platter because a plate wouldn't hold it, Holman looked fondly at the six hot cakes and the dozen fried eggs. The eggs were well cooked but not burnt and all the yolks stood up unbroken. He let his pleasure show at last, in his face and voice.

"By God, she *is* a home!" he said.

"She ain't much to look at, but she's a home," Restorff agreed. They were all grinning at Holman, sharing his feeling.

"Looks like you got competition, Harris," Wilsey said. "Harris is the chow hound on this mess," he told Holman. "He'll try to ruin your appetite with filthy talk at dinnertime, so there'll be more for him."

"He used to drive old Pitocki away from the table sometimes," Farren said. "Harris is the foulest-mouthed bastard alive."

"Prong you and all your relations and all your ancestors back to George Washington," Harris told Farren amiably, between clicking bites of ham.

"You see?" Farren said. "That's the only way Harris knows how to say good morning." He grinned through his beard.

"I got a cast-iron gut," Holman said. He was dabbling hot cake in egg yolk and eating it. "I'm going to like this ship."

"She ain't much on liberty, but she's sure enough a home and a feeder," Burgoyne said.

Outside the bugle blew officers' call and then assembly and they all trooped aft to stand quarters for muster. The sun was bright on the brown river and many brown junks and sampans were out there. The *San Pablo* deck coolies were working in undress whites without insignia, and Holman felt he looked more like the coolies than like the real sailors in their shorts. He would have to have some shorts made for himself.

"We fall in here, to starboard," Burgoyne said.

The whole crew made only one double rank across the fantail, with the needle nose of a one-pounder gun projecting over their heads from the boat deck rail above them. At their backs, doors led into the head and washroom and a central hatch led down to the Chinese quarters in the hull. A wooden grating two feet above the deck filled the semicircular stern and covered the rudder quadrant. The captain, a short, dark, stern-looking lieutenant, stood on the grating against the varnished wheel with the bare flagstaff angling up behind it. A bigger, awkward-looking ensign stood on deck with the backs of his legs against the grating and out in front of him three chiefs faced the sailors.

"Fall in, sailors!" each chief said separately to his gang. "Atten-*shun!* Answer up to muster!"

The sailors wore black shoes with white socks rolled to their shoe tops. The chiefs and officers had white shoes and ribbed white socks that came up to their knees. That, and their regulation uniform caps, was their only difference from the white-hatted sailors. Lynch, the chief machinist's mate, was a man who looked big more with whisky bloat than with muscle, and his face had a flabby, sagging look. He was being very military.

"Burgoyne!"

"Here, sir!"

"Holman!"

"Here . . . sir."

You were not supposed to have to say "sir" to a chief after boot camp. Holman hated to say it to anyone. It was his private trouble to hate everything like this muster and not be able to explain why even to himself. But he could stand it for a while, and then he would have his way of getting out of it. On the stone-faced river bank to his left Holman saw from the corner of his eye the mob of watching coolies, all brown skin and blue rags and gaping faces under broad bamboo hats or head rags. The Chinese were always gaping at the ocean devils. Ordinarily, Holman could ignore them as completely as other sailors did.

"Front and center!" the ensign barked. When the three chiefs heel-clicked to attention in line before him he snapped, "Report!" and each chief saluted and reported all hands in his department present or accounted for. The ensign returned each salute and said, "Very well!" and then about-faced and saluted and told the captain what the captain could not help already knowing.

"Very well!" the captain said, saluting down at the ensign.

The ensign about-faced. "Posts!" he snapped, returning the chiefs' triple salute, and the chiefs ran off their clean, brisk, square-cornered little dance in reverse and all was as before.

Maybe that's it, Holman thought. From the first "Here, sir!" they had all been telling each other what everybody already knew, and it had to be very serious and set and precise, as if it meant something important, but it did not mean anything at all. It was like extra rocker arms and idler gears in a machine, to click and spin and bob and make a show, and do nothing except soak up power that should go to the machine's real work. Well, at least it's a show for them coolies, Holman thought. Thank Christ it's over.

It was not over. A quartermaster came on from port, with a seaman and a Chinese trailing him. The seaman held the colors in their triangular fold, breast high in two hands, and the Chinese had a shiny bugle under his arm. The quartermaster stepped up on the grating and saluted the captain.

"The clock reads eight o'clock, sir," he said.

"Make it so," the captain said.

Almost instantly eight bells began striking from the bridge and the Chinese bugler snapped his bugle to his lips. On the last bell, he blew attention.

"Atten-*shun!*" all the chiefs barked.

Chiefs and officers about-faced and stood at salute. The bugler blew colors and the quartermaster hoisted the colors quickly to the peak of the staff, where the river breeze caught them and streamed them rippling toward the watching coolies on the bank. The quartermaster stood at salute until the bugler blew *carry on*. Then he fell back into ranks.

This was battleship stuff. The rule was that the smaller and more isolated the ship, the less you had of military crap, and this ship should have least of all. But here they were pulling battleship stuff.

"Take stations for physical drill," the ensign ordered.

Holman set his jaw grimly. They were not going to leave out anything. He hated physical drill. The men opened out and spaced off with extended arms. Two of the chiefs and the ensign stood to one side and the big chief boatswain's mate stepped up on the grating to lead the drill. He had a tanned, open face and a powerful voice and yellow hair thick on his arms and crowding out the open neck of his shirt. His name was Franks.

"Jumping jack!" he said.

They all jumped and clapped their hands together above their heads twenty times. Then he gave them the windmill and touch-toes and twist-belly, each one twenty times, slashing with his hairy arm as he counted cadence in a great voice, starting with a roar and trailing off, "ONE . . . *two* . . . three . . . four," over and over. The captain stood quietly watching it, and he made a picture against the big wheel with the flag streaming above him. Franks gave them push-ups on a two-count and they all brought their faces right down to the deck, still damp from scrubbing. They finished with stationary double time. Franks started it as mark time, and he marked time himself, not counting, and all the sailors kept pace with him. Franks raised it slowly through quick step to double and to double-quick, they all following the rhythm of his feet, then faster still, as fast as they could run in place, knees pumping, elbows jogging, teeth bared, Holman with a growing ache in his side, no voices but the sob of breath and the slap of many feet building and building a stupid thundering stampede going nowhere faster and faster until Jake Holman could not stand it any longer and Franks roared, "Ship's compan-EEEE . . . *halt!*"

The ensign came forward. "Resume ranks!"

They fell in, red-faced, puffing, tucking in shirt tails and wiping sweat. The coolies on the bank probably figured it was some kind of joss pidgin, Holman thought. Chinese believed all ocean devils were crazy, and stuff like this gave them a right to think that.

"Fall out!" Lynch said.

Franks sounded his bosun's pipe. "Now d'ye hear there, fore and aft, all hands turn to!" he bellowed. "Commence ship's work!"

It made no difference that all hands were right there in front of him and he could have spoken in an ordinary voice.

They broke ranks and headed forward. Lynch held Holman for a handshake and a short talk. He did not ask the usual things about past experience with machinery and so on. He only said welcome aboard and we really been needing a man to take old Pitocki's place and you got yourself a real pair of man's shoes to fill on this ship, Holman. Holman was still burning inside from the drill.

"How come good old Pitocki ever left this ship?" he asked.

"He died last winter in Changsha. Typhus, they said." Lynch's manner turned cold. "Pitocki had twelve straight years aboard this ship. He could've retired, and he wouldn't. He wouldn't even go up for chief."

"Oh. I'm sorry," Holman said. He was not really sorry.

"Well, take today to get settled in," Lynch said. "Tomorrow we'll look around the engine room and get you squared away down there."

A fat little Chinese in a black skull cap and gray gown popped out of the hatch behind them. "Ho, you, Ho-mang," he said. "Must makee sew sew pidgin."

"This is Sew Sew," Lynch said. "He wants to take a template off you, for your uniforms. You need shorts."

"A template?" Holman stared.

Lynch laughed. "How we do it on here. Well, take it easy."

He went forward. Sew Sew had a narrow board with a set of strings dangling from it. It had a big Chinese character in red at one end and smaller ones in black above each cord peg.

"This befoh time belong P'tocki," Sew Sew said. He held it at arm's length and looked from the dangling strings to Holman and back again. "My tinkee you litee bit all same P'tocki," he said.

Each cord was a body part measurement. One by one, Sew Sew tried Pitocki's cords on Jake Holman's body and he snipped pieces off the too-long ones, and when they were too short he made new ones. It felt weird to Holman. He was bigger than Pitocki around biceps and chest, but Pitocki was longer in arm and leg and bigger around the belly. It built up a weird feeling of standing inside Pitocki's ghost, with here one of them sticking out and there the other. Sew Sew muttered each time he had to change a cord. To him, all sailors were lumpy, forky objects to be covered smoothly with cloth and it would be very nice if they were all exactly the same size and shape. Sew Sew finished his template and held it up and gazed at it and he looked pleased. He said he would make six suits of shorts and they would be in Holman's locker the next morning.

"Make four suits of dungarees, too," Holman said.

Sew Sew looked doubtful. *"Sampabble* any man no wanchee too much dunglee," he said.

"My wanchee foh piecee dunglee," Holman said firmly.

When he made himself the place he wanted on this ship, he was practically going to live in dungarees.

In the captain's day cabin Lt. Collins and Ensign Bordelles sat at the round, green baize-covered table. They had cups of coffee on the table and the various parts of Holman's service record lay spread out before them.

"Tom, I doubt the man," Lt. Collins said. "I never saw this pattern before in a service record." He tapped a sheet with a pencil. "Eight ships in eight years. Only bad apples get bounced around like that."

"Bad apples don't get four-oh marks and letters of commendation," Bordelles said.

"He's been commended for difficult emergency repair jobs. No doubt he's a fine engineer. But why the low marks in leadership?"

"And only in leadership."

"Precisely!" Lt. Collins took a sip of coffee. "Not in conduct. He has four-oh conduct. If he had a string of mast reports and court-martials, I'd call him a good man forthwith."

Bordelles shook his head and raised his cup to drink.

"Tom, these service records don't always give a complete picture of a man. Men like Pitocki was, yes. This man Holman . . . I wonder." Lt. Collins' thin, dark face was thoughtful and he shuffled the papers before him restlessly. "A ship's company is like an orchestra. A big ship can absorb a few sour notes and put on the kind of pressure that can change them," he said. *"San Pablo* is just not that big. I saw you watching Holman at quarters. What's your subjective impression of him?"

"Hard. A bruiser. Good man in a football line," Bordelles said. "I couldn't tell anything from his face."

"Hides his feelings. I thought I saw a trace of sullenness," Lt. Collins said. "Or it might have been quiet contempt or secret triumph. It was just enough to make me uneasy, even before I looked at his record."

"We've only a few days. If we start the summer cruise with him, we're stuck for a year."

"See what the chiefs think of him, in the next few days. I'll have a talk with Holman myself."

"Yes, sir." Bordelles gulped the last of his coffee and stood up. "It's almost time for battle drills, sir. What shall we run today?"

"Repel boarders. Starboard," Lt. Collins said.

Sew Sew ducked back down the hatch and Holman started forward. A bugle blasted and he heard Chief Franks' voice from the boat deck, "All hands! Repel boarders, starboard! Repel boarders, starboard!" Sailors exploded out of the compartment and all over the ship feet thudded as they ran to their stations. Holman tried to get into the engine room to get out of the way and he met Burgoyne coming out, dragging a steam hose. Then Lynch grabbed him.

"Stand by here, Holman. You're in the waist party."

They stood by on the triangular quarterdeck. The arms locker behind the ladder to the boat deck stood open. Lynch snatched a riot gun, handed it to Holman, and motioned to him to join the men kneeling along the bulwark. The gate in it was closed and the short gangplank pulled inboard. Holman knelt and Burgoyne knelt beside him and balanced the steam hose nozzle on the steel bulwark. It was a valve and a short piece of pipe wrapped in gunny sacking.

"Waist party ma-a-anned and ready!" Lynch yelled. He had a husky voice. The bow and stern parties reported manned and ready.

Holman glanced around. A big flat-faced sailor was holding the bight of the steam hose waist high with heavy gloves. Lynch had a pistol in his left hand and a shiny cutlass in his right. He frowned and motioned with his cutlass for Holman to face outboard. Holman did, and noticed that the other men's faces were keen and tense and their eyes were scanning back and forth. In addition to Burgoyne there were the pleasant-faced kid, Wilsey, with a riot gun, and the old electrician, Harris, scowling down the barrel of an automatic rifle, his coarse white hair bristling. Holman sighted along his riot gun and felt stupid. A riot gun was a kind of sawed-off shotgun that fired buckshot. Holman had never fired one.

The same crowd of brown, ragged, cone-hatted coolies was up on the bank watching, all along the brick wall where Holman had stood, and twenty or more were down on the pontoon gazing stupidly into gun muzzles almost near enough to nudge them. Hard to figure what they made of it all, Holman thought. Probably not much. Ensign Bordelles came down the ladder to the quarterdeck. Lynch said, "Manned and ready, sir." Holman felt the ensign's eyes on his back.

"One of your riot guns has no reserve ammunition," he said.

"He's a new man, sir, not instructed yet."

"Very well. Why haven't you steam to the hose nozzle?"

"Condensation would start leaks in the hose, sir," Lynch said. "I can't drain it and warm it up on account of the slopeheads on the pontoon."

"This is not Long Beach and it is not even Hankow," Bordelles said sharply. "When *San Pablo* holds a drill it is always in Hunan Province and it is always in deadly earnest. You know that, Chief. Now bear a hand and get steam on that hose!"

"Aye aye, sir! Stawski! Cut in the root steam."

"Chien! Steam on the deck valve!" a voice yelled.

"Belay that! This is a battle drill, Stawski. *You* cut in that steam!" Lynch said angrily. "Crack it in slow. Frenchy, aim the nozzle down the side." Lynch came to the bulwark and waved his cutlass. "*Cheelah!* Stand clear, you slopeheaded bastards!" he yelled at the coolies on the pontoon.

They stared stupidly and did not move. Stawski cut the steam in fast. The steam came pushing a plug of hot water ahead of it and the hose jumped like a snake and almost got away from Burgoyne. Scalding water sprayed out with a spluttering roar over the coolies and they pulled back with wild yells of fear and pain. Then steam came in a roaring, billowing cloud that hid the scrambling coolies.

"Maskee. Throttle off, Frenchy," Lynch said.

Someone laughed on the boat deck. Bordelles ran up the ladder and snapped, "Silence during drills!" The steam cleared off and the last of the scalded coolies were still running up to the bank. The coolies up there were laughing and pointing fingers. They thought it was a good joke on the scalded coolies. The steam hose humped across the pulled-in gangplank, leaking badly even after being drained. It was made of interlocking brass strips wound in a spiral, with asbestos packing between the turns, and it was supposed to be self-tightening under pressure. But steam feathered all along it and it made the whole quarterdeck hot and wet and steamy.

When they secured, Lynch told Holman that he would be second in command of the waist party. He gave Holman a key to the arms locker, the same key Pitocki had carried for twelve years. Holman was going to have to co-sign all the Title B cards with Lynch, for the stuff in the locker. There was a lot of stuff, including a box of grenades and a dozen cutlasses. It was not good news to Holman.

"Chief, do you have quarters and battle drills like this every day on here?" he asked.

"All but weekends. Some days we skip the battle drills."

Holman did not let his dismay show on his face.

It was not until after dinner that Holman could get into dungarees and into the engine room. He sniffed in the smell, and his heart beat faster. Seven or eight half-naked coolies were scrubbing and shining. One was Po-han, and Holman winked at him. He started at once to learn the plant. The main plant was the two boilers, the engine, the main condenser, the main circulating, air and feed pumps, and all the piping that served them. The auxiliary plant was the dynamos and the remaining pumps and heat exchangers and piping. The piping was hardest to learn, and almost all navy engineers figured they knew it when they knew all the key valve combinations for routine operating. On any ship the piping had hundreds of valves and fittings and it branched and snaked behind things and through bulkheads and in and out of the bilges until a man's eyes became lost and dizzy trying to trace and remember. On an old ship there would always be hidden cross connections and plugs and blanks and drain valves, put in for some forgotten purpose by men long since dead or transferred, and no one would even know they were there. No one but Jake Holman. It was part of his secret to take all of the piping, clear and sharp in detail, inside his head.

He started with the steam at the boiler shells and traced it through every branching to every outlet and memorized the position of every valve. Then he went to the log desk and sketched the system from memory and checked his sketch against the actual piping, and he had it, all right. He took up the exhaust system. The tracing took him all around the engine room and he could feel the coolies watching him and not liking it and the boss coolie liking it least of all. The boss coolie wore a black jacket with cloth buttons to show that he did not work. He was old, with a bony, cruel face and a few long hairs on his chin. Holman knew that feeling from his other ships, although it was strange to feel it from Chinese. There was always a clique of old hands in an engine room, and they always wanted a new man to learn from them as much as they wanted him to know and wait his time for admission to the clique. It always disturbed them to see Jake Holman learning by himself. They were afraid he would learn too much and have power over them, and they were right. It was rough on them. They couldn't try to learn more themselves, because they had spent too many years pretending they already knew it all. They couldn't openly stop Holman from learning, because learning the plant was supposed to be good. So they always tried by the weight of their silent disapproval to force Jake Holman to stay as fumbling and ignorant as they were, and nothing in the world could spur Jake Holman on more than that silent disapproval. The machinery was always on Jake Holman's side, because machinery was never taken in by pretense and ignorance.

Holman could not really believe he was going to be in a struggle with the coolies. They were just coolies and even Stawski, the fireman, could give them orders. Holman finished the feed system and he was ready to start tracing lines in the bilges and he needed help. Po-han and another coolie were scrubbing the white round of the auxiliary condenser.

"You, Po-han. You, Joe," Holman said, pointing at them. "My looksee bilge side. Take up floh plate. You sabby?"

"My sabby. Catch fye sclapah," Po-han said.

He dropped his rag in the bucket and went around the engine to the workbench. The other coolie just stared at Holman. The boss coolie came up. He was angry.

"Bilge pidgin no can do," he said. "Lynch speakee me washee poht side."

"My talkee Lynch by-m-by," Holman said.

"No can do bilge pidgin!"

The old man's voice rose high and cracked and he had spittle on his lips. The coolies had all downed rags to watch, and now face was involved. Holman had to save both their faces. He tapped his chest.

"My do bilge pidgin. Looksee pipe, larn pidgin all pipe, you sabby?" he said mildly, wanting all of them to hear. "Must have one man floh plate pidgin."

"One piecee man can do," the boss coolie said grudgingly. "Two piecee man, no can do."

He was willing to save face, but he was still angry. Holman shrugged. Po-han came with a file scraper and Holman had him lift a floorplate beside the main air pump. He found it dark and hard to get around in the bilges. The main engine foundation ran along the keel like a wall and heavy I-girders ran curving down and across from the bilge stringer to the engine foundation. Fore-and-aft brace and tie plates between the girders made a honeycomb of what were called bilge pockets. Along the side were the auxiliary machinery foundations and the water ends of pumps. Holman had to squirm across the tops of the girders, between the light angle-iron framing that supported the floorplates.

He grunted and squirmed along. It was hot, hard and dirty work, and just because of that, the bilge piping was always the least known. Most of the piping ran on top of the girders, but some went lower, through the limber holes of the girders, and Holman looked at every inch of it and ran his hands along the sides that he could not see. He did not want to miss any hidden fitting or cross connection. Even if it was only an ear left on a gasket, he wanted to know about it.

Po-han was a good helper. Whenever Holman tapped on the underside of a floorplate, Po-han was right there to lift it and let light flood in. The bilges were very dry and clean, for bilges, and they smelled cleanly of paint and oil. Everything was painted with red lead except the bottom plating, which was coated with black bitumastic. In places the plating bulged inward and even some of the girders looked slightly askew. There was no dirt or rust. But red lead in bilges never gets quite dry and down beside the engine oil had rotted the bitumastic, and when Holman came out to make his first sketch he was dripping sweat and smudged from head to foot with red and black.

Po-han took sharp interest in the sketch. He pointed to the crosses and said, "Wowel? B'long wowel?" until Holman understood he meant "valve" and nodded.

Holman worked across back of the engine and along both sides and finally across the front. He was getting very tired, and part of it was the mental concentration of so much learning. The pockets across the front were the worst of all, with heat from the steaming boiler softening the bitumastic and a tangle of hot drain lines to dodge, but quite a bit of light came down the backs of the boilers and there was no need to lift floorplates. He had just traced a feed suction line over to a hydrokineter when Chinese yelling broke out above him and someone cried, "Jehk! Jehk!" and a slug of hot water hit him on the back of his legs. He scrambled into another bilge pocket just in time. Steam roared and blasted where he had been and came through the limber hole beside him very hot and choking.

"Turn off that steam! You sons of bitches, turn off that steam!" Holman yelled.

It stopped. Holman was shaken and angry. He crawled back to where a floorplate was up and came out. Someone had blown down the boiler water glass, but no one was near it now. The coolies were all going up the starboard ladder.

"Stop! Which one of you bastards blew that glass?" Holman

yelled through the engine at them.

They went on up. Holman ran around the engine and got control of himself at the foot of the ladder and stood there fuming. Po-han, his face a blank, stood over by the workbench. He would not meet Holman's eyes. Holman calmed himself down. He knew that boss coolie had blown the glass. Po-han had objected and had tried to warn Holman, but Po-han probably had good reasons for being afraid of the boss coolie. Po-han was still all right.

"Holman! What the hell happened to you?"

Wilsey was coming down the ladder, clean in white shorts.

"Been in the bilges," Holman said. "That Goddamned bone-faced boss coolie blew the glass right on top of me!"

"Old Chien? Well, we always blow the glass when the watch changes." Wilsey stopped at the foot of the ladder. "None of us ever goes in the bilges," he said. "Chien probably didn't know you was there."

"He knew. He knew, all right. Then they all hauled ass."

"They always knock off at four o'clock, and Chien always blows the glass then," Wilsey said soothingly. "Chien's a good old guy. If you treat him right, he's always respectful and does what you tell him." He edged past Holman and went to the log desk. "We couldn't get along without old Chien," he said.

"By God, I can get along without him!"

Wilsey turned. His round, pleasant face looked annoyed. "Just what in hell were you doing in the bilges in the first place?"

"Tracing lines."

"I'd've been glad to show you where the valves are. On this ship, only coolies go bilge crawling." He looked Holman up and down and frowned. "We all lose face when a white man gets as filthy and dirty as you are right now. If you want Chien to respect you, just stay out of the bilges."

"I don't give a shit about your face," Holman said. "Chien don't have to respect me, but he better God damned well not cross my bow again. I just want to learn this plant, and nothing's going to stop me!"

Wilsey shrugged and turned his back and began writing up the log. Holman scowled at him a moment, then shrugged too and went back into the bilges. He did not have much more to go. When he finished and came out, Wilsey was gone.

"Good job. Make finish," Holman told Po-han. "Come on. We knock off now. Clean up." He made hand-washing motions.

"Hab got watch," Po-han said.

That meant he would have to stay down there until eight o'clock. Holman stayed and talked for a few minutes to let Po-han know by his manner that he did not blame him for the steam blast. Then he headed for the washroom. He was pig-dirty and bone-tired, but he knew the piping.

Taking clean clothing from his big, new locker and walking through the clean, spacious compartment cooled Holman's temper. So did the washroom. It was all enamel and shiny white tile, with four spigots along the trough and a shelf and mirrors above it. The two showers were inboard and they had steam connections of eighth-inch tubing and a cock, so you could set the water as hot as you liked. The windows and the door to the fantail were open and a cooling breeze blew through.

As he showered, Holman thought about the washrooms in Fleet ships. They were hot and crowded. You got a ration of one bucket of water to shave, brush your teeth, wash your clothes and take a bath. You bathed squatting on a tile deck with other naked men around you so thick that the saying was you had to scrub three strange asses before you came to your own. If you wanted a bath too often, they sneered at you for being too lazy to scratch.

He was shaving when the little man came in and undressed, dumping his clothes on the bench. Holman had met him that morning, but he could not remember the man's name. On a new ship it always took Holman a long time to connect up names and faces, especially if they were not engineers.

"Hi, Holman." the little man said. "Sunburned already?"

"Sunburned?"

"Backs of your legs all red."

"Oh. I got hit in the ass with a steam blast."

"Watch it when you first put on shorts. New guys always get sunburned."

"I'll watch it." Holman kept on shaving.

The little man started the shower splashing and got under it. In the mirror, Holman could see the man eying him. He had bright red hair and pinched-in, elfish features under a bulging forehead. He was a wiry, fair-skinned little man.

"Holman!"

The little man's voice was a whipcrack. Holman turned around, surprised.

"What's my rate?"

"Storekeeper," Holman guessed.

"Yeoman. Ship's writer, to you. Now what's my name?"

"I don't know." Holman almost said he didn't give a damn, but the little man intrigued him. "I heard too many names today," he said.

"I'm the Red Dog. Red Dog Shanahan. Red Dog Bite-'em-on-the-ass Shanahan, and nobody's ever supposed to forget my name. I'm a dangerous and desperate man."

Holman grinned. "I'll remember it now," he said. He turned back to shaving.

"Nobody ever shaves themselves on this ship," Red Dog said. "You're breaking Clip Clip's rice bowl."

Clip Clip was the Chinese barber. "Let him charge me double for haircuts," Holman said. "I like to shave myself."

"We don't even sell razor blades and shaving gear in the canteen."

"You got a canteen on here?"

"Yeah. It opens whenever somebody can get Duckbutt Randall off his ass."

Holman finished shaving and ran his fingertips over his face and started to leave. Behind him the little man snapped, "What's my name?"

"Red Dog Bite-'em-on-the-ass Shanahan," Holman said.

"Arf! Arf! Good man, Holman!"

Holman walked back to his locker grinning.

After supper he went below again, in clean dungarees, to check some of his sketches. Po-han followed him and he would point to one of Holman's sketched crosses and then to a particular valve and ask, "Same? B'long same?" Po-han was always wrong, but he knew that there was something very wonderful about those marks on paper, if he could only grasp the secret. He worked his lips and screwed up his features and he looked about to cry. Holman could read that expression and he had often known in himself the painful, tantalizing feeling behind it. Something in Holman answered to the young bilge coolie.

He tried to explain, but the pidgin English they shared was not enough. Po-han could not get the idea of breaking down the great mass of piping into separate systems. He could not say what was moving in what direction through any of the pipes that Holman pointed out. He did not even have the idea of stuff moving through pipes. All of Holman's doubts came back. How could these bilge coolies ever tend machinery?

"Come over here," he told Po-han.

Po-han followed him over to the feed pumps. Holman choked the throttle on the duty pump and dropped the pressure fifty pounds.

"You fix," he told Po-han.

Po-han eased open the steam inlet and restored the pressure. The hot well stood just aft of the pumps. Holman knelt and opened the rundown valve. Po-han watched the water level drop in the gauge glass with his Chinese eyes as wide and round as he could get them. Just as the water went out of sight, Holman closed the rundown valve.

"You fix," he said.

Po-han practically flew to the make-up feed pump and set it clacking. He watched tensely until the water level built up again and then secured the pump. Holman tried him on several other operations and questioned him on them all. Po-han knew what to do, but he did not know what it was that he did. He knew in a vague way that steam and water moved through pumps and valves, but when he twisted a valve he did not realize that he was opening or closing it. To Po-han, all that he did was isolated little magics that moved a pressure gauge pointer or a water level back to the right place. What he had glimpsed in Holman's sketches, what his eager, wistful eyes were reaching out for, was the big magic that would make a living whole out of all the little magics. Well, some navy engineers he had known were not much better off than Po-han, Holman thought. He decided to try to show Po-han the steam cycle. He started at the boiler.

"Inside b'long steam. Live steam," he said, thumping the boiler shell. "Strong steam."

Po-han nodded. They traced the steam from the boiler shell to the feed pump throttle, and Po-han could not understand the difference between live steam going in and exhaust steam coming out. He just did not have the basic words and saying "exhaust" to him did not give him the idea behind the word. It was no good showing him pressure gauges. Po-han thought fifteen pounds on the exhaust gauge was "moh plashah" than one hundred thirty pounds on the steam gauge, because the exhaust gauge and its numerals were physically the larger. He could not read the numerals and he did not know the meaning of "pressure."

"Jesus. I don't know how to tell you, Po-han," Holman said.

Disappointment began dulling the eager pain on Po-han's face.

"We'll try a different way," Holman said.

This time Holman acted it out. He was live steam, coming along the line snorting and bulging his muscles, and the live steam did work in the feed pump, Holman reaching in to the crosshead with both arms, grunting heavily, pretending to lift the piston rod up and down as it stroked, and then the steam came out the exhaust valve wheezing, drooping, muscles slack, staggered over to the condenser and went to sleep, Holman's folded hands beside his head.

Po-han went through the same act. His eyes never left Holman's face. He understood that the steam got tired in the pump, but he thought it died in the condenser.

"Maskee. This side steam makee dead," Holman said, slapping the condenser shell. He knelt and bled water from a cock on the air pump discharge. "Before steam, just now water," he told Po-han. "Water belong dead steam."

"Stim dead! Stim dead!"

Po-han knelt with the water flowing over his fingers and his eyes sparkled. He knew fire turned water to steam in the boiler, but apparently he had never realized that a flow of river water through the condenser turned steam back into water. The thought excited him. Holman became water and made undulating motions along the condensate discharge line to the hot well. Po-han followed, undulating too. At the hot well he pointed to the water in the gauge glass.

"Stim dead!"

Holman nodded and grinned. He undulated from the hot well along the feed suction line into the water end of the feed pump. Po-han followed. Holman came out of the feed pump still undulating silently, but stiffly, fists clenched and muscles bulging to indicate increase in pressure. Po-han followed suit, but he looked puzzled. He did not understand pressure. Holman undulated stiffly through the feed heater and began making a sizzling noise.

"This side makee hot," he told Po-han.

He had Po-han feel the temperature difference between inlet and outlet. Po-han understood. Holman sizzled and undulated along the feed line to the feed check on the boiler shell, pushed open an imaginary trap door, clacked and went into the boiler. Po-han clacked and went in too.

His face was like a searchlight. He looked at Holman and tapped the bottom of the boiler gauge glass. "Stim dead!" Then he tapped the steam space above the water in the glass. "Stim live! Stim live!" It was wonderful to see his face. He was just realizing in his own fashion the life-and-death cycle of the steam, endlessly repeated, and how it tied together pumps, piping and heat exchangers into the big magic. He looked like Columbus discovering America.

Suddenly, his Chinese face alive with joy, he began acting out the steam cycle again, as Holman had done it. Holman followed, grinning. When Po-han came back as water to the feed pump, his face shadowed and he stopped.

"This side . . . how fashion . . ."

He didn't know how to ask and Holman didn't know how to tell him.

"Pressure," Holman said. "Makee pressure."

"Plashah." It was just a noise in the air to Po-han.

"Push. Workee," Holman said. "Inside boiler live steam have got too much pressure. Suppose water wanchee go inside boiler, no have got pressure, no can open door."

He imitated the clack of the feed-check valve. Po-han was trying very hard, almost crying, but he couldn't get it. Holman dropped the feed pressure by fifty pounds and tapped the gauge.

"You belong water. Just now no have got pressure," he told Po-han.

He motioned Po-han to come along the feed line and Po-han did, undulating stiffly and doubtfully.

"My belong live steam, have got too much pressure," Holman said.

He began snorting and grasped Po-han's bare, sweaty shoulders and pushed him backward, sliding on the oily floorplates, to beside the feed pump. Then he stopped and raised the feed pressures back to normal and tapped the gauge. The feed check on the boiler began clacking again.

"*Now* you have got pressure!" Holman put Po-han's hands against his shoulders. "Now push me, pushee live steam!" he said. Po-han pushed weakly. "Workee! Have got too much plashah!" Holman said. Po-han pushed harder and Holman's feet began to slide. He slid backward, his hands resting lightly on Po-han's shoulders, and he saw the pure light of joyful learning come back into Po-han's face. This time he really had the idea, with no dark spots left in it anywhere.

"Plashah! Plashah!" Po-han cried.

"Pressure!" Holman echoed him, grinning happily too, and then he saw somebody in white watching them from the gratings. He dropped his hands, feeling foolish and embarrassed. Po-han, unseeing, went on to clack once more into the boiler.

The man in shorts came on down. He was the other watertender, the one junior to Burgoyne. Holman did not remember his name.

"I got to write up the log," he said. "I didn't want to break up anything."

He had a perky, sparrowy manner, to match his long nose and beady eyes, and a nasty little grin.

"I was teaching him the steam cycle," Holman said.

"That what you call it?"

He did not quite dare make the wisecrack he wanted to. Holman set his jaw.

"He don't know enough English. He didn't know what 'pressure' means," Holman said. "I had to act it out for him. How would you do it?"

"I wouldn't bother. He already knows all he needs to know. They're all too stupid to learn anything."

Holman flushed. "What's your name?" he asked. "I forgot your name."

"My name's Perna."

"Well prong you, Perna!" Holman said harshly. "Everybody's got a right to learn. Whoever wants to learn what I know, I'll teach 'em!"

"You don't have to get your bowels in an uproar about it," Perna said. He made a face and went around the engine to the log desk.

"I won't be surprised if I end teaching this coolie a damned sight more than you got brains enough to learn!" Holman called after him.

He went up the ladder, angry again. He had met that kind on other ships. He knew them now by their very tone of voice and manner. They sat on a nickel's worth of knowledge as if it were the great Inca treasure, and if anyone junior to them learned something, they thought they were being robbed. Nothing in the world delighted Jake Holman more than bankrupting a son of a bitch like that.

He could not go to sleep. Shadowy pipe and valves and fittings kept sliding across the dark gray screen of his closed eyelids. He had an angry knot left in his stomach and he could hear a faint buzzing behind his left ear. It had been a long while since he had heard that buzzing. It came only when he was very tired or worked up about something, something like the clash with Perna. It always led his mind back to where it had first started, and he could only get rid of it by going back there. It was not a very nice place, back there.

He had wanted very badly to finish high school, so where he had finished was in the jail in Wellco, Nevada, because that was how things worked in Wellco, Nevada. The town marshal was beating him up in a little room with a rough cement floor. The marshal had a blackjack swinging from his wrist, but he only used his fists. Holman could not seem to fight back. At sixteen, he was too near being a man to break and cry and not yet man enough to go for the throat and die fighting. His ears were ringing and he was losing the feel of his body and he could only keep getting up again from the floor that smelled like carbolic acid. The marshal's face never changed, lean and leathery, not angry, not enjoying it, just doing a job in the same way he some-times broke remounts for the U.S. Cavalry in the pole corral at the edge of town. And so he broke Joris K. Holman down at last to his hands and knees in a mess of his own blood and vomit sharp and burning in his throat.

Holman shuddered convulsively in his bunk. He was sweating all over.

It was easier in court. The buzzing made a kind of dream screen between Holman and the rest of them. Garbage Tin, the school super-intendent, was there, his eyes still blacked. Judge Mason would not take Holman's word against Garbage Tin's, about the lie. But Judge Mason did fix it up about Holman's age and got him into the navy. To the end Garbage Tin held out for reform school.

Holman relaxed slightly.

The navy was a lot like reform school, but they paid you for it. They made Holman a fireman, because of his husky build, and when he got a ship he could go ashore with a little money in his pocket, for the first time in his life. He made no friends on the ship and he avoided civilians ashore. He hated civilians. He found a pock-marked Mexican whore on Pacific Street, with a kind, sweet face, and she could make the buzzing go away for hours, sometimes for days. He kept going back to Maria. Aboard ship he hated all military crap and he hated personnel inspection most of all. You had to stand at attention with your eyes fixed on an imaginary spot three feet ahead and six inches up while the captain talked about you to your division officer as if you could no more see nor hear than a piece of machinery. At those moments the buzzing was very bad. They were all excited because they were Making the World Safe for Democracy. Holman did not care about that. The posters of Uncle Sam pointing and glaring reminded him too much of Garbage Tin. He heard that in the Asiatic Fleet there was a lot less military crap. Out there, the guys said, they were only keeping China safe for Standard Oil, Robert Dollar and Jesus Christ. All old Asiatic sailors were supposed to be crazy. Holman's shipmates thought he was dim-witted, and sometimes they called him Asiatic. He decided slowly that he wanted to go to China, but he found it very hard to take initiative in anything in those days. Then his division officer dumped him in a China draft, to get rid of him, and so he went to China anyway.

Holman sighed and relaxed quite a bit. His stomach was easing.

It was much better in China. The whores were all like Maria, and the Japanese girls were the best ones of all, and they soothed and healed Jake Holman. The buzzing softened down and he began coming out from behind his dream screen. He liked it ashore. He liked junks and sampans and rickshaws and pagodas and tiled roofs with upturned corners. He liked the noisy, crowded, smelly streets of open-front shops full of everything from dried duck gizzards to lacquered coffins. He loved the hanging red-and-gold signs he couldn't read and the yelling Chinese arguments he couldn't understand and the twangy, jangling music that did not sound like music. It all made him know that he was a hell of a long way from Wellco, Nevada. He began taking more interest in his work aboard ship, and then he discovered the big secret.

Holman relaxed altogether. He could barely hear the buzzing be hind his ear.

The secret was simple. They could not get along without the

machinery. If it did not run, the ship would be a cold, dark, dead hulk in the water. And it did not work with engines to order them to run and to send down the marines to shoot them if they did not run. No admiral could court-martial an engine. All machinery cared about a man was what he knew and what he could do with his two hands, and nobody could fool it on those things. Machinery always obeyed its own rules, and if you broke the rules it didn't matter how important or charming or pure in heart you were, you couldn't get away with it. Machinery was fair and honest and it could force people to be fair and honest. Jake Holman began to love machinery.

It brought his mind alive again. Just as it had been with him in high school, he found that he could learn the inner secrets of machinery faster than anybody else. Just as it had been with his high school teachers, he discovered the basic ignorance of his senior petty officers, and of course they hated him for that. But they were also accountable to their officers for the machinery, and they were all secretly afraid of their machinery, and when they were convinced that Jake Holman knew more about it than they could ever learn, they were happy enough to let him take care of it and keep them out of trouble. The only favor he wanted in return was to be excused from all musters and inspections and topside military crap. That was an easy favor to grant, and they always granted it. Whenever he could, Holman always transferred to a smaller ship. The smaller the ship, the less they had of military crap.

Holman yawned and stretched his arms and the buzzing was all gone. This ship was the smallest yet, and it had as much military crap as a battleship. But they still had to have the machinery. And she really was a home and a feeder. He would worry about the rest of it tomorrow. He went to sleep.

3

For turn-to next morning Holman walked around the engine room with Lynch. He was wearing his new white shorts and he felt very silly dressed like that in an engine room. This first walk and talk about the machinery on a new ship was always a kind of mental wrestling match, with the new man trying to show the chief how much he knew. Lynch wouldn't wrestle. Holman scratched his thumbnail on pump rods and commented that they were steam cut. He shook valve gears and the loose bushings rattled. Lynch just grinned.

"She steams," he said. "That's all we give a damn about."

The other engineers were all down there too in shorts, and their day's work was only a gesture. Burgoyne looked around the fireroom while Perna checked the bunkers, and then they both made out the coal report. Stawski followed two coolies around and watched them jack over idle pumps with a crowbar. Wilsey watched a gang of coolies jack over the main engine. The jacking gear was a removable worm that engaged a worm wheel around the shaft just aft of the engine. They turned the worm with a long ratchet bar, and it took three coolies hauling at it with a rope and singing, "Hay ho! Hay ho!" while a fourth coolie squatted and threw the bar clicking back after each heave. Holman could barely see the balanced tons of metal move.

"Are them coolies dogging it, or is she really that stiff?" he asked Lynch.

"She's stiff. The dockyard rebabbited all the bearings," Lynch said. "She'll free up, with a day's steaming."

Chien followed them around the engine room. He ignored Holman. He was very attentive to Lynch. Lynch told Chien various small cleaning and repair jobs to do. Holman simply could not draw Lynch into technical talk.

"There ain't no blueprints. Nobody ever knew the valve settings," Lynch said. "Chinamen in Hong Kong built her for the Spaniards, Christ knows how long ago. So long ago her frames and plates are all wrought iron."

"I been noticing the dents."

"You ought to see her in drydock, all humps and hollows. She just ain't got the springback steel has," Lynch said. He laughed. "She's a beat-up old bitch, but by God she's a home!"

After battle drills Holman had to go with Lynch again, to sign Title B cards in the CPO quarters. The quarters were aft on the boat deck, in a block that also held the sick bay and a small stateroom for the Chinese pilot. There were wicker armchairs outside under the awning and broad-leafed plants in green wooden tubs, and the Chinese mess-cook was sitting in one of the armchairs shining shoes. Inside, the CPO bunks had blue spreads, but otherwise the place was no more clean and spacious than the crew's compartment, directly below it on the main deck.

"Lemon! Catch coffee!" Lynch told the messcook.

They were alone at the round table inside. Holman had a big stack of cards to sign. On each one he had to cross out Pitocki's name. Lemon brought coffee in a porcelain pitcher and set out two of the CPO cups with handles. Lynch leaned and pulled a bottle of rum out from under a bunk. He held it up and sloshed it.

"You'll have some, won't you?"

"Sure. And much obliged," Holman said.

Lynch splashed rum in the cups. He filled his own half full. He did not look good. His face looked puffy and yielding, like wax that was too warm, and his brown hair was very thin on top. The hot coffee in the rum made an aromatic smell.

"Here's how," Lynch said. He tossed off half his cup and snorted.

"Ain't how for me," Holman said, grinning. He sipped at his cup.

"Needed that!" Lynch said. "Holman, I hear you locked horns with old Chien yesterday."

Holman went on guard. "It wasn't much. We both saved face."

"Well, you know how slopeheads are about face and old custom," Lynch said. "I got to cut you in on how we do things on this ship. It ain't like the Fleet ships you're used to, not a bit."

When you wanted something with a bilge coolie you always went through old Chien, he said. Same with the deck coolies, you went to Pappy Tung. You never got familiar with deck or bilge coolies. It was all right to kid with the compartment coolies, because they knew their places. And you never wore dungarees except to stand a steaming watch.

"Like you yesterday, in the bilges and all dirty," Lynch said. "It made it look like you didn't trust Chien, so he lost face. And you lost face for being so dirty."

"That's how it is on here, huh?"

"That's how it is."

Lynch poured more rum for himself. It was putting a sparkle in his pouched eyes and his face looked firmer.

"No, thanks." Holman waved away the bottle. "What work do we do, and what do they do, down in that engine room?"

"They do the coolie work, the dirty stuff and the mule hauling. We give 'em the jobs, supervise and inspect. And we keep up the paper work." Lynch squinted at Holman. "Oh, we make the big decisions, and we'd take over in any emergency, but for routine stuff Chien carries the load."

"Whatever happens down there that ain't routine?"

"Nothing! Nothing, by God!" Lynch leaned back and laughed. "Old Chien's been aboard more than twenty years and not much *can* happen he ain't seen and handled before. That's what's good about it."

Holman poured himself more coffee. He kept his face straight.

"Keep old Chien happy, give him what he wants, and you can just forget about the Goddamned machinery," Lynch said.

It was clear enough that Chien had the place on this ship that Holman wanted for himself. But how could he ever ease Chien out of it if all engine work was coolie work and he was not a coolie? He saw Lynch eying him oddly and he tried to grin.

"Get out of that Fleet way of thinking," Lynch said. "We ain't in no engineering competition. We ain't got any division maneuvers or drill schedules to keep up. No admiral is going to chew the Old Man's ass if we break down. We don't even have typhoons and we ain't never out of sight of land. Engineering just ain't *important* on this ship."

"I guess you're right," Holman said sadly.

"What is important is face and old custom." Lynch sipped at his coffee royal. "Take shaving. It's old custom that Clip Clip shaves all hands." He rubbed his jaw. "Hell, I'd feel abused if I had to shave myself. I probably forgot how."

"The coolies get paid by squeeze, huh?"

"And how, they squeeze!" Lynch nodded vigorously. "On coal and stores and chow—oh, I could tell you some stories. But you'll see." He chuckled. "It all goes to Lop Eye Shing. Sew Sew and Press Press and Clip Clip's take, the tips, everything goes to Shing and he shares it out again."

"Shing. Who's he?"

"Number one boy for the ship, been aboard twenty-five years," Lynch said. "He's half paralyzed, you don't see him on deck much. But he'll be up tomorrow for payday."

Holman stood up. "I got 'em all signed," he said, pushing the cards toward Lynch. "Thanks for the rum. And for the good advice."

Lynch waved a hand. "Good for us both."

In the compartment they were drinking coffee at the mess tables and waiting their turns for a shave. Holman poured a cup and sat down and Burgoyne shoved a paper at him.

"Put your name down for your turn," he said.

"Don't need a shave right now." Holman knuckled his jaw. He had a stubble, but he knew it was too light in color to show much.

"Ought to have a clean shave to take the quarterdeck," Farren said. "You got the twelve-to-four."

Farren made out the watch list for Holman's section. Holman looked at Farren's beard.

"Maybe I'll grow me a beard," he said.

"It's a free country," the gunner's mate said.

They were not as friendly as yesterday. On any other ship Holman would not have cared about that, because he would have the machinery to back him up. He did not know about this ship. I will get shaved, he thought, and then, no, God damn them, shaving was a man's own private business.

They left Holman out of the talk. They were all kidding Clip Clip, talking about bending him on like a messenger and discussing his good and bad points as a piece of *duhai*. Clip Clip was a nervous, wizened old Chinaman in a white U.S. Navy surgical gown, and he was very fast and expert with his shaving. He shrilled and chattered back at the sailors, making a great show of anger, and they all laughed at him. A big, sloppy seaman named Ellis, with a half-round scar on his cheek, sneaked up and goosed Clip Clip. The old man jumped and squealed and turned, waving his razor.

"My cuttee you neck!" he shrilled.

Ellis retreated, to a burst of laughter.

"Every time you goose him, he adds twenty cents to your bill," Farren told Ellis. "Serves you right."

"Aw, you reckon he'd do that? You reckon old Clip Clip'd do a thing like that to a shipmate?" Ellis said.

They all laughed some more. After a while Wong, the messcook, started putting out the mess gear for dinner.

Bronson was a fleshy, important-looking first-class quartermaster. He stood stiffly on the quarterdeck and reeled off the watch dope to Holman: ships in port, senior officer present, weather. . . . Holman hardly listened. He was hating it already and thinking how you relieved a steaming watch in an engine room. You went down early and checked the machinery and when you knew of your own knowledge how things were, you went to the throttle and told the guy, "Okay, I got it." He did not understand half of what Bronson was saying. He did not know anything about this topside military crap and he did not want to learn. He was wishing that he had never put his name in for the U.S.S. *San Pablo*.

"That's the information, up to the moment." Bronson stood waiting.

"Okay, I guess I got it," Holman said.

"You're supposed to salute me and say, 'I relieve you, sir.' "

Rage rippled over Jake Holman. "It ain't regulation for enlisted men to salute each other," he said, trying to control his voice.

"On this quarterdeck we're both junior officers of the deck," Bronson said. "It's how we do it on here, Holman."

"If you was sitting in God's own armchair, you'd still be an enlisted man." Holman's voice trembled. "I won't salute you. I never did believe in that kind of crap."

Bronson turned pale. His lips pinched in and he looked at Holman in silence for almost a minute. Then he saluted and said, "I hereby turn the watch over to you, sir."

Holman checked his impulse to salute back. He turned his guilt to anger. "Okay, I got it," he said, more surly still. "Give me that Goddamned peashooter." His face was burning.

Silently, Bronson unbuckled his pistol belt, and silently Holman buckled it on himself. Bronson went away. The pistol lay heavy and accusing against Holman's thigh and the Chinese messenger was looking at him curiously. Holman knew he had gone too far. He had long known that his dislike of military crap was like a private disease, which no one else could understand. Other guys hated it and said so, but it did not curdle the inside of their bones. New panic tried to rise in him. He felt like a dog on its hind legs. Like a whore in church. He stood at attention and looked down at his hairy bare legs and saw that his knees touched and his ankles touched and there was a long, narrow, figure-eight gap between his knees and his ankles. He had never noticed that before. He did not know whether he was knock-kneed or bowlegged. What am I doing here, he thought. Jesus Christ on a crutch, what am I *doing* here?

An old help he had once used came back to him. They could command you what you had to do, he thought, but they could not command you how you had to feel about it, although they tried. So you did things their way and you felt about them your own way, and you did not let them know how you felt. That way you kept the two things separate and you could stand it. Slowly, Holman began getting hold of himself.

He was able to return the salutes when he checked out the liberty party, one of whom was Bronson. Chief Franks was senior OOD, and he came down and stood most of the watch with Holman. He was breaking Holman in, instructing him in the watch duties without seeming to, just passing along information while he talked casually about things. Franks was probably not trying to sound out his attitudes, Holman decided. Franks had a plain, straight manner, and he was not one of the sly, watching kind. It turned out to Holman's relief that he would not have to know anything about seamanship.

"Pappy Tung looks after all that stuff without anybody telling him," Franks said. "He's the best seaman aboard."

Pappy Tung seemed to have the same position on deck that Chien had in the engine room. He was a short, sturdy old Chinese with a dark face that seemed carved out of wood. Like the other deck coolies, he wore navy undress whites without insignia, but he also wore a black neckerchief to mark his rank.

"That's good. I sure ain't no seaman," Holman said.

The important thing was the smart appearance of the ship, smart side and boat courtesies and, most of all, exchanging salutes with passing ships. Bugle calls, hand salutes and color dips had to be timed and spaced exactly right. Lt. Collins had a very raw nerve for passing honors, Franks said, and if they did not go off exactly right he would raise hell. Franks handled the ceremony for the several ships that passed, to show Holman how to do it. They only exchanged salutes with treaty power flags. A few rusty steamers flew the five-barred Chinese flag, but they did not make dips. The big junks did not bother with flags, unless you could call a white cloth with the skipper's name in Chinese characters a flag.

"That's the kind of flags most of the warlords down in Hunan use," Franks said. "The slopeheads just don't savvy flags, is all."

Junks did have a kind of passing ceremony, when one junk over-hauled another one, and Holman and Franks walked over to port to watch one on the river. The faster junk was trying to cut sharp across the bow of the slower one and they were neck and neck and curving in toward the bank. On the smaller, slower junk the crew was scream-ing and beating gongs and shooting firecrackers.

Franks chuckled. "That big boy's trying to unload his devils on the little fellow."

Holman knew about that. They believed that devils held hands and tailed on behind a junk, more and more of them as time passed, and the only way to get rid of the devils was to cross the bow of another junk. If you could force another junk to cut through your string of devils, your cut-off devils would join his string and you went on your way bobtailed and lucky again.

"We keep a tub of spuds on the bridge to throw at 'em, when they try that stuff on us," Franks said. "Ignorant bastards, ain't they?"

"I guess it's real to them," Holman said. He could see that the small junk was going to get a new load of devils, for all their noise and try-ing, and he felt a bit sorry for them.

His other watch duties were to keep the log and carry out inport routine, sweepdowns, sick call and so forth. Most of the things had a bugle call attached and the watch messenger was also the bugler. There were four of them aboard and they were all named Fang.

"So you don't have to worry about telling 'em apart," Franks said.

The four Fangs were Lt. Collins' addition to the ship. He had had Lop Eye Shing hire them away from the warlord army in Changsha. Paying them had raised the squeeze quite a bit and cigarettes and beer had each gone up a dime.

"I had to let 'em squeeze all the canvas I was going to use for new awnings," Franks said.

"Was the ship as regulation military before Lt. Collins came aboard as it is now?" Holman asked cautiously.

"Just about. It always has been." Franks looked out over the pontoon. "He's hot about it, all right. He can get kind of mystical about it and make you feel funny. But he's just the right skipper for down in Hunan Province."

By the end of the watch Holman was almost at ease. There was a signal watch on the bridge and a roving sentry and when they reported, on the hour, Holman exchanged smart salutes with them. When Farren relieved him at four o'clock, Holman said all the right things and exchanged salutes with Farren. He had the split set up in himself again, and it was working all right.

From the quarterdeck he went down into the engine room to write up the log there, because he had also been standing the engine room watch officially on paper. It still seemed like a fantastic joke. Chien and his coolies were knocking off and Chien blew the boiler glass just as Holman came down. They exchanged blank looks. Holman checked the plant and everything was all right. He felt slightly like an intruder when he went around to the log desk.

He entered the four o'clock temperature and pressure readings in the various columns of the log sheet. Then he filled them in for the three previous hours, and he felt like a sneak. Faking readings like that was called "radioing," and it was an engineering sin. He signed his name to the log, and his name was a lie. Because the coolie who had really stood the watch was not even aboard, officially on paper, and he was only represented on the log sheet by tally marks in the margin for the buckets of coal he had burned. Well, that was how they did it on the U.S.S. *San Pablo.* That was what it meant to be a Sand Pebble.

At sunset Franks mustered the duty section on the fantail and they made evening colors. Coolies watched it from the bank, but it was not much of a show. Holman turned in early and the Fang called him for the watch at midnight by tapping on his bunk frame. The deck coolies were never supposed to touch you. There was nothing to do on the quarterdeck watch at night, except to write up the log. The Fang squatted and went to sleep beside the boat deck ladder and Holman was alone. He looked up the bank to the corner of the brick wall where he had stood and had his first look at the *San Pablo* two nights ago, and he shook his head.

The deck log was a lot different from the engine room log. You had to put in the deck log what ships were in port and what kinds of clouds were in what parts of the sky and the direction and force of the wind. Holman had to search for the north star, finding the Big Dipper first, and he had not looked at the stars in years. The high, strung-out clouds drifted among the bright stars as if a strong wind blew up there, but there was only a light breeze on the river. The river was black and it whispered and chuckled. It was a big river, already a mile wide six hundred miles from the sea. A few lights bobbed on it and there were more lights on the far bank. There was a pagoda over there, and an old walled city named Wuchang, but at night they blended with the dark, humpy hills.

"High, scattered, moving clouds all over the sky," he wrote in the deck log.

He logged the air temperature and pressure from the barometer and also the river temperature and depth. Those were temperatures and pressures and water levels, just as you logged them in the engine room, he thought, but up here you could not adjust them if they were wrong. You could not know when they were wrong. Down below even the illiterate coolies knew that much, from red limit marks on the pressure gauge dials and pieces of string around water-level glasses. It was much better down below. You did not care which way was north; you went by port and starboard, fore and aft. You did not care whether it was day or night or what the weather was, unless it got rough enough to pitch the screw out of the water or ship a sea down the skylight. In the engine room you had control of things.

Holman paced across to the port side and back again, several angry times.

Well, with the bugle you controlled a lot of what people did from the quarterdeck, he thought. What the ship did as a ship, as in rendering passing honors. The gangplank was there. It was a kind of gate or threshold, the place where the ship officially touched the world. The gap in the bulwark was flanked by two big wooden slabs with eagles carved on them. Lots of ships in China had those slabs; they were made cheaply ashore in the same shops that made chests and coffins. There was another eagle slab fastened to the bulkhead above the log desk and a long, narrow slab slung from the overhead just inboard of the light. It had a carved dragon and the ship's name in block letters. There were a brass clock and a name board mounted on the slab above the log desk. Something made the quarterdeck sacred, so that anyone coming on it always had to salute. But the Chinese did not have to salute the quarterdeck.

The thing is to act like it's sacred but not believe it, Holman reminded himself.

Because after all it was only a small, triangular area of deck where the midship passageway met the starboard main deck gallery. Its only furniture was the arms locker under the boat deck ladder and on the other side the varnished log desk up against the white wooden bulkhead that enclosed the crew's compartment. Almost all of the ship's superstructure was wooden, and it had been built on the *San Pablo*'s wrought-iron hull after she had come to the river. She was much too topheavy ever to go to sea again. The log desk stood on high legs and you wrote standing up. The slanting top lifted up and inside were spare pencils, a pair of binoculars, a box for liberty cards and boxes of sanitubes and condoms for the men going on liberty. That was all there was to the quarterdeck.

There was no machinery. Well, that brass clock is a kind of time-chopping-up machine, Holman thought. The pistol on his hip was a kill-people machine. But the pistol was more like a power tool and so were all the other guns in the arms locker, and the cutlasses in there were hand tools. The name board beside the clock was like a status board in a big engine room, with pegs or tags to tell you at a glance what pumps were on and what important valves were closed or open.

The name board had twenty-four names, each on a separate little stick that slid in a groove. There were parallel columns for "Aboard" and "Ashore" and you slid the sticks from one to the other as the people came and went. The top name was Lt. William Collins, USN, Commanding, and he was ashore. So was P. A. Lynch, CMM, ashore. They said Lynch was gone on a Russian cabaret girl. One of the names was C. J. Pitocki, MM1/c, and he was aboard. They had all been telling him what a fine old guy old Pitocki was, Holman thought. They didn't want Jake Holman on their ship. They wanted some nameless, faceless raw material that they could nudge and pinch and shape into another Pitocki. It was a weird, lonely night notion, and it bothered Holman. He tried to scratch out Pitocki's name and broke his pencil point on the transparent tape guarding it. Pitocki was unscratched. Sure, old Pitocki's aboard, Holman thought. You don't get rid of a twelve-year plankowner just by killing the bastard.

The panic he had felt at noon began creeping over him again. He tried to visualize his own face, and he could not. He knew he had a firm, squarish face and a strong jaw and gray eyes spaced wide under bushy eyebrows, but he could not make himself see it. All he could get was magnified glimpses of the corner of his mouth or the point of his jaw, with lather and a razor scraping, or his hand with a comb parting his short, sandy hair above a vague, wide forehead. He was about to go aft and look in a mirror when the dozing Fang jumped to his feet. Holman saw a slim, erect figure in service whites walking briskly down to the pontoon. It was Lt. Collins.

Lt. Collins returned the new man's salute and started up the ladder to the boat deck. On impulse he stopped and turned, standing with his face in shadow and looking down at the new man, Holman, in the light beside the log desk.

"Holman, how do you feel about this ship by now?" he asked. "Do you think you'll like this duty?"

"I like it fine, sir."

They always said that. They thought they had to.

"Are you sure? Don't be afraid to speak up." He made his voice friendly and reassuring.

"I never had living conditions so good in all my life, sir," Holman said. "I can't hardly believe yet how good it is on here."

"I mean the whole ship. The duty. Do you think you will be happy in this ship?"

Holman licked his lips. "When I get used to these topside watches, sir—I'm more used to things down below—I guess I will, sir."

He was not being candid. Lt. Collins began questioning him. He wanted to discover that puzzling something hinted at but not revealed by Holman's service record. The man had grown up in a poor family in a small Western town. He had dropped out of high school to join the navy during the war. It was a perfect background for a career man. His frequent transfers Holman explained by saying that he wanted experience with new machinery plants. All his transfers had been at his own request. It did not explain his low marks in leadership contrasting with almost perfect marks in the other categories. There was no direct way to ask him about that.

"Can you say what you really feel about machinery, Holman?"

"It's real, sir."

"What do you mean?"

The man pondered. "Well . . . other ships I been on . . . military stuff, drills and inspections . . . in the end, somebody gives you a mark on it." He was grasping painfully for words to clothe his thought. "I mean, it's always inside somebody's head, like. But machinery runs good or bad or it don't run at all. You can't fool yourself or anybody else about it. It's just . . . *there*. The same for everybody." He was red and sweating from effort.

"In the end the test of the military stuff is life or death in battle and possibly freedom or slavery for the country which gives one life."

He said it gently. The man seemed honest in his confusion. Here on my own quarterdeck I meet it again, Lt. Collins thought. There were the men who gave and took death in battle. There were the other men who shuffled papers and cooked beans and such, logistic support for the fighters. The army could keep them separate. In a ship, they all went into battle together. You could not make the distinction between man and man. It had to be made within each man, and each man had constantly to make it for himself. Military ceremony was a powerful help in that. The distinction was built into a man in his boot training and the military ritual thereafter maintained it.

"You know the twofold nature of duty."

"Yes, sir. Military is most important."

He knows it as a verbal formula, Lt. Collins thought. Unconsciously he probably rejects it and that shows up in his behavior in some way that earns him those low marks in leadership. Lt. Collins made his voice firm but kindly.

"*San Pablo* is not a Fleet ship, Holman. In Hunan Province it is only by keeping instantly ready to fight and die that we avoid having to do so. No man can be excused."

"Yes, sir. I never meant—"

"Anyone can learn technical skills. In *San Pablo* Chinese do the dirty work and routine drudgery. Military duty demands a certain spirit of instant readiness to deal in life and death. Only the very best men, and no Chinese, are good enough for that."

"Yes, sir."

"The men in *San Pablo* are that kind of men. They are all old hands. If you feel that you are not their kind of man, now is the time to say so."

Holman said nothing. He could probably not admit a thing like that, even to himself. But a strained look was growing on his face. The shoe was pinching.

"We start summer cruising Monday. I still have time to swap you back to the Fleet, if you feel you will not be happy in my ship."

"Please, no, sir!" Holman said. "I'll learn what I need to. I'll measure up, sir."

It was clear that he meant it. Lt. Collins smiled slightly.

"Very well. I may talk to you again, in a few days."

He went on up the ladder and stopped outside his cabin, at the boat deck rail. The talk had begun a train of thought in him. That often happened, and he had no one with whom he could talk out such trains of thought. You should keep a journal, he told himself.

The key was death. In Cromwell's time everybody knew about

death. The church saw to that. But now the people did not like anything that reminded them of death. The naval uniform marked men whose primary purpose in life was to deal in violent death. People would rather not have to know that, even some who wore the uniform. A few years back Josephus Daniels had put chaplains and paymasters into the same uniform as line officers. He was trying to mask the face of death. The current recruiting slogans were pure Josephus Daniels: *Join the navy and learn a trade. Every battleship a school.* It was no wonder the men tended to forget the primary purpose of their lives.

The only true recruiting poster was one they did not use any more. It was Uncle Sam pointing and saying *I need you.* Any man who wanted a better reason than that did not belong in the navy.

Well, the men in *San Pablo* were all right. Chinese handled their logistics and the Sand Pebbles could be pure, dedicated fighting men. If Holman was not one of them, they would know it and they would reject him. *San Pablo*'s isolation was a protection. But the way the times went, with the smart ones back in the States mocking their own history, Holman's basic confusion could creep unseen into any man. Lt. Collins meant to call all hands aft for a talk before they started the summer cruise. This was the thing to talk about, he decided.

He drummed his fingers on the rail and looked out across the dark water. His mind began forming simple phrases. He went into his cabin to jot a few of them down before he went to bed.

On the quarterdeck, Holman paced anxiously. He had not thought before that he might be shanghaied off the ship. He did not want to go. He did not want to lose that bunk and locker and mess table. So he had lied to Lt. Collins.

Well, he would just have to make it true. If they had no use for him as an engineer, he would have to become a good topside sailor. He resolved to give in on the shaving and do everything else he could to get on the right side of his shipmates. He was going to need their good will after all.

He recognized the scared, qualmish feeling in his stomach. When you had something to lose, they had a way to put the fear of Christ into you. He could not stop pacing. He was remembering what had happened the only other time in his life when he had had something to lose.

4

At breakfast Holman talked and tried friendly jokes and after drills he had Clip Clip shave him. The sailors drinking coffee were talking about Red Dog Shanahan, who had just finished two weeks of restriction for getting into a fight with Fleet sailors in Hankow.

"You look pretty rugged," Farren told Holman, in the barber chair. "You think you and me could take the Reg Dog for a run ashore and keep him out of trouble?"

"Be glad to try," Holman said.

"One of you can hold his mouth shut and the other one can hold his arms," Wilsey said. "But who'll hold his feet?"

"We'll go to the Hole in the Wall. That's just up the bank here, beside the dockyard," Farren told Holman. "We'll wear shorts, and then we can't change our minds and go to Hankow. Hankow's where the Red Dog runs wild."

The liberty uniform in Hankow was dress whites, because Fleet ships were in port and all sailors ashore had to be dressed alike.

"Sounds good. I'll go," Holman said.

"You guys are my elders, if not my betters," the Red Dog said. "I put myself in your hands."

"I'll bet anybody ten dollars you all come back under arrest," Restorff, the gunner's mate, said.

"Oh, no, no, no, Gunner!" Farren said. "The gunner always wins his bets," he explained to Holman. "Don't bet, Gunner!"

"Can't pass up easy money," Restorff said.

Everyone laughed. "I'll take a dollar of that, Gunner," Harris said. "I like to see guys get in trouble."

"Thanks, you kind-hearted shipmates," Farren said sarcastically. "Harris, you cheap son of a bitch, you could at least of bet him the whole ten dollars."

"I'll bet you the other nine, Gunner," Holman said. He leaned forward out of the barber chair to shake on it.

The Hole in the Wall was a rough, stuffy little board-and-brick leanto and all they had was Horsehead beer served by two dumb and dirty Chinese girls. You could take the girls in back if you wanted to, Farren said. Who the hell wanted to, the Red Dog said. Holman did not talk much. He felt strange, being ashore with two topside sailors, and he knew that being accepted by the crew depended a lot on how he behaved on this first liberty. He would have to be agreeable, spend freely, and be game for anything. The beer was just cool, Limey fashion, and the girls brought chunks of ice to put in the glasses. The Red Dog picked up a chunk of the ice and squinted at it.

"I can see the cholera bugs winking at me," he said. "They all got slant eyes."

He began talking about the ice in Hankow. It was clean and cold and crystalline. It tinkled in the glass like the bells of fairyland. The Scotch whisky was smooth as a maiden's brow and of a flavor so delicate that even the vast vocabulary of Red Dog Shanahan could not do it justice.

"Belay that talk," Farren said. "We got to make him stop that, Holman. He's trying to undermine us."

"Cool, beautiful young Russian princesses. Virgin princesses. Green-eyed and graceful as cats." The Red Dog sketched them with his hands in the air above the table. "Firm, rose-pointed breasts. Skin like white rose petals. Curly, warm nests." His voice and face were ecstatic.

"Holman, we just got to put a sack over his head. We got to, or we're lost," Farren said. "He'd get Jesus Christ in trouble, if he had him ashore."

Holman laughed. Farren reminded him of a big St. Bernard and the Red Dog of a fierce, yapping little terrier.

"You know, I'm awash to the gunwales with this damned warm beer," he said. "I'd like a shot of whisky."

"If you great, monstrous bastards are awash, how do you think I feel?" the Red Dog said.

Farren stroked his beard. "Maskee, let's go back to the ship and change into dress whites," he said. He leaned to Holman's ear and whispered, "We'll shackle the little bastard to his bunk and go without him."

"Arf! Arf! Arf! I heard that!" The Red Dog jumped up on his chair and pointed accusing forefingers. "It's mutiny!" he cried. "Shame on you selfish sons of bitches!"

"I was joking. We'll take you," Farren said. "Come on aboard and change uniform."

"I don't trust you. You ain't going to trap me back aboard that ship." The Red Dog turned to Holman. "You look like an honest man with no crap in your blood, Holman," he said. "Let's go up to Hankow and leave this bearded traitor here to founder himself."

"We'd be out of uniform. How about the shore patrol?"

"We'll go in a car, to the Green Front," the Red Dog said. "It's up an alley, and we can hire a kid to watch for the patrol."

"Okay, I'm game," Holman said. He stood up.

"We'll be sorry," Farren said, standing up too. "You don't know this little pint of piss yet, Holman. He's a devil."

They each took a beer to drink in the car, and it was cooler in the moving car with their shorts and short-sleeved shirts and their white sun helmets with the ship's name across the front. The driver cursed and honked his way past brown-legged coolies pushing wheelbarrows and files of coolies with broad bamboo hats and twin baskets of green vegetables slung jouncing from shoulder poles. The road ran along the river bank and into Hankow along the broad, tree-lined bund. To the left, walkways ran down to pontoons with moored steamers and clusters of small craft. Most of the business buildings were of brick, several stories with arcaded verandas, and some had walls around them with gardens inside. It was a big, busy city, and there were many Sikh cops, as in Shanghai. There were five concessions in a row along the river, Farren said, but the German and Russian concessions belonged to the British now, on account of the British won the war. There was a victory monument for the war on the British bund, a lady angel on a pedestal, like the one in Shanghai, and beyond the British bund was the native city. Along the native bund the junks were three and four deep.

The Green Front was a small place with a row of tables along one side and a bar along the other. The floor was damp and it smelled cool and beery. Five sailors in dress whites were eating a meal at one of the tables and no one was at the bar.

"Roll in, you Sand Pebbles!" the bartender yelled when he saw them. "Hi, Farren. Red Dog, who let you out of your cage?"

He was a fat, pink man with thin white hair and a white shirt open at the neck. They introduced him to Holman as Nobby Clarke, a retired machinist's mate and an old-time river rat. The back bar was stacked with bottles and there was also a stuffed pheasant and a photograph of an old sidewheeler.

"That's the old *Monocacy,* first gunboat on the river," Farren told Holman. "When you see them wheels start to go round, it's a sign you had enough and it's time to go back to the ship."

"I steamed her, when I was a kid," Nobby said. "She was a man-killing bitch to steam, but she was a home." He looked fondly at the picture.

The Red Dog was standing between Holman and Farren. He thumped the leather dice cup on the bar and rolled five aces.

"You got the devil on your side, Red Dog," Nobby said.

"He's my uncle. When he dies, I'll inherit hell."

"What'll you do with hell?" Farren asked.

"I'll sell it to the missionaries for a million dollars."

"You think you're joking, but I believe you, you Irish peckerhead," Farren said.

"It's true," the Red Dog said. "Roll 'em, boys!"

Holman lost. He called for a new bottle of White Horse and said to leave it on the bar, which meant he was buying the bottle. The white-coated bar boy set up the drinks. In China, the white bartenders never mixed or served drinks.

"Sure you're that flush, Holman?" Farren asked.

"I'm going to win nine Mex from the gunner," Holman said.

"Ho ho ho!" Farren said. "That's what you think."

They drank and talked and laughed, the Red Dog grinning up impishly from under his sun helmet cocked askew. They were all feeling the whisky and it was going to be one of the happy, floating drunks, Holman could tell. Some drunks were wild and jumpy and some were morose and savage and Holman's drunks by himself were always sad and gloomy ones, but this drunk was floating. It was a knack the Red Dog had, to lift and carry a drunk. The Fleet sailors had finished their chow and were drinking at their table, talking in bursts and then falling silent, with morose faces, as if they could not get their drunk off the ground. They were from the U.S.S. *Pigeon,* a minesweeper. The Red Dog had taken the spirit of the place away from them, and they did not like it.

"How come you guys up here out of uniform?" Nobby asked.

"We're in uniform," the Red Dog said. "We're river rats, and this is our proper uniform."

One of the Pigeons started to sing "Subic" and the others joined hoarsely and they all went flat and false and petered out on the first verse. They were pretty drunk, but it was a heavy, lumpish drunk. The burly shipfitter they called Buffalo slapped the table.

"God damn it!" he roared. "Boy! More drinks, you slant-eyed son of a bitch!"

He was a hulking man with a scarred, beaten-up face, probably a fighter. Holman knew how they were feeling; they would not get drunker, they would just get meaner. One or another of the five kept scowling at the Red Dog. They thought he was too cocky and happy.

"Lynch was in a while back," Nobby said. "With that Russian."

"She's a cow," the Red Dog said. He hunched his shoulders and squeezed spurts of milk from imaginary breasts.

"Red Dog, where's them Russian princesses?" Holman asked.

"Right now they're taking baths in donkey milk," the Red Dog said. "They're very special gear, Holman. They're all directly descended from Ivan the Terrible. They won't come in till the rabble clears out."

A chair scraped behind them. "Hey, you guys," Buffalo said.

The Sand Pebbles swung around. Farren squeezed the Red Dog's arm and frowned a signal to be quiet.

"Seen any elephants today?" Buffalo asked.

"Not today," Farren said.

"Wearing them hats, I thought you might be hunting elephants. Want me to tell you how to catch a elephant?"

Holman squeezed the Red Dog's other arm. "All we're hunting today is white horses," he said. "We already caught one." He motioned his head at the bottle, almost empty now.

"You want to catch a elephant, the first thing is, you show him your pretty white legs," Buffalo said.

The other Pigeons laughed jeeringly. They meant to start a fight. Nobby Clarke hurried around the bar.

"Hold it, you guys! Have a drink on the house," he pleaded.

"We're the experts on elephants," the Red Dog said. "We know elephants always come back to crap in the same place. So we find five piles of elephant crap and then we wait for the elephant."

Farren laughed and Holman joined him. They exchanged a look above the Red Dog's head. We'll take 'em, the glance agreed. It was a sudden warm bond between them and they turned the Red Dog loose.

"Listen, slow down, take a turn, you guys! Take your Goddamned argument outside," Nobby was saying.

"I saw some elephants over in the Jap Concession," Buffalo said. "I think you better go over there."

He meant it to be a bluff-out, a forced runout, Holman realized. He set himself to take that Buffalo, when the thing blew. He knew his own quick, terrible strength could take down almost any man, and he feared an angry fight. But this would be a happy fight.

"In case you elephant hunters lost your compasses, I'll be glad to show you where the door is," Buffalo said. The other Pigeons laughed nastily again and eased back their chairs. Their faces were ugly.

"Oh, pee on you, John," the Red Dog said in falsetto.

Farren and Holman roared. It was a masterstroke of wit. The *Pigeon's* Fleet nickname was *Pea John* and the Red Dog had insulted both the men and their ship. It stopped them cold. But, from their faces, in another heartbeat the air was going to be full of flying furniture. Nobby ducked behind the bar. Holman tensed for it.

Footsteps sounded, the door opened, and four British sailors came in. They wore shorts and sun helmets. The Red Dog snatched off his own helmet and swept out a grand bow.

"Dr. Bangerknox, I presume," he said.

"As I live and breathe, it's Milord Red Arse Bite-'em-on-the-dog Shanahan!" the foremost Limey said. "Hello, Farren."

He was a square, ruddy man of about Holman's build and he was half drunk, but his gray eyes went keenly back and forth. He knew something was wrong.

"We been hunting elephants and we caught a buffalo," the Red Dog said. "What do you bold hunters know about buffaloes?"

"They're vicious brutes. They charge with their eyes open," the ruddy man said.

"This buffalo's up a stump. We can't make him charge."

"Not sporting to shoot unless he charges." The Limeys were spreading out and balancing on their toes, siding with the Sand Pebbles without question. "Might take a reef in his tail," the ruddy man said.

"I'll spit in his ear." The Red Dog began hawking his throat.

They all chimed in with unprintable suggestions. The big ship-fitter's lips were working and he was ready to go it blind mad. His shipmates could not face the sudden change in odds. "No, Martin. The hell with it, Martin," they said, getting up. They did not call him

Buffalo any more. They got him moving toward the door. "Come on, Martin," they said. "Let's find an honest American place to drink."

"Arf! Arf! Arf!" the Red Dog barked after them. All the river sailors laughed.

They were all at the bar with fresh drinks and the drunk was floating higher than ever. The ruddy man was Banger Knox, an engineer, and they were from H.M.S. *Woodcock,* which also cruised in Hunan Province. That made a bond between the two ships and they would always stand together against any Fleet ship or even a main river gunboat. The Hunan Chinese were much tougher and fiercer than the tame main river Chinese, they explained to Holman. The *Woodcock*'s nickname was *Timber Dick*, and the sailors were Timber Dicks, and in any main river port the Timber Dicks and Sand Pebbles always stood together. Farren told about the Red Dog's stroke of wit against the Pea Johns and he had to explain it before the Limeys could laugh.

"Fair baffles me how you blokes can twist a name into an insult," Banger said. "You've a low, nasty sort of talent for it."

They shouted each other down telling Holman about a fight last winter in Changsha. The Red Dog had begun calling the Limeys Limber Dicks, and after it had been explained to them they had all had a very good fight in a place called the Red Candle.

"We tried for a fortnight after to hit on a good insult for Sand Pebble," Banger said. "The best we could do was *simple apple.*" He looked pleadingly at Farren. "I hope you find that just a wee bit insulting?"

"I've heard of bad apples and horse apples." Farren stroked his beard judicially. "I don't know about simple apples."

"We'll consider it a mortal insult, just to be friendly," the Red Dog said. "Nobody but our fellow Hunanese can call us that."

Banger raised his glass. "Thank you, Milord Red Arse."

"But the Hunanese are the natives," an English sailor said.

"All right, we're Hunaneers," Holman said.

"Us Hunaneers, we got no fears," the Red Dog said. He began to sing, in a clear Irish tenor:

> *Us Hunaneers, we got no fears,*
> *We do not stop at trifles;*
> *We hang our balls upon the walls*
> *And shoot at them with rifles.*

The Limeys thought that was very good. They explained that what made it so funny was that you could not really hang them upon the walls, you know.

Holman began blanking out and coming back. Things were disconnected. They did a lot of singing. The Limeys had a good song about the old barstard from Kent. Two more bottles of White Horse were on the bar and Nobby Clarke floated around back there like a pink balloon with sparse white hair. It was a very happy, high-floating drunk. Holman talked very earnestly to Banger Knox. He had a profound new idea. Some men composed poems and some composed music, he explained to Banger, but Red Dog Shanahan was the world's finest artist at composing drunks. It was a shame the world did not know that about him. Too bloody right, Banger agreed. The Red Dog should be buried in Westminster Abbey. They decided solemnly to crown him drunkard laureate and they pulled tail feathers from the stuffed pheasant to stick in his helmet band as a crown. But the Red Dog thought that made him an Indian and he climbed on the bar and warwhooped and wardanced the length of it.

There was shouting outside in the street and a bar boy went out to check and came in to say there was trouble.

"Hey, you guys! Hey, you guys!" Nobby was saying. "If there's trouble, you better go down to the bund and stand by."

"Let these main river people look after their own trouble," Farren said. "We love everybody."

"We're Hunaneers," the Red Dog said. "We're just visiting up here."

The thing about a floating drunk was that you were detached. You did not have to care about rules. You were floating so high and happy that the sad, serious people only laughed at whatever you did. It made them a little bit happy just to watch you and know how you were feeling and nobody wanted to shoot down a floating drunk.

Far off a power plant siren let go in short, fast hoots, on and on and on. Suddenly Nobby was wearing one of the washbasin British steel helmets and he was banging on the bar with a rifle butt.

"Come on! Come on! That's the emergency signal for the Volunteers!" he was saying. "Come on, sailors! Shove off down to the river!"

They were following the Red Dog down a wide street and Chinese in blue gowns and rags were running both ways. The store windows were all broken and so much torn white paper was on the street that it looked like snow. Two coolies were smashing a heavy iron grating edgewise down on new bicycles. Holman and Banger took the grating. They were much stronger men than the coolies and they could bring the grating thundering down like a Nevada stamp mill and bend a new bicycle almost double. The coolies kept pulling away the smashed bicycles and feeding in new ones.

The crowd was thicker and it blocked them. The shaven Chinese heads were close together like cobbles in a pavement that also surged and heaved like a sea and a trapped rickshaw was like an island in it, shafts high, the fat Chinese passenger leaning forward onto the puller's skinny brown shoulders. The Red Dog still had his feathered helmet and they followed it through the packed crowd. Veins throbbed and swelled in the temples of the shaven heads and the mouths were open, screeching, and showing teeth and fluttering tongues. They pushed through into an open space and Farren still clutched a bottle of White Horse. It was about one-third full. He beckoned grandly with the bottle.

"All hanje," he said. "Time for lil drinkee."

It was a half-circle open space around the entrance to a cross street, and across the entrance was a line of Sikh cops and helmeted white civilians with rifles. They were yelling and motioning. One white man stepped forward.

"Come inside, you drunken fools!" he said. "They'll kill you!"

"Not ush," Farren said. "We're Hooney—we're Hunaneers."

"Come inside! That's an order!"

The man pulled at Banger's arm. Banger jerked away and looked very dignified.

"You talk like a bloody Yank, chum," he said. "You can't give orders to a Hunaneer, you know."

The Red Dog began to sing.

> *Us Hunaneers, we shed no tears,*
> *We give no damn for riches;*
> *We prong our wives with butcher knives,*
> *Us hardy sons of bitches.*

More men came out and pushed and tugged them singing inside the line. Come on, you buccaneers, your officers are going to hear about this, the men said. Come on, for Christ's sweet sake, before we all get killed! They went along the street, staggering and stumbling, and firemen in red helmets were running past them the other way, unreeling white hose. They were going along beside a brick wall covered with stucco that had fallen off from big, scabby patches and a file of British sailors came by on the run and somehow carried off the Timber Dicks in their wake. Holman stopped.

"You know, thish serious," he said.

They all stopped and looked back. Their drunk was coming down to earth. The yelling at the head of the street was louder, a great screeching, and white plumes of water shot up there. Further back, the British sailors were making a barricade of planks and a dismounted gate. The wall beside the barricade had sharpened bamboo stakes along the top and a big tree bushed greenly out over the wall. A woman with a pad and pencil came up from somewhere. She was not very young, and she looked frightened.

"I'm a reporter," she said. "Do you think they'll try to storm the armory?"

"Oh yes. They always storm the armory," the Red Dog said.

"Oh, you're drunk!" she said. She sounded disgusted.

The woman went up to the barricade. The British sailors were lining out kneeling and they had a machine gun on a tripod and a young officer stood behind them with a sword. The plumes of water were falling back along the street and they wavered and stopped and the firemen fell back through the barricade. After them came the Sikhs and Volunteers, all soaked with water, and they all went inside the compound. The woman went in with them. She turned in the gate to look back at the Sand Pebbles and the Red Dog threw her a kiss.

"Krishe! Gotta heave!" Farren said. His eyes were bulged and glassy.

The waving arms and shaven heads came down the street slowly as a tide makes and their frantic screeching filled the street. The young British officer walked back and forth slapping his leg with his sword. Above the shaven heads was a big sign for Three Castles cigarettes and the sudden crackling, volleying fire chopped through it and down into the crowd. The tripod danced and the machine gun throttled off the screeching like hands around a throat. The crowd was gone except for flopping, lumpish bundles criss-crossing each other on the street, and the firing ceased with a few after-pops.

Farren was heaving and strangling, bent over, hands on stomach, his beard all foul. The sight and smell of it made Holman's stomach knot and rise. He was not drunk any more.

"Red Dog, take his other arm," he ordered. "We got to get the hell out of here."

Around the second corner they ran into the American shore patrol.

The drunk ended officially next day on the quarterdeck. Everyone not concerned with mast kept clear, but the ragged coolies on the pontoon watched it without understanding, as they watched everything on the *San Pablo*. The three prisoners stood in line, hats in hand, facing the log desk, which had been moved across to stand right against the foot of the boat deck ladder. On the back of the log desk, ordinarily hidden, was a weather-stained card lettered: *Shame on you bastards*. It was an old *San Pablo* joke, but the three prisoners and the three chiefs standing in line inboard were very quiet and solemn. Lt. Collins came down the ladder and the chiefs saluted him. The prisoners did not have the privilege of saluting.

Lt. Collins stood on the bottom step, where he could look down on the prisoners across the log desk. He gave them each in turn a cold, sharp stare. Then he turned his thin, dark face down to the paper on the desk before him.

"You men are all charged with being drunk and out of uniform and with insolence to the shore patrol," he said quietly. "Have you anything to say?"

Farren spoke for all three. "We just had too much to drink, sir, and we're sorry now."

Franks stepped forward. "Farren is a good man, Captain," he said. "He's always clean and sober aboard and attentive to duty and very reliable."

In turn, Lynch and Welbeck stepped forward to say the same things about Holman and Shanahan. Lt. Collins turned his eyes back to the bareheaded prisoners and they were very cold eyes.

"You are not specifically charged with what I consider your most serious offense," he said. "There was a dangerous riot in progress. You should have placed yourselves under the first military command you encountered. Drunk or sick or asleep, no matter what, you are fundamentally on duty every minute you draw breath." His voice rapped harsh and cold at them: "There is *no* relief and *no* escape from your military duty!" He slapped the desk for each *no*. "Do you clearly understand that?"

"Yes, sir," they all said humbly.

"Very well, then." His voice lost its edge. "Holman, I am sorry to have to spoil your clean record so soon. Farren, your record already leaves much to be desired." He looked at the Red Dog, dwarfed between Farren and Holman, and a twinkle came into his eye. "Shanahan, it is impossible for you to shock me any more, but I continue to be mildly disappointed in you," he said. "I have no doubt whatever that, if the truth were known, you started that riot all by yourself." He paused. "Stay aboard three weeks, all three of you." A shadowy smile crossed his face, but he quickly hardened it and snapped, "Mast dismissed!" and went back up the ladder.

A few minutes later, drinking coffee in the compartment, Holman knew he was in. They were all calling him "Jake" and wanting to hear the story of the big drunk again and what the captain said at mast. A well-composed drunk like that one always became a sea story, to be told and retold for years, and Jake Holman was already solidly a part of *San Pablo* folklore. He was a true Sand Pebble and there would be no more question of the captain swapping him back to the Fleet.

5

It was their last day in Hankow and the skipper was going to make a talk after quarters.

"He gets right fancy in them talks of his," Burgoyne told Holman at breakfast. "You don't know how to take it sometimes."

"Last Thanksgiving he told us how China is like Indian country in the old days in the States," Farren said. "The businessmen and the missionaries are the settlers."

"We're the U.S. Calvary on the plains of Texas," Wilsey said.

"Prong the U.S. Calvary," Harris said. "I hate dogfaces."

"I knew an old soldier once that was an Indian fighter," Holman said. "We got lots of Indians back where I come from."

"Prong Indians too," Harris said. "Pass that jam."

"It just now strikes me, the treaty ports and concessions are like Indian reservations," Holman said. "Only it's the palefaces that are on 'em."

"All but the missionaries," Farren said. "The biblebacks are scattered all over hell's half acre. They're the ones give us all the trouble."

"Prong all missionaries twice," Harris growled.

Wong brought Holman his dozen fried eggs. He explored the new thought as he ate the eggs. He liked new ways of looking at familiar things. He began looking forward to the captain's talk.

After they made colors Bordelles put them at parade rest and Lt. Collins came to the edge of the grating to talk. As before, Holman was struck by the picture he made in white and gold against the great varnished wheel with the flag rippling red and white above it. Lt. Collins looked down, his thin face unsmiling.

"Tomorrow we begin our summer cruising to show the flag on Tungting Lake and the Hunan rivers," he said. "At home in America, when today reaches them, it will be Flag Day. They will gather to do honor and hear speeches. For us who wear the uniform, every day is Flag Day. We pay our honor in act and feeling and we have little need of words. But on this one day it will not hurt us to grasp briefly in words the meaning of our flag. That is what I want to talk about this morning."

He paused. Chinese quarreled noisily on passing junks. As always, ragged coolies watched from the bank.

"Our flag is the symbol of America. I want you to grasp what America *really is,*" Lt. Collins said, nodding for emphasis. "It is more than marks on a map. It is more than buildings and land. America is a living structure of human lives, of all the American lives that ever were and ever will be. We in *San Pablo* are collectively only a tiny, momentary bit of that structure. How can we, standing here, grasp the *whole* of America?" He made a grasping motion. "Think now of a great cable," he said, and made a circle with his arms. "The cable has no natural limiting length. It can be spun out forever. We can unlay it into ropes, and the ropes into strands, and the strands into yarns, and none of them have any natural ending. But now let us pull a yarn apart into single fibers—" he made plucking motions with his fingers "—and each man of us can find himself. Each fiber is a tiny, flat, yellowish thing, a foot or a yard long by nature. One American life from birth to death is like a single fiber. Each one is spun into the yarn of a family and the strand of a home town and the rope of a home state. The states are spun into the great, unending, unbreakable cable that is America."

His voice deepened on the last words. He paused, to let them think about it. It was a new thought and it fascinated Holman. Just by living your life you wound and you wound yourself into the big cable. The cable grew and grew into the future like a living thing. It was a living thing. The thought fascinated Holman.

"No man, not even President Coolidge, can experience the whole of America directly," Lt. Collins resumed. "We can only feel it when the strain comes on, the terrible strain of hauling our history into a stormy future. Then the cable springs taut and vibrant. It thins and groans as the water squeezes out and all the fibers press each to each in iron hardness. Even then, we know only the fibers that press against us. But there is another way to know America."

He paused for a deep breath. The ranks were very quiet.

"We can know America through our flag which is its symbol," he said quietly. "In our flag the barriers of time and space vanish. All America that ever was and ever will be lives every moment in our flag. Wherever in the world two or three of us stand together under our flag, all America is there. When we stand proudly and salute our flag, that is what we know wordlessly in the passing moment."

Holman's eyes went to the flag. It looked almost alive, streaming and rippling in the breeze off the river. He felt that he had not ever really looked at the flag before.

"Understand that our flag is not the cloth but the pattern of form and color manifested in the cloth," Lt. Collins was saying. "It could have been any pattern once, but our fathers chose that one. History has made it sacred. The honor paid it in uncounted acts of individual reverence has made it live. Every morning in American schoolrooms children present their hearts to our flag. Every morning and evening we render it our military salutes. And so the pattern lives and it can manifest itself in any number of bits of perishable cloth, but the pattern is indestructible."

A foul smell blew across the fantail. It was from a passing string of barges taking liquid Hankow sewage back to the fields that fed

Hankow. Sailors called them *honey barges*. The foul breeze made no difference in the bright, rippling appearance of the flag.

"For us in *San Pablo* every day is Flag Day," Lt. Collins went on. He was talking easily but earnestly. "Civilians are only morally bound to salute our flag. We are legally bound. All Americans are morally bound to die for our flag, if called upon. Only we are legally bound. Only we live our lives in day to day readiness for that sacrifice. We have sworn our oaths and cut our ties. We have given up wealth and home life, except as *San Pablo* is our home. It marks us. It sets us apart. We are uncomfortable reminders, in time of peace. Those of you who served in the last war will know what I mean."

Heads nodded along the ranks. Holman nodded too.

"It is said there will be no more war. We must pretend to believe that. But when war comes, it is we who will take the first shock and buy time with our lives. It is we who keep the faith. We are not honored for it. We are called mercenaries on the outposts of empire. But I want to speak for you an epitaph written for an army of mercenaries such as we in *San Pablo*."

He cleared his throat and spoke solemnly:

> *These, in the day when heaven was falling,*
> *The hour when earth's foundations fled,*
> *Followed their mercenary calling*
> *And took their wages and are dead.*

He paused again. There was some foot shuffling in the ranks. They did not want to take this stuff too personally, Holman knew. Lt. Collins hardened his expression. His eyes bored at them. He seemed to loom above them on the grating. His voice rang harshly.

"We serve the flag. The trade we all follow is the give and take of death. It is for that purpose that the American people maintain us. Any one of us who believes he has a job like any other, for which he draws a money wage, is a thief of the food he eats and a trespasser in the bunk in which he lies down to sleep!"

It shocked them. Holman felt his cheeks burn. That was not the idea he had of himself. All along the ranks they were looking down at their feet.

Lt. Collins talked on, his voice quiet again. He talked about the flag code. There was a lot of it. The honey barges moved by and the air was clean once more. The flag was a Person, Lt. Collins said. The union of stars was the flag's honor point, its sword arm. You always displayed the flag so that it faced the beholders. There was only one time when the flag turned its back on the beholders. Lt. Collins' voice became hushed.

"That is at a military funeral, when one of us who has lived and died honorably goes to join the staff of the Great Commander," he said. "Then our flag lies face down on the coffin and clasps the dead man in its arms. I am not ashamed to believe that in that moment the spirit of the dead man passes directly into our flag. That is our special reward, who keep the military faith."

He said it quietly, looking at them quietly, and went right on.

"So may we all live and die honorably, each in his own time," he said. "And now in closing, I want to read you what Calvin Coolidge, our Commander in Chief, has to say about our flag."

He pulled a white card from his pocket and read: "Alone of all flags, it represents the sovereignty of the people, which endures when all else passes away. Speaking with their voice, it has the sanctity of revelation. He who lives under it and is loyal to it is loyal to truth and justice everywhere. He who lives under it and is disloyal to it is a traitor to the human race everywhere. What could be saved, if the Flag of the American Nation were to perish?"

He sighed and put the card away. He seemed abruptly smaller and less intensely present. He went forward, walking rapidly and looking at no one. Bordelles took over to dismiss the formation.

Afterward, the men stood around on the fantail. They were oddly quiet. Holman waited for someone to say something sarcastic. When men had been touched underneath, that was how they put themselves right again. Holman did not want to be the one to start it. No one started it.

"Let's go see what Big Chew's fixing to feed us today," Burgoyne proposed.

He and Holman walked forward. The galley was built in above the engine room on the port side. Its door opened on a triangular deck space that was the counterpart of the quarterdeck on the starboard side. One or both of the galley helpers, Small Chew and Jack Dusty, usually sat outside the door preparing vegetables. This morning it was Jack Dusty with red cabbage and green peppers.

"Smells good, whatever it is," Holman said.

A swab was propped across the galley door. Holman peered in. It was a long, narrow space with a white tile deck. A sink, a worktable and a black coal range stood along the inboard side. The range had two nickeled oven doors and pots and skillets hung on the bulkhead above it. Big Chew was stirring some pots on the range top. He saw Holman and turned, waving a spoon.

"No can! No can!" he said sharply. "Makee splice!"

Holman stepped back hastily. Big Chew was both fat and muscular under his white apron. He had a shaven bullet head and bold black eyes and a manner that said he knew he was boss in that galley.

"Splice what?" Holman asked Burgoyne. "The mainbrace?"

"He means surprise. We're going to have a holiday dinner."

The two men stood back at the rail, sniffing the good smells. They heard the oven door click and slam closed and a hot, spicy smell drifted out to them.

"Wonder what he's making?" Holman said.

The Sand Pebbles did not have names for Big Chew's dishes. No two of them were ever quite the same. They were all the best food Holman had ever eaten. He had already noted how the crew respected Big Chew. They would come to the galley and tell him how good the food was, but they would never think of joking with him as they did with Clip Clip.

"Any chow on here's better than a holiday dinner in the Fleet," Holman said.

"Ain't it the truth! She's a home and a feeder!"

Stawski and Ellis came up, sniffing, and Big Chew drove them off. Holman knew he was not going to feel like a thief when he ate that chow. The other men still did not mention the speech. Holman began to wonder if he was the only one disturbed by the speech.

All but Harris were quiet at dinner. Harris talked more loudly and obscenely than ever. Holman had always disliked foul talk at the mess table, and he had never once eaten a meal aboard any ship without it. The meal was baked ham and roast chicken, with vegetables and sauces, and the surprise was a special cake at the head of each table. The one between Holman and Farren was square, with white frosting, and decorated with a crude U.S. flag in red and blue sugar paste. The stars were a scatter of blue plus marks and below the flag Big Chew had put a Chinese character in red that meant good luck.

"Pass the pronging chicken," Harris said.

"All we got here's eating chicken," Holman said.

Harris scowled and reached a long arm for the chicken.

"You know, just for today, Harris ought to talk clean," Farren said.

"You want the poor bastard to strangle?" Wilsey said.

"Only way he knows how to talk is dirty," Burgoyne said.

"Prong you and all your relations, Frenchy."

"You forgot my ancestors back to George Washington."

"Prong them three times," Harris said. "All the way back to Miles Standish." He had a long, lopsided chin that almost met his sharp nose when he had his false teeth out. He always turned his head sideways to bite at his food.

"Harris learned all them words in his cradle," Restorff said. "His mother spoke them words over him when he was an innercent little baby."

It was a long speech for Restorff. Suddenly, like a fire in dry grass, they were all ganging up on Harris. Harris felt it, and his coarse white hair seemed to bristle more wildly.

"Harris never had a mother," Farren said.

"He wasn't a baby. He was a pup or cub or something," Holman said.

"He wasn't even born," Wilsey said. "He just crawled up out of the bilges one day and put on a white hat."

Harris stopped eating. He glared at them and his wide slash mouth grinned at them like a shark.

"Up all you bastards with a cargo hook," he growled. "I can talk decent, when there's any decent people to hear me."

"How do you know, if you never once tried?" Farren said. "I'll bet you can't."

"What'll you bet? How much?" Harris thrust his face at Farren.

"I'll bet you my ration of that cake."

"Bet money, you cheap bastard."

"We'll all bet you our cake rations," Wilsey said. "How about it, guys?" They all nodded. "How about it, Harris?" Wilsey said. "That's five to one odds for you. That's how sure we are you can't do it."

"Tell us a nice, clean sea story," Burgoyne said.

Harris slapped the table. "Maskee, I'll do that! I'll show you God . . . *blessed sailors!*" he said through his teeth. "Some of you maybe heard this story, but I was there and saw it happen. It was years ago, on the old . . . *South Dakota.*"

They all grinned, as Harris narrowly avoided the obscene nickname they all used for that ship.

"I had a kid striker in the electric gang, name of Arthur Lake," Harris said. "Arthur was a very clean kid. He wouldn't say . . . honey . . . if he had a mouthful. He had rosy cheeks and he wrote letters home and he kept his mother's picture inside his locker door. He went ashore to the Y to swim and sing songs. He was always cleaning his fingernails and he stoled our battery water to brush his teeth when water hours was on. When he scrubbed his clothes he wouldn't hang 'em in the uptakes, like the rest of the black gang. Oh, my no! He hung 'em topside with clothes stops, like the deck apes had to, because he said the sunlight made 'em smell clean and fresh. When he took a—I mean when he went to the head—he always used nine fathoms of . . . of . . . *toilet paper!*"

"Watch him sweat for them clean words," Wilsey said.

"Gettin' 'em, ain't I?" Harris was eating again, chewing and talking and glaring at each of his messmates in turn.

"One day in Shanghai Arthur and me and two watertenders was waiting for a sampan to come alongside so we could go ashore. Arthur kept looking down to where his skivvy shirt crossed the V of his dress white jumper and he would pull his jumper out with his finger and sniff. I guess he liked the clean smell of himself. Well, we got a sampan, and the old woman sculling it wanted a dollar to put us ashore. The tide was running out very strong and we drifted a long way downriver before we could make her take forty cents. Then she landed us on the outboard side of a whole mess of barges and she was clear before we found out all the inboard boats was loaded honey barges. Of course the old . . . lady . . . done it on purpose."

"Jesus!" Holman said.

"Watch it, Holman! You got to talk clean too," Harris said.

"I'm sorry," Holman said. "Go on."

"Well, it's easy to walk a honey barge gunwale most times," Harris resumed. "Only these all had dried mud dikes built up a foot high along the gunwales so they'd hold more. And they was level full, all greenish-brown and covered with flies and bubbles rising and breaking in the hot sun. Me and the watertenders went across, but Arthur was afraid. We joshed him about it, and the slopeheads was all watching and laughing, like they always are, and finally Arthur started across." Harris closed his eyes and threw back his head. "I can see him now. He come slow and careful and on his right that . . . stuff . . . was even with his shoe soles. It stunk so bad you could almost *hear* it stink and, I swear, it *drew* him. He had his arms out sideways and a awful look on his face and he'd sway out over the stuff and then right himself and sway out over the water, and he was like a drunk man in slow motion. Once he froze, and his face was as white as his jumper. Then he started coming again and halfway across he fell into the stuff. He went clear out of sight under it. Then he come up all dripping and in one smooth motion, like a porpoise jumping, he went over the side into the river. We waved money and yelled Joe Min and the slopeheads hollered and looked all around, but them tide currents had Arthur, and nobody ever seen him again."

Harris opened his eyes and grinned sharkishly along the table.

"There, by God! I guess I proved to you bastards I can talk clean."

"You son of a bitch!" Farren said. "You everlasting son of a bitch! You win, all right!" He shoved the cake down in front of Harris.

"We're sorry we doubted you, Harris. We learned our lesson," Wilsey said. "Now how about being a good shipmate and sharing that cake with us? You'll get a bellyache if you eat it all "

"Prong you hungry bastards." Harris plunged his fork into the cake and lifted a chunk to his mouth. The cake was reddish-brown under the white frosting. "I'll eat it all myself," Harris said, chewing. "What I can't eat, I'll spit on."

6

Show-the-flag cruising was very pleasant. They did not get underway until after quarters in the morning and they anchored before supper at night. Whenever he could, Lt. Collins anchored near a village or town and he would always spend several days at the walled cities. Hunan Province was hilly and green. There was the pale, feathery green of bamboo groves beside white farm compounds and the flat jade green of young rice fields and the glossy dark green of camphor and pomelo trees. In some places whole hillsides were pink and white with flowers and the breeze off those hills came fresh and pleasant across the decks of the *San Pablo*. Rocks and cliffs were olive green with moss and ferns and the bare earth of landslips was red.

Tungting Lake was like a huge pond with green, rocky islands in some places, and vast mudbank shallows and reed marshes in others, and clouds of white water birds that flew up screaming as the *San Pablo* thumped by their feeding grounds. In most places the lake had no definite shore, instead grading off into reed marsh, but near the Chien River the hills came right down to the lake, very steeply. They said the lake was really a big overflow basin for the rivers and it almost dried up in winter. The currents ran brown along the drowned river beds but in the shallows the mud settled out and the water was blue or green, depending on how the sunlight hit it. Breezes could roughen the water in little skipping dark spots here and there and a wind could roughen the whole surface and pick up a million glints from the sun, but there were no waves. It was very different from cruising on the ocean. The ocean was serious. The Chinese thought there were mermaids in Tungting Lake, but Franks said he had seen them and they were white porpoises. No one knew what porpoises were doing there, so far from the ocean. Probably the fresh water had bleached them. It was supposed to be bad luck to sight a white porpoise.

The *San Pablo* passed many junks in the rivers and on the lake and swarms of sampans with men fishing or shrimp trapping, and there were mat huts and fishtraps all along the shores. Sometimes they passed long timber rafts with matshed villages on top of them and children playing around the huts. Occasionally they would meet H.M.S. *Woodcock* or the Japanese gunboat *Hiro* and then they would man the rail and exchange formal passing honors. They carried a Chinese pilot and much of the time in the lake he kept two deck coolies in the bow sounding with bamboo poles and singsonging water depths in high Chinese voices that blended with the bird screams. The lake was tricky. Sometimes they would see long-beaked herons wading and fishing only a hundred feet from the ship and that would be the only way they could know there was a mudbank there.

Everywhere they went the Chinese looked at them with a special unwinking, jaw-hanging kind of look. They gaped from junks and sampans on the lake and from their fields along the river banks, faces shadowed under conical bamboo hats, and from their creaking treadmill pumps that lifted river water to the fields. The treadmill coolies would turn facing the river, five or six abreast with their shoulders against the wooden bar, never breaking the rhythm of their creaking, endless climb. They would watch the *San Pablo* thump and waddle past them, high and white and blocky, smoke trailing from her single tall stack, and it was not possible to tell from their faces what they were thinking. People would come out of the walled cities to stand and watch or to move slowly along the stone-faced river bank, with the same dumb looks. They would watch the Sand Pebbles at their musters and drills and calisthenics. For show-the-flag cruising, the bugling for drills and ship's routine was done by all four Fangs at once, and it made a hellish racket, because they were not good enough to stay together on the calls. But loud bugling made military face in China and warlord armies in the walled cities seemed to bugle day and night. The *San Pablo* had to outbugle the warlords. It was not possible to guess from their faces what the Chinese thought about it all.

There were some who watched without showing their faces. On the second day in the lake, passing a bluff headland, Holman heard Franks roar from the bridge: "All hands, take cover! Clear port side!" and a scatter of distant pops and the close-up hum of rifle bullets sent Holman running to the quarterdeck with his heart jumping. Stumpy Restorff was there beside the open arms locker, cleaning and oiling guns on a greasy hammock spread on deck. Ellis, the scarfaced seaman, was helping him.

"It's only a *toofay* salute," Restorff told Holman.

He was not excited. Bells jangled below and the fire doors clanged and the engine thud slowed. Ellis slipped a clip into a rifle and stood up.

"I'll try for a potshot from the galley windows," he said.

He left. Machine-gun fire crackled sharply from the bridge and then stopped. Pappy Tung and all the deck coolies had crowded into cover aft of the quarterdeck.

"What's *toofay?* Who the hell's shooting at us?" Holman asked.

"*Toofay*. Bandits," Restorff grunted.

The machine gun on the bridge cut loose again briefly and Ellis fired rapidly from the galley. After a long pause, the *San Pablo*'s whistle sounded. The little gunboat had a deep, hoarse whistle that would better have suited an ocean liner, and Burgoyne said it dropped the steam ten pounds every time they blasted it. Bells jangled again and the engine thud picked up and the deck coolies scattered back to their painting and scrubbing. Ellis came back with his rifle and a pot of steaming water.

"Damn it, now I got to scald it out," he said. "Thought I saw something move in them bushes, but likely I didn't."

The *San Pablo* exchanged salutes with the *toofay* about once a week. Every town and district of Hunan was controlled by different groups of armed men. If they obeyed the treaties and did not interfere with treaty people, they were warlord troops. If they shot at gunboats and robbed such palefaces as they could catch, they were bandits. They all treated the civilian Chinese about the same, and that was not very well. Some of the minor warlords were supposed to be subordinate to the big warlord in Changsha, but for the most part each one was king in his own area. A great part of Lt. Collins' job was dealing with warlords.

Each steaming day Holman spent four hours on throttle watch, with Burgoyne tending water. He liked that, he and Burgoyne in dungarees and stripped to the waist, hand rags dangling from hip pockets and sweat towels around their necks, and the main-drive machinery talking and moving all around them. They steamed an easy five or six knots in the rivers and three or four knots in the lake and it was easy steaming. Too easy, Holman learned on his first watch.

He kept the log and handled the throttle and Chien had charge of everything else. The old man moved all day between engine room and fireroom watching his coolies stoke furnaces and feel bearings and oil down and swab rods. When the low-pressure crank bearing ran hot it was Chien who gave it the emergency treatment with brown soap and water and came to the throttle station and told Holman he would have to slow the engine by ten revolutions. Chien had the only authority that counted, the authority to make decisions about the machinery and to carry them out. But Holman signed the log and he had the official responsibility. Old Chien could not have that, because he had no legal existence for the navy. Holman went to see Lynch.

"I want a real steaming watch," he said. "I know they got to be Chinamen, but I want the same ones each watch and I want to know who they are and I want to train 'em and know I can trust 'em."

"You can trust Chien. You see anything wrong before Chien does, you just tell him," Lynch said. "Hell, Jake, it's easy as driving a car, way it is now. Why look for trouble?"

"Because I feel like a dummy down there," Holman said.

The throttle was the honor point. No Chinese was permitted to touch the throttle. But in effect they had everything else, and it was a stupid honor. Holman wrangled carefully with Lynch, not revealing all that he felt.

"All right, I'll settle for one man, to be my oiler on the main engine," he said at last. "That coolie, Po-han. Reckon that'd hurt old Chien's feelings too much?"

"I'll talk to Chien," Lynch said.

Chien gave in on Po-han, but he didn't like it. It was all unofficial, of course. Chien called Holman "Mastah" when they spoke, which was seldom. Scuttlebutt sprang up that Holman and Chien were feuding. That was probably Perna's work, Holman thought. Perna was a sly bird. He and Wilsey and Stawski stood their watches in the old way, often one man tending both throttle and feed checks while the other was cooling off topside. Perna pretty well led Stawski, the big, stupid fireman, on a leash. There was one other fireman, a kid named Waxer, who did not stand steaming watches. He was a striker to Harris and also to Waldhorn, the radioman. One of Chien's coolies named Chiu-pa seemed to do all the electrical work.

Holman began to like Burgoyne. He was mild and easy-going, willing to let Chien run the fireroom, where Burgoyne was in charge on paper, but he sympathized with Holman's desire for more control in the engine room. The throttle station was a brightly lighted angle formed by the log desk, with the gauge board up behind it, and the forward part of the engine. It was like a quarterdeck for the engine room. Burgoyne would stand there, drooping his lean, tattooed weight by one hand from an overhead valve wheel, legs crossed, smoothing his drooping mustache with his free hand, under lip bulging with the Copenhagen which he spat at intervals into the trash bucket beside the log desk. He was a simple, pleasant, unhurried man and a good watchmate. Sometimes he would sit on an upended bucket, elbows on knees. Holman invariably stood balanced easy and ready on both feet, watching the many-formed motions of the engine and listening to all the machinery sounds, even as he talked. Po-han ranged along the engine and back into the shaft alley on his oiling duties, and he was always coming to the throttle station to ask questions. Po-han was afire to learn.

"I swear, Jake, Po-han's the little image of you," Burgoyne said one day. "Same square build and all the muscles, only his skin's darker." Burgoyne looked from Holman to the cheerful, grinning coolie. "I *do* swear it! Stands like you and cocks his head the same— Jake, he's studying to ape you."

"Let him," Holman said. "He'll be a good engineer."

Po-han's English got better every day. He was still linking up all the little magics into the big magic and he wanted to learn names. *May . . . stim . . . stah . . . wowel!* he would say, for *main steam stop valve,* his eyes shining with joy in a new name learned. He was fitting what he learned into a very weird scheme of his own that Holman drew out of him one afternoon on watch. Po-han spoke as much of it as he could and acted out the rest. They laughed, watching him, and Po-han laughed too, because they were all friends. To Po-han, the engine was a metal dragon. The dragon ate steam and excreted exhaust steam to the condenser. The air pump and feed pumps were metal coolies and boatmen who returned the digested steam to the fields. The boilers were the fields and the stoker coolies out there were farmers who had captive suns in their furnaces. They were continuously raising a crop of steam which Holman, as throttleman, continuously harvested and fed to the dragon. It was honorable to be a steam farmer, but the greatest honor was to attend the dragon and massage his limbs and oil his joints. Po-han was very pleased and excited by his scheme.

"Who'd ever guess he was thinking like that, watching him work? Pure wonders you, don't it?" Burgoyne shook his head. "Steam farm. The sun in a cage." He laughed. "You could sure God get sunburned by them suns, all right."

"It ain't just funny," Holman said. "He's got to make it hang together best way he can. Don't you, Po-han?" He slapped the coolie's shoulder and grinned at him. "You know, Frenchy, coal was moss and ferns a million years ago, and it took sun to grow it. When you burn coal, it's like turning that sunlight loose again. When you blister your arm on a steam valve, you really are sunburned, in a way of figuring."

"A funny way of figuring. I'll have to study that."

"It is, Frenchy, you think it through." The notion was exciting Holman. He pointed to the electric light above them. "That's million-year-old sunlight," he said.

"You're bad as Po-han," Burgoyne said. "How do you guys think up stuff like that?" He grinned and spat in the trash bucket. "Steam farms. I'll have to tell Perna that."

"No. Perna'd make a nasty joke out of it," Holman said. "Po-han trusts us, to tell us things like that."

"You're right. I won't tell Perna."

Through all their steaming watches Chien's coolies worked on cleaning and minor repairs and old Chien drifted around watching everything. He always wore his shiny black, close-buttoned jacket and he never had sweat on his bony face. Holman seldom spoke to him and he often felt the old man's hostile eyes on the back of his neck. It would be no use to ask old Chien what scheme he had to hang the plant together. Probably he did not have a scheme, Holman thought, and he did not want to see Po-han gain one. Whatever the reason, Chien neither liked nor trusted Holman and Po-han.

Holman found some eighth-inch copper tubing and wound it into a steam coil and hooked it into the back pressure line to the feed heater. He got a gray enamel pitcher and some mess cups from Wong and began making engine room coffee. The smell of the coffee, added to the odors of hot oil, hot metal and scorched rubber packing, made the engine room smell right to him for the first time. You always put a big pinch of salt into a pot of engine room coffee before you boiled it, to make up for the salt you lost in sweating. It gave the coffee a special flat, oily kind of taste.

"This is right good," Burgoyne said, tasting his first cup of it. "I like to forgot how black gang coffee tasted."

At first the other watch would not make any coffee. They kept on sending to the galley for it. Po-han did not drink any of it, because Chinese did not like coffee and because it was strictly against old custom for them to use crew's mess gear. Even when Wong and Clip Clip ate leftovers from the crew's mess, they always used chopsticks and tin pieplates. One morning Lynch sniffed the coffee smell from above and came down for a cup.

"Ain't smelled that for years," he said. "Makes me hungry for a cup." He sipped at it. "Ain't no coffee like shaft alley coffee," he said.

On other ships all the engineers believed that. After a week or so Perna and Wilsey and Stawski also began brewing and drinking engine room coffee.

The summer cruising shook Holman down to the ship's routine. There were the daily drills and musters. Every Friday there was lower-deck inspection. Lt. Collins and Bordelles and the chiefs, all in white, walked through the engine room and fireroom with old Chien hovering along in their wake to take their praise of how clean and shipshape it all was. They never asked how well it ran. Saturdays they had personnel inspection and Holman hated that as much as he always had. It was really no strain. The compartment coolies shined shoes the night before and laid out clean uniforms in the morning and Oh Joy always made a great chattering fuss about each man looking just right before he went out. It was the simple standing there and being looked at like a thing that Holman hated. After personnel inspection came inspection of topside and living spaces. It was a royal progress of Lt. Collins through the ship, accompanied by Bordelles and the chiefs, the Red Dog to take notes, Farren bearing a flashlight, one Fang in the lead to bugle *attention* when they came to a place, and another Fang in the rear to bugle *carry on* when they left it. Holman had to stand by the quarterdeck arms locker for topside inspection. They never inspected the Chinese living quarters, in the old iron hull of the ship, below the main deck.

About every ten steaming days they coaled ship, usually from Chinese barges. Chanting coolies streamed aboard with the coal in flat baskets on top of their heads and dumped it down the deck scuttles. Other coolies below in the bunkers leveled and trimmed and the work went fast. The *San Pablo* had one thwartship and two wing bunkers, boxing in the fireroom, and they held about ninety tons. Lynch always took Chien's word for tonnage and quality.

"Chien's the guy that's got to burn it, he'll look out for slate," Lynch told Holman. "Don't worry about it."

Bordelles would pay whatever Lynch said to pay, and coal was one of the big sources of the squeeze that paid all the coolies. Bordelles always paid in silver Mex dollars because they did not trust paper money in Western Hunan. There were no banks there, and Bordelles had to carry enough silver for the whole summer. They said he always left Hankow with his bathtub so full of silver dollars he could not take a bath until the Fourth of July. As soon as the coal was aboard, Pappy Tung and his deck coolies would go after the coal dust with hoses, scrubbers and rags, and in an hour or two the *San Pablo* would be as brass-gleaming white as ever.

Payday was every other week and it involved more of the things Jake Holman did not like. Bordelles knew every man in the crew, yet he had to countersign each pay receipt as witness of the man's signature and then watch each man put his fingerprints on the back of his pay receipt to prove that he was really the man he was pretending to be. They had to file past the mess table to draw their money with their hats clamped under their arms, and the only other place you had to carry your hat that way was in officers' country. Welbeck and Bordelles, wearing pistols, sat in Burgoyne's and Harris' places at the mess table, and behind them Duckbutt Randall, also armed, guarded a dishpan full of reserve Mex dollars in brown paper rolls. Lop Eye Shing sat next to Bordelles, in Farren's place, to collect each man's coolie bill.

The first payday was Holman's first sight of Lop Eye Shing. He was tall and robust, with a big nose for a Chinese, and he did not look as old as he must have been. His paralysis gave his face a sad, sinister look, the left eyelid drooping—that was why they called him Lop Eye—and the left corner of his mouth drooped. The right side of his face was firm and bold. He talked good English, slurring some words, and when he talked little flickers of life ran through the left side of his face, but they never quite caught. He had a deep voice for a Chinese and he always wore a black skull cap and a gray gown and he walked with a gold-mounted cane. It was very plain that the other coolies were afraid of him.

Shing collected a lump sum that covered laundry and barber and tailor bills and tips for Wong and Oh Joy, and it came to about ten percent of each man's pay. No one ever asked for a breakdown. Shing dumped the dollars clinking into a basket on deck beside the table and they made quite a heap when it was all there. Then Clip Clip and Oh Joy would carry the basket aft and down to the Chinese quarters while Shing shuffled behind them with his cane. After payday the men who did not have liberty would gamble, rolling dice or playing blackjack, and sometimes poker. Restorff was usually the big winner.

When they were not steaming, Holman took his regular turn at quarterdeck watches. He learned to stand them well, disliking them but never hinting it. All the ship's traffic funneled across the quarterdeck, and at times it was interesting. The big event each day at anchor was when the chow came aboard. Big Chew would go over to market, importantly in a gray silk gown and carrying a fan and parasol. At the walled cities, he would always have a sedan chair to carry him, while Small Chew or Jack Dusty ran alongside. Having selected the food, Big Chew would come back alone and shortly afterward his helper and the market people would bring the food down. The food had to be inspected on the quarterdeck and the Sand Pebbles liked to gather and watch it and speculate on how it would taste.

Jennings, the pharmacist's mate, inspected the food. He took all his responsibilities very seriously and he was never known to laugh. He was a blond man with close-clipped hair and a rosy face and large, solemn pink eyes behind steel-rimmed glasses. He would kneel and look at the profusion of fruits and leafy vegetables in straw and wicker baskets and then look up at Big Chew.

"Chew, you must wash all this very thoroughly in permanganate solution," he would say.

Then Jennings would stare dubiously at the meat, usually pork and chicken, poke it, smell of it, and make fussy worry-sounds.

"Chew, you must cook this meat very, very thoroughly," he would say.

Big Chew never washed anything in permanganate, but he cooked it all Chinese fashion and no one ever got sick. The *San Pablo* did not have refrigeration and, except for dry stores, they had to live off the country. Away from Hankow the food was almost wholly Chinese. It was roast duck and chicken and pork and ham cut up small and sweet little shrimps stewed or boiled or fried with rice and all manner of vegetables and spicy, gingery sauces. Every meal was different and each one was an experience to remember. Bordelles always paid without question whatever Big Chew said it cost, and that was another big source of squeeze.

"Who cares, so long as Big Chew stays inside the ration and keeps the troops happy?" Welbeck would say.

Big Chew kept the troops happy, all right. After every meal someone or other was certain to lean back and pat his stomach and say, "I can't give her much on liberty, but by God she's a home and a feeder!" He would be speaking for all of them.

She could not be very much on liberty in Western Hunan, because there were no treaty ports with bars and whorehouses for the ocean devils. Off duty, the Sand Pebbles flaked out in their bunks or played cribbage and acey-deucey at the mess tables or stood on deck and stared back at the Chinese. Out in the lake, they sometimes went ashore to explore islands or hunt or fish through the mud flats and the reed marshes. There were millions of birds, but they lost most of those they shot, and they were always talking about getting a ship's dog.

They could go ashore sightseeing in the walled cities, but they had a rigid rule not to get drunk. The Hunan coolies were not as tame as the treaty port coolies and there were no Sikh cops to keep them in line. The old walled cities interested Holman. They lay along the rivers, with a paved bund and flights of stone steps leading down from it to the water. The walls were old and crumbling and gray, with embrasured parapets, but with lines of laundry flapping up there instead of knights in armor. The gate houses had heavy, curving tiled roofs, like temples. All day long files of water coolies yo-hoed and slopped their way up the steps from the river with wooden buckets of water at the end of carrying poles, because the cities had no other water system. They had no electricity either, and the only lights at night were bobbing paper lanterns.

They did not even have rickshaws. People who rode inside the cities had to ride jouncing in sedan chairs carried by coolies who never stopped screaming for gangway. Holman liked to walk through the narrow, crowded streets of open-front shops and stop and watch the work going on in back—woodcarving with the clean smell of camphorwood, chopstick splitting with the smell of varnish, the beating out of silver into the thin foil they used to make money for dead people in an endless shower of hammer *tinks*. The Chinese stared back at Holman, and he was a show to them. He wandered long, smelly, stone-paved streets narrow enough to span with his arms and roofed into dim tunnels with bamboo and matting. He always went into the temples and stared back at the fierce guard-gods with black beards and glaring eyes, and he nodded at the fat, calm Buddhas and smiled back at the gravely smiling Kwan Yins. He always left his money in Kwan Yin's offering box. He was struck again and again with the thought that up until now he had never really been in China, but only in the treaty ports, which were a kind of bastard China.

Sometimes in the cities he would meet other palefaces, walking or in chairs, and they would pretend not to see each other. It was well known that missionaries despised sailors. They thought sailors set bad examples and cut down the local recruiting for Jesus, and the scuttlebutt was that they wanted all the gunboats taken clear out of China. Ensign Bordelles always had to call on the missionaries and see if they were having any trouble. Lt. Collins would not see them unless he had to. But he always called on the local warlords and went to their feasts and invited them and their staffs aboard the *San Pablo* for dinner in the wardroom. They would come down to the ship in chairs, some wearing civilian gowns and some in uniform, and the Sand Pebbles always put on a smart show of saluting and bugling. Big Chew would feed their enlisted bodyguard outside the galley. Warlord soldiers never looked very military. They were scrawny men in sleazy gray cotton uniforms and straw sandals, and in full kit they would have a teapot hung from their belts and a paper parasol. It was common knowledge that they never fought battles, but only made a great looksee pidgin of yelling and shooting in the air, while their warlords fought the real battle with silver bullets.

The *San Pablo* carried a locked storeroom full of beer in brown quart bottles, bought with the welfare fund. Several evenings each week Oh Joy would hire a sampan or wupan to lie alongside and the liberty men would go down into it to drink beer, because it was against regulation to drink beer aboard. They had to pay Oh Joy for the beer, and the profit went into the general coolie fund. Oh Joy would keep the beer in a tub with gunny sacks and pour river water over it to cool it as much as he could. He was a spry, dry, chattering old Chinaman with big yellow front teeth, and he looked like a wise, wicked old rabbit.

Every payday they would have what Jennings called a "biological." They always arranged to be at one of the walled cities, and Holman's first one was at Changteh on the Yuan River, when he was still restricted from the Hankow trouble. Oh Joy and Clip Clip went ashore to line things up and the hired junk came alongside right after breakfast. Drills went sloppily that morning because the Sand Pebbles were trying to catch glimpses of the women and they were all kidding Jennings. He would go aboard the junk and take smears and paint iodine numbers on their bellies so nobody could switch them on him when he came back to run his clap tests in the *San Pablo* sick bay. It would have been easier to bring the women to the sick bay, but there was a regulation against that. The Sand Pebbles always accused Jennings of turning down the young, pretty ones and keeping the old and ugly ones with bound feet.

Excitement would build up and just before dinner Red Dog Shanahan would always put on the same act in the open space by

the barber chair, which they called the bull ring. Red Dog would
sketch out with gestures a woman on the deck and pretend to be
Jennings examining her. Here now, down with the trousers, he would
say, pulling them down, and up with the jacket, rolling it back, and he
would paint the iodine number on the imaginary belly with pursed
lips and sweeping flourishes. Sometimes the woman didn't understand
and the Red Dog would assure her that it was only doctor pidgin.
Then he would poke and prod and sniff and squint and wrinkle his
nose and make worry noises, exactly as Jennings always did when
he examined meat on the quarterdeck. The Sand Pebbles at the mess
tables would hush laughing as Crosley began sneaking up behind the
Red Dog. Crosley would wait until the Red Dog had his head right
down in there and then he would make to push it while they all held
their breaths and, after a few false starts, he would push it. The Red
Dog would pretend his head was caught and he would lunge and buck
and strangle while everybody roared. Finally he would get his head
out and then reach in after his imaginary glasses and begin wiping
them off.

"Crosley," he would say solemnly, "you must be sure to prong
this meat very, very thoroughly."

That always brought the most thundering laugh of all.

At Changteh, when dinner was finished, Franks sounded his bosun's
pipe on the quarterdeck and passed the word: "Awa-a-ay *boarders!*"
The liberty men climbed across to the foredeck of the junk, where
there was room for Clip Clip tending a tub of beer and room to roll
dice for drinks. They also rolled to see who went first on the women
and who took wet decks, and there was much laughing and despairing
and arguing. The junk was the middle-sized kind, with three cabins
in the low deckhouse amidships and a narrow walkway along each
side. Oh Joy squatted on top of the deckhouse and collected two
dollars from each man who entered one of the low, sliding doors.
There was a standing argument about which was best, to keep going
back to the best-looking girl or to take each in turn. Crosley, Ellis,
Stawski and Perna formed what they called the Clean Sweep Club, and
the last one to make a clean sweep had to buy beer for the others.

The duty section men stood along the bulwark and watched enviously. When one of the liberty men had enough, he could come back aboard and stand by for a duty man, and before the day ended all hands except the restricted men had a crack at it. For the first one, Holman was glad that he was still restricted. The junk was hired for the day by Oh Joy and the women were from someplace on the beach; the people who owned the junk and lived aboard it stayed inside the stern castle. Twice a little boy got out and wanted to play on deck and his mother scolded him and dragged him howling back inside. Wong kept handing more beer across to Clip Clip and taking the empties aboard. They were singing and having a very good time on the junk. The best-looking girl was in the center cabin and she got most of the repeat trade. Late in the afternoon she began crying and wailing inside the cabin and shortly afterward Bronson came out and went forward.

"What'd you do to that pig, to make her cry like that?" Harris asked Bronson. "You ain't hung as heavy as all that."

"She dropped her shoe in the piss pot," Bronson said. "Hell of a thing to bawl about, ain't it?"

She was still crying inside there when the junk pulled away, after evening colors. It cut down her trade a lot, but Oh Joy climbed down off the deckhouse with a whole sack full of Mex dollars. Clip Clip had a smaller sack full, from the beer. The profits from the biologicals went into the general coolie fund.

In spite of the comforts and interests topside and ashore, Holman still loved the engine. On a steaming watch he would often lose the thread of Burgoyne's talk as his eyes and ears drifted off into the engine, into the maze of oil-shining brass and steel higher than a man's head and twenty feet long and all in whirling, stroking, rocking, lawful motion. The three piston rods stroked up and down out of the overhead cylinders, driving the crossheads to bend like giant knees. The crossheads drove the conn rods like thick legs striding and the cranks went round and round like ponderous feet and ankles. Beside each crank, driven by it, the twinned eccentrics jigged their diverging rods to each end of the rocking, overarching link bars, which in turn drove slender valve spindles back into the cylinder casting to measure and control the flow of power to the cranks. It was all flowing power, tons of sculptured metal in cyclical, patterned motion, and the light played through it in a pattern of rhythmic gleam and shadow. The manifold, repeating sounds of it flowed into Holman's ears. The vibrations came in through his hands and feet and the smell of steam and hot oil and burnt packing filled his nostrils. It was all inside of him in a pattern of blood-pulse and nerve-thrill.

Then he knew the engine was a blind, bolted-down giant doing a tireless three-legged dance. On his starboard side the main circulator *chuck-chuck-chucked* rapidly, pushing the cooling river water through the condenser tubes, and on his port side the main air pump plunged and wheezed and gasped, starting the condensed steam on its way back to the boilers. Aft and away, whirling whitely through spring bearings and the squat thrust block, the shaft ran into the gloom of its long tunnel.

Holman was tuning his ears to hear the individual sound of each working part of the engine and of each pump and, while he talked absently to Burgoyne, he would practice picking each one out separately with his ears. Within a few watches he had added an ear picture to the eye picture already inside his head, and he could make an inspection tour of the engine room with his ears alone, without leaving the throttle station. Whatever was going wrong, he would know it. That faculty with his ears was what had made men on other ships think Jake Holman had black magic with machinery. He began teaching it to Po-han. He was increasingly pleased with how Po-han could learn. The eager young coolie was teaching himself, and when Holman opened a new door for him, Po-han knew how to explore the room for himself. He was always surprising Holman with how much he had learned. Burgoyne praised Po-han and took pride in him too, because they were all watchmates.

Holman's ear picture was ugly because of the *thud* in the low-pressure crank bearing. Something was wrong with the L.P. and old Chien and his coolies had to refit the bearing about every five steaming days. The first day it would run almost quiet, but also hot, having to be nursed with soapy water and oil flooding and reducing speed until it wiped itself enough clearance to run easy. But then would begin the muted *thud* each time the great crank came round, and the shiver that ran dumbly through the ship. By the fourth day the *thud* would be loud and jarring and, to Holman, dangerous, although no one else minded it. Then Chien would refit it again.

Chien did not want Holman to watch the bearing work. He and his coolies would hunch over it and conceal as much as they could, and it was not often that Holman's topside military duties gave him time even to try to watch. Chien never asked Holman to inspect and approve a bearing job or any other repair job. He would get anyone else who had paper authority, even Stawski, rather than Jake Holman. It irked Holman to see a stupid fireman like Stawski gravely inspecting and approving a job he could not possibly have done himself. Holman ached to refit the L.P. crank bearing with his own hands, coolie work or no. He was sure that after a few such refits he would begin to see a wear pattern that might tell him what was wrong.

"It has to be out of alignment some way," he told Lynch one day. They were drinking coffee at the throttle station.

"That thump's been in there for twenty years and nobody's ever been able to take it out," Lynch said. "It ain't alignment. I've seen that engine in dockyard stripped to the soleplate with piano wire through every cylinder. Nothing's out of line."

"I bet I could take out that thump, or else find out exactly why I can't," Holman said. "There ain't no mysteries about machinery."

"Big talk, Jake."

"Give me a chance to prove it, Chief."

"Oh hell, old as this ship is, ready for the scrap heap when they commission the new ones—" Lynch gestured impatiently and spilled his coffee. He was irritated. "Let old Chien handle it. Hell, she steams, don't she?"

"Chien'll keep her steaming," Burgoyne said. "He always has."

Holman dared not press it, because Lynch had already cautioned him several times about cutting in on Chien. The old man had been complaining. Scuttlebutt persisted that Holman and Chien were feuding. Yet all that Holman did was to walk around on steaming watch inspecting, and learning the plant with his ears, and teaching Po-han. Chien didn't want anybody to learn. He wanted Holman to stay by the throttle and exercise only paper authority while Chien himself kept the real authority, the only kind of authority that the machinery acknowledged, and the only kind that was real to Jake Holman.

Chien was always around, working his coolies, and his blank old face and stiff shoulders expressed disapproval whenever Holman left the throttle station. Po-han would not talk about Chien. He was very much afraid of Chien. Holman sometimes worried that Chien might strike at Po-han, who was a very junior coolie. But Chien struck in other ways. Small things began to go wrong on watch. Holman would pick them up with his ears as often as with his eyes and go directly to the trouble and set it right. Then he would show Po-han, and that was how he struck back at Chien. It was a feud, but a very strange one. Once the vacuum began dropping, which meant an air leak, and Holman's ears picked up the tiny, trilling whisper clear across the engine room and through all the greater noise. It was an old hidden, forgotten valve on the air pump suction line, which had probably been a gauge connection many years ago. Holman went to it and reached under the floorplates and closed it in one sure motion, without even looking to find it. Then he rose and turned to meet Chien's stare. The old man's yellowed teeth were bared, and his face expressed pure terror.

Often on a steaming watch Holman would lean with his hands on the protecting handrail and watch the L.P. crank as it thumped around. He knew there was misalignment, whatever Lynch said, and he hoped he might spot it with his eyes. He would watch the ton of moving metal sweep out its thirty-inch circle, half its orbit above the floorplates and half down in the crankpit, like rolling day and night. He could not spot anything. But his ears picked up an almost inaudible whispering. It seemed to shift and vary and came from everywhere at once. His ears could not pin it down and identify it. It was a tiny, fretful web of little mutterings and it was trying to tell him something.

He would stand there for long minutes straining to interpret it. Then he would feel the hair bristle on the back of his neck and he would turn and Chien would be looking at him with that flat, bony old stare.

7

One morning in mid-August a white porpoise crossed their bow. An hour later they got orders from Comyang in Hankow to go at once to Paoshan on the Chien River, where antiforeign riots were supposed to be in progress. They were already on their way to Paoshan and all it meant was raising speed to the maximum of eight knots, which would get them to Paoshan in late afternoon instead of next day. No one was very excited.

The drill that morning was landing force, and they rolled full packs. Holman was in Bordelles' section, with Farren as squad leader and Crosley, Shanahan, Ellis and Tullio as squadmates. They fell in on the fantail and it was the same as always, Bordelles inspecting gear and arms and taking a swallow from someone's canteen to make sure the water was clean and fresh. Then he went to the bridge to report.

"Farren, you figure we really got to go ashore and shoot somebody?" Holman asked. He wanted them to show the same tension that he was feeling.

"Not shoot," Farren said. "The warlord'll stop it. Maybe General Pan's men will have to shoot."

They all explained to Holman. Warlords sometimes had reasons for not stopping riots, but when they could save face by blaming it on a gunboat, they would usually stop them. They would explain to the people that if they did not more gunboats would come and kill everybody. Just the presence of the *San Pablo* moored under the wall with its flag and guns would probably calm Paoshan right down, Farren said.

"They're beating up native Christians and looting 'em," Crosley said. "Likely Pan wasn't squeezing enough protection money and he just wanted to put the fear of Christ in 'em, to up the squeeze."

"Yeah, but what if he won't stop it? Or can't?"

"Then we'll stop it," Farren said.

"But how do you stop a riot?"

"Walk at 'em with guns," Crosley said. "If they don't give ground, fire over their heads. Then they'll break and run."

"They'll be howling in Chinese," the Red Dog said. "You won't understand it, Jake, but what they'll be yelling is: 'Here comes the great and terrible Red Dog Shanahan! Run for your lives and hide all your virgins!' "

"Hide all their *samshu,*" Ellis said.

"Arf! Arf!"

"No, but God damn it, I mean, what if they shoot back?" Holman persisted. "Come at us?"

Farren shrugged. "We'll make the best fight we can. We'll mow the bastards like hay, while we last."

They all nodded. It made Holman know how deadly seriously they took all the drills that were only an irksome make-believe to him. He still did not believe he was to going to shoot anyone, or be shot at. He looked across the rail at the river and the green, swampy delta land from which white birds were flying upward screaming. He did not want to look at their faces. He did not know these shipmates of his.

"Hell, don't talk like that, Jake," Tullio said. "They won't come at us."

"They'll run," Crosley said. "Slopeheads always run."

"Silence in ranks!" Bordelles had come back to dismiss them.

"Chief Franks' section will go ashore with the captain," he said. "We'll stand by in reserve aboard. Leave your packs and your guns on your bunks."

It was just like any other drill to all of them but Holman.

When Holman took the steaming watch after dinner, Wilsey was making eight-point-two knots and the thump in the L.P. was worse than Holman had ever heard it. The greater power was wiping and pounding the soft metal more rapidly, and the more the clearance increased the worse it pounded, and it was like a snowball rolling downhill. At one o'clock Holman sent for Lynch.

"Chief, we got to stop and take some clearance out of that bearing," he told Lynch.

"I heard it that bad before." Lynch was scornful. "We only got about three more hours."

"She won't make it."

"Chien says she will. I already told the skipper she will."

Lynch went up angry. The knock became worse. It took on a sharp, bone-thudding quality that made the floorplates chatter and the wrenches behind the workbench jump in their hangers. Old Chien hovered near the L.P., watching it narrowly. He was acting worried. So were Po-han and Burgoyne worried, and Holman's nerves fined to a wire edge. At two o'clock he sent for Lynch again.

"I'm scared, Chief," he said. "I'm going to cut to half speed."

"Make your turns."

"She's about to carry away, Chief," Holman said. "She'll blow a head and scald us. She'll flail the rod through the bottom and *sink* the Goddamned ship!" He reached for the fireroom annunciator. "I'm going to slow down."

Lynch blocked his hand. "No, you ain't! Make your turns! By God, that's a military order!" He was frowning and his lips were pooching in and out. He was angry and afraid too, and he was being stubborn.

"Put that in writing!" They had to shout at each other above the engine racket. "Put that on paper, with your name under it, and

I'll do it," Holman shouted. Lynch shook his head. "Okay, then, take this throttle!" Holman yelled. "You and Chien can have the watch, you're so Goddamned sure about it! Come on, Frenchy!"

He made to leave and Lynch stopped him. "We'll secure," he said, and walked around the engine. "Chien! Burn down your fires!" he yelled at the old man. "Pretty soon makee stop."

Lynch went up and Chien went to the fireroom. Holman began easing in the throttle. Lynch came back down with Lt. Collins, who looked angry and impatient. Chien came back and his coolies laid out wrenches and a sledge. The job would not take very long. Wilsey and Perna and Stawski came down in whites and drifted around. They wanted to make a show of concern and being useful, because the captain was down there.

When the steam was low enough they anchored. It seemed very quiet, with the jarring thud stopped. Holman stayed at the throttle to position the L.P. crank, which would have to be at top center. The control lever worked a small reversing engine that could slide the great, curving, double-bar links back and forth through the main engine and hold them at any point. When they were in mid-position the three slide valves were supposed to be closed and the engine stopped. But the valves leaked and, even with the steam shut off at the throttle, air leaked up the piston rods to create a pressure imbalance with the vacuum in the condenser, and the engine would still run. It would lie quiet until enough air leaked in and then it would suddenly jump, one way or the other. To hold the L.P. on top, Holman had to keep jiggling the lever very slightly across midposition. The tremor of the control lever was magnified to an oscillation of several inches in the links and the great crank rolled ahead and checked and back and checked and Holman held the engine rocking there, all the trembling tons of it instantly responsive to his hand, and it felt like an extension of his own bone and muscle. He was showing Chien how well he could control the engine. Then they put in the jacking gear, pinning the worm in place engaged with the worm wheel on the shaft, and the engine was in a secure mechanical lock. Holman locked the control in mid-position and went around to watch the job.

The crank was still trying to roll. It was working through the backlash of the jacking gear with sharp clicks each way, but the gear held it. The crank bearing was like a beer barrel split lengthwise and clamped around the crankpin with two big bolts on each side. They would have to back off the nuts enough to drop the bottom half slightly and take out a thin metal shim from each side and reduce clearance, and then slug the nuts up tight once more. It was emergency procedure and the coolies were not used to it. They were all afraid to get down into the crankpit and hold the wrench. Chien shrilled at them and they screamed back.

"Why don't they begin, Lynch?" Lt. Collins asked. "You told me ten minutes."

"I'll get down there and hold the wrench," Holman said.

"My takee lench! My takee lench!"

Chien did not want to lose face by working, but even more he did not want Jake Holman getting in on any repair job. He took off his black satin jacket, to keep it clean, and his bony old man's chest was hairless and smooth and showed every rib. He climbed down and held the wrench and the work went fast. The heavy-set coolie named Chiu-pa swung the sledge. When the shims were out he slugged the nuts up full due again and Chien handed out the wrench. Chien was tightening the set screws that locked the nuts when the crank came grinding at him with a high, dry squeal.

Holman flew to the control lever. He heard the one great scream as the crank crushed the old man's chest and drove his air out, and then he had the crank checked and trembling back on top center. Chien slid down out of sight, to the bottom of the crankpit. They were all running and yelling now. Lt. Collins started into the crankpit and Lynch pulled him back. Wilsey was prying up a floorplate. They were going to go into the bilges and pull Chien out through the manhole in the soleplate and that would twist and wrench hell out of the broken old man.

"Lynch, come here!" Holman yelled. "God damn you, Lynch, *come here!*"

Lynch came. He was pale and staring. Holman pulled Lynch's hand to the control lever.

"Hold her on top!" he said, and ran.

Chien was doubled over flat in the crankpit, head between legs. Holman straddled him in the slippery oil and water and reached between his own legs to grasp the skinny arms at the shoulders. He straightened up, lifting Chien carefully, and the crank kept nudging the back of his head with short, dry squeals. Lynch could not hold it as steady as Holman had. Lt. Collins leaned down to take Chien from Holman, and the old man's face passed an inch away from Holman's face. The eyes were open and the pupils very large and there was no expression in the eyes. Chien's mouth was open and bubbly blood came out of it and his chest was all torn and bloody. Jennings was on the floorplates with blankets and a stretcher, and when Holman climbed out of the crankpit they were already carrying Chien up the ladder.

Holman looked at Lt. Collins. Neither spoke. They both had blood on them. Holman knelt and took out the jacking gear. He could see that the shaft had turned inside the worm wheel. He stood up again and he was beginning to shake.

"I guess we can get underway now, sir," he said.

Lt. Collins seemed to jerk. "Yes. Yes, we can," he said.

He went up the ladder and Holman went around to the throttle. Lynch's face was working and he had tears in his eyes. "I wouldn't trust you to hold it," he kept saying, half to himself.

"Nobody had time to think," Holman said. He took the control from Lynch.

"I guess I'll go stand by the sickbay, see about old Chien," Lynch said.

He went up. He would stop for a slug of rum first, Holman knew. They were all clearing out, even the coolie work gang. Holman started to open the throttle bypass, to let warming steam into the engine, and found it already open. He knew he had closed it. His arm muscles remembered closing it. But it was open, and that steam might have been just the extra push . . . It shook Holman. He didn't know what to do. Finally he pretended to open it, and he did not think Burgoyne noticed.

They got underway and the L.P. still thumped, but it would take them to Paoshan. Burgoyne had to keep going out to the fireroom to check the stoker coolies, because Chien would not be doing that any more. Po-han did his oiling and tending, but he walked wide as he could of the L.P. crank. Nobody wanted to talk. Once Burgoyne said, "God damn it! You know, just God damn it all to hell! Poor old Chien," and then he packed his lip nervously with snuff. They worked up to eight knots and moored to the Paoshan pontoon at about five o'clock, and Lt. Collins went ashore with Franks' landing force section while Pappy Tung was still doubling up lines.

Holman ate a late supper in dungarees and came out on deck. Bordelles told him to bear a hand and shift uniform and fall in with the reserve landing section. Farren and the others were already standing by under arms on the quarterdeck. Lynch was there, with the OOD duty.

"I got to repair the jacking gear and refit a crank bearing," Holman said.

"The bilge coolies will do that," Bordelles said.

"I don't think they can, without Chien," Holman said. "What do you think, Chief?"

"I don't know about them other ones, how much they know," Lynch said. "Maybe Jake better supervise it, Mr. Bordelles."

"Why can't you do that?"

"Got the duty." Lynch slapped his pistol.

"Well . . . all right." Bordelles didn't like it.

Holman told Po-han to round up four coolies and put them to unbolting the big L.P. cylinder cover and wiping out the crankpit. He and Po-han repaired the jacking gear. The worm wheel fit over a collar on the shaft and it was meant to be locked in place by two square keys. Both keys were gone. One had been gone a long time and paint was so thick over the empty keyway that it was hard to tell it was even there. The other key had worked out with the jarring vibration that day, and nothing but rust had been holding the worm wheel when old Chien had gotten down into the crankpit and trusted his life to it.

That was how it was with machinery, and Holman explained it to Po-han. If you were sloppy and ignorant with machinery, sooner or later it would kill you. It didn't matter how well you meant or how pure your heart was. But if you knew how and did take care of machinery, you were safer than you were in church. Old Chien was still alive up in the sickbay, holding on like a cat, Jennings said, and they would try to get a missionary doctor for him. But old Chien was through in the *San Pablo* engine room.

"My sabby, Jehk," Po-han said solemnly.

Holman found keystock in the rack under the workbench and they cut and fitted two new keys. With a light chisel, Holman upset the collar and gear metal over each end of each key, to hold them in place no matter how much the shaft vibrated. When they had more time, they would put a countersunk machine screw through each key, he told Po-han. Po-han nodded eagerly. He understood the principle.

Holman watched the four coolies work. They were suddenly friendly and anxious to please him, instead of being hostile and suspicious, and he was hoping to make the same kind of contact with them that he had with Po-han. They knew the job. They made up their beam clamps solidly and ran their eyebolts all the way in and they were clever riggers with their slings and chainfalls. They lifted aside the big cylinder cover and hoisted the piston and rod assembly and they walked the two bearing halves out on the floorplates very nicely. Chiu-pa seemed to have charge of them.

The bearing looked terrible. In some places the metal was black with burnt oil and in others it was pounded smooth and silvery. Black and silver needles of wiped metal filled the oil grooves. Holman worked on the bottom half; he could not hold off any longer. He cleaned out the oil grooves with a cape chisel and scraped the carbonized patches until the metal stopped coming off as gray dust and curled away in clean, silvery flakes. His hands enjoyed it and his eyes enjoyed seeing the bruised and dirty metal turn clean and frosty with scraper marks. It was like healing something ulcerated, making it whole and sound again. He began taking spots with the mandrel and scraping for a fit. Chiu-pa was scraping the top half and Holman saw that he was going much faster than Chiu-pa. He stopped to show Po-han how to scrape.

Po-han was awkward. The scraper was a large three-cornered file with four inches of the small end ground smooth and grooved along each flat and the edges stoned sharp and smooth. The right hand had to learn a special rock and draw and the left hand had to learn how to pivot and tilt the edge for depth of cut. Holman could nip off a flake the size of a pinhead or curl off a long, broad shaving, without thinking how he did it, but he broke it down to fundamentals to show Po-han. The idle coolies squatted around grinning and watching and Holman had them all try their hands at it. They laughed and kidded in Chinese at each other's fumbles. The one called Pai was pretty good with a scraper.

They were all clever to pick up the how of it, but only Po-han could handle the why. They had a hollow steel mandrel the same size as the crankpin and they would coat it all over lightly with Prussian blue and roll it sliding around in a clean bearing half. When they lifted it out, blue would show on the contact points and they would scrape bearing metal off only under the blue highspots. After each scraping and test, the blue spots were bigger and there were more of them. Holman tried to explain about even distribution of load in the bearing so that no one area would have too big a share of the load and squeeze out the oil film and wipe. Po-han had to help the others in Chinese, because their English was not as good as his. Each blue spot was like a coolie who helped to hold the load of full engine power, Holman told them; so the bigger the coolies and the more of them and the better spaced they were, the better they could hold the load. Pai and Dong and Chiu-pa did not get it. They could see the little blue coolies in the top half taking the gravity load of the piston and rod assembly, but they thought the coolies in the bottom half were loafers. They simply did not have the basic idea of energy flow.

Po-han got it. He acted it out, fisting his arms around like a crank and saying, "Pushee pushee! Pullee pullee!" while the others looked at him in wonder.

Yet Chiu-pa could spot and scrape and fit a bearing almost as skillfully as Holman. He did not need to know why he was doing what he did. It was just old custom. The stuff about little blue coolies was no more than a pleasant story to go with a piece of old custom. Well, they were all older men than Po-han, Holman thought. Maybe you had to be young.

It was not old custom with Chiu-pa to round the edges of oil grooves, but when he saw how Holman did it he was willing to do the same. They put the refitted bearing back in place, working very handily, and slugged it up with lead wires squeezed inside to measure the oil clearance. When Holman wanted to take out shims to set the oil clearance at six thousandths, Chiu-pa objected. He was very sure that if it were not set at ten thousandths the bearing would burn out. He did not think of it as a figure or any kind of measurement, but only as matching scratch marks, probably made by old Chien, on the micrometer barrel and spindle. Well, if the engine was out of line, you would want more clearance to allow for that, Holman thought. There was something to be said for old custom, after all. He set it at ten.

When the job was done and all of them had gone up except the watch coolie, it was nearly midnight. Holman felt tired and good. He felt satisfied at finally getting his hands on the machinery, and he was not going to let it go again. He made a pot of coffee and sat on the workbench drinking a cup of it. Wilsey came down in whites to write up the log. He spread out a rag and sat beside Holman on the workbench and had a cup of the coffee. They talked about Chien.

"Them keys gone. Who'd ever've thought about that?"

"Everybody, after today," Holman said.

"Yeah, I guess. But you just never know, do you?"

"You can know if you want to," Holman said.

They heard noise topside. The landing force was back. Perna and Stawski came down and poured coffee and sat on the workbench. It was the first time they had ever come down off watch to drink engine room coffee. Wilsey told them about the keys.

"It was them keys gone, huh, Jake?" Stawski said. "You sure it was them keys gone done it, huh?" He was eager about it.

"Sure. Hell, yes," Holman said. "What else?"

"It was them keys, all right," Stawski said.

"All shows to go you," Wilsey said.

"We brought a missionary doctor back to look at Chien," Perna said. "He's up there now."

"They was all holed up in their compounds and the doctor didn't want to come out," Stawski said. "The skipper really blistered his ass for him, way Bronson tells it."

"Wish I'd heard it," Wilsey said. "Prong missionaries."

"I was just thinking, working on that bearing," Holman said. "Any of you guys ever figure out just what it is you do, when you fit a bearing?"

"You spot and scrape and take leads," Wilsey said.

"Yeah, but why? What do you *mean* by *fit?*"

"Well, *fit.* Everybody knows that." Wilsey waggled his foot out in front of him. "Just *fit.* Like your foot in a shoe."

"In a bearing, it means equal distribution of load," Holman said.

"So what?" Perna said.

They didn't want to talk about bearings. Perna told about the rioting. The mob was out in the streets, all right, yelling and milling, but the Sand Pebbles had gone right on through to the warlord's *yamen.* Lt. Collins had offered very politely to help the warlord stop the rioting and the warlord had declined politely and sent out his soldiers to do it alone. In a few hours they had the streets clear and quiet. The Sand Pebbles had gotten a good chow out of it, but Franks would not let them drink the warlord's *samshu.* Afterward, they had checked all the missions. No palefaces had been hurt. Only a few native Christians had been killed.

"One mission, they offered us all a glass of milk," Stawski said.

"What started them rioting anyway?" Holman asked.

"Some slopeheads claimed they saw a missionary woman boiling babies," Perna said. "So they all went wild."

"Them missionaries ought to be more careful who they let see 'em, when they're boiling babies," Wilsey said.

8

Chien still had life in the morning, like an ember in ashes. The mission doctor wanted him to die on the *San Pablo*. When a Chinese died in a mission hospital, a story always started that the missionaries had murdered him so they could use his eyes to make camera lenses. If Chien died ashore, it might renew the rioting.

After breakfast Bordelles took his landing force section on a boat trip to a rural mission about fifteen miles from Paoshan. The city looked normal, gates open in the gray stone walls and the line of water coolies chanting and slopping up the stone steps from the river. Not far above the city Farren turned the motor sampan into a broad creek. With his red beard under his white sun helmet and his strong, tanned bare legs, Farren looked like a pirate at the tiller. Bordelles sat beside him. Holman, Crosley, Tullio, Red Dog and Ellis sprawled on the thwarts in the waist.

"You're gonna light a fire under China Light, huh, Mr. Bordelles?" Red Dog said.

"Going to try," Bordelles said. "Anyway, it won't hurt to show the flag and a party of armed men to any bandits down off that mountain today."

Holman sat up straight. China Light was Miss Eckert's mission. He wondered if he might see her. He wished he had not spoken so harshly that last time they had talked.

It was a clear, sunny morning and they had a lunch packed under the stern sheets. It began to seem like a picnic to Holman. The creek wound through green fields. It was stone-banked much of the way and overhung by drooping willow and mulberry trees. Children rode on water buffaloes that grazed along the bank. Other children tended duck flocks. They beat the ducks with bright rag scraps at the end of strings dangling like whips from long bamboo poles. The ducks quacked, but it did not hurt them. The children ran and hid and the buffaloes tossed their heads and snorted, when they saw the boatload of armed ocean devils. Then the children peeped out again, very curious. But the grown people working in the fields or floating down to Paoshan in sampans filled with garden stuff only stared with blank faces.

Away from the ship, Bordelles was quite democratic. He was tall and gawky, with a big nose and chin that would make a fine admiral's mask someday. Holman began asking him questions about China Light. He learned that it was more than just a church and a school. It owned a lot of surrounding farmland. Hundreds of Chinese lived there, and about a dozen palefaces. It was supposed to be under the fat warlord in Paoshan, but it was also claimed by the bandit chief on the mountain, who was squaring around to fight the warlord.

"A few more years and he'll be the warlord," Bordelles said. "Poor old General Pan will be going hungry up on the mountain."

The men laughed. The mountain was a long purple wall off to the left. It came down steeply, without foothills, to the river flood plain. They were getting near enough to make out steep ravines, blue-shadowy with timber. A lot of camphorwood and tung oil came from the mountain, Bordelles said.

"Tell him about Old Man Craddock," Farren said.

"I seen him," Holman said. "He was on the steamer I rode up from Shanghai."

"Did he speak to you at all?" Bordelles asked.

"Once or twice," Holman said. "Not very kindly."

Bordelles chuckled. "He wouldn't. Not old Craddock."

Craddock was a leader of a group which blamed all anti-Christian trouble in China on the treaties and gunboats, Bordelles explained. He had started a petition to have the *San Pablo* kept out of Tungting Lake. The people at China Light had notified the consul in Changsha that they were renouncing their personal treaty rights. They wanted no gunboat protection and no reprisals or indemnities, whatever might happen to them. Of course they could not do that. As American citizens, they were as much bound by the treaties as the Chinese were. The consul had told them so.

"They know it and they like it," Crosley growled. "They're just making looksee pidgin for the slopeheads."

China Light was an independent mission. There were no higher echelons to bring pressure on Craddock, Bordelles went on. The China Light people would probably refuse to obey an evacuation order, if the consul had to send one out. So Lt. Collins had composed a waiver they would all have to sign individually.

"They're good. Read 'em one, Mr. Bordelles," Red Dog urged.

Bordelles read one. It stated that the undersigned chose to ignore consular advice to evacuate in full knowledge of the risk of harm to himself and embarrassment to the United States of America. "I swear before God that this is my own uninfluenced private and personal decision, and I hereby release the U.S. Government from all further responsibility for my welfare," the waivers ended.

"They sign *after* they've had a warning," Bordelles said. "Might not be so easy, then. I have to make old Craddock sign a receipt for these and a promise to mail them to Changsha, if they ever refuse to evacuate."

"He'll give you a bad time, Mr. Bordelles," Tullio said.

"I'll give him one right back."

"They'll run from real trouble, Craddock out in front," Crosley said.

"Don't be too sure about old Craddock."

Bordelles told them about the file on Craddock in the consulate at

Changsha. His mission up north had been wiped out in the Boxer. His wife and several others had been killed. He got a big indemnity for them out of the Boxer Settlement, which also opened Hunan to missionaries. He married again and led the rush into Hunan, founding China Light in the same year the *San Pablo* had come to Tungting Lake. He was wiped out again in the 1910 riots and with the indemnity for that he bought enough local farmland to make the mission self-supporting. He owned it like a ranch.

"Give him his due, he's a tough old devil," Bordelles said.

They tied up at a stone jetty near a cluster of huts in a bamboo grove. Farren and Ellis stayed as boat guards. Bordelles led the four others in single file, arms slung, along a raised flagstoned path that was like a dike through fields blue with fat cabbages. The mission was about a mile away. It was a very long brick-walled compound with tiled roofs and treetops showing above the wall and the U.S. flag on a pole rising highest of all. Chinese huts scattered off from one end of it, into the fields. Bordelles took a branch of the path that led to the other end. It was hot walking under the high sun and dust stuck to their sweating bare legs and arms. Farmers in the fields watched them pass from under wide bamboo hats. They crunched across packed gravel and stopped before big wooden, ironbound double gates. The gates were closed. Bordelles knocked on the small side door. No one answered. Bordelles frowned and spat.

"Not a word out of you men from here on," he said. "You in particular, Shanahan."

"Arf arf, sir!" the Red Dog said softly, and they all grinned.

Bordelles drew his pistol and fired a shot into the ground. An old Chinese opened the side door, but he kept it on a chain and he could not understand anything. Finally a bearded white man came and flung the door open and stood there.

"You are impatient, Mr. Bordelles," he said. "I wish you had not done that."

He was Craddock. He was tall in a black suit, with a beak nose and fierce eyes deepset under shaggy eyebrows. His black beard was streaked with gray and he radiated power like an admiral. Bordelles was not abashed.

"And I wish you had answered my knock," he said. "I've come on duty, Mr. Craddock. To check your safety and discuss changes in our evacuation plan."

"We are in God's care here and we are all right." Craddock had a deep, harsh voice. "All you accomplish, by coming here with your arms and your uniforms, is to imperil our standing with the Chinese. And we will never evacuate China Light, sir!"

"So you wrote the consul. That's why I'm here, sir." Bordelles was being very formal. "Is there somewhere we can talk?"

"We are talking."

"I have papers you must read. I would prefer to talk privately, indoors."

Bordelles took a step toward the door. Craddock did not budge.

"No doubt your arms are your warrant for forcible entry," he said.

Bordelles flushed scarlet. "Not at all, sir," he said tautly. "My men are tired, hungry and thirsty. I thought you might have a sterilized stone you could give them."

"You are pleased to mock me, sir. Very well, come in." Craddock stepped aside from the door. "I must ask you to leave your arms and cigarettes in the gate house."

They went in. "Put your cigarettes on that shelf, men," Bordelles said.

"The arms too, if you please, sir," Craddock said behind them.

"I am not free to please, sir. We are ashore on duty under arms," Bordelles said. "Go ahead through, men."

It was abruptly cool and clean and green inside the wall. Three big white clapboard houses with green shutters lined each side of a flagstoned street. They were set back among trees and rose arbors and flower beds on neat lawns marked off by white picket fences. All the houses had downstairs and upstairs verandas with white railings and rocking chairs. Nobody was in sight except some coolies sprinkling water on flower beds and borders. It was a sharp change from the hot, dusty cabbage fields.

"This way, please."

Craddock passed them with quick, chopping strides, stiff and angry, and they followed him up the path to the first house on the right. A house servant in a gray gown came out and Craddock gave him sharp orders in Chinese. He led the sailors around by the side veranda to a back porch and pointed to some benches. He was being very snotty, in a Chinese way. They sat down, leaning on their rifles upright between their knees, and looked at each other disgustedly.

"I guess we ain't going to get any chow," Crosley said.

"Don't look like it," Holman agreed.

Crosley was a signalman, a squat, ugly little man with a big head, pop eyes and a wide mouth like a frog. He had a hoarse, croaking voice to match his face.

"That cheap, biblebacked old devil!" he said.

"Bordelles broke a few off in him," Tullio said. "He's giving him hell in there right now."

From time to time they could hear voices rise angrily somewhere inside the house. A servant came at last, with a basket of damp towels and bowls of tea. The sailors swabbed their faces and arms and legs with the towels, for momentary freshening. The towels were tepid instead of hot. They were getting second-chop treatment. Crosley scowled at his bowl of tea.

"Don't drink this slop, guys," he warned. "They prob'ly pissed in it."

"Watch it!" Tullio whispered sharply.

Shirley Eckert was seated at her desk in the faculty office when she heard the shot. She went to the open window and saw Mr. Craddock stride angrily across to the gatehouse. She knew the gunboat was in Paoshan and the danger was supposed to be past. She was still nervous. Then armed sailors in white sun helmets and shorts came through the gatehouse. They swung along jauntily. Mr. Craddock took their officer into his house and sent the sailors around to the back veranda. Shirley lingered at the window.

"I hope you're not alarmed, Miss Eckert."

She turned. Mr. Gillespie had come in. His brown hair was rumpled and his tanned, pleasant face looked concerned.

"I thought that shot might have alarmed you," he said. "It's only a bit of navy arrogance. Mr. Craddock will soon get rid of them."

"He'll be rude to them, you mean?"

"Well . . . very formal." Gillespie smiled. "Their coming here is deliberate provocation, you understand. They know they're not wanted here."

Shirley was not sure she did not want them. Gillespie noted her hesitation.

"Our only chance to carry on our work in China lies in breaking the association in Chinese minds between gunboats and missions, at least China Light," he said. "That officer could just as well have come alone, in civilian clothes, if he had to come at all. He is deliberately trying to strengthen the association."

"I know," Shirley said.

They had all been telling her about it. It was true enough. But something was not right.

"All right, Mr. Craddock will be rude," Gillespie said. "The Chinese will see and talk about his rudeness. Thus he makes this visit weaken the association rather than strengthen it, as they mean it to."

She nodded. Gillespie sat on a desk corner, one leg dangling.

"The men. The sailors," she said. "They can't help it. They have to obey orders."

"They're hard men who have chosen a hard life."

"They'll think we despise them."

"We must persuade the Chinese that we do." He leaned forward. "They come flaunting rifles," he said. "Rifles are for killing people, killing Chinese, in this case. How could we honestly welcome them, even without Chinese watching us?"

Mr. Gillespie was an evangelist, not one of the teachers, but he had been quietly attentive and helpful to Shirley in getting settled at China Light. She did not want to disagree with him.

"I think I will just go down and see if they want water," she said.

"I'm sure Mrs. Craddock will have tea and towels sent out to them."

If she dares, Shirley thought. Mr. Craddock utterly dominated his fragile wife.

"Then just to say hello," she said. "One friendly word."

He stood up, frowning slightly. "I'll go with you."

"No. Please," she said. "Not against your convictions, Mr. Gillespie. I'm new and ignorant. It won't spoil anything, if I go."

He protested. She went out alone, taking stock of herself. She had on a tan dress with long sleeves and of course no makeup. She was having to let her hair grow out and she had scarcely enough yet for the skimpy knot she kept it in. Loose wisps straggled. She had to walk slowly so that perspiration would not soak through her dress. She was not going to charm anyone. But she could speak a friendly word.

As she went down the side veranda of the Craddock house, she heard the old man's angry voice inside. On the rear veranda one of the sailors whispered, "Watch it!" fiercely, as if danger threatened. The four men jumped to their feet facing her, each with his rifle. It was awkward. She scanned their faces and words would not come. Then, with a small thrill, she recognized the big, square man.

"Mr. Holman!" she said. "I'm so glad to see you again!"

"Miss Eckert. Hello there."

She had not meant her greeting to be so warm. Holman named off the other men for her like objects. They grinned, very ill at ease. It was hard to make talk. The nice-looking Italian boy was from Brooklyn. The impish redhead was a Californian. The froggy little man was from New Jersey. She felt they wished she would go away and leave them to their man talk. She started to excuse herself.

"If you'd care to walk through the grounds, I'll be glad to show you around," she said, instead.

Dutifully polite, they mumbled thanks and began to sling their rifles.

"Oh, you'd have to leave your rifles here," she told them.

"Then we can't go," the froggy one said.

"I'll go," Holman said. He leaned his rifle on a bench. "Take charge, Crosley," he told the froggy man.

"You can't! You're on duty!" Crosley objected.

"If any enemy attacks, you guys just open fire," Holman said. "I'll be back here before you see the whites of their eyes."

"It ain't funny, Holman!" Crosley said angrily.

"Let's go, Miss Eckert."

They walked away. "Arf! Arf!" one of the men said softly behind them. Holman grinned.

"We call that one Red Dog on the ship," he said.

"I hope you won't get in trouble, leaving your rifle."

"They all make-believe with guns," he said dryly. "Soon as they pick one up they're John Paul Jones defending the Alamo, or something."

"And you don't make-believe?"

"Not with guns. I'm an engineer." He glanced around. "These houses and lawns and flowers sure look nice."

"They're for the American staff. Most of them are away now, at Kuling for the summer."

They came into the grassy quadrangle with the flagpole in its center. Holman looked husky and sunburned and much more sure of himself than he had seemed on the steamer from Shanghai.

"That's the middle school, where I will teach," she told him, pointing. "And that's the chapel and that one is the student dormitory. And down at the other end is the hospital."

They were handsome two-story brick buildings with arcaded verandas and Chinese roofs, quiet because of summer vacation. Only the hospital had its verandas crowded and people coming and going. She told him about the Chinese doctor and nurses and all the work they did.

"They have to send serious cases, like major surgery, to Paoshan," she said. "But they do a lot of good."

"I'll bet they do," he agreed. "Say, you know, this is a pretty place." He was sniffing the air and looking at the flowering shrubs and borders. "It's like a park," he said.

She led him on through into the Chinese section of low houses in walled courts, all whitewash and gray-tiled roofs. The streets there were busy with cart and coolie traffic and children scrambling. She nodded and said hello to several Chinese wearing gowns.

"They're native staff—I mean, not servants," she explained. "I don't know them all apart yet. They live in these houses."

"This is a big place."

He was looking all around. Just inside the shop and storehouse section she halted.

"I don't know what all is in here," she said. "It goes on outside the gate. Some of the people are staff and some rent their shops and stores from the mission and work on their own."

"Like a little town, ain't it?" The high chatter of voices and the tool noises of men at work came through the sour-smoky smell. He sniffed. "It even smells like a Chinese town," he said.

"It's not dirty," she said defensively. "It's the food and cooking oil they use, and incense. Lacquer and camphorwood in the workshops."

"Hell, I like it!" he said. "I'm sorry if you thought—I mean, I know Chinese ain't any dirtier than they're forced to be."

"Those long buildings, godowns," she said. "The mission takes a share of the crops for land rent. Mr. Craddock keeps a reserve in those godowns, for bad years. No one ever starves around China Light."

"Like in the Bible. The skinny cows," he said. "You know, this is all right. I guess I always thought missions only saved souls."

"They do, but that's not in my department," she said. "Mr. Craddock has all sorts of plans for China Light. He has some machinery set up to make sugar out of beets, but nobody can make it work right. He has an electric light plant, still in the crates, someone told me."

"Whereabouts?"

"Somewhere in there." She waved vaguely. "It's too hot here. Let's go on."

She led him to what had already become her favorite retreat, a stone bench in a nook among trees around the little American cemetery. Climbing roses covered the rough stone wall and tinged the air with delicate scent and color. Bees and one little bird were busy there. He sat beside her and fanned them both with his sun helmet. It had the name U.S.S. *San Pablo* in gold on a black ribbon sewed across the front brim. She looked at his face, strong, blunt and honest. He looked at her and she became abruptly conscious of her appearance.

"I'm letting my hair grow out," she apologized. "It's at its most wretched stage now." She tried to tuck away stray wisps. "They don't want me to wear most of the dresses I brought."

"You're so young and pretty, nothing could spoil how good you look."

He said it honestly. She was not pretty, but if he thought she was, that made her so for him. She warmed to him.

"Thank you, Mr. Holman."

Delicately, she tried to excuse Mr. Craddock's bad manners. "He has strong opinions," she said. "I'm afraid he's right. Only I wish it didn't have to make such a difference between people. That's why . . . what I . . ."

"I know," he said. "The guys felt it. They won't blame you."

"Not just me . . ."

She couldn't discuss it. She told him how she was studying Chinese six hours a day with Mr. Lin. She would have one class, of senior students who spoke fair English, when school started. By the next year she would know enough Chinese to take a full teaching load.

"How long they got you signed up for?" he asked.

"Seven years."

"We ship for four at a time," he said. "I been in China a little over seven years."

"Without going home?"

"My ship's home. That's how it is with us."

"Mr. Craddock says it will be that way with me at China Light," she said. "It isn't now. I wonder how long it takes?"

"Depends on the person, I guess. For me it was quick."

They talked about the riots in Paoshan. He was not pressing any claim. Still, she could not deny that the riots had sprung up in the gunboat's absence and stopped with its arrival. She confessed to her own fear during those two days, and her relief when the gunboat came.

He smiled. "I'm glad we came."

One of the Craddock house servants found them and chattered in Chinese. They stood up.

"Your officer is ready to go," she told him. "I hope he won't be angry with you."

"I don't think so."

Constraint grew between them. She wondered if he was remembering how he had taken leave of her that other time. Suddenly he had both her hands. She realized she had held them out, slightly and involuntarily.

"Good-bye, Miss Eckert," he said. "I don't feel any danger here. But if there ever is, we'll be back."

He pressed her hands and dropped them. She watched him walk away behind the servant, husky and red, erect and square-shouldered. She did not feel any danger, either. She sat down again.

Sometimes you met people and something flashed across, she thought. It was over in a flash, and you only knew about it afterward. This was the second time with Holman.

The first time was on the steamer from Shanghai to Hankow. Riots were going on in Shanghai, with people killed. The passengers on the steamer were nervous and angry and they quarreled terribly. Holman took no part in it. The others talked of past wars and massacres and they were making her very fearful of China.

It had been warm and sunny also, that other day. They were just passing a wooded bluff with gray walls and towers, very Marco Poloish in the watery sunshine. From nowhere the American destroyer came like a long gray spear flying. Brown smoke rolled from its four rakish stacks, sailors in white stood by the deck guns, and a string of colored signal flags danced gaily above the bridge. It was beautiful and deadly and it brought a catch to her throat. The steamer, rocking in its wake, was instantly all alarm. Men shouted and ran and clanged shut the steel doors penning the Chinese on the lower decks. Mr.

Craddock hustled her to her cabin for safety. There would be shooting, he said.

Alone there and fearful, she peeped from her window as the steamer rounded the wooded point. Gray walls slanted across a green hill and dark tiled roofs curved above them. Brown junks lay all along shore. The anchored destroyer swam into view, guns trained ashore. Two power boats filled with armed sailors drew V's in the brown water, heading in past some wooden ship hulls with house roofs above their decks. Buildings showed through trees along a stone embankment. Black smoke rose above the trees. She heard a distant noise of shouting.

Distressed and fearful, vaguely not wanting to be alone, she had slipped out on deck. She saw Holman there, sturdy with his rifle. The sight brought the same catch to her throat that the destroyer had. Then he had pointed his finger through the bars and her focus had widened out to include the three Chinese children.

"Bang bang, you're dead," the sailor said gravely.

The children hesitated and then smiled. One pointed and said, "Cah! Cah! Cah!" in an excited voice. Holman grinned at them.

The little play changed everything. Her sense of danger vanished. It all seemed a game in which no one really hated and feared anyone else. That was in the smile they exchanged when he turned, startled and guilty, to meet her understanding smile.

A short while afterward she was in the saloon with the refugee women. They came aboard off the hulks with amahs and crying children and tales of outrage. They had shrill voices and strained angry faces and the cords stood out in their necks.

"Of *course* they run away when the sailors come, the cowards!" one woman said. "Tie them to the cannon's mouth, *I* say!"

"Whip them! Make their bones drop out!" another shrilled.

Shirley could not hope to tell them what she knew. Nor could she tell the men, at an ensuing dinner-table argument. Mr. Craddock, not too gently, pointed out that the missionaries in Chinkiang had not been molested. They lived out among the natives and they had stayed quietly at home in prayer. The people from the foreign concession, businessmen and the collectors of customs, salt tax and postal revenues, had fled to the hulks and sent for the destroyer. Their homes were looted and some houses were burned. Mr. Outscout, the chronically angry Englishman, had countered with an attack on Christian education in China.

"Your schools. Put notions into Chinese heads. Democracy. Lincoln and cherry tree, that rot," he said accusingly. "How d'ye know what's already in the heads, eh? You're all fools playing chemist." He fountained with his hands. "Heads pop! Burn! Fizz over!"

It was a great embarrassment, Shirley knew, that mission-educated students were the most virulently anti-Christian. They were so despite considerable missionary support for Chinese independence. The business faction, which clung to the unequal treaties, enjoyed taunting the missionaries about it.

"Christian education!" Mr. Outscout tossed his gray hair scornfully. "Told Graves a few days past in Shanghai. Parade your very campuses, I told him, and for every placard denouncing the treaties there's another maligning your Christ. Where's your profit, eh? Eh? Graves couldn't answer!"

"Our Christ, Mr. Outscout! Will you deny Him, sir?"

The other men calmed the two. Holman, as usual, took no part. She no longer thought it was apathy. He simply did not think it was important. But it was very important to Mr. Craddock, who expected Shirley to side with him. On the trip to Hankow she had learned how deep and angry was the gulf between the two factions of foreigners in China.

Many missionaries believed that the unequal treaties impairing Chinese sovereignty should be canceled. The most visible symbols of the treaties were the gunboats. Gunboats infuriated Mr. Craddock. They made it seem to him that he was preaching Christianity figuratively at gunpoint. He had not liked her talking to Holman.

"The saintliest spirit, if unguarded, may take a coloring from a troubled spirit which comes too near," he had warned her once, in attempted delicacy. He did not speak to Holman himself.

Since her arrival at China Light, she had wondered more than once whether Mr. Craddock's spirit was not troubled. He loved fiercely. He trusted God rather than gunboats with emotional speech and gestures which made God seem very like an invisible gunboat in the sky. Shirley did not want to take a coloring from Mr. Craddock.

Gillespie was altogether different. He did not get excited.

"The Chinese are the most civilized people on earth," he had told her. "Too many of us approach them as if they were tribal Africans. I hope you will not." He also wanted to get rid of the treaties and gunboats. "The Chinese have a fundamental sense of decency and justice," he said. "The gunboats only outrage it. We'd be safer without them."

Shirley found that reasonable. She liked Gillespie. She thought Holman might have been a man much like Gillespie, if chance had not cast him as a sailor. Each man in his own way gave her comfort.

She stood up, abruptly lighthearted. She began picking roses for her desk in the faculty office, where she must go now for her Chinese lesson with Mr. Lin. He was an elderly, dignified man and very patient with her. No one could help but trust and respect China in the presence of Mr. Lin. He gave comfort, too.

9

Bordelles spoke sharply to Holman about abandoning arms on duty. Craddock had left him in a bad temper. Once back in the boat, however, he softened. Red Dog urged him to tell about his fight with Craddock. Bordelles made a good story of it. Craddock, being independent, was hard to deal with. By the same token, he could not exert anything like the political influence back in the States that the mission board people could. All the Americans who put pennies in the plate to save the heathen could also put votes in the box to sink a Congressman. It was dangerous for a naval officer to cross a mission board. It was not very dangerous to insult Craddock.

"You think they'll really run the gunboats out of China, sir?" Tullio asked.

"Not a chance. They don't want to," Bordelles said. "They only want to be on record with the Chinese pretending that they do."

"What you think we're building that new flotilla for, Tullio?" Farren asked. "Right now, down in Shanghai."

Lynch was waiting for Holman on the quarterdeck. "Jake, come below," he said. "We got troubles, boy."

Holman followed him. "What happened?"

"The engine's haunted."

"Haunted!"

"The coolies think it is. Chien's dead and his ghost is in the L.P. crankpit. The coolies are scared to come down here."

The engineers were all in dungarees, sitting on the workbench with a fresh pot of coffee. Lynch and Holman poured themselves cups and Lynch explained what Lop Eye Shing had told him about Chinese ghosts. It was very complicated. Dead Chinese left three ghosts. One of Chien's was in the sickbay and one had gone ashore with his body, but the most dangerous of the three was the one in the crankpit.

"Lop Eye says a Chinee ghost after while splits into little ghosts, and they split again, and after a month or two they ain't no more trouble than mosquitoes," Lynch said.

"We can't wait that long. We can't get underway without the coolies," Holman said.

"Lop Eye's ashore now lining up some holy man to come aboard tomorrow and run the ghost off the ship," Lynch said. "We'll have to stand the auxiliary watches tonight, though."

Haythorn, the coxswain, came in on the gratings. "Hey, you bilge rats," he called down. "How about some water in the washroom?"

Stawski slid off the workbench. "God damn it, I been filling that gravity tank every half hour," he said. "What you deck apes doing with all that water?"

He went over and opened the steam inlet and started the fresh water pump clacking. Holman walked over beside him.

"Keeping the water end lined up, eh, Ski?"

"Hell yes, every half hour, why not?"

"The water chest valves leak. Your water's draining back through the pump on you," Holman said. "Close the discharge valve and it won't be every half hour."

Perna bounced out of the fireroom. Coal dust and sweat smudged his face and he was angry. He choked in the feed check.

"You stupid Polack, watch how you take on feed!" he told Stawski. "You're killing my steam!"

"Come out here and tend your own God damned water," Stawski

said. "You're a watertender, ain't you?"

"Damn right I am, and that means I'm a rated man and not a coolie," Perna said. "You come out and pass coal for me."

"Like hell! I ain't no coolie either." Stawski turned to Lynch. "Chief, why don't you fire them stupid coolies, if they won't work?"

"And then where'd you be?" Lynch said.

"You figure two men on watch, do you?" Holman asked Lynch. "One man can stand this watch. Hey, Frenchy?"

"Don't reckon as I want to, myself," Burgoyne said.

"I won't stay down here alone at night," Perna said. "Neither will Ski. We already talked about it."

"You mean both you guys believe in ghosts?"

"Not in American ghosts," Perna said. "You can't tell about slope-heads. They're sneaky bastards."

"If they think they got three ghosts, they might really have one," Wilsey said. "Where there's smoke there's fire, Jake."

Burgoyne knuckled his mustache. "When I was a kid we lived in a house once where things come knocking on the door at night," he said. "It bothered the womenfolk right much. We moved out of that house."

"Well hell," Holman said. "We lack one man for a two-man watch list. How about Harris?"

"He swears he won't come down here except for electrical emergencies," Lynch said. "And don't look at me like that, either. Take Waxer."

"He know anything?"

"No. But he'll be company."

"I'll take the midwatch by myself," Holman said. "If you'll leave me a clean fire and a coal pile, Frenchy."

"I'll sure do that," Burgoyne said.

After supper Holman talked with Farren and Bronson about taking engineers off the topside watch list. They sat at Bronson's mess table with their watch lists.

"Why can't you just let things slide down there, till the coolies come back?" Bronson asked.

"There'd be no water and the lights'd go out," Holman said. "You think you get them lights as natural as sunshine?"

He did not like Bronson. Petty officers who worked on the bridge, close to the officers, often acted as if some of the glory rubbed off on them. Bronson was very much that way. He was a fat, pompous man.

"Farren's only losing two," Bronson said. "That's all I'll give you. I'll give you Perna and Stawski."

"I'll take them and Wilsey too," Holman said. "You ain't giving me nothing, Bronson. I'm taking my own men down where they belong."

"And I'll take 'em back," Bronson said. "You don't have the right attitude, Holman. I've heard the officers worry about you. Why don't you get wise?"

"I'm wise to you. Prong you."

"Take it easy, Jake," Farren said.

"And I'm wise to you," Bronson said. His face was red. "That coffee pot you started down there. The whole ship knows you rigged things to get Chien killed."

"Say that again!" Holman stood up, leaning with his hands on the table. "God damn you, say that again!"

"That's the scuttlebutt," Bronson said defiantly. "You got some pet coolie down there you want to put in Chien's place."

"Who told you that?"

"It's just scuttlebutt."

"Scuttlebutt travels on words." Holman's voice was shaking. "You tell me one man you heard say that, or I'll beat your fat face in!"

The other men were gathering around. Bronson had turned pale and it was very quiet in the compartment.

"Hell, you know how scuttlebutt is, Jake," Farren said. "It's just talk, all a joke, what the hell?"

"Not when it calls me a murderer, it ain't no joke!" Holman looked at them all. "Any of you guys tell Bronson that?" They all shook their heads. "Somebody has to say a thing for the first time. I think you just done that," Holman told Bronson. "Now you come with me to the skipper and prove what you just said, or else you take it back!"

"I was hasty," Bronson said. "I guess I take it back."

"You mean you ain't sure?" Holman leaned nearer Bronson.

"I'm sure. I take it back."

"Well, see that you stay sure and you keep it back!" Holman stood erect. He was trembling. "If I hear that story again from any-body, I'll come beat *your* lying teeth down your throat!"

He walked back on the fantail, to be alone. Strangely, Stawski came back to reassure him. Holman brushed Stawski off. He didn't want to have to talk to anybody for a while.

Wilsey and Burgoyne turned the watch over to Holman at mid-night. It was in excellent shape. The steam was up and the fire cleaned and dampered and he would not have to tend the fire for at least an hour. He paced the floorplates restlessly, drifting around and looking at everything in just the way old Chien had used to do. Well, Chien was dead. Dead. The engine room was already looking untidy. Water beaded the oily floorplates around the firemain pump and dirty rags hung here and there. The drip pan under the condensate pump was half full of water and smeared with swabbing oil. Holman began tidy-ing and wiping, to keep his mind busy.

For some reason he kept remembering old Ed Gard. He had not once thought about old Eddie in many years.

When he was eight he had a red coaster wagon to fetch the dirty clothes home and to deliver the clean laundry, all over town. Some-times the nice ladies gave him old clothes for him and his little brothers. They always showed him how strong and good the clothes still were and he was trained to say thank you to the nice ladies. It was hard to be friends with the other kids at school and around, when they laughed at him for wearing their old clothes, and the only friend he had was old Eddie.

Eddie had a white mustache and bristling eyebrows and he worked with horses at the feedyard on the edge of town, across the road from Jorry Holman's house. Eddie had been in the Civil War and fought Indians afterward and he had a Pension. It was his plain duty to marry some good, Christian woman and let her take care of him, so that she could have a Widow's Pension when he died. Jorry's mother was one of the good women. But Eddie loved only horses and he would not even speak to any woman.

He lived in the grain room and kept his clothes in a brown canvas warbag. He always wore khaki shirts and blue Levis. Sometimes, when he was working on harness with a bottle beside him, he would sing to himself, and he did not mind Jorry Holman watching and listening. He could not sing very well. One of his songs was:

> *Oh, I'm goin' away to the Filla Pie Neens*
> *To fight for my country and to live on beans.*

Sometimes it was the Filla Pie Noons and he was going to live on prunes. Jorry Holman hoped he might go too.

Jorry liked to get old Eddie talking about fighting Indians. He had fought them all over and he had been in a big Indian fight right where Wellco was now, only then it was only sagebrush and a few willows and cottonwoods along the creek. He had taken an arrow through his cheek and the scar still showed. Eddie did not remember how the arrow tasted, but he said it hurt like billy hell when the whisky they gave him ran out through the hole.

"What did you do with the arrowhead?" Jorry asked. He wanted to see it, and to hold it in his hand.

"I spit it out," Eddie said.

Eddie divided Indians into *friendlies* and *hostiles,* but he said they were all hostiles under their plagued red skins. Everybody knew the only good Indian was a dead one, but now they were living off the government up in Duck Valley and breeding like flies, and someday they would try to take the country back again.

Jorry liked to think about old Eddie when he pulled his red wagon around Wellco with the laundry. He never knew but what right where he was standing maybe old Eddie killed an Indian on that spot before there were any houses in Wellco. One day, out in the sagebrush close behind his house, Jorry found a pure white arrowhead. He kept it and believed it was the very one which had gone through old Eddie's cheek. After all, Eddie had had to spit it out *somewhere* nearby.

The summer Jorry was ten years old Eddie took sick. The good women brought him soup and stuff, but he would not take any of it. His cheeks sank in and his nose sharpened and he looked like a fierce old bird. When he got too weak to go to the toilet, he stopped eating. The other men at the feedyard knew what he wanted and they stopped cursing and kept their voices low and stayed away from the grain room. Only Jorry Holman could go in there, to bring water and mix it with whisky in Eddie's old tin cup. Eddie lay wrapped in a gray blanket leaning back against the fat-eared, dusty oat sacks. He sipped the whisky and stared all day at a shaft of sunlight that speared in through the high-up little window. It danced and dazzled with bright specks of grain dust. The snuffling and stamping and whickering of horses came through the partition, and Eddie listened to the horses, but he never spoke a word. Jorry thought he lay all night like that, too, his eyes fierce and bright as a hawk's eyes.

The good women thought it was a sin and a shame, but they could not make the men do anything. On the third afternoon Jorry's mother and two other women forced their way into the grain room. Eddie cursed them in a low, clear voice and they went away, crying and angry. In a little while they came back with two extra women and a preacher. Eddie cursed them again, very terribly. The preacher was half crying and he said, "Brother Edward, you are about to pass into the hands of the Living God. Oh, I beseech you, soften your heart!" They all flopped down beside the oat sacks to pray and Eddie cursed God in a voice dry as a snake rattle. He said what the preacher probably did with the women when he had them alone. They got very angry and his mother ordered Jorry to go home and Jorry told her to go to hell. They went away talking about Judge Mason and the town marshal and Jorry thought they were going to have him and old Eddie both put in jail. But nothing happened. It got dark and there was only enough whisky left to fill two more cups. Eddie spoke again. He said to put it all in one cup and leave out the water.

"They took a lot out of me, but I'm going to hold on till morning," he said. "You're a good kid. You can pull stakes now. Tell 'em the last thing I said was that they could all go piss up a picketrope."

Jorry did not go home. He went out into the sagebrush and part of the night he just walked and part of the night he lay on his back looking at the stars. All that night the coyotes howled along the rimrock. He cried some, but mostly he just felt a pain in his throat and belly and the tears ran down his face in silence. After that night he never cried again. When he went home in the morning his mother tried to scold him, and he told her to go piss up a rope.

Well, back there now in Wellco, Nevada, they were all pissing up ropes, as far as Jake Holman was concerned. He was going to serve out his twenty years in China and retire in China and he was never going to see Wellco, Nevada, again.

As he paced the floorplates, Holman noticed that he was swinging clear of the L.P. He noticed that whenever he stopped he was putting his back up against something. He had a crawling feeling along his back. Something wanted into his mind. He set his jaw and let it come in.

It was the memory of Chien's eyes two inches from his own. The pupils were very dilated, but the eyes were not angry or accusing. They were not concerned about anything. That was how it was when you were dead. You were not concerned about anything.

I didn't do it, Holman told his memory of the eyes. *All I did wrong was not to be sorry.*

The eyes began to fade.

I wish the old man didn't have to die, Holman thought. *I didn't want him hurt. I don't want anybody hurt.*

He walked over and gripped the handrail and looked down into the crankpit. The crank was on the starboard quarter and it was shadowy down there. Holman spoke in a low voice.

"Chien, if there's anything left over of you that can hear me, I want to tell you that I didn't mean you any harm," he said. "And I'm going to take the knock out of this L.P. engine. I'm going to do that, old man."

He felt silly after he had said it. He felt better, too. Miss Eckert at China Light came pleasantly into his mind. He thought about how surprisingly extensive that mission was and all the things they did there besides church stuff. He wished he might have had a look at the sugar beet machinery that wouldn't work. He knew the bar he had tried to put up between himself and Miss Eckert was down again. He did not feel any duty to put it back up.

10

Lt. William Collins knew his men said of him that he wore gold braid on his pajamas. He did not mind. They said it approvingly and, in the figurative way they meant it, it was quite true. A career naval officer, he felt, had to subordinate his private life to his official life; that was his sacrifice on the altar of his country. Lt. Collins had a private life of sorts, in abeyance now back in the States, and someday he would take it up again, perhaps even marry, although he did not like to think of that part. She would have to be some officer's daughter, who would know how to be a navy wife. But now it was very good not to have a wife. As soon as he had taken command of *San Pablo* and realized the potentially desperate situation he faced in Hunan, he had known that his official life was going to take all of his time and energy. That was when he had sewed the figurative gold braid on his pajamas.

In some ways it was very stimulating and rewarding. A commanding officer went ritually by his ship's name. "*San Pablo* leaving . . . *San Pablo* passing . . . *San Pablo* boarding . . ." were the various navy regulation hails that accompanied Lt. Collins in his comings and goings. He insisted that they always be made. He had strongly the old navy sense of a ship as a living person. One did not put *the* before a ship's personal name and one did not serve *on* a ship, he served *in* it. All of the Sand Pebbles were collectively *San Pablo,* but Lt. Collins looked out the eyes and bore the name. It was his fancy sometimes to say *we* instead of *I,* but the referent of both pronouns was *San Pablo.* He rather enjoyed being *San Pablo* in his pajamas.

Now he sat, a slight, dark man in crisp whites, waiting to see Lynch and Holman in his day cabin. It was a small room on the starboard side of the boat deck, with inner doors leading to his bedroom and to the bridge. A red Peking rug covered the deck and his small rolltop desk stood neatly in one corner. He sat facing the door across the round, green-baize-covered table on which the clean cups and saucers sat waiting too. In *San Pablo,* coffee with the captain was a rare and calculatedly ritual occasion.

Lynch came in first, snatching his hat off his balding head. Holman followed. He wore clean dungarees, a breach of ritual. At Lt. Collins' invitation both men sat down, holding their hats in their laps. Lt. Collins studied Holman as Yen-ta came in and poured the coffee and went out again, leaving the silver pot in the center of the table. Holman had the sullen air very strongly. It was a felt thing, because the man's square face was impassive, as always. Lt. Collins tried to put both men at ease with a few remarks about the accident. They were an unofficial board of inquiry into the cause, he told them.

"What do you think, Chief?"

"Well, sir, it was them keys jarred out."

"Why did they jar out?"

Lynch shrugged. "The vibration, sir."

"And why the vibration?"

"From the bearing knock. Chien was going to refit it that night, if we could've got into port on it." Lynch glanced at Holman.

Always at some point you had to stop asking why, Lt. Collins thought, or you would go all the way back to creation. But a man had died, and some account had to be taken of it.

"It is normal for an engine with the links in neutral to turn with that much power?" he asked Lynch.

Lynch began explaining about the vacuum in the condenser and air leaks up the rods. The links were never exactly in neutral, he said, because you had to run the link blocks in or out to balance the engine, and there was no truly neutral position. Lynch warmed up, and something of the practical man's irritating condescension was coming into his manner. Lt. Collins could not follow the words clearly. He was trying to remember his classwork on marine engines. There was something called a Zeuner diagram in which valve action was translated into neat arcs and angles on a sheet of paper. But a sheet of paper could not kill a man. Lynch talked on. Holman was studying the golden eagle and anchor crest on his coffee cup, apparently not listening.

"It was just an act of God, Captain," Lynch finished huskily, at last. He was pleased with himself and he made free to pour himself another cup of coffee.

"I can't report this officially, because Chien had no official existence aboard," Lt. Collins said. "But I don't want anything like it to happen again. If any personal responsibility can be fixed, I would like to know about it unofficially."

Lynch pouted. Lt. Collins looked at Holman.

"Do you call it an act of God, Holman?"

Holman started. "I don't think God's got much to do with machinery," he said, sitting upright. "Men are responsible for machinery, and you can always find out who."

"All right, whom do you say?"

"Whoever should've took that knock out of the L.P. when it first started," Holman said slowly. "And if he couldn't, he should've worried about vibration and inspected things regular and pinned whatever might come loose. That man was Chien. He killed himself."

"He worked under supervision."

"Not really. We got too many military duties. We can't spend enough time below." The man's sullen aura spread across the table, but his face did not change. "We lose face if we go bilge crawling and get dirty. We're supposed to stand back cool and clean and military and supervise for a few minutes every day. It won't work, sir! You have to get right close up and mix yourself with machinery, if you want to know about it and control it."

"Well!"

Lt. Collins drummed his fingertips on the green baize. The man's whole manner was a sneer at military duty. But not his words. It was probably unconscious. And it was undeniably convenient to blame Chien's death upon Chien himself, error and correction in the one event. He decided to change the subject.

"I've invited Shing to call on me," he said. "We will discuss a replacement for Chien. Have you any recommendations, Lynch?"

"Pai, maybe," Lynch said. "Or old Ping-wen, the boilermaker. They're both old timers. I'd settle for either one, sir."

"Can I say something?" Holman asked. Lt. Collins nodded. "Most of the work is cleaning work. I never saw a cleaner plant," Holman said. "But most of the pumps just barely run, and you know about the main engine. Other accidents could easily happen. I'd like to have the new coolie boss run just a cleaning gang and set up another special little gang for nothing but machinery repair."

"Good idea," Lynch said.

"There's one coolie named Po-han. He's different from the rest." Holman spoke rapidly, as if he feared being cut off. "The other ones learn kind of monkey-see monkey-do, and whatever they know, they know like that, like old Chien. But Po-han sees steam pushing pistons and metal pushing metal and water lifting valves and springs closing them and all like that, the whole plant all of a piece and working together . . . it's a kind of picture . . . and a feeling. . . ." He had outraced his words.

"I know what you mean," Lt. Collins said.

"I mean, that kind of guy, he can learn new things by himself, figure out troubles, look ahead, not like old Chien—"

"Chien was a good old man, Jake. Don't blacken his name," Lynch broke in, frowning. "This coolie of yours, he's too new aboard to take charge of a repair gang. If that's what you're getting at."

"I been training him on steaming watches and he already knows a lot, sir." Holman's manner was becoming animated. "I'd like to take personal charge of the repair gang for a while, to train Po-han, train 'em all. I was hoping I might get excused from drills and topside watches for a while, sir, to do that." His eyes pleaded.

Lt. Collins shook his head. "No one may be excused from his military duties, Holman."

He would have to reassess Holman's effect on the ship, he thought. There was the coffee mess he had started in the engine room, to split the black gang off from the unitary crew. Was that conscious? How much of his motivation in this repair gang scheme was conscious? Yet it was a plausible scheme, and the only doubtful element was Holman himself. The sullen aura was surrounding the man again, like a cloak.

"Yes, sir. I'd like to try anyway, sir, what time I can find, do the best I can, anyway," he said, his face expressionless once more.

Make me feel guilty, will you? Lt. Collins thought. I neither like nor trust you, Holman. I'm afraid of what you might do to *San Pablo*. He stood up, to signal an end of talking. Holman and Lynch jumped to their feet.

"I'll talk to Shing about it," Lt. Collins said.

Outside by the tall stack, Holman asked Lynch, "Chief, why's he got to ask Shing about a repair gang? Don't he run this damn ship?"

"Well, old Lop Eye sort of runs the coolies," Lynch said. He was looking up at the bund. "Here they come to get Chien's ghost," he said.

A dozen of them in loose gray or yellow robes came down to the pontoon, surrounding a red sedan chair. Lop Eye Shing came out to meet them with deep bows. They had beads around their necks and some wore skull caps and some had bare, shaven heads with scars on them. The holiest one of all, in the sedan chair, wore a kind of peaked cap, and his skin was like yellow-waxy paper plastered tightly over his face bones. Lop Eye Shing bowed very low to him.

Holman joined the other Sand Pebbles on the main deck, to watch them come aboard. The old holy man was named Wing and he starved himself every other month, Clip Clip told them solemnly. The old man walked feebly. Two younger ones helped him up to the quarterdeck and down into the engine room. Two more came behind carrying a bronze urn with carvings on it. The others had gongs and drums. It was a wholly Chinese affair. They were alone in the engine room for nearly an hour, gonging and clanging and singing and popping fire-crackers, and a strong blue haze of burning joss sticks came up. The Sand Pebbles were impressed. They knew something pretty big and mysterious was going on down there. When the party left the ship, some of the Sand Pebbles thought they had Chien's ghost in the bronze urn. Oh Joy said no, the urn was only to burn joss sticks. A Chinese ghost was not something you could put in a box, he said. What they had done was to break the ghost up into little pieces that the wind would blow away.

Holman and the other engineers went below. The engine room smelled strongly and strangely of incense and powdersmoke. Bits of red paper from the firecrackers flecked the oily machine parts. The coolies were back on the job and Ping-wen seemed to be in charge. He was a thin old man, much like Chien, but with a sly, merry look. Wilsey kept turning and looking around and working his arms and shoulders as if he were trying the fit of a coat.

"You know, it feels like nothing ever happened down here," he said. "It feels just like it used to. It feels all right again."

"It sure enough does," Burgoyne agreed.

Holman could feel it too. There was something to that joss pidgin, he thought. He did not see Po-han, and wondered where he was.

"I'll make us a pot of coffee, to celebrate," he said.

Yen-ta opened the door for Lop Eye Shing. Lt. Collins stood to greet him, with repeated slight bows, and offered him a covered bowl of tea with both hands. Shing propped his stick against his gray gown and took the bowl in both hands. He had to support both his left hand and the bowl with his good right hand. Very carefully, he pivoted to set the bowl on the table and, at Lt. Collins' repeated in-vitations, seated himself.

They talked about each other's health and the weather. Shing seemed at ease, but Lt. Collins was not. It was something like conferring with a warlord, but there were no treaties and body of diplomatic correspondence in the background to structure the situation. Shing had no legal existence in *San Pablo.* Yet when Lt. Collins worked out something new with him they were, in a sense, writing unwritten laws. It was not comfortable.

Neither man touched his tea. Lt. Collins could not read Shing's feelings. The sagging left side of Shing's bold face gave him a leering, sardonic look that seemed to belie his words and smuggle sinister import into the blandest phrase. In due time they got around to Chien. There was no precedent for handling a coolie death. Lt. Collins was afraid that Shing was going to demand an indemnity, which could not legally be paid. He explained very carefully about Chien.

"It was Chien's own fault, you see, because he did not inspect those keys," he finished.

Shing nodded, leering amiably. "Chien, Ho-mang make fight," he said. "Ho-mang kill Chien. *Mei yuh fah tzu.*" It was a verbal shrug.

"What do you mean, Holman killed Chien?"

With some difficulty, Shing made it clear that it was a spiritual fight. The engine had intervened to decide it in favor of Holman. All the Chinese were taking the engine's judgment as final, Shing indicated. The Chinese mind, Lt. Collins thought. Who will ever civilize them? But he felt relieved.

"Any man say Ho-mang belong teach-man," Shing went on. "He have got plenty face. Oh, just now, too much face! Any Chinese man say fight-man *bu hao,* teach-man moh bettah."

Lt. Collins frowned. Chinese values, he thought. It was hard to think of Holman as a teacher, that sullen, indrawn man. But it was a title of respect in China and the way was open to suggest Holman's idea of a separate repair gang. Shing did not accept the idea readily. He did not want the coolie Po-han to be boss of it. Lt. Collins tried to explain what was special about Po-han, and it seemed to be the very reason Shing was opposed. Finally he gave in, but very delicately he demanded a balancing concession in Lt. Collins' sphere of authority. He wanted a promise that Holman would be transferred before Lt. Collins himself was relieved of command.

Lt. Collins thought about that. Would he lose face, set a dangerous precedent, if he agreed? He wanted to agree. Did Shing, too, sense an undefined menace in the man Holman? He asked Shing for reasons. Shing was evasive.

"I think bye-m-bye *Sampabble* moh bettah, suppose Ho-mang go Shanghai moh fah," was all that he would say.

"All right," Lt. Collins said at last.

Shing smiled, as well as he could. His sardonic, permanent half wink seemed to make them fellow conspirators. Lt. Collins resisted an urge to squirm. The tea was still untouched. Shing, as guest, had the initiative. Lt. Collins looked pointedly at the tea bowls. Shing took up his bowl in both hands and drank, and the visit was formally ended.

When he had bowed Shing out, Lt. Collins found that he was sweating. "Phew!" he said, shaking his head, and went into his bathroom to wash his face and hands. When he came out, he called Yen-ta.

"Tell Holman to come up here," he ordered, in a voice firm and sure again.

Holman, still in dungarees, sat woodenly in the same place, across the green-topped table. There was no coffee. Lt. Collins told him it was all set for Po-han to head a special repair gang. Holman's face did not change.

"Yes, sir. Thank you, sir," he said. "That's good."

"I'm going to relieve you of topside watches for the time being, until you can get the gang organized and trained."

The face became alive and friendly. "Yes, sir! I'll work with 'em, to fix everything that's wrong now. Then they can keep it up to snuff by themselves." He actually grinned.

"That pleases you?" Lt. Collins smiled. "Is it getting to the machinery, or getting away from military duties?"

"Well, sir . . . both, I guess." Holman's voice was guarded. "I wouldn't mind the military duties so much, if I knew everything was all right down below."

"But you still wouldn't like them?"

"Well, they still wouldn't come quite natural, I guess. But I'd carry 'em out, good as anybody, sir. If I knew things was okay below."

"I want to make us both clear on your attitude to military duty, Holman," Lt. Collins said. "I want to go back to something you said this morning, about the Chinese learning machinery monkey-see monkey-do. How do you know you haven't learned military life that way? How do you know military life is not all of a piece, all connected sense, if you could only understand it?"

"I've tried, sir. If it made that kind of sense, I'd have it doped out by now. But it don't."

"Hmmm. It doesn't, eh?" Lt. Collins thought a moment. "All right, what's the derivative of pv with respect to $t?$"

Holman shook his head dumbly. His face was wooden.

"It's part of understanding machinery, but you'd have to have a couple of years of college math and physics before I could begin to explain it to you. Does it make sense to you now?"

Holman scowled. "If I knew it, what could I do down below that I can't do now?"

"You could design new machinery."

"If I could've gone to school, I'd know that! I'd know ten times more'n that by now, and things nobody ever knew before!"

Obviously, it was a sore spot. Lt. Collins held up his hand.

"All right, Holman! All I'm trying to say is that somewhere along the line every man must accept his limitations. I am no exception, and neither are you."

"I'm sorry," Holman said. "Sure, I'm stopped on machinery, and I know where. But on this other stuff, I'm stopped before I even start." His face was suddenly clear and open. "If it makes sense, can you give me just a start on it?"

"Think of it this way." Lt. Collins steepled his fingers. "The crew of a ship must be designed, just like the machinery which powers the ship. Captains before me designed *San Pablo* for the very special job we have. But the human spirit will not hold a permanent shape, like steel or brass. Our design is process, dynamic, like a pattern of juggling eggs." He made juggling motions. Fascinated interest marked Holman's face. "We have to refit ourselves into the design every day," Lt. Collins went on. "That is the purpose of our military ceremony and all that we do in *San Pablo*. Does it make a glimmer of sense to you now?"

"I can't see how it works. Can you show me just a little bit how it works?" Holman was leaning forward in a strained anguish of curiosity.

"You saw it work here in Paoshan, two days ago. But I'll give you a textbook example. Last year at Wanhsien, in the gorges, junkmen rioted and killed an American. H.M.S. *Cockchafer* was in port. Her captain ordered the warlord to behead two junkmen on the bund and to walk himself in the American's funeral procession, in full uniform and on foot while the white people rode in chairs. The warlord obeyed. It was a terrible loss of face, and he took it out on the junkmen later, but there will not be any more trouble in Wanhsien."

"I heard about that, down in Manila," Holman said. "I wondered if the two they beheaded were the ones that did the actual killing."

"Who could know? Presumably they were part of the mob."

"They'd know. But that's off the track." Holman was searching for words. "I don't see any connection between that and . . . and salutes and colors and stuff. The quarterdeck stuff."

Lt. Collins clasped his hands. "Consider this. The warlord had ten thousand soldiers ashore, to *Cockchafer*'s fifty men. He had field artillery to outgun her twenty to one. He would never have surrendered face to another Chinese, with odds like that in his favor."

"He was scared of what would come after. All England. The Royal Navy. Marines."

"No. No." Lt. Collins shook his head. "Wanhsien is above the rapids. He knew all the treaty powers together couldn't get enough force up there to match him. But he obeyed."

"He was bluffed? You mean—"

"*Not* bluffed!" Lt. Collins slapped the table. "That warlord obeyed a certain *moral* authority that is really in the British flag, do you see? The kind of virtue we maintain in our flags by our military ceremony, by the way we live our lives." He paused, gazing keenly at Holman. The man was chewing his lip and straining to comprehend. His spread, blunt fingers clawed gently, unconsciously, at the green baize. Black grease outlined the fingernails. "Moral authority," Lt. Collins repeated. "Like the power of a man's eye over a dog's eye."

The hands made fists. "The warlord wasn't a dog. He should've told them Limeys to go to hell!" Holman said.

Lt. Collins stifled a surge of anger. You fool, to try explaining, he told himself. It was the man's eagerness to know, and his own urge to communicate this thing he felt, that had betrayed him.

"I guess the warlord had military fear," Holman said heavily.

That was an enlisted man's phrase. It meant moral authority which the man obeyed unwillingly, sweating and tongue-tied and radiating unconscious hostility in the presence of officers. You could not help despising such a man, because he was despising himself. But when the man accepted moral authority, he found his pride and self-respect, and relations were easy and pleasant. It was easy and pleasant with all of the Sand Pebbles except Holman. Enlisted men did not have a phrase for the good feeling, but you might almost call it military love.

Abruptly, he looked directly into Holman's gray eyes. Holman dropped his eyes, and the square face went impassive. The sullen aura spread across the table.

If they did not break his gutter spirit in the big ships, we can't break it in *San Pablo,* Lt. Collins thought. Shing was right. Well, wrap it up now. Break off this misguided effort.

"Holman, no man alive understands the mechanics of how we put moral authority into our flags," he said slowly. "Mechanics is not the word for it. No word has been coined for it. I can perhaps follow a causal chain more deeply into that mystery than you can, but I reach my own limits." He was trying to keep the distaste he felt out of his voice, and to keep the corners of his mouth up. "I accept my limitations, as you must, as all men must. In the end, I have to take it monkey-see monkey-do. But a nicer word for it is faith. You will be a much happier person when you learn to have faith."

"I want to know," Holman said. "I can't stand feeling like a monkey."

Lt. Collins stood up, feeling his face flush. Holman scrambled clumsily to his feet. Lt. Collins made his voice officially impersonal.

"I am not in the habit of justifying myself to enlisted men, Holman. You may know this much: the *esprit* of the marines is partly due to the fact that they can all be fighting men, because the navy handles their logistics. In *San Pablo,* the Chinese boatmen handle our logistics, and I insist that we must all be fighting men. That is all the reason you have any need or right to know." He was lashing the man with his flat, impersonal voice. *"San Pablo* is not a Fleet ship. As long as we move and smoke boils out our stack, we will make the impression I wish on the Hunanese. Engineering is going to remain coolie work in *San Pablo*. It is going to remain work done by second-rate, inferior men of whom no courage or honor is expected. You may do such work for as long as it takes you to train your man to replace Chien, but you must not glorify what you do, and when you have it done I will transfer you back to the Fleet."

"Aye aye, sir!" the man said thickly, flashing teeth.

He put on his white hat and saluted, clumsy as a bear, and almost bolted out the door. Lt. Collins relaxed his fists. He had not realized they were closed. He rang for Yen-ta and ordered coffee.

He poured another cup. They all lived it without having to think about it, he thought. Even Tom Bordelles, who would go far with the blind, straight, wordless drive he had. There was no one to talk with about these thoughts. Except, incredibly, the man Holman, who wanted to know. Lt. Collins wryed his mouth. Holman's analytical tools were a sledge hammer and a cold chisel. He could only destroy the thing he wanted to take apart. But even the finest tools, the most subtle mind, would destroy it. The act of observing altered unpredictably the thing observed. It was wrong to try to look.

That was the flaw in Holman. Only I must look out the eyes, Lt. Collins thought. And I look at it and it squiggles away. From me alone it squiggles away.

You had to take the world as you found it. When *San Pablo* first came to Hunan, China was still an empire. What hurt one part hurt all. The memory of the Boxer Suppression was painfully fresh. They had good physical reasons, when they saw the flag on the Hunan rivers, to tremble and obey. Now China was a crazy-quilt turbulence of big and little warlords, but they still obeyed. It was old custom. They obeyed the moral authority of the treaty power flags.

Coldly, alone at his table, he faced it. As a fighting machine, *San Pablo* was a joke. In a genuine battle he could not whip even General Pan's ragtain army, let alone forty million Hunanese. He was a man with a kitchen chair in a cage full of tigers.

But in another part of his mind he knew that Chinese could not fight a genuine battle. Bordelles and the Sand Pebbles had a blind faith in that. It was justified. Chinese made pariahs of their armed men. No people who believed so could win any battles, except among themselves. Once we commission the new flotilla building in Shanghai, he thought, we can bring a thousand men to Paoshan. We can bring enough gunpower to pulverize the city. I have to hold the fort until then.

Faith made *San Pablo* invincible in Hunan. Faith kept the tigers believing that they were house cats. Nothing must shake that faith.

But someone had to look out the eyes.

He turned abruptly and pulled open a drawer of his desk and took out a pair of Chinese baby shoes. He set them on the green baize. They were blue, with crude U.S. flags embroidered in white and red on each toe. They spoke something wordless of what that symbol could mean in the Chinese mind.

In Hunan many Chinese displayed imperfect U.S. flags to protect their property from warlords and bandits. In the strange Chinese mind they were protection against more than just human predators. They drew good luck, and the smile of heaven. They warded off

Chinese devils. A missionary had given Lt. Collins the baby shoes, as a heathen curiosity. One of his woman converts had made them for her child, substituting the foreign symbol for the traditional tiger head. The missionary had called it superstition and taken them from her. But he displayed that same flag prominently above all his mission property.

The ignorant mother was wiser than the missionary, Lt. Collins thought. And the speechless child was wisest of them all. Only the simplest minds could touch the highest truths. You look at it and it squiggles away. You cannot know it, you can only feel it. As mother and child felt it . . . nothing special . . . just a feeling that everything is all right. All . . . all . . . all . . . all right . . .

Footsteps on deck stopped before his door. Hastily, Lt. Collins put the shoes back into his desk. But the footsteps went on, into the bridge.

Holman almost ran down to the engine room. It was his sanctuary. Courage and honor be damned, he thought. Whichever way you turned it, the military crap was still being a monkey-on-a-stick. He looked at the engine and it soothed him. You know how to deal with the monkeys, don't you, Engine, he thought. Well, he was going to lose the best ship for living aboard that he had ever had. The faster he trained Po-han, the faster he would be putting the skids under himself. Well, he would teach Po-han all he knew, everything, and when they shanghaied Jake Holman he would leave behind him a man just like himself. They would not get rid of Jake Holman as easily as they figured.

He spotted Po-han among the coolies and called him over to the workbench. Po-han said he had been ashore. He had uncles and many cousins in Paoshan. Holman told him about the new repair gang. Po-han was doubtful until he understood that Holman would work with them, and then his whole face beamed delight. They decided on Pai, Chiu-pa and Lung for the rest of the gang. Holman felt the tension of the interview with Lt. Collins leaving him. No more topside watches, he thought happily. No more drills. He felt good and easy with Po-han, better than with anybody else aboard. For a while at least, it was going to be all right. He squeezed Po-han's shoulder and shook him gently.

"Maskee? Can do, Po-han?"

"You, me, can do, Jehk," Po-han grinned back.

11

It was very good to be with the machinery again. It was like coming home from the wars. Holman's hands became hard and grimed and his dungarees oil-stained and his steaming shoes oil-soaked and molded very comfortably to his feet. He got along well with his repair gang and began learning a kind of pidgin Chinese in order to talk and joke with them. They kidded each other just like sailors, but you had to understand how a turtle was a particularly bastardly kind of bastard in order to appreciate their insults. They all had their individual laughs and grins and gestures and so much play and expression in their faces that Holman wondered why he had ever thought that Chinese faces were blank. He would not let them call him *Mastah* or *Sheensheng,* so they called him *Ho-mang* and Po-han called him *Jehk*. None of them would make their jokes at Holman, and he often wished they would.

Ping-wen took over smoothly, for cleaning and boiler work. He and Holman were respectful to each other, and the cleaning coolies still had blank faces. The ship was underway most of the days and the repair work had to be done in the evenings. Wilsey and Burgoyne often came down to drink coffee and watch the work. Burgoyne was proud of Po-han, who was still oiler on the steaming watch. Perna and Stawski would come down to drink coffee, but they did not have any interest in the repair work.

The topside sailors did not like it, for Holman to be off drills and deck watches. They did not say much, but Bronson and Crosley began calling him Ho-mang, and they meant it as a dig. Holman just grinned at them. Ho-mang was as good a name as any other.

He was not really training anyone, except Po-han. Pai and Chiu-pa and Lung were old hands, and every operation on the pumps was something they had done before and they were satisfied with their understanding of it. They were careful, steady workers and they had a grave respect for their tools and the machinery, such as few sailors had, and Holman respected them for it. It did not matter that they thought of pump parts in terms of kidneys and livers and such. When they spotted and scraped in a steam pilot valve, the pump stopped stalling; it was all right if Chiu-pa thought he had smoothed the wrinkles in the pump's worried brain. But Po-han could see beyond it to a steam-bound auxiliary piston, which he acted out by hissing and pressing his palms together, and he knew a pump stalled because it couldn't help it and not because it was too worried to keep its mind on the job. If spotting did not cure it, he could go on to renew the rings or rebush the gear. Whenever Po-han learned something new he was so delighted that it made Holman glad too.

The Sand Pebbles thought they knew all about the coolies and they did not know anything, Holman decided, after a while. Men like Pai and Chiu-pa were not bilge coolies at all; they were skilled workmen, even if they had screwy notions of what they did. But the Sand Pebbles called even Lop Eye Shing a coolie. For them, Ping-wen had one face for all the bilge coolies and Pappy Tung one face for all the deck coolies. They goosed Clip Clip and kidded with Wong and Oh Joy and they would stop by the galley to tell Big Chew the chow was very good, but they did not know even those house coolies. Their jokes, all they said and did, it was the same over and over, like parrot talk. It was old custom to goose Clip Clip. It was old custom for Clip Clip to jump and squeal and chatter, and for all hands to laugh.

For the Sand Pebbles, the coolies were collectively a kind of machine that kept the *San Pablo* clean and shipshape. The house coolies, which included Sew Sew and Press Press, and Captain Doo, who cleaned the head and washroom, were a part of the machine that kept the living quarters clean and neat, bunks made up, shoes shined, lockers always full of good, clean clothing, and the best chow in China on the mess tables three times a day. It was just old custom. It was also by far the best life Jake Holman had ever had, and when the thought came that he was going to have to leave it he would frown and shake his head and think about something else.

He was amazed at the extent of squeeze. They did not overlook anything, not even pencils from the ship's office, salt from the galley, and aspirin and pink lady from the sick bay. Every quarter the *San Pablo* had a shipment of stores sent to her by commercial steamer from the navy godown in Hankow, and half of it was for squeeze. Farren always ordered four dozen paint brushes. Holman learned he had to order enough brass and steel stock, sheet lead and copper, zinc plates and spelter and other metals, to supply a ship four times the size of the *San Pablo*. The coolies took the whole of the welfare fund, profits from the ship's store and beer sales and biologicals. The Sand Pebbles called it the "coolie fund." Whenever a sailor's shoes or clothing became a bit worn they would be squeezed and replaced by new ones and the cost would be in the mess bill which Lop Eye Shing collected on paydays. It was almost a kind of taxation, Holman thought. Like all sailors, the Sand Pebbles would curse and cuff and kick coolies around on the beach, but they did not kick the ship coolies. If one of them forgot and did, his next mess bill would be several dollars more than usual. He would know why, and no one would be sorry for him.

The coolies lived their life very much apart. They came and went across the rail aft, to keep from cluttering up the quarterdeck and also to let the squeeze go ashore unofficially. Lt. Collins never inspected their quarters below the main deck. None of the Sand Pebbles ever went down there. After the crew's payday Lop Eye Shing would pay off the coolies and they would gamble all night, the sound of their quarreling coming up through the deck, and often enough the heavy, sweet smell of opium came up through the hatches. They would get drunk and scream and fight down there and be around the ship next day with black eyes and scratched faces, but no one ever took official notice of it.

Holman asked questions and collected all the scuttlebutt he could about the coolies. There was not much. The Sand Pebbles believed that Lop Eye Shing kept exactly half the squeeze money for himself. He was supposed to have a big house and half a dozen pretty wives in Changsha and to be the social equal of the warlord. The Sand Pebbles were not interested in how things on the *San Pablo* had come about. It had always been that way and it was old custom and that was enough. Po-han also seemed unwilling to talk. He did say that there was a feud between Big Chew and Shing and that Big Chew would like to ease Shing off the ship and be number one himself. Big Chew had some of the other house coolies on his side, and also the four Fangs. They had been warlord soldiers and were supposed to be very tough. But Big Chew was afraid of Shing's gangster connections in Changsha. Po-han said frankly that he was afraid both of Shing and Big Chew, and he did not want to get mixed up in anything, even by talking.

Lt. Collins had said that the crew, everybody aboard, had been *designed* for their special job. The thought nagged at Holman. No one could tell him how. Finally, in an argument with Chiu-pa, he found one clue.

They were going to pack the fire and bilge pump and Chiu-pa wanted to soak the square, laminated Tuck's packing in water overnight and then step-cut it with a close clearance. Holman wanted to butt-cut the dry packing with a half-inch clearance to allow for swelling and put it in right away. Chiu-pa explained that if the belly snakes were not drowned first, they would bind the pump and break the follower plate. Holman said that water did not drown the belly snakes, it only made them grow, and all you had to do was to leave them enough room to grow in. Chiu-pa became excited and waved a turn of the old, step-cut packing in Holman's face.

"Olo custom! Olo custom!" he said.

"I makee new custom," Holman said.

Po-han was grinning. Pai and Lung were not.

"Befoh time P'tocki doee olo fashion, plopah fashion!" Chiu-pa insisted.

Holman pinned him on that. Yes, many a time Pitocki had packed that pump with his own hands, Chiu-pa said, and always he soaked and step-cut the packing. But when Holman tried to find out how and when pump-packing had become coolie work, Chiu-pa turned vague. Holman had Po-han put the packing in dry and butt-cut. For days afterward Chiu-pa watched the pump suspiciously, waiting for it to groan with a bellyache and then bind and break something.

The clue was that once Pitocki had packed pumps, and later it was coolie work that no white man could do without losing face. Holman built the rest up in his mind, from what he had seen happen on Fleet ships when they stayed a month or two in a Chinese port.

First the sampans would cluster around the slop chute and the Chinese in them would scream at each other and fight with dip nets for the garbage. So the cooks would give one sampan the garbage contract and people from that sampan would come aboard to collect it. Very quickly, that extended to scraping plates at the mess tables and then to washing them, and in a week or two every sailor-mess-cook would have his Chinese helper who did all the work. In the galley they would peel potatoes, and the cooks would be careful not to notice how they peeled them much too thickly and also dumped all the big, outside leaves of the cabbage into the garbage, which was their only pay. They would also shine the range and clean pans and coppers and they would take to sleeping on gunny sacks in the galley passageway so that they could be on hand early in the morning.

At first one or two would squat in a corner of the crew's washroom and scrub clothes for a few clackers a bucketful. The sailors would be a bit ashamed to squat there too, scrubbing their own clothes and feeling cheap because they were only saving a clacker. So very soon the Chinese scrubbed all the clothes and they would set up an ironing board with a big charcoal iron in some corner and at night one or two would sleep on mats under the ironing board.

Certain big, dirty jobs, such as chipping and painting sides and peak tanks for the deckforce or cleaning bilges and boilers for the engineers, would be saved until the ship came to China. Labor contractors, paid by the welfare fund, would bring hundreds of coolies aboard and do the jobs in a few days. A few deck and bilge coolies, the quick and handy ones, would stay on to do routine dirty work. They would be paid with brass shavings from the lathe, dirty wiping rags, old clothes, oily kerosene, all the stuff that would be thrown away in any other port but had value in China.

Within a month they would be all over the ship, humble, crouching in corners, ready to do any dirty, irksome thing that sailors did not like to do, and do it cheerfully and well. They were like water seeking its level, patient, not pressing, always ready when the chance came, making life smoother and easier for everybody with their Chinese magic, and all they wanted in return was trash and leavings and a few clackers now and then. What kept it from going too far on Fleet ships was that in time they always went to Manila, which was American flag country, and all Chinese had to get off.

But the river gunboats never left China and the *San Pablo* hardly ever left Hunan. Lop Eye Shing had come aboard twenty-five years ago as a garbage coolie and he was still aboard. And now, if scuttlebutt had it right, he made a lot more money every month than even Lt. Collins made.

Holman could see how it would all happen. They would build the wooden superstructure to give the crew healthier living quarters in the tropical summers. A river boat did not have to be seaworthy. Then there would be no reason why the Chinese should not take the old quarters. They would reduce the crew a man or two at a time, because the Chinese were doing all the hard work, and it would also make more living space for the others. When Pitocki packed the water end of a pump, at first the coolie would only hand him tools and wipe up after the job. Then the coolie would bolt and unbolt, then make the gasket, learning the job step by step, monkey-see monkey-do. It was dirty and uncomfortable under a pump, with water dripping in your face, and sooner or later old Pitocki would let the coolie do the whole job. Then it would be coolie work, and Pitocki would lose face if he packed a pump himself. He would be breaking a coolie's rice bowl.

So they had learned it monkey-see monkey-do in stolen bits from lazy machinist's mates until they could monkey-do it all, after their fashion, even such highly skilled jobs as refitting bearings. Sailors came and went and the bilge coolies stayed on and they made all the work coolie work. All the sailors had left was control of the throttle and feed checks underway and making out and signing the log sheets.

Well, nobody designed that, Holman thought. It just grew. Or did the Chinese know what they were doing? Had Lop Eye Shing designed it? It was hard to say.

It was the same topside. There, all the sailors had left was the guns. No Chinese could touch a weapon. Restorff was the only petty officer who still had the whole of his work to himself. Almost every day he would have a greasy hammock laid out somewhere on deck, cleaning and oiling guns, and all of the seamen helped him. Restorff had been aboard almost ten years, longer than any other Sand Pebble, and from him Holman got the second clue.

"When I first come aboard here, back before the war, the old *Sand Pebble* was the easy-go-sloppiest ship on the river," Restorff said one time.

"What changed her?" Holman asked.

"Lieutenant Von Bredow," Restorff said.

There were a lot of officers with German names on the China Station then, Restorff went on. The scuttlebutt was that the navy wanted to get them out of the way, in case they might be disloyal in a war against Germany. They had all been pretty touchy about it. Lt. Von Bredow came to the *San Pablo,* and maybe he was taking his resentment out on the sailors or maybe he was just trying to demonstrate his loyalty, but he began turning it into a battleship with uniform of the day and drills and quarterdeck ritual and inspections and all manner of military ceremony. He was a tall, hard, sharp man who never smiled, Restorff said.

"She was a madhouse for quite a while," Restorff reminisced, smiling ruefully. "Lots of the guys couldn't stand it, and they got swaps or transfers."

That was probably when Pitocki gave over the pump packing to Chien, Holman thought. And bearing fitting and everything else, because the topside military stuff had begun taking all of his time.

"Now it seems like it's always been that way," Restorff said. "The guys like it that way. And it makes face with the slopeheads."

Well, it was a design, all right, Holman thought, but it was hard to say who designed it. It was a design, and there was no place in it for Jake Holman, and so they were going to get rid of him. Whenever that thought crept up on him, he would clamp his teeth and grimace.

He still enjoyed the steaming watches with Burgoyne and Po-han, but the useless entries in the log began to bother him. The *San Pablo* used standard navy log sheets and every hour the throttleman had to report to the bridge the temperature of the river water and the average revolutions of the engine. The temperature would tell a deep-sea ship whether it was in or out of some current like the Gulf Stream and warn of icebergs nearby. They used the average RPM for navigation. But there were no warm currents or icebergs in Tungting Lake and the Chinese pilot could always tell exactly where he was by looking ashore, and it did not make sense to log those readings. When Holman griped about it to Burgoyne, the lean watertender only grinned and shrugged.

"Hellfire, they got a column in the log for it. Ain't that a reason?"

The RPM had to be reported through the voice tube in one of the many verbal formulas they used on the *San Pablo* that had seemed funny to somebody once and now were like fossilized jokes. You tacked on "up and down, up and down." One day the L.P. was thumping louder than usual and it was on Holman's nerves, because he still had not found out what caused it. Crosley called down from the bridge for the hourly readings.

"What you makin', up and down, up and down?"

Angrily, Holman varied the formula. "Forty-seven, roundy-go-round, roundy-go-round," he yelled back.

"Roundy-go-thump," Crosley said.

Holman heard them laughing on the bridge. It was a joke. They did not often have a new joke on the *San Pablo,* and they made the most of it. "Whatcha makin', roundy-go-*thump,* roundy-go-*thump?*" they would call down after that. Somebody was always repeating the phrase spontaneously, on deck or in the compartment, and it always got a laugh.

"I been hearing that thump for years and I never really noticed it until now," Farren told Holman. "Now I hear it all the time, seems like."

"I'm going to do something about it this winter in Changsha," Holman said. "They better have their fun while they can."

He didn't know just what he was going to do about it, and it bothered him. He knew that Bronson and Crosley and quite a few others were keeping the joke up just to needle him. They had found a good way to get under his skin, all right. Increasingly, he grudged the time it took to refit that bearing every few days. He winced every time he heard the joke phrase.

One day at the noon meal the L.P. was thumping worse than usual, enough to rattle mess gear on the tables. Bronson said, "Roundy-go-*thump!*" and they laughed. Crosley said "Roundy-go-*bang!*" and they were all laughing and coming into it at the other two tables, roundy-go-*boom, crash, pop, thud, bong,* everything they could think of, in time with the slow engine beat, and howling their laughs. It flared up sudden and weird, like fire in dry grass. They were all chanting hoarsely in unison, stomping their feet and slapping the tables in time with the engine beat, with their eyes bulging and their faces red.

Holman did not know how to take it. At his table his messmates were trying to be loyal to him and not join in, but Restorff and Harris were slapping the table softly in the rhythm and it was all they could do to hold off.

"They're going nuts!" Farren muttered. "Somebody throw a bucket of water on 'em." He was embarrassed.

"Maybe I better go below," Holman said.

Suddenly Red Dog stood up on his chair and began a high, shrill yapping. The Sand Pebbles looked at him, but they did not cease the chant. Red Dog jumped down and went around the table and lifted his leg suggestively behind Bronson. A beatific look came slowly over his pinched-in features and the chant began to hush and grow ragged.

"Arf . . . arf . . . arf," he said comfortably, and lowered his leg.

The chant died away and the Sand Pebbles were all laughing normally and happily at Bronson. He turned around in his chair and he was furious.

"You little redheaded son of a bitch!" he told the yeoman.

"Arf! Arf! Arf!" Red Dog barked delightedly.

The Sand Pebbles laughed all the harder.

After that incident, Holman studied the engine in a kind of desperation. He had to discover what made the L.P. wear so rapidly. It still eluded him, and time was running out. The lake shrank and the *San Pablo* was forced back into the drowned river channels. Vast mud flats emerged, stinking brown and yellow with drying water weeds, and millions of white birds screamed all day harvesting them. The Sand Pebbles began to talk about wintering in at Changsha.

"It's a big place, a treaty port, Jake," Farren said. "Nothing like Hankow, but it's civilized enough to have bars and one good whorehouse."

Near the end, Holman stopped thinking. He would stand beside the L.P. and strain to hear the myriad tiny voices, trying to empty his mind except for the tiny voices, hoping that the answer would just come to him. He had solved some very tough problems that way.

No answer came. On their last day of steaming they were headed up the Siang River to Changsha, and Holman felt he was whipped. He wandered the topside aimlessly, watching the scenery. It was rather open country, rice stubble yellow on the flats and low hills far back. The Siang was a broad river with a maze of channels through long white sandbars. Roundy-go-*thump!* it kept coming up through Jake Holman's feet and into his bones. He could not enjoy the new scenery.

He went below and stood beside the L.P. Perna and Stawski had the watch. They were talking and did not see Holman. They never looked at the engine. Holman watched the great crank come round and round. He should be able to catch some hint, from the play of the bearing between the crank webs, as to where the misalignment lay. It was no good. It was too dark down in the crankpit. If he could only see it against light, instead of against darkness, he thought.

Before he knew it, he had picked up a ball peen hammer and slipped into the bilges beneath the main condenser. He did not raise a floorplate, because he did not want any light down there. The engine soleplate was in three parts, flanged and bolted together, and also bolted through chocks to the ship's structure. Each part was like a big, square cast-iron box and the inside of the box was the crankpit. In the cool darkness the oval manhole into the L.P. crankpit was like a huge eye of dim light winking fifty times a minute as the crank swept by it.

Holman lay on his back and prepared to ease his head in through the manhole. The oil-rotted bitumastic stuck to his shirt and there was water all around, but none where he lay. He eased his head and shoulders in very gingerly. He knew he was safe, but something in him did not know it. He kept wanting to jerk his head away as the great crank plunged down at him and the end of his nose tingled and itched. The crank passed about four inches above his nose and he could feel the wind of its passage like fingers stroking his face.

He forced himself to stand it. His hair was a mess of oil, but if he raised his head the crank would tear his face off. I'd really lose face, he thought. The grim humor steadied him, and he began to observe. The crank slapped back and forth between the webs, all right, and he could see its complicated sequence more clearly than he ever had, but it told him nothing. The tiny, whispering voices were all around him, almost in his ear. He emptied his mind again, waiting patiently. He did not know how long he waited. . . .

It was a bead of oil that came and went and came again. In the tail of his eye. One of the tiny voices. He cut his eyes to focus on it. It was at the joint between the soleplate and one of the chocks. It meant movement, where there should be no movement, movement so tiny that only magnification of it by the oil droplet made it possible to be seen at all. He searched for other oil droplets and found them. All the tiny voices began to talk sense.

They had a big thing to say. Easing out of the crankpit, listening, Holman scarcely heard the thunder of running feet on the floorplates above his head. The voices spoke of a long-ago grounding that had bent the soft wrought-iron structure of the ship itself. It had skewed out of plane and parallel the two channel beams to which the soleplate was bolted. It was not much, and all the bolts had drawn and yielded just enough among them all to accommodate and permit the engine still to turn.

"God almighty!" Holman said softly, crouching outside the crankpit. He was very happy and excited.

No wonder they could not find any misalignment in the dockyard. They lined each cylinder on its soleplate section. They took it for granted that the rigid soleplate was as true as the keel beneath it. But the soleplate was not rigid and the keel was not true. There was a shifting, twisty hump beneath the L.P., distributed across all the loose bolts and chocks that complained in their tiny voices, and that was what made the L.P. wear. It was what had killed old Chien.

Holman took his hammer and began sounding bolts, to verify what he already knew. They all gave him back the dull thud of a bolt loose and working rather than the sharp *ping* of a tight one. He heard feet above him again, and cursing, and someone lifted a floorplate. Holman looked up, blinking in the sudden light. A pistol was pointed at him. Lynch's face behind the pistol looked popeyed and terrible.

Holman stood up, alarmed. Lynch lowered the pistol. Stawski, his face pale and small eyes bulging, was twirling a crowbar as if it were a bamboo stick. Lynch was working his lips silently, as he put away his pistol with shaking hands.

"Jake! Jesus Christ, Jake!" he managed to say. Then angrily,

"Come out of them bilges, you God damned fool! I almost shot you!" Then tremulous, shaking his head, "Jake. Jesus Christ. We thought you was old Chien's ghost."

Holman climbed out. Stawski replaced the floorplate and went sheepishly back to the throttle. Chiu-pa had seen Holman's face in the shadowy crankpit, Lynch explained. Perna and Stawski would not believe it, but when they saw for themselves they panicked. All of the Chinese had followed them topside and the plant had steamed unattended for almost ten minutes.

"You'd think they'd recognize my face," Holman said.

"Not down there under that crank," Lynch said. "Under a horse's tail, maybe yes."

He was shaking with reaction and beginning to be angry again. Suddenly it tickled Holman. He found himself laughing uncontrollably.

"Shoot a ghost! Ho ho ho, shoot holes in a ghost!" he laughed. "What good would that do, with a ghost?"

"Well, what the hell would you do with a ghost?" Lynch said.

"Jesus, I don't know, Chief. I hope I never have to find out." Holman could not stop laughing. "I guess I'd just pretend he wasn't there."

"Ah, you're crazy with the heat!'

Lynch went up, feeling insulted. Holman tried to calm himself down and stop laughing. He was starting to shake, and he was just realizing how very near he had been to death.

12

The Siang River was wide and shallow at Changsha. Across the river a mountain rose up, yellowy-orange around the base with autumn leaves, and the sun always set behind that mountain. The river had many long, white sandbars and across the main channel from the city was a very big sandbar where the important treaty people had their houses. The big houses were behind dikes and walls and surrounded by trees. Changsha had a higher and longer wall than Paoshan but you could not see it as well, because the bund was built up with tin-roofed godowns and foreign brick buildings. One hotel on the bund was always lit up at night and music came from it. The river bank was a sheer wall of masonry with stone steps inset here and there and slanting down to the sand uncovered by the receding water. The Chinese dumped rubbish and garbage down on the sand and it would build up and stink all winter until the spring flood swept it away, Burgoyne told Holman. Junks and sampans of brown-yellowy, bare oiled wood crowded three and four deep all along the river bank except where there were pontoons for the commercial steamers. Much of the city was outside the walls. To the south rose the tall smoke-stacks of an antimony smelter and to the north there was much missionary property. The Japanese Consulate was outside the city to the north, with the Japanese gunboat anchored offshore.

The river ran north. It seemed backward to Holman. He always thought of north as being uphill. North was a high place.

When the river was full, an eddy kept a deep pool scoured out near the north end of the city. At low water the pool stayed full, but it had only a very slow eddy current in it. It was the *San Pablo*'s anchorage. Trash and turds from the head would drift very slowly two or three times around the ship in a kind of continuous moving wreath before it got into the sluggish current of the main channel. The Sand Pebbles called their anchorage the goldfish bowl. H.M.S. *Woodcock*'s berth was upriver and across the channel, abreast His Majesty's Consulate on the big sandbar.

All day every day blue-clad coolies swarmed in the junks and along the bund, pushing wheelbarrows and pulling carts, five or six men leaning and straining along ahead of the heaped carts like hitched horses. Changsha had electricity but no running water, and lines of water coolies slopped along all day between the river and the city. They had five-gallon kerosene tins at each end of their shoulder poles, instead of wooden buckets, as at Paoshan, and that was as near as Changsha had gotten to civilizing its water supply. The coolies sang their work chant all day, *hay ho, hay ho,* and it made a happy sound in the crisp, smoky autumn air.

Changsha was a treaty port and foreign businesses could own property there. Their buildings were all along the bund—oil companies, steamship companies, export and import agencies. Each company had its own house flag which flew all day above each building and on the many honking launches which took the businessmen back and forth between the city and their homes on the big sandbar. They flew the company flags on their homes, too. On Sundays they replaced all the company flags with national flags. But the consulates and missions and gunboats flew the national flags all through the week.

From the first, there was a drop in military tension on the *San Pablo*. Only one Fang at a time made bugle calls. Franks shortened the calisthenics and they only held battle drills every other morning.

Liberty started every day at one o'clock. Restorff, Harris, Vincent and Haythorn were shacked up in the city, but the other Sand Pebbles made their liberties in the Red Candle Happiness Garden. It was in a cluster of Chinese buildings outside the wall, where the liberty men could hear the ship's siren sounding the recall, if trouble broke. One petty officer always went along on shore patrol and he had to stay sober and keep order and be ready to get the drunks back to the ship in a hurry. Jennings examined the girls every week and kept a pro station stocked in the head and nobody ever got set up in the Red Candle. They could not get trapped inside the walls by sudden trouble, and it was a very convenient arrangement.

A Portygee half-caste named Victor Shu owned the Red Candle. He was seldom there, and a Chinese woman ran it for him. The Sand Pebbles called her Mother Chunk. Shu had a ship chandlery business in the city and he was in with the warlord. He was supposed to have a tie with the river gangsters who levied toll on Chinese cargoes and pirated junks that would not pay, and he was said to be a good friend of Lop Eye Shing. Every year some of the local missionaries tried to make the Red Candle close down, and every year Victor Shu outmaneuvered them.

A favorite story on the *San Pablo* was about the time the missionaries had a project to win the Sand Pebbles away from the Red Candle. They were supposed to come to another place and play tennis and croquet and drink lemonade and cocoa and meet some nice girls. The project fell through when Jennings showed up ahead of time to examine the girls.

Holman went ashore with Burgoyne on the first liberty of the season in the Red Candle.

"This is the garden, hey?" Holman said.

"Might could call it that," Burgoyne said. "The bar's over here."

The small stone-paved courtyard had some dusty shrubs in green boxes. They crossed the courtyard and went into a large square room with half a dozen round wooden tables. Sand Pebbles in white uniforms sat already at several of the tables, drinking the first whisky they had had for months, and heavily made-up Chinese girls sat with them. The first drunk in the Red Candle was always a wild one, Burgoyne told Holman.

"I sure don't envy Bronson tonight," he said.

Bronson had shore patrol. He sat importantly by himself at one table, looking around and fingering his club and pistol and brassard. A barboy in a white coat came to Holman's table and they ordered whisky. The boy brought the drinks from in back somewhere; there was no bar in the room. It had a low ceiling with one bare bulb dangling from a cord. The bulb burnt feebly red in the smoky haze, because the voltage was always low in Changsha, Burgoyne said. The floor was dusty, splintery wood, damp here and there with drink slops, and Chinese theater posters hung all around on the gray plaster walls. They were of pretty Chinese girls in red and green and gold and some had bare breasts. None of the girls at the tables were as pretty as the ones on the posters.

"That's Mother Chunk." Burgoyne pointed.

She had a broad red face and gray hair pulled back tightly and she wore a black silk jacket and trousers. She was swapping obscene insults with Crosley, Vincent and Waxer at the table next to Holman's, and she was giving better than she got. They were trying to give her a bad time because she did not have any new girls in since last year.

"You all same goddam *Sampabble* sailah, whassamattah no likee all same gel?" she said. She whirled away from them, to Holman's table. "Ho, Flenchy!" she greeted Burgoyne. "Whassamattah no takee gel topside?"

"Give me time, Mother. After while," Burgoyne said.

"I tinkee you olo man, no can do."

She made an obscene gesture. She had rings on her fingers and natural feet. Burgoyne grinned at her.

"I ain't either," he said. "You want to feel, Mother?"

She grabbed at him under the table and he pushed her laughing away. She turned her gaze on Holman.

"You belong new sailah," she accused him. "What name you?"

"Holman."

"Pitocki's relief," Burgoyne said. "He all same Pitocki."

"Ho-mang." She studied Holman. "Long time P'tocki come this side." She lowered her voice. "Have got one piecee new gel topside. She jus' now makee pitty." Mother Chunk pantomimed powdering her face. "Young gel, school gel, too much flaid. Suppose bye-m-bye she come you table? Maskee?"

"Sure, maskee," Holman said.

Mother Chunk winked at him and went on to trade insults with Farren and Red Dog.

"You're in, Jake. Mother likes you," Burgoyne said. "She always favored old Pitocki, too."

They ordered new drinks. Rain started drizzling outside and it became darker, drunker and smokier inside. The Sand Pebbles had chow brought to their tables and they took the girls topside and came back and drank and ate some more. The room grew noisier with chairs scraping and falling over, voices quarreling, dice cups thumping and dice rattling as they rolled for drinks. Someone was always slapping a table and shouting "Boy!" Holman began feeling his whisky and thinking about chow. He noticed a civilian had come in and was sitting alone in one corner, at a table partially masked by a screen.

"That's one of the German engineers from the smelter," Burgoyne said. "We call that the German table."

Some of the Germans in Changsha had houses at the upper end of the big sandbar, Burgoyne said, but they could not go to the club because they were not treaty people. They had lost their treaty rights in the war and now they were something like White Russians. They did not lose face if they came to the Red Candle.

"Kind of no-account, you might say," Burgoyne said. "That old boy's name is George Scharf, and he comes here right much. He's a crazy old coot, you get him drunk enough to talk."

"Talks English?"

"Better'n you and me. He's educated."

The German was drinking whisky and watching the sailors with a small, amused smile. He was tall and elderly, with thin brown hair and a long, lined face that looked sad behind his smile. He had character, Holman decided. The room was quieting. Nobody had a girl topside. Holman wanted to eat, but not at the Red Candle. He felt restless.

"I feel like going someplace else," he told Burgoyne. "Walk off a little of the whisky."

"Ain't no place else."

"Well, just a chow joint. Know any good ones?"

"Stick around," Burgoyne said. "The guys are petering out. This is just the time Mother Chunk always pulls something."

"All right. One more drink."

"Don't forget what Mother promised you, Jake."

She was young and very pretty and afraid in a sleeveless yellow dress. Heads turned to look at her as she came toward Holman's table. She had a handkerchief crumpled in her left hand and she looked straight ahead. Holman felt oddly embarrassed. He started to get up but Crosley was ahead of him, catching the girl's arm and pulling her to a seat between himself and Waxer. Holman settled back.

"You missed out, Jake," Burgoyne said. "You got to be right fast on your feet in this place."

Holman shrugged. The girl had bobbed hair, shingled in back, and she was speaking very good English. Her voice sounded tight and artificially held low.

"I should warn you, I get a commission on what I drink. All I drink is cold tea, but you will pay for whisky."

"Boy! Catch foh piecee whisky!" Crosley yelled.

Delight was all over his frog face. He knew the other Sand Pebbles were watching and envying him. The girl sat stiffly, her left hand in her lap, wearing a fixed smile that did not look natural. She had smooth, clear skin and a pretty, oval Chinese face with large, clear eyes.

"What the hell, Jake?" Burgoyne whispered. He tugged his mustache, his eyes on the girl.

"My name is Maily. I keep books for Mr. Shu and act as hostess," she was saying. "I'm *so* pleased to meet all of you."

"I'm Crosley. This here's Waxer, and that's Vincent across the table," Crosley said. "Never mind them bastards at the other tables. Tonight you're mine, Loveyduck."

"Hey, I want seconds!" Waxer said.

He was a very blond boy with pale eyes and no whiskers and he was always making a great show of proving his manhood on the whores.

"I'll think about it," Crosley told Waxer.

They questioned her. She wouldn't say how she learned English or where she came from. "My secret," was all she would say, with that smile. She did not act like a Chinese girl. She held her head high and showed her teeth when she smiled and talked. Except for her face, she was absolutely an American girl, Holman decided, pretty and clean and decent and scared, and that was what made the excitement in the room. It was like electricity in the smoky air.

Crosley had an arm around her, playing with her breast. She seemed to be pretending it was not happening to her, but her smile kept slipping and she would have to put it back. She had learned that Crosley was from New Jersey and she was trying to talk about Trenton and Washington crossing the Delaware. Of all things to talk about, Holman thought.

"That was before my time," Crosley said.

Burgoyne was scowling. It was the first time Holman had ever seen him look angry. Waxer put his arm around the girl.

"As hostess, I'm supposed to divide my time among all the tables," she said shakily. "It's been very pleasant, but I must go now."

She tried to get up. Crosley pulled her back down.

"Not till we been topside a couple of times, Loveyduck."

"I don't go upstairs. I'm only a hostess."

Her bright, forced smile and voice seemed to be her only defense. Waxer and Crosley each had one hand under the table. She gasped and jerked and lost her smile and put it back again. She looked at Holman and Burgoyne and all around the room. There was no hope in her eyes.

"Jake, we got to get her loose from them bastards," Burgoyne whispered.

Holman nodded. It was very old custom that you did not interfere with a shipmate and his woman. Guys off other ships, yes, and that was how many fights started. But not a shipmate. Burgoyne was an old-time Sand Pebble. It would be best to let him take the lead and then back his play, Holman decided.

The girl gasped and jerked again. "Please don't do that, Mr. Crosley," she said. Her voice was like a spring wound tight to snapping.

"Ah, now, Loveyduck," Crosley said. His face was red.

Burgoyne stood up. "Let her come over here, Flagbag," he said harshly. "It's our turn now."

"Go to hell, Frenchy," Crosley said. "You won't even get a wet deck on this little pig, not tonight you won't."

Holman stood up. He wanted to pick up Crosley and throw him twenty feet. "You heard Frenchy. Let her go," he said. He put his feeling in his voice.

"Easy there, you two!" Bronson said. "Stand fast, Ho-mang!"

He moved in, twirling his club. He was Crosley's buddy and his brassard made him navy authority for the moment. Holman looked at Bronson's fat, important face and hated him.

"Enough's enough, Bronson," he said. "You get that girl away from 'em, then."

"This is a whorehouse, Ho-mang, in case you didn't know," Bronson said. "Whores got duties, just like sailors, in case you didn't know that either."

"You won't always have shore patrol."

"I got it now."

"Please! I can't stand it!" the girl said.

All three chairs scraped as she struggled. Crosley laughed. Burgoyne cursed and started around the table. Mother Chunk burst through the Sand Pebbles, all standing now. She was shrill-voiced and angry.

"Whassamattah you, Closs-eye? You wanchee *duhai,* pay money, go topside!"

"I'll pay, Mother," Crosley said. "I'm ready for a cruise topside. I got one a cat couldn't scratch."

He clinked two Mex dollars on the table. Mother Chunk pushed them away scornfully.

"This gel first time piecee," she said. "Mus' pay two hundah dollah."

"Oh, for Christ's sake!" Crosley didn't want to believe it. "I'll pay ten Mex. Maskee?" He dug in his pocket.

"Shu talkee two hundah dollah!" Mother Chunk insisted. "Golo money!"

"Two hundred dollars *gold,* for God's sake?" Crosley's frog face and hoarse voice were outraged. "Nobody's *ever* going to have that much money, Mother," he said plaintively.

"Bye-m-bye somebody catch," she assured him.

"Well, God damn it!"

Crosley looked around for sympathy. The Sand Pebbles were beginning to smile. Crosley looked at the other girls, but his gaze did not linger on them. His face was turning ugly.

"Well, by God, she can still drink with me!" he said.

"She go oddah table now."

"You can't change house rules like that, God damn you, Mother! Long as I got money to buy her drinks, I keep her!"

"She's coming to my table," Burgoyne said.

"Like hell!" Crosley said.

"Watch it, Frenchy! You too, Ho-mang!"

Bronson laid his club like a bar across Holman's chest, nudging him back. He had little pale dimples at his mouth corners. The girl was standing up, with her frozen smile, and Burgoyne and Crosley each grasped one of her arms. The air was very tense again. Red Dog came up and patted the girl on the head.

"That's the Seal of the Red Dog," he told her. "Now if anybody so much as puts a hand on you, something terrible will happen to 'em." He turned to Crosley. "Hands off her, Flagbag!"

"Stand clear, Shanahan! You too, Burgoyne!" Bronson snapped. "That's a military order! You want to be put under arrest?"

Crosley screamed and jumped forward, releasing the girl. He turned, rubbing his buttocks with both hands, and glared at Red Dog.

"Arf! Arf! Arf!" Red Dog said.

Crosley lowered his head and rushed, fists milling. Red Dog darted out an arm and Crosley stopped. He sank slowly to his knees, hands waving feebly. Red Dog was pinching his nose, and it was hurting him so badly that it took his strength away. His eyes were popping and his loose-lipped mouth gaped and he went "Ah . . . ah . . . ah . . ." in a high, strangled tone.

"Stop that, Shanahan! You're under arrest!" Bronson roared.

"Will you protect me from this violent person, sir?" Red Dog asked. Impish delight was all over his face.

"I'll club you down!"

Bronson raised his club. Holman set himself to intercept it. Red Dog twisted and pushed and then stepped back, his hands up. Crosley arose, breathing hoarsely through his mouth. All his fight was gone. He raised his hand unbelievingly to his nose and blood gushed out of his nose and down the front of his white jumper, as if he had opened a tap. Mother Chunk laughed. Then they were all laughing, howling and roaring off the tension. Bronson led Crosley back to the head. It was all over.

She sat at Holman's table, between Farren and Burgoyne, and they laughed about Crosley. They were all being careful of their language, and it did not seem like a whorehouse any longer. She could not talk naturally, and neither could the sailors. She smiled and talked like someone reciting from a history or a geography book. But she was exciting them just by her clean, strange presence, and the fact that she was a virgin in a whorehouse. All the Sand Pebbles tried to crowd chairs around the one table and one by one they slipped away again to take one of the other girls for a cruise topside. They were all drinking freely and the room was once more full of happy noise.

Holman was not happy. He was excited, but when he looked at the other girls they looked frowzy and flabby and not clean enough. Crosley came out with cotton stuffed in his swollen nose and left without looking at anybody. The girl tried to talk across the table to Holman, asking about the geography of Nevada, and he gave her short answers. She seemed to be trying to pay him special attention, and he could not respond. Too much whisky on an empty stomach, he thought. He called the boy and ordered shrimps and rice.

When the boy brought the chow, it was too crowded to eat at that table. Holman stood up, and all the other tables were dirty with spilled food and drinks and cigarette ashes. The only clean one was the German table. Holman walked over there.

"Mind if I eat some chow at your table?" he asked the German engineer. "It's the only clean place left."

"Of course not," the German said. "Please sit down."

Holman ate in silence. The German watched the sailors with his one-sided little smile. Red Dog had started them all singing. Holman finished.

"Have a drink with me?" he asked Scharf.

"Thank you."

They drank in silence. Red Dog had even Bronson singing. It was all good shipmate spirit again in the Red Candle.

"That girl, Maily," Holman said at last. "You know anything about her?"

"Victor Shu brought her here a week ago. She is a mystery." Scharf pronounced all his words more distinctly than he needed to. "One drinks and looks on and the people are all mysteries," he said.

The words kindled Holman. Sometimes when he was drunk he would feel that he was right on the edge of unrolling the master blueprint of creation. It was just a way of looking at things, a sideways slant of the mind's eye, that he could only get into when he was drunk, and he would always pass out before he got drunk enough really to see anything. But it was more exciting than a woman. Whatever he said and what other people said seemed loaded with strange and wonderful meaning. He listened to himself as to a stranger.

"You're a mystery. You're an educated man," he told Scharf. "What are you doing in a whorehouse?"

"I am watching the world end."

"The world's a whorehouse."

"This is a temple," Scharf said. "I watch you sailors at your rites."

Holman grinned at Scharf. He signaled the barboy and told him to bring a bottle of whisky to the table.

"You are like the old monks who ended their world a thousand years ago," Scharf said. "You are a monastic brotherhood vowed to poverty, obedience and unchastity."

"All I do is take care of machinery."

"Our German priests are in disgrace," Scharf said sadly. "We Germans are only ordinary people now."

Holman poured more whisky. "I wasn't in that war, not to fight," he said. "I never hated Germans. I'm ordinary people, too."

"You are strong. It is your duty to despise." Scharf sipped whisky, with his mocking little smile. "It is hard to despise in weakness. One must hate and fear. The coward must despise himself."

"Chinese don't. They think it's human nature to be cowards."

"Ah!" Scharf set down his empty glass and peered keenly at Holman. "The Chinese are the only ordinary people," he said. "I wish I could be Chinese."

"So do I, sometimes." Holman refilled both glasses. "How's the world going to end, Scharf? Burn up?"

"I think we will just all slide quietly under the tables."

"You and me'll be the last ones."

Scharf's blue eyes crinkled. "Drink to that!"

He raised his glass. Holman clinked glasses so hard that Scharf's glass broke. The German's little smile faded. He wiped his hand on his sleeve.

"It is an omen," he said mournfully.

"Omen of a new drink," Holman said. "Boy! Boy, there! Catchee moh one piecee glass, chop chop!"

He got very drunk and blanked out at intervals. He came out of it for a moment when Bronson was getting them all on their feet to go back to the ship at midnight. They were milling around among the tables. The girl Maily swam in front of him.

"I'm sorry we didn't have a chance to talk more, Mr. Holman," she said. "I am very pleased to have met you."

She looked very clean and nice and she was smiling naturally at him. He groped drunkenly for her hands and she gave him the right one.

"So'm I," he said. "Take care of yourself, Maily."

"Come on, Jake." Burgoyne tugged at his elbow. "We need your beef. Help us carry Farren."

"Sure." Holman looked around. Scharf was asleep with his head on the table. "Where's Farren?" Holman asked.

"Over here under the table," Burgoyne said.

13

Chill, damp days began to spoil the fine autumn weather. The commercial steamers still ran from Hankow and Holman waited impatiently for the water to drop low enough to stop them. Then the *San Pablo* would be trapped for the winter in her goldfish bowl and he could disable the engine long enough to realign the foundation. It would be a very big job, and the thought of it excited him, but he did not talk about it. He worked with his repair gang on smaller jobs and they were getting very good at working together. The plant was in fine shape, all but the L.P. engine.

The steamers from Hankow brought letters to Lynch that had all the Sand Pebbles arguing. No one was supposed to have a private life on the *San Pablo*. Lynch's Russian woman had a chance to buy a small bakery and teashop in Hankow. She would put up the money, but she wanted Lynch to go partners with her, because he was treaty people and his name on the papers would ensure gunboat protection for the property. Lynch did not know what to do. He did not want to stick his neck out. He was going to retire in a few more years and he had been thinking vaguely that he would buy a share in the Green Front and relieve Nobby Clarke behind the bar. He did not know about a teashop.

"A guy my age, he's got to think about the future," Lynch kept saying.

The big mess table topic, however, was the new girl at the Red Candle. It was a week before someone discovered that the last two fingers were missing from her left hand. She was very clever at hiding it with a handkerchief that she seemed only to be holding. The Sand Pebbles speculated on who could possibly get two hundred dollars gold and take her topside. A big winner in a poker game, they thought. Or one of the chiefs; scuttlebutt said Lynch had some liberty bonds. But the chiefs did not go to the Red Candle. They would take a room at the bund hotel and have girls brought in. White hat sailors could not afford that. The Timber Dicks, from H.M.S. *Woodcock,* sometimes came to the Red Candle, but they had less money than the Sand Pebbles. The Sand Pebbles were going to be very jealous of whoever first took Maily topside. They would not gamble any more after payday, for fear someone would win too much.

Maily had a strange effect on the Sand Pebbles. They tried to talk decently at her table and the sober ones made the drunken ones keep their hands off her. They all went along with her pretense that she was only a hostess and as soon as she had saved enough money to buy a ticket she was going down to Shanghai and get an office job. She asked almost as many questions about Shanghai as she did about America. But all hands knew, from Mother Chunk, that Maily was going deeper in debt to Victor Shu, and there was only one way she was going to get the money to go to Shanghai.

They respected her desire to keep her secret. It made her even more exciting to them, not knowing. The other girls wore Chinese clothes, but Maily had many different dresses and she looked pretty and young and clean in all of them. Listening to her voice (like an American girl's, if you closed your eyes, Wilsey said) with an occasional tremor in it (that twanged a string inside you, Farren said) or watching her eyes bright with hidden terror (like a little rabbit about to be caught, Crosley said) charged up a man's batteries until he couldn't stand it, Stawski said. So they would take one of the pigs topside and it would be no good and an hour later they would do it again and it would still be no good. But it was a very good business for Mother Chunk's department and if Maily could have been taking a commission on that, as well as on drinks, she would already be in Shanghai, Duckbutt Randall said.

One cold day Holman put steam for the first time on the brass radiators in the compartment. They banged and thumped and the acrid smell of metal polish baking off filled the space and a furious argument about Maily grew up while the men were eating dinner.

"I bet she ain't even cherry," Crosley said. "I bet she's just a trick Victor Shu thought up to keep all the guys horny."

Perna agreed. A dozen men howled down the idea. They all wanted to believe that Maily was a virgin.

"Ask Doc. He inspected her. Ain't it so, Doc?" they all appealed.

"She's a virgin," Jennings said. "I'm sorry I insisted on examining her."

"How could you tell? What's one like?" Crosley challenged.

"One what?"

"A maidenhead. What's it look like?"

"Oh," Jennings said. "It's just a membrane. You probably wouldn't recognize it, unless you knew what to look for."

"Well, I don't see where she's worth two hundred gold, or even ten," Crosley said. "One of them things is one of them things, if it's hung on a cow. I ain't gonna let her get me bothered."

Laughter swept the tables. They knew Crosley was the most bothered one of all. He could not forget that one time he had had his hands all over Maily.

"It ain't just popping the cherry that you pay for," Farren said. "It's a special feeling that goes with it."

"Yeah!" Bronson slewed his chair around. "It's like you had to wear second-hand clothes all your life and here you got something new. You're making it second-hand for all the bastards that are going to come after you."

"That's it," two or three agreed.

"Bilgewater, Bronson!" Harris snorted. "You never popped one, that's plain to see!"

"I suppose you did, huh? You know all about it, don't you?"

"Damn right, and it's worth the price, and I'll tell you guys how it is," Harris said. "They're scared. They watch you and their face and eyes ain't going to look quite like that again in their whole lives. It makes you God for them few minutes. And afterward their hand comes up and touches your cheek to see if you're real."

He glared at Bronson. No one spoke. It was very quiet.

"You guys keep talking, I'm going to start raising me two hundred dollars," Harris said.

"You're shacked up. You're out of it," Crosley said.

"I'm hell out of it!"

"You got to be able to raise something else besides money, Sam," Wilsey said.

"I can raise that, too!"

Burgoyne was frowning. "I swear, I wish someday I could eat one meal on this ship when all Harris talks about is chow," he said.

"Harris thinks he's talking about chow," Wilsey said.

"Wong!" Farren yelled. "Bring Harris a plate of bearded clams on the half shell!"

"And a bottle of red lead!" Stawski shouted.

They all chimed in. Harris bristled his white hair and howled curses at them. The compartment rang with laughter. It was always a lot of fun to bait Harris.

An hour later, alone with Holman on deck, Burgoyne seemed embarrassed. "Jake, I got to tell you I'm saving my money to buy Maily," he said. "But I won't take her topside. I'll just let her go on down to Shanghai."

"What the hell, Frenchy?"

"Something Harris said. But don't tell nobody. They'll think I'm crazy."

"I won't tell. But I mean, why tell me?"

Burgoyne dug out his can of Copenhagen. "Because she favors you, Jake. If you're studying to buy her, I'll stand aside. I'll even loan you money."

Holman felt very uncomfortable. "Hell, I ain't talked half as much to her as the rest of you," he said. "I think she likes you best,

Frenchy. You're the only one ain't been going topside. I'll loan you money."

"You're wrong, Jake." Burgoyne worked his lips and spat over the side. "But if that's how you feel about it, then thank you kindly."

The Sand Pebbles changed into blue uniforms for winter. Misty rains drove the Saturday personnel inspections to the shelter of the boat deck awnings. After the inspections, Ensign Bordelles always read aloud a portion of "Rocks and Shoals." That was navy regulation, dating back to a time when most sailors could not read the posted copy. Duckbutt Randall was the only Sand Pebble who could not read and write, but it still had to be read. "Rocks and Shoals" listed twenty-two different offenses for which you could suffer death or such other penalty as a court-martial might direct. The Sand Pebbles liked best the one about pusillanimously crying for quarter. Bordelles always stumbled over that word.

The Friday lower-deck inspections were the only times that Holman talked to Lt. Collins. He would meet the inspection party inside the engine room hatch, salute and report ready for inspection. Then he would stay at Lt. Collins' elbow, to answer questions, as they walked around the gratings and then around the engine on the lower level. Everything was always very clean, with the engine shined and oiled and complexly gleaming down the center of the engine room. Lt. Collins looked and nodded and felt for dust on ledges and he did not ask any questions. Somewhere at random he would stop and point to one of the slick, worn old floorplates and Holman would pry it up. It was always clean and dry in the bilges underneath. Just before the party went on into the fireroom, where Burgoyne would be standing by, Lt. Collins would nod firmly and say, "Your station looks very well today, Holman."

"Yes, sir. Thank you, sir," Holman would say, saluting. "I'll pass the word on to the men, sir."

He would boil up a pot of coffee and drink it with relief, after the inspection was secured. He hated inspections. Ping-wen and his coolies cleaned the engine room, and Holman hated to pretend to take the credit for it. But it was that way all over the *San Pablo,* for inspection. Tullio stood by in the crew's compartment, Stawski in the head, and Duckbutt Randall in the galley. Only Restorff honestly stood by his own work for inspection.

The commercial steamers stopped running. Changsha was cut off, except for the railroad that ran one train a day to Hankow. The *San Pablo* was wintered in. If there was trouble somewhere, she could not go. Everyone relaxed even more. They did not expect any trouble in Changsha. The warlord, General Chao, had been there several years and he was all settled in. He held an occasional head chopping on the bund and here and there in the city you might see his soldiers "protecting" a shop while the Chinese sat inside idle and looking unhappy. But by and large the squeeze on the merchants was fixed and regular and General Chao kept the students firmly in line. He would let them parade along the bund to blow off steam, but only against the Japs. They were trying to promote a boycott of the Japs. They would come chanting down the bund, straggling lines of boys and girls in white robes and dresses and even little bare-kneed kids in blue-and-white school uniforms. Their signs were always anti-Jap, but they would stop and shake them at the *San Pablo* anyway. One sign read: *Imitation Devils, Go Back to Japan!* The Sand Pebbles laughed at that one. They thought it was a good name for the Japs. One or two squads of soldiers always shadowed the parades. Everyone said General Chao was a good warlord.

Holman went to talk to Lynch in the CPO quarters. Franks was there, and he had a coffee royal with them. Holman asked permission to disable the engine and take the knock out of the L.P. He explained very carefully what he had discovered.

"It's in line," Lynch said. "I *seen* 'em point the rods in Hankow."

"Sure, each cylinder's in line with its own crank," Holman agreed. "What I mean is, the cranks ain't in line with each other."

"They got to be. That's built in."

"But they ain't." Holman explained again about the grounding. It wouldn't happen to a steel ship, with some spring to the hull, but the *San Pablo* was wrought iron, he reminded Lynch. "If you want to come down in the bilges with me, I can *show* you what I mean, better'n talking," Holman said.

Lynch looked hostile. "I ain't going in them bilges," he said. "For Pete's sake, Jake, what you talking about? That's *hull,* boy, Title A! You can't fool with stuff like that!" He waved his hand impatiently.

"You guys are over my head," Franks said. He finished his coffee and went out.

"Even supposing you're right, what could you do?" Lynch said. "You got a drydock in your pocket, or something?"

"I figure the H.P. soleplate and the thrust foundation are still in original line with each other," Holman said. "I want to center a wire between 'em and then take out the L.P. chocks and file 'em to bring the L.P. soleplate back down true again. Then I'll bolt the whole thing up rigid and true, and she'll be all right."

Lynch pondered. "We ain't got the lifting gear. We ain't got the tools," he objected. "Nor the men, neither. It's a dockyard job, even the way you figure."

They wrangled about gear. Lynch did not have a very clear idea of what was on hand, or what would be needed.

"It's dangerous," he said. "You'll kill somebody. Like . . ."

"Like what?"

Lynch didn't answer. He had his hands flat on the table and he was pooching his lips in and out and squinting at Holman.

"I know I can do it, Chief. Like I know I can walk across the room." Holman stood up and walked up and down the room and sat down again. "Like that," he said.

Lynch shook his head slowly. "That kind of work ain't for ship's force," he said. "I'm scared you might just make it worse. What if we couldn't even get underway when the floods come?" His face darkened. "Who'd have to answer to Comyang for that, hey? Me and the skipper, that's who! Not you and your slopeheads!" His voice rose and he pounded the table. "No, by God! You leave that engine alone! It's all right the way it is!"

"It ain't all right the way it is. You seen it kill a man," Holman said. "Okay, you're the boss. But I wish you'd let me do it."

Lynch stopped glaring. "I just got an Irish feeling all up and down my back that it'd be bad luck," he said. "Let sleeping dogs lie. She steams, don't she? Hell, they'll scrap her in another year or two. Why bother?" He wanted to smooth things over.

"Yeah, I guess. Well . . ." Holman stood up.

"Have another cup." Lynch reached for the bottle.

"No thanks. I have to get ready for patrol."

Holman went out. He was very disappointed. He was wondering if he dared to go to Lt. Collins, over Lynch's head.

Since talking to Burgoyne, Holman had not been making every liberty at the Red Candle. When he went there, he talked to Scharf, if there was no other German at that table. Several times he talked with Banger Knox of the *Woodcock,* who sometimes came in. He avoided Maily. He did not believe she favored him, but Burgoyne's saying that had made him feel dimly responsible for her, and he did not like it.

On his shore patrol, forbidden to drink, he watched her with the others. She had a few shared jokes with them by now, but she never once put aside her forced smile and her false hostess manner. It was her armor. Late in the evening Holman ordered a supper of shrimp and rice and pork bits and asked Maily to share it. It would save her owing Shu that much more, he thought.

"I'll be delighted, Jake," she said.

They ate at the German table, because no one was using it. She wore a warm-looking brown dress with a white lace collar and she kept up her bright, false screen of chatter. She wanted to know all about the Nevada desert.

"I don't want to talk about Nevada," Holman said. "I hate Nevada."

"I hate Hunan," she said. "I hate China."

"I like Hunan. What do you hate about it?"

"Oh . . . many things. Because it's where I am, I suppose. And I can't get away."

Her screen was breaking down. Her voice was different, sad and tired, and she looked very soft and helpless with the new look on her face. He thought she wanted to tell him something, but when he drew her to the point she recoiled.

"I did something very bad. Don't ask me where or what," she said. She was looking down and pushing shrimps around in her bowl. "I believe this is my punishment. This is hell."

"Punishment! I think you're good," he said. "Good people ain't supposed to go to hell."

"I'm bad. But you're good." She raised her eyes. "You're strong and good. Why are you in hell?"

"I'm bad." He could hardly meet her eyes. "I belong in hell. I like it in hell."

She dropped her eyes. "If you could have anything you wanted, Jake, what would it be? Do you know?"

He thought about that. "I guess to know everything there is to know. Or fly to Mars, like John Carter," he said. "But if you mean what's possible, I'd like to do a certain repair job on the main engine, out on the ship."

She smiled faintly. Before he knew it, he was pouring it out to her, all about Po-han and Chien and the engine and what he had to do and how they wouldn't let him do it. She did not understand the technical part, but she was very sympathetic. It made Holman feel better. He scowled when he saw Perna coming toward their table, carrying a drink. Instantly, Maily put on her hostess face.

"What do the camels eat, in the Nevada desert?" she asked.

"Let me tell you about the grizzly bears on Boston Common," Perna said.

It was a standing joke to kid Maily about America, because she asked so many questions. Holman did not speak to her again that night until he was rounding up the liberty party at midnight. Then, fleetingly, she gave him her natural smile.

"I'll pray that you get your chance, Jake," she said softly. "Goodnight. And thank you for the dinner."

His chance came a few days later. Lynch got another letter and he could not stand it any longer. He applied for twenty days' leave to go up to Hankow and see about that teashop and decide one way or the other. His going left Holman senior engineer aboard. Holman thought about it for a few hours, long enough for Lynch to get safely out of Changsha, and then he went to see Lt. Collins. He stood stiffly just inside the door, holding his hat, and asked permission to disable the main engine. He explained the job and Lt. Collins understood without trouble. But he bit his lip and would not give permission.

"Isn't that a pretty big job for ship's force?" he asked.

"It's a lot of work. It'll mess the place up for a while," Holman said. "But it's all work we're able to do, sir."

"I wonder Chief Lynch didn't mention it."

"He knows about it, sir," Holman said hastily. "Him and me talked it over, what gear we had, how to do it. But Lynch has sort of had his mind all took up lately, sir. . . ."

Lt. Collins half smiled. He knew about Lynch's troubles.

"It'll cut repair work next summer almost in half, lining up that soleplate," Holman said. "I'll guarantee a smooth-running engine and two extra knots all next summer, sir."

Lt. Collins hesitated. He still had a slight frown.

"It's the last and biggest repair job left to do down there, sir," Holman said. "When it's done, the plant will be in perfect shape and Po-han and the rest of 'em will be plenty ready to keep it steaming. They won't need me any more. I'll be ready to come back on deck."

Lt. Collins nodded. Holman knew they were both thinking the same thing. He had said he was going to transfer Holman when that time came.

"Permission granted," Lt. Collins said.

14

Holman started the job next morning. He felt filled with power and joy and it spread to his men. He told them they were going to drive out the devil that made the engine sick, and winked at Po-han. The engine seemed to cooperate. The big nuts broke easily and the pistons broke free of the rods with one smashing sledge blow on the pullers. Holman and Po-han did the sledge and wrench work. Pai and Lung and Chiu-pa did the rigging. They were good at it. They could walk a ton of metal to wherever they wanted it without banging anything and with almost no halting to shift purchases. All day their chain hoists rattled. They worked at a dead run, Holman whistling cheerfully, Po-han wailing snatches of song, and all of them shouting happy insults at each other. It was as good as being drunk. By five o'clock all the crank bearings and crossheads and conn rods were out and littering the floorplates. Above on the gratings the valves and their spindles, pistons and cylinder covers lay heaped in a jungle of metal. The wash-wash coolies going to hang clothes to dry above the boilers had to pick their way between the heaped metal on one side and the deep, empty cylinders on the other. Pai and Chiu-pa and Lung sat sweating and tired in the L.P. cylinder, like three men in a barrel, and grinned up at the laundry coolies and called them turtles. They did not know what they were doing, but they had caught Holman's feeling of power and accomplishment. Holman came and looked down at them, dirty and sweating himself, and made the double thumbs-up sign.

"*Ding hao!*" he said. "Knock off now. Today make finish. Tomorrow take out crankshaft."

Oddly, it seemed to dampen their cheer. They looked at each other and climbed stiffly out of the cylinder.

After supper, Holman and Po-han worked on. The others had gone ashore, but men who felt about machinery as Po-han did never worried about working hours. He and Holman took out the link bars and drag rods and eccentric straps and rods and piled them on the heavier pieces. They finished near midnight, both very tired. Heaped engine parts filled both sides and the only clear space in the engine room was inside the gutted engine. The twenty-foot, flatiron-shaped cylinder block still ran overhead and from it three paired, square columns came down like open archways to rest each on its own section of the soleplate. The heavy crankshaft ran nakedly along at floorplate level with the metal guards off the big coupling flanges between each crank and only main bearing caps left in place. Holman and Po-han stood at the forward end and looked through the empty archways to the white bulk of the main condenser. Po-han had lost his cheer.

"Hey, Po-han! Whatsamatter you?" Holman rallied him.

"I flaid, Jehk. Heart no good." Po-han patted his chest.

It was the stripped engine, Holman thought. The engine parts, each with its place appointed relative to all the others, and the way they lay heaped now in upside-down, criss-crossed confusion. It clashed with the memory of them all in ordered, living motion. Po-han was thinking that this was a serious thing to be doing to the great metal dragon. Holman tried to reassure Po-han.

"Must fix foundation," he said. "After, put back, same same. L.P. no more makee trouble. You, me, engine, all happy."

Po-han grinned weakly. He was still disturbed. Perna came down to write up the log. He looked around and whistled.

"Holy Joseph!" he said. "Looks like a typhoon hit this place!"

"Me and my two-legged typhoons." Holman grinned. He even liked Perna, at the moment. "We're taking the knock out of the L.P."

Perna scratched his long nose. "Won't be like the same ship without that knock," he said. He looked around doubtfully. "Think you'll ever get it back together again?"

He was as disturbed as Po-han, in his own way.

Next morning Ping-wen's coolies were all at work, but of Holman's men only Po-han sat forlornly on the workbench.

"Chiu-pa stop homeside. He sick," Po-han told Holman.

Something was wrong. Po-han was trying to blank his face, but a misery showed honestly through it. Pai and Lung had to visit sick parents, he said. He did not know when any of them would be back.

"I sick too. Must stop homeside litee bit," Po-han said sadly.

Holman knew it was very serious. He stifled his anger. "You, me, long-time friend," he said gently. "You speakee me proper."

Po-han did not want to. Slowly, Holman drew it out of him. They were all frightened, Po-han too. They thought disturbing the engine foundations was bad joss. Lop Eye Shing thought that, and it was his orders to go ashore and stay lost until Holman gave it up. Shing was ashore too. It would not do any good to talk to them, even if Holman could find them, Po-han said miserably. Holman had to keep choking back his anger. Po-han revealed that it was possibly also a rice bowl matter. The constant bearing refits while the ship cruised made up a good third of the repair work. For a wild moment Holman wondered whether Chien had not known all the time what ailed the L.P. He felt sick and angry and helpless.

"We'll do it alone," he said. "You, me, Po-han."

"No can do, Jehk. Lop Eye Shing makee me tlobbah."

Shing would fire him, Holman gathered. He explained that Lt. Collins had approved the job, wanted it done, and he would not let Shing fire Po-han. Lt. Collins could fire Shing, if he wanted to, Holman said. Po-han would not believe that Lt. Collins had any power at all over Shing. Holman's arguing and pleading only made him more ashamed. Finally he crept miserably away.

Holman was alone. He raged inside. He thought of Shing's sardonic face, with its leering wink and drooping mouth corner, and he smashed his fist into his palm. He was stopped. Wilsey and Stawski would refuse to help. The engine was no concern of Burgoyne's. It would be no use to ask Ping-wen for help, not against Shing. Lt. Collins would almost certainly tell him just to give up the job. And there was no time. He had to get the root of the job done, at least, before Lynch came back.

He went over to the engine and put a wrench on one of the big coupling nuts and slugged at it one-handed. The sledge just bounced off. He braced the wrench with his knee and slugged awkwardly with both hands. The wrench slipped off and skinned his knee and fell into the crankpit with a mocking clatter. He went back and sat on the workbench.

He sat there for an hour. He was whipped. He would have to put the engine back together, all hopes gone to hell, all yesterday's good work useless, and all next summer it would be roundy-go-*thump* again. He sat staring bitterly at his two empty hands.

"Jehk."

Holman looked up. Po-han had a shy, boyish look on his face. His head was up and his eyes were steady.

"Inside litee bit hot now," he said, putting his hand on his heart. "I can do, Jehk. I no give goddamn, Lop Eye Shing makee me tlobbah."

Holman jumped grinning off the workbench. He could feel the fires blazing up in him again.

"You, me, Po-han! We'll whip 'em all!" he said. "If we have to, we'll make Lop Eye Shing so much trouble he'll turn sky-blue pink!"

Po-han grinned, but not very strongly. He was still afraid.

The engine fought back. The coupling nuts would not come loose. There were thirty of them, ten to a flange, each nut four inches across, and they were welded in their threads by the rust of fifty years. Po-han held the wrench steady and Holman swung the twenty-pound sledge until his wrists felt wooden and his fingers trembled and he could hardly close his hands. In two hours, they got one nut off.

"Po-han, we got to get smart about this," Holman said.

With ball peen hammers they beat the paint off all the nuts, hoping by the repeated small shocks to loosen the rust-bind in the threads. They dripped kerosene on the exposed bolt threads, hoping it would seep inside the nuts to loosen and lubricate. Then Holman sledged again.

There was an art to sledging. Amateurs used a full-arm swing, and it was mostly noise and show. The best way was to move the sledge only about a foot, arms rigid and your right hand only a few inches from the hammer head, and you swung your whole body from the ankles. You made your whole body into a battering ram with the sledge as striking point, and you poured the fused momentum of bone, muscle and steel into what you hit. If what you hit did not yield, all the energy reflected back into you, and it jarred you to your heels.

The nuts would not yield. They tried each nut in turn, jacking the shaft to get at the lower ones, and stopped to ball peen again and drip more kerosene, and sledged over the nuts a second time. Holman sledged with an increasingly desperate, blasting anger, and with each blow he could feel in his right hand the back jar of unavailing force re-enter him. Steel on steel struck sparks and added a sulfurous flavor to the steamy, damp kerosene smell. Both men dripped sweat. By suppertime they had loosened one more nut.

"Ain't much, for a day's work," Holman said wearily.

Po-han grinned. He was happy about that second nut. He thought they had all winter. He did not know about the time pinch.

After supper Holman went to the sick bay and got small bottles of oil of peppermint and oil of wintergreen. He had heard that they were more penetrating than kerosene. He tried to explain to Po-han, as they dripped the smelly stuff on the bolt threads. Po-han thought about it and became very excited. With some difficulty, he told Holman his idea: castor oil, then, should be best of all. Holman laughed and explained again about viscosity and why castor oil would not work on rusted steel threads. It cheered him.

The cheer did not last. By midnight the engine room smelled like a candy store and Holman's arms were numb and aching to the shoulders and they had not loosened one extra nut. Haythorn came in on the gratings and yelled down.

"Hellfire, Jake, you gonna keep up that pounding all night? There's guys up here want to sleep."

"I'm just now knocking off," Holman said.

Po-han was concerned about Holman. "Tomollah plenty can do," he said. He patted Holman's shoulder. "I burn joss stick, Jehk."

"You do that, Po-han," Holman said. He was ready to try anything.

In the morning Holman's right hand was sore and badly swollen. He could not close it. He had to hold the wrench and let Po-han sledge. He coached Po-han on form, and Po-han learned it rapidly, but he was just not heavy enough. There was a saying: the smaller the man, the bigger the hammer. But the navy did not have sledges bigger than twenty-pounders. Holman made Po-han cushion his hand well with a rag, to soften the back jar, as he should have done himself the day before. They went over all the nuts again and did not loosen a single one of them. Holman sighed.

"What the hell we going to do, Po-han?"

"Hammah!" Po-han said. "Hammah hammah hammah!" He grinned at Holman.

"By God, that's the spirit!" Holman said.

They started over the nuts again. Lt. Collins came down and stood on the bottom step of the ladder and looked around. His face did not like what he saw. Holman stood up respectfully.

"Just what is it you plan to do?" Lt. Collins asked.

Holman explained again. With the engine stripped and the floor-plates up alongside it, they could see the slight bulge in the bottom plating. A wetness of water in the bilge, with kerosene iridescent on top of it, made a dry black island of the bulge. There was no denying it.

"I hadn't realized it would take all this." Lt. Collins motioned in distaste at the piled engine parts. "Don't let any silly professional pride lead you to taking any risks, Holman. Give up the job, if it seems too much for you."

"We'll do it, sir. We're going right along with it," Holman said.

Through the gratings he watched Lt. Collins go out of sight. He knows about Shing's boycott, Holman thought. You can't keep nothing from scuttlebutt on this ship. Why in hell didn't he order me to stop? Holman would have been almost glad to have been ordered to stop, just then. But he would not stop of his own accord.

"Well, let's get at it," he told Po-han.

They dripped more kerosene and candy oil and sledged all around and no nuts would budge. Po-han streamed sweat, and his breath whistled. Holman felt grim. He wired a rag to a steel rod and soaked it in gasoline and lit it. Then he held it to one of the nuts, hoping the heat would expand the nut and break the rust bind, but the flame was not concentrated enough. Flaming gasoline dripped and set fire to the kerosene in the crankpit and they had a bad few minutes putting it out with gunny sacks. That put an end to that scheme. Don't take any risks, Lt. Collins had said.

They went over the nuts again. None yielded. Holman tried to put on a good face at dinner.

"You better have Doc look at that hand," Burgoyne told him.

"It's all right. I'm not using it."

"Want I should come down and help this afternoon, Jake?"

"No thanks, Frenchy," Holman said. "Extra hands ain't what I need just now. But you ain't got a blowtorch in your locker, have you?"

" 'Fraid not." Burgoyne laughed. "Well, I'll go ashore then."

That afternoon Po-han seemed willing to go on hammering forever. It was no good. Holman decided to chisel off the nuts, although he did not have enough hex stock to make all new ones. And if the coupling bolts would not come out, as they probably would not, he would by God drill them out. They could send to Hankow for stock to make new ones. He would settle just for having the foundation aligned by the time Lynch got back.

Po-han whaled happily away at a cold chisel. Holman knew it was foolish, but he got another chisel and worked himself. His hand hurt and he could just barely manage a ball peen hammer with it. It went painfully slowly. After supper they each had one nut split along the flat, spread and backed off. Holman's hand throbbed and hurt all the way to the shoulder, and he could not do another one. It was no good. Po-han might get another one by midnight—

"Hello, Jake!"

It was Banger Knox, red-faced and grinning at them, dressed in a pale blue one-piece boiler suit.

"Fair got it all in pieces, haven't you?" he said, looking around. "Frenchy told me about your trouble, at the Red Candle."

Holman saw the blowtorch he was holding. "God bless you, Banger!" he said. "Why didn't I think to check with your ship?"

Expanded by the pale blue concentrated flame, the nuts came loose. Not easily, screeching and groaning in ancient, rusty protest, but off they came. Holman plied the torch, Po-han held the wrench, and Banger was an absolute artist with the sledge. The engine room filled with the smell of gasoline, scorched paint and hot metal and it rang with exultant British, Chinese and American yells as each nut yielded. Duckbutt Randall came in on the gratings.

"Hey, you guys," he called. "What's coming off down there?"

"Nuts!" Holman whooped in sheer delight.

"Nuts to you, too," Duckbutt Randall said indignantly. "I think you're all nutty as a fruitcake!" He went back to the quarterdeck.

Shortly after midnight, the nuts were all off. Banger was dirty and sweat-soaked. Holman made coffee and they all drank it and felt good together.

"You saved my life," Holman told Banger. "I was about whipped."

"No whip!" Po-han was indignant.

"Hammah hammah hammah." Holman laughed at him.

"Hammah hammah hammah!" Po-han grinned proudly.

Holman showed Banger what he planned to do. The British sailor saw it instantly. He whistled.

"You've a bloody bold notion there, chum," he said admiringly. "I don't see why you can't bring it off, though. D'ye mind if I stop by now and then to watch the work?"

"God, no!" Holman said. "Come any time. Jesus, Banger, I wish I could give you the ship."

"I would like a go at this job. I would indeed," Banger said. "Fair down to first principles here, you know."

"I know," Holman said.

The hand throbbed and kept him awake. He went to the sick bay after breakfast. Jennings had him soak it in hot water and then bandaged it and put it in a sling.

"Be sure to keep it elevated," he said. "Don't try to use it."

"I'll be careful, Doc," Holman said.

"I mean it! You could lose that hand, if you get a bone infection!"

"Sure, Doc."

Holman hurried below. He was very impatient with his hand. Po-han was waiting. The next step was to drive out the coupling bolts. Po-han tried several, sledging as hard as he could, and they would not start. The bolt metal just splayed out. They had to stop and make a socketed brass drift to protect the bolt ends. Po-han was too slow on the lathe, so Holman took his hand out of the sling to make the drift. He tried to use only the tips of his fingers. Then he held the drift while Po-han slugged at it. No bolts would start. They were body-bound, a tight, driving fit when they were installed fifty years ago, and even a little rust could bind them absolutely. It was going to be a worse ordeal than the nuts had been.

"We can't bull 'em out. Let's get scientific," he said.

He tried the blowtorch. As he had feared, the big coupling flanges soaked off the heat so fast that it did not help. They dripped oil of wintergreen, but it could not possibly seep through eight horizontal inches, and all it did was smell the place up. Then they slugged over all the bolts and not a one would start. Holman shook his head. His hand hurt and he felt dizzy. He had a feeling of the great, dumb, massive invincibility of the steel and the soft, weak, hurtingness of flesh. He wished incongruously that he had some candy to eat, the thick, pink, disc-shaped candies kids got back in Wellco, Nevada.

"Hammah hammah hammah!" Po-han said.

"Hammah hammah hammah!"

They went round again. Po-han sledged beautifully, but he was just not heavy enough. Holman thought that if his hand was all right he would sledge those bolts with such wild fury that they would all pop out. No bolts started.

He went up to dinner. They all knew he was in trouble and none of them were sorry for him. Bronson kidded him about the hammering.

"You sound like the village blacksmith down there, Ho-mang," he said. "You going to keep it up all night again?"

"The muscles of his scrawny arms are strong as rubber bands," Crosley said.

After dinner, Holman gave up on the sledging. He had Po-han saw one bolt off flush with the flange and they rigged a drilling post and he had Po-han start drilling the bolt out. Holman began sawing off another bolt. He favored his hand all he could. Po-han seemed tireless. He turned the drill with the ratchet lever and fed it heavily with his left hand and the chips came out smoking.

"Drill drill drill!" Holman said, grinning at him.

"Dlill dlill dlill!"

Burgoyne came down quietly in dungarees. "What can I do, Jake?" he asked.

"Spell Po-han on that ratchet handle, if you want to," Holman said. "But you ain't got no call to do engine work, Frenchy. You got the boilers."

"You let me study out what my calls are." Burgoyne grinned his slow, easy grin and knuckled his mustache. "I ride on this ship, don't I?"

"Well . . . I'll be much obliged, Frenchy."

Holman felt weak and foolish inside. He bent to his hacksawing, to hide his feeling. They all worked steadily. After supper Banger came aboard again. He had another drilling post with him.

"I thought you'd never start them with the sledge," he said.

By midnight they had three drilled out. Each bolt meant hand drilling a two-inch hole through eight inches of steel. It was mankilling. The others were dirty and tired and cheerful. They didn't know about the time pinch.

"Good show, mates," Banger said. "Leg over leg, the dog got to Dover, as you might say."

"Dlill dlill dlill!" Po-han said.

They all laughed with him.

"Jake, you got to take better care of that hand," Burgoyne said. "You take my patrol tomorrow and let me work down here."

Holman tried to argue.

"Lie up a day. Don't be a bloody fool," Banger said.

"All right," Holman said.

The hand would not let him go to sleep easily. He lay in his bunk and thought about them. They were all good guys. They were all very good guys.

Jennings was angry about the hand. "It's worse. It's dangerous," he said. "You could lose it, you know."

"I won't lose it, if I can help."

"It's not yours to lose! You're government property and I'm responsible for you!" Jennings said sharply. "You stay out of that engine room, understand? Or I'll ship you over to the mission hospital!"

"I'll stay out. I got patrol today, Doc," Holman soothed him.

It was rather quiet in the Red Candle. Scharf was not there. Holman asked Maily to have supper with him again, at the German table. She was wearing the same brown dress. They ate fried pork bits with sweet peppers in a gingery sauce, a dish Holman especially liked, and fluffy white rice. He had to eat awkwardly, with his left hand. She was worried and solicitous about his hand. He told her about the job and how it was going and she worried about that too. He could not understand how anybody in a spot such as she was in could possibly worry about anyone except herself. But her whole face and the scared brightness of her eyes were softened, and she was not thinking about herself.

"Hell, Maily, you're in worse trouble than I am," he said. "I wish there was something we could do about you."

Her voice turned bitter. "No. I'm a mistake in the world. I was meant to be eaten by pigs," she said. "I'm an American in a Chinese body. I'd rather not talk about it."

"Maybe we could get you out of here. Frenchy would help."

"Frenchy. He's nice." She smiled sadly and shook her head. "No one can help. It's God's will. My punishment."

"Punishment!" Holman hated that word.

She was twisting her handkerchief. "I ran away from a . . . a place. I stole some money. I was going to Shanghai and find work and return the money as soon as I could save it. But bandits in the hills robbed me."

"Well, if bandits—"

"God moves in strange ways. I prayed and He told me to go into Changsha and find work and return the money." Her voice was low and toneless and she was not looking at Holman. "The first office I went into was Mr. Shu's. I know God led me there, because Mr. Shu advanced me the money and I could sent it back right away."

"Did Shu tell you what you had to do?"

"You mean go upstairs, when someone could pay?" Her face was very pale. "Yes. That is how I know God guided me to him. Because it fits so perfectly the . . . the reason I ran away."

He was glad she did not raise her eyes. Anger boiled in him. All he knew about God was that you could not talk about God to people who believed in that stuff without hurting their feelings.

"How do you know you ain't been punished enough already? How much do you owe Shu?"

"Nearly a hundred dollars, gold."

"We could raise that much in time, me and Frenchy," he said.

"We'll buy you out of here, Maily." She was blushing. "I mean without touching you," he added.

"It would be evading God's will for me." She was blushing even more. "But I had hoped it might be. . . ."

She could not go on. Holman didn't know what to say. He was glad to see Scharf come in.

"May I join you?" Scharf asked.

"It's your table," Holman said. "I was hoping you d come in."

Scharf wanted to know about the hand. Holman told him about the job and how it was with engineering on the *San Pablo* and about Lop Eye Shing's boycott. Scharf sipped whisky and kept nodding.

"I hear all the talk, Jake," Maily said. "They think you brought your trouble on yourself. Bronson is the worst, but I think they all want you to fail. Or at least don't care."

"I know. I ain't going to fail, though."

"Bronson and some of them really hate you," she said earnestly. "They think you want to change things and get yourself out of military duties and you don't care enough about how they feel."

"Why should I? I don't give a damn how they feel!"

"Please, Jake. Don't push them too far."

"They can't help resenting you. You cheapen the thing they live by," Scharf said. "How do you really feel about the martial spirit?"

"I think it's stupid!" Holman stretched out his leg and patted the holstered pistol on his hip. "I couldn't close my fingers enough to fire this thing. But here I am with it."

"I do not know how you get away with it," Scharf said. "You would not in a German uniform."

"They got to have the machinery. So they got to take guys like me along with it." Holman chuckled. "They'd like it better if all they had to have was a piece of sharp rock to cut throats with."

Scharf smiled. "Be careful of your own throat, with thoughts like that. You are pretty much alone, with thoughts like that."

"I got machinery." Holman nodded. "I know what you mean, though. You got to have a gang. A man alone ain't got a chance."

"I think if you have just one person," Maily said.

"Then what?"

"Then you're not alone."

"It's a somewhat relative term," Scharf said.

Maily had to go back to her hostess duties. Another German came in. He could not speak English, but he made it plain enough that he resented Holman's presence at that table. Holman moved off alone and thought about things. When he said goodnight to Maily, he tried to express his thinking.

"Try to stop believing that God stuff, Maily," he said seriously. "Look where it's got you."

She was shocked. "Oh, don't say such things, Jake!" She looked around nervously. "If I couldn't believe in God, I'd just have to kill myself," she whispered.

They drilled all day. Banger came aboard. They would not let Holman work, although his hand felt much better. He was miserable, just watching. It was going to take a week of steady drilling, and he could not spare that much time.

"Ho-mang, come up! You got a visitor!"

It was Crosley, yelling from the quarterdeck. Holman went up. Scharf stood there, beside the biggest sledge hammer Holman had ever seen.

"George!" Holman said. "Jesus, that sledge! I didn't know they made 'em that big!"

"In Germany. We use it at the smelter to break up molds," Scharf said. "It weighs about fifty of your pounds."

"Well, God bless you for it!" Holman picked it up with his left hand. "Come on down."

"Hold it!" Crosley said. "I ain't so sure that's regulation."

"I'm acting chief engineer, while Lynch is gone," Holman said. "I'll be responsible. Come on, George."

"Beetle!" Banger yelled, when he saw the sledge.

He and Po-han took turns with it. They swung with clenched, bared teeth. Po-han had become a master sledger. Bolt by bolt they came out shrieking, with little clouds of reddish dust. All the men hated the bolts, and they jeered each one's defeat. A fever was on them all and when the bolts were out they went on to lift the main bearing caps and rig to lift out the cranks. Scharf worked as hard as any. Holman worked left-handed at whatever he could do. He had the driving, joyful feel again, as on that first day. About ten o'clock they had the cranks out, and only then they rested. They sat around the edge of the L.P. crankpit with their feet dangling, because that was the only clear space left in the engine room. Scharf's thin, sad face looked almost merry. He had a smear of grease on his long nose.

"Well, Banger, you can take your old man home again," Burgoyne said. Banger looked blank. *"Old man,"* Burgoyne repeated. "Your drilling post."

"Oh!" Banger grinned. "You mean my drilling *pillar*. Now *we* call that a *john bull*."

They began kidding Banger about the words he used. A key was a *feather,* the reversing shaft a *wyper,* and a bearing pedestal was a *plummer block*. Po-han was taking it all in. He was always anxious to learn new names, but he could not make much of their joking talk. Holman held up a monkey wrench.

"What do you strange people call this thing?" he challenged Banger.

"The only proper name for that there tool—" Banger paused, his gray eyes twinkling— "is a *Clyburn spanner*."

"It's a Spanish open-end wrench," Burgoyne said.

"In Germany we call such a wrench an *Englishman*," Scharf said. *"Ein Engländer."*

"What's it in Chinese, Po-han?" Holman asked. "Chinee man, what name speakee?"

Po-han said it was a *turtle beak* because "no have got teeth." He clashed his own white teeth to illustrate. They had a good laugh at that. While they were laughing, Jack Dusty came down with a tureen of food and some bowls and forks. He uncovered the tureen and it was steaming ham and rice and onions and it smelled very good.

"Big Chew makee you chow," he said simply.

Holman and Burgoyne looked at each other. "Big Chew's breaking the boycott!" Burgoyne said. It was the first time anyone had mentioned the boycott. "Well, they say of all of 'em aboard, he's least afraid of Lop Eye."

"God bless Big Chew," Holman said. "Fall to, guys. We all earned it."

They were all hungry. Sweaty and unwashed, they sat around the edge of the crankpit and ate bowl after bowl of it until it was all gone. They were feeling good and happy and satisfied together. They talked about what came next. It would take time and patience and some very skilled work and judgment, but it would not be a man-killer, like breaking those coupling flanges. When they were ready to go up, Po-han stopped them. He held up the monkey wrench.

"What name this? What name *plopah?"* he asked.

Burgoyne laughed and laid an arm across Po-han's shoulders. "You're an American, Po-han," he said. "You're supposed to call it a monkey wrench."

"Monkey lench! Monkey lench!"

They all went up laughing.

The wire was a long, bright gleam through the empty archways and above the gaping crankpits. It marked the true axis of the crankshaft and they had to reposition the L.P. soleplate section to line with it. They unbolted the section. They strained and hauled at it with chain hoists and screw jacks and turnbuckles and steel wedges, checking the bearing beds with straight edge and calipers, and discussing how much to file off which chocks. Scharf and Banger were just as careful as Holman to make sure Po-han understood what they were doing. They would let the weight back down on the filed chocks and take more caliper readings from the wire. The readings would be changed, but they would not be right. So they would do it again. They filed too much off some of the chocks and had to shim them.

Patience was the word. Holman's hand grew steadily better and he could use it for light work. The time came when the soleplate rested true and Po-han wanted to dance and shout, but Scharf stopped him. They tightened a few bolts, and it pulled off skew. Out came the chocks again, cast-iron spacer squares with holes in their middles, shiny with filing, each one familiar as an individual human face. It would be another long cycle of trial and error.

Every night near midnight Small Chew or Jack Dusty brought down covered bowls of the spicy Hunanese food Holman liked so well. They all sat around the crankpit and ate and were happy together. After that first time, Holman had gone to the galley to thank Big Chew. Big Chew had grinned, burly and bold-eyed, and patted his ample belly under his soiled white apron.

"Suppose workee too much, any man mus' have chow," he said.

Nobody on earth ever had better chow than Big Chew could make, Holman thought. It was like a pat on the back every night. It helped a lot.

Then one evening, after a week of steady work, they tightened a few bolts and checked and it was still in line. They looked at each other, no one wanting to speak, and took all the bolts up snug. It was still in line. Dumbly they went back into the bilges and slugged every nut up full due, until each one *pinged* to a hammer blow. Holman handed Scharf the calipers. The German checked gravely, interminably, and at last turned with his face impassive. Then his smile broke through.

"You may dance now, Po-han," he said.

Holman and Banger danced too, grinning and bashing each other's shoulders, while Scharf and Burgoyne smiled at them.

All next day they bedded the cranks, scraping or shimming main bearings to bring the coupling flanges fair and true, and before they ate chow that night they had the coupling flanges bolted up again. Po-han seemed unusually quiet and thoughtful as he ate.

"Chiu-pa, oddah man, come back workee now," he said.

"How do you know?" Holman asked him.

"I know."

Banger put down his bowl and patted his stomach. "Well, it's been a bit of a go, mates, hasn't it?" he said. "George, we needn't stop by for the rest of it, I suppose."

"I want to thank you guys. I don't know how to say what I feel,"

Holman said. "If I can ever help one of you guys like you did me, I sure as hell will."

"Wanted to try my hand . . . learn a bit. . . ." Banger was very red. "Oh hell, Jake. They say blood's thicker than water."

"If I can ever help *anybody* the way you helped me, I'll do it!" Holman said. "I think that's how I feel."

He was afraid he was going to cry. It was a strange, almost forgotten feeling. It would not do at all. He got up hastily and went to make a pot of coffee so that he could snap out of it.

Pai, Chiu-pa and Lung went calmly to work as if nothing had happened. Before the first day ended, they were laughing and joking. Holman led them in refitting each bearing as they rebuilt the engine, pointing the conn rods to meet each crank fair and central, and day after day the heaped engine parts went back to their appointed places. The empty archways filled up with piston rods and bulky crossheads and connecting rods. Between them, eccentric rods forked up to either end of the double-bar links that curved across like steel rainbows to carry the slender valve spindles. Holman worked in a driving fury and he carried the others with him. All the heaped and rusting confusion moved back into place and order, with every nut snugged up and locked and every part fitted easy and true to every other part.

Ping-wen moved in his coolies to clean and polish and paint and the engine stood bravely new. On the evening of their last day of grace, Holman put steam on the engine to test it. He and Po-han and the watch coolie were alone in the engine room.

It tested out beautifully. It did not stick in any position. It was instantly responsive to light finger pressure on the control lever. Light gleamed and glanced as the shining tons of metal moved smoothly and silently. Holman showed Po-han how to control it. Po-han trembled with fear and eagerness. Holman brewed a pot of coffee and drank a cup and smiled to see Po-han get the hang of it. It was a sense of the engine as an extension of your own body, a feeling that you could close your eyes and still know where every part of the engine was, the way you knew that about your body. You felt a joyful, enormous, tireless power in yourself, and there was nothing on earth to match the first time you felt that. It was coming over Po-han. His face was shining.

"Same me! Same me!" he cried.

"You're graduating, Po-han," Holman told him.

He told Po-han that he was going back on deck watches. Po-han would have charge of the repair gang on his own. Po-han got a cup of coffee and they stood by the throttle and talked about it. Holman did not say that he was probably going to have to leave the ship. He did not want to think of that. He did not want to leave the ship, and friends like Burgoyne and Po-han. He knew now that he had never had any friends before.

Loud voices sounded from the quarterdeck. The liberty party was coming aboard.

"Hell, he's getting underway!" somebody said. "Hey, Ho-mang, got any coffee down there?" someone else yelled.

"Fresh pot!" Holman shouted.

Perna and Stawski came down in blues and peacoats, damp with rain, swaying a little. They were mean drunk, not happy drunk.

"Who's your new throttleman, Ho-mang?" Perna jeered. Po-han stepped away from the throttle, still holding his coffee cup. "What's his rate?" Perna asked.

"We're just testing," Holman said. "Try the engine, Ski."

Stawski was snuffling and blinking and turning his head. Words did not come easily to him, even sober. "Prong the engine!" he said. "Prong the pronging engine!"

Po-han was still grinning and admiring the engine. He was too happy to understand.

"Ask the new throttleman if you can have some coffee, Ski," Perna said. "Say *sir* to him. Maybe he'll let you use his cup."

Stawski's flat face screwed up. He flew into a drunken, crying rage. "You slant-eyed son of a bitch!" he howled. He knocked the coffee cup from Po-han's grasp. "You slopeheaded bastard!"

He began slapping and kicking Po-han. Po-han cowered back, arms shielding his face. Holman grabbed Stawski's peacoat collar and jerked him back and around.

"Knock that off, you drunken ape!" he said.

Stawski howled and swung at him. Holman slapped the distorted face twice hard and then slugged him in the belly. Stawski sat down in the spilled coffee, legs sprawling, tears on his cheeks.

"I'm gonna get up and kill you!" he sobbed.

"Get him out of here! Put him to bed!" Holman snapped at Perna.

"We'll get out, all right," Perna said.

Holman saw pure hatred in the little watertender's pointed face. He looked more than ever like a rat. Holman shook with sudden anger.

"I savvy you, Perna. You ain't as drunk as you're making out," he said. "You put Stawski up to that, God damn you!"

"We'll get out of *your* engine room, Ho-mang!"

"And don't come back," Holman said. "We can get along just fine down here if we never see you two bastards again."

He kicked the blubbering Stawski to his feet and started the two men up the ladder. Perna looked down from the gratings, showing all his teeth.

"You ain't heard the last of this, Ho-mang," he said.

15

Breakfast was an angry hush. No one but Burgoyne would talk to Holman. Holman knew he had to square things.

"I'm ready to go back on deck watches," he told Farren.

"All right. You'll have the mid," Farren said curtly.

Holman went to quarters and calisthenics and afterward drew Burgoyne aside. "What's so Goddamn wrong, Frenchy?" he asked.

"Po-han hit Stawski. He raised his hand to a white man," Burgoyne said. "They're blaming you. Maybe they're right."

"I hit Stawski."

"Perna says Po-han did. And Po-han was drinking coffee and handling the throttle."

"Perna's a liar!" Holman didn't know what to say. "What's wrong with *you*, Frenchy? You and me both been drinking coffee with Po-han."

"Well, things was all tore apart and upside down then." Burgoyne's lean face looked distressed. "God damn it, I'm pulled both ways, Jake," he said. "I like Po-han. I know Perna's a sneak. But guys have got feelings, too." He dug out his round tin of Copenhagen. "You and Po-han just ride out the storm, Jake. Maybe something'll happen to take their minds off it."

Something did happen. Lynch came aboard, red-eyed and weary. He had lost weight and the skin sagged along his jaw. He went up to the CPO quarters and scuttlebutt had the story within the hour. He had been drunk the whole time in Hankow. He had married the Russian woman and cashed in his liberty bonds and they had bought the teashop. He was not happy about it.

"I went to sleep on the train coming down here and I dreamed it wasn't so," Lynch said. "Then I woke up and it was so." He looked at Franks and Welbeck, across the table from him. "What am I gonna *do?*"

"Why the hell did you ever do it?" Franks asked.

"Oh God, I don't know! It was like I lost all my backbone." Lynch cradled his head in his hands. "She kept feeding me vodka and orange juice. That stuff dissolves your brains, boys. Don't ever touch it!"

"She's a White Russian, so she doesn't have a passport. That makes her Chinese, to American law," Welbeck said. "And it's against the law to marry a slopehead. I don't understand how the consulate would give you a license."

"I don't remember getting one."

"Then you *ain't* married, Lynch, old boy, old boy!" Franks said.

"She says I am. And I remember being in a church." Lynch rubbed his forehead. "There was singing and silver and gold. And a priest in robes and a big beard. He kissed me and I slugged him."

"Without a license, you ain't married," Welbeck said firmly. "The church boloney don't count. Only the law counts."

"You're still a free man, Lynch," Franks said. "Brace up, kid! You're free!"

"But she's got my money! She's sitting and grinning right now up there on top of that teashop!"

Lynch would not be comforted. The Sand Pebbles laughed about his trouble at dinner and it eased the tension. They agreed that Lynch was not really married, he had just been taken for his money. He had lost liberty bonds but not liberty.

"I had her out once. Her name's Looby," Wilsey said. "She's one of the coal heavers."

It was a legend that White Russian women worked their way down from Vladivostok to Shanghai on the coastal steamers. The tall, muscular ones with their hair in thick blond braids were said to have stoked boiler furnaces. They were all supposed to have been princesses in the old days.

"She's big enough to handle poor old Lynch," Farren said.

Holman stood his quarterdeck watch very correctly. When Lt. Collins went down to his gig to go ashore, Holman saluted smartly, and he put his lungs into passing the word: *"San Pablo . . . leaving! San Pablo . . . leaving!"* Then for good measure he ran up to the boat deck and shouted, "Bridge, there! Bear a hand hoisting that absentee pennant!" Holman was being very military. Lynch was senior OOD. He came on the quarterdeck only once. He looked sourly at Holman.

"What did you do to the engine?"

"Lined up the foundations. It's all back now. Tests out perfect."

Lynch glowered a long moment, grunted and went away. Holman shrugged. Just before he was relieved, Lop Eye Shing went ashore. Because of his paralysis, he was the only Chinese permitted to come and go across the quarterdeck except on duty. Shing greeted Holman courteously and they talked for a few minutes. Watching him being sculled away in his hired sampan, Holman thought that Shing was taking his loss of face like a man. When Holman went below to write up the engineering log, Po-han told him that he would not be aboard the next day. Shing had fired him. Po-han's face was very blank.

Holman raged. "He can't do it!" he swore. "That lopeyed son of a bitch! I won't let him get away with it!" He insisted that Po-han must stay aboard. "I fix! I speakee you proper, Po-han, I fix!" he kept saying. Po-han agreed to stay, but his face was still blank.

Holman went to the CPO quarters. Lemon was setting the table for Lynch's supper. Lynch was lying in his bunk with his eyes closed.

"Lynch!" Holman said. Lynch opened his eyes. "Lop Eye Shing wants to fire Po-han," Holman said. "And Po-han is just now all set to take over down there, like Chien used to have it. Will you tell that droop-faced bastard where to get off, or shall I go tell him?"

"I told Shing to fire him. The whole crew wants to get rid of that coolie." Lynch rose up on his elbow. "If I could, I'd fire you too. God damn you, you disobeyed my orders! Something could've happened!"

"It was my neck out. You was clear," Holman said. "Anyway, nothing happened."

"The blazing hell nothing happened!" Lynch swung his legs over the bunk side and sat with fists on thighs. "I got married and lost my money! You call that nothing?" He glared accusingly. "Don't try to look innocent! You drew down bad luck, just like I said you would, and I'm the one got hit!"

Holman didn't know whether to laugh or curse. "Well, you don't have to take it out on Po-han," he said. "He only done what I told him."

"I guess you told him to hit Stawski."

"That's Perna's lie! *I* hit Stawski!"

"Well, *I* fired Po-han for it!" Lynch said. "And now get the hell out of here!"

"One man for request mast, sir. Holman," Bordelles said. "It's about that coolie who hit Stawski."

"Bring him to my cabin," Lt. Collins said.

He sat sideways at his desk to face the two men. Holman was in undress blues, very neat, as if for inspection. He looked tense.

"Well, what is it, Holman?"

"Lop Eye Shing is trying to fire Po-han, sir, you know, the one I trained to replace Chien," Holman said. "Shing ain't aboard this morning. But I want to ask you to overrule Shing, so I can tell Po-han."

"Do you know Shing's reasons?"

"I think so, sir. His real reason." Shing had a vested interest in keeping the engine misaligned, Holman said, to make more repair work. He had ordered the coolies to boycott the job. Po-han had disobeyed Shing, for the good of the engine and on Holman's promise that Lt. Collins would protect him. Holman expanded on Po-han's skill and intelligence and devotion. He was very tense and earnest about it and he made it a plausible story. "We just got to keep Po-han aboard, sir, for the good of the ship!" he finished.

"The ship is more than just the engine." Might as well let the man down easy, Lt. Collins thought. "Your trouble is in letting something specific and concrete blind you to the larger view of things," he said. "This coolie you speak of is a kind of unofficial contract laborer. Shing is the unofficial contractor. He has all the authority in the case. Do you see?"

"I see it ain't fair to Po-han, sir," Holman said stubbornly. "Do you mean you don't have any authority over Lop Eye Shing?"

Bordelles frowned at Holman, in warning.

"Of course I have! Shing's authority is delegated!" Lt. Collins paused to control his anger. Somehow, he was peculiarly vulnerable to this man Holman. "I am just as pleased as you are to have the engine reliable," he said. "I am not pleased with the way it was done. You withheld information from me, just as you think you are doing at this moment." He let anger edge his voice. "You disobeyed Lynch. Your coolie disobeyed Shing. You encouraged your coolie to violate the customary pattern of behavior in the engine room and in the end he struck a crew member. In short, you gravely misaligned the structure of authority in this ship. Shing's action is the cheapest and easiest way to set it right again, and it has my full approval."

He turned back to his desk. The interview was over.

"That don't make it fair," Holman said. "Po-han didn't hit Stawski. *I* hit Stawski."

"Perna and Stawski say differently," Bordelles said sharply. "That's two men's words against yours, Holman."

"That don't make it true. Ski was drunk and Perna's a liar."

"So you say. Come on, get out of here."

"It's true, Mr. Bordelles! Po-han *didn't* hit Stawski!"

Lt. Collins turned back to face them. "Of conflicting stories people tend to believe the one that pleases them most," he said. "The crew believes Perna. Whether it is justified or not, their belief is itself a *fact* in the situation. I consider Shing to be acting on that fact, with my approval."

"Well, does that answer you, Holman?"

Bordelles was motioning Holman toward the door. The man's face was red and desperate and he was crunching his white hat.

"Listen. When I told Po-han you'd protect him, he didn't believe you could," Holman said. "None of the Chinese believe you can overrule Shing. But if I get the crew to agree to keep Po-han, will you do it?"

"Come on! Get out of here!" Bordelles shoved Holman.

Holman resisted. "If you never have overruled him, how do you know the coolies ain't right?" he challenged. "He lives down there in the Spanish cabin, bigger quarters than you got! He draws more money than you! How does anybody know the coolies ain't right?"

"Silence!" Bordelles shouted.

His face was white. He was trying to shove Holman out the door.

"No, wait!" Lt. Collins stood up. "Holman, if you can persuade the crew to want to keep Po-han, I will overrule Shing," he said.

"Aye aye, sir!" Holman said.

The door closed behind Holman. Bordelles was still angry.

"The insolent bastard!" he said.

"Sit down, Tom." Lt. Collins motioned to a chair and sat down himself, with his elbows on the table. "That Holman. He should never have been enlisted," he said musingly. "He's a dark, angry question unable to receive the answer. He's a Caliban. I don't know what he is."

"He's a troublemaker!" Bordelles hesitated. "Do you really think it was advisable . . ."

"To promise to overrule Shing?" Lt. Collins smiled. "It was impulsive, I admit. I don't know. It might be good policy to overrule

Shing openly, just once. I have never thought out clearly the nature of his authority in the ship." He drummed with his fingers. "Personal authority is always delegated. The person to whom it is delegated is always accountable to higher authority for the way he uses it. The supreme, undelegated authority in *San Pablo* rests in the American people collectively. Through a chain of command it is delegated to me; I exercise it in their name; and back through the chain of command I am responsible to them for what I do. That is why I must never let my authority even seem to be impugned from beneath. That is why mutiny is punishable by death." He broke off, to smile at Bordelles. "Excuse me, Tom. I'm thinking out loud."

"Go on, sir," Bordelles said.

"I also delegate authority within my ship. It is possible to see *San Pablo* as a working structure of authorities, down to the level of seamen and coolies who control only their own behavior. It is necessary to allow each man a graded leeway in his use of authority, because it is a dynamic structure, not a static form. I am guided in that by navy regulations. Unfortunately, we have no written regulations governing the Chinese boatmen. All we have is a body of custom and usage. I have no *official* authority over Shing." He frowned.

"You can throw him off your ship. You can break his rice bowl."

"Yes. And his face is involved here. He may feel he has to break his own rice bowl, if I overrule him."

"They say Big Chew wouldn't mind replacing Shing."

"Lynch's face is involved, too."

"Poor Lynch." Bordelles chuckled. "Do you consider he's really married, sir?"

"Of course not." Lt. Collins smiled.

"Well, Holman is not going to swing the crew over," Bordelles said. "They feel very strongly about it. Many of them have never really accepted Holman."

"I simply have to get rid of him. There may be a place for him in a big ship. But not in *San Pablo*."

"Bronson has hinted to me of something unhealthy in Holman's relationship with that coolie."

Lt. Collins shook his head, frowning. Homosexuality was a nasty, ever-threatening danger aboard ship. That was why the men had to be given periodic access to women, whether the missionaries approved or not. Under the right circumstances a commanding officer could simply write out an Undesirable Discharge for a man, from which there was no appeal, and set him ashore. But it was not a power to be used lightly.

"I'll arrange a transfer when we're in Hankow again," he said.

"Do you have to wait, sir?"

"I feel I'd better. Otherwise government funds would be expended in transportation. It would all have to be down on paper." He looked up and smiled. "And frankly, Tom, I wouldn't know what to write. I'd rather handle it by word of mouth."

"Yes, sir, I see that," Bordelles said. "Well, Holman is not going to change the crew's mind. Rest easy on that, sir."

Holman went down to the main deck. He was trying to think hard and coldly. Burgoyne called him aside.

"I was talking to Scharf last night, in the Red Candle," he said. "He's ready to fix Po-han up with a job in the smelter."

"No, by God!" Holman said. "Po-han earned his place on here. I ain't going to let 'em take it away from him!"

He told Burgoyne what Lt. Collins had promised. Burgoyne was certain the Sand Pebbles would not be swung over. He urged Holman to drop the notion and let Po-han go to the smelter. Holman would not consider it.

"Okay, if I lose," he said. "But I ain't lost yet."

He talked to Big Chew, alone with him in the galley. Without either man actually saying it, they agreed that they might cost Lop Eye Shing so much face that Big Chew could get his job. Holman said he would talk to the crew after dinner and it would help if it was a very good dinner. Big Chew's eyes gleamed.

"Apple pie," he said. "Lemon. Wine. I glate gingah."

The dinner was exceptionally good. Holman did not try to join the talk. All morning they had been grinning and watching him covertly, waiting for him to show some sign of distress, some admission of defeat. The food took their minds off it. There was hot, clear chicken soup with Chinese cabbage and lean beef stewed tender with several vegetables and hot biscuits with pots of strawberry jam. Wong put two pies on each table, and they were masterpieces. Criss-crossed strips of cheese were half melted into the flaky brown crusts and inside grated ginger and lemon peel gave a hot, spicy tang to the mixed cheese and apple and other nameless, delicate flavors. The perfume filled the compartment and every man ate two pieces. Then they leaned back in their chairs with coffee and cigarettes and they were all in a very good mood.

Big Chew had done his part. Holman stood up. He stepped into the bull ring and stood facing them, arms out and braced against the white stanchions on either side. The Sand Pebbles hushed their talking and eased their chairs around to face him back.

"Guys, I been all wrong and I'm sorry," Holman said. "I'm back on deck watches now and I'll stand by for any man that asks me until I make up every watch I missed. Things I said that I shouldn't, I'm sorry about them, too."

They did not have much expression. He told them about Po-han disobeying Shing for the good of the ship and how it was not fair that Shing should make him suffer for that. A few heads nodded.

"I say Lop Eye Shing don't have any right to fire somebody, if the ship loses by it," Holman said. "Everybody knows there's bad blood between Lop Eye and Big Chew. If Shing gets away with this, he's liable to fire Big Chew next."

"He'll play hell!" Duckbutt Randall exclaimed.

Heads nodded and a growl ran along the tables. They were coming around. Then Bronson raised his hand.

"Why tell us? Go talk to the skipper."

"I did. Shing's pretending it's because the crew wants to get rid of Po-han," Holman said. "If I can tell the skipper that ain't so, he'll overrule Shing. He told me he would."

Bronson smiled nastily. "Well, you know, Ho-mang, it is so."

"For the good of the ship, Bronson. Po-han's trained up and

ready to replace Chien, and he's the only Chinese aboard that is. With him down there, I can stay topside just like Pitocki did. It can be like old times again."

"Balls, Ho-mang!" Bronson was enjoying it. "Your pet coolie was using mess gear and he hit a white man. Next thing we know he'll be up here after a bunk and a place at the mess table."

A mutter ran along the tables. Yeah! That's telling him, Bronson! Their faces were like curtains coming down on rows of windows. Holman clenched his teeth.

"I was cold sober that night and I know what happened," he said. "I was the one hit Stawski. Po-han was drinking coffee, all right, but he had it in one of their tea bowls."

"He *was* using a mess cup!" Perna jumped up. "That's really true about the mess cup! I seen it!"

"But the part about hitting Stawski ain't true, is it, Perna?" Holman asked softly. He could see it register on all the closed faces. "All right, Bronson, he used a mess cup. Stawski broke it. And I'll guarantee Po-han won't never use another one. Is that one thing enough to cancel out all the good he done, and what he can still do, for the ship? Do you think that's *fair,* Bronson?"

The fat face took on a cautious look. Bronson knew he had become a spokesman. He glanced at the other Sand Pebbles and back to Holman.

"Well, considering the difference between a slopehead and a white man, Ho-mang, yes. Yes, I think it's fair enough," he said.

Perna, Crosley, Randall and others nodded agreement. Sure it's fair. Tell him, Bronson. Holman iced his temper.

"What kind of difference you figure makes that much difference, Bronson?" he asked evenly.

"Slopeheads just ain't Americans and by law they can't ever be Americans," Bronson said.

"You mean being fair only counts between Americans?"

"Well, white men." Bronson shifted in his chair. "I mean, fair's different with slopeheads. They're sneaky. They lie and steal. They're dirty. Their yellow goes clear to the bone. There ain't one in all China with guts enough to stand up and fight like a man. Fair's different, with people like that." He glanced around, and heads nodded.

"None of that's true about Po-han."

"He's a slopehead, ain't he?"

"Bronson, would you personally fight Po-han? To prove what you just said?"

"Why should I? Everybody knows that!" Bronson said angrily. "I don't need to prove it!"

"I don't know that personally about Po-han, and neither do you," Holman said softly through his teeth. "Are you game to prove that about Po-han personally? I'm asking you."

Bronson colored. "Oh, I could. I could, all right. But I don't see why the hell I should oblige you."

"How about Stawski fightin' Po-han?" Burgoyne said.

All heads turned aft to Stawski's table. The suggestion pleased them. Yeah, yeah, let Ski fight him. Stawski stood up, grinning.

"Sure, I'll fight him," he said. "I'll beat his goddamn eyes around to slant the other direction." He was pleased with the attention.

"If Po-han shows enough guts standing up to Stawski, we'll let him stay aboard," Burgoyne said. "How about it, guys?"

"No! No, by God! Only if he wins the fight!" Bronson stood up. "A slopehead would let you beat him to death, if there was any money in it. Winning is the only thing that counts!"

They were all agreeing with Bronson. Holman knew it was the best he could do, just now. Po-han couldn't win, of course. But if he took a beating and showed real guts, it would touch them, and that would be the time to try again.

"It's a deal," Holman said. "Only if Po-han wins."

He sat down and poured a cup of coffee. He was surprised at how tired and trembling he was. Talk about the fight buzzed at all the tables. They decided to stage the fight at the Red Candle on the next payday, which was a few days off. Bronson turned to face Holman's table.

"You want to bet any money on your man, Ho-mang?"

"What odds?" Holman asked.

"Even money. You rate slopeheads even with white men using your mouth, Ho-mang. You got the guts to do it with your money?"

Several men laughed. It's really me they want to hurt, more than Po-han, Holman thought. If I lose some money to 'em, and be a good sport about it, it might help when I try again.

"Okay, even money," he said.

"How much?"

"Eighty Mex. That'll be my whole payday."

"I want twenty of it!" Crosley yelled.

They shared it out among them, arguing excitedly. They were like sharks smelling blood, Holman thought. Perna was very bitter because he did not get any of the bet.

"Bet the payday after, Ho-mang!" he urged. "I'll give you two to one."

"I don't like to be in debt," Holman said. "One payday's enough."

"Three to one," Bronson said. "Still scared, Ho-mang? How about four to one?"

"Five to one, you cheap bastard!" Perna yelled from his table. "You got shit in your blood, Ho-mang?"

"I'll take them odds, Perna, if you're so anxious to bet," Burgoyne said.

"How much?" Perna was taken aback.

"All you got, boy. All you can borrow."

Perna hesitated.

Burgoyne grinned and tugged at his mustache. "You smelled of your own blood lately, Perna?"

"All right, forty Mex," Perna said. "I'll take your money, Frenchy. It'll spend as good as anybody's."

Then they were all after Burgoyne, shouting and waving arms. The fever had them. Burgoyne bet all he had. Restorff was fidgeting.

"I'll take some of that five-to-one money, if there's any left," he said, not too loudly.

"You already bet the other way," Farren said.

Restorff hushed him. He went over to the nonrated table looking for bets. After a moment Farren followed him, to hedge his own bets.

"You really figure Po-han's got a chance?" Holman whispered.

"He's got anyway one in five," Burgoyne said. "At least he's hard and tough. Ski's soft, and he's got mud in his blood."

"Po-han's got fire. You know, I think he *will* win!"

"If he's willing to fight."

"Sure, he's willing!" Holman said.

16

Holman and Burgoyne took Po-han to the Red Candle shortly before eight o'clock. It was a clear, cold night. The two sailors were nervous and jumpy, but Po-han was calm. Holman thought it was a kind of false calm, and it worried him.

"Remember, Po-han, you got to *fight!*" he said for the tenth time, as they crossed the courtyard. "You got to hit him! hurt him! hit him! hurt him!"

"Can do, Jehk."

Po-han had been that way ever since he had agreed to fight. He had not wanted to fight. He said that he was afraid of Stawski and he could not fight him. Holman and Burgoyne had had a long argument with Po-han, down by the workbench.

"Too much cold this side," Po-han kept saying, patting over his heart. "Suppose cold this side, any man no can fight."

"You before plenty time fight Chinese man. One time you fight Fang, makee him black eye," Holman urged. "How fashion no can fight Stawski?"

"Ski no same!" Po-han was very earnest. "Too much no same! I flaid Ski."

"I think he means he's got military fear for Americans," Burgoyne said.

Military fear was a kind of built-in cringe. They built it into you in boot training and afterward you could never get rid of it. If you thought you did, you were only leaning too far in the other direction trying to fool yourself. They could call it military pride and loyalty up and down all they wanted to, but when you looked at it closely it was still a cringe. It bent a man, and he could never be straight again. You could not just talk him straight.

"Listen, Po-han," Holman said. "You hit Ski, makee bleed little bit, I think you heart plenty hot." He patted his own heart. "I already speak you fight Ski. Suppose no fight, I lose face."

Po-han gave in. "You no lose face, Jehk. I fight Ski."

They had drilled Po-han on only a few simple things: to keep his left out, his chin in, and to work on Stawski's gut. They didn't want to confuse him. They began to think that Po-han would have a real chance if he would only fire up. But he would not fire up.

The dressing room was across the court from the bar. It was small and cold and bare, with Jennings' medical stuff on a table. In one corner Perna and Crosley were getting Stawski ready. They had drinks and Stawski was complaining because they would not let him have one.

"After the fight I'll buy you all you can hold," Perna said. "With Frenchy's money."

The two sets of men did not talk to each other. Po-han stripped down and put on a pair of Burgoyne's white summer shorts. He shivered. Burgoyne went out to get a *pukow* from Mother Chunk. Farren and Jennings came in and they measured off four long, equal strips each of linen bandage and adhesive tape. Farren had the gloves. He was going to be referee. Burgoyne came back with two Chinese quilts and threw one to Stawski.

"Thanks, Frenchy," Stawski said.

Holman and Burgoyne bandaged and taped Po-han's hands. He had much smaller hands than Stawski and the same length of tape would go around several more times. Holman worked carefully, laying firm figure eights around wrist and knuckles and criss-crossing

the back of the hand, casing and bracing all the wrist and hand
bones, trying to build striking points solid from knuckles to elbow.
Farren watched. Burgoyne talked in a low voice.

"They're right drunk already, over there," he said. "Shing and
Big Chew are there. There's a table of oil and tobacco men, too."

News of the fight had seeped all over Changsha. Businessmen could
not ordinarily come to the Red Candle, because they would lose face.
But it was all right to come to see a fight.

"They got Maily with 'em and a couple of bottles on their table,"
Burgoyne said. "They're out to make a night of it."

Holman was lacing up the gloves. Po-han sat hunched under the
pukow, still with that false calm.

"I guess we're all set," Farren said. "Take your man in first,
Holman. He's the challenger."

"Let's go, Po-han," Holman said.

It was warmer in the bar, very noisy and smoky, and the light was
dim. The tables were jammed into one end and two strands of heaving
line ran across to make a boxing ring of the blind end. It was about
twenty feet square of splintery board floor. All the posters were off
the walls. A yell went up as they led Po-han across to a chair in one
far corner and made him sit down. Burgoyne had a bucket of water
there, and a stack of short-time towels and bottles of ammonia and
vinegar.

Holman went over the few simple things again with Po-han, in a
low voice. He kept glancing at the tables. The businessmen were at
far left, five men in the khaki and boots they wore when they went
upcountry. They were pretty drunk. Maily had on her brown dress
with the round white collar. A tall, good-looking man whom the
others called Van was making Maily drink whisky he poured from
one of the bottles on their table.

"Them bastards," Burgoyne said. He was watching too.

The Sand Pebbles had the two tables on the right, and they were
very drunk. Franks and Welbeck were there. Duckbutt Randall, on
patrol, walked importantly back and forth swinging his club. He was
a fat, fair man and he always waggled his rump when he walked.

"That's Victor Shu, at the center table," Burgoyne whispered.

It was Holman's first sight of Shu. He was a big, coarse, dark man in dark European clothes, with a gold watch chain sagging between his vest pockets. Lop Eye Shing and Big Chew, in Chinese gowns, sat at Shu's table. Shing had been made stakeholder for all the bets. Holman caught Big Chew's eye and winked. Then the big yell went up.

Stawski was pushing his way through the girls and barboys behind the tables, Mother Chunk clearing a path for him. Stawski came grinning through into the ring and let the *pukow* slip from his shoulders and shook hands with himself over his head. He was big and pink and slabby with muscle, but not very hairy, for a white man. He pawed with his feet and thumbed at his nose and snorted. He was enjoying it. Perna and Crosley pulled him to the corner by the Sand Pebble table and sat him on a chair.

Red Dog was at that table, with a kettle and a big spoon. He was timekeeper. They were all yelling. Farren came over to Holman.

"Sure your man savvies all the rules, Jake? You ready?"

"He savvies. We're ready."

"Then send him out fighting."

Farren signaled Red Dog, who said "Arf! Arf!" and whanged his kettle. Burgoyne lifted the *pukow*. Holman slapped Po-han's shoulder.

"Fight! Hit, hurt! Hit, hurt!" he said urgently.

It was no fight. Stawski clowned it. He was calling his shots, light, glancing blows on Po-han's face. He started Po-han's nose bleeding and cut his lips and they were laughing at all the tables. Po-han was not fighting. He bounced and jumped and flailed and slapped with open gloves and Stawski would brush them aside and land wherever he pleased. Po-han kept turning his head to look at Holman, and Stawski could have taken his head off at those times, but he did not want to win that way. "Hey! I'm the guy you're fighting!" he told Po-han once, and it drew a big laugh. Stawski did a lot of fancy dancing and at the end of the round he went back to his corner puffing and grinning.

Holman and Burgoyne stopped Po-han's nosebleed. They talked

fiercely to him. They could not stir him up, and they shook their heads at each other.

The next two rounds were about the same. Stawski was slowing, but he had Po-han bleeding above both eyes. Blood was all down Po-han's front and all he could throw was looping, clubbing downswings that did not bother Stawski at all. Mother Chunk and the girls and the kitchen help crowded in between the tables and they made a solid wall of people yelling there. Farren kept the fight in the center of the cleared space. Po-han's blood was all over the dusty floor and their leather shoes thumped and shuffled and Stawski's gloves *splat-splatted* steadily on bloody flesh. Through all the noise Holman could hear Stawski puffing. Holman had insisted on three-minute rounds, hoping for that.

Perna and Crosley looked worried. They sent Stawski out to finish it in the fourth round. He began hitting Po-han as hard as he could. He was big and slabby and gasping and unmarked, except with Po-han's blood. Po-han's muscles were cleanly rounded, like separate living things under his blood-smeared skin, and he still bounced like a red rubber ball. Stawski was landing hard, knocking Po-han down now, but Po-han would not stay down long enough for Farren to start a count. He spat out a tooth and his eyes were so swollen that he probably only saw Stawski as a blur, but he landed several solid right hooks to Stawski's ribs. They were the first real blows he had struck.

"Frenchy! If he can only keep up them hooks!" Holman said.

"Kill him! Kill him!" they were yelling from the tables. Stawski had his lips skinned back and his nostrils splayed and he was trying. Po-han caromed off the gray plaster, leaving bloody marks, and he rose from the bloody, splintery boards with slivers in his flesh, and Stawski slammed him down again. Po-han rose, windmilling blindly, not even facing Stawski. Stawski shrugged and looked at Farren. Farren walked over to raise Stawski's hand and Red Dog whanged the kettle.

"You son of a bitch!" Perna screamed.

"Arf! Arf! Arf!"

Holman and Burgoyne worked on Po-han with towels and ammonia. There was no use trying to stop the blood. Po-han spat out another tooth and he was trying to say something through his pulped lips.

"Hammah hammah hammah," he was saying.

Farren came over. "Throw in the towel, Jake," he said. "Your man's dead on his feet."

"No."

"Then I'll stop it. I don't want him killed. I'm responsible."

"Po-han's just starting to fight," Holman said.

Red Dog banged the kettle. Holman shouldered Farren aside and pushed Po-han out on the floor.

"Hammah hammah hammah!" he told him.

Stawski was shot. He could hardly keep his arms up. Po-han began the right hooking, and even when Stawski took it on his forearms it *thugged* and hurt. Stawski could not get set. It came to Holman what was happening. Po-han's body was fighting, without any hindrance from his brain, and it was *sledging* Stawski. All the way from the toes, with the fist as striking point, it was pouring its momentum into Stawski and it was killing him. Po-han drove Stawski blindly, gasping and eye-bulging, against the walls and into the tables, spilling drinks, and they were smelling blood and death at the tables. "Kill him! Kill him!" they screamed and the room was one great, smoky scream as they danced and howled there. Stawski went to hands and knees for a nine count and got up again. Po-han doubled him over and, blindly as a machine, sledged him in the jaw. Stawski went down with a *crack* and a *thud*. It was very clear that he was not going to get up again.

Holman half carried Po-han across to the dressing room. Jennings, looking worried, was working on Stawski. He had someone call rickshaws and he took Stawski away to the mission hospital with a broken jaw. He did not have any time to look at Po-han but Tullio, his seaman striker, came to help. Tullio was half drunk but he was very careful and gentle as they sponged Po-han off and stopped the bleeding with collodion and gauze and bandaged him where they could. Tullio pulled out all the slivers with tweezers.

"He'll have to have a dentist look at that mouth," Tullio said. "I can't do anything about that." He was worried about Po-han. "I wish he'd come out of it," he said. "He may have concussion."

They got some whisky into Po-han's battered mouth, but he would not come out of it. He could neither see nor talk, but he seemed to know Holman and he would do what Holman wanted him to do. They got him dressed and standing outside in the courtyard. It was very noisy across the way in the bar.

"Where can we take him?" Burgoyne asked.

"Back to the ship, I guess," Holman said. "You want to stand by him while I round up rickshaws?"

Big Chew came out of the bar, walking with a roll and looking very happy. *"Ding hao!"* he said. "I sabby you luck-man, Ho-mang! Long time I sabby!"

"Must take Po-han shipside," Holman said. "He no good."

"How fashion shipside?" Big Chew was a bit drunk. "Takee home-side! He wife catch Chinee doctah, fix evahting!"

"Po-han's got a wife?"

"Shoo, hab got wife! I sabby what side. My cheh takee he."

Big Chew called out in Chinese and the two coolies squatting beside one of the sedan chairs at the upper end of the courtyard rose and brought it down beside the group. Big Chew gave them directions in Chinese and they had a noisy argument. Holman had not known that Po-han had a wife. He felt he should go along, but he would not be able to talk to them, and Po-han's wife would probably be very angry. Or she might cry.

"Help me get him in the chair, Jake," Burgoyne said.

As soon as he felt Holman's hands, Po-han climbed obediently into the chair. The coolies hoisted it and moved off.

"Frenchy, I hate to just leave him go like that," Holman said.

"He maskee!" Big Chew said. "Come inside, talkee Shing, catch money!"

"That's right. Lop Eye's holding stakes," Burgoyne said.

"I jus' now catch plenty money!" Big Chew patted his waist.

"Did you bet on Po-han? Who with?"

"I bet Lop Eye Shing," Big Chew said. "I takee all he money."

"I hope not quite all," Burgoyne said. "Come on, Jake. Let's us go get ours."

The bar had a hair-trigger atmosphere that Holman didn't like. They were all glassy-eyed and all talking at once in voices hoarse from yelling, and they were not listening to each other. Shing was still at Victor Shu's table. Shu was leaning back and smoking a cigar, his thumbs in his vest pockets. Pleasantly enough, Lop Eye Shing paid off. He gave Burgoyne almost a thousand Mex in new Hankow bills. At one of the Sand Pebble tables someone noticed, and a yell went up.

"Frenchy's going to buy Maily!"

"Let's all of us take 'em topside and put 'em to bed!" Perna said.

"Shivaree! Shivaree!" Vincent yelled. They were all on their feet and yelling. "Make 'em dance in their skivvies!" Crosley shouted. They were all ready to go, like gunpowder. It was ugly.

"Get her in back, quick, Frenchy!" Holman said. "I'll hold 'em here, if I can." He turned. "Frenchy's buying drinks for the house!" he yelled. "All you want, on Frenchy! Sit down, guys! Order up!" He waved his arms.

They did not sit down. Holman remembered a glimpse of Maily's face during the fight, horrified and yet fascinated, and a kind of looseness about her mouth. They had been making her drink. He turned, and Maily was standing up. Her face was white and scared. Burgoyne had one of her wrists and the tall one, Van, had the other.

"Not so fast. Not . . . so . . . fast, sailor!" Van was saying. "She's going to a hotel with us, when we break up here." Burgoyne said something. "How do you know we won't pay two hundred and ten?" Van asked.

"I spoke first and the price is already set," Burgoyne said.

"Prices are set by competition in a free market, eh, Quinn?"

"You tell 'em, Van!" a chunky, snub-nosed civilian said. "You got yourself some competition, sailor," he told Burgoyne.

"How about it, Mr. Shu? Two-ten takes her, right?" Van said.

Shu rolled his cigar. "Maybe the sailor can pay that much. He did speak first."

The Sand Pebbles were crowding in close, jostling Holman. All the khaki-clad civilians were standing up, bunching behind Van. Only Shu's table separated them. It was not good. Duckbutt Randall pushed through and beat on Shu's table with his club.

"All right, all right, break it up!" he shouted. "Spread back, you guys! Let go of that girl!"

"You got no authority over me," Van told Duckbutt. "This is still a free country."

Duckbutt sputtered. "This is a free and independent whorehouse and Victor Shu owns it," he said. "What Mr. Shu says goes. Anybody don't like it, they can go back where they come from!"

He scowled at Van. He knew civilians had no business in the Red Candle. Duckbutt liked to feel important, and he was in his glory.

"All right, I'll pay two-ten," Burgoyne said angrily.

"Two-twenty," Van said.

"Auction! Auction!" Quinn yelled. "How about it, Mr. Shu? Make it an auction?"

Shu puffed blue smoke and shrugged. "Why not?"

It took the Sand Pebbles' drunken fancy and the explosion faded back. "Hey! Hey! Auction!" they yelled, and helped Quinn pull a table out into the cleared space. They lifted Maily up on it and Quinn climbed up beside her. Maily's lips were trembling and she kept closing her eyes. Burgoyne looked very angry.

"Hey day! Hey day!" Quinn shouted. "Just *look* at this merchandise! What am I bid for this fine piece of girl flesh?"

"Two-thirty," Burgoyne said.

"And forty," Van said.

"Three hundred," Burgoyne said.

They loosed a cheer. Maily had her hands clenched beside her, her head back and her eyes closed. She had blue cloth shoes and no stockings and her knees were trembling. All eyes were on her and Holman felt the change in the crowd. They were remembering all over again that she was a virgin in a whorehouse. Van was hesitating.

"*Three* hundred gold dollars!" Quinn shouted. "That only buys one leg, boys!" He twitched Maily's brown dress above her knee. "Clean, fresh, brand-new goods, untouched by human hands!" He passed his hands in the air near her, outlining her breasts and hips. "Hey day! Bid her up! Show your red American blood, boys!"

"Three-fifty!" Van said.

The crowd cheered again. Burgoyne, white-faced, was smoothing his mustache savagely. The gunpowder feeling was coming back into the air and they were all crowding the auction table. Holman looked around and caught Red Dog's eye. Red Dog made a pinch motion and Holman nodded. He didn't know what Red Dog meant, but something was due to break in seconds. Van took a drink from the bottle he was holding.

"Give up, sailor," he told Burgoyne.

"Four-fifty," Burgoyne said, through bloodless lips.

That was about all he had. Holman pushed through and grasped his arm. "You can have what I got, Frenchy," he said. Burgoyne's arm was like iron and he did not answer. They were all whistling and cheering, with a high, howling note in their voices, and their faces did not look good. Quinn was shouting, red-faced and eye-bulging. Holman could not hear what he said. Quinn went down on one knee and began raising Maily's dress slowly, in teasing jiggles. Her face was absolutely bloodless, and she swayed, eyes still closed. She must feel awful alone up there, Holman thought. He had his fists clenched and every muscle tense, and the mob lust was exciting him too, and he didn't know what to do.

The mob roared in outrage. Maily had on Chinese underwear, loose blue drawers that came halfway down her shapely thighs. "Undress her!" Vincent screamed and they were all shouting hoarsely, "Strip her! Strip her!" Quinn stood up and ripped savagely and her dress fell down around her hips. The fire was in the gunpowder.

Red Dog barked high and sharp and Holman took it as a signal. He kicked fiercely at a table leg and caught Maily as the table tilted her down to him and passed her to Burgoyne, shouting, "Outside, Frenchy!" Then he slugged Quinn and turned to see Van scream and plunge forward with Red Dog riding high on his shoulders and yapping frantically. Red Dog snatched down the overhead light and

Holman bruised his way through screaming darkness to the door, hurling them aside each way like a snowplow. He saw Burgoyne and Maily in the courtyard and ran to join them. Behind him in the darkness a roaring, howling, wood-splintering fight of all against all raged on. The Red Candle had finally exploded.

"Run, Frenchy!" Holman said. "Some of 'em may come after us!"

Someone did, shouting in Chinese behind them as they ran down narrow streets and around twisty corners, working inland from the river. Maily could not run fast.

"Go on with her, Frenchy," Holman panted. "I'll wait and stop that bastard behind us."

He turned with fists ready, catching up breath, and it was Big Chew who came pounding along. As he gasped and puffed and tried to talk, his two coolies with his sedan chair loped up. Holman turned and cupped his hands.

"Hey, Frenchy, wait!" he hailed. "It's friends!"

Lights were coming on behind barred and latticed windows. They were making too much noise. Big Chew made them walk on quietly and slowly until they came to a silent, deserted street. He was still drunk and happy that he had gotten so neatly away from the fight. Maily had to keep holding her dress up, hands crossed to shoulders. She was shivering and Burgoyne had his arm around her.

"We got to take her someplace," he said. "Some safe place."

"How about the bund hotel?"

"Shu'll find her there. He'll get her again."

"Can he, though? I mean, there's Chinese cops, ain't there?"

Burgoyne laughed bitterly. "There ain't no law in China, Jake, only warlords. And Shu's in with this warlord."

"Let me go back to the Red Candle," Maily said in a broken voice. "There's no hope. It's just God's will."

"No it ain't God's will!" Burgoyne said, with fierceness strange to him. "Tomorrow I'll go pay Shu exactly what you owe him and not a clacker more. And then we'll get you on the train for Hankow." He hugged her against him.

"How fashion speakee?" Big Chew said. Holman explained and

Big Chew nodded thoughtfully. "Mus' hide she," he said. "Shu makee looksee, this side, that side, no can find. She stop by Po-han, I tink all maskee."

Maily rode in the chair. Chew was probably right, Holman thought, on the way there. It was a poor section of twisty, narrow lanes, mud walls and low tiled roofs over near the railroad cutting, very confusing. Po-han lived in one room of a small courtyard with a tree, and a dim light was on inside. Big Chew went in first, talking rapidly to a pale, pretty little woman who bowed to him. Both ends of the room were curtained off and there were only a chest, a clay stove, a table and one chair in the middle part. A small, smoky kerosene lamp burned on the table. They all came inside except the chair coolies, and it was quite crowded.

Po-han's wife was putting wisps of grass in the stove and blowing and she got a fire going under a tin pan of water. A thin, waspish older woman came out and Big Chew talked to her. They argued back and forth. Maily's head was drooping and Burgoyne was half supporting her. Big Chew seemed to win the argument.

"Maskee," he said, grinning. "Gel can do, stop this side."

The older woman was Po-han's mother, he told them. Po-han was asleep on opium pills. The Chinese doctor had just left and Po-han was going to be all right. Holman had been expecting both women to spit curses at him, on account of Po-han, but the mother ignored him and the little wife was only shy and nervous, working up her modest fire under her pan of water. She murmured something and slipped out into the courtyard.

"Here, you better sit down, Maily," Burgoyne said.

Maily was shivering again. Po-han's mother spoke soothingly to Maily and led her behind one of the curtains. Sleepy child voices sounded back there, and Maily began a quiet sobbing. The three men talked about Po-han and the brave fight he had made. They were all standing, because there was only one chair. Po-han's wife came back with some tea bowls she had probably had to borrow. She was red-cheeked and kept her eyes down as she brewed tea.

"She tink Po-han too much lose face, no hab got cheh, teacup," Big Chew said quietly.

Holman looked around again. It wasn't much, earth floor, no ceiling except the tile roof, whitewashed walls and one glazed-paper window. But it was simple and decent and good, he thought, after the Red Candle. She ought to spit in my face, he thought, blame me for Po-han. But she gives me tea. Po-han's mother came back out and they all drank tea. She said something to Big Chew.

"Olo woman speakee mus' pay litee money," he said.

"I'm going to give Po-han half of what I won," Holman said. "No, by God, every clacker of what I won!"

He began laying bills on the table.

"I'll give him half of mine," Burgoyne said.

Burgoyne began counting off bills. Big Chew explained to the women. There was quite a volley of Chinese back and forth with the old lady. Big Chew took out a sheaf of bills and added a generous portion of it to the little heap on the table.

"Same me," he said jovially. "You luck-man, Ho-mang. Po-han too much luck, too much money, jus' now. You makee he velly big man, Ho-mang."

Po-han's pretty little wife suddenly began to cry.

17

Next morning the Sand Pebbles proudly displayed black eyes and fat lips and skinned knuckles and Duckbutt Randall had a piece bitten out of his ear. They were all friendly to Holman. A good fight cleared away nastiness and resentment just as the spring flood swept away the winter garbage along the riverfront. A good fight, win or lose, settled things in a way a man could accept with an easy heart. And it had been a magnificent fight. The businessmen had been beaten to a pulp and forced to crawl on hands and knees across the courtyard. Lop Eye Shing and Victor Shu and most of the girls and the kitchen help had also been beaten up in the wild darkness. The Red Candle was a glorious, absolute wreck. The Sand Pebbles would tell and re-tell that fight for years to come, as a part of their folklore.

Even Lynch took it for granted that Po-han would stay aboard. Lop Eye Shing took his loss of face and did not quit. The *San Pablo* was too good a rice bowl to give up. Big Chew did not seem disappointed. He hinted to Holman of some kind of plan.

"I speakee somebody Hankow," was all he would say about it.

Burgoyne went into the city and paid Shu a hundred dollars gold. He told Holman about it the next day in the engine room. Shu had insisted that he must have four hundred and fifty, Burgoyne's last bid, and if Burgoyne would not pay it, then Maily would have to come back and work it off.

"The greasy bastard!" Holman said.

"He tried right hard to fish out of me where Maily is," Burgoyne said. "He told me his men were watching the trains and the riverfront and if she tried to leave town he would have her arrested."

"He can't do that!"

"She says he can. She's Chinese, Jake." Burgoyne spat in the trash can. "Victor Shu can do just about anything he wants in Changsha."

Holman stood quarterdeck watches every night, as his part of the general settlement. He became more aware again of the world outside the engine room. It was a dreary world of dull skies and misty rain and the mountain black across the river shrunken to steel-gray channels between the sandbars. Changsha crouched old and gray and smoky above its garbage and the *San Pablo* floated in its fish pond surrounded by a wreath of its own garbage. Burgoyne went ashore nearly every night to see Maily and he said she kept asking why Holman did not come over.

"Tell her I'm standing by for everybody, paying off watches," Holman said.

He was obscurely glad of an excuse to stay aboard. Po-han was mending rapidly, Burgoyne reported. He had enough money to buy the whole courtyard where he lived and become landlord to the other tenants. He had thrown the tenants out of the rooms on either side of his own and put his mother in one room and rented the other to Maily. Burgoyne had been helping Maily pick out furniture and gear and she spent her time fixing up the room.

"You ought to come see it, she's that proud of it, Jake," Burgoyne said. "She thinks you're sore at her, or something."

"Pretty soon," Holman said.

He was just as happy to have Burgoyne grapple with the problem of Maily. Life aboard was smooth and easy. Chiu-pa took care of the machinery well enough, and Holman had lost interest in it. He knew it was in fine shape. He began rather liking the quarterdeck watches. Stawski came aboard with his jaw wired up, thinned down from living on liquids, cheerful and reconciled. Then Po-han came back to duty, very proud of two shiny gold upper teeth he had had put in. He was bouncy and cocky in the engine room, but he stayed away from the throttle platform and the coffee pot. Perna and Stawski treated him as they had old Chien. The fight had canceled everything, as if it had never happened, and it all went smooth and easy again. It was clean and warm and dry inside the ship and Big Chew's chow was better than ever.

Burgoyne went ashore with Po-han almost every night and came back around midnight. He was afraid Victor Shu had found Maily. Some Chinese men in the street had tried to make her go with them. She screamed and a crowd gathered and she got safely back to the courtyard. She was afraid to go out again, except with Burgoyne. Then one morning the men had come into the courtyard and had only gone away after Po-han's mother had cursed them and screamed up a crowd of neighbors. Burgoyne and Po-han and Holman had a conference about it beside the workbench. They were a gang of petty racketeers who hung out in a teahouse near his place, Po-han said, and they might well be working for Shu. The whole neighborhood was afraid of them.

"I'll go ashore with you today, Frenchy," Holman said. "Let's take a look at that teahouse."

Po-han knocked off early to go with them. The district was a spill-over of mud walls and shacks outside the city wall, toward the rail-road, narrow, dirty streets jumping with noise and people. When the three men approached the teahouse the people cleared away, as if they smelled trouble. Po-han led the way inside, not stopping, to a table at the back where five of the tough guys sat. Two were in Western clothes, the others in gowns, and they hardly had time to stand up before Po-han was at them, punching silently and savagely. Holman and Burgoyne jerked and slapped and cuffed them and there was a lot of high-pitched squalling, but it was not a fight. The men slapped and scrambled and squalled, but they did not really fight. One of them pulled out a pistol, holding it as if just to show that he had it, and Holman took it away from him without resistance. The floor was slippery and crunchy with spilled tea and food and broken crockery. They kicked the gangsters into the street with blood on their faces and people came out of doors all along to point fingers and laugh and jeer. Po-han, puffing and happy, left a message with the teahouse proprietor for the gangsters who had not been present. Burgoyne gave the man some money for the broken furniture.

"Tell him if we have to do this again we won't pay next time," he told Po-han.

It had been very quick and easy and they all felt good about it. Holman put the pistol in his peacoat pocket. It was a cheap, nickeled Belgian revolver, and it was loaded.

"You know, we ought to go into the city and put a bug in Victor Shu's ear, while we're at it," Holman said.

"Let's go," Burgoyne said.

The people cheered them as they passed. The gang had long been running a clacker-level squeeze racket in the neighborhood, Po-han said. Now they had lost so much face that people could refuse to pay. It was a good feeling, being cheered. They walked through North Gate into the city, striding along three abreast, and everyone got out of their way. Shu's office was up a side street. It had a big red-and-gold sign in Chinese and a smaller one in English that said "V. Shu, Ship Chandler."

Holman led the way in. It was a long place, dark-shadowy in back, with boxes and tar and oil smells, and there were three desks up front behind a wooden railing. Shu sat at one of them. Holman kicked open the low gate and walked in and looked down at Shu across the desk. Shu looked mildly surprised.

"We just beat up some gangsters out on North Terrace," Holman said. "We thought you might like to know."

"Very interesting," Shu said politely.

He was not letting much feeling show on his big, coarse face, but his eyes were narrowed and watchful. Po-han and Burgoyne closed in on either side of Holman.

"They were bothering Maily," Burgoyne said. "We'll really get mad if it happens again."

Shu poured himself a cup of tea from the pot on his desk. "A man must always be ready to protect himself and his property," he agreed amiably. He pulled open a desk drawer and laid an automatic pistol beside his teacup. "You see I am ready."

Holman took out the Belgian pistol and balanced it in his hand. "We make 'em all sizes in America, up to sixteen inch," he said.

Shu raised his eyebrows. "I do not think you can get the big ones into Tungting Lake," he said easily. "Neither do I think you can claim consular protection for the girl Maily. She is Chinese."

"We won't bother the consul," Holman said. "We'll just come ashore with whatever men and tools we need to do the job."

Shu gave up the sparring. His face muscles set harshly and his voice turned hard. "Changsha is not a foreign concession. Chinese law applies here," he said. "The girl is Chinese. There is nothing you can do about that."

"Inside a couple of days she's going to be my legal wife," Burgoyne said flatly.

Shu's eyebrows raised again. "Oh well, if you can do that . . ."

He shrugged and put away his pistol. Then he studied some papers on his desk, sipping tea and ignoring his visitors. Holman looked at Burgoyne and noticed that a dozen Chinese had come up softly to stand just behind them. The back of his neck felt strange. He jerked his head toward the door.

"Let's get some fresh air," he said.

It was pretty feeble. They walked back, not swaggering, all of them knowing that Victor Shu had had very much the best of it. Burgoyne's statement had jarred Holman. He was thinking about it.

"Frenchy, you meant that, about marrying Maily?"

"I purely do. I been after her all last week to marry me," Burgoyne said. "I thought it was the only way to make her safe, and now I know it."

"Well, hell!"

"It ain't only that. I want to. I think about her all the time," Burgoyne said. "She's so decent and helpless. Jake, I'm that pushed and twisted and hauled and squeezed around inside I ain't a mite myself any more and sometimes I think I'm crazy. What do you think?"

Holman didn't answer. He didn't know what to think.

"I keep having the feeling it's the biggest, onliest chance of my life and I got to take it if it kills me. I got to do it right," Burgoyne said. "Jake, what *do* you think?"

"I think maybe you're in love," Holman said. "Whatever that means."

They came home to Po-han's courtyard like conquering heroes, all the same. The neighborhood people were shooting firecrackers to celebrate the rout of the gangsters. They bowed and called out to Po-han and he visibly enjoyed it. He had much face. He was a property owner with two gold teeth and a son and ocean devil friends to stand by him, and things were all right with him. It made Holman and Burgoyne feel good too and they swaggered again, grinning as they swung into Po-han's courtyard, with its single tree. Maily came running to meet them.

"Jake! Jake!" she cried. "I'm so glad to see you!"

"I'm glad too, Maily." He clasped her hand. "You're looking good."

She wore a black embroidered Chinese jacket and trousers and she was very excited and pretty with no strain and only natural color in her face. They all had tea in Po-han's main room and Holman learned that the wife's name was Mei-yu and he should call Po-han's mother Tai-tai. The two children were shy of Holman and would only peep out from behind the bed curtain. The bed had been cleared out of the other end of the room and there were two tables, half a dozen chairs, a new and larger stove, and quite a lot of other new gear. Po-han was so very proud of it that he could hardly pretend not to be when Holman praised it.

Then the men had to go and have more tea in Maily's room, and show it to Holman. It was smaller, freshly whitewashed and cheerful, with a red-and-white-striped bed curtain and green rush matting on the floor. She had a small table and two chairs and a chest and she would not sit down herself because she had to brew the tea. She had Mei-yu's old clay stove and a basket of grass and weed stems to feed the fire.

"Hey, it looks good and clean and happy in here, Maily," Holman said. "It's just like you."

"Thank you, Jake." She blushed and she was very pleased. "Frenchy helped me pick everything," she said. "He paid for it all, too."

"You'll civilize him yet, Maily."

Burgoyne chuckled and tugged his mustache. "The little gal has got herself a great big job there, don't you think, Jake?"

They drank tea and laughed and talked. Po-han was left out of much of the talk because his English was not good enough, but he grinned and was happy along with them, all the same. He caught Holman's remark that it was too bad they had not stopped to buy some bottled beer along the way.

"I sabby shop hab got plenty beeah," he said.

Burgoyne stood up. "No, sit down, Jake," he told Holman. "You're company. You and Po-han are having supper with us tonight, and I got to get stuff for that, too."

Maily, flushed and happy, whispered to Burgoyne what to get, because it was to be a surprise for Holman.

"You sit here and talk to Maily, Jake," Burgoyne said. "She ain't seen you in a coon's age. We'll only be gone a few minutes."

As soon as they left, a discomfort filled the room. Holman half expected Maily to put on her hostess manner and ask him about Nevada. But she sat down in the other chair, her manner very earnest.

"Jake, Frenchy wants me to marry him. I don't know what to do."

"Yeah. Frenchy told me."

"I owe him everything. He's simply *good,* Jake, I think more than anybody I ever knew. But I don't think I love him."

"I don't know much about love." Holman squirmed. "I don't believe much in love."

"I'd do anything for him, even die. I've told him I'd just live with him, as his wife." She was blushing. "That's his right, now."

"Well, ain't that love?"

"It's love . . . but it's not love, either. I can't explain. It's something you just know."

"I don't know," he said heavily. "I think Frenchy loves you."

"I know. He demands me silently . . . to love too . . . and I can't. Nothing I ever read in novels or magazines says what to do . . . what happens then."

She talked about love, all she had read, in uneven bursts of talk. Holman listened uncomfortably. Love happened to you like a whirlwind and changed you and made the world around you into heaven, she said. True love always won out. Holman did not believe that stuff. Women grabbed just whomever they could grab, and that other was only a smokescreen. Maily was a fool not to grab Frenchy, Holman thought. She had never seen movies, or she would be talking about them too. She kept talking and Holman only half listened.

He was thinking it must be tough to be a woman. They had to have stuff around them, a room and furniture. They were all needs and wants and wishes and the only real trade they had was going to bed. They did not have a place where they could live safely and do what they pleased outside of that place. They were out in the middle of it, and when they grabbed a guy to save themselves, all they could do was to pull him out in the middle of it too. No wonder they made up that love crap, Holman thought. It was their way of getting drunk and forgetting their troubles.

"For Christ's sake, marry Frenchy, if he wants that!" Holman said at last, to stop her.

"I don't want to hurt him," she said. "I'm afraid I'd be evading my punishment. God's will for me. I don't want to involve Frenchy."

"You been punished enough already to satisfy any decent god," Holman said. "Forget that stuff. Load it all off on Frenchy, if that's what he wants."

"You think everyone is as strong as you are." She was twisting her handkerchief around her left hand. "Frenchy's good, but he's not strong. Not the way you are."

"He's as good a man as anybody I ever knew," Holman said. "Marry him and let him worry about it."

He felt very uncomfortable. None of the talk made sense. There was no sense in it. It was woman stuff. Something was pushing at the door and he got up to open it. It was a very little girl in padded red jacket and trousers and tiger shoes.

"Su-li!" Maily said.

She brought the child in. It was Po-han's daughter, she told Holman. Su-li was just learning to talk and she was always in mischief of some kind. The little girl skirted Holman at a safe distance, watching him with fear and fascination, while they talked about her. Then she was at his knee and in a few more minutes in his lap and pulling at his nose to see if it was real.

"She likes you, Jake," Maily said.

Holman made up a game with Su-li. She had her hair in a pigtail tied with a red string. He would pull her pigtail gently and say *ding ding!* as if ringing a bell. After a while, when he tugged it, she would say *ding ding!* She would look pleased when Maily and Holman laughed and then turn shy and press her face into Holman's chest while he patted her in reassurance. They were still playing the game when Po-han and Burgoyne came back with the beer. Su-li would not say *ding ding!* when the other men pulled her pigtail, and it pleased Holman.

They ate supper in Po-han's main room, pushing the two tables together. It was the pork bits with sweet peppers and gingery sauce that Maily knew Holman liked. Mei-yu had helped her cook it, but it was not as good as Big Chew's version. Holman praised it anyway. Maily ate with the men, but Po-han's women would not sit down. Maily's easy laugh and free manner contrasted with Mei-yu's modesty. The old lady had a bold eye. She was wispy and straight and dignified. The children called her Nai-nai.

After supper they drank more beer and talked and it was very cozy. Holman had the little girl on one knee and he tried to coax Po-han's son onto the other one. The boy, Ah Pao, was about four, crop-headed and moon-faced and much more shy than his little sister. He stayed close to Po-han, who plainly liked him best. Finally Holman got the boy on his knee also.

"Look what I got," he said. "You're out in the cold, Frenchy."

"That's what you think," Burgoyne said.

He unbuttoned his cuffs and began rolling up his sleeves. At once the children wriggled off Holman's lap and ran to trace their chubby fingers over Burgoyne's tattoos. Holman had to laugh.

"If you took off your jumper, you could be the Pied Piper," he said. "You walking picture book, it ain't fair."

There was an awkward moment when Holman remembered the Belgian pistol and offered it to Po-han for protection of the house. Po-han took it, but his women began a furious chattering in Chinese. The children, frightened, ran behind the women, and Po-han sadly gave the pistol back to Holman. He explained that when warlord soldiers looted, they always pretended to be looking for arms. Wherever they found them, that house and all the people in it were forfeit. If it was a rich house or had pretty women, they would often pretend to find one of their own pistols, so they could loot and rape. At such times pretty women put on rags and smeared dung and soot and ashes all over themselves, so they would not be attractive to the soldiers.

The talk made an ugliness in the room. They could not get back all of their good feeling. But when Holman and Burgoyne decided to go back to the ship, Holman tugged Su-li's pigtail again and the tiny girl unexpectedly said, *"Ding hao!"* It made a good laugh to say goodnight on. Burgoyne lingered in the courtyard to say goodnight to Maily privately and Holman waited for him in the street. He waited quite a while.

They were almost to the river before Burgoyne spoke. "Maily said she'd marry me." Their footsteps on gritty stone scuffed loudly.

"I don't know what to say, Frenchy," Holman said. "I hope it works out good."

No one was on the streets. Somewhere back in the dark alleys a watchman beat bamboo sticks together and sang out in Chinese.

"How does it feel? All jumping around inside?"

"I'm like to busting inside," Burgoyne said. "I couldn't be no more scared if I was facing a firing squad."

18

Snow was falling on China Light. It hurried whitely across the class-room windows, dry and cold. Shirley Eckert's ankles felt cold, under her neat table. She wished the stove coolie would come by on his rounds to shake up the grate and add coal to the small heating stove halfway down the room. Dignity would not permit her or her students to do it.

The room held thirty desks. Her eight students had taken the ones nearest the stove this morning. She felt removed from them. They were busy with paperwork she had set them. They had about ten minutes to go before the reading period. Cho-jen, as usual, had already finished. He seemed restless, leafing through the text and then glancing at the snow dance in the windows.

She was afraid of Cho-jen. She wondered, as on all the other mornings, if this would be the day.

It was a large white-plastered room with a blackboard and maps of China and North America on the side wall. Behind her back, on the front wall, were U.S. and Chinese flags and portraits of Lincoln and Washington. The students wore padded gray or blue Chinese gowns, all but Cho-jen. He affected European suits, poorly cut and gracelessly worn over his lithe young limbs. This morning he wore a red scarf, which he kept fingering.

She felt his eyes on her and met his gaze. Unabashed, he studied her, as if she were a museum exhibit. She smiled slightly. He did not respond. Finally, carelessly, he dropped his eyes to the text.

It will be today, she thought.

They had warned her about Cho-jen. He was a brilliant student who delighted in making fools of his teachers. His attacks were unpredictable and devastating, they said. Once he began on a teacher, he did not stop. He would destroy all discipline in a class. As much as they could, they kept him in classes taught by native staff. But for Shirley's first year they were forming this special class of advanced students who could be taught wholly in English. Cho-jen, for all his youth, was easily the most advanced student they had. He would have to be in her class.

Mr. Mills, the principal, had told her about Cho-jen in the faculty office before school opened. He overpolished his glasses in unconscious agitation and his face pinked with the shadow of old angers. He hinted that her predecessor, Mr. Morgan, had broken his contract as much because of Cho-jen as of poor health. He had made Cho-jen seem evil and dangerous.

"But, Mr. Mills, what is it that he does, really?" she asked.

"He asks questions. Not for information. Bedeviling, *leading* questions," Mr. Mills said. "He'll cross-examine you like a shyster, if you let him. You must not let him. Hold fast to the text."

Shirley nodded. That was not how she meant to teach.

"His father is very influential," Mr. Mills said. "And after all, the boy is brilliant. Erratically brilliant. But I wish his father would let us send him on to a university."

Mr. Gillespie had been more helpful. "I've talked to the boy a few times. From all I can gather, he's an authentic genius," he said. "It needn't be a disgrace if a boy like that outpaces his teacher mentally."

"Some ordinary person had to teach Leonardo," Shirley said.

"Don't antagonize him," Gillespie said. "Don't pontificate. Never bluff. Don't try to crush him with authority and the great weight of your learning." He chuckled gently. "I'm afraid poor Morgan was prone to that."

"I'm sure I'm not. Whatever other faults—"

"Christian humility," Gillespie said. "We can all use more of it. It is a saving grace, Miss Eckert."

Mr. Mills designed the course for her and chose the material. They would get an hour of grammar and composition each morning, followed by an hour of literature. They were to learn all the poetry by heart and recite it in unison.

"Will that help them to fluency in English?" she asked doubtfully.

"It trains tongue and ear. It is a link to the old Chinese way, and they are used to it," Mr. Mills said. "You must have them read the prose aloud, also."

She had found Cho-jen in person no monster at all. He was younger and slighter than the other boys, yet clearly the dominant one among them. He had clear skin and delicate, mobile features and rather large, un-Chinese eyes. His manner was one of subdued restlessness, as of volcanic energy waiting release. The older boys were quite limited in English. Cho-jen spoke it almost perfectly. He was an attractive boy.

She was prepared to meet him with disarming honesty. He gave her no chance. He was aloof and respectful. He did his classwork perfectly, with bored ease, asking no questions. He made her feel futile and useless as a teacher. Mr. Mills thought that might be a subtle attack.

"He's fiendish. He's waiting for you to let your guard down," Mr. Mills said.

Shirley did not think she had a guard up. She knew Cho-jen was giving Mr. Mills a bad time in trigonometry. After several weeks, in an effort to reach Cho-jen, she disobeyed Mr. Mills. She decided to experiment with having them paraphrase the poetry they recited. It would train them in linking thought with English words. She explained and asked Cho-jen to do the first section of the day's assignment.

"His friend walks around town and hears the soldiers getting ready to march," Cho-jen said easily. "Then he climbs up in the steeple. He frightens the pigeons who live there. It is dark and gloomy. He looks out over the town, in the moonlight."

"Very good!" Shirley said. "Tao-min, will you do the next one?"

Tao-min was an earnest, pudgy boy with steel-rimmed glasses. He looked upset. "Soldiers are below," he said hesitantly. "They have many houses, soldier houses. I think . . . many are dead?" He wanted her to signal approval. "They are . . . ghosts?" he asked.

"No, Tao-min." She did not smile. "He looks down at a graveyard. Some places in America we bury people all together, beside the church. It is an analogy with a soldiers' camp."

She could not explain analogy to them. Tao-min was red and leaning forward and straining to understand. The others squirmed in sympathy. Desperately, Shirley reduced her English almost to pidgin. She made pleading, frustrated gestures with her hands. She knew she was red as Tao-min. Her experiment was failing at first trial. Then Cho-jen spoke a few words in Chinese. The faces cleared. All the boys sighed with relief. So did Shirley.

"Analogy!" Tao-min said proudly, understanding.

"Thank you, Cho-jen." Shirley said from her heart. They had set a pattern. At crucial moments thereafter she would look at Cho-jen and he would clear it up in concise Chinese. Fine autumn days went by. Wintry rains came, and closed windows and the inadequate stove. The other boys were very noticeably improving their English. Cho-jen was really the teacher, Shirley knew. Just last night she had talked to Gillespie about it in confidence.

"He may just be fattening you for the kill, although I hate to think that," Gillespie said. "You have let yourself become dependent on him. That in itself is a subtle loss of face, for a teacher."

"It's clearly the best way to teach the class," Shirley said. "They are all really learning."

"Just the same, it's not old custom."

It was probably cat-and-mouse, he warned. In time, Cho-jen would try to humiliate her publicly. He told her, also in confidence, how Morgan had gone to Craddock and said that either Cho-jen must be expelled or he, Morgan, would break his contract. Morgan had gone. Only Craddock knew who Cho-jen's father really was, but he was clearly a man not to be offended.

The stove coolie came in with his scuttle to fix the stove for the next hour. Shirley glanced at the snow-whipped windows. It was almost time to begin the reading.

It was strange how one boy could have everyone upset. Leah, Shirley's Chinese maid, said firmly that Cho-jen's father was the bandit chief on the mountain. It might well be true. All the Chinese deferred to Cho-jen. He had a personal servant, a huge, scar-faced man named Wang, of whom all the mission servants went in terror.

Uneasily, she knew that she had not yet met Cho-jen, for all the talk in class. He had kept his strange brilliance shielded. It had been a remote and delicate fencing between them. She did not think it was just because she was a woman.

Cho-jen was studying her again, with that cool impersonality that had no tinge of insolence. She cleared her throat.

"All right, boys, it's time for our reading," she said. "Tao-min, will you gather the papers and bring them to me, please?"

The reading went well at first. The rule was that a boy who wanted a phrase explained held up his hand and the boy who was reading paused. Shirley told them she thought *"non mi ricordo"* was "I do not remember" in Italian, but she was not sure. Monongahela and Bourbon were kinds of whisky, but she had never tasted either. When Cho-jen began reading, Fu-liang held up his hand. Cho-jen read on. Fu-liang shook his hand. His gaze appealed to Shirley.

"Please, Cho-jen," she was forced to say.

Cho-jen stopped, looking annoyed.

"Break on wheel?" Fu-liang asked.

He was a tall, pale, literal-minded boy. Shirley explained what little she knew about breaking people on the wheel.

"Do you in America—did President Jefferson break them on the wheel?"

"Oh no, Fu-liang! It is metaphor again, with irony," she said.

"Look down the page—Cho-jen has already read it—'The big flies escaped.' That is metaphor too. It means the important people, the leaders of the plot, were not punished at all."

Fu-liang nodded. They all understood metaphor now, but often they found the associations very strange.

"Please go on, Cho-jen."

Cho-jen picked up in mid-sentence just where he had paused. ". . . when the president of the court asked him at the close whether he wished to say anything to show that he had always been faithful to the United States, he cried out, in a fit of frenzy, 'Damn the United States! I wish I may never hear of the United States again!' "

Cho-jen cried it out too, his face suddenly twisting and his hand slamming down the book. The other boys looked shocked and frightened. Shirley felt a thrill of fear. The room was very still.

"Reading that makes me a bad feeling, that I do not like, in my stomach and my back," Cho-jen said evenly. "When I read the end, I wanted to cry. I do not wish to cry about a stupid man. What kind of story is this to teach to Chinese boys?"

"It is just to help you learn English, and about America."

He stared coldly. He was not answered.

"It is really a simple story, for children in America," she said. "They are the best stories to help learn a new language. I am trying to learn Chinese. Mr. Lin has me reading such a story, the story of Mo-lan."

"Yes, it is such a story," Cho-jen agreed. "But everyone has a father."

Shirley could say nothing. She knew Cho-jen was launching his attack. He stared bleakly.

"The story says this man was least guilty of all in the plot," he said. "Even the leaders were not punished for the plot. This man was punished *only* for the words he spoke."

"Yes."

"Afterward he repented, truly, from the bottom of his heart."

"Yes."

"He did good works. He risked his life. He fought bravely in a victorious sea battle."

"Yes."

"Everyone pitied him. Powerful people tried to have him pardoned. They could not. No human agency could get him pardoned."

"I'm not so sure—" Shirley leafed rapidly through her copy. "I would like to read it again, before we discuss the whole story," she said. "You know, Cho-jen, the others have not read it all."

"Would you say he could not be forgiven, in this world or the next? Does not the story say that?"

"I don't know, Cho-jen. You must let me read it again."

She shrank from the fierce intensity in the boy's face. He was like a swordsman poised for a lunge, merciless. She had never imagined he could look so.

"The man was shut out of heaven. He was in hell. I have talked to Mr. Gillespie about your hell. He told me the fire is metaphor for agony of spirit. Do you agree the story says the man was in hell?"

"I can't say yes or no, Cho-jen," Shirley pleaded. "I never thought of the story that way. You must give me time to read it again." His fierce gaze did not soften. "If you will wait after class, you can show me the places and I will read them and tell you what I think," she said. "I am not afraid. I will be perfectly honest."

"I will wait until after class."

He took no further part in classwork. Shirley's mind raced, as she went on with the lesson. Cho-jen studied her impersonally, waiting. She felt as if huge old China had suddenly opened two of his many-millioned eyes and fixed them upon her.

The students filed out. Cho-jen came toward her table. She stood.

"Let's both sit nearer the fire," she said. "I've been very cold here."

She sat in Tao-min's place, beside Cho-jen. He was poised to begin. She forestalled him.

"Remember the story was written during the Civil War," she said. "People's loyalties were divided. They were confused. It was terribly important then to stress national loyalty."

"Why?" He looked up at the map. "What if someone on the other side had said 'Damn Texas!' Would that have been a sin?"

"The Texans would have thought it very wrong."

"Damn Mexico?"

"Mexico was a different country."

"Here. Look." He opened his book to the introduction. "Here he speaks of Jesus praying for all men to become One. Now here—" he turned the page— "he says you are making that happen. You have made all the Indians One. In your Civil War—does he mean that it is bad to make several nations out of one, but good to make one nation out of several?"

"Let me read it." She read it slowly. "Yes, I think he means that," she said.

"The United States and Mexico?"

"Oh no. Mexico is a separate country. They speak a different language."

"Then Canada?"

"It belongs to England."

"Why was it not a sin for the United States to separate from England?"

"The English thought it was. But we wanted freedom."

"Did not Texas and Alabama want freedom?"

"They said so."

"What *is* freedom? Who is judge of what is freedom?"

"Cho-jen." She put her hand on his arm. "I don't know. No one knows. Those are matters of opinion. No one knows the truth." For the first time his eyes softened, but not much. "Whatever I might say would only be my opinion," she said. "It would be no better than your opinion. Would you ask Tao-min such questions?" He shook his head. "Then why do you ask me?" she said.

"Because you are a teacher."

"You are more teacher than I in this class," she said. "I teach only English grammar. And literature."

"This is literature." He flipped pages. They were heavily marked. He must have studied it line by line. "Here," he said. "Read that."

She read the underlined passage aloud. "In that war it is time again for young men and women, and old men and women, for all sorts of people, to understand that the Country is in itself an entity.

It is a Being. The Lord God of nations has called it into existence, and has placed it here with certain duties in defence of the civilization of the world."

"In your opinion, is the United States a Being?" he asked.

"It is a personalized abstraction. It is only a poetic figure of speech," she said. "Remember, we studied that. Remember, 'When Freedom from her mountain height,' and so on?"

"Is the Lord God of nations a personalized abstraction?"

She felt herself pale. She kept her eyes steadily on his.

"I don't like to think so. But I don't know."

He closed the book. He seemed suddenly satisfied. The poised-hawk glitter was gone from his eyes. He looked more boyish than she had ever seen him.

"You are like Mr. Gillespie," he said. "He is honest, too."

She let the implication pass in silence. Cho-jen was staring at the flying snowflakes. His eyes pursued some dream in their white dancing. His delicate features were smooth and relaxed and his lips parted. He looked very young, a frail vehicle for the genius striving to feed and form itself. She yearned to help him to his full and just magnificence of stature.

"You are right. It is not a good story to teach Chinese boys," she said.

"Mr. Mills chose it. I know," he said. "Mr. Mills is stupid. He knows mathematics only by rote, the way he makes us learn poetry. He wants us to learn mathematics that way."

"I don't approve of learning even poetry only that way."

He turned his face from the window to face her smile. He gave her a quick, mischievous, sharing smile.

"Let's not do it, then."

"But after all, Mr. Mills—"

"I'll tell you a secret. Many students at China Light are secret members of the Kuomintang," he said. "I am one. If General Pan knew, he would send soldiers to kill us."

"Oh, Cho-jen! Surely not!"

"He would. If Mr. Mills knew, he would tell General Pan."

"I'm sure he wouldn't. But I won't say anything." She felt frightened. "If you're right, you shouldn't tell me such things."

"You are good. All the boys want to love you." A sparkling, elfish look was growing on his face. "We have groups in both schools in Paoshan, too. I am the leader of all of them. Wang carries messages for me."

His restlessness overcame him. He stood up and walked to the window and back. She watched him, smiling fondly. She knew it was boyish showing off. She did not know how much of it to believe.

"I want to make a student strike this winter," he said. "I think I will make it about the poetry." He was tugging at his scarf. "Do not fear Mr. Mills, Miss Eckert. Perhaps I will make him go away and demand that you be principal."

"Oh no! I couldn't possibly."

"You could. Mr. Mills is stupid."

"Many good people are going to seem stupid to you, Cho-jen. You are a rather special person."

"I know I am," he said seriously. "But you are not stupid."

"What is the Kuomintang?" she asked.

His face lighted. "It is the People's Nation Party," he said. "We have secret student groups everywhere in China. Soon we will make China into a Being, too. We will sweep away all the warlords." He paced again. He could hardly contain the excitement the thought roused in him. "We will send away all the foreign gunboats and soldiers. We will make the same kind of laws against Americans that America makes against Chinese. We will send away all the criminal and stupid and greedy Americans."

"I wish you luck. I hope you can do it, Cho-jen."

He put his foot up on a chair and rested his arms on his knee. "You must stay and help us, Miss Eckert. We make plans at night. We want to make all the big American staff houses into a girls' school, so our sisters can be educated too. We have begun to think of you doing that for us." His smile was serious now, but unreservedly warm and friendly. She felt strongly the foreshadowing of his inborn power to command the spirits of other persons. "We will protect you," he said. "From Mr. Mills and from Mr. Craddock too. Many of the Chinese staff are with us in secret. We are already more powerful than you would believe."

"I believe." She could not help believing. "I want to stay and help," she said.

"I must go. I am very busy."

He picked up his books. He was all a boy again, careless and happy. He went out the door, smiling back at her and raising his hand. On boyish impulse . . . or was it the calculation of genius . . . he had spilled his treasure of secrets out before her and she knew she was bound to absolute secrecy. She could not even mention it to Mr. Gillespie. Cho-jen was more than just a boy. He would not fit any ready-made category. He left her feeling somewhat as if huge old China had regarded her gravely and found her good.

She knew she was going to treasure that feeling.

19

The Sand Pebbles thought Burgoyne was crazy because he had not collected his purchased due from Maily. When they learned that he intended to marry her, they knew that he was crazy. It was the sole topic at their forum around the mess table for a whole week. Burgoyne took all the joking with his customary mild good humor.

"It's like a time's come for me. A bell struck," he said once. "I got to do it. That's all."

"Frenchy's in love," Farren said.

"He's kept it in his pants too long and his brain's addled," Harris said. He turned to Burgoyne. "Plug her a couple of times and you'll be all right," he told him.

"Sam, what does a crude bastard like you know about love?" Wilsey asked.

Harris bristled. "I know all about love. Love is just a mental hard-on," he said. "Any old whore can cure it for you."

"No joking, Frenchy, why don't you just shack up?" Farren said. "You know they ain't going to change a United States law just for you."

"I want a preacher to say the words over us," Burgoyne said.

None of the Changsha missionaries would say the words. They all wanted a paper from the consulate or the ship granting civil or military permission. That was against the Asiatic Exclusion Act, and Burgoyne could not get permission. The fight over Maily was a scandal all over Changsha. The missionaries knew about Maily.

"They all figure Maily's a whore, and they treat me like I wasn't no better," Burgoyne told Holman.

It was old custom for missionaries to despise sailors. The navy would not let an enlisted man marry until he was a second-class petty officer, and by then he was supposed to be seasoned enough to know better. If he didn't, he had better not expect any official favors just because he had a wife. Good sailors were supposed to make do with whores. That was one reason the missionaries despised them. But most sailors considered that the navy was protecting them.

Burgoyne's troubles revived the argument as to whether or not Lynch was really married. The Sand Pebbles did not think so. Just saying the words over a couple did not make them married, not *Russian* words, anyway, such as were said over Lynch. There was some doubt about English words.

"Well, what is it makes you really married?" Holman demanded.

Nobody could say. Then Restorff cleared his throat. "I think you ain't really married unless the woman can have you put in jail if you don't give her money," he said.

"Gunner, you're the only sensible man at this table!" Farren said.

Burgoyne wanted the words said over them anyway. The missionaries would not say plainly that they were forbidden to say the words without a license, Burgoyne told Holman, but they acted as if that were so.

"There's one guy out south of town said he wanted to think it over, pray on it, he told me," Burgoyne said. "I'm going out there this afternoon. He's my last chance."

"I'd like to go with you," Holman said.

The Reverend Mr. Partridge talked to Holman and Burgoyne in a small room with a rag rug and a sign on the wall stating that God was Love. He made them sit in rocking chairs while he paced up and down and explained that his conscience would not let him perform the ceremony without civil permission. He was a kindly, pink-faced man with a clipped gray mustache and a gray coat. Burgoyne looked defeated. Holman spoke up.

"Would you get in trouble if you did it anyway?"

"Yes. With my conscience. I've explained that."

"I mean with American law."

"I don't think so."

"I want to understand something," Holman said. "Can I ask you some questions?"

"Please do." Mr. Partridge went on guard.

"All right." Holman leaned forward. "If you did speak the words, would that make them really married?"

"In the eyes of God, yes."

"Suppose they were going to live together anyway. How would that be, in the eyes of God?"

Mr. Partridge paced with tightening lips and thought about that. Then he stopped, hands clasped behind him and bouncing slightly on his toes.

"It would be breaking the Seventh Commandment," he said. "But to enter into a vowed marriage knowing that it cannot endure and be fruitful is to make a false personal pledge before God, and that is a greater sin." He pursed his lips. "Now that I think of it, I am not at all sure such a marriage would be valid in the eyes of God, Who knows all the secrets of men's hearts."

His posture and manner irritated Holman. "Suppose Frenchy and the girl believed in their hearts, as deep as even God can see, that they would stay married till they died," he said. "Would it be a greater sin then? If you did say the words?"

"Yes, and I would share it!" His voice was sharp. "Because I would know! And your friend knows too, because I've explained to him."

Burgoyne stirred. "Nothing you told me makes any difference," he said. "I'm going to retire and live in China like lots of other sailors do. I want to be married to my woman is all."

"I see it's no use explaining."

"Can I pin just one thing down, Mr. Partridge?" Holman said. "What is it really makes you married, God or American law? What if they disagree?"

Mr. Partridge was trying very hard to continue looking kindly. "If you are honestly interested, I will be glad to instruct you," he said. "But you would have to start with simple things." He tried another smile. "We must all learn to walk before we run, mustn't we?"

Holman hid his anger. "Please tell me the answer like you would if I was ready to understand," he said. "If I don't, I don't. We'll shove off. But please let me try."

"All right." Mr. Partridge paced again, throwing out short sentences. "Marriage is not an indulgence. It is a sacred privilege. Yes, and responsibility. There is something called moral fitness and readiness for marriage. Marriage and the rearing of lawful children. Part of it is a sober regard for the opinions of one's fellow countrymen. That, and a willingness to obey the laws they make to govern themselves." He stopped and rocked on his toes. "Is that clear to you?"

"Just like crystal!" Holman stood up and tugged Burgoyne to his feet. "So Congress outranks God," he told Mr. Partridge. "Thanks for the dope."

"Here now, let's not have any mockery or blasphemy under this roof!"

Holman laughed into the red, angry face. "If I was you, Partridge, I'd get out of the God business and go run for Congress," he said. "Come on, Frenchy."

The Reverend Mr. Partridge slammed his door very emphatically at their heels.

They stopped in the bar of the small hotel outside the south gate and ordered whisky. They were alone in the place.

"He just rubbed me the wrong way," Holman said. "One of them fat, pink, kindly important bastards that run the world and heaven and hell to boot. He reminds me of somebody. Bronson?" He drained his glass and beckoned the bar boy. "Who ever gave them bastards charge of the world?"

"God did, I guess," Burgoyne said. "Jake, I was just thinking how-come I first joined the navy. It was to get away from a little old gal back in Carolina that claimed I knocked her up. Maybe I did, but there was twenty other boys had their crack at it too. She was a real whore, and they was going to *make* me marry her."

"That's how the sons of bitches work," Holman said. "It was a judge put me in the navy. It was that, or else reform school."

"What'd they have you for?"

"Beating up—say! Now I know who Partridge reminds me of!"

Holman sketched out the story. A boy had brought a bottle of whisky to a class wiener roast and some of them got drunk and in-sulted girls and fought. Holman had been expelled for it. He had gone to the principal's office and begged for another chance.

"School was the first thing I ever had to lose," he told Burgoyne. "That principal—Partridge reminds me of him. The kids called him Garbage Tin."

Garbage Tin had plainly enjoyed making him grovel. It was a nasty, squirmish thing. Then Garbage Tin had promised to cancel the expulsion if Holman would sign a paper saying how sorry he was that he had brought the whisky to the party. He had not brought it, but he couldn't rat on the boy who had, and he finally signed the paper for the sake of getting back in school. The next day he found that he was still expelled. Garbage Tin said he had only promised to reconsider his decision, and he had done that, and it was still the same decision. Holman did not have anything left to lose. He had gone at Garbage Tin like a wildcat and driven him under a desk.

"Didn't you have any kin to stand up for you?"

"Only my mother," Holman said. "She didn't count for much in that town. She did housework by the hour and took in washing."

"That's nigger-woman work in Carolina."

"The kid that brought the whisky was Bill Mason. He was the judge's son."

"They had to save his face so he could be a judge someday," Bur-goyne said. "Well, that's how the sons of bitches work, all right. Well, I guess you don't have to love 'em for it."

"They expect you to," Holman said. "They think they're the most loving and lovable bastards alive."

The two men drank in moody silence. Holman was thinking.

"Frenchy, why not have a Chinese priest marry you?" he said. "They got all kinds of gods."

"I never thought." Burgoyne tugged his mustache. "I wonder . . ."

"There's one they call Kwan Yin. I like her statues," Holman said. "I tell you, let's ask Po-han about it when he comes home."

"Let's do that!"

They bought bottled beer on the way. The day was cold and early dark. They met Po-han in the street, just coming home. The women were all in Maily's room putting up wallpaper. The men helped finish the job by lamplight, while the children laughed and played with scraps of paper. The paper was a silvery gray with a wide-spaced pattern of green leaves and red berries and they all thought it looked very good. Then Po-han's women went home, taking the children and their lamps.

"Sit down, Po-han. Have a beer," Burgoyne said.

"I'm all smeared," Maily said. "Excuse me while I wash my hands and change clothes." She had on a plain blue coolie outfit.

"No. Sit here beside me, on the chest."

Burgoyne shifted to make room and pulled her down beside him. The room seemed dim and shadowy with Maily's one little lamp. They all sat at the table and drank beer and Burgoyne asked Po-han about getting married in a Chinese temple. The talk seemed to embarrass Po-han. He said Chinese did not get married in temples. He did not think Burgoyne and Maily could be married the Chinese way.

"He's right, Frenchy," Maily said. "It just isn't meant to be."

"Well, how *do* Chinese people get married?" Holman asked.

With Maily's help, Po-han tried to explain. Burgoyne had his head in his hands and did not seem to be listening. Neither gods nor law had much to do with a Chinese marriage, Holman gathered. You worried about stars and lucky days and there were special presents and ceremonies between the families, and the ancestors on both sides came into it too. Po-han seemed to think you could not be married unless you had a family to do the special things.

"What I want to know is what *does* it?" Holman said. "What's the precise second you change from being single to being married?"

"It doesn't happen in any precise second," Maily said.

"Then there'd have to be a time when you was a quarter-married or half-married, and that don't make sense," Holman objected. "I mean, what's the point of no return? Like when you hold up your hand and swear, when you join the navy."

Maily had to confer with Po-han in Chinese. The idea was new to both of them. Po-han's broad, honest face wrestled with the thought the way it did with a new engineering idea. You could leave any part of it out and you would still be married, Po-han said. What you left out just made it less lucky for both families, and you needed all the luck you could get when you were married. He finally got the idea through to Holman. It was like grafting between fruit trees. They cut the girl off from her own family and grafted her onto her husband's family. But you could not graft one loose twig to another loose twig. Po-han was delighted with Holman's final comprehension.

"So mus' have olo mama, olo papa, too much all fashion people belong he." Po-han grasped in widely with his arms.

It saddened Holman. "Well, I guess you really are whipped, Frenchy," he said soberly.

Burgoyne raised his head. "No, I ain't whipped," he said. "I been studying out what it means while you was arguing. Marrying is mixing two lives together, like creeks joining up."

Holman did not expect that kind of talk from Frenchy Burgoyne. "Can you mix people's lives like running water?" he asked.

"You run between high banks, Jake. Maily and me don't. The time's come for us."

He had a light in his gaunt face and his voice and manner were strangely solemn. They were all a bit afraid of him. He pulled the concealing handkerchief from Maily's left hand and folded both her hands between his own large, hairy hands on the table top. He looked down at her.

"We're mixing our lives together, Maily. We'll never be able to unmix them again, and we'll never want to." His voice was strong but tender, and he was smiling down at her. "I take you for what you are and all that you are and mix you with all of me and I don't hold back nothing. Nothing! When you're cold and hungry and afraid, so am I. When you're happy, so am I. I'm going to stay with you all I can and take the very best care of you I can and love you every minute until I die." He took a deep, slow breath. "Now you say it."

"I will always love and honor and serve you, Frenchy, and stay as near to you as I can, and do everything I can for you, and live for you, and I won't have any life except our life together. . . ." Tears welled out of her eyes but she smiled steadily up without blinking. "I will just love you, Frenchy, all of me there is just loving you forever."

Burgoyne bent his head. They kissed. Holman looked at Po-han. Po-han looked awe-struck.

"Now we're married," Burgoyne said. "You guys want to each put one hand on top of ours? For luck?"

Holman and Po-han stood up and did so. "I hope you have luck," Holman said. "I hope it goes smooth and easy for you."

He looked at Po-han and they both went out silently into the courtyard and closed the door behind them. They looked at each other again in the darkness. They both knew something terribly important had just happened in there.

"I burn joss stick," Po-han said.

"Yes," Holman said. "I wish I knew something to do."

He walked back to the ship alone in the cold, quiet night. The last time along those streets Burgoyne had been with him. He felt sad and alone and it was a feeling he knew well but seldom as strongly as he felt it now. He crossed the bund and saw the ship bulking darkly out on the dark water. Light glowed warm at its windows and he knew it was warm and dry inside the ship. The men on duty were there. He did not want to go back to the ship. But he was barred from the Red Candle and there was no place else for him to go.

20

The Sand Pebbles considered that Burgoyne was just shacked up. He went to request mast and asked that Maily be named as his next-of-kin in his service record. When a man died, his next-of-kin got his personal effects and back pay and also a death gratuity equal to six months' pay. Both Bordelles and Lt. Collins told Burgoyne that he was not officially married and it was impossible.

"Can I just call her a friend, then?" Burgoyne asked.

"As long as you have any blood kin, you can't have a friend," Bordelles said.

Burgoyne's next-of-kin was an uncle. "He's a hell-shoutin' Baptist preacher and he thinks I'm dirt," Burgoyne told Holman. "I hope I never see him again."

The only official acknowledgment he could get of Maily's existence was a safe-conduct pass. These were primarily for the ship's coolies, to protect them from forced labor for warlord soldiers, but long ago a form had also been worked out for shack women. It was known that Lt. Collins did not approve of shacks, because in an emergency it was much easier to get the men aboard if they were all in the Red Candle, but he abided by the old custom. Red Dog made up the paper. Yen-ta put the Chinese writing down the left side and Red Dog typed the English crowded over on the right. The English text read:

The bearer, Maily Burgoyne, is employed in the household of Francis Marion Burgoyne, WT 1/c, United States Navy, serving in U.S.S. *San Pablo.* Any unwarranted interference with bearer, when busied upon her lawful occasions, will be considered the indirect harassment and annoyance of a United States Citizen within the meaning of the treaties governing relations between the United States of America and the Republic of China and will be dealt with accordingly.

All the passes had a colored U.S. flag on gummed paper pasted at the top and Lt. Collins' signature with the ship's seal over it at the bottom. They were mainly looksee pidgin, meant to impress ignorant warlord soldiers. Red Dog made a special addition to Maily's pass. At the bottom he typed in: "This woman is married to the favorite nephew of Calvin Coolidge, Supreme Warlord of the United States of America. For every finger that touches her, one thousand heads must roll. Tremble and Obey!" He signed underneath in great, leaping letters, "Red Dog Shanahan," and sealed red wax over a twist of red ribbon. With a pair of scissors he delicately forked the ends of the ribbon.

"There! That's my wedding present to you and Maily," he told Burgoyne.

Maily laughed when she saw it. "Our marriage certificate," she told Burgoyne. She could not have a wedding ring, because she had no finger for it. She was very happy in those first days and she would lean up against Burgoyne and look at him in a way no woman had ever looked at Jake Holman.

Holman made all his liberties in Po-han's courtyard, because he was barred from the Red Candle. He would bring candy for the children and they learned to climb over him and search his pockets for it. He became acquainted with the three tenant families across the courtyard and the children from that side would search him for candy too. All the children called him *Uncajehk,* for *Uncle Jake.* Little Su-li remained his favorite, and she knew it. She was a princess, when Uncajehk came visiting.

With Po-han's help Holman worked out a wedding present. They had the dry pond under the single tree cleaned out and Holman contracted with one of the tenants, a water coolie, to keep it filled. Then he bought the two most expensive goldfish he could find in Changsha, graceful black ones with long, lacy fins, and put them in the pool. It was only about four feet across and two feet deep, with a border of rough, natural rocks. Maily was delighted with the fish.

The tree in the courtyard began to leaf out in delicate yellow-green. When it was not raining, they would put a table and chairs under it and drink beer there. They did not get drunk and yet, to Holman, there was a drunken, happy feeling about just being there. The goldfish learned to come when Maily trilled at them. She would kneel, dimpling the water with a piece of rice cake, and the fish would nibble at it. She was very pretty kneeling by the rough rocks and when the fish curved their bodies gracefully in sunlight they were purplish-red on the curves.

Holman bought cheaper, golden goldfish, one for each child, and the children clustered around the pool to watch them. One time Su-li fell in and Mei-yu and Po-han's mother chattered and fussed. They always had a smile and a bow for Jake Holman, however, and he was happy there. He considered the pool was really his present to the whole courtyard, because he was so happy with them. It was something very new in his life. The tree kept leafing out and the flower buds on it were swelling.

"Pretty soon it'll be time to start the summer cruising," Burgoyne said one evening. "Jake, I wish I didn't have to go."

Unexpectedly, in March, Changsha got a new warlord. There was some shooting in the hills south of town, to save face, but General Chao was outgunned and he knew it, so he took a bribe and pulled out peacefully. That was called fighting with silver bullets, and most warlord battles were fought that way. Everyone knew that Chinese soldiers couldn't really fight. At the mess table they talked about the last time a rival warlord had challenged General Chao, two years earlier. His men had trenches on the sand flats across the river and they wanted to cross over to Changsha. For weeks they potshot at Chao's positions on the big sandbar while the Sand Pebbles guarded the big treaty houses, which were also on the big sandbar. Then one day the attacking soldiers just got up and walked across the sand into Chao's machine guns. They went down in heaps and windrows and in a few minutes the challenging warlord no longer had an army.

"That wasn't fighting, that was just being crazy," Farren said.

"Well, weren't Chao's men fighting?" Holman said.

"They didn't know what else to do."

Lt. Collins stopped liberty for several days during the change-over. The city was all shuttered up and the bund almost clear of coolies. A warlord change-over was always a time of looting and killing. The *San Pablo* coolies either stayed aboard or ashore inside their homes, because their safe-conduct passes were not much good at those times. Burgoyne had to stay aboard and Po-han stayed home in the courtyard. Holman and Burgoyne worried about them, but there was nothing that they could do.

There was very little looting. Chao's men had to get out too fast, and the new men did not loot, which was almost unheard-of. They wore tan instead of gray uniforms and their general was named Tang. The gunboat captains and the consuls all exchanged calls with him and the city unshuttered itself and Lt. Collins granted liberty again. Everyone said it was a very peaceful change-over.

Everything was all right in the courtyard. Po-han had pasted paper American flags above all the doors on his side of the courtyard. On the other side they still had tigers above their doors. Po-han said everybody thought the new warlord was better than the old one.

"New sojah man, any time he takee, he pay," Po-han said.

Life in the courtyard was even better and happier than before. Holman made up a new game for the children one day, when Ah Pao dropped a fragment of rice cake in the pool and the goldfish began to nuzzle at it, pushing it this way and that. He laid goal threads floating on the water on either side of the pool. When the fragment bumped a thread, it was a score for that side of the courtyard. Each child knew his own goldfish and they screamed with excitement when their fish were pushing the wrong way. All the grownups came out to watch the children and the bright little fish and to laugh at the game. Po-han bet with the water coolie. Su-li's fish scored the first goal for her side, and she was almost frantic with joy.

"The children love you, Jake," Maily said. "They'll miss you when you go cruising."

Maily's two black ones did not join in the game. They were aristocrats and would only eat from her fingers. They knew her by sight now, and she did not have to trill at them any more.

Spring was all over both banks of the river in a yellow-green mist of new leaves and spotty patches of pink and white flowers on the mountain. When the wind was right, it smelled of flowers. The warming weather raised nasty smells and swarms of flies from the winter's garbage along the foot of the embankment. Then one morning the river was suddenly rising as they watched it, rolling powerfully muddy brown with yellow foam on top, eating away the sandbars and the piles of rubbish. Now and then a junk along the bank would carry away its moorings and go careening downriver while all hands aboard it yelled and screamed and tried to get it back to the bank. Pappy Tung had to keep veering out more chain as the water rose. The anchor dragged and Holman and Po-han warmed up the main engine and steamed ahead slowly, just enough to ease the strain. The engine worked beautifully. The smell and sight of the steaming engine room excited Holman. He had almost forgotten about the engine.

In a few days the water dropped again, almost as low as before, but the river bed was clean with fresh white sand. It had been what the Sand Pebbles called the false flood, the Siang's personal flood, which all ran away in a few days into Tungting Lake and hardly wet the bottom. The real flood would come later, when the mighty Yangtze flooded and backed up into Tungting Lake. The false flood was a signal to get coal and stores aboard and prepare for summer cruising. The ship came alert. There were more drills, and military tension picked up noticeably.

General Tang was much easier on the students than General Chao had been. They held more parades along the bund, with more life and spirit in them. Buglers always headed the parades, sounding reveille over and over, very off-key and squawky. The students, cued by section leaders, shouted slogans in unison, like cheering sections at a football game. They had thin, screechy voices, even for Chinese, because they were so young. They were bolder with their signs. Some read: DOWN WITH IMPERIALISM! and CANCEL UNEQUAL TREATIES! The Sand Pebbles laughed at one placard which read: GUNBOATS, GO HOME! For more than twenty years Changsha had been official home port for the U.S.S. *San Pablo*. The Sand Pebbles considered that they were home.

The student parading and street corner speeches inside the city made many people nervous. The students were harmless, but they could get a mob of coolies all worked up, and that was how riots got started. It made an uneasy feeling among all the treaty people. General Chao had known how to keep the lid on things, they said. He was an old, experienced warlord. The oldest hands among the Sand Pebbles were not perturbed.

"This Tang bastard won't last long," Restorff said sagely.

Tang lasted hardly a month. He went as quietly as he had come, early in April, just before the true flood. General Chao had gotten more troops from General Wu, who owned Hankow, and the word was that Wu was going to get a cut of the Changsha squeeze money. The Wu men were very rough. Fires glowed ashore at night and there were shots and screaming most of the night. Po-han stayed home and Burgoyne had to stay aboard again. On the second day of the looting Bordelles' section of the landing force went ashore to stand by the U.S. Consulate on the bund. Wu's men were not anti-foreign, but when warlord soldiers got drunk on loot and blood and helpless women they were liable to do anything. There was a lot of blood. They held head choppings every day on the bund and threw the bodies over the embankment, to lie where the garbage heaps had been.

The worst was over by the fourth day. That morning Bordelles got a trouble call from a mission school inside the city. Warlord troops were trying to billet themselves in the school, which was full of woman refugees from the looting and raping. Bordelles led his section in to throw the soldiers out.

It looked bad inside the walls. No one was on the streets except soldiers in baggy, dirty gray uniforms and a few coolies hauling loads under guard. The shop fronts were all shuttered with vertical planks and most of them had holes broken through. The Sand Pebbles passed a number of headless bodies, with blood and flies clotted black on the flagstones.

"They been having themselves quite a time," Crosley commented.

They passed one execution team. The officer was young and neatly dressed and he carried the red-and-yellow paddle that meant he had the power of instant life and death. The executioner walked just behind him, in a red hat and red sash, with the big shiny chopping sword on his shoulder. The sword had a long red tassel on its handle. A squad of riflemen in fairly good formation brought up the rear. They came straight down the middle of the street, the young officer proud and haughty and not seeing the Sand Pebbles. Involuntarily, the sailors made way.

"Jesus Christ, there goes death walking!" Farren said.

About thirty soldiers were milling around in the courtyard of the mission school. The missionary was a fluttery little man with rimless glasses. He was sweating and arguing in Chinese with the soldiers. They were grumbling and beating their rifle butts on the stones but, when they saw the Sand Pebbles, they became quiet. The missionary came over.

"Please just wait a bit, Mr. Bordelles," he said. "I'm about to convince them that their billeting order is for the native school over in the next block."

"Which one is their officer?"

"They don't seem to have one."

The missionary hurried back to argue some more. Bordelles winked at Red Dog and turned his back to study some shrubbery. Red Dog held his riot gun at port and went behind the gray soldiers and began kicking them. When they turned, he shoved the gun broadside at their faces and said, "Arf! Arf! Arf!" They didn't know what to make of it. Red Dog was herding them toward the gate. It worried Holman.

"Stand easy," Farren told him, laughing. "If you take 'em serious they're liable to take themselves serious, and that's the only time you have trouble."

"Here now! Stop that!" the missionary told Red Dog, fluttering hands at him.

"Arf! Arf! Arf!" Red Dog said cheerfully.

He tried to sidle behind the missionary, who kept turning to protect his rear. Some of the gray soldiers began laughing. Red Dog got behind the missionary and landed a gentle kick. All the warlord soldiers began laughing and going out the gate. The missionary was very indignant. He complained to Bordelles, who was still admiring the shrubbery.

"It was the best way to handle it, Mr. Ingram," Bordelles soothed him. "It's a joke to them now. They won't bear you any resentment."

Outside in the street again, Holman asked Bordelles a favor. "We're not too far from where Frenchy Burgoyne's woman lives," he said. "Could we just stop by there and see if she's all right?"

Bordelles said yes. He wanted to look around anyway, to make a report on the state of the city. They went out the north gate. Po-han's district was a poor one and it was not very torn up. There were no bodies in the streets, but soldiers roamed there and many gates were broken open. Po-han's gate was broken open. Only Po-han and Maily came out to talk to them. Maily was pale and thin in ragged, stinking Chinese clothes. Soldiers had come in three times, Po-han said, but he had scared them off with his and Maily's safe-conduct passes. He was quite cheerful. He thought this visit of armed sailors in uniform would make him plenty of face and he would not have any more trouble with the soldiers.

Holman talked privately with Maily. She insisted that she was all right and not afraid any more. Soldiers had done bad things in the courtyards on either side of them, and they had had to listen to it, but she thought the worst was over now. She asked them to wait while she wrote a short note for Burgoyne.

"I'll take that and deliver it," Red Dog said. He was the *San Pablo* mail clerk. "I don't remember old Frenchy ever getting a letter before."

Very few of the Sand Pebbles ever got letters.

Changsha settled down quite rapidly. General Chao had just been teaching them a lesson. When he called the soldiers off, they did not want to stop, and the last several days all the heads lopped off on the bund were soldiers' heads. A few shops opened and farmers began bringing in stuff to the markets. For a few days Duckbutt Randall went ashore with Big Chew to buy chow and then it was safe for Big Chew to go alone. Lt. Collins started liberty. Holman went ashore with Burgoyne and very shortly it seemed just the same as ever in Po-han's courtyard. Po-han had gained much face in the neighborhood and his tenants across the courtyard had pasted paper flags over the tigers above their doors.

The true flood came quietly in the night. It was a slow, steady rise of water with lazy back eddies and an actual slackening of current, but it covered and carried away the stinking corpses along the foot of the embankment. It was Yangtze floodwater from melting snow on the great mountains of Tibet, backing up the Siang and filling Tungting Lake for the summer. Silently, hour after hour, day and night, the broadening brown river swallowed sandbars and crept up the stone embankment fronting the city until the chanting water coolies had only a few steps to climb with their slopping pairs of tins.

The gunboats did not start their summer show-the-flag cruising until it was certain that Changsha had settled down. They were very busy getting ready aboard the *San Pablo*. Pappy Tung and his coolies were painting the blocky topside a fresh, gleaming white. Ping-wen and his coolies were up in bosun's chairs tarring the stack guys and painting the tall black stack. They shined the brass siren and the great, hoarse whistle to sun-winking radiance. Everything was ready in the engine room. Then Holman was shocked to learn that Po-han did not want to make the cruise. He told Holman, with considerable embarrassment, that he could live on his rents from the courtyard and he wanted to stay home and take it easy.

"Well, damn it! Well, *hell,* Po-han!" Holman said.

He felt betrayed and disappointed and more nearly angry at Po-han than he had ever been. Po-han was ashamed. Holman talked earnestly to him, recalling their work on the engine and how the summer cruise was going to be the payoff, and Po-han changed his mind. As soon as he did, he was very cheerful and happy about it.

The weather warmed suddenly and the uniform changed to whites. A few students tried to parade and General Chao arrested all of them. The soldiers whipped the boys with bamboos. They stripped the girls and led them naked around a barracks square, to shame them, but they did not kill or rape. The Chinese were strongly against killing students. That was the mistake the British had made in Shanghai the year before.

Everyone said that, with a really big warlord like Wu behind him, Chao was safely settled in Changsha. H.M.S. *Woodcock* and the Japanese gunboat sailed. The *San Pablo* was to sail on Monday. Holman spent Sunday afternoon and evening in the courtyard. That morning Po-han and Burgoyne had gone to a temple to burn joss sticks for luck on the cruise. Maily had been shocked.

"I figure Chinese good luck is as good as any other kind," Burgoyne said. He leaned forward and tousled Maily's hair. She smiled at him.

"It's the best kind, in China," Holman said. "I wish I'd gone."

It was very fine sitting and drinking beer under the tree in the courtyard. Petals were falling from the tree's pink, trumpet-shaped flowers. They littered the fish pool and some of the graceful little fish nuzzled at them. The air was faintly perfumed. They were going to have a gala farewell supper brought in from a restaurant later on and all the children felt the holiday spirit. They ran and shouted and chased each other around the courtyard. Su-li tired sooner than the older children and she came and climbed into Holman's lap. She laid her cheek against his chest and traced her tiny finger around the blue eagle and chevrons on his white jumper sleeve. He felt a surge of warm feeling.

"You know, Frenchy, this is good," he said. "It's just . . . well, *good!*"

"I wish we didn't have to go cruising," Burgoyne said.

"Same me!" Po-han looked a bit defiantly at Holman.

"Well, I'm kind of anxious to see how the engine's going to hold up," Holman said. "Cruising's good, too."

They did not answer. Holman grinned at them.

"You home guards!" he said. "I'm the only honest-to-God sailor in the crowd. But I know how you feel."

He tugged Su-li's pigtail. The little girl looked around mischievously. She remembered how to get her laugh.

"Ding ding," she said. *"Ding hao!"*

21

From the start of the cruise there was no bearing trouble and all hands commented on the smoothness of the engine. To Holman's ears, however, it was still discordant. He and Po-han worked on it during their steaming watches while Burgoyne stood by the throttle. It was good, being all three together there with the engine and the memory of the courtyard in Changsha shared among them.

Holman had to teach Po-han about horsepower. For real smoothness, the power developed in each cylinder had to be equal. Power distribution was controlled by a screw adjustment that changed the position of the drag-link pins on the rock shaft, and you could link in or out while the engine was running. You were supposed to have indicators, which drew graphs of the changing pressures in the cylinders, as a guide to that. The *San Pablo* engine had never had any indicators. Holman had to make rough calculations of the correct receiver pressures and run the links in or out until he got them. When they began it, Po-han sprang a surprise. During the warlord change-overs in Changsha he had learned Arabic numerals from Maily, and all of the simple arithmetic she knew as well.

"She thinks Po-han's a natural-born genius," Burgoyne said.

He had been sharing the secret with Po-han. The pressure calculations took inverse proportion, and Po-han learned that in about fifteen minutes. But it was only monkey-see monkey-do with marks on paper, and he could not relate it to the engine. He looked beseechingly at the receiver pressure gauges, mounted three in a row on the board above the log desk, and shook his head in perplexity. Holman tapped the I.P. gauge. It read twenty pounds.

"Wanchee more horses, this side," he said. He tapped the L.P. gauge, showing seven pounds. "This side have got too many horses."

They went to the L.P. and he had Po-han ease out the L.P. link a fraction of an inch and they both felt the vibration smooth out a bit. Then, back at the log desk, Holman pointed to the twenty-five pounds on the I.P. and five on the L.P. and tried again to explain about the equal sharing out of horses. Po-han could not get it. It seemed to him that horses were pounds and the biggest cylinder should have the most pounds, not the fewest. He slapped his palms against his temples and his face twisted.

"Head no good, Jehk," he said. "Head no goddam good!"

"Hell, Po-han, I don't savvy it either," Burgoyne said, grinning. "That's only for special nuts about engines, like Jake."

"Steam do work, same horse," Holman said. "Little bit steam, same one horse. Plenty steam, same plenty horse."

"Steam *pushes,* like a mule against a collar," Burgoyne said. He pushed Po-han. "Steam *pushes* the ship."

Po-han was groping for a deeper understanding than Burgoyne had, Holman knew. Po-han could not rest on words. They went on with the fine adjustments, making them cut and try, judging with ears and fingertips, and they worked the last remnant of pulse and raggedness out of the engine vibration. Only they two knew they had done it; even to Burgoyne it seemed the same as before. All the while Po-han wrestled with horsepower.

He had the notion of heat energy, but he thought the horses died in the main condenser. He was stopped by the thingness of steam, Holman knew. He could not mix time up with thingness and pull out the notion of pure energy.

"Suppose one horse run very fast, he same two horse," was the best Holman could do to clarify that mystery.

Po-han's broad face was often an agony of fruitless concentration. He could take the readings on clock and counter and pressure gauge and he could count the horses as he might catties of rice. He knew and felt the power of that, but it was still monkey-see monkey-do with marks on paper, and it was not enough. It was already more than Perna or Wilsey could do, and they would have hated Po-han for learning that much, if they had known. There was not a drop of dog-in-the-manger envy in Burgoyne. He was as proud of Po-han as Holman was.

"Tell Po-han to give up. He's gonna bust," Burgoyne said.

"I'd give a year of my life if I could get it across to him," Holman said. He meant what he said.

"I swear, he'll bust his head wide open," Burgoyne prophesied.

Po-han's illumination came without warning. He was staring at the engine and he began bridling and jogging his elbows and prancing like a horse marking time.

"Whoa, there!" Burgoyne said, laughing.

"White hoss! Too much white hoss!" Po-han yelled.

Then he was off, galloping down the port side of the engine room and back again, unable to stop. "White hoss! White hoss!" he kept exclaiming. Burgoyne looked disturbed.

"What the hell, Jake?" he asked.

"He's all right. He's breaking through," Holman said.

He felt very good about it. It was not something that Burgoyne could understand. Po-han bent with his hands on the thrust block and kicked his heels aft like a frisky colt. "White hoss! White hoss!" Finally he calmed a bit and came back to the throttle platform. His face was shining.

"I sabby hosspowah, Jehk," he said solemnly.

Holman nodded. "You sabby, Po-han."

"I swear, I never seen it turn a guy into a horse before," Burgoyne said. "You sure you're all right, Po-han?"

Po-han wanted to talk about it. He was still so excited that his pidgin English poured out of him like unbroken horses and Burgoyne could scarcely follow. But Po-han had it, all right. He had the pure notion of energy, and his world would never be the same again.

The steam came aft through the main steam line like wild white horses. The throttle and the slide valves were gates and the horses ran invisibly down the connecting rods and out along the whitely spinning shaft. Only their pale ghosts went to the condenser. When there were too many horses in the boilers they kicked open the safety valves and charged off into the sky in a great, white, trumpeting host of horses. If the horses could not escape that way, they would kick the boiler apart and sink the ship.

"He beats hell, don't he?" Burgoyne marveled.

The most wonderful thing of all was that the horses could not die. They ran aft and kicked themselves free off the screw, and they became the motion of the ship and the turbulence of the wake, but they did not die.

"Nevah make finish!" Po-han said. "White hoss nevah die!"

"Never die," Holman confirmed.

Their eyes shared that knowledge and they loved each other in that moment. Burgoyne was left out of the deeper part of it. But there was not a scrap of jealousy in Frenchy Burgoyne. He was a rare, fine shipmate, Holman thought.

After that it was not the same on watch. There were tricks with tools that Holman could still teach Po-han, but otherwise he had taken Po-han as far as he could go himself. Once he saw Po-han with a lump of coal in his hand, staring at it. Po-han had the strained, aching look on his face. He was trying to understand how wild white horses could be locked up so cool and safely in a black stone. Jake Holman could not tell him. He had often looked at a lump of coal like that himself. "Coal burns" was no answer. It was just words. How did the wild white horses from the sun ever get into the coal? But it was still very good on watch. It was just pleasant, steady steaming.

Well, it was pleasant. They would stand on the throttle platform, Burgoyne chewing snuff and hanging leanly from an overhead valve wheel, and Holman standing erect and balanced on spread legs, in the way he had, and they would just be there. Over on the port side Po-han would be standing balanced and ready also, although he had never been on a sea-going ship that might roll and pitch him into the machinery, and he would have his eyes closed. He was listening.

It was the hushed rubbing sound of oil sliding through oil on a score of bearing surfaces. The slide valves and piston rings made a drier, muffled whispering. Steam blowing through ports and receivers roared hollowly far off, like a million hoofs drumming a distant prairie. The scores of valve gear bushings made a lisping, oil-muted chatter. All the sounds sang together. The quick, light throb of the circulator rustled cooling water through the condenser tubes like a woman walking in silk. The air pump plunged and all its bucket valves clanked shut and it rose straining and gasping to sluice the condensed steam to the hot well for the groaning feed pumps. Air wheezed out of the hot well vent with the wet smell of steam and the wet hay smell of oily loofa sponges, and it mixed with the burnt rubber smell of hot packing and hot swabbing oil. From the fireroom came the hiss and the sulfur smell of coal smoke and water on hot ashes, the scrape of shovels and the clang of fire doors, and the shrill voices of the stoker coolies calling each other lazy turtles. All the voices sang with the engine. And then, standing with eyes open, to stride with the rods and plunge with the crossheads and jog with the valve gear and catch the intricate play of light and shadow as the wild horses spun whitely aft into the dimness of the shaft alley. And to take in through feet and fingertips the same white horses, transmuted by screw thresh, spreading from the thrust block to join the slower, smoother engine vibration feeding down through the sole-plate chocks. To have knowing in their bones the same vibration that trembled water in glasses topside, and rattled loose windows, and worked rivets and stringers and frames minutely rubbing and creaking and whispering the old ship's secret life through all its structure, there knowing and controlling and almost being the source of the ship's life—that was how it was.

That was what they had that Frenchy Burgoyne could not share with them. Burgoyne liked to joke about it. He would blow the glass on one of the boilers. Steam would roar under the floorplates and feather up through the cracks.

"How many horses in the bilges, Po-han?"

"I tink one dog powah," Po-han would say scornfully.

They would all laugh. But Po-han shared with Burgoyne something in the memory of the courtyard in Changsha that Jake Holman could not fathom.

"If we was in Changsha, I'd be getting home about now," Burgoyne said one day. "If it was Saturday, I'd have all day tomorrow at home."

"You got it bad, Frenchy," Holman said.

"I got it bad, Jake. I don't care who knows it."

"What you like number one, Po-han?" Holman asked. "Stop homeside? Run engine?"

"I likee stop homeside!"

"That's the boy!" Burgoyne slapped Po-han's shoulder. "You and me both, Po-han!"

Po-han knew Holman's feelings were hurt. "Suppose have got home, any man mus' wanchee stop homeside," he tried to explain. He said a lot of other things and made sleeping and eating gestures, but it all boiled down to that. He was trying very hard to make Holman understand. Burgoyne understood, all right. Well, Po-han knew about the engine too, and he was the one to judge, Holman thought. He grinned at the two men.

"You're just a pair of bloody homeguards," he said.

"That's all we want to be," Burgoyne assured him.

Homeguards or not, they were still the two finest men Jake Holman had ever known. It was very pleasant on the steaming watch.

Holman liked almost everyone that summer. He strolled the top-side like the other Sand Pebbles and he began feeling curiously detached from the engine room. Po-han down there was so much like himself with the machinery that it was like being in two places at once. Holman would stroll the boat deck and look in on Waldhorn in the radio shack, shoot the breeze with the chiefs in their wicker armchairs under the awning, and move on aft to the sick bay to talk with Jennings about chlorinating water. On the main deck he would stop to joke with Red Dog and Duckbutt Randall in the ship's office, hunch down to watch Restorff and his helpers clean guns, drink coffee and wait for his shave in the crew's compartment. He met everyone squarely and talked easily.

He knew most of the Chinese by name and he would nod and grin at them. On the first meeting of the day he would exchange slight bows and a few words with the important Chinese. Lop Eye Shing was always very pleasant. Nearly every day Holman drank a bowl of tea in the galley with Big Chew. He liked and respected the bold and burly cook. Except possibly for Clip Clip and Oh Joy, he respected all the Chinese. They treated him with a seriousness that they did not show to the other Sand Pebbles, and it made him feel solid.

Holman was trying to be a good topside sailor. He was hoping that Lt. Collins would forget about transferring him. He got back on fair terms with Lynch and Bordelles. Lt. Collins remained very formal and military with Holman, as he was with everyone, but several times he had commented favorably on the engine. None of them could deny the engine. It could hold ten knots all day with only a smooth vibration, and one time they caught up with and passed the Japanese gunboat, crossing her bow delicately, and gaining much face thereby. There was quite a saving in coal, too, but Ping-wen took that in extra squeeze. Holman did not want to leave the *San Pablo*. When the thought worried him, he would look fondly at his bunk and locker. He would experience anew the pleasure of his real chair at the solid table and order a dozen fried eggs for breakfast, as if to remind himself of all that he had to lose.

He was taking pleasure in the simple flow of things: eggs and meat and vegetables across the quarterdeck, into the galley, to the mess tables, and the bantering talk there. Coal down the bunker scuttles, heaped on the floorplates, blazing on the grate bars, ashes whipped up and over the lee side to stain the wind and water. Clothing from locker to body to wash-wash coolie and back clean and fresh in the locker. The flow of activity: Restorff's weekly round of the guns; the drills and inspections; Pappy Tung's coolies holystoning, scrubbing, painting, shining; Oh Joy and Wong shining shoes, making up bunks, changing linen, waxing and polishing the red linoleum; Ping-wen's coolies up on the stack every morning shining the whistle and siren and the flaring copper mouth of the safety valve blow-off. It was a sense of the ship constantly renewing itself. The flow of the ship through the brown water: bow wave curling off like the point of an arrow; cream-coffee wake stretching aft like the shaft of the arrow; black smoke rolling out the stack and the flag fluttering in the breeze of motion; engine vibration thrumming the rigging and the stack guys; catching and passing junks and sampans, rocking them with the bow wave, and now and then the whistle *oonging* monstrously at junks and timber rafts up ahead hogging the fairway. That was part of how it felt to be a Sand Pebble.

It felt meaningful and important. Boatmen and fishermen turned to watch their passing; brown, stooping farmers straightened to stare; white birds flew up screaming and buffaloes snorted off in terror across green fields. At the cities and market towns the people came down to the bund to stare. Lt. Collins dealt directly with the warlords of life and death in those cities. If the ship was to stay for several days, as was usual, they would charter two sedan chairs for official calls. The ship had special curtains with eagles embroidered in gold to replace the regular curtains on the chartered chairs. It made face for all the Sand Pebbles when Lt. Collins rode up the bund in one of those chairs behind an honor guard of warlord soldiers. Underway or at anchor, the Sand Pebbles ran slashingly through their drills, and they strolled and lounged along the clean teak decks, themselves neat and clean in white shorts, barbered and well-fed and rested, watching the swarming Chinese life all around them on land and water with a comfortable feeling of being in control of things. That was another part of how it felt to be a Sand Pebble.

Holman was learning to see the ungainly white upperworks and tall stack and the puny three-pounder in the bow without the urge to laugh. His memory of the ocean and of the lean, low destroyers was fading back. The trick was to see the *San Pablo* as the Hunanese saw her, who had never seen other kinds of warships. The trick was to forget about the world outside Hunan. Then you were a Sand Pebble in your heart. But sometimes without warning the absurdity of the fat, waddling gunboat and its extremes of military ceremony would flood Jake Holman like sudden sickness, and he would know that he was not quite yet a Sand Pebble in his heart.

The bridge was the ship's high and holy place underway, as the quarterdeck was at anchor. The ship's bell hung there, so often polished that the Spanish words on it were half worn away. They struck the bells every half hour, day and night, on that ship. Holman began going up into the bridge, when Farren had the watch, to see how they did things.

The bridge was thirty feet from wing to wing, where canvas-covered machine guns were mounted on universal joints, and about ten feet fore and aft. The deck was teak. The flying bridge made an overhead, and a steel bulwark ran waist-high along front and sides. Doors on either side led through the after bulkhead to the boat deck and two inboard doors led one to Lt. Collins' quarters and the other to a small chartroom. There was not much gear: the high, brass-mounted mahogany wheel amidships; the bank of brass voice tubes and the engine order telegraph stumpily on one side of it; the magnetic compass like a little man with fists on the other side; against the after bulkhead a varnished wooden arms chest and a signal flag locker. Beside the flag locker a ladder and a trapdoor led to the flying bridge, where signals were made.

It was a high place, open on three sides to the world. It was all space and sunlight and natural air blowing, unlike the stuffed and cluttered engine room.

What was on the bridge, primarily, was people. Bordelles or Franks always had charge underway, with Farren or Bronson as junior watch officer. There were seamen for relief helmsman and lookout and a signal watch. But the Chinese really stood the watch. The Chinese pilot stood beside the wheel and gave orders to the coolie helmsman, and if the water was tricky he would have two more of Pappy Tung's men in the bow sounding with bamboo poles and singsonging up to him in Chinese. The pilots came aboard on contract and they changed from time to time. They had their own cabin just forward of the CPO quarters. There was always a duty Fang on the bridge, with his bugle, and another Fang for messenger.

Holman found it pleasant up there talking to Farren and watching the passing show. When the helmsman spun the wheel, he liked hearing the familiar rattle of the steering engine down below and watching the ship's bow swing over at the same time. You missed that last part, when you were on the floorplates. When they made a speed change, he liked to hear the familiar shovel scrapes or slam of ashpan doors, as the case might be, and at the same time see the smoke thin or boil freshly and note the change in wake and bow wave. It was only from the bridge, he was learning, that he could catch the feeling of the ship as a whole.

Holman was on the bridge one afternoon when they were on their way to Paoshan to see about unrest reported there. They were skirting Ta Island. It was all ponds and bayous and tall, hummocky stands of reeds. They could see bamboo and white mud walls and a few real trees far inland. An angry mosquito buzz crossed the bridge and aft another bullet *spanged* on metal. Far back in reeds to port, a faint *pop pop* sounded.

"*Toofay* salute." Farren grinned. "They hit the stack again."

It was a legend that the stack was all they ever did hit. It was covered with small sheetmetal patches. The Chinese did not believe the legend. They all ran into the chartroom. Vincent took the wheel. Bordelles slowed to one-third speed. Farren passed the word.

"Take cover! Clear port side!" He jerked the canvas housing from the port machine gun and peered over it at the reeds. "One more shot, you *toofays*. Please shoot, you nice little *toofays*," he said. "Let me spot you."

Holman could not see the answering *pop,* but Farren opened fire. It was very loud, and the gun shook his shoulders like silent laughter. The air was suddenly sharp with powder fumes, and bright, empty cartridges tinkled on the white deck. Farren turned and grinned through his red beard.

"That ought to hold 'em, Mr. Bordelles."

Bordelles rang standard speed and pulled the overhead whistle cord. The whistle blasted hoarsely. Crosley, beside the flag locker, shook hands with himself in the air.

"Another redskin bit the dust!" he said, and a bullet rang the whistle like a bell and glanced off shrieking. Crosley's eyes popped. "Them dirty sons of bitches!" he said indignantly, glancing around for agreement.

Bordelles, scowling, slowed again. "Get up on the crosstrees and spot!" he snapped at Crosley and, to Farren, "Put a couple of pans into 'em this time!"

Crosley scrambled up the ladder. More men came on the bridge. They were grinning and eager and walking springily on their toes.

"Hey! Hey! I see 'em!" Crosley yelled from above. "Fire a burst, Farren!" Farren did so. "Left about fifty! Down fifty!" Crosley guided him in. "Now you're on! Right on, boy! Mow 'em down!"

Farren stood spring-legged and hunched and his body moved in a slow, stationary dance. He was lashing the target area in a figure-eight pattern. Holman could not see much. The tall reeds swayed and broke under the storm of bullets. The area took on a dark, mottled look against the lighter green. Oil smoked off the machine gun. It was too far away to see much.

"All right. Cease firing," Bordelles said at last.

They waited a few minutes to be sure the *toofay* had enough. One of the Fangs came out of the chartroom and began gathering up the cartridge cases. They would go for squeeze. Another bullet whined over and the Fang scuttled back into the chartroom.

"Hey! They aimed that one at *me!*" Crosley shouted.

Lt. Collins came into the bridge through his private door and all the men snapped to attention. He was cool and crisp and half smiling.

"Can you see figures? Are they in uniform?" he called up to Crosley.

"All I been seeing is reeds waving, sir," Crosley said. "There's a shack in there, too. I can see the roof tiles."

"Call the men to general quarters, Mr. Bordelles," Lt. Collins said.

That was a slow-clanging gong and a ragged bugle call. Holman had to go below and take the throttle. Lynch came down. He only came to the engine room when drills required him to. They spent an hour working on the *toofay*. The ship had a different, lively, springy feel to Holman and his ears brought him the picture of what they were doing up there. The machine guns mowed several acres of reeds and Haythorn probed with the three-pounder for the hidden hut. It barked sharply, much like Red Dog. Sweat beaded Lynch's puffy face and he kept slapping his pistol. There were a lot of bells and maneuvers with the engine, to hold station in the sluggish current. When they finally secured and whistled and steamed on, a scattering of shots still came from the reeds to send them on their way. Lynch was disgusted.

"It ain't like the old days. We been getting soft since the war," he grumbled to Burgoyne. "I tell you, it's damned bad luck not to have the last shot!"

22

The water was very low in the Chien. After they left the delta, Lt.
Collins had to climb with his binoculars to the flying bridge to see
well across the banks. He saw women out sweeping the rice fields
with twig brooms. They made reddish dust swirls in the light breeze.
Reddish streaks showed through the whitewash on the mud-walled
farmsteads. They were drying and crumbling under the clear, bright
sky. The bamboo groves around the farmsteads drooped sadly. Along
the banks groups of ragged farmers in conical bamboo hats climbed
endlessly on the treadmills that drove their groaning pumps. All that
morning the sound of the pumps had followed *San Pablo* like a re-
proach. Or menace. The farmers leaned on the bar and climbed with
thin brown shanks and they did not turn, as they usually did, to
watch *San Pablo* steam by them. The river swirled clear above white
sand in the shrunken channel. It should have been muddy brown
and running from bank to bank.

Lt. Collins climbed down, stopped for a word with Bordelles, and
went back into his cabin. He had not seen anyone fishing all morning. He did not like the seeming of things. Paoshan was the furthest
reach of his responsibility in Hunan, and he was never sure of it.

He came out when they tied up to the Japanese pontoon in Paoshan, right after the noon meal. A plank led from the flat steel pontoon to a sandy foreshore that stretched a hundred feet to the stone river embankment. Water should have been lapping the stone. Chinese were massed all along the bank and more were up on the gray, crenelated city wall and a crowd hum filled the air. People were all over the river sands. One group of warlord soldiers was tending a fire and another group of priests and soldiers was slaughtering animals at the water's edge. They had a bull, a sheep and a pig. The pig squealed and resisted and made a nasty business of it.

"All lines doubled up, sir," Bordelles reported. "I think I'll go aft and watch the show, if it's all right."

"I'll go with you."

The chiefs and a few others were by the sickbay. They cleared a space along the rail for the two officers. Most of the crew was on the fantail watching. The priests were clipping and shaving the animals. A stocky Chinese in a gray gown waded out and began to declaim above the river with flinging, emotional gestures.

"Sir! That's General Pan!" Bordelles whispered.

It was indeed the Paoshan warlord. If that fierce, jolly, hardheaded man would put off his uniform and behave like this, things had to be very wrong. The sailors on the fantail had begun laughing. Word came up that General Pan was confessing his sins to the river god. Oh Joy was translating for the sailors, and they were laughing. Lt. Collins sent Franks down to stop it and to quiet them.

"Tell them it's religious. They have to respect it," he said.

General Pan was a kind of an officer and a kind of a friend, and Lt. Collins did not want to know about his sins. They were best left in Chinese. When Pan went back into the city, Lt. Collins would call on him at the *yamen* with all due ceremony and then he would learn what the trouble was. By then the chartered sedan chairs would be rigged. Abruptly, he turned and went forward. Bordelles followed.

"The Chinese are a very ingenious people," Bordelles said.

It was one of the ensign's favorite joking remarks, and sometimes it irritated Lt. Collins. It irked him now. It did not seem in good taste. It did not seem at all a time for joking.

He rode through noisy, smelly streets in the sedan chair, from the *yamen* to the mission compound, still shaken by what General Pan had told him. He kept his curtains down and peered through the cracks. He did not like the crowd faces. A sedan chair with curtains up passed him and the passenger was a squealing pig dressed in silken robes. Waves of jeering laughter followed the pig. He had to wait at the main street until a procession passed. They were men and women with headdresses of woven willow branches and they carried smoking joss sticks. They had straw pads strapped to their knees and every third step they would go down and beat their foreheads on the filthy stones. They all had blood on their strained and staring faces.

At the mission he drank tea in a dowdy American parlor and talked to Reynolds, the senior missionary. He was a stooped, worn man with sparse hair and rimless glasses and a gentle manner. He was very reasonable, for a missionary. He was not one of the anti-gunboat fanatics, like old Craddock at China Light. The two younger men present let Reynolds do the talking.

"Thank God our womenfolk are at Kuling for the summer," he said.

"How about the women at China Light?"

"Some are still there, I'm afraid."

Lt. Collins frowned. It was always simpler if there were no women and children.

"Mr. Craddock feels safe that far from the city," Reynolds said.

"What's your estimate, Mr. Reynolds?"

"I . . . don't quite know, sir. This is very unusual."

"General Pan says the countryside will rise *en masse*." Pan had been deeply disturbed. He had tried hard to make Lt. Collins understand that this was something radically out of the ordinary. "What do you know about this man Wing?" Lt. Collins asked.

One of the younger men jumped up, flushing. "He's a servant of Satan!" the man said harshly. "He thinks he can coerce the Almighty! He means to blackmail very God Himself!"

"Please, Mr. Baker," Reynolds said. "Wing is a native holy man," he told Lt. Collins. "He's behind the trouble, all right."

They had had a series of bad years in the district and a small famine last year, Reynolds explained. They were weakened. If it did not rain soon they would have a big famine this year and they would all die. So they had begun to make heaven lose face, to force rain. They believed in a vague, impersonal heavenly power that could be symbolized in many ways and influenced, even coerced, by the way they treated the symbols. They had begun to outrage decorum and to beat and revile their wooden idols. That much was old custom in China.

"Then Wing began preaching that the Christian God was the one inhibiting the Rain Dragon," Reynolds said sadly. "The people began demanding that we humiliate and coerce our God."

Lt. Collins raised his eyebrows. Of course the notion was preposterous, Reynolds went on, but it was hard to make that clear to ignorant Chinese. What they had done was to begin holding every day at noon a mass public prayer for rain, on a bell signal from the mission, as a token of good faith and concern. But Wing had begun a fast, pointedly and publicly aimed at the Christian God. Local geomancers had concurred in a prediction that if it did not rain by a certain day it would not rain all summer. Then Wing had announced that if it did not rain on that day he would burn himself alive on the river sands and the Christian God would have no face left at all.

"The day is Friday," Reynolds said. "Today is Tuesday."

"General Pan expects them to go berserk and kill all the Christians in the district," Lt. Collins said. "What do you think?"

"You must not let Wing burn himself!" Baker exclaimed. "It's repugnant to all civilized opinion!"

"That part is a purely Chinese affair. I have no authority, under the treaties, to interfere."

"You could order General Pan!"

Lt. Collins checked his anger. It was the anti-gunboat missionaries' habit of siding with Chinese complaints of arbitrary high-handedness which had so gravely undermined the structure of gunboat authority in China since the war. But these men were not anti-gunboat.

"General Pan expects his own soldiers to join the mob, Mr. Baker," he said. "He fears for his own life and I have offered him refuge in *San Pablo* Friday."

"We must simply pray for rain and trust God's mercy," Reynolds said.

"I can take you and the China Light people to Hankow. You can collect an indemnity later, for property damage."

"What about our native Christians? What about their property?" Baker wanted to know. He was a chunky blond young man.

"I am only responsible for American lives and property," Lt. Collins said. He was deciding that he did not like Baker. "I'll take as many as I have room for." He turned to Reynolds. "I want to ask a favor, Mr. Reynolds. Will you go to China Light and persuade them to come in and take refuge on the ship before Friday?" Reynolds looked dubious. Lt. Collins smiled grimly. "I know," he said. "But you will be more likely to persuade them than I would be. At least the women and children."

"I'll try," Reynolds said.

"Good! And thank you for it!"

Lt. Collins finished his tea and stood up. The other men rose.

"What about our native Christians?" Baker pressed.

"Most of them can take shelter with relatives in the country," Reynolds said. "This is China, Mr. Baker. We'll build up again."

"They can bring death on their relatives in the country!" Baker would not smooth it under. "You and General Pan simply have to do *something,* Lt. Collins!" he almost shouted.

"I'm not God. I can't make it rain," Lt. Collins told him evenly. "Good afternoon, gentlemen."

On the way back he heard the drums and gongs all around him in the city. People still crowded the bund. Over their heads he could see the ship, solid and gunned and comforting. His chair tilted down the inset stone steps to the sands, the bearers yelling for gangway and jostling the water coolies trying to come up with their yoked wooden buckets slopping. He got out of the chair on the pontoon, beside the small office-waiting room with the Japanese flag atop it. The sailors were all along the rail aft, watching another ceremony. Even Randall, on the quarterdeck watch, was too busy staring at it to know that his commanding officer had returned.

Chinese with wild, angry faces were holding over the fire a bamboo platform with a wooden god image on it. The god's paint was blistering and the crowd shrieked and howled. They moved the god off the fire and seized buckets of water from the water coolies and doused him. Their yelling and drumming and gonging rose in crescendo. They flung the empty buckets away and the water coolies went humbly to refill them. The sailors were all pointing and laughing. Lt. Collins caught Randall's eye.

"*San Pablo* . . . boarding!" Randall cried in confusion.

He ran to the gangway to salute. Lt. Collins brushed angrily by him and went to his cabin and sent for Bordelles.

"Muster the men aft. I want to talk to them," he said.

He had a few minutes to plan what he would say. The men probably had a garbled story by now, but they had no sense of the gravity of the situation. In a way, that was good. He did not want to shake their superb confidence.

Facing them on the fantail, he told them what he thought they should know. "The people know they are all going to die and it affects their minds," he said. "The least we can do is to respect their ceremonies and humor them in anything they think might help. General Pan has ordered that no animals be killed for food, no fish caught and no eggs broken, until it rains. We can only get vegetables from the beach." He paused. They were taking it well. "I expect you all to keep a decent silence about the decks during their ceremonies," he went on. "I want the deck watches doubly alert. We must be prepared for unexpected outbursts."

They nodded gravely, glancing at the mob along the bund. They were good, steady men. Lt. Collins dismissed them and went to the bridge and called a repel boarders drill. He thought it might have a good moral effect on both sides. It went very nicely, as *San Pablo* sprang to arms. The bugle sang high and clear, running feet thudded, guns swiveled, cutlasses flashed on the main deck, and steam roared and billowed amidships. One by one in hearty voices the shouted reports came in. Bordelles made the rounds and returned smiling.

"Perfect, sir. They're really on their toes."

"Very well. Secure from all drills."

In his cabin, with coffee, they talked it over. Bordelles did not think the China Light people would come in to safety. Craddock would just say, as he was so fond of saying, that he dared to trust God rather than guns, implying that whoever did not was both cowardly and heathen.

"I'm glad it's Mr. Reynolds going out there and not me," Bordelles said.

"Well, I hope they come in."

"So do I, sir, but they won't." Bordelles shook his head. "Maybe it'll rain. I hope it rains."

"Double up all sentries tonight, Tom. Give them a pep talk."

Lt. Collins took a turn around the boat deck before he went to bed. There were still a few people on the bund, with bobbing paper lanterns, and drums were going in the city. The fire on the sands burned redly, soldiers crouched beside it. He could just make out the sacrificial animals in the glow of the ship's stern light. They lay side by side on a low platform, their legs folded neatly beneath them, and willow branches had been stuck into the sand all around them. They were clean-shaven, except for their heads. The water chuckled along in front of them and they looked cool and pale and peaceful there together.

He could not go to sleep. The mock fire danced shadows on his window. Drums and the far, ceaseless groaning of the treadmill pumps assailed his ears. He pondered what General Pan had tried so hard to say in his inadequate English.

They were all going to die and they knew it. There was a heavenly order that sent rain and an earthly order that died if it did not get rain, and the two were tied together. The people pleaded and they died patiently and when they had had enough of that, they struck. They mocked heaven and scorched their wooden idols. Wild, angry destruction of all earthly authority symbols to wound their heavenly counterparts. General Pan was such a symbol. So were all the missionaries, with their treaty privileges. So, pre-eminently, was *San Pablo*. It was a tortured, irrational Chinese version of the rational doctrine that all authority was coupled with a commensurate responsibility.

They could not come to grips with the Christian God. There was just no way of getting at Him. He did not have to give a damn about Chinese or anybody else, unless He pleased to. He could only be supplicated, never coerced. Or *could* He? *Did* this holy man Wing know what he was doing?

A sleep-edge vision shaped itself: the great, collective beast refusing death, rising to rend with powers and methods unthinkable— Lt. Collins was jolted fully awake. He turned on his light and smoked a cigarette.

It was blank nonsense. Nonsense, but their acts based on it would be real. Stick to that level. He had to get the Americans out safely. That was all his responsibility. He would get the China Light bunch aboard somehow, if he had to go out there and plead with each one individually. He would hate that, but he would do it. Their lives were his responsibility.

Firmly he lay down and turned off the light. Firmly he stopped his thoughts and listened to nothing but the tread of the deck sentry. Quite soon he drifted off and slept soundly.

He slept late. Crackling rifle fire brought him out on deck in his pajamas. A file of warlord soldiers on the city wall was firing into the sky to stir up the Rain Dragon. They were doing that every morning, General Pan had said, to comfort the people. Franks and Bordelles came up, worried, and Lt. Collins explained about the Rain Dragon. He sent Franks down to reassure the men on the main deck.

"Pan hinted that I should fire my guns every morning too," he told Bordelles. "I think Pan half believes that stuff. He's nervous."

Bordelles chuckled. Down on the main deck the sailors were laughing.

Lt. Collins ate breakfast alone in his cabin. Yen-ta brought him scrambled eggs and a glass of milk. Mr. Reynolds was trying to break down the Chinese prejudice against milk and he was very proud of his little dairy run by native Christians. He always sent out a quart of milk every morning that the ship was in Paoshan. Lt. Collins pointed at the milk.

"Take away!" he told Yen-ta. "Throw away!"

He did not like milk. It was from the glands of female animals. The Chinese were right about milk. It was unmanly stuff. He did not want the eggs, either. If the crew was going to have to do without eggs, he did not want any being saved back for the chiefs and officers.

"Can catch plenty egg," Yen-ta assured him. "Evahbody catch plenty egg."

It was a nervous day. Muster and drills ran off snappily, with a bit too much vigor. Chinese still moved restlessly on the bund and down on the sands. Only the everlasting water coolies were behaving normally. A few high white cumulus clouds drifted across, trailing cool shadows, but they were not going to rain down any rain. They had slowly shifting, fantastic shapes. Perhaps that's where the Chinese get their notion of a Rain Dragon, Lt. Collins thought.

He spoke to Welbeck about the crew's mess. *San Pablo* did not have refrigeration and they had to buy fresh stores as they used them. Welbeck said Big Chew could make out very well with vegetables and dry stores for a few days. One of the engine room coolies had relatives in Paoshan and he was smuggling eggs out to the ship. The hens were not obeying the warlord's order, Welbeck said, chuckling. The coolie was the same one who had made all the trouble in Changsha; he was coming in handy now. Shortly afterward Lt. Collins saw the coolie, Po-han, come aboard with a heavy basket. On impulse, he stopped and commended him. The coolie grinned proudly, showing two gold teeth, and Lt. Collins felt good about it. He did not remember ever having commended one of the Chinese boatmen before, but that fellow had real ship's spirit.

In the afternoon he sent Bordelles ashore to see if Reynolds had come back from China Light, and what the word was. If it was bad, he would have to go to China Light himself next day, the last day of grace before the burning. Bordelles had not been long away when the mob thickened on the bund. Shots and a confused crowd clamor came from the city. It could be trouble. General Pan had said he had no reliable troops left. Lt. Collins thought about sending Franks and his section of the landing force to the mission but, given the mood the people were in, that might precipitate a lot of needless killing. He cursed missionaries under his breath and tried to look calm when Franks came up, also worried about the tumult in the city.

"It's probably just another rain magic ceremony," Lt. Collins said. "Let's go out and have a look."

Fortunately, it was that, and Lt. Collins felt Franks' unspoken admiration. It was the Rain Dragon himself, greenly winding out of the city and many-legging it along the bund while a shouting, gonging troupe ran with him shooting firecrackers. He was made of green cloth that came to the waists of the twenty-odd men who were his legs. His big spherical head, with green whiskers and bulging eyes, bobbed and turned. He came curving and humping down to the sands, driven by his attendants. They were trying to make him cross the fire, and he did not want to. He tossed his head angrily and dodged and doubled and they headed him back with gongs and firecrackers. Everyone along the bund screamed when he crossed the fire. Each pair of legs jumped high and landed running with short steps and it was like a hump traveling along his back. Then he stood trembling and wrinkled and telescoped into himself with his goggle-eyed head on the sand, and all the spirit and life were gone out of him. The attendants began splashing him with buckets of water. It revived him. Slowly his head came up and he stretched out again sleekly green and dripping and he went cavorting back up to the bund while the crowd cheered.

"Well, sir, I hope that gives him the idea about a little rain," Franks said.

"I hope so too, Chief. It would make things a lot simpler."

Bordelles did not come back until almost sunset. He had had to wait for Reynolds. The news was not good. The China Light people refused to evacuate, but Mr. Craddock would come in in the morning.

"You're in for a rough time, sir," Bordelles said, trying not to grin. "Mr. Reynolds says old Craddock's mad as a split snake because we even came here. He's going to order us back to Hankow."

Lt. Collins smiled grimly. It was still a joke to the rest of them.

He talked to Mr. Craddock alone in his cabin. The old man was angry in black, his gray-streaked beard like a club, his eyes and manner more bold and fierce than ever before. Lt. Collins had decided that a soft-spoken disdain would be the best counter.

"I came here under orders and I will have to stay through the crisis," he said. "I can't leave while American lives are in danger."

"It is you who make our danger, sir!" Craddock launched into the anti-gunboat credo. The unequal treaties and the gunboats in Chinese inland waters made a mockery of the Christian spirit. They sparked and fueled the native anti-Christian feeling. Lt. Collins listened patiently, toying with his tea bowl. "The Chinese do not distinguish between your people and mine, sir!" Craddock rumbled across the green baize. "They think we are all Christians."

"Well, aren't we?"

"Ask yourself, sir. All the Christians in this district have been praying publicly for rain every day at noon. Have you and your men?"

"No. We have no chaplain."

Craddock looked his contempt for that excuse. Lt. Collins was thinking. The praying was in part, as General Pan would say, a show to comfort the people. No doubt *San Pablo* was spoiling the moral effect. And there was just a chance—

"In times of great stress the Chinese attack their authority symbols," Craddock said. "Your ship, sir, is a very hated authority symbol and we are all perforce associated with it in the Chinese mind. The best thing you can do for us is to sail away from here at once."

"I will have my men pray on deck this noon," Lt. Collins said. "Would you be willing to lead them in prayer, Mr. Craddock?"

"I would be glad to." His manner gentled notably.

"In order to associate the ship more clearly with the local Christian effort, do you suppose I might give the prayer signal with the ship's whistle?" Lt. Collins pursued his thought.

Craddock considered. "Yes. Yes, a good idea," he decided. "I have time still to go ashore and arrange it with Mr. Reynolds and his people."

"What do you think about tomorrow, the crisis? Would it help if all the Christians in Paoshan were here aboard, at the crisis scene, so to speak, to pray together?"

"It might indeed. Yes, I think it would." Mr. Craddock stood up. His manner was wholly changed and mollified. "I'll arrange that too," he said. "I'd better get ashore now, Lt. Collins."

Lt. Collins saw him off the quarterdeck. So far so good, he thought. When he had them all safe behind the guns, his duty would be done. The next step, and not an easy one, was to get the crew ready for prayers. They were probably more profane and irreverent than even the usual run of peacetime professionals, and they had the China sailor's traditional dislike of missionaries as well. He had them called aft for another talk and he phrased it carefully. He had to leave them room to take the prayer as a joke, if they liked, and yet not seem facetious himself. Predictably, several of the sea lawyers objected. They knew that they could not, under navy regulations, be forced to pray. Holman, surprisingly, was not one of them. Holman had been doing very well lately.

After dismissal, he planned it with Bordelles and Franks. Harris could be stationed in the bridge to blow the whistle. The other conscientious objectors could take the deck watches. Navy regulations prohibited men on duty under arms from taking off their hats or assuming undignified postures.

"Old Craddock'll raise hell," Bordelles warned. "He'll say kneeling is a perfectly dignified posture."

"We are still bound by navy regulations," Lt. Collins said.

The prayer went clumsily. Bordelles mustered the men and spaced them out in the pattern for physical drill. The men had dogged red faces. Harris blew the whistle in a vindictive, overlong blast that sent a cloud of steam drifting above the sands.

"Ship's company . . . *uncover! Two!*" Bordelles said. "Ship's company . . . *kneel!*"

They all knelt, hats beside them, except Craddock. An air of embarrassed constraint hung over the fantail. The men would not look at each other. Some knit their fingers and some steepled them. Craddock raised his hands and his bearded face to the sky and led off the prayer.

He prayed very loudly, asking God to forgive them all for their swinish lusting after drink and harlots, for all their love of blood and violence, and to relent and send rain. The men were scowling and stirring. Just in time Craddock saw the danger signals and switched to Chinese. He raised his great voice to full register. God and the Chinese out there alone knew to what nameless sins he was vicariously confessing *San Pablo*. The sailors subsided. It was all right, in Chinese.

He thundered in Chinese for ten minutes, until Harris cut him off with another long whistle blast. The men did not wait for dismissal. They stood up and bolted for the crew's compartment, where they would swear and growl themselves back into their accustomed and comfortable state of grace. Craddock went up to the boat deck with the two officers. He was going to take tiffin aboard. He was strangely affable. He had had a chance to launder some very dirty souls and he had scrubbed hell out of them and he was feeling good about it. Bordelles loyally played up to him.

"I feel a lot better about things now, Mr. Craddock," he said. "Maybe I'm foolish, but I wouldn't be surprised if it rains before tomorrow afternoon."

"It rests with God's infinite mercy," Craddock said.

Just before lunch a new crowd clamor broke out. It sounded like jeering laughter and the three men went out to see what it might be this time. Two Chinese in white dunce caps, one at each end of a bamboo ladder, were crossing the sands. Seven or eight dogs, fastened upright between the ladder rungs, were forced to skip and hop along on their hind legs. Each dog was dressed in a crude white sailor suit and they had crude flags tied to their flapping forepaws, variously Japanese, French, British and American. Craddock began laughing.

"That's a shame-heaven show," he explained. "Everyone is supposed to laugh."

The old devil was laughing from more than a Chinese sense of decorum, Lt. Collins thought. Someone in that town had a nasty turn of humor. The dogs howled and hopped along. They twisted their heads and snapped at each other and showed big white teeth. A high, sharp yapping broke out on the lower deck.

"Get in step, you mangy sons of bitches!" Shanahan's voice rose clearly. "You're a disgrace to the tribe!" The sailors were all laughing on the lower deck. "Arf! Arf! Arf! Eyes . . . *right!*" Shanahan shouted.

He was pretending that the dogs were passing in review. The dogs *were* ludicrous. Suddenly Lt. Collins and Bordelles were laughing too, helplessly swept away. The whole ship was laughing, to match the laughter of the Chinese on the bund. When the dogs were out of sight, the laughter subsided in red-faced, wheezing chuckles.

"The Chinese . . . are a very ingenious people," Bordelles gasped happily.

The mood lasted through tiffin. Craddock seemed actually human. He left in a good mood, promising to return with all his juniors the next morning. The prayer had indeed been a success.

Later in the day Lt. Collins learned from Yen-ta that the Chinese on the sands had been greatly impressed by the prayer. Twice the steam cloud from the whistle had drifted over the sands and drops of water condensed in it and fell hissing on the fire. The Chinese thought that was very potent rain magic. Lt. Collins chuckled privately at the irony. It made him feel better about Mr. Craddock.

Jake Holman had been getting more tense every day. He could not forget what Lt. Collins had said so matter-of-factly: *the people know they are all going to die.* He felt that he was the only man on the ship who appreciated what was going on. *It affects their minds.* The people were trying to take God by the throat. They were going to have rain, if they had to wring out heaven like a swab. It was an enormous thought, and Jake Holman could not shake it off. He would like to take part in a project like that. He suspected that the other Sand Pebbles were afraid underneath also, just not wanting to admit it to each other. They were only covering with their jokes and swagger.

On Friday the whole world felt like a loaded gun on a hair trigger. The same tantalizing spun-sugar clouds floated around up there in the dry, bright sky. No one had much to say about the decks. During drills the warlord and some of his officers and women came aboard, with bales of gear. They were like rats leaving a sinking ship, the Sand Pebbles said uneasily. Shortly afterward, the missionaries came aboard. Burgoyne spat over the side.

"Their ship's sinking too," he said.

It was old custom that the missionaries took the boat deck and the Sand Pebbles stayed on the main deck, like oil on top of water. A baby was crying up there, and it sounded very out of place. The men had to watch their language so closely that they could hardly talk at all and they could no longer come from the washroom out on the fantail with no clothes on. They drifted uneasily along the main deck, resenting the missionaries. The crowd up on the city wall and along the bund was thickening. Near the fire on the sands priests had built a small mat shed. On a shelf in front of it they had wooden drums shaped like fish and some joss sticks smoking. Soldiers dumped the animal carcasses into the river and they floated away. The priests were sticking fresh willow branches into the sand around their mat shed.

Holman watched it all. Steam was up in both boilers and they were ready to go in the engine room; Po-han was looking after that. Most of the crew was back on the fantail watching the sands. Clip Clip had to come back there to call them for their shaves. Above them on the boat deck the missionaries were watching too. The two groups did not look at each other. The sailors knew the women up there despised them. The women probably considered, quite correctly, that the sailors had impure thoughts about them. Holman saw Miss Eckert up there, in a gray dress. She caught his eye and smiled.

"Hi!" he said. "Hello there."

"Hello, Mr. Holman." She came to the rail, looking down.

He could not talk to her there, in the quick chill of embarrassment and resentment among the Sand Pebbles. Through the open door of the head he could see Harris sitting on the trough. Harris grinned at Holman and began to sing, in a high, mocking voice:

> *I am Jesus' lit-tull lamb,*
> *Yes, by Jesus Christ, I am. . . .*

Holman waved his hand vaguely at her and bobbed his head and almost ran forward. He had to get out of there. On the way forward he thought of an excuse and went up the ladder to the boat deck. He began testing the stack guys. She came forward to meet him.

"I'm slacking the stack guys," he said loudly.

"It's very high." She looked up at the smoke drifting away.

"That's to make a good natural draft through the furnaces." He slapped the guy. "These cables keep it from falling over. With all the fires lit, it gets hotter and has to expand," he said. "We got to slack the guys, or it would buckle." He was saying it all for Crosley's benefit, down on the quarterdeck. "This is a turnbuckle," he went on. "It's got right- and left-hand threads. When I turn it this way, they both screw out. You see?" She nodded, puzzled at his manner. "Now I'll get the forward ones," he said.

He went forward, out of Crosley's hearing. She followed. Her hair was well grown out, knotted back and smoothly pretty in the sunlight. She smelled clean, like Ivory soap.

"How are things at China Light?" he asked her.

"Oh, wonderful! I enjoyed my first school year," she said. "I love China, now."

"All shook down, huh?" He smiled. "I'm glad."

"Some of the boys have such quick, eager minds," she said. "One named Cho-jen is a true genius. I'm beginning to understand China, Mr. Holman. I'm never afraid any more."

"There may be shooting here, before today ends."

"I hope not." Her face shadowed.

"So do I."

He was suddenly and unaccountably very glad that she was safe aboard. She was thinner and her skin was rougher than before. American women always looked big and coarse to him, compared with Chinese girls, but he did not feel that about Miss Eckert.

"Do you think the old monk has a chance to win?" he asked her.

"Mr. Craddock says it is heathen spiritual arrogance," she said. "We are to pray that it not be punished as it deserves."

"That means for it to rain?"

"Yes."

"I guess it depends on how you look at it."

She looked concerned. "Mr. Craddock really does a lot. He has food stored at China Light for all our people. And he has his farmers plant sugar beets in some of the high fields. They send roots way, way down to reach water. They're thriving."

"That machinery," he said. "They got it working yet?"

"Not the way it should. They can make a kind of crude molasses."

"If I could talk Chinese and had time and the chance, I could show these farmers along the river how to get up twice as much water with them treadmill pumps," he said.

"Could you really?"

"I'd true up the flumes and polish 'em. Put low-friction packing on them wooden vanes," he said. "Metal bearings, with oil."

"I wish you could have the chance."

"Sometimes I think about a fleet of barges, with boilers and steam pumps," he said. "I could teach Chinese to run 'em and take care of 'em."

She smiled. "You have the missionary spirit, Mr. Holman."

It shocked him. He stared at her. She read his thought.

"Not all missionaries are evangelists. There are medical and teaching missionaries," she said. "You could be an engineering missionary."

"Is there such a thing?"

"I never heard of one. But there could be."

It was an absolutely new thought to him. She moved to the rail and he followed her. A ventilator and a boat made a private little alcove for them.

"Chinese can learn engineering," he said. "I know." He began telling her about Po-han and the other Chinese. He knew he was like a little boy turning handsprings to show off, and he couldn't help it. He knew also that she would understand and not laugh at him. He told her all about the ship and what he had done. "Except for the guns, us sailors are just passengers," he finished. "And that Po-han—if there was only a few thousand like him in China . . ."

"There are many millions like him in China," she said. "All they need is a chance."

"I'd like to see 'em get a chance."

"You're a teacher too. You are already an engineering missionary."

They looked at each other. The quarterdeck bugle blared mess gear. It saved him. He was about to say something foolish.

"I have to go eat now," he said. "Afterward we have to stand by repel boarder stations. I won't see you again until after . . . after whatever's going to happen."

They both looked at the sky. It did not look any different.

"I'm just not worried," she said. "I feel it will rain."

"It will, if hoping helps. I sure been hoping."

He went lightly down to the main deck. So you could be a missionary without fiddling around with souls. You could be a teacher. A teacher *too.* How about that?

The waist party stood by on the quarterdeck, beside the open arms locker. Lynch paced nervously and slapped his pistol and they talked in very low voices. The missionaries on the boat deck were going to pray straight through and they were making all the noise on the ship. The men up there took turns leading the praying and now and then they all stopped for a hymn. The high, cottony clouds were heaping and piling behind the city. The wall and bund were solid with people. Soldiers and monks were building a pyre on the sands.

"They could go hermentile any second. This could get pretty nasty," Lynch kept saying.

Burgoyne was nervous too. He had an extra large lipful of snuff and he kept crossing the quarterdeck to lean out and spit and look aft.

"If there is a God, and He knows how to make it rain, I don't rightly see how He can hold out," Burgoyne said.

"Hah!" Harris said.

"Harris don't believe in God," Wilsey said, winking.

"I believe in admirals," Harris said.

"Harris is going to hell."

"I'll worry about that when I get there."

"Harris is a bad influence on us kids," Wilsey said. "No wonder we're so sinful that God won't let it rain."

Stawski snickered. Harris bristled.

"You got something, Wilsey, you say it to me, not just about me!" he demanded. "I'm here, too."

Wilsey put his lips to Harris's ear. "Prong you, Harris," he whispered.

"Prong you and all your relations clear back to Judas!"

"Pipe down!" Lynch snapped. "Cut out that kind of talk!"

"You believe in God, Chief?" Wilsey asked.

"Times like this I do," Lynch said. "No use guys pushing their luck, times like this."

The missionaries started on "Rock of Ages." The flurry of talk on the quarterdeck died down. The great crowd of Chinese ashore was hushing, also.

At three o'clock they brought the old man out of the city. They were having a hard time getting him through the crowd on the bund. Holman could see the sedan chair, high and tossing like a ship. Bordelles came.

"Stand to your guns," he said. "Put steam on the hose."

From their positions along the bulwark they watched the sedan chair working down to the sands. The great crowd was absolutely quiet. The whole world, except for the missionaries on the boat deck, seemed to be holding its breath. It was a very tremendous feeling and Holman's stomach muscles ached with tension.

"Jake, I'm scared," Burgoyne whispered.

"Who's scared of a million slopeheads, on the wrong side of eight machine guns?" Harris asked. His craggy face was bitter with contempt.

"That ain't what I'm scared of, Harris."

"Pipe down!" Lynch whispered harshly behind them. "I mean it, God damn you guys! Next one goes on report!"

The bearers set the sedan chair on the pyre. The old holy man was moving inside it. He raised a hand. He was probably saying something. A priest brought a burning stick from the small fire and pushed it into the pyre. A thread of smoke went up. A vast, low murmur rose from the crowd. It was like the whole air speaking.

The missionaries started on "Lead, Kindly Light."

The smoke went up thinly, with little red flames at the base, and the blue column of smoke wavered and broke at the top. The missionaries choked off and the world was absolutely still. The daylight was going dim and queer. Holman saw gooseflesh on his arms. The crowd seemed to growl deeply in thousands of throats, and Holman shivered in the sudden dusking chill along the deck.

"Jesus, Mary and Joseph," Stawski whispered.

Holman tore his eyes away from the pyre. Vast, blackening clouds were boiling over the city and pale lightning played jaggedly through them. The nearing roll of thunder blended with the crowd growl, seemed to rise out of it, grew irresistibly to a great world-roaring. Wind came in pats and slaps and gusts. The light went still more dim and queer. The air had a sharp, wet smell that tingled in the nose. Then rain in splats and patters and a gusty, threshing deluge that drove under and up and across and filled the air with flying water.

Holman could not see anything on the sands. The thunder was a solid roar. The waist party pulled inboard, wet to the skin, up to their ankles in water that the scuppers could not carry away fast enough. The river was a mass of whitecaps stippled and flattened with rain splash, a ghostly froth of air and water. The ship rocked and creaked. Farren and Haythorn came down to double up the moorings again. Farren grinned through his dripping red beard as he crossed the quarterdeck and Holman grinned back at him. Things fell into place.

It was only a thunderstorm, but it was a regular cloudbuster. It was nearly an hour in passing over and it left a fine rainbow behind. The fires were out on the sands and the crowd dispersed. They began celebrating inside the city with firecrackers, and it sounded like the Battle of the Marne. Holman did not see Miss Eckert before the missionaries went ashore. Word went around the ship that the missionaries were praising God for having answered their prayers.

The Sand Pebbles snorted over that at supper. They wrangled about it, and a general opinion took shape. It was just a thunderstorm that would have come anyway. The priests in the city were smart and they had smelled it and rushed the old holy man down there in time to claim the credit. Holman stayed out of the argument. He thought the old holy man had won an honest battle, and he was happy about it.

A few days later the regular soaking summer rains began. The city was quiet and General Pan was back in control. The rain more than made up for lost time. The land greened lushly almost overnight and it began to be moldy and miserable in Paoshan. The Sand Pebbles wished they were back on the lake again, where there was often a breeze. They were very pleased when the supercargo of an oil company junk came aboard with a breathless tale of piracy on the lake.

23

The junk had been bound for Paoshan loaded with tinned kerosene. It was under charter to the oil company and so permitted to fly the U.S. flag, and that made the piracy a legal outrage. The *San Pablo* got up steam at once.

"We captured a mess of pirates down there in 1920," Restorff said.

"Ten of 'em. It was September and the water was so low they didn't think we could steam this end of the lake," Harris said. "We fooled 'em."

"What did you do with 'em?" Holman asked.

"Brought 'em to Paoshan. The warlord had their heads off inside of a half hour, right down there on the sand."

"You can sure-God think of some nice, juicy things to talk about at chow, Harris," Burgoyne said.

"Too bad about you delicate bastards," Harris jeered. "Let me tell you about a slicing I saw once, up at Wanhsien."

"Permission not granted," Wilsey said. "Slice *you*, Harris."

"Slice you too, and all your bloody ancestors!" Harris said.

They found the pirated junk late on the second day, dismasted and partly burnt and derelict in the lee of a rocky islet, in the em-

bayment of a vast reed marsh. Bordelles and a party boarded it. The
kerosene was gone. The bodies of the crew were there, bound and
mutilated. The flag was there, torn in two and befouled with blood and
filth. They brought the flag back with them and Crosley took it below
and burned it decently in one of the boiler furnaces.

The pirates were probably watching from the reeds, but there was
no hope of catching them. Lt. Collins decided to sink the derelict
with gunfire, as a moral show of force. The three-pounder barked
repeatedly and Lt. Collins closed the range until they could see the
splinters fly, but the junk would not sink. Its timbers had inherent
flotation. It was very frustrating and in the end they had to board
again, drench the splintered timbers with their own kerosene, and try
to complete the burning. The gunfire had made quite a mess of the
bodies.

"I told Franks you can't sink a Chinese junk that's empty," Restorff
grumbled.

The *San Pablo* sailed away just at sunset with the junk wreckage
flaming redly against the reeds. The Sand Pebbles were disgusted. But
a thrill ran through the ship when they learned Lt. Collins' plan. As
soon as it was full dark the *San Pablo* crept back again, with not a
light showing, and lay to under cover of the rocky islet to avoid the
noise of anchoring. Before daylight the full landing force would go in
to search the reed marsh and possibly to catch the pirates off guard.

Each section went in one of the ship's two sampans. They hoisted
the motors inboard and poled with bamboos, careful not to splash or
talk or clink weapons. Franks went south half a mile, but Bordelles
went right in past the smoldering wreckage, which smelled very foul.
Once inside the reeds it was absolutely dark and they settled down
to wait for daylight. They cursed in whispers and slapped mosquitoes.
With dawn, a thin, misty rain began. They ate some of their sandwiches and started their search.

The reeds were like very tall corn, with narrow green leaves and
reddish-green stalks. The air was hot and dead and green-rotten-
smelling and there was long green grass under the water. Farren

crouched in the bow with the machine gun. Holman and Vincent poled. It was hard work and they had to keep backing out of blind reaches. Gnats joined the mosquitoes whining about their heads. They kept getting fouled in beds of the broad-leaved rushes that the Chinese wove into mats. They saw many long white snakes in the water.

"Them are good eating snakes," Farren whispered once. "We ought to catch some, for Big Chew."

"Pipe down!" Bordelles whispered behind him. "It's pirates we want to catch."

They could not help making noise. Holman did not think they were going to catch any pirates. He was soaked with rain drip from outside and sweat from inside and he poled doggedly in the dim, greenish light. After four hours of it, he was sick of the whole business. The others were still excited and alert.

Then they stumbled into a thinning in the reeds and a slightly higher hummock with several hundred square feet of almost dry ground. Bordelles signaled *Halt!* and they all seized weapons. There were two small mat sheds on the hummock and several small sampans drawn up and the coarse grass was all trampled. Farren readied his machine gun.

"One of them walls is moving," Crosley whispered. It did seem to be shaking. "They're poking rifle barrels through, Mr. Bordelles!" Crosley whispered urgently.

Bordelles made up his mind. "Rake 'em, Farren!" he said aloud. "Pole on in, Holman!"

Farren chopped back and forth through the two huts. Holman drove the boat in powerfully and they all splashed ashore yelling, weapons ready, Red Dog leading the pack. Holman brought up the rear. He was so excited that he came ashore with his bamboo pole instead of his rifle.

They did not notice that fumble, in their disappointment. No one was in the huts. There were five tins of kerosene in one of the huts. Four of them were punctured by bullets.

"Well, I guess we give the show away for nothing," Crosley said.

"Maybe not," Bordelles said. "Tear down one of the huts and make a smudge fire, to guide Franks here."

Franks would be coming to the sound of the guns, of course. The smudge helped with the gnats and mosquitoes, but the smoke did not rise well in the misty air. It spread out and hurt their eyes and made them cough. Bordelles kept wiping his face with a dirty handkerchief. His face was red and lumpy with bug bites. While they waited, he told about his plan.

The hummock was obviously a staging point for moving the kerosene inland in the small sampans. Very likely the pirates had not gotten it all safely away yet. Somewhere further in there would be a secret channel that led to the pirates' shore base. When Franks came they would split into four search groups, each in one of the small captured sampans. Whoever found the channel would signal with shots and flares and they would rejoin and all go in and smoke out the pirates. They would probably not catch any pirates, but they might recover a good part of the pirated kerosene.

"Mr. Bordelles, you're really smart!" Crosley said.

When Franks came he approved the plan and they worked it out in detail. Perna caught the job of staying behind as beach guard, and he was very unhappy about it. They all refilled their canteens from the waterbreakers. It was only eleven o'clock, but they ate the rest of their sandwiches and they were ready to go.

"Good-bye, Perna! Keep the home fires burning, Perna!" they all jeered at Perna, as their small sampans snaked easily away into the reeds. Almost at once they lost sound and sight of each other.

Holman was in Bordelles' boat, with Crosley and Tullio. He would rather have been with Farren and Red Dog. He poled again, and Crosley watched in the bow with his automatic rifle. Bordelles stood up and pushed reeds aside and signaled the way to Holman. The little sampan slid along easily. After a while they came into what seemed a twisting channel. They went about a hundred yards along it and Bordelles halted.

"I wonder if we should call in the others," he said. "What do you think, Holman?"

"I think yes," Holman said. He wanted them all there, with both machine guns.

"Let's go just a bit further," Bordelles said.

Around the next turn, the channel pinched out. In the next hour they found two more blind reaches like that. When they found the true channel they went more than a mile along it before they were ready to believe it. But it was unmistakably a channel, with reeds chopped out and sedge dug away, a long, winding, green-shadowy tunnel. Holman stopped poling and Bordelles looked at him.

"Ain't it about time to call in the other sampans?" Holman asked.

"We're very close in now. We might give up the chance of a surprise," Bordelles said.

"This rain would've muffled them shots we made," Crosley said. "Let's sneak on in and surprise 'em. We can take 'em, Mr. Bordelles."

"We'll scout on in," Bordelles decided. "No more talking."

Holman poled, his eyes on the water, until he was surprised to see tree tops to port. Then there were trees above the reeds to starboard also, and a clear current that waved and rippled the water grass, and the reeds were thinning out. They were going up a creek. Bordelles, his pistol ready, stared keenly ahead. He kept waving Holman on. Then he snapped his hand around with the fingers spread, and that meant *stop!* Holman stopped. They drifted silently back with the current for a hundred feet and Bordelles had them secure the sampan to the bushes on the port margin.

"I saw the stern of a boat," he whispered. "A big one. Who wants to scout the place?"

"Let me, sir," Tullio said.

He eased ashore and worked carefully along the bank, not making much noise. He was gone about twenty minutes and came back excited and eager.

"There's a stone jetty and a big wupan, nobody in it, and it's got kerosene in the bilges," he said. "There's a farm compound up the bank. The gate's closed. I didn't see anybody up there, no smoke or anything."

"Very well done, Tullio!" Bordelles said. "We'll have a look inside that compound, I think. You lead the way."

Tullio flashed his white teeth in a smile and slipped over the side again. They followed him through knee-deep, sludgy water to a dirt bank covered with moss and ferns. They went through willows and past real trees with dark, waxy-green leaves. It had almost stopped raining and watery sunlight hit the wupan. An iridescent oil scum floated on the water in the bilge. Bordelles nodded vigorously.

"We will indeed have ourselves a look inside that compound," he whispered. "You walk directly up to the gate, Holman. We'll cover you. If firing starts, sprint *for* the wall, and take cover at its base."

"Aye aye, sir," Holman said.

Crosley and Tullio went off to either side. Holman walked up the path. The whitewashed wall was about eight feet high, with a closed wooden gate in the center, and gray tiled roofs showing above it. He felt numb. He didn't know what he was going to do when he got there. Bordelles yelled and there was red-shot smoke and a slap on Holman's left jaw and his body was crawling on hands and knees into the shrubbery. Black smoke rose above the wall. Crosley's BAR chattered and the bullets made red splotches on the wall. "Hold high, Crosley!" Bordelles yelled. He ran past Holman, pistol in hand, and crouched at the base of the wall.

Holman had blood in his mouth and his teeth wouldn't line up. He was afraid to clamp them together. He wished Farren and Red Dog were there. Crosley was still firing short bursts. Bordelles stood up flat against the wall and tossed something over to right and to left. There was a double explosion inside. Bordelles lunged with his shoulder at the gate. That was something he could do, Holman thought. He picked up his rifle and ran to join Bordelles, and his solid weight crashed the gate open.

"Give me your grenades!" Bordelles said. "Cover me!"

He ran to the biggest house, at the left. A man was down, crawling feebly in front of it. Bordelles tossed a grenade through an open window and ran around to the side and there were more explosions back there. Crosley shot the creeping man in the head. He and Tullio ran back to join Bordelles. An old woman was spreading a quilt over a heap of something to the right of the courtyard. She jerked and worked frantically.

Bordelles and Tullio came back through the big house. They walked springily, in a slashing, dashing way. Holman was standing there.

"They all got away out the back gate," Bordelles said. "Say! You're hit!"

Holman tried to say it was nothing. He could not talk well. Tullio tore open a first-aid pack. Rifle shots sounded in back and Bordelles snapped, "Spread out!" and they did. It was only Crosley. He came out grinning all over his frog face.

"I was just killing them pigs back there," he said. He darted his eyes around the courtyard. "What about that old woman?"

"For God's sake, Crosley! Don't kill her." Bordelles laughed. "Let her go. She can't hurt anything."

"I didn't mean kill her," Crosley said.

The old woman crept away. Tullio sprinkled powder on cotton and packed it in Holman's mouth and put a clumsy battle dressing on the outside. Crosley and Bordelles found about a hundred tins of kerosene under the quilts. All the bedding in the place was piled on top of it. Maybe it was the old woman's way of hiding it under the bed, Holman thought. She just wanted to help. He had a dull ache in his jaw. He felt as if he were one or two moves behind in a game he didn't know how to play in the first place. The others were pulling the unpunctured cans out of the heap. Kerosene was slopping and spreading on the damp clay.

"Take the good ones down and load them in that wupan," Bordelles said.

Tullio started down with two of them. A spatter of shots from the woods drove him jumping back.

"They've circled around!" he said.

"They'll get our sampan!" Crosley was unslinging his BAR. "We're cut off!"

"Don't get excited, men," Bordelles said. "Farren and Franks are coming. They'll take them in the rear." His happy grin was gone, however. "Count your ammunition," he said tautly. "We'll have to go easy, now."

Crosley had only two magazines left. Holman had not used any of his. They refilled two magazines for Crosley from Holman's and Tullio's stock. "Wasting shells on pigs!" Tullio sniffed. "The other guys are coming," Crosley said. "They couldn't help but hear our fire. All them grenades." "Of course they're coming," Bordelles said. He spread them out, to watch both gates. It was seeming longer than it was, Holman knew. From time to time bullets from the woods whined across the wall. Then, very far away, they heard the *San Pablo*'s siren going in short, screaming pulses. It was the emergency recall signal.

They clustered around Bordelles at the front gate. "What if the other parties go back to the ship, now?" Tullio asked.

"They won't, if they heard our firing."

"If." Crosley started and swore angrily. "That old woman!"

"Find her!" Bordelles snapped.

Hastily they searched the pens and shacks, but the old woman was gone. She would tell the pirates there were only four ocean devils trapped there and it would make them bold enough to attack. All of a sudden it was very bad.

"I should've let her have it!" Crosley said bitterly. "The only good ones are dead ones."

"We'll have to fight our way out of here before they can react," Bordelles said.

They all jumped to his crisp orders. They slashed the good cans with bayonets and they set fire to the kerosene and the soaked bedding. "Too bad these damned mud houses won't burn!" Bordelles said. The fire caught and *whooshed* in a roaring column of flame and smoke. Crosley jumped out the gate and crouched and sprayed the woods blindly with bullets while the others ran down to the jetty. Then they fired, while Crosley ran to join them. They all crashed along the creek bank, careless of noise, and their sampan was where they had left it. In seconds they were in the sampan, Holman and Tullio both poling vigorously, and in a few minutes they were well out into the reed marsh. It had all run off very smoothly, like a drill.

"Well done, men! Very well done!" Bordelles said.

They were all grinning at each other, except Holman. Far behind them, the pirates were still shooting at nothing. Black smoke was billowing high above the trees back there, rolling, outfolding, shot through with red.

"They'll see *that* from the ship!" Crosley said proudly.

They met Farren in the channel and the two sampans went back in company, shouting the story back and forth, and Red Dog yapped triumphantly. When they shifted to the ship's boat at the hummock, they began being solicitous of Holman. They would not let him pole. He felt dizzy and nauseated and his jaw hurt badly. He was thirsty, and when he tried to drink from a canteen he spilled most of it. He kept thinking about ice-cold, very sweet lemonade.

In the sick bay, Jennings fussed and clucked about Holman's jaw. Holman could feel the ship getting underway, even as they hoisted the boats in. Jennings cleaned out Holman's mouth with an alcohol swab and packed the jaw with medicated cotton and it hurt very much.

"It looks pretty clean. I won't probe," Jennings decided. "We're going straight to Changsha, and I'll take you to the mission hospital for that. They have x-ray there."

Holman was sicklisted. He had to take a shower in the sickbay head and put on pajamas and turn into one of the sickbay bunks. He was glad to lie down. The Sand Pebbles began coming back to see how he was and to congratulate him. Both Lt. Collins and Bordelles stopped by with cheerful words. All the chiefs looked in. Even Pohan came up, full of admiration. Big Chew made beef broth and brought it up personally for Holman's supper. Holman drank it through a bent glass tube and it was hot and rich and good. He winked at Big Chew and wished he could tell him that he appreciated the soup more than all the other attention he had been getting.

In the evening the Sand Pebbles came back again, by twos and threes. They wanted Holman to have all the dope. General Tang was back in Changsha with some other warlord to help him, and they were pushing on down the river. They were supposed to be trying for Hankow also, and there was real fighting going on all along the lower Siang. For some reason Comyang was very excited about it and Waldhorn was glued to the radio receiver. All sorts of stuff was coming in coded and Bordelles would be up all night decoding it.

"Clear out of here, you men!" Jennings said at last. "Can't you see he can't talk? He needs rest."

It was peaceful, alone in the dark. General Tang had been all right before, and they would be all right in that courtyard in Changsha. Holman drifted uneasily toward sleep. He had not liked all the attention and praise. He had not done anything in that fight, except to get wounded. But that made him the *San Pablo*'s walking battle scar, and that was what they were proud of. They did not give any more of a damn for Jake Holman than they ever had. Except for Burgoyne and Po-han, they did not even know Jake Holman.

All next day they steamed across the lake. Holman was feverish and he slept most of the day. The ship buzzed with scuttlebutt. One of the new orders from Comyang was that gunboats could no longer shoot back when they were fired upon unless they could clearly see and identify who was shooting at them. But you could never see that. His shipmates came to cheer Holman and stayed to wrangle with each other. The new order meant they would just have to run out of range when they were fired upon, and the *San Pablo* would lose more face than it could stand losing. Half asleep on laudanum, Holman listened to them argue. Some thought it must be a mistake in decoding. Some thought it would be only for a day or two. Some thought Lt. Collins would just pretend to see the *toofay* and they would go on shooting back.

"Not that Collins," Harris said. "He thinks orders are sacred."

It was the nearest thing to a gripe about Lt. Collins that Holman had ever heard. The wrangling went on and on. No one could understand why Comyang was so worked up about Changsha. No one had ever heard before of the new warlord who was teamed up with General Tang. The new warlord's name was Chiang Kai-shek.

24

They turned up the Siang channel early in the morning and at once began meeting junks headed downriver loaded with soldiers. Ordinary warlord troops seldom had flags around, but these junks had big flags. Being Chinese, they had to do it bass-ackward, as Farren said, and the flags were in the bow. They were bright red, with a blue field that held a white, serrated disk. No one had ever seen that flag before. The soldiers wore a strange green uniform. They seemed mostly scrawny kids, and they looked across from their junks to the *San Pablo* with bold, black, measuring eyes. They did not look at all like sloppy, hangdog, happy-go-lucky warlord soldiers.

Quite often they sighted green troop columns marching north along the banks, with the new flag out ahead of every unit. The whole countryside seemed excited and moving, streaming northward toward Hankow. There was supposed to be a big battle going on at the foot of the lake.

Twice before dinner the *San Pablo* was fired upon from ambush. Both times it was a low and deadly fusillade that smashed windows and drilled through the wooden superstructure. Both times Lt. Collins personally rang up flank speed and they ran out of range without

shooting back. Holman felt weak but clear-headed and he dressed
and went down to the crew's compartment. Farren and several others
were lashing mattresses across broken windows. Tullio was sweeping
up glass. They were angry and ashamed.

"He takes the wheel himself and makes everybody else on the
bridge squat down behind the bulwarks," Farren told Holman. "He
keeps his face as blank as a flange."

"He don't like it any better than we do," Vincent said.

None of Pappy Tung's men would work on deck. Fortunately, the
galley was included in the steel engine room and bridge portion of the
superstructure, and Big Chew stayed on the job. Holman had his
soup at the mess table with the others. Only about half of the crew
sat down to the meal. They had barely started when more firing
broke out.

"Take cover! Clear port side! Clear port side!" Franks' voice
sounded from forward. "All guns, hold your fire! Hold your fire!"

Bells jangled below and the ship picked up speed. The men at
Holman's table looked at each other. Glass tinkled and bullets
thudded into wood and mattresses. Duckbutt Randall, at Bronson's
table, took his plate aft to the nonrated men's table, which was
flanked by double-deck bunks.

"Hell with it. Let's eat chow," Farren said.

Holman worked on his soup. He was unpleasantly aware of the
door open to the port side, just behind his back.

"Them green soldiers are all *toofay*," Restorff growled. "Them
and their warlord with 'em. All *toofay*, by God!" His blunt, brown face
was angry.

"I don't get them orders," Farren said. "When we tuck in our
tails and run, we're just asking for more of it."

"We'll get more," Restorff said.

"Prong orders!" Harris said. "Let's shoot the bastards!"

"These come right from Coolidge," Red Dog said, from the other
table.

"Prong Coolidge! What's he know about China?"

Harris hurled his fork across the compartment. He went into a frenzy of cursing, tossing his white hair, scrawking his voice, bulging his outraged eyes, outdoing himself. He howled new and strange obscenities. The other Sand Pebbles forgot the bullets and listened with wondering admiration. Harris cursed Coolidge and China and missionaries and most of all the new warlord, whom he called, in a strangled, throat-tearing shout, that green-assed, baby-raping, mother-defiling *Chancre Jack!* The possibly accidental nickname delighted the Sand Pebbles. The cursing was almost as satisfying as a sixteen-inch salvo in among the ambushers. When Harris subsided at last, puffing, his craggy face a dull red, the firing had stopped. The *San Pablo* had run out of range again.

"Arf! Arf! Arf!" Red Dog barked happily.

"Chancre Jack," Farren mused, with relish. "That's his name, all right."

They ran a gantlet of bushwhacking rifle fire more or less all afternoon. Someone, afterward no one could remember who, coined a nickname for the hateful new flag: *gearwheel flag,* for the serrated white disk it bore as emblem. It was a good nickname, that could be growled deep in the throat. The last flurry of fire came only ten miles from Changsha itself.

The *San Pablo* anchored in her regular place. There would be no liberty until Lt. Collins came back from the consulate. Changsha was swarming like an anthill. Green uniforms were everywhere along the bund. It was a weekday, but all the treaty business places had national flags flying above the company flags. They were almost lost in the great show of gearwheel flags along the top of the city wall. Changsha was a city of flags.

A huge gearwheel flag floated from the top of the bund hotel. After sunset the hotel blazed with light and rang with music. Crosley turned the long glass on the roof garden and reported that they were all gearwheel officers up there, dancing with Chinese girls. Even some of the girls wore the green uniform. It was very gay and festive. A military band alternated playing "Onward, Christian Soldiers" and "A Hot Time in the Old Town Tonight."

It was a very cold homecoming for the Sand Pebbles.

Lt. Collins came back, looking stern, and went straight to his cabin. Word came down that there would be no liberty until further notice. Red Dog came back with mail and the Sand Pebbles gathered around him in the compartment to hear the scuttlebutt.

"The Red Candle's closed," he said. "They got Victor Shu in jail. They say he's an enemy of the people."

That hit them hard. The missionaries had never been able to close the Red Candle. No one spoke for a moment.

"Well, I guess the missionaries are all getting their guns over that," Wilsey said at last, somberly.

"I hear a lot of 'em favor the gearwheel, all right," Red Dog said. "Damned if I know why, though. I hear the town's full of missionary women and kids from upcountry. The gearwheels are raising hell with the missions upcountry."

"What doing?"

"Taking 'em over for troop quarters," Red Dog said.

They were putting their horses in the churches, he went on. They tore out crosses and holy pictures and put up their gearwheel flag and pictures of Sun Yat-sen. All the people, missionaries included, had to come in and bow to the flags. They were doing the same thing in the heathen temples.

"Well, but God damn it!" Farren said. "You'd think the biblebacks would be screaming for blood."

"They ain't, though," Red Dog said. "From what the clerk at the consulate told me, they're the ones behind the no-shoot-back order."

The Sand Pebbles cursed and wrangled over that mystery until taps.

After breakfast Holman had to go ashore with Jennings. When he took a dress white jumper out of his locker he found that a spent bullet had driven wood splinters into it, but the cloth was not harmed. The sampan coolie demanded a dollar and the rickshaw coolies on the bund wanted a dollar each to go to the mission hospital. It was far too much. The coolies would not bargain. They spat curses and turned their backs and an unfriendly crowd began to gather.

"Hell with 'em, Doc," Holman said. "Let's walk."

They walked. The rickshaws in Changsha were no good, anyway. They had wooden wheels and hard rubber tires and no springs and all the important people rode in chairs. It was a pleasant morning for a walk. All the shops were open and the streets thronged and gearwheel troops were moving through. Holman was struck sharply by the difference. Warlord soldiers straggled on the march, slouching and slovenly and hung with strange gear such as teapots and umbrellas. Or they loitered along the streets with a sly, sullen, hangdog look that marked them more surely than their uniforms. The people feared and despised them. The people smiled and waved at the gearwheelers. Little boys ran shouting after them, clutching paper flags. The soldiers marched briskly along in step, fairly neat, heads up, and more often than not they were singing. Holman saw several girls swinging along in ranks with the soldiers.

"They're all just kids," he said.

"Cantonese all look like kids," Jennings said. "It's Malay blood."

Holman tried to place his feeling. He was feeling *left out,* he thought, wondering. He had not felt that, to care a damn about it, since years ago in Wellco, Nevada.

The hospital was a big brick building with a Chinese roof. There were other brick walls and buildings and trees and neat green lawns and tennis courts and it was an extensive place. They had a gearwheel flag and a U.S. flag side by side over the main building. Inside it smelled of ether and iodoform, and people in white, most of them Chinese, were very busy. They all knew Jennings. It was strange to hear Doc Jennings called "Alfred."

After the x-ray Holman had to sit a long time alone with Chinese patients on a wooden bench in a passageway. A Chinese nurse had a desk at one end. People in white, and some in the gearwheel green, kept passing. They looked curiously at Holman. He felt like a strange specimen with his sailor suit and his bandaged jaw.

Jennings came and led him to a small white side room and he sat in a dentist's chair while a pretty Chinese nurse took off his bandage. He had whisker stubble under it. The doctor was a thin, fussy little man in a white gown. He studied the x-ray plate and asked Jennings how it happened. Jennings made it sound as if Holman had been storming the Halls of Montezuma, because that was how they were telling it on the ship. The doctor sniffed.

"Chiang Kai-shek is going to do away with all that banditry and piracy," he said. "There won't be any excuse for gunboats being here."

"Who'll keep Chiang in line, if we go?" Jennings asked.

"You're as bad as the oil company people, Alfred." The doctor pressed fingers along Holman's jaw. "Does that hurt, sailor?"

"Little bit."

It hurt like hell. They had to put in a metal prop to help him keep his mouth wide enough open. The doctor was after a piece of metal with probe and forceps. He kept talking to Jennings about the new warlord. Sweat streamed down Holman's face. The nurse kept wiping his forehead with gauze and the touch of her fingers helped him. The doctor was not feeling anything. He was just doing a job with tools.

"Got it!" he said. He took the prop out of Holman's mouth. "Rest a while," he told Holman. "Rinse your mouth."

The nurse held a basin for him. Holman's head cleared and he tried not to pant audibly. His calf muscles were trembling.

"No, Chiang is not another warlord," the doctor was telling Jennings. "China is becoming a nation, being newly-born as a nation, all around us. Can't you feel it in the streets and see it in people's faces?"

"No," Jennings said. "What's China been all along, then?"

"A geographical expression." The doctor turned back to Holman. "This is what hit you," he said. It was like a blunt tack. "What sort of guns do they shoot these in?" the doctor asked.

"A big two-man shotgun, kind of a blunderbuss," Holman said.

He remembered the gun lying in the courtyard. Crosley had thrown it into the burning kerosene.

"You were lucky the whole charge didn't hit you," the doctor said. "Well, shall we get on with the rest of it?"

"What do you mean, the rest of it?"

"A molar has to come out. I'll have to probe for broken roots."

"Jesus Christ," Holman said. He should not have begun letting down.

"Oh, come now, no profanity, please," the doctor said. "We pulled a tooth for General Chiang last week, over at his headquarters. He only took five minutes off work."

"You know what we call him on the ship?" Holman said. "We call him Chancre Jack."

The nurse hid a smile. "Do you?" the doctor said. "Open up, please," he said.

It was very, very bad. Holman stood it by hating the doctor. He would not give that son of a bitch the satisfaction. But it came over him in waves and it was the nurse's fingers that held him in place. Her fingers, and glimpses of her soft mouth drooping in pity. She carried him through the red haze of it and then they had him resting there with his head down on his knees and their voices sounded far off.

"I'd rather not give him a bed," the doctor was saying. "We already have the wounded coming in from the fighting around Yochow. You can take care of him in your sickbay, can't you?"

"I'm all right," Holman mumbled. He raised his head, hands on trembling knees. "Let's go back to the ship, Doc," he said to Jennings. He stood up. He was groggy, but he felt strength coming back. "Let's go, Doc," he said thickly, around the cotton in his jaw.

"You ought to rest an hour or two," Jennings said.

Holman turned his back on the doctor. "Thank you very much," he told the nurse, and tried to smile at her. She smiled very sweetly at him. "See you aboard," Holman told Jennings.

He walked out. Jennings caught up with him and took his arm. "You have to rest a little first," he insisted.

"Not in this God damned place," Holman said. "I'm going around by the railroad and stop and see how Maily is. I'll rest there." Jennings didn't like it. "You don't have to go with me," Holman said. "I don't even want you along."

Maily was all right. She was in Chinese rig and her room was clean and neat. She made tea, and it warmed and firmed Holman's stomach. She was sympathetic about his jaw and she wanted to know all about the trouble at Paoshan. She was very curious about Paoshan. Holman kept waiting for the children to come laughing and scrambling in.

"How's Su-li?" he asked, finally.

"She's well. She's a little darling," Maily said.

She said it strangely. Her eyes were shiny and sad. Holman was feeling stronger.

"Let's go out and feed the fish," he said.

The black ones came and ate rice cake from Maily's fingers, and it was just like before under that friendly tree, except that nobody else was in the courtyard. They all had tigers back above their doors, Holman noted. Then a woman came out of one of the rooms across the court. She came and spoke to Holman in Chinese and her voice was shrill and angry. Holman did not know what to think.

"What's wrong? What's she saying?" he asked Maily.

"She's Ling's wife, you know, the water coolie," Maily said. She was blushing. "She says you owe Ling money for water for the fish-pond, ten dollars."

"I already paid him for all summer," Holman said.

"I know. He raised the price." Maily was embarrassed. "The students have been telling them they should charge more for work, for everything, if it's for rich people."

"I'm rich, for God's sake?"

"Well, all treaty people . . ."

Maily seemed scared. Mrs. Ling—Holman recognized her now—was still jabbering. For Maily's sake, Holman gave the woman twenty dollars. She took it and shut up, but she did not bow or smile.

"Thank you, Jake," Maily said softly.

The door scraped behind them and Ah Pao came out. He was chubby and pouting in red. Su-li came behind him. They did not run to Holman. They stopped short and stared at him with big eyes. He thought it was his bandage, and the medicine smell. He squatted down and held out his arms.

"Su-li," he said. "How's my girl?"

Su-li wavered and tears came in her eyes. She was biting her hand. She shrank behind Ah Pao.

"Su-li," Holman said. *"Ding ding."*

"*Bu hao!*" the little girl said.

She turned and ran back inside her open door. Ah Pao went to Mrs. Ling. He looked over his shoulder at Holman and jabbered to Mrs. Ling. The coolie woman began to laugh. Holman stood up and looked his question at Maily. She would not meet his eyes. Po-han's wife came out, with a frightened smile and a bow at Holman, and snatched Ah Pao away. She scolded the little boy and dragged him wailing back into the room and shut the door. Holman took Maily's arm.

"Maily! What's it all about? What's wrong with everybody?"

"Please come inside again, Jake," she said.

They sat down at her table and she told him about it. The gear-wheelers—she called them *Kuomintang*—were preaching hatred for the treaty people. They were supposed to be oppressing and ex-ploiting the Chinese under the unequal treaties. The gearwheel was against all rich people, who were supposed to be automatically on the side of the ocean devils. You didn't really have to be rich to be in trouble. Po-han was in trouble, because he was landlord of the court-yard and because he worked on a gunboat. That was why Mei-yu was so frightened. The gearwheelers had cut all rents in half, not that it helped the tenants any, because they had to give the other half for a tax. It all came out of Maily in a rush.

"What was Ah Pao saying?" Holman asked.

"He was asking Mrs. Ling when the green soldiers would come to put you in the fishpond." Maily smiled sadly. "The street orators have been saying that the treaty people will all be pushed into the sea. Ah Pao has never even seen the river. It's the only way he can under-stand it."

"Jesus," Holman said. "Even the little kids. Even *babies!*"

"It's like a sudden poison."

Maily began to cry silently. Holman reached across the table and patted her shoulder.

"Are you . . . are they giving you a bad time, too?"

"They overcharge me, on our street," she said. "Mei-yu has been buying for both of us."

"It's more than that." His voice roughened. "What the bastards been doing, Maily? Tell me!"

"Nothing, really. It's just a coldness. I feel that I'm being . . . left out . . . shut out . . . pushed away, somehow."

"I know. I been feeling that all day."

"You're an American. But if I'm pushed away, where is there for me? If I'm not Chinese, what am I?" Her voice was breaking.

"You're Frenchy's wife," Holman said. "He'll take care of you, Maily. I'll help all I can. Don't you worry now."

"I can't help it. I worry what will happen to Frenchy." Her face was all broken up with her crying. "I'm just God's curse to myself and everybody," she said. "I wish I were dead!"

"Maily! Don't say things like that!" Holman slid his chair around to where he could put an arm around her shoulders. There was nothing nasty about it. "You ain't told me everything," he said. "What you told me ain't all that bad. Come on now, what's the rest of it?"

Crying into his shoulder, she told him. She was going to have a baby. She had been very happy about it and suddenly it was . . . all wrong, a danger, not fair to Frenchy, he might hate her for it, she couldn't say all the ways it was wrong.

"Everybody in the streets is so happy and hopeful and I'm . . . I'm . . ."

He smoothed her hair. "It's all right," he kept saying. "I'll get back to the ship and tell Frenchy he's just got to get special liberty and come over here. You just need Frenchy with you."

She stopped crying and he prepared to go.

"I won't tell Frenchy the news. He'll want to hear it the first time right from you," Holman said. "He'll be proud, I know. He really loves you, Maily."

That started her crying all over again.

25

Franks' landing force section was standing by at the consulate. There had been no trouble right in Changsha, but everyone expected it. Gearwheel agitators were making speeches on street corners and they held rallies on the bund every day. They were forming everybody into unions and making fantastic promises of how good it would be when they won their rights and blaming all their troubles on the unequal treaties. It was bound to lead to riots.

The shackmasters, Burgoyne among them, were granted special liberty. They understood it would be canceled the first time any one of them got in trouble. Holman's jaw healed rapidly and he was busy every day fastening the engine room floorplates around the bridge for makeshift armor. He had plank walkways down below in place of the floorplates, revealing everywhere the raw red lead of the bilges, and the engine room looked ripped open. Po-han worked at the job. The way things had changed ashore made him value his job aboard a great deal more than being a landlord. But he was also worried about the ship.

"Evahbody speak, all gunship go, nevah come back this side," he told Holman.

"No, no, Po-han," Holman assured him. "Right now we makee plenty more gunship in Shanghai. Pretty soon we have two, three American gunship this side."

Holman had never seen the Sand Pebbles so uneasy. They watched the troops passing downriver and repeated all the scuttlebutt. The commercial steamers were being fired upon. They came into Changsha with armor around their pilot houses and sand bags piled along their cabin decks and almost all the paleface women and children were leaving for Hankow. The consul sent out word to evacuate Western Hunan and all the Americans left the Chien Valley except the people at China Light. The China Light people did not send in their waivers. The Sand Pebbles cursed about that and seemed to take it as a bad sign. They were very touchy. Word came of a big gearwheel victory near Yochow. General Wu's men were said to have been undermined by propaganda and their officers bought with silver bullets. The Sand Pebbles repeated that. They did not want to believe that any Chinese could really fight. Word came that the gearwheels had mined the river in the Chenglin narrows and all commercial steamers stopped running into Hunan. Gearwheel troops monopolized the railroad. Changsha was more cut off than in the wintertime. The days were hot, sultry and electric, and no one knew what to expect.

One day they were eating their noon meal when they heard a far, strange noise. Wong dropped a tureen clattering on deck and burst into the compartment, very frightened. "Topside sampan! Topside sampan!" was all he could say. They all went out on deck curious to see a wonder and it was only three airplanes flying low over Changsha. They had the gearwheel on their wings and tails.

"First time I ever seen one of them infernal machines," Restorff grunted.

"It's Russians flying 'em," Crosley said, with assurance.

Bolshevik Russians were known to be with the gearwheel troops. The planes made much face for the gearwheel in Changsha. They added to the unease on the *San Pablo*. England and Japan and America had thousands of airplanes, but they did not have any in Hunan Province.

The students paraded along the bund nearly every day, very bold and noisy, with a forest of placards denouncing the treaties and the treaty people. According to scuttlebutt, many were the sons and daughters of big landlords and merchants who were in gearwheel prisons or who had even been shot. It was a thing unheard-of in China, where they worshiped ancestors. It was the student parades, more than anything else, that rasped the nerves of the Sand Pebbles. But they always watched them, in the way a man's tongue will seek an aching tooth.

"What the hell *are* the unequal treaties, anyway?" Wilsey said once.

"They give us our treaty rights," Ellis said. "We got to stand up for our rights."

"What the hell *are* our rights?"

"I don't know. I guess the officers know," Ellis said. "Ask Bordelles, if you really want to know."

Crosley aimed an imaginary gun at the line of students. "Boy oh boy, just like ducks in a row!" he said. He closed one eye and clicked his tongue rapidly. "Ducks in a rain barrel," he said. "Bet you they'd knock off that sign crap, quick enough."

"You can't shoot students," Ellis said.

"Old Chao stripped the girls and led 'em around in front of the soldiers," Crosley said. "I bet them soldiers liked that."

"I'd like it," Ellis said. "I bet some of them young ones are real tender gear."

"Hot damn!" Crosley snorted and pawed with his foot.

"You guys been aboard too long," Wilsey said. "Too bad you ain't shackmasters."

The shackmasters were not having it easy. All of them except Burgoyne were arranging to send their women to stay with relatives in the country, until the storm blew over. Maily had no relatives. The others urged Burgoyne to unshack, but he would not consider it. He was looking worried and not saying much. He had not told Holman about Maily being pregnant, and Holman did not mention it.

"I guess they say things in Chinese that hurt her feelings," Burgoyne said. "I can tell that much from faces. But nobody offers to hit her, or anything. But they overcharge her and Mei-yu both, now. They got to go clear over by South Gate to buy at a decent price."

"How about you?" Holman asked. "They give you a hard time?"

"Well, not right out in a way you could understand it that way." Burgoyne's face twisted and he tugged his mustache. "Maybe they cuss me, but they don't throw rocks, I mean. It's just a feeling so strong you could nearabout cut it with a knife."

"Well, piss on 'em!"

Burgoyne shook his head. "Po-han feels it, too. We don't never sit out by the fishpond any more. Him and me sneak home like it was a crime for us to have a home."

"How's Maily taking it?"

"She makes out to be cheerful." Burgoyne dug out his snuff. "But she cries in bed, when she thinks I'm asleep. And she's back on that crazy stuff, that God hates her."

"You got to get her to Hankow, Frenchy."

"I know that. I know that, now."

They talked about it. The only way was to go by junk. The word was that all junks were being commandeered by one side or the other, in the fighting above Hankow. It was not safe, but neither was Changsha safe. Po-han had offered several times to arrange a junk passage to Hankow for Maily.

"Makes me wonder, is it his way of hinting that Maily is bringing extra trouble on him?" Burgoyne said. "And she is, all right."

"I don't get it. Why in hell should she?"

"Account of me. And she's American too, and they know that, too." He pinched out some snuff. "I don't know what her raisings were, for she won't talk about that, but she's more American than you or me."

Holman felt an obscure warning signal. "No, Frenchy, she's Chinese," he said.

"Only on paper."

"Paper's what counts. It's down on paper that no Chinese can ever be an American."

"How about Chinatown, in Frisco?"

"They ain't Americans. We had Chinese in my home town, but even when I was a little kid I knew they wasn't Americans," Holman said. "Not any more than the Piutes up on the Duck Valley Reservation."

"Maily's always been American to me."

"You come from the wrong part of the country."

"Well, I got to get her out of this part of this country," Burgoyne said. "By the Lord God, I hope General Wu up there kills half of them gearwheelers and runs the other half clean out of China! Things was real good here, till the gearwheel came."

Bordelles took his section to the consulate to relieve Franks' group. It was easy duty. They slept on cots on a screened side veranda and stood two-hour sentry watches at the front gate. There were a deck of cards and a few old *Country Gentleman* magazines for the men off duty. The head was poor: a room off the kitchen with several big slop jars and a circular pottery tub four feet across and a foot deep. Coolies had to bring water in buckets. The consulate food was not half as good as Big Chew's meals. It was easy duty, but they were standing by for trouble, and a small noise at night would bring them all awake.

Trouble was in the air. The consul was deep in *walla walla* with the gearwheel people over mission property upcountry. It was almost a relief when the alarm came one sunny afternoon that gearwheel troops were trying to move into a mission school right in Changsha, the same school Bordelles had cleared of Chao's soldiers in April. They marched to the scene with the feel of springs unwinding.

Holman and Farren headed the double file behind Bordelles and they swung along in step, arms at right shoulder, washing the people aside like the bow wave of a destroyer. The school courtyard was full of green soldiers and carrier coolies with baggage. Two missionaries were talking to a little knot of gearwheelers. Bordelles barked, "Detail . . . *halt!*" and their feet went *one . . . two!* "Order . . . arms!" and they brought them down with a slap and a jingle. Bordelles stepped forward.

"Hello, Mr. James, Mr. Ingram," he said cheerfully. "Little trouble, eh?"

"A small misunderstanding, I'm afraid," the older man said. "Ensign Bordelles, may I present Major Liu of the National Chinese Army?"

Bordelles in his white and gold bulked much larger than the slender Chinese officer in neat green. No one moved for a second. Then, to avoid saluting first, Bordelles held out his hand. Treaty people did not salute warlord officers. Bordelles went up on his toes, leaning a bit, in an effort to crush Liu's hand. Liu's face did not show anything.

"What is your mission here, Mr. Bordelles?" he asked.

"My mission is to ask you that, Mr. Liu," Bordelles said. "This compound is American property. You can't just *lafoo* it."

"The English word is 'commandeer,'" Liu said. "This is Chinese soil. I have already shown Mr. James my authority under Chinese law to commandeer his school for a battalion headquarters."

His voice was quiet, but he was tense. It was very tense and quiet in the courtyard. Mr. James said something about the Chefoo Convention. Bordelles stepped nearer Liu and looked steeply down on him.

"May I see your authority?" he asked, just as quietly.

"No." Liu stepped back. "You have no right even to be here, in uniform and under arms," he said. "I will have you and your men escorted back to your consulate. If necessary, I will post a guard to see that you stay there."

Bordelles jerked visibly at almost every word. His eyes stared and his lips tightened. The Sand Pebbles shuffled their feet, getting set. All the colors were brighter. Bordelles spoke slowly.

"Let me warn you, Mr. Liu. Any interference on your part with me and my men in the performance of our lawful duty will constitute an act of war against the United States of America." He paused, to let that soak in. "If your superior officers are not prepared to go to war against America, they will probably disavow your action and make amends." His eyes holding Liu's eyes, Bordelles drew his forefinger slowly across his throat. "It has happened before," he said.

Liu was pale, too. He did not flinch. Holman felt numbly that two great, groping giants were touching fingertips. When Liu spoke, his English was slurred from tension, but his voice was still quiet.

"All too often before, but we have had enough of that now," he said. "I will quote your own history to you, Mr. Bordelles. If you mean to have a war, let it begin here."

You know, it could, Holman thought suddenly. Bordelles' nostrils were white and flaring and all his cheerful farmer look was gone. Liu spoke a command and the green-clad soldiers began to form up. They all had rifles and the noncoms had Mauser machine pistols in the wooden scabbards. There were at least four squads of them. *Custer's Last Stand,* Holman thought. *Remember the Alamo.* It did not seem to have anything to do with him personally.

"You may have your men sling arms, or you may have them lay down their arms," Liu said.

Bordelles was silent as stone. *Please. Please, gentlemen,* the two missionaries were saying. *Be reasonable. Make allowances.*

"You may go under escort or you may go under full arrest," Liu said. "That is all the choice I will give you, and you must make it now."

The missionaries slipped away. Bordelles stood frozen. Time seemed stopped. Liu spoke in Chinese. The noncoms echoed and the green soldiers fixed bayonets. The sudden hedge of bright, sharp steel was like an electric shock that started time again. A veil came over Bordelles' face. He turned half left.

"Sling arms," he ordered, in a choked voice.

One squad of gearwheel soldiers walked ahead of them and another came behind. All the street people knew. They pointed and taunted and jeered and they came out on narrow balconies and looked out of upper windows to laugh. Some spat or threw melon rinds and street filth. The gearwheel sergeant had to keep shouting at the people to stop it. It was a great, numbing wind of laughter. Bordelles walked sturdy and straight as a mast just ahead of Holman. His uniform was turning slimy. Holman heard it and felt it all, his gunsling chafing and the thud of his own marching feet, but he did not seem to be involved in it personally.

It was much better when they got outside the wall, on a wider street. The escort halted smartly at the consulate and the sailors went on through the gate. Bordelles went to his room. Without speaking or looking at each other, the sailors threw their guns on their cots and went to the washroom. The coolies had to bring a great deal of water. Afterward, dressed in clean uniforms, they were still silent. The laundry coolie came to pick up the dirty uniforms.

"No good. Throw away. Makee cumshaw beggar man," Farren told him. "Nobody can ever wash them clean enough again for me to wear."

Heads nodded slowly. They were all in a kind of shock, Holman realized. They were like women who had just been raped. He did not feel badly about it himself. He had the familiar feeling of a dirty job well done, a boiler cleaned or a stretch of bilge mucked out and painted, and he was all cleaned up again and that was behind him. He wished that he were a ready, fun-making man like Red Dog, to cheer the others up. He went over and stood behind Red Dog and squeezed his shoulder.

"Arf! Arf!" he said.

"Go to hell," Red Dog said.

He did not even look up to say it. Holman went to his own cot and sat down and read a *Country Gentleman*. In about an hour Franks came to take them back to the ship. There was not going to be any more landing force at the consulate.

Once aboard, they began coming out of it. When the feeling was spread over all the Sand Pebbles, it did not weigh so heavily on the men of Bordelles' section. Harris cursed furiously, and it raised all their spirits. The incident had been reported to Comyang in Hankow and it would probably go all the way to Coolidge in Washington. There would be a very big flareback, the Sand Pebbles told each other. More American gunboats, and very likely British and Japanese gunboats too, would come to Changsha. There would be a showdown with the gearwheel and they might even shell the city. Talking about it, they grew almost cheerful again.

But Farren sent Oh Joy to fetch Clip Clip. He had Clip Clip cut off all his hair and beard and then shave it all to smooth, white skin. He kept testing with his fingertips.

"Shave against the grain," he told Clip Clip. "Get this little patch here. And here. And here."

Farren looked like a pale stranger when it was done. He had a strong, handsome face. There was a dimple in his chin that no one had ever seen before.

For three days they waited for the big flareback. Radio traffic was heavy. Lt. Collins seemed to spend half his time ashore. On the fourth day he had the crew mustered aft for a talk, and they knew they were finally going to get the dope. Facing them from the stern grating, framed by the big hand-steering wheel behind him, Lt. Collins looked very serious.

"Men, we are plunged into a new and strange situation," he began. "The first thing we must do is to try to understand it. The students are the key to it. I want you to understand about the students."

Chinese respect for the students was a hangover from the old Imperial days, when scholars had been the most powerful and important people. It was a kind of superstitious worship of learning. It had some weird angles. Ignorant coolies thought the printed word was sacred. Everywhere in the cities they had stone receptacles for waste paper with words on it and someone would take the words away and burn them reverently. Missionaries had been mobbed and even killed when they used newspapers for toilet paper. But the weirdest thing of all was that the Chinese believed anything in print had to be true.

"The students are supporting Chiang Kai-shek," Lt. Collins said. "They put lies in print and send the material ahead to the army. Other students read it to the people and even to General Wu's soldiers and they believe it. They are undermined before they go into battle. They desert or surrender. General Chiang has done very little honest fighting in this campaign."

Heads nodded. That explained a lot of things, in a way.

"Now about the particular lies they use," Lt. Collins went on.

They blamed all troubles, droughts, floods, epidemics, bandits, famines, locusts and warlord battles on the treaty powers. They were promising the people a kind of Chinese heaven-on-earth as soon as they canceled the unequal treaties. All warlords who obeyed the treaties were running dogs. The students spread fantastic lies about the treaty people.

"For instance, our little sortie against the pirates last month," Lt. Collins said. "They fired first, and we killed only one pirate. But the consul has a clipping from a local newspaper stating that we killed thirty unarmed people, including women and children. They have suddenly begun making similar fantastic charges against gunboats on the main river. That is why we have the new orders not to fire back blindly against ambushers, because if we do the students will make another big lie of each occasion. We are up against lying as a matter of planned strategy, and it forces a new counter-strategy on us. Because you cannot stick a bayonet into a lie."

Farren muttered. Lt. Collins looked sharply at him.

"What did you say, Farren?"

"You can always stick a bayonet into a liar, sir," Farren said.

"Yes, and the unkilled liars will call him ten women and children." Lt. Collins shook his head. "We are fighting lies now, not armed men. It is an accident of history that we in *San Pablo,* here in our home port of Changsha, are the first American armed unit to come face to face with this new thing. How we face it can make it our great honor or our disgrace. I intend that it shall be our honor. Now, then!"

He slapped fist into palm and scanned them all. Holman stiffened involuntarily. All the men stiffened.

"It is our military honor to obey orders without question," Lt. Collins said soberly. "I will not go further into the background of our orders. I will say only that our government has decided for the present not to treat the current fighting as just another warlord squabble. For the time being, we will treat it as an authentic civil war in which we must be very carefully neutral. We will avoid the least shadow of suspicion of interference in any purely Chinese affair. We will cruise only between treaty ports and we will put armed parties ashore only in concessions. We will not use force to protect American property. We may use force to protect American lives, but only American lives, and only when it is not possible to protect them in any other way."

He paused for breath and wiped his face and hands with a handkerchief. It was very warm, but he was sweating more than he needed. Holman could feel the stir of dismay running along the ranks.

"Some of you, our shipmates, as we all know—" He stopped and coughed. "It was an unpleasant experience. But it was not dishonorable. Understand that. It was highly honorable. It was a magnificent display of moral courage. I am proud of every man who took part in it. I want you all to understand about moral courage. I know it is not easy. We are trained to fight men, not lies. We are trained to face death and wounds, not public scorn. But to win this fight against lies, we must find the moral courage to endure public scorn and even personal indignities without flinching or retaliating. That is the sacrifice the service of our nation demands of us now. I know we all have the moral courage to make it. And that is all I have to say to you. Are there any questions?" His eyes swept the ranks. "Yes, Farren?"

"You're saying there ain't going to be any big flareback, ain't you, sir?" Farren said.

"Not for the time being. I've explained, it's not that kind of struggle."

They broke ranks and all they carried away with them was the heavy knowledge that there was not going to be any big flareback. The whole ship was feeling dismally like that hour or so on the consulate veranda, Holman thought.

"This is a council of war, gentlemen." Lt. Collins smiled wryly. "The new kind of war." Bordelles and the three chiefs sat around the table with him. They all had coffee. "Franks, how would you say the men are taking it?"

"Not a bit good, sir." Franks shifted. "I hear a lot of griping, the bad kind. They been shoving and kicking the ship's coolies around. I've had to raise hell with Ellis and Stawski about that."

"How do we know them coolies ain't all pulling for the gearwheel, behind them stupid, flat faces they got?" Lynch asked.

Franks smiled grimly at Lt. Collins. "You see?" his eyebrows said.

"Now that the *Woodcock*'s in port, they'll open their canteen at the British consulate," Bordelles said. "The men can go there and drink beer, get off the ship, anyway."

"Won't help, sir, not if I know sailors," Franks said. "They'll just pick fights with the Limeys."

"Well, what do you suggest, Chief?"

Franks scratched his head. "Can't think of anything, here in port, sir," he said. "But next time we go cruising and get shot at, it would help a lot if we fired back."

"Provided we can see our targets."

"We can always pretend we see them," Bordelles said.

"We are presumably men of honor," Lt. Collins said coldly. He had been expecting one of the chiefs to suggest that, but not Bordelles.

"We don't all have to see 'em, sir," Franks said. "We could put somebody up in the crosstrees, somebody with sharp eyes and a good imagination."

Bordelles smiled. All the heads nodded. Lt. Collins frowned.

"No," he said. "In this ship we will obey orders to the letter."

Franks shrugged. There was a painful silence. Then Welbeck spoke.

"It would help if they knew what was coming. If they could see an end to it," he said. "It would help my morale too, if you want the truth, sir."

Lt. Collins steepled his fingers. "I don't know what's coming," he said. "I've talked several times to the new Hunan Commissioner for Foreign Affairs. I think he wants to be decent and reasonable. But he seems to have little authority over the troops and even less over these worker and peasant unions they are forming. If that goes on, I don't know what's coming."

"Well, then, damn it!" Lynch said. "Excuse me, sir."

"Their Bolshevik advisers," Bordelles said. "Bolshevism is what's coming."

"A possibility." Lt. Collins nodded. "The problem seems to be, what strategy will best prevent that? Not all their leaders are Bolshevist. Chiang certainly is not. But he is strongly nationalist. He will abrogate the treaties if he is not stopped, make no mistake about that."

"Bolshevism is Russian nationalism," Bordelles said.

"They are trying to make it seem Chinese nationalism. The consul is sending urgent reports. No one at home—" Lt. Collins broke off. He was not going to criticize the government.

"I don't savvy that stuff, sir," Franks said. "Neither will the sailors. For them, it's got to be simple."

"You're right, Chief!" Lt. Collins nodded vigorously. "It's beyond all our competence. We will simply carry out our orders."

"Hell, maybe Wu will kick the tar out of the gearwheel up at Hankow," Bordelles said. "The other northern warlords are moving troops down. We don't have to assume Chiang's going to win."

"That would sure fix things, wouldn't it?" Welbeck said hopefully.

"Yeah, but Wu's still losing, from all the scuttlebutt," Franks said. "The guys got to see some clear way out of all this, sir. Even if it's pulling the ship clear the hell out of China, the way the missionaries want. Even if it ain't true. But they need to see some kind of end, sir."

Lt. Collins thought about that. An idea was forming. It took shape as the council dragged on. The sailors were what they were, very fine men of their kind, but they needed help in this strange situation. As he thought out a possible help, it began to seem more and more pleasing and plausible even to himself. It was indeed a help. He grew impatient and dismissed the council.

"Wait a moment, Chief. I want to talk to you," he told Franks.

The chow was very good, but they were all griping. They were beginning to repeat themselves, Holman noted.

"Us moral heroes!" Harris sneered. "I'm a moral coward, myself. I say kill the slopeheaded, gearwheeling sons of bitches!"

"If we got to run when we get shot at, let's run all the way out of China," Farren said. "Might as well, all the good we can do."

"This ship can't go to sea," Burgoyne said. "It ain't seaworthy."

"We ought to put in for a transfer, every last bastard of us, and sign it in a round robin," Wilsey said. "That'd make Comyang take notice."

"Speak for yourself," Burgoyne said. "Put in for your own transfer."

Harris slammed down his coffee cup, slopping it. "You want to go back to scrubbing your own clothes, Wilsey? Eating beans and diving your own bilges? Sleeping in bunks four high with somebody's dirty ass in your face every which way you turn?"

"No, I don't," Wilsey said. "I just meant——"

"Then stick it out with us moral heroes!" Harris said. "Let's fight for what we got, any way we have to."

Chief Franks came into the compartment, husky and cheerful looking, and stood between the two stanchions forward of the mess tables. The men all stopped eating and looked at him.

"Sailors, I got something to say," Franks began. "It ain't official. I'm an enlisted man, just like you are, and what I got to say is only my idea of what the score is. But I don't want it repeated, and I don't want the wrong people to hear it."

His serious manner impressed them. "Get out of here, Wong!" Bronson ordered. Men got up and closed the doors and stood by them. Others pulled down windows. Franks nodded approval.

"All right, here's how I figure it," he said. "These gearwheelers are all Bolsheviks and they sprung up out of nowhere without warning. They don't give a damn about human life and we do, and that's why they got us by the balls. Because we got missionaries, with a lot of women and kids, scattered all through China, and if we start anything now, the gearwheelers will take it out on them. But once we got all our sheep in the barn, it'll be a different story. I guess you all heard something about Plan Red?"

Heads nodded eagerly. Plan Red was an old scheme for all the treaty power gunboats to work together in case of another emergency like the Boxer Rebellion.

"Well, I'll tell you about Plan Red," Franks went on. "First, everybody pulls in to the treaty ports. If it's real bad, we give up

Chungking and Changsha and fall back on Hankow. But we can get the whole fleet up to Hankow. We put in troops to hold the concessions there and we got China split from Hankow to the sea. Then we counterattack, back to Changsha and Chungking, and we'll see who's got who by the balls then." He grinned fiercely. "That'll be the day, sailors!"

"Us and the Limeys, hey, Chief?" Bronson said.

"The Japs, too. And the Frogs and Wops. All of us." The men began talking and Franks waved his arms. "Keep in mind, this ain't official," he said. "Might nothing come of it. General Wu at Hankow is on our side and he could still win up there. But the missionaries are trickling in to the treaty ports, not too fast, I figure so as not to tip our hand, and maybe the day's coming."

"A lot of the biblebacks are for the gearwheel, so I hear," Bronson said. "You figure they might hold back, just to foul up Plan Red?"

"Them at China Light," Crosley growled.

"They might," Franks agreed. "I think when we're sure about that we'll just go ahead and let 'em take what's coming to 'em."

All the men began talking excitedly. Franks went out. He left a wholly different spirit behind him. Things made sense again to the Sand Pebbles.

"I bet the skipper put Franks up to telling us that," Farren said. "He couldn't say a thing like that himself, if it's a military secret."

"We got to keep it secret," Restorff said.

The men nodded, grinning at each other. Excited talk was going on at all the tables.

"Plan Red is really short for Plan Red Dog Bite-'em-on-the-ass Shanahan," Red Dog shouted. "Arf! Arf! Hear that, all you Sand Pebbles?"

"Arf! Arf!" many of them barked back at him.

"Say, this is damn good chow!" Wilsey said. "I'll have to stop by and tell Big Chew how good it was."

"I want more. Where's Wong?" Harris said. "Wong, you slant-eyed son of a bitch, come in here!" he shouted at the closed door.

Plan Red made the whole world look different and better. Pappy Tung's men had the windows reglazed and the bullet holes puttied and the whole topside repainted. The days continued hot and sultry, with occasional thunderstorms. The Sand Pebbles watched the student parades with indulgent amusement and stared back contemptuously at green-clad soldiers in passing junks. Word came that General Wu had lost Hankow, but he was still holding the walled city of Wuchang across the river. The concessions at Hankow were safe, of course; they were foreign soil, just like consulates. A landing force was ashore guarding them and Fleet ships were gathering at Hankow. It was all going according to Plan Red.

Things became worse ashore in Changsha. The many small unions —they even had one for whores—were lumped into one big worker-peasant union that took more and more unofficial power. They had strike pickets, who wore a dark uniform and carried six-foot bamboo staves, and they were a kind of unofficial police force. One day they arrested Po-han and took him before a kind of kangaroo court. Po-han's neighbors and tenants all testified that he was a good land-lord and had not been one for very long and he got away. Other landlords were not so lucky. They were fined and some were beaten to death. Po-han worked harder than ever aboard ship. He was quiet and worried. So was Burgoyne.

"It gets worse every day," Burgoyne told Holman. "If we pull out of Changsha, that Plan Red stuff, I'll just have to get Maily to Hankow."

He was more hopeful about junks getting through, now that the main fighting had moved downriver from Hankow. He was not a man to be bitter and angry, but he often cursed the gearwheel in his quiet way.

"People want to be friendly and they're scared to. They'll get them-selves in trouble," he told Holman. "We're just poison now."

There were not many gearwheel soldiers in Changsha any more. They had all gone on downriver to the fighting. But the worker-peasants were setting up a militia. They were just ragged coolies and farmers with red armbands and not one in ten had a gun. They carried big swords and spears and tridents and halberds, stuff left over from the old Empire, and one day a gang of them hauled a small brass muzzle-loading cannon along the bund. The militia often marched in the student parades and they were always good for an extra laugh.

Holman went several times to the Royal Navy Canteen to drink beer. It was a kind of godown shed behind the British consulate on the sand island, with several tables and some old magazines and a dart board. There was very good spirit among the sailors. The Limeys knew about Plan Red too, of course. Some of the younger business-men would drop in and contribute a bottle of whisky. The treaty women were almost all in Hankow and there was no longer a social schedule in the Changsha Club. Some of the businessmen were the same ones who had been beaten up in the Red Candle, but that was all forgotten. They were a band of brothers against the gearwheel. As Crosley liked to say, "Times like now, all us palefaces got to stick together."

One day Holman was drinking beer with Farren, Restorff and Banger Knox and two businessmen came in. One was the tall man named Van.

"Sure. Sit down here," Farren said.

They had a bottle of Peter Dawson. The smaller, kewpie-faced man was named Wilbur. They were wearing tough khakis and leather boots. Farren admired their boots.

"I'm glad the women are gone so we can dress the way we please," Van said. He stretched out one long leg. "I like boots. They're heavy on the feet and they clamp close around the leg," he said. "You feel you could stomp and kick and not get hurt yourself."

"Like tight leather gloves," Perna said, at the next table. "In Seattle the cops wear leather gloves with a patch of sheet lead under the backs. They backhand you and it's lights out, boy!"

The Peter Dawson went around and was quickly emptied. Van and Wilbur talked about their troubles with strikes and pickets. They were very bitter about the gunboat orders, especially the part about not protecting property. They thought it was just an invitation to the gearwheel to loot the palefaces. They were most bitter against the missionaries.

"They send lies back to the States and get their church people to write letters to Congressmen," Wilbur said. "Nobody in Washington knows what the score really is in China."

"The missionaries have 'em thinking this Chiang Kai-shek is another George Washington," Van said. "They want to pull the gunboats out and just turn China over to him. If we had our way, there'd be more ships in here and we'd enforce the treaties to the hilt."

The strange thing was that the missionaries were taking a worse beating from the gearwheel than anyone else. Van and Wilbur explained that, getting angry, interrupting each other, each one anxious to say it his way. Less than one percent of Chinese were Christians and most of them were rice Christians, Van said, but the missionaries made out back home that all China was on the verge of turning Christian. The missionaries had a soft life in China and damned few of them would even be able to make an honest living on their own, and they knew if they told the truth about China they would break their own rice bowls.

"They want to throw the rest of us to the wolves, to save their rice bowls," Wilbur said.

They blamed the anti-Christian troubles on the treaties and the gunboats, Wilbur went on. They were trying to make points with the gearwheel. They were trying to pretend that they never had had any part in the unequal treaties. That made the two men angriest of all.

"They came in under the treaties as forcibly as opium ever did!" Van said. "They grabbed themselves a damned sight better deal under the treaties than we've ever had!"

"They're not fooling the students for a minute," Wilbur said. "The students say Buddha came to China on a white horse and Christ came on a cannonball."

Holman had heard that before. He laughed just the same. Van and Wilbur went on talking. The people to consider were the ninety-five percent of Chinese who never thought about flags and treaties and only wanted to go on farming and working and doing business in peace. They were the real Chinese. The civilians were more worked up about it all than the sailors were, because they didn't know about Plan Red.

"It's a time to close ranks and the missionaries won't close up on us," Banger summed it up. "Very kittle folk they are, you might say."

"I wish Harris was here," Van said. "I dearly love to hear him take off about the missionaries." He was scowling and somber.

"It can't just go on forever," Farren said. He was growing his beard again and he was red-fuzzy all over his head and face. "Sooner or later something will happen to blow the lid off."

"The shooting will start and the missionaries will just have to take their bloody chances," an English sailor said.

"And I do hope it's bloody!" Van growled.

The lid blew off at Wanhsien, in the Yangtze gorges. The news came to Changsha in late afternoon and the city boiled with excitement. So did the *San Pablo*. H.M.S. *Cockchafer* and two other British gunboats had fought the Wanhsien warlord, who was not a gearwheeler. It was a hundred and fifty sailors against fifteen thousand troops and it was a great victory. Later in the evening word came that the British had been driven off with a quarter of their force killed or wounded, but they claimed two thousand Chinese casualties. The French gunboat *Gree* had stood by through the whole fight and done nothing to help. That last seemed a bad omen to the Sand Pebbles.

"Them Frogs will all get the moral Croyx de Garry," Harris sneered.

In the morning Burgoyne came aboard with mud splashed on his white uniform and he was bleeding from a cut above his eye. He had had to run from a street mob. "They're crazy mad over in town," he said. He told Holman privately that during the night someone had pitched Maily's two black goldfish out of the pond, to die on the dirty stones.

"Just her two," Burgoyne said. "It's a sign, Jake. I told Po-han go ahead and fix up a junk passage for her soon as he can."

The student parade that day lasted all day and it was frenzied. They stayed on the bund opposite the gunboats screaming and shaking insulting signs. One was a crude cartoon of a sailor with a baby stuck on his bayonet. The signs claimed twenty thousand people killed at Wanhsien. That was how they lied, the Sand Pebbles commented. The right way was always to claim the other side got hurt worse than you did. It threw you off when they claimed that themselves and even beat your claims. Chinese had no pride at all.

More news came in. The treaty power consuls were calling all Central China missionaries in to the treaty ports. All Western China was exploding with rage. The British scaled down their claim to about two hundred enemy casualties at Wanhsien. Women and children were to be pulled back all the way to Shanghai. It seemed to be Plan Red, all right. All day the Sand Pebbles stayed on deck, ready for anything. Lt. Collins would not let Burgoyne go ashore. It would have been suicide to climb up on the bund in a navy uniform. Po-han went ashore.

During the night a few holdout missionaries sneaked into Changsha, disguised in Chinese clothes. American destroyers reached Hankow and the large gunboat U.S.S. *Duarte* was ordered from Hankow to Changsha. The crippled British gunboats with their wounded aboard were turned back by gearwheel artillery fire at Hanyang, just above Hankow. The American destroyer U.S.S. *Stewart* had steamed up there and blasted the gearwheel guns to bits and brought the little gunboats safely into port. The Sand Pebbles repeated that proudly. It was the real Plan Red spirit. Late in the day a telegram came to the consulate from Paoshan. The China Light people were afraid for their lives and they wanted a gunboat to come and take them out.

"Wouldn't you know it!" Crosley said in disgust.

No one thought the *San Pablo* would go. Paoshan was not a treaty port. The water was very low in that end of the lake in September, perhaps already too low. The China Light people had had their warning and their chance to get out while commercial steamers still ran, and it would serve them right to be left there. Holman worried to himself about Miss Eckert. He was glad when orders came from Comyang the next morning for the *San Pablo* to get the China Light people and take them to Hankow.

It was a frantic day. They began raising steam. A number of

civilian passengers came aboard. One was Wilbur. Bales and boxes of merchandise lined the main deck on both sides. They would make good bullet shielding for the superstructure. Ping-wen had trouble getting enough coal. Big Chew was ashore trying to get extra food. Po-han was still ashore trying to get Maily aboard a junk for Hankow. When the coal was aboard and steam raised, Lynch wanted to report ready to get underway. He and Holman were in the engine room.

"Let's hold off awhile, Chief," Holman said. "Po-han ain't back. Frenchy's up on deck watching for him."

"We can steam without Po-han. This is war, boy!" Lynch rubbed his hands. "Plan Red! I'll report ready." He did so.

"Stand by and rock engines for the time being," Bordelles called back. "We have to wait for Big Chew to come aboard."

Holman gave Wilsey the throttle and joined Burgoyne on the main deck. Burgoyne was very nervous. He was tugging his mustache and working the snuff in his lower lip.

"The hell of it is, Po-han don't know we're sailing," he said. "He might just wait till morning."

There was nothing to do but watch and hope. Big Chew and Jack Dusty came aboard, with only one basket of vegetables, and there was not much hope left. On the bridge they tested the whistle and siren with a hoarse blast and wail, the signal for getting underway. Pappy Tung and his men went forward to raise the anchor. The anchor windlass began to clank and the hoses were going. Pappy Tung was cursing in Chinese.

"There he comes!" Burgoyne shouted, and began coughing.

Po-han was on the stone steps, waving his arms and arguing with a sampan man. Burgoyne was choking and coughing. He had breathed in some of his snuff. Po-han came alongside just as the anchor broke water and the screw began to thresh. Holman and Burgoyne reached down hands to pull him scrambling aboard. He came up grinning, showing his gold teeth.

"I heah whistle," he said. "I sabby ship go. What place go?"

"Paoshan," Holman said.

Po-han said he had just put Maily and her gear aboard a junk that would sail in the morning for Hankow. He pointed it out, but it was too far up the bund for them to be sure which one. Burgoyne had tears in his eyes from his coughing spell. He was getting control of his voice.

"Well, thanks, Po-han," he said. "You're a real shipmate."

"Laodah have got Kuomintang papah," Po-han said. "I think go Hankow no tlobbah."

"We're going to Hankow too, Po-han," Holman said.

"I just wish I'd had a chance to say good-bye to her," Burgoyne said.

"She'll be all right. She'll be waiting for us in Hankow, Frenchy," Holman said.

He was thinking that Po-han had not had a chance to say good-bye to his family, either. That was how it was with sailors.

26

In places the lake bottom lay almost bare, green-slimed mud and coarse grass sallowing. *San Pablo* followed the drowned channel and her bow wave crumbled mud from the banks. Fish teemed in the shrinking patches of water. Chinese in hundreds of sampans competed with millions of white birds at harvesting the trapped fish. The breeze brought human yells and bird screams and a smell of greenish rot.

Lt. Collins spent his days on the bridge. He was depressed. Under the new ruling *San Pablo* had no right in that end of the lake any more. He was to get the missionaries out quietly, avoiding incidents at all costs. He thought of how *San Pablo* had first opened up the lake with a famous cruise to Paoshan. China was still a shadowy Empire in those old days and they had protested it was a breach of the treaties because Paoshan was not a treaty port. Fighting Bob Evans was C-in-C Asiatic. He had said his interpretation was that the gunboats could go anywhere in China they could find water to float their keels. He had made it stick and the right automatically extended to the other treaty powers; it had been a factor in opening up Central China. It was *San Pablo*'s modest mark on history and now history was erasing it. This would be *San Pablo*'s last cruise to Paoshan.

In the Ta An narrows they passed a stranded timber raft. The people would have to live in the matshed village on top of it until the spring flood floated them again. Not far beyond the raft they were fired upon from ambush. They got up the hinged armor flaps and ran out of range. Most of the bullets hit the stack. It was probably all of the ship that could be seen from the ambush. The tall stack was covered already with patches over bullet holes. It was weakened by rust inside that fretted all the way through in places, and it was just one more sign that *San Pablo* had almost lived out her days.

The sailors on the bridge took the ambush well. Plan Red was sustaining them. But one of the passengers, Wilbur Venn, was on the bridge, and he would not let it go.

"Great stuff, hey, Bill? Something to write home about!"

Lt. Collins smiled sourly. He did not like to be called "Bill" on his own bridge.

"I'll fight too, if you have to fight," Venn said. "So will Pollard. We know your orders and all that but, I mean, if it's forced on you, just give us guns."

Lt. Collins nodded. He hated warlike civilians almost as much as he hated belligerently peaceful missionaries. Fighting was for professionals. Venn would not stop talking.

"It's just not natural, Chinamen shooting and white men running," Venn said. "It's against nature. Next thing you know, this guy Tunney's going to beat Dempsey." He waited for a response. "Bill, I'll bet you ten and the drinks Tunney wins," he said. "We'll settle at the club in Hankow."

"No." Lt. Collins turned his back. He despised Venn.

"Hey, Wilbur, I'll bet you ten on that," Crosley said.

"You figure Dempsey'll take him, do you?"

"Nobody living can beat Jack Dempsey," Crosley said scornfully. "He'll beat the meat off the bones of that damned gyrene."

Venn went over to talk boxing with the sailors. Lt. Collins went back to his thoughts. They were not any more pleasant.

In the delta the rice tops had a silver-frosty bloom. The patchwork fields rippled in the breeze like greensilver pools. Blue hills to the south grew more clear, with red-orange patches of autumn leaves and the dark green of camphor, the lighter green of tea groves and bamboos, red earth and whitish rock. Beyond the delta the banks rose high on either side and many white sandbars humped above the clear water. The sandy foreshore at Paoshan lay white and bare. The bund and the city wall were almost deserted. Only a squad of Pan's gray soldiers were on the pontoon and the Japanese flag was gone from the pontoon office.

"I see the missionaries inside, through that window there," Bordelles said as they were tying up. "Under guard, I suppose."

Lt. Collins went down to the quarterdeck to receive them. Packing cases cluttered the area and he saw with annoyance that an oil leak from one of them was staining the white teak. The box was labeled GRAHAM EXPORTS. The missionaries came out of the shack. The three men had no coats and they had blood on their shirts. Their faces were cut and swollen. The two women were not marked. They came aboard first. The younger one with the two children was hysterical. Loose hair straggled down her contorted face.

"We've been robbed and beaten and insulted!" she shrieked accusingly at Lt. Collins. "My babies have had nothing to eat since yesterday!" They were not exactly babies. The girl was almost old enough to interest the sailors, who watched curiously from aft. "It's all your fault, up there at Wanhsien!" the woman cried. "Innocent babies have to pay!"

"It was the British at Wanhsien, ma'am," Lt. Collins said. "We have the honor to be Americans."

"You're all the same wicked men of force and violence!"

Lt. Collins beckoned Jennings over. "Take them topside, do what you can for them," he ordered. They would berth in the sickbay. He turned to the three men. "This isn't all of you," he said. "Where is Mr. Craddock?"

"They remain under the sheltering hand of our Lord," one of the men said. "We who fled have already been punished for our little faith."

Lt. Collins felt dismay. "How many stayed?" he asked crisply.

"Four. The Craddocks, Miss Eckert and Mr. Gillespie."

"Did they send their waivers with you?"

"They sent no waivers. They trust a stouter shield and a more dreadful sword than yours, Captain."

A sailor snickered. Lt. Collins frowned.

"Go with the others. I have no more time for you," he told the men. "Farren, take them to the CPO quarters."

Farren grinned his sympathy. "Up the ladder, you guys!" he told the missionaries, shooing with his hands.

Pan's soldiers were still on the pontoon and their officer was talking in Chinese to Shing. Shing turned, balancing on his cane, and said the officer had an urgent message from General Pan.

"Genlah Pan speak ship go othah side chop chop," Shing interpreted. "He speak you, no sailah man, come shohside."

Lt. Collins asked questions. It turned out Kuomintang agitators were in town inflaming the people over Wanhsien. The ship was strictly boycotted. It was clear enough that Pan was preparing to submit to the gearwheel and he did not want to be compromised by a courtesy visit from his old friend Lt. Collins.

"Tell him I understand," Lt. Collins said.

He went up to his cabin. He had a decision to make. If they had only sent their waivers, he could leave them at China Light with a clear conscience. He thought he had never loathed missionaries more than at this moment. They all wanted to play Christ and suffer for the sins of other men—*wicked men of force and violence*—but what they suffered was only the consequences of their own vanity. Stupidity. Cunning and bad faith. Not sending those waivers was no oversight. He slapped his table and thought about it. Then he rang for Yen-ta.

"Ask Mr. Bordelles to come here."

"Tom, you'll have to take the motor pan to China Light," he told Bordelles. "Get those people or get their signed waivers. Take four men, armed of course."

"I'll just hustle 'em all down to the boat," Bordelles said cheerfully. "I'd like that."

"No. They're still citizens of a free country," Lt. Collins said. "But try to persuade them. And don't lose any time."

Bordelles went out. It was late afternoon. It would be almost morning before he could return, at the best. At the worst . . . Lt. Collins drummed with his fingers. Someone knocked at his door.

"Come in," he said.

It was Chief Welbeck, looking harried. "Sir, they're all griping," he said. "That woman's on my neck for milk and eggs for her babies. Jennings put her on me, damn him!"

"She's hysterical. Give her canned milk."

"She knows they got fresh milk in town, at that Christian dairy," Welbeck said. "Nobody can shut her up. God and President Coolidge, not to speak of Comyang, are going to hear about it, if she don't get milk."

Lt. Collins smiled. "You'll just have to grin and bear her, Chief. Don't try to shift her to my neck. Tell her we're boycotted, and that's that."

"Lop Eye Shing wants to send that bilge coolie over to get milk," Welbeck said. "You know, sir, the one that got eggs for us last summer. He was raised here and he's got relations in the city."

"Why tell me?"

"I thought I better, sir. I don't know what the score is."

His impulse was to forbid it. Damn the yapping woman! But it would be ignoble, their kind of mean and narrow action, if he had no better reason. If the coolie wanted to go ashore, he had every right to. It was really Shing's responsibility.

"I suppose the man wants to go?" he said.

"He's scared but willing," Welbeck said. "He acts kind of proud to be singled out for it."

"He wants to visit his relatives and pick up the milk while he's at it?"

"Something like that, I guess, sir."

"Well, he's Shing's man. If it's all right with Shing, it's all right with me."

"Yes, sir," Welbeck said. "I'll tell him go ahead."

After a moment Lt. Collins went out on deck. He was uneasy. Pan's soldiers were gone. Shing was aft, at the boat-deck rail. Lt. Collins joined him. Shing verified that the man really wanted to go. Together they watched him cross the sands, shoulders square, swinging a basket. He was dressed like any other coolie, in an open jacket and the droop-seated black trousers. He got up on the bund and into the tunnel-like city gate with no trouble.

"I don't like it," Holman said. "Things ain't right here."

"He was proud to go," Burgoyne said. "Po-han likes to help."

They were sitting on the workbench. Holman rattled the vise handle.

"I wish I'd been there. I'd've stopped it," he said.

"What's that noise?" Burgoyne said.

It was a crowd yelling. Lt. Collins went into the bridge. "Call Franks!" he snapped at Crosley. People were boiling out the city gate and running from either side along the bund. *The boat party,* Lt. Collins thought. *Nine people.* "Repel boarders! On the double!" he snapped at Franks.

"Hell!" Holman slid off the workbench.

"Repel boarders! *Repel* boarders! *Jump,* you bastards!"

Holman ran topside. Lynch was jerking open the arms locker. A black tongue of people was thrusting out the arched gateway. All along the bund they were streaming in to a center. The center was somebody running.

Po-han!

He had lost his jacket and he ran swinging something white and they poured down the stone steps after him like a stream of cannibal ants. Their shrill, high, screaming "Sa-a-ah! Sa-a-ah!" was like a fiery wind. Feet pounded the boat deck. Someone thrust a riot gun into Holman's hands. "Over their heads if they touch the pontoon! Shoot to kill if they cross it!" Franks roared. "Wait the word! Wait the word!"

Sand slowed Po-han. He labored leaping. A stick thrown like a spear struck his legs. He fell and the mob flowed over him.

"*Hold* fire! *Hold* fire!"

The mob swirled and milled. They had the coolie on his feet, jerking and slapping him. Many were gray soldiers. Strangely, Shing came on the bridge. He was a godsend. Lt. Collins thrust the hailing trumpet at him.

"Offer ransom!" he said. "Speak I pay money. One hundred dollar."

Shing shouted in Chinese. *Purely Chinese affair. Orders. Neutral. The boat party. Wanhsien. Women aboard.* Lt. Collins thought in flashing atoms. Soldiers with long poles, bark still on them, pushed through the mob. *Ransom the only way. No official funds.* They were daring the ship to shoot, Shing said. *Wanhsien!* The soldiers lashed their poles into a tripod and hoisted the coolie with a rope to his hands bound behind him. *Out of my own pocket, then.*

"Tell them two hundred!" he snapped at Shing.

Po-han dangled, pitching forward. Holman could see the strain in his ridged belly muscles, arms and shoulders. He was looking at the ship. Someone on the bridge was yelling in Chinese. Three soldiers grasped Po-han around the waist and legs and surged their weight on him. He dropped abruptly as his shoulder joints burst, and he screamed.

Someone on the bridge screamed, "You dirty sons of bitches!" Another cracked voice, Lt. Collins: *"Back,* Haythorn! Back from that gun. God damn your soul *don't fire!"* Franks roared a caution aft. Holman's ear buzzed. His guts were frozen. He was paralyzed.

"Five hundred! *Tell* them, Shing!"

The coolie hung nearly straight, twirling slightly. A red-sashed soldier climbed on a boulder and beat at his mouth with a knife handle, then dug with the point. *Gold teeth.* Lt. Collins signed Crosley to take Haythorn's machine gun. *Wanhsien. Boat party. Orders. Crosley's steady.* The coolie was bending his head back and back but he could not get away from the knife.

"Oh jesus oh jesus oh jesus," Burgoyne was saying.

"Steady!" Lynch said. "Keep station, Jake!"

"Go to hell."

He ran up the ladder and forward and into the bridge. Bronson stopped him.

"Get out of here, Holman! Back to the waist party!"

"Go to hell. We got to shoot. Do something."

"He ain't American. We got our orders."

"He's a shipmate."

Their faces were chalk white on the bridge. Lop Eye Shing was hailing with the trumpet. Po-han screamed again and again. The red-sashed soldier was pulling off a thick strip of skin and muscle slanting down Po-han's left ribs. He was tugging and cutting. Po-han's face was one bloody scream.

"Offer a thousand!" Lt. Collins told Shing. He turned inboard, white, sweat-streaming. "Holman, get back to your station!"

"Go to hell. Shoot. Do something."

The officer drew his pistol. "Go below or I'll shoot you for a mutineer!" He whispered it hoarsely. His eyes were terrible.

Bronson was tugging at Holman's arm. Holman slammed his gun butt into Bronson's belly and the quartermaster went down.

"Shoot, God damn you!" Holman said. "Shoot *somebody,* you yellow son of a bitch!"

He could feel his flesh reaching out for the healing bullet. He locked on Lt. Collins' eyes and he could hear Po-han wailing and wailing in half-voiced words. They were all frozen there. Then Lop Eye Shing turned around, evil-faced, saying something.

"Po-han talkee too much no can," he said. "Po-han talkee some-body shoot he."

"Oh God!" The pistol lowered. "Yes. Yes." Lt. Collins looked around the bridge. "Who—"

"I will, sir."

Crosley was holding a rifle. Holman jerked it away from him.

"Not you, Crosley," he said.

He chambered a cartridge and took aim with the bridge rail as rest. He followed Po-han's head with the beaded foresight, rolling, rolling, and Po-han saw him and held his head still. Holman sagged his stomach muscles and in a quiet place far back in his mind he said

Good-bye, Po-han. He squeezed the trigger. He saw the head jerk and he knew that it was all right now.

He stood erect, trembling. Bronson was still down, gasping and retching. Weakness washed through Holman. No one spoke. He crossed the bridge and threw the rifle out into the river. The splash seemed to release him. He ran for the engine room.

They anchored again in midstream to wait for the boat party. Holman ran everyone out of the engine room. They were afraid of him.

He tended the fires and water. He oiled and rocked the engine. He did not want to stop moving. The planks bridging the naked bilges were slippery with oil. He sprinkled more sand on them. Sand was in the bilges, all along the bare, red-leaded ribs of the ship. That sand was going to wear hell out of the bilge pump.

Burgoyne came on the gratings and said, "Chow, Jake," quietly. After a few minutes he went away.

It was dark. He heard them talking on the quarterdeck. They were pulling themselves out of it in the only way they knew. *That sign on him says "running dog," Oh Joy told me.* Crosley's frog voice. *He sure didn't run fast enough that time.* Harris. A general laugh. Stawski? *Arf! Arf!* Someone shushed fiercely and the voices faded. The buzz behind Holman's left ear did not fade.

Franks stood at the head of the port ladder. "Jake, you got the eight-by on the quarterdeck," he said. "Double guard tonight."

Holman looked up. "Not me," he said. "I got the watch down here."

"We all know how you feel. Duty's the stuff to take your mind off it." Franks' voice was kindly. "You got to do your duty, Jake."

"All I got to do is die someday. I'll never stand a topside watch again. Nor go to quarters. Not on this ship."

"However you want it, Jake. For now." Franks went away.

Taps went. He sprinkled more sand on the planks. He cleaned the fires savagely, slicing clinkers, hoeing ash and red coals out on the floorplates. He made a sulfurous hell with the cooling hose and gulped it into his lungs. The choking burn relieved him.

Burgoyne was on the throttle platform. His face was sad.

"It's midnight, Jake. Give me the watch. Turn in."

"Get out of here, Frenchy."

"It had to be, Jake. Orders. It'd been sure death for the boat party, maybe all hands. Remember Wanhsien." Burgoyne gulped. "Po-han understands, wherever he is now."

"Where he is now. Where is he? Get out, Frenchy!"

"I loved him too. I loved him like a brother."

"You can't— *Get out,* or I'll slug you!"

"It happened, Jake. It's past and done. You got to let it be a thing that happened."

"You want to know something ain't happened yet?" Holman breathed through flared nostrils. "Maily's knocked up."

Burgoyne flinched. "Jake! What you saying? That ain't so."

He put out a hand. Holman struck it down.

"It's true. She told me herself, that first day in."

"She would've told me first of all." Burgoyne's face was working. "If it's true, why didn't she tell me?"

"You figure that out," Holman said harshly. "Go topside to figure it out. God damn you, now maybe you'll leave me the hell alone!"

Burgoyne went up, his shoulders drooping. Sometime later Big Chew came down quietly and left a covered bowl of food beside the hot well. Holman threw bowl and all into the trash can.

All night he moved like a prowling animal, keeping his hands busy, and it was right behind him. If. If. A chain of ifs, from his first hour aboard.

Po-han was still there, in the smooth, quiet stroking of the pumps he had rebushed. The quick, pulsing throb of the dynamo. The high, sculptured steel- and brass-gleaming engine. Deep in the foundations of the engine, Po-han was there.

Hammah hammah hammah.

He saw Po-han in the curling flames and heard him in the whispering steam and the trickle of water into the hot well. It all came from the sun and it went where everything went. Along the way it shaped itself so you could know it, in a laboring engine or a warm and breathing man; you joined and mixed and knew. But you could not stop or hold it. It never ran backward. It went where everything went because it was everything.

Wild white horses. Wild white horses.

You could not repair a dead man. The engine was only metal. He groped his hands along the smooth, hard links and rods and columns and he could not touch Po-han. He struck the engine column until his knuckles bled, soothed by the pain, but the engine did not feel anything. It was just metal. It could not give anything back.

Po-han was not there. He was not anywhere. They should name a destroyer after him, but they did not even have his name written down on paper. They never would have. Tonight they laughed and tomorrow they would hardly remember. Po-han was a coolie. One grain of sand.

Po-han would never be there again, smudged and oily and grinning, his eyes dancing with a new idea. Po-han was alone on the dark river sands, hanging from broken shoulders. His fires were out, his wild white horses charged off and lost in the big, dark sky.

You, me, can do, Jehk.

Can do. Can die. Must die. But everything else is voluntary. All night the buzz behind his left ear did not stop once. *Can die,* it was saying.

Near morning Bordelles came back with the China Light stragglers. Holman let the steaming watch come down and they got underway at dawn. He kept the throttle. He would not eat or drink or speak to anyone. They all kept clear of him. It was plain that they thought he was crazy. He found a kind of wild, pleasant freedom in being crazy. He had not filled in the auxiliary log sheet all night and he did not start a steaming log. At the end of the first hour Crosley whistled the voice tube.

"What you making, up and down, up and down?"

"I don't know," Holman said. "What do you care? You know where you are."

"I got to have it for the log."

"Wipe your tail on the log. We'll still get there."

"Well, by God—"

Someone hushed Crosley. They did not call down for readings again. By the end of the day Holman was feeling groggy and weak and all the lights had colored haloes. He knew he could not last through another night. After they anchored, Jennings came down. His eyes looked round and solemn behind his rimless glasses. He let Holman's bitter words just slide off him.

"You're sick. You're in a nervous state," he said. "I'm only doing my duty."

"I know. I'm government property," Holman said. "I'm on your Title B cards, ain't I?"

"You have to eat and rest. I'm responsible for you."

"You think I'm crazy, don't you?"

"No. If I did, I'd bring men down to overpower you for your own good," Jennings said. "Prove you're not, by coming up with me."

"Well, I am crazy, Doc. It's a great feeling and you ought to try it yourself," Holman said. "Maskee, I'll come up. But you tell them bastards to keep clear of me. Tell 'em not to cross my bow."

"Nobody will bother you, Jake."

No one was in the washroom when he took his shower. He shaved himself, for the first time in many months. His face had fierce red eyes and hollow cheeks and a puckered scar on the left cheek that was tricky to shave around. He could not shave there as smoothly as Clip Clip could. Wong put a big plate of meat, rice and vegetables in Holman's place, and a pitcher of coffee. The Sand Pebbles were all at the other two tables, pretending to watch a couple of acey-deucey games and keeping their voices down. The food stuck in Holman's throat, but he drank a cup of the coffee. Then he sat on his bunk.

They all wanted to help him and he hated them. He hated them for being alive. He hated himself for being alive. That was crazy. It was all right, being crazy. If you killed somebody, it wasn't murder. That was why they were afraid of you. They didn't know who you'd kill next. Yen-ta came in and whispered to Burgoyne. Burgoyne came over.

"Jake, the skipper would like to talk to you."

"I don't need any of his moral courage right now."

"It ain't an order," Burgoyne said. "You don't have to go."

"Then I'll go," Holman said.

It was clear and dark and warm topside, with all the stars out. Lt. Collins looked pale and tired. He tried to explain about Po-han: the orders to shoot only to save American lives; how the not-shooting was what had really saved the American lives, women, children; it would have been another Wanhsien fight; Comyang's neck was out for their even being at Paoshan; the big lie the gearwheel would have made; the propaganda harm to America and to the navy. Holman would not sit down, but he listened quietly. He knew it all already. The raw edge in him seemed dulled at last. He did not want to lash out.

"All that's true. Po-han's still dead," Holman said. "I killed him."

"I know," Lt. Collins said.

That was all. Outside, Holman stopped by the rail, the same place where he had talked to Miss Eckert. He looked at the dots of light, fishing sampans, shrimp trappers, all over the far dark water like fallen stars. He listened to the buzzing behind his ear. Sometimes he could almost make words out of the buzzing, like seeing faces in clouds. Two dark figures came forward, past the engine-room skylight, and the bearded shape of one of them was Craddock. They stopped, facing Holman, and the woman was Miss Eckert.

"Mr. Holman," Craddock said. Holman just looked at him. "Our mission is to all burdened spirits," Craddock said. "We can help you find peace. Please let us help you." His voice was deep and dark as the night over them.

"Didn't they tell you I'm crazy?" Holman said. "Ain't you scared?"

Craddock's hands wrestled with each other. "It was God's merciful hand acting through you. By prayer you can know that in your heart and forgive yourself."

Holman thought about Craddock's rain prayer of the past summer. His head felt cool and clear and crazy and his ear buzzed.

"All God is on this ship is a word to swear with," he said. "What I want to know I want to know in my head. Why Po-han? *Why Po-han?*"

"God's ways are unsearchable. We are all His instruments and we must not question Him." Craddock intoned the words.

"Because he don't know the answers?" Holman laughed bitterly. "From the way he takes care of his tools, I wouldn't let him run an engine room, let alone the world."

The girl just stood there. Craddock stiffened. "No matter how blasphemous your words, no matter how ugly and vicious the life you lead, you cannot forfeit one atom of the great love God bears you," he said coldly. "You need only fall on your knees and repent and you will find a joyous peace you cannot even imagine."

He said a lot more, wrestling his hands and cracking his knuckles.

"You came to me. I didn't send for you," Holman said. "You despise me, don't you? You want to smear God on me the same way you'd smear blue ointment on a chancre, don't you?"

The beard jutted. "I hate the sin and love the sinner."

"People are what they do. The sinner is the sin," Holman said. "I'm a murder, not a murderer. You can't hate ideas, you can only hate people. The thing you kill is people." He laughed again, coldly crazy. "I hate you too, Craddock. You're phony as brass and glass. I ain't your kind and never want to be."

"Say what you will, you are still God's child! You cannot escape His love!" Craddock pronounced it like a sentence to the gallows, with fierce relish.

"Tell my father next time you see him that I said to stow all missionaries in the double bottoms of hell."

Craddock turned his back. "Come away, Miss Eckert," he said harshly. "We can do no good here."

She followed the old man obediently for a few steps and then halted. After a moment, she turned back. Holman relaxed his fists. She was about the only person alive he did not want to hurt.

"He was trying to help you in the only way he knows," she said softly. "We feel guilty. If we had not stayed behind—"

"I already iffed all the ifs. Po-han's still dead."

"Yes. Talking won't change that." She leaned on the rail and he turned to lean beside her. "Many Chinese Christians have been tortured and killed this past week," she said. "One of our Chinese pastors was tortured and killed, when the news from Wanhsien came."

"Po-han wasn't a Christian."

"He was off your ship. They make no distinction."

"Craddock does. Why didn't they kill Craddock? Why Po-han?"

"China is becoming a nation."

"I heard that before. I don't know what it means."

"It means being Chinese in the same way you are an American."

"I don't know that either."

"I'll tell you how Cho-jen understands it."

Cho-jen was her brilliant student. Her Po-han. He said China's weakness was in believing that all men were brothers. In a true nation only your fellow citizens were brothers and everybody else was fair game if they could not defend themselves. The Christian God was really a set of tribal deities, one for each treaty power flag. Christianity denationalized the Chinese by making them feel American and despise China. But they were barred absolutely from America as an inferior race, so they were being taught to despise themselves. Yet any American who wished might come to China and live there outside of Chinese law under the protection of his own armed forces. Cho-jen said China had to become a nation in self-defense.

"Nationalism is a deep, intense feeling," she said. "Can you see how the sight of foreign flags and gunboats, so long taken for granted, can be suddenly infuriating?"

"I guess I can. It don't help a bit about Po-han."

"Not your grief. But you said you wanted to know in your head."

"I don't know. Why Po-han? Why not old Craddock?"

"Mr. Craddock is only their enemy. But Po-han, and all like him, are suddenly traitors in the new light of nationalism." She looked out across the water. "Think of a Japanese gunboat at St. Louis, in defiance of our wishes. And an American who worked aboard it, caught ashore. . . ."

"Yes."

"In my home town, during the war, they killed dachshunds."

"Yes."

"I thy Flag am a jealous Flag, and thou shalt have no other flags befcre Me. Cho-jen is fond of saying that." Her voice was very sad. "Cho-jen says treason is the modern sin against the Holy Ghost. He says the Chinese must become the Chosen People of their own tribal god, if they are to survive in the modern world."

"I understand now," Holman said. "It don't help a bit."

"Not your grief. I wish I could share that with you."

She moved nearer. The night was warm and dark around them. The only noise was the buzzing in his ear. He wanted to touch her hands, beside his on the wooden rail. As if she knew, she put her left hand on his and he put his other hand on top of it. He felt her warm, unjudging nearness and the iron clamp around his chest eased up.

"It ain't that I shot Po-han, my finger on the trigger," he said at last, haltingly. "It ain't only that."

She said nothing.

"I knew our orders," he said. "I'm an American. I could've run down there and made it legal to save us both." His throat was tight. "I was afraid," he whispered. "I stayed aboard."

She was silent. Her hand lay warm and unflinching between his hands. The strident buzzing back of his ear softened. He swung his head against her shoulder.

"All the time I was being glad it wasn't me," he whispered.

Her free hand came up and pressed his head against softness under the rough texture. Afterward he could not remember how long it was they stood that way. The cold craziness and the red-hot hurt beneath it and all the shame and hatefulness of everything drained out of him into her and he could breathe without the ache in his throat. The buzzing behind his ear stopped. They stood that way a long while and parted at last without saying anything more.

27

When he woke up in the morning, it felt like coming off a drunk. He could remember all he had done and said, and he was ashamed of most of it. The only part of it that he wanted to remember was that with Miss Eckert. He was not ashamed of that.

The men avoided him in the washroom. At the mess table they spoke in low voices and did not look at him. He did not like it.

"How long till we get to Hankow?" he asked Farren.

Farren looked surprised and pleased. "Three days, if you give us the turns," he said.

"We'll give you the turns," Holman said. "Won't we, Frenchy?"

"Sure enough! We sure will, Jake!" Burgoyne said, grinning.

"Want me and Perna to take the first watch?" Wilsey asked.

"Yeah, will you? I want to flake out again," Holman said. "I still got a headache to sleep off."

He half slept for several hours. Then he got up and had Clip Clip shave him and he felt pretty fair. He was able to shoot the breeze casually with the men drinking coffee. He stopped by the galley and had a bowl of tea with Big Chew. Nobody mentioned Po-han.

In the afternoon he and Burgoyne took the steaming watch and at first it went pretty hard. Chiu-pa was oiler. Holman heard a tiny steam blow start down the air pump rod. Chiu-pa was wiping over by the feed pumps and he did not move. The steam blow became louder. It rasped Holman's nerves. He began hating Chiu-pa for a stupid idiot.

Po-han would have heard it instantly and been over there to set up on the gland and swab the rod. Many a time he had done it, grinning happily . . . holding his head so . . . reaching in so. . . . Suddenly a rivering sense of loss surged at Holman and just as suddenly it seemed to pass him. He had a feeling of Miss Eckert in the darkness and how friendly everyone had been all day.

"Chiu-pa!" he called. "Catchee air pump gland!"

After that he tried not to listen to the small things. Chiu-pa was a good man and he would catch anything before it became serious. At the end of the hour Crosley called down hesitantly for the readings. He did not say *up and down, up and down.*

"Sixty-two, up and down, up and down," Holman shouted into the voice tube. "More to spare, if you want 'em!"

"Gotcha, Jake!" Crosley said.

What it took was not paying very close attention to the machinery. By the end of the watch he had the hang of it. It was going to be all right.

Each day after that it was easier. Holman stayed on the main deck. He caught glimpses of Miss Eckert on the boat deck, but he did not try to talk to her. He would not have known how to behave. That talk in the dark had changed things between them, but he did not know just how. He did not know how she felt about it.

Often she was with one of the men missionaries who Lynch said was named Gillespie. He was a well-set-up man of medium height with a strong chin and a sure, pleasant look about him. The men missionaries bunked in with the chiefs and Lynch had all the dope on them. Gillespie was the only one Lynch respected. Lynch said Gillespie came from a rich family and he was only being a missionary for the fun of it.

～〇

All hands manned the rail when the *San Pablo* steamed into Hankow. They were excited. They passed the native city first, to port, the bund six deep in junks and boiling with people. The gearwheel flag floated from every high place. It was worse than Changsha. Across the river the walled city of Wuchang was under siege. General Wu's five-barred flag floated from a hilltop inside the walls. On Pagoda Hill back of Wuchang a gearwheel battery was firing into the city. They fired about one shell every five minutes and a smoke haze hung above the gray walls.

The big white stone Customs House marked the beginning of the foreign concessions. That bund was wide and tree-bordered, with pontoons for steamers. Treaty power flags and company house flags flew in profusion from every building, as if they were trying to match the gearwheel show in the native city. But what outmatched the gearwheel was the long gray line of warships down the middle of the river. They were sited so that their big guns could fire straight up the streets. As the *San Pablo* passed each ship, the sailors along the rail saluted in unison to bugled signals. The Sand Pebbles stood proudly and they snapped their salutes. They passed H.M.S. *Cockchafer,* shot full of holes and covered with glory, and they waved their hats and cheered.

To Holman everything looked scaled up. The destroyers looked like cruisers and the cruisers like battleships. Once Hankow had looked pokey to him, after Shanghai. Now, after Changsha, it looked like New York City.

"God, ain't they pretty?" Duckbutt Randall kept asking, as they passed each warship. "That gearwheel. Huh! It ain't a fart in a typhoon!" He spoke for them all.

The *San Pablo* anchored off the ex-Russian Concession. Sampans came out to take off passengers. Holman knew that refugees were being funneled down to Shanghai. He did not expect ever to see Miss Eckert again and he had to say at least good-bye. He pushed through the crowd on the quarterdeck.

"Good-bye, Miss Eckert," he said.

She smiled and said good-bye. That was all they could say. Sailors and missionaries both stared, as if it were wrong and unheard of. Only Gillespie did not look upset about it.

All the ships had landing force ashore. There was no liberty. Lynch went ashore on special liberty. He said he was going to get his money back from that Russian woman or know the reason why. He was gone all night. He came back in the morning drunk and happy.

"That teashop's got rooms topside and in back," he told them in the CPO quarters. "She's got 'em all rented to rich slopehead refugees. She's even got the passageways rented."

"Making money, you mean?"

"Almost three hundred Mex a day," Lynch said happily.

Welbeck whistled. Franks stood up and walked a circle around Lynch, grinning and sniffing.

"Becky, he smells just like a rose," Franks said.

"I got me a gold mine, boys," Lynch agreed.

He told them about it. The gearwheelers were shooting landlords and moneylenders out in native territory. Thousands of them with their families and money were jamming into the concessions for safety. They would pay almost anything for a place to stay while they tried to bribe their way aboard a treaty-flag steamer to Shanghai. Chinese passages on those steamers already cost ten times as much as saloon passages, Lynch said, which were still reserved for white people.

"Stand by for me, Becky. I got to go back over tonight," Lynch said. "She needs a man there. All she's got is a pimple-faced kid cousin named Valentine." He slapped his hands together and rubbed them. "Come visit us, when liberty starts again," he said. "Harbin Teashop, on Rue Krassof. There'll always be an open bottle, boys!"

"We'll do that, Lynch-boy!" Franks said. "Say hello to Looby for us."

"Her name's *Liuba*." Lynch looked annoyed. *"Lee-oo-bah.* It means *love* in Russian."

Franks' landing force section took the first week ashore. Red Dog went over every day for mail and he brought back newspapers and scuttlebutt. Maily had not shown up at the Green Front, he said. Coolies from the dockyard came aboard and measured to make armor flaps for the bridge and all the superstructure windows. Ping-wen brought the floorplates back to the engine room. All the white paint had to be scraped off them. The coolies worked very slowly at it.

"Pappy Tung's coolies are dogging off, too," Farren told Holman. "It's all them signs and propaganda."

Sampans with big signs went up and down the river. They tried to come close enough to harangue the ship coolies in Chinese. The ships kept fire hoses led out, to wet down and swamp the sampans if they came within range. One sampan went round and round *H.M.S. Cockchafer* all day long. Its sign read: DAMN EYES KILL BABY BRITISHER, GO HOME!

The line of warships made a brave show all day. Signal flags fluttered from yardarms, power boats shuttled back and forth, bosuns' pipes and bugles shrilled and blared. Commands rang out for battle drills. For colors every morning all hands on a mile of warships stood at hand salute while the bands on the two cruisers played their way through five national anthems.

The chief pastime aboard was watching the siege of Wuchang. One day two Wu gunboats came upriver to shell Pagoda Hill. They were small, white and rusty and they steamed up and down behind the screen of treaty power warships with their deck guns barking. The ships went to battle stations. People ashore crowded rooftops along the bund to see the show. They all cheered when Wu's popguns raised dust on Pagoda Hill.

The gearwheel guns began firing back and making splashes in the water. They were trying to pot the Wu ships as they crossed the gaps between the treaty power ships. On the *San Pablo* everyone was certain that as soon as a gearwheel shell hit one of the treaty ships it would be legal to shoot back. Then the cruisers would take the whole top off Pagoda Hill. After a while the British admiral told the Wu ships they would have to get out in the open river. They went back downriver instead. As soon as they were clear of the concessions, small-arms fire whipped the water white around them. Crosley watched through the long glass.

"Jee-*zuzz!* We just think we been shot at!" he said that night at the mess table.

At the mess tables they repeated the same things that were in the newspapers. Things were hopeful. Wu had stopped fighting in the north. All the northern warlords were coming south to gang up on the gearwheel. People were calling them "The Allies." Northern Chinese ate noodles made of wheat flour. That was supposed to make them more noble and tough than the sneaky rice eaters from south of the Yangtze. Big Chew fed the Sand Pebbles rice every day of their lives, and they could still believe a thing like that.

"Once up in Chefoo I kicked a rickshaw coolie and he knocked me on my ass," Harris said. "He did! Course I was drunk."

"That's them noodle eaters for you!" Restorff said proudly.

Often over by Wuchang there was the rattle of small arms and the sight of little men running. One by one the buildings outside the gray walls were being burnt in attacks. They said many thousands of civilians were trapped inside the walls and starving because the defending soldiers had all the food. Missionaries were trying to arrange a truce and get them out.

The Wu flag looked lonely and gallant above the city, ringed round by the many gearwheel flags outside. All night every night the guns on Pagoda Hill flashed like the lightning of a distant, grumbling storm. All night the low red glare of fire rose somewhere above the walls. And every morning the five-barred flag still floated above the highest hill inside the city. It was the first thing the Sand Pebbles looked for when they came on deck in the mornings.

Bordelles' section relieved Franks' section. Landing force headquarters was the YMCA. They had one day of lectures and drills on street fighting. The next day Holman and Tullio were part of a detail sent to one of the power plants. The Fleet sailors in the detail were happy about it. They said it was better than patrols in the bundocks, where you got spit on and hit with rocks and could not do anything about it. Inside the concessions proper it was home soil, just like the grounds of a consulate.

The power plant was a brick-walled compound with tall stacks and brick buildings inside. Riley, the CPO in charge, took the new men on a tour of the guard posts. After the tour he talked to them in the squadroom where they had their cots.

"Gearwheel agitators are trying to pull our coolies out on strike," he said. "Our job is to keep our coolies inside and the gearwheel outside." He was a stumpy, grizzled torpedoman, and he talked from the side of his mouth. He was very earnest about it. "Our coolies ain't prisoners," he said. "They just got to pretend they're prisoners. If they don't, the gearwheel will call 'em running dogs and take it out on their families." He paused, looking at each man in turn for emphasis. "They even got to pretend with each other," he went on. "Because some of 'em might be white rats."

"What could one do if he really wanted out?" Holman asked.

"He'd be pretending," Riley said. "Everything's a lie, sailor. That's how it is in China now."

Holman stood corporal of the guard and made the rounds once an hour when his watch was on. Off duty, he sat in the squadroom and drank coffee. Some of the Fleet sailors were old shipmates. One was a tall, black-browed coppersmith named Roach. The Fleet sailors were not very hopeful about Plan Red. They were almost as disgusted with the businessmen as with the missionaries. All they wanted was to get back to salt water.

"This stuff's for the marines!" Roach growled.

The Fleet sailors had their sights set on the really big fight that would come someday with the Japanese. Holman had almost forgotten how they felt in the Fleet. He had become a river rat, as the Fleet sailors called the Yangtze Patrol men. On the river the Japs were allies.

The third afternoon Tullio called Holman to the main gate.

"She wants to talk to somebody," Tullio said. "She won't go away."

She was a girl activist, in green blouse and skirt and canvas shoes, standing saucily alert under the brick archway. She had bobbed hair and a cute, perky face and clear black eyes that stared right back at Holman.

"I have a message for Wang Chung-fu," she said. "His wife is very ill. She wants him to come to her."

"Why don't you smuggle it in with the coal or chow, like you do the other stuff?" Holman asked her.

"Wang might not believe it then. This is true."

Holman grinned. "I'll have somebody tell him."

"I want to tell him myself. I don't trust you to tell him."

"I'll see what I can do. Wait here."

The red-faced civilian engineer on duty said they had tried before to get at Chung-fu. He was shift boss on the boilers and a leader among the coolies.

"Tell the wee bitch to bugger off," the engineer said. "Nip her one on the rump. That's the way to rout 'em, lad."

Holman went back to the gate. "I'm sorry. They won't tell him," he told the girl.

"Will you tell him, then? I think I trust you."

"Not against orders," Holman said. "I'm sorry."

She left. An hour later Tullio called again. The girl was back and Miss Eckert, in the same brown dress, was with her. Electricity ran all over Holman.

"Hello!" he said. "I thought you'd be in Shanghai by now."

She smiled. "We have to wait our turn. There's a long list."

"I'm glad. I mean, only in a way . . ." He was confused.

"We may not go at all," she said. "But the reason I'm here is to verify this girl's story. We have a physician's statement."

She held out a paper. Holman would not take it.

"I believed her the first time," he said. "It's just orders."

"Whose orders?"

"Just orders. You can't do anything about orders."

"Somebody gives them," the Chinese girl said.

"I can do something about them," Miss Eckert said, rather sharply. "This is a clear humanitarian case."

"Well . . ." Holman looked at Tullio.

"Go tell him." Tullio grinned. "I won't rat on you, Jake."

"No. I don't want you boys to get in trouble," Miss Eckert said. "I'm free to make the trouble. Let me speak to your officer."

Holman sent Tullio for Riley. Miss Eckert said she would just work her way up the line until she found an officer able to countermand the order. If he would not, she and the others would write about him to the newspapers in America. Riley came and listened grimly to Miss Eckert's request.

"Why don't you people stop making us trouble?" he asked. "I can't let no propaganda come in here. I got orders."

"At least read the doctor's statement."

She thrust it at him. He pushed it away.

"Lady, right now in China wives ain't near as important as electricity," he said heavily. "Give it up, why don't you? You ain't being loyal to your own people."

"I'm loyal to human needs!" She had color high in her cheeks. She was not a bit afraid of Riley. "May I have your name, sir?" she asked.

Riley scowled. "Never you mind my name, lady. You just bring me a written order from the O-in-C at the Navy Y. Go work on him."

"I will!" Miss Eckert said. "Good-bye, Mr. Holman."

The Chinese girl smiled at Holman and Tullio, as the two girls turned away. Riley looked suspicious.

"You know that fleabag, Holman?"

"We brought her up from Hunan."

"Should've left her there to rot!" Riley growled.

After supper the duty engineer caught a coolie slacking a plug to start a slow oil leak in the dynamo. Riley called Holman in. The coolie was a skinny, shrinking young fellow, very scared.

"Pick a couple of your men and work him over out in the coalshed," Riley ordered. "Don't kill him. Just make him wish you would."

"Not me," Holman said. "Get somebody else, Chief."

"And why the hell not you?" Riley shot out his jaw. "Them's orders!"

"Give 'em to me in writing. Sign your name under 'em."

Riley looked at Holman thoughtfully. His anger changed to contempt.

"Weak stomach, hey?" he said. "All right. Send Roach in."

They were making quite a bit of noise back in the coalshed. Holman went to a small office down the hall, where two Chinese clerks slept, and told them about Wang Chung-fu's wife. They poured him a cup of tea and did not say much. When the midnight shift went on, Chung-fu was missing. Roaring with rage, Riley broke out the whole guard. He doubled the interior guard for the rest of the night.

The next day British sailors relieved them. The American landing force was being withdrawn to the ships. Everyone blamed it on missionary dirty work in Washington. The American sailors lost face. One good thing came of it, however. Comyang started liberty. A small landing force went back ashore, to patrol the streets in squads of riflemen. Technically they were only shore patrol, to police the men on liberty.

Holman made his first liberty with Burgoyne. They were both worried about Maily, who had still not reached Hankow, but they pretended that it was all right. The rickshaw coolies at the French jetty all wanted triple prices and they would not argue about it with the usual Chinese good humor. The coolies ashore were all in unions and asking enormous prices and being nasty to the treaty people.

"Hell, let's walk, Jake," Burgoyne said. "What's wrong with 'em, anyway? It don't seem like China."

They walked a few blocks. Flags hung out along all the streets. Some corners had sandbagged gunposts. There were many Chinese police in blue. The tall, khaki-clad Sikhs, with their neat turbans and bearded grins, carried carbines. They all said, "Hi, Johnny," to the two sailors, who said, "Hi, Johnny" in return. Sikhs and American sailors were friends and they called each other "Johnny." Coolies and American sailors called each other "Joe."

"Hey, Joe! Wanchee rickshaw?"

There were two of them and they would go to the Green Front for only double the right price. Holman and Burgoyne each took one.

"This is kind of more like it," Burgoyne said.

Burgoyne's coolie took the lead. They went a roundabout way, dodging through alleys. They kept looking around and jabbering at each other. They passed Lynch's teashop. It was a dingy place with one dirty show window and a big U.S. flag above the sign. In the next block the pullers turned down another alley.

Halfway down it, several men blocked them. Holman's man stopped, shafts high, and tried to turn around. Coolies were running from that way, too. The rickshaw went over, Holman with it. They were beating the rickshaw coolies with bicycle chains, *thunk, thunk,* peeling their shaven scalps off. Burgoyne was yelling and kicking. Holman got to his feet. Both coolies were on hands and knees, trying to pull their heads beneath them like turtles. It was all very sudden and fast and without any noise except grunts and groans and foot shufflings and the sudden *pops* when they took pliers and wrenched out the valves of the rickshaw tires.

"Knock it off, damn you!" Holman yelled.

He began slapping and grabbing. A whistle shrilled and the strange coolies ran. Sikh cops came in both ends of the alley, trapping them in their turn. The Sikhs slapped them and kicked them and roped them together. They did not resist. The Sikhs led them off, seven men, ordinary ragged coolies. The two pullers had to go along, blood streaking their dumb faces, pulling their flat-tired rickshaws. A British police inspector lingered, writing in a small notebook.

"Now you see 'em and now you don't," Burgoyne said, smoothing out his mustache. "I swear. That was right fast, Jake."

"No harm to you two lads, I take it?" the inspector said.

"No," Holman said. "What was it all about?"

"They wouldn't join the union. We give them all the protection we can." The inspector shrugged. "You see how it is."

"What'll you do with them guys you caught?"

"Knock them about a bit and let them go. The jails are full."

"Come on, Jake," Burgoyne said. "We'll walk for sure, now."

They walked along Honan Road. Rickshaw coolies cursed them in English and Chinese. That was how it was. If you would not pay the fantastic new prices, then you were breaking rice bowls. You could not win. A fat white man up ahead was having it even worse. He was carrying a heavy suitcase and losing face with every step. He wore a straw hat and he was sweating through his white coat. His left arm stuck out stiffly, to balance the suitcase. Yapping coolies followed him. One ran in and kicked the suitcase and it spilled open. The coolies began snatching and throwing socks and drawers and paper. They were not stealing it, they were just throwing it around. The man went to his knees, trying to grab his gear and repack it. A laughing crowd formed. The man saw the sailors.

"Mariners! Aid me! Aid me!" he called to them.

He was some kind of foreigner, a fat, pink, very distressed man. Some Hankow Volunteers clattered up on horseback, yelling and waving sabers. Holman held Burgoyne back.

"Let them Volunteers take care of it," he said. "We ain't on duty."

Inside the Green Front things were right. Sailors and girls sat at the tables and more sailors lined the bar. They were all talking and slopping drinks and rattling dice. It smelled cool and beery. Holman and Burgoyne squeezed in and a barboy brought them whisky. As soon as he could, Nobby Clarke came down.

"Your woman ain't checked in yet, Frenchy," he said.

They talked about Maily. An *Elcano* sailor up the bar, a bald-headed coxswain, was listening. He came down.

"Hi, Frenchy. Heard you talking," he said. "I started my pig down from Ichang on a junk ten days ago."

"Hi, Fischer. You mean she ain't got here yet?" Fischer said no.

"Well, you know, them junks ain't never in a hurry," Burgoyne said. "They'll stop a week, two weeks, any place they take a notion."

He and Fischer reassured each other. Fischer had been trying to rent a room. Rents were much too high in the concessions, but he had been dickering for a room above a bicycle shop in the native city.

"Ain't it dangerous over there?" Burgoyne asked.

"They ain't bothered me none. Only thing is, you got to dodge our shore patrol to get over there."

The native city was out of bounds. The room was twelve Mex a week and that was damned high too, Fischer said. But the way the gearwheel had people feeling, old Tung Li was sticking his neck out in renting to a paleface at all.

"We might take that room together," Fischer suggested. "It could be for whosoever woman gets here first."

"Yeah!" Burgoyne thumped down his glass. "That's something a man can do, ain't it?"

"Maskee! Let's go close the deal!"

Burgoyne grinned, for the first time in days. He and Fischer went out, striding briskly. Nobby Clarke watched them go and shook his head.

"Poor bastards. They'll never see their pigs again," he said. "Lucky if they don't, you ask me."

"You figure it'll get worse here?"

"It'll be hell, come low water and the cruisers have to go. I'm glad I got my woman and the kids down to Shanghai while I still could."

"They can send their women to Shanghai."

"Not a chance!" Nobby said. "No sailor's got the kind of money that costs now."

Nobby had to go back and roll dice with some destroyer men. Holman had another drink. He kept wanting to think about Po-han. A civilian in a gray suit pushed in beside him and ordered a whisky sour. Holman saw only the arm and hand, cameo cuff links, long, well-kept fingers, an onyx signet ring, on the polished bar. Nobby bustled up.

"Yes, sir!" he said. "Anything I can do, sir?"

"I want you to set up drinks for the men of the *San Pablo,* as they come in," the man said. "Can you do that?"

The hand laid bills on the bar. Nobby scooped them up.

"Yes, sir! Here's one right beside you, sir," he said. "What'll it be, Jake?"

"More White Horse."

"I'm Ed Graham."

Holman looked up. The man had a long, elderly horse face with a kindly expression. "I'm Jake Holman." Graham had a warm, firm handshake. "How come the drinks?" Holman asked.

"You brought some stuff up from Changsha for me, after the steamers stopped running," Graham said. "I tried to give your captain a case of whisky and he wouldn't take it. So I thought of this way."

Holman remembered those Graham cases on the quarterdeck. Heat from the engine room had fried a stinking oil out of them. It had stained the planking and made Farren very angry.

"Guys'll be obliged," Holman said. "I remember them cases. What was in 'em?"

"Women's hair. Compressed and baled."

"What do you do with it? How's it used?"

"I send it to the States," Graham said. "They use the best grades to make hair pieces for women who don't have enough of their own. The poor stuff is used in making newspaper mats."

"You ought to pick up a lot of hair now, all these gearwheel gals bobbing their hair."

"You'd think so, wouldn't you?" Graham agreed. "But it's made the market worse. Short hair is a badge of this so-called revolution. Women are afraid to cut their hair. They're afraid of what will happen to them when the loyalists come back."

Holman swirled his drink. "You figure Wu's coming back?"

"More likely Chang Tso-lin will come," Graham said. "The Japs are backing him heavily. And our money's on Sun Chuan-fang. Wu's about done for."

Kai-shek couldn't last, Graham went on to say. No Chinese could hold out very long against either lead or silver bullets. It would take a while. Graham had already sent his wife to Shanghai. He was closing out all his Central China business and he would go to Shanghai himself before long. It was going to be pretty rough around Hankow.

"I know how you boys feel, your neutrality orders and all," he said. "You will just have to be patient, like the Chinese."

"I saw some today wasn't acting very patient," Holman said.

Graham went out. Holman had several more drinks. Po-han kept coming into his mind. He could not summon his memory of Miss Eckert in any effective way. It was as if she could not be with him in a place like the Green Front. And now Maily was lost somewhere along the way. He would never see Maily again either. Nobby came back.

"That was Mr. Graham. He's a *taipan*," Nobby said. "What was it you Sand Pebbles done for him?"

"Brought some stuff up from Changsha," Holman said. "God damn it, Nobby, it don't seem fair."

"Ain't *fair!*" he cried, hours later, and slapped the red-checkered tablecloth. He spilled his drink.

"Itt somethings," the large, blonde Russian woman across from him said. "You vill be sick." She spoke in Chinese to the boy who came to mop at the tablecloth.

"This honey barge world vill be sick," Holman said. "Want 'nother whisky."

She was feeding him with a spoon. It was rice and something. "Goot! Goot!" she kept saying. "You itt, beb-bee."

Whenever he tried to talk, she had that spoon right in there.

"Got 'nough, you big white bitch!" he choked at last. "You eat it! Want 'nother whisky!"

"Please, no more vis-kee. You be no goot to me, beb-bee."

"I never been any good to any son of a bitch on earth," he said bitterly. "Boy! More one whisky!"

It was a small room just big enough for the bed. The walls kept going round. She helped him get his uniform off. It was a rocking, pitching small room in a big rough sea. It was no good. She did all the things they knew how to do and it was not any good at all. She pulled his head between her breasts.

"You vant to cry," she said softly in the darkness. "To cry is better than the vis-kee."

He rolled his head dumbly.

"You cry, sailor," she whispered. "Here is nobody to laugh at you."

He could not cry. After a while he went to sleep.

28

The Alliance Hostel was not a pleasant place. It was crowded with refugee missionaries violently torn from their past and fearful of their future. Children picked up their parents' anxiety and quarreled and cried all day. The place ached with doubt and indecision and public heart searching. They talked interminably.

Shirley sat at a table in the lounge, trying to answer Cho-jen's letter. She felt like two persons when she wrote to Cho-jen, and one of them was a traitor. She reread his letter, boldly drawn with the pen rather than written in script. That was like Cho-jen.

The Kuomintang had the Chien Valley, he told her. He was president of the student union and he meant soon to become a power in the master worker-peasant council in Paoshan. He knew his own worth. He was full of plans for China Light.

"Please come back, Miss Eckert," he wrote. "Mr. Gillespie can come, if he will teach instead of evangelizing. I do not want any of the others."

Except for the Craddocks, the other families had already gone to Shanghai. Mr. Craddock had given them each a year's salary from the China Light reserve funds in Hankow. It did not leave much, and no more would come from China Light. Cho-jen now had effective control of the mission finances.

Querulous voices reached her from the dining room. They argued all day in there, in the smell of tea and boiled cabbage. They were telling each other they had not fled from personal fear or lack of trust in God. Many had the same story: their native staff had asked them to leave because their presence infuriated the heathen Chinese, who would take it out on the native Christians. Unspoken in each story was the ugly suspicion that the native staff only wanted to get administrative control into its own hands.

It had been so clearly at China Light. She remembered that terrible night, the naval officer curt and contemptuous, Mr. Lin and Pastor Ho speaking blandly, and Mr. Craddock obdurate as flint. But Cho-jen had told her privately and candidly of their aim, knowing that he could trust her, and she had tipped the scale. She had persuaded Gillespie to go and all of them together had overborne Mr. Craddock.

I was like a Judas goat, in reverse, she thought. Now Cho-jen wants me to come back. What will I tell him?

You could hear every shade of opinion at the Alliance Hostel. Most of them agreed that association of missions with gunboats in Chinese opinion had to be broken, or Christianity was through in China. The unequal treaties had to go. The treaty powers had most of the exploiting privileges of colonial masters but none of the responsibilities for human welfare. A few missionaries agreed with the business faction that the treaties could not be given up until China had a responsible government.

Mr. Craddock could be scathingly eloquent on that. So much of Chinese sovereignty was taken away by the treaties, he said, that the Chinese could not form an effective government. And to the contention that the United States was bound by the Nine Power Treaty not to make changes in her own treaty with China except with the consent of all the other treaty powers, Mr. Craddock would explode. That was giving nations like Belgium and Portugal veto power over the United States, and it was intolerable.

"No man who favors the unequal treaties has the right to call himself a Christian!" Mr. Craddock liked to thunder.

Yet Shirley knew from Mr. Lin that Mr. Craddock had only come to that conclusion a few years ago.

Many missionaries thought they should all go home until China was granted equal status as a nation. Then those of them whom a sovereign Chinese government would permit to do so might return. Only so, they said, could they be in China in honest good faith. Cho-jen asking me to come back is something like that, Shirley thought.

But there were Christians at the Alliance Hostel who did favor the unequal treaties, in the face of Mr. Craddock's thunder. They talked openly of armed intervention and of something called Plan Red. There was old white-haired Mr. Eustace, who lived wholly in the past, to the despair of his daughters. At least once each meal he would pronounce sententiously: "It is time for the Society for Propagation of the Gospel to step aside. It is time for the Society for Propagation of Cannonballs to bring them to their senses." Then he would dribble food down his shirt front.

She bent to her letter. She did not know what to say.

"Hello, Shirley. China Light mail?"

She looked up. "Hello, Walter. Nothing new." Gillespie looked pale, almost ill. He had gone with a truce team to try to get starving civilians out of Wuchang across the river. "Did you have any luck?" she asked.

"A few thousand. We filled six lighters," he said. "Then they clubbed them back and closed the gate. It was very bad, Shirley."

They were skeletons, without strength, he said. They jammed in the narrow gate, desperate to escape. Mothers held their babies above the press until their strength failed. Then both went under. He had counted more than two hundred of the weakest, trampled to death in the moment of liberation.

"Unspeakable things are going on in Wuchang," he said.

A hundred thousand civilians were starving. The defending general in Wuchang would not let them go. He wanted to put the onus on the Kuomintang, if it would not lift the siege. He was swearing to defend Wuchang to the last man. He was said to have refused an enormous personal bribe. Gillespie shuddered all over. He cleared his face with an effort.

"Well, we have to carry on. I'll bathe and change," he said. "Then how about the show at the Victoria? It's De Mille's *Ten Commandments,* and there's a matinee."

"Maybe tonight," she said. "I want to go for a walk."

She wanted to think it out about Cho-jen. She wanted to be alone in the little public garden she had found in the native city.

On the ships uniform changed to blues to match the crisping weather. Destroyers came and went, convoying commercial steamers filled with refugees. They were constantly fired upon. Propaganda sampans plied along the line of warships with signs and shouted slogans. Suspicion rose up nastily between the Sand Pebbles and the *San Pablo* coolies. Lop Eye Shing was dickering with Lt. Collins for more money. Everybody knew the ship could not stand any more squeeze. Clip Clip raised shaves by a nickel and haircuts by a dime. Ping-wen's men did a very poor job of scraping the white paint off the floorplates.

"Place looks like it's got leprosy," Lynch said ruefully, one day after lower-deck inspection.

"They're slacking all along the line," Holman said. "I was waiting for the skipper to blast about it."

"He knew he'd just lose face," Lynch said. "There's times you got to look the other way."

Lynch was in good humor these days. He had paid off the mortgage on the teashop and he was talking about selling it to some rich Chinese who wanted a safe investment out of reach of the gearwheel. They were offering plenty, Lynch hinted, but Liuba was holding out for more. She'd get it, too.

Wuchang held out gallantly. Day and night the grumbling guns fired into it. A smoke haze hung above it all day. The two Wu gunboats came back upriver, but this time they flew the gearwheel flag and fired into Wuchang. Their captains had been hit by silver bullets. The newspapers said General Liu inside Wuchang had turned down sixty thousand dollars. He was going to fight to the last man. The Sand Pebbles were getting sentimental about General Liu. They could really take it, in Wuchang. Every morning the five-barred flag still flew above Dragon Hill.

Big Chew did not change. He turned out better food than ever. He made flaky roast duck and spiced fish and ham and pork and vegetables a hundred ways. If such a thing were possible, he was outdoing himself.

Holman went into the native city with Burgoyne to see the room for Maily. There was a permanent British guardpost where they crossed Taiping Road. It was a big matshed, with sandbags and barbed wire. The British sailors did not try to stop them. In China, every nation was its own law. The room was above a kind of hard-ware store, with the stairs inside. It was small and shabby and the single window had no glass. Holman opened the wooden shutter and looked down into a short blind alley filled with beggars. Burgoyne closed the shutter.

"I don't like looking down there," he said. "It gives me the creeps, someway."

He had a clay stove and a rickety table but no chair yet. He had some clay pots and mats and his prize was one of the thick white quilts they called *pukows*. Fischer had gone back to Ichang and Burgoyne had the room by himself. He sat on the floor with his back against the wall and clasped his bony knees.

"Sit down, Jake," he invited.

Holman paced back and forth. "What the hell, Frenchy, do you just sit here like that?" he asked.

"I think how it'll be with Maily here," Burgoyne said. "Once in a while I go out and buy something more that we can use."

"Well, Jesus Christ."

"Sometimes I sleep all night on the mat, with my head on the *pukow*," Burgoyne said. "But I never unroll the *pukow*. That's for when Maily comes."

There was something unbearable about it. It was almost nasty. Holman knew he had to get out of there.

"It's a good place. Maily'll fix it up real nice," he said.

He made excuses and went out. He did not dare to tell Burgoyne that Maily was never going to come.

The narrow flagstoned streets were crowded and noisy. Here and there students were making speeches to small groups. There were gearwheel soldiers in green and other soldiers in gray, with red, white and blue scarves around their necks. The gray ones were deserters from the Wu forces. They were all kids. Strike pickets in dark green marched along, with their bamboo staves. Pretty little girl activists in lighter green bounced along in tennis shoes. There were throngs of ordinary Chinese, mostly coolies.

It felt like a holiday. Holman drifted along, idly watching them. He began to have the *left-out* feeling that he had had in Changsha. They all had purpose, he thought, going somewhere, working together in a big, exciting plan. It made every day like a holiday. When they looked at each other, that jumped between them. But when they looked at Jake Holman nothing jumped. All they saw was something cluttering up their way. He was just a sailor killing time by walking because he did not want to go to a bar and get drunk again.

He walked a long way, past fine houses behind brick walls and across railroad tracks. He was lost. It was a fine, clear day to be lost in. He came into a kind of park on the shore of a small lake. It had trees and shrubs and graveled paths and lotuses floating in the lake. Only a few Chinese were strolling there. In one place beside the lake were several of the hollowed, fantastically shaped rocks they liked in China. Holman liked them too.

A white woman, the first he had seen all day, stood looking at them. He waited behind a shrub for her to move on. She wore a brown woolen sweater with the elbow out. Then he glimpsed the curve of her cheek and something bright shot through his sadness. She was Miss Eckert.

"Hello!" he said cheerfully.

She whirled. "Mr. Holman!" Then she smiled.

From the first, he felt easy with her. She said she was not going to Shanghai. She was going back to China Light as soon as it was safe.

"I think it's safe now," she said.

"That ain't how I hear it," he said doubtfully.

"There's a lot of hysteria about danger. A few treaty people have been beaten and humiliated," she said. "But no one's been killed. The Germans have not been bothered at all."

"You're treaty people."

"I know," she said sadly.

"Maybe you're right." He wanted to cheer her. "I just been walking all over the native city. I didn't feel in any danger. All I felt was left out."

"You feel that too?" She smiled again. "Aren't they full of joy and energy, though! At China Light I could be part of it."

"If they want you there."

"They want me!" She changed the subject. "I love these rocks," she said. "They're so wild and romantic, and yet Chinese."

The rock was high as their heads and grayish-white. It was a stony froth of big and little hollows with sharp edges. Some of the holes went all the way through it. Holman stroked his fingers in one of the hollows.

"They make me think of steep waves in a strong wind," he said. "You can never really see them. They change too fast. They make you wish you could stop time for just a second. That's the feeling these rocks give me, that time stopped."

"They are a kind of frozen time, aren't they?" She put her hand on the rock.

"How do the Chinese ever chisel 'em out like this, know just *how?*"

"Oh, they don't! They have to be natural," she said. "They're waterworn limestone. Cho-jen calls them footprints of the river dragon."

"That's your student? I'd like to meet a kid like that."

"I wish you could. Cho-jen would approve of you." She looked at him apologetically. "That sounds backward, but that's how I think of Cho-jen. He's extraordinary."

"You told me."

"Not by half."

Every true teacher dreamed of finding a genius-potential mind among her students, she said. Just once in a lifetime. Her face grew radiant as she talked. He began to understand how it felt to be a teacher. Cho-jen was such a genius, she said. He was only a boy and he had the leader force of an Alexander. He would be a very great man in China someday.

"And of course I feel all his other teachers misguided him," she said, smiling. "Only I understand him."

She was pretending to mock herself, but she meant it.

"I used to think I could learn anything," he said. "All I ever learned was machinery. But I know more about machinery than most men ever learn." It sounded like brag and he changed the subject. "These rocks," he said. "You know what happens, when I look long enough at a rock like this one?"

She smiled encouragement. "What happens?"

"I shrink. I get the feeling I'm small as an ant," he said. "I get the feeling of high cliffs and deep caves and hollows like ranches. I start climbing with my eyes."

"I'd be dizzy."

"I get dizzy. But I have to keep looking and climbing until I find my home place."

She took her hand off the rock. "Where is it on this one? Or should I ask?"

"I never looked at this one before," he said. "Sometimes it's hard to find. It's always high up and dangerous to get to."

"I grew up in flat country," she said.

She started them talking about their homes in the States. They were exploring each other. He told her about sagebrush and rimrock and crystal air and coyotes howling at night. About storms at sea and volcanoes and earthquakes and steam and engines. He did not mention any people. He kept his eyes on the rock.

She talked of Minnesota and her parents and her big brothers Tom and Charley and so many friends and schoolmates that the names jumbled. She made him see her warm, bright house with books and music and rugs on a polished floor. In the summers they had a log cabin beside a lake. They were always clean in good clothes in that house, and they loved each other. Her face was soft and happy, remembering.

Everything she said put the Great Wall of China between her and him. It did not seem to matter, beside the rock. She pressed him to talk about his family. He would not.

"I left all that," he said. "I'm going to serve out my time and retire in China. Lots of China sailors do that."

She glanced at the sky. He followed her eyes. It was a very pretty red and orange sunset. They had talked for hours.

"Oh my! I have to go!" she said. "I have an important letter to write."

"I'm lost," he confessed. "Can I walk with you, far as the British Concession?" He took a last look at the rock.

"Of course," she said.

It was a pleasant walk. When they came to Taiping Road he saw an American patrol coming and he stopped.

"Can't let that patrol see me," he explained. "The native city's out of bounds to us. Supposed to be dangerous."

He stood against a shop window. She stood in front of him. Some coolies loitering there were curious. She explained in Chinese why Holman was hiding. They laughed and stood closer, to help make a screen. The patrol thudded by, arms swinging, bayonets bright above them.

Once across Taiping Road, Holman told her goodnight. It would not do to walk together in the concession. When people saw a girl on the street with a sailor, they figured she also went to bed with him. Everybody knew that was the only use sailors had for girls.

Lynch was looking well. His face firmed up and he walked jauntily. He smoked cigars and he had good French brandy to put in his morning coffee. He seldom went into the engine room, but he would call Holman up for coffee royal and get the dope. He was not concerned about how sullen the coolies were getting. He would lean back with a shine in his eyes and the new, firm look about his mouth and wave all that grandly away.

"Baby 'em along, Jake. They'll get over it."

Through some roundabout Irish superstition he had once blamed Holman for getting him married. Now he seemed grateful.

"Liuba's the best thing ever happened to me," he would say, puffing blue smoke. "You ought to get yourself a good woman. I mean it, Jake!"

Downriver the rice eaters were still defeating the noodle eaters. Liuba had a plan. They would sell out in Hankow for a big killing and buy property in Shanghai. When the gearwheel moved in around Shanghai, they would make a really big killing.

"All the money in China will be in Shanghai then," Lynch said.

Over in Wuchang they were still holding out. All the buildings outside the walls were burnt and most of them inside, most likely, from the angry red glare of fire that rose every night under the intermittent shelling. Several gearwheel airplanes showed up and dropped bombs on the city. That seemed to the Sand Pebbles to be just too much. But every morning on Dragon Hill the five-barred flag was still there.

Burgoyne did not look well. He lost weight. He turned morose and cursed the gearwheel bitterly. He made all the other Sand Pebbles uncomfortable. He would not look for sympathy, but neither would he give up hope. His hope was hideous, like a mangled snake that would not die.

The little public garden became Shirley's refuge from the emotional jangling of the hostel. She went there every afternoon. When he had shore leave, Holman came there. It was not by verbal prearrangement. They were always pleasantly surprised at meeting.

She became very much interested in Holman. The garden freed him from constraint. *No-man's land,* he sometimes called it. He was plainly happy there. He was as glad to get away from his ship as she from her hostel. She felt free also. Her shabby sweater did not matter. But when they walked back to the concessions, the constraint came between them once more.

One evening she told Gillespie about Holman. They were having hot chocolate and pastries in a small bakery-tearoom crowded with White Russians.

"It's my teacher's instinct, I believe," she said. "There is a good man hidden in him, even from himself."

"If I'm going to teach at China Light, I suppose I should cultivate my own instinct," Gillespie said. "Is that how it works? Seeing the form in the block of stone?" He smiled. "It sounds ambitious."

"Oh, not like that!"

Good teachers were like gardeners in a human garden, she explained. They helped human personalities find their most happy and attractive growth. Where they saw need, they had to help. As a gardener would stop for a moment to prune and straighten a wayside shrub. Gillespie looked doubtful.

"I'm afraid I've always dismissed gunboat sailors as a group," he said. "They've made their life choice."

She nibbled a pastry as he talked. He suggested gently that she felt guilt, because if they had not remained behind at China Light then Holman would not have had to shoot the coolie who was his friend. She nodded. She did feel guilt.

"So do I feel guilt," Gillespie said. "But I wonder if it is helping the man to open new windows for him? He's chosen his life."

"He hasn't!"

"What makes you so sure?"

She could not say, instantly. It was a cumulative impression. It was in his attitude toward the Chinese, his seeing no essential difference between himself and them. It was in his dislike of military pomp and ritual. *It's stupid. It's like you choose up sides and kill each other,* he had said once.

"He seems to have no *limiting* sense of himself," was the best way she could sum it up.

It intrigued Gillespie. He asked questions.

"He's had some high school, I think," she said. "He's very intelligent, but the only outlet he has found for it is machinery. He has made a kind of poetry of machinery."

She could tell Gillespie nothing of Holman's background, except that there was something painful in it which made him reticent. She realized that she knew less of Holman than she had thought. Gillespie sipped chocolate and kept his eyes inscrutably on hers. Unlike the others at China Light, he had always treated her as adult and responsible. She hoped he was not going to become fatherly now.

"What will become of him? What's his aim in life?"

"He doesn't seem to have any," she said. "He means to retire and live out his life in China. He told me he would not be a bartender. Beyond that, he has no idea."

"Most of them do become bartenders."

She drank off her chocolate, as Gillespie talked. A black sludge was left in the bottom. She ate bits of it with her spoon. It was faintly bitter. Retired enlisted men in China also became bouncers in cabarets and armed guards at gambling places, Gillespie said. Some became bodyguards to rich Chinese. A lucky few got on as police or as outside men in the customs service. But for the most part they became subsidized beachcombers.

"I wonder if the brutalizing effect of the life they lead may not be a kind of merciful natural anesthesia," Gillespie finished.

"They can change their lives."

"Not easily." He waved his hand at the White Russians seated at small tables all around them. "These are people with changed lives," he said.

The Russians were all drinking strong brown tea from glass tumblers. They looked beaten and sad. Two ragged, bearded old men were playing chess. They might have been noblemen once.

"I don't think it's the same thing," she said. "I intend to go on seeing Mr. Holman."

"I was not suggesting that you stop. Just be thoughtful."

"Let's pay and go back to the hostel," she said. "This place is depressing."

They walked back in silence. She thought about Holman. He

would often forget himself in talking to her and the hard, square lines of his face would soften. He had eager smiles and wistful smiles and a whole gamut of natural expressions which he probably never used, except with her.

It was like bringing a statue to life. She could feel him reaching out to her for form and direction. It was her teacher's instinct. You could trust an instinct.

Holman knew it was against all the rules. It could not last. He did not think about that in the garden. He just added each time with her to all the others in the place in his memory.

It rained one afternoon and they went to the teahouse in one corner of the garden. It was a noisy, sloppy, happy place, for all its red lacquer rails and pillars and screens of glazed paper set in geometric designs. She spoke in Chinese to the waiters and he felt welcome there. They had a kind of booth that looked out on the garden in the rain.

"I didn't see any other girls in there," he said. "You sure it's all right?"

"It's all right. It goes with my sweater."

She still had the hole in her elbow. Someone had given her the sweater. Most of her clothes were still at China Light. They drank tea and ate sweetish rice cakes. The breeze brought a cool, damp, green smell to their table.

"I've heard the other sailors call you Jake," she said. "Is your first name Jacob?"

He grinned. "That's a nickname. For my initials. My real name's Joris Kylie."

"Joris? Is it for some relative?"

"No. Nobody ever had a name like that. It sounds like a girl's name."

"Not to me." She closed her eyes. "Joris. Joris. It makes me see a laughing man on horseback, with a sword and soft leather boots and a gay white plume in his hat."

"Jorse, Jorse, ride a horse." He laughed. "That's what the kids used to yell at me in grade school."

"You see? It's in the name."

"They were making fun of me. I never have liked that name."

"I've never heard of another girl named Shirley. My mother found it in a Brontë novel," she said. "I used to think it was a tag-along imitation of my big brother Charley. The boys used to tease me and call me *Chirley,* because I tagged after them."

"Shirley." He closed his eyes, just as she had. "Shirley. Shirley." He felt his cheeks warming with the pleasure of saying it. All it made him see was her sitting beside him, her eyes soft and smiling, just as if he were still looking at her. "Shirley. Shirley," he repeated, and opened his eyes. "All it makes me see is you."

"Because it's my name."

"I'd like to call you Shirley. And you call me Jake."

They called each other Jake and Shirley the rest of that afternoon. Holman felt a tingle to it each time, like fingers touching flesh. They did not talk about serious things. But when they walked back into the British Concession at dusk, the enchantment vanished.

"Goodnight, Miss Eckert," he said.

She marveled at the speed of his transformation. He did not yet know himself how he had changed. But she knew. His shyness was gone. They could talk candidly, without fear of offense. When he spoke of his shipmates, what had once been irritation was now more like compassion.

"This never-fight-back stuff. It's breaking their hearts," he said. "You know, I never saw it that way before."

It was not breaking his heart. But he was going to be less happy than ever aboard his ship now, she knew. He still lacked much. He had no sense of religion and no developed interest beyond machinery. She could see the rising question and search behind his puzzled eyes.

They went every afternoon to the teahouse and had a modest meal with their tea. Their private booth above the garden took on a shared intimacy. She told him all about China Light and her duplicity with Cho-jen. She spoke of the emerging Chinese nation and the part Cho-jen would play and her own part in helping Cho-jen and the other boys. She was trying to reveal to him the central theme of her life, to form that concept in him, so that he might find his own central theme.

"I know," he said thoughtfully. "You need a reason for being alive. Machinery ain't—isn't enough."

It was raining that day and they had unconsciously moved closer for warmth. She saw the question in his eyes that he could neither formulate nor she answer. She yearned to answer it for him. Somehow, their shoulders touched. His arm went round her waist. She began to melt into him. Then she stiffened.

Instantly they were several feet apart and staring strickenly at each other. He was pale.

"I didn't—it happened—I didn't mean—"

He was pathetically anxious that she not think he had been trying to treat her as a sailor's girl. She had to reassure him.

"I know. It surprised us both."

Her heart was thumping. She saw the same fearful understanding in his face.

"We mustn't let it go on."

"No." He was red now.

"Perhaps we shouldn't see each other again."

"I'll stay away." He stood up. "I'm sorry. I never wanted to spoil this garden for you."

"It's my fault." She gulped and breathed in deeply, to hold back tears. "I thought I was being a teacher," she said. "But I was only being a woman."

"I guess people can't really unmix themselves," he said.

Then he was gone, quickly and quietly. She felt she had wronged him. My dedication is to Cho-jen, she reminded herself. Cho-jen, who is to be one of the great trees of China. She caught one glimpse of Holman crossing the garden in the rain. She began quietly to cry.

It was just as well, Holman thought next day. Liberty was stopped for all hands. Wuchang had fallen. The gearwheel flag flew on Dragon Hill. It was the old Chinese story of sellout. Some of the defending troops had mutinied and opened the gates. The Sand Pebbles were very gloomy that day.

Over in the native city they were going crazy with joy. People thronged and danced along the bund. Flags and paper lanterns bobbed above them, and poles with strings of popping firecrackers. Boats of all sizes plied back and forth from Wuchang. As the day passed, the mood ashore turned ugly. Thousands of people had starved to death in Wuchang. Agitators were said to be parading bony corpses, with teeth marks on them, through the native city, to inflame the people.

The forces ashore manned the perimeter defenses. The Americans stood by under arms aboard their ships, ready to land instantly. There was bitter talk on the *San Pablo* quarterdeck. To the Sand Pebbles, how they could blame the starvation in Wuchang on the palefaces was beyond all sane conjecture.

That was how things stood about suppertime, when a runner came off to the ship with a note for Frenchy Burgoyne. Maily was waiting for him at the Green Front.

29

"There is no legitimate reason for which I can grant you special liberty, Burgoyne," Lt. Collins said.

The man, standing beside Bordelles and twisting his white hat, looked dumbly, whitely desperate. He was getting ready to plead. That would be sticky.

"However . . ." Lt. Collins wrote a few lines asking about an ammunition order, folded the paper and sealed it in an envelope. He wrote: "Guard Mail: Navy Godown" on the envelope and handed it to Burgoyne. "Put on a guard belt and take this to Navy Godown," he said. "How long it takes you and the route you go are your own responsibility. You must take all the consequences if a patrol catches you misusing it."

"I do thank you, sir!"

Burgoyne went out, trembling with relief. The two officers looked at each other.

"A mistake, Tom."

"I'm glad you did it, sir."

"But a mistake. A small evasion of duty." Lt. Collins swung his chair around. "Sit down. This is an ugly thing already. Tell me all you know about it."

All hands had been assuming the woman was lost on the way from Changsha, Bordelles said. They thought Burgoyne should have unshacked in Changsha, as the other men had. Anti-foreign feeling was building to a crisis in Hankow; Burgoyne was in for more trouble with her. But the crew thought Burgoyne was soft in the head. It was not a general morale threat; it was Burgoyne's private trouble.

"The trouble simply is, he seems to love her," Bordelles said.

Lt. Collins frowned. Love was not as common a hazard in China as syphilis, but it could destroy a good man much more surely. With sixteen years of four-oh service, Burgoyne should have been immune.

"He'll be tempted to jump ship. He needs protection." Lt. Collins drummed with his fingers. "I could have him transferred to Shanghai with the next convoy."

"You saw how he was, sir. It would break his heart."

"He'd get over it. But I don't want to lose an experienced engineer, the way things are shaping with our Chinese. That's why I've kept Holman."

"He might send the woman to Shanghai," Bordelles suggested "Hmmm."

No junks could get through the war zone. Chinese passage on treaty steamers was impossibly expensive, because of the squeeze the native staffs were taking from rich refugees. But he had heard that a few Chinese passages were kept available at regular prices for servants of saloon passengers. He suggested to Bordelles that someone might take the woman down that way.

"Let's both ask around about it ashore," he told Bordelles. "It's a bother. But it might help save a good man."

Things became worse ashore. Up north Feng, the Christian warlord, came out for the gearwheel. He stabbed Wu in the back. Wu was out of the game. It made the Chinese very cocky in Hankow. They began tearing down the ancient wall around Wuchang. The cruisers had to drop downriver. The U.S.S. *Duarte,* a large gunboat, went to take winter duty at Changsha. The *San Pablo* would winter in Hankow. Liberty started again, but only for chiefs and officers. Petty officers could go to the Royal Naval Canteen.

Burgoyne found a way to jump ship from the canteen and get to the native city without being caught by patrols. He would come aboard in early-morning darkness. The quarterdeck watch had to cover up for him, checking him in on the log and the nameboard. If he were caught, it would go to Comyang, and a lot of men would be in trouble. The Sand Pebbles grew resentful of the accumulating risk. They could not reason with Burgoyne. He rebuffed fiercely every suggestion that he unshack. He was getting a dark, wild look.

"I don't want to get anybody in trouble. I ain't asking you to cover up for me," he said. "Log me absent. But I got to keep going over, long as I ain't stopped cold."

He wanted no sympathy from them. He would talk about Maily only to Holman. She had been held under arrest by gearwheel agents in Ta-li, he said. They had not hurt her, only asked questions every day.

"Or so she says. She's almighty changed, Jake," Burgoyne told Holman. "She's quiet and sad and peaked in the face. She's back strong on that God stuff."

"How are things going with you ashore?"

"Worse than Changsha. It's that same being pushed back and froze out." Burgoyne tugged savagely at his mustache. "Tung Li already raised our rent five a week. He's got to pay off the block warden, account of us."

"You got to get her to Shanghai someway. I got some money I could throw in. The guys would help."

"I ain't a beggar!" Burgoyne flared. Then he slumped. "Well, maybe I am. But the skipper's working on it for me." He told about Lt. Collins' plan. "We just got to hold on until he finds somebody."

"I'll jump ship with you tonight. I want to see Maily."

"No. It's a miracle every time I get away with it," Burgoyne said. "Maily worries enough about me. She already told me not to let you take the chance."

"Well, tell her I wanted to. Tell her I wish I could come."

The coolies were squeezing unmercifully and doing less work every day. Permanent gear was disappearing from all over the ship. Clip Clip raised haircuts to a dollar and no one joked with him any more. Propaganda sampans hung off the *San Pablo*. The coolies seemed afraid to go ashore, except to the concessions. Two of the Fangs had been arrested in the native city. They were still gone.

"Too much tlobbah come," Big Chew told Holman. The burly cook was worried. He said they were all going to have to join the boatmen's union. "By-m-by no can," he said, shaking his head. "Tlobbah come, Jehk!"

Holman took all of Burgoyne's shore patrol duties in addition to his own. That put him ashore every third day tramping the streets in a squad of riflemen. When he had the dawn patrol, he always worried that his squad would be the one to catch Burgoyne sneaking back to the ship.

"I won't surrender. I'll make the bastards shoot me," Burgoyne had said.

They were called shore patrol, but their real purpose was to back up the police. They marched with fixed bayonets, to make a better show. Often Chinese hooted and spat at them. It was dismal work. The streets were littered. Broken windows had paper or rags stuffed in them. It was often rainy and cold. When they tramped jingling past the Alliance Hostel, Holman always looked for Shirley. He never saw her.

He thought about her very often. He could remember every one of her changing expressions and every tone of her voice and everything she had said. His cheek remembered that first time, the softness of her breast, and his guilty arm remembered the last time. He could still sweat with the sudden fear that had stricken them both. He did not have any opinion about it. He just went over and over it in his mind.

One cold, wet day Riley was the squad leader and Holman was the senior petty officer in the squad. Riley took note of that, not happily. He remembered Holman from the power plant. Soon after they began their patrol, a police messenger on a bicycle called them to trouble in the ex-German Concession. They followed the messenger at double time for six blocks and halted, puffing, on a corner.

A dozen tall, bearded Sikhs were waiting there, with Chinese assistants. The Sikhs grinned and said, "Hi, Johnny." Halfway down the block a ragged blue coolie mob was surging and yelling under a sign that read GRAHAM EXPORTS. Glass tinkled and torn white paper snowed out the windows. Riley squinted, sizing it up. Then he spat tobacco juice into the gutter.

"Automatic riflemen, fall out. Come with me across the street," he said. "Holman, take the rest of the squad in and break 'em."

"Form single rank," Holman told the remaining five men. "Ready bayonets. You know how to do it."

He took the place nearest the wall. He had not done this before, but he knew how to do it from the lectures and drills at the YMCA. You walked steadily at them with your bayonets aligned at throat level and you fixed your eyes on the place where the bayonet would go in, if they did not give way. You walked right for that exact spot. It was supposed to break their nerve.

"Forward . . . *march!*" Holman said shakily.

He stepped out with them. The coolies faced around, yelling and shaking fists. Some of them tore open their jackets and stuck out their skinny chests. The sailors walked steadily. Over the tip of his bayonet Holman could see the brown, curving ribs and he saw the spittle fly as the coolies screamed. They were not giving way. Holman did not like it at all. The line of sailors slowed.

"Step *out,* sailors!" Riley roared from across the street.

It galvanized them. They lunged. The coolies flinched and broke back. Instantly with deep shouts the Sikhs charged through, kicking and clubbing. The mob had changed to single coolies darting every which way like frantic rats. It was just as they said in the lectures at the YMCA.

Holman went in the door, past Chinese streaming out. Behind a wooden railing Graham was standing knee deep in torn paper. Blood ran down his long face and dripped on his gray suit. Desks and filing cabinets lay on their sides, with drawers pulled out. Holman went behind the railing.

"They hurt you, Mr. Graham?" he asked.

"I don't feel anything."

Graham dabbed his fingers in the blood on his face and looked at them. He sat down shakily on the one desk still upright.

"It's only a small cut," Holman said, looking at it.

"I know you. You're Jake Holman," Graham said.

He was still groggy. He was leaning down and trying to pull a desk drawer open. Holman opened it. Graham took out a bottle of White Horse. Riley and several sailors came in.

"How'd this riot get started?" Riley asked.

"I had to fire them all weeks ago. They've been making the usual fantastic demands for severance pay." Graham was saying it to Holman. "Well, Jake!" he said. "You boys came just in time. You look like God's own angels to me. Have a drink!"

He was coming out of his shock. He held out the bottle.

"Sorry. Can't drink on duty," Holman said. "Thanks, anyway."

"I'll set up drinks in the Green Front. By God, I *appreciate* you boys!"

"The Green Front's closed," Riley said. "Nobby Clarke's gone to Shanghai, the lucky bastard."

"Well, I'll think of something, Jake," Graham said.

Sirens sounded outside. Some British police came in. Riley made his report to the inspector. Their job was finished.

"Fall in outside, sailors," Riley ordered. He was angry because he felt bypassed. When they fell in outside, he scowled at Holman. "You know everybody in this rat's ass town, don't you?" he asked sourly. "You river rats, huh? I'm a Fleet sailor, myself."

It was cold and raining and the river was gray as steel. Lt. Collins was returning in his gig from an unhappy talk with the Flag people. The day before Pappy Tung, Ping-wen and Oh Joy had started ashore in a hired sampan. A gearwheel police launch had swooped in and taken them only a hundred feet from the ship. It had gotten away with them upriver to the native city before a ship's boat filled with cursing Sand Pebbles could rescue them.

"And a very good thing for you your men did not catch them," the Flag Lieutenant had said. "This river is like the high seas. We use it. But we don't own it."

Things seemed closing in. Lop Eye Shing had hinted sullenly that with enough money he could buy the men free. But there were no official funds for that. Shing had gone ashore and had not come back. The gig circled to make the gangway. *San Pablo* looked dingy. It would get worse, with Pappy Tung no longer on the job.

"They're Chinese. You know the orders, Bill," the Chief of Staff had said. "Any official interest we might show would probably only make it worse for them."

"*San Pablo* . . . boarding!" Haythorn cried, on the quarterdeck.

On the boat deck rain thrummed the awning. Burgoyne was waiting outside the cabin door. He squared up and saluted.

"Do you wish to speak to me, Burgoyne?" Lt. Collins asked.

"Yes, sir. If you've got time, sir."

"Come inside."

It was warm and dry inside. Burgoyne stood uneasily, twisting his white hat. He wanted permission to put in his papers to retire on sixteen years. It came as a shock.

"That's not much of a pension, Burgoyne," Lt. Collins said. "I've always taken you to be a thirty-year man."

"Always figured I was, sir. But now I got a wife and I got to find something ashore."

She was not his wife, but it would only hurt his feelings to keep telling him that. There was no use asking how things were. From the man's gaunt, desperate look, they were obviously much worse. Lt. Collins knew that Burgoyne was jumping ship. Sooner or later, it was bound to come to his attention officially.

"I haven't had much luck finding her a passage to Shanghai," he said. He checked his wry smile. The story was going around the clubs that young Bill Collins was infatuated with a cabaret girl and was concocting a wild story to get her down to Shanghai. "Have you thought about her taking a junk passage down?" he asked Burgoyne.

Burgoyne's head snapped up. "I won't never let her ride a junk again!" he said fiercely.

"Has she tried the mission refugee shelters?"

"Yes, sir. They're all full up."

They were having to turn away thousands of heartbreaking cases, Lt. Collins knew. They would not consider a sailor's shack girl a deserving moral case, he also knew. It would be a very sticky, distasteful business, pleading her case to them. Because she did not really have a case.

"I'll talk to some of them myself," he said. "But I want to remind you again, Burgoyne, of the oath we have both sworn. We are in a new kind of war here, a war in every sense but shooting. It may demand new kinds of sacrifices, our deepest feelings, perhaps even personal honor."

He paused. A red glow was coming into the man's somber eyes. He knew where that talk was leading and he would not go there.

"Yes, sir," he said. "About putting in my papers, sir. Is it all right?"

"Have Shanahan make them out. I'll approve and forward them," Lt. Collins said. "They'll have to go all the way to BuNav. It will take several months."

He dismissed Burgoyne. That was what it could do to a man, he thought. One of the finest, the kind of man who was meant to serve out thirty years and cry on the quarterdeck when his shipmates mustered to row him ashore for the last time. That was what it could do. And it was infectious. He had temporized too long. With a strong feeling of revulsion, he decided that he would have Burgoyne transferred to Shanghai with the next convoy.

Shirley had a plan. Walter Gillespie had accepted it, with misgivings. It remained to broach it to Mr. Craddock. They sat in the Craddocks' small room, three of them around the table. Mrs. Craddock sat back and did not join in the talk. She had no substance. It was as if her powerful old husband lived with the vitality of both their lives.

"We must all buy Chinese clothing to wear on the trip," Craddock said. "Good-quality, padded things. It will be like the old days." He brushed a hand over his hair. "I wore a queue in the old days."

"I think we face a different kind of hostility now," Gillespie said. "It's the young people, the students. They wear foreign clothes themselves."

"It's what we do, not how we look," Shirley said.

The junk was chartered. They were going back to China Light against consular advice and without notifying the consulate. Nightly at the hostel a mixed group had been praying that England and America would give up the unequal treaties as an act of faith in China. Mr. Craddock became wrathfully impatient with his government. He meant his return to be his personal act of faith.

"We have to show ourselves useful to their plans," Gillespie said.

Gillespie was going to take a teaching post. Mr. Craddock did not like it that Cho-jen was setting conditions on their return, nor that Cho-jen wrote to Shirley instead of to himself. She knew Mr. Craddock thought he would resume administrative control. He did not yet understand that it was a revolution.

"We must exert moral control and guidance," he said. "We must keep them in the faith."

"Yes, sir. By our example," Gillespie agreed. "But the coercive power is in their hands now. Unless we seem useful to them on their terms, they will just send us away again."

Craddock nodded agreement. Shirley took her chance.

"What if we could take someone with us to be mission engineer? To make the sugar mill work and set up the electric light plant?"

"He would be a godsend," Craddock said simply. "But I could never find such a man."

"I think I have. Let me tell you about him, Mr. Craddock."

She told him about Holman's gift for friendship with Chinese, a teacher's gift. She told about his devotion to machinery. She dwelt on his aversion for the military aspect of his life, and how he had cut all ties with home and cast his lines in China. Craddock looked very sternly at her.

"I think he's in or moving into a crisis in his life, Mr. Craddock," she finished. "He doesn't know it yet. But coming to China Light would give him the aim and purpose he needs so badly."

Mr. Craddock pondered. "Would he be morally suitable?"

"Yes. He's a good man."

"Could he get a discharge?"

"Probably not. I think he would just come."

"Have you spoken to him about it?"

"No. I've discussed it with Walter. We wanted to ask you, first."

Craddock looked at Gillespie. "The man would be deserting," he said. "That is a very grave thing."

"I've told Shirley we must not try to persuade or entice him," Gillespie said. "Just tell him of the opportunity."

"We are going back against the expressed will of our government," Shirley said. "How would he be different?"

"He has sworn an oath on the name of God."

"To serve his country. By your own reasoning, wouldn't he be serving his country more truly at China Light than aboard his gunboat? Wouldn't his personal act of faith be even more significant than ours? Or at least seem so, to the Chinese?"

"Let me think," Craddock said.

He bowed his lionlike head in his hands. It was his mode of brief, silent prayer. After several minutes he looked up.

"We have prayed and God has given us His answer in our hearts," he said slowly. "If the man could do that, be answered so . . . does the man pray? Is he even a Christian?"

"I think he would just wish he knew what to do and after a while something would seem right to him," Shirley said.

"Does not God speak in all deeply sought moral decisions, whether or not called on by name?" Gillespie asked.

Craddock was not sure. They talked about it. Shirley could see that the old man was terribly divided in his own mind. His own dreams for China Light were involved.

"Mr. Holman could train Chinese on the machinery," she said. "It could be the start of a vocational program."

"I will pray tonight and think about it again in the morning," Mr. Craddock said at last. "We have a week yet."

"Whatever seems right to you, Mr. Craddock," she assented.

She meant it, she realized suddenly. She did not need Craddock's consent. Cho-jen was anxious to have an engineer at China Light. But it was indeed a grave matter. For the first time since she had known him, she felt gratefully dependent on Mr. Craddock's moral judgment. She would be ruled by it.

Red Dog gave Holman a letter. It was the first he had ever gotten on the *San Pablo*. Before he could wonder about it, Farren called him to the quarterdeck, and he stuffed it into his pocket. Bronson and Wilsey were with Farren. They were a delegation.

"You're the only one Frenchy will listen to," Farren said. "You got to talk him into unshacking."

"He's killing himself. His head's a skull," Wilsey said. "It hurts me to look at him."

It had to stop, they had decided. Burgoyne had pushed his luck far past the danger point. He would get them all in trouble. They seemed to hate Maily, for what she was doing to Burgoyne. *That damned pig,* Bronson called her. When a guy went crazy, there came a time when you had to take hold of him, for his sake and your own.

"Harris and Doc want to go right to the skipper about it, officially," Farren said. "You tell Frenchy it's his last chance, Jake!" He thumped the log desk.

Holman knew Burgoyne was sleeping on the workbench. He went below and woke him. He did not know how to start.

"How's it going now with you and Maily?" he began.

"Mighty bad. We got to find another place, come the end of the month."

The native city had been organized into block societies, he said. He and Maily could not belong. They were being squeezed out of their block and they could not squeeze into any other block. Tung Li was helpless.

"You got to move her into the concessions, no matter what it costs," Holman said. "I'll talk to Lynch."

"Lynch is selling out in the next day or two. Even if I could find a place and afford it, the patrol would get me there."

"Well . . ." Holman told him what Farren had said. "I don't know what to say, Frenchy. Seems like it's just got to end."

"It's got to end," Burgoyne agreed.

"Then let her go, if it has to be."

Burgoyne's face set hard as iron. "That's what she keeps telling me. She wants to take it all on herself." He slid off the workbench, fists clenched. "Jake, I'm honest to tell you. I never go home that I ain't afraid she won't be there. Or else she will be, with her throat cut."

"*Christ,* Frenchy!" Holman gritted his teeth. "But how would it help her any, you getting a court-martial, maybe going to prison in Cavite?"

"That'd just be the chance of things, like getting killed in a war. I could stand that," Burgoyne said. "Don't you see, Jake, it can't be *me* that does it! It's got to come from outside."

"I guess I see," Holman said.

He walked around behind the main condenser to look at his letter. It was only a line.

Dear Jake,
I would like to talk to you again. Could you come Tuesday?
Shirley

He whistled soundlessly. He did not know what it meant. But today was Tuesday. Burgoyne was still standing like a statue beside the workbench. Holman went back to him.

"Frenchy, I want to jump ship along with you this afternoon."

"Jake, I told you—"

"This is my own private business. It's important."

"Well, sure, then."

30

They split a beer in the canteen and then walked back past the head and into the kitchen. A bearded Sikh watchman got up off a stool and said, "Hi, Johnny." Burgoyne gave him a dollar. He led them between bales and drums and crates in a big, dark, tar-smelling warehouse section and let them out a small door that opened on Poyang Road. They cut through alleys to Boundary Road, checking each cross-street for American patrols before darting over. They walked boldly into the native city past the British guard post, with its White Ensign flying above the sandbagged matshed. A short way beyond, Holman stopped.

"Thanks, Frenchy. I turn off here."

"Remember, go all the way to the Jap Concession to get a sampan back," Burgoyne cautioned him. "Our patrols don't cover that bund."

Holman hurried his own way. It had stopped raining, but everything was cold and damp. He did not recognize her at first, beside the stone, because she was wearing lightly padded blue Chinese jacket and trousers.

"Jake," she said, smiling. "It's really me."

"Well, so it is! You look good in that rig."

They were both tense, on guard against themselves. She and three others were leaving for China Light in the morning on a chartered junk, she told him. She insisted they were not going into any danger.

"All I hear's the other way," he protested. "It's worse down there."

"We have permission to come back," she said. "It won't be like before, our being there without even granting them any say about it." She told him about Cho-jen being in effective charge of everything. "We're trying to give up the unequal treaties in our own actions," she said. "We're not even informing the consulate."

She wanted his approval. He had many doubts. He was afraid for her.

"You know what they say on the ships, about missionaries who won't come out? Or who sneak back?"

"What do they say?"

"That they're being hostages to the gearwheel. To keep us from fighting."

"Nonsense! Jake, you can't believe that!"

"Not about you, I guess. But suppose it did come to fighting? You'd be bad off."

"Not at China Light."

She explained carefully. As long as the unequal treaties remained in force, they meant to dissociate themselves from their government. They would not even let the consul know they were there. They were going to show their personal good faith to China as individual men and women.

"I'm even prepared to become Chinese, if I must," she said.

"What!" Then he laughed. "Oh, you mean on paper. But that's still serious."

"I'm sure it won't come to that."

"Sometimes I wish I could be Chinese. Born to it, I mean."

"That's why I wanted to see you."

She told him that he could be the mission engineer, look after the sugar mill and set up a light plant. She spoke of a training program for young Chinese. Her voice was strange, flat and fast, and her expression curiously wooden. She kept her eyes on him. He could see what she meant. It hung together. It made sense. He wondered why he had never thought of it himself.

I will! he thought, and his hands tingled.

She paused, waiting for him to say it. He knew he was staring at her. She was rosy and pretty. She dropped her eyes. He searched for thought.

"Craddock. He hates sailors."

"Not you. He's prayed about it. And you wouldn't be a sailor, then."

"That's right. I got almost two years to do." He bit his lip. "I couldn't get a special order discharge now." She was silent, her eyes still lowered. "If I went with you now, I'd have to desert," he said.

The sound of the word in his own mouth chilled him. A deep, vague fear displaced his glow and tingle. He felt a sudden anger, as if he had been offered something wonderful and then had it snatched away.

"I'll have to serve out my time. I suppose that'd be too late."

"Maybe not. Cho-jen knows about you. He approves."

She kept her eyes down. Her mouth was drooping. Something desperate flared along his nerves.

"Shirley, do you want me to come? Really want me?"

"Not for my sake. For yours, I think." She raised her head and looked at him steadily. Her face was pale. "It must be your own un-influenced decision, Jake. Don't think of me. Think only of the need you will find there of the work you know best how to do."

"How can I help but think of you?"

"You must try. Pray, if you can." She was very serious. "Mr. Craddock says that's how it must be. He wouldn't let me tell you until today."

"I don't know how to pray. Let me think."

The more he thought, the more hopeless it was. He could not believe that they would not catch him, any place on earth that he might go. If he were in Shanghai, he might buy a Cuban passport to protect him. But you could not do that in Hankow. He wished that she had never given him the thought. He knew it was going to haunt him with its allure and its hopelessness.

"It's no use, Shirley," he said at last, miserably.

"I shouldn't have said anything."

"I'm glad you did. In them few minutes—I know now I won't ever ship over in the navy."

They tried to talk. It did not go very well. He had a strong, sad feeling that he would never see her again. It was almost dark before she finally said it.

"I suppose we'd better say good-bye. Shall I go first?"

"No. I will," he said. "I want to remember you standing here beside the rock. Like the first time."

He walked a few paces and turned around. She was just standing there smiling in her soft blue Chinese rig. He took her into his eyes and swallowed and raised his hand.

"Good-bye, Jake," she said.

"Good-bye, Shirley."

He said it so low in his throat that she probably did not hear. Then he turned and walked away. He felt like a wooden man.

He got hold of himself somewhere along Ho Kai. The shops were lighted and people were all around. He stopped to get his bearings. He was almost under the hanging bicycle wheel he remembered as marking Tung Li's place. He verified it by the little blind alley just beyond. Then he went inside and up the stairs and knocked on Burgoyne's door.

No answer. No slightest stir inside.

He knocked again, sharply. A woman's voice spoke in high, breathless Chinese.

"Frenchy!" Holman said. "It's me. Jake."

"Jake!" two voices exclaimed.

A chain rattled. Burgoyne opened the door. Maily, behind him, said, "Jake! Oh, Jake!"

"Hello, Maily." He took her hands. They were cold.

"Come aboard, boy!"

Burgoyne pulled him inside and closed the door. The room was dark, cold and lamp-smelly. Maily turned up the wick in the tiny kerosene lamp and the shadows pulled back into the corners. Burgoyne had on a ragged Chinese coat and trousers. His bony wrists and ankles stuck out of them.

"I wear 'em here around home," he said. He rattled the one chair. "Sit down, Jake. We call this the emperor's throne." Holman didn't want to. "Come on. You're company," Burgoyne said. "First we ever had here."

Holman sat down. The room was dismal. Patches of the brown wallpaper hung loose. Maily had hung up a few bright scraps of cloth. She knelt by the clay stove lighting a fire to make tea.

"I'm sure glad to see you again, Maily," he said lamely.

"I'm glad too, Jake."

She was thin in the face and her hair was growing out. She wore a padded blue cotton jacket that flared at the hips, above padded blue trousers. She was trying not to let him see her from the side.

"Maily's purely busting to talk to somebody besides me," Burgoyne said. He paced back and forth. "We got to celebrate this," he said, and slapped his leg. "Maily, we got to whomp us up a company chow!"

He knelt beside her. They opened the chest and whispered. What they had, what they could afford, Holman thought. He knew the shops overcharged them. They were probably almost broke.

"I meant to bring a basket of chow with me, only I was afraid I might not find you," he said. "I'll go get it now."

"No. You're company." Burgoyne stood up, holding a basket. "And I know right where to go."

Holman stood up. "Let me, Frenchy. I want to."

"I'm dressed for it. They don't like the uniform around here," Burgoyne said. "Besides, you're company. So damn it, *be* company! Talk to Maily."

"At least let me pay for it."

"I got enough."

"If I'm company, you got to humor me," Holman said. He stuffed some Mex bills into Burgoyne's jacket. "All right, damn it, *humor* me!"

They all laughed. Burgoyne went out.

Holman knelt beside her. "How are you, Maily? How is it, really?"
She waved. "As you see. Only worse."

The *pukow* was rolled out and rumpled. They had been in it when
he knocked, for warmth. Maily was blowing at the charcoal sticks.
Her thin, smudged face was blotched with red spots and her hair was
stringy. Her little hands were grimy and thin as bird feet. He remembered her firm roundedness and perfect, blooming skin. Now she was
a coolie woman.

"I'll tell you how it is. It's like a story I read once, by Edgar Allan
Poe," she said. "There was a man and they hypnotized him and he
died, but they wouldn't let him die."

"I never read it."

"Frenchy's fighting God's curse," she said. "I brought it on him."

"Oh *hell,* Maily!"

"It's true!" She sat back on her heels, eying the fire. "It would
comfort me if I could convince you, Jake. I've never told this before."

He paced and listened. She was raised as their own child by a
missionary couple who had no children of their own, she told him.
The man had found her as an infant abandoned on a winter hillside,
wrapped in a straw mat and being rooted at by pigs. Frost took several
of her fingers and toes, but they had saved her life.

"I used to think the pigs had bitten them off," she said. "At the
same time I didn't really believe the pig story. I thought it was a kind
of stork story."

She loved her foster parents. Somewhere along the way she learned
that she had a Chinese body. She did not learn surely that she was
not an American on paper until she was eighteen. The mission's
Chinese doctor was discontented and talked of going to Shanghai.
They had to have the clinic in operation to keep down native
hostility. Then the doctor fell in love with Maily.

"They didn't tell me directly. They just made me know indirectly
how important it was to the mission to keep Dr. Wing," she said. "At
prayer meetings they talked about pigs and God's grace that preserved
me. They kept urging me to search my heart in prayer. I pretended to,
but I didn't."

"Well . . . wouldn't a doctor be a pretty good deal?"

"I didn't love him!" She sat up straight. "All my life I'd been hearing them condemn and try to break down the Chinese custom of arranged marriages." She slumped again. "Besides, I didn't want to shift from being American staff to being native staff. It makes a big difference in how you live." She looked around. "Now look how I live. Now I know that they were right."

She held out a long time. Then she stole money and ran away.

"You know the rest of it, Jake. I owe my life to God's grace and I evaded His will for me. Frenchy is a good man, the best man I ever knew, and I have brought God's curse on him."

She was crying. She bent to blow the fire. Holman wanted to rage against her foolish belief. But it was a kind of comfort to her. And he had absolutely no other comfort to offer in exchange.

"There comes some one time in your life when God calls on you to pay the debt you owe Him. That was my time, and I failed." She looked up, tears streaming. "Oh Jake! When your time comes, don't fail! Don't fail!"

She put her hand on his knee, beseechingly. He moved away.

"Maily. Oh *hell,* Maily!" he said. He felt like crying himself.

"Don't tell Frenchy," she pleaded. "He's so bitter already. Something dark and burning is in him. I'm afraid, Jake."

They heard Burgoyne's footsteps on the stairs. She bent hastily to blow the fire again. She was wiping away the tear tracks with her grimy jacket sleeve.

The two men drank tea at the table. The little lamp shadowed the hollows of Burgoyne's cheeks and gleamed on skin tight over bone. Maily was making chopping and mixing noises behind Holman.

"It's a surprise, Jake. Don't look," she warned him.

Burgoyne was curious about Holman's reason for jumping ship. Holman sketched out the story about Shirley and the offer to make him mission engineer. As he talked, the wild, joyful, jump-off-the-edge feeling rose again in him.

"Right this minute they're aboard some junk along the native bund.

They won't sail till morning." He leaned across the table. "Frenchy, let's go find 'em! You and me and Maily. I bet they'd take us all. What do you say?"

"You mean desert?" Burgoyne stared at him. "Jake! You crazy, boy?"

"Hell yes! Why not desert?"

"I got in my papers to go out on sixteen," Burgoyne said. "I can't throw that away. And besides, it's *wrong!*" He was leaning back and staring unbelievingly at Holman. "And besides that, it'd be going over to the enemy," he said accusingly.

"The Chinese ain't our enemy," Holman said. The chill was coming back over his spirit.

"The gearwheel's our enemy!" Burgoyne said. "They're trying to run us all out of China. God damn it, *I* ought to know!"

"You got it figured wrong, Frenchy."

"I hell got it wrong! They're poisoning China!" Burgoyne relaxed his manner. "Chinamen ain't the way they are now by nature, Jake," he said plaintively. "You purely know they ain't."

"They're turning into a nation," Holman said. "They can't stand to have foreign gunboats in their rivers and people like us ashore in uniform, without their permission."

"But we're *Americans*," Burgoyne protested. "They know we don't want their territory. We're just protecting our own people."

Holman felt hopeless again. He changed the subject.

"That smells good, Maily."

"Don't you dare look!"

"I can't help smelling. It smells good."

When Maily served the food, it was rice and fried peppers and pork in the gingery sauce that Mei-yu had taught her to make. It was very good and it brought back old times. Both men praised her and she smiled and cried. They had only the chair and chest to sit on, so Maily ate standing, bowl and chopsticks in hand, like a Chinese woman. She brought them acrid Chinese wine, heated. The hot food and wine made the room steamy warm and good-smelling.

"You got the best cook in China, Frenchy, and the prettiest one,"

Holman said. "You better be good to her. You better not turn your back."

Burgoyne pulled Maily against him and she smiled down. "Anybody gets this gal, it'll be over my dead body," he said fondly.

It was one of their old jokes from Changsha. They drank hot wine and talked about Changsha and it brought those old days back for them very powerfully.

Leaving, Holman turned in the hall, to face them both in the doorway. He put one hand on each of their shoulders and pressed them together.

"I had a good time," he said. "It was just good, being here with you."

"Thank you for coming, Jake," Maily said. "Goodnight. God bless you."

He left them smiling.

In the street, he did not smile. It was dark. The drizzle had started again. He turned up his peacoat collar. A gust of unconsenting rage at his helplessness shook him almost physically.

He walked along. Two uniformed pickets walked at him. He gave way. Half a block further along he gave way for three others, and they shifted too. They were trying to force him into a filthy puddle. It was too much. It triggered him. He turned and shouldered between them and swept both arms out powerfully.

They tumbled and splashed. A shout went up. It was the thin, screechy Chinese mob shout. Holman's hair bristled. He faced around.

A line of men had formed across the street. Almost like magic, the street seemed solid with angry, yelling faces. Windows opened. Heads peered down, between potted plants on window balconies.

The line moved slowly toward him. He gave ground backward, fists ready at hip level. You could always face down a Chinese mob, they said. It was the power of the eye. You had to face them down. The danger lay in running. That was what they said. Holman whirled and ran.

Stones overtook him and thudded on his back. The screech raced by him like fire in treetops. The street ahead filled with men. Holman burst through them, elbowing, shouldering, fists lashing out for his life. Far ahead he saw the brighter lights of Taiping Road and the White Ensign flying above the guard post.

Chest aching, feet pounding, he ran for it. Whistles shrilled ahead. British sailors deployed from the guard post with bright bayonets. Holman threw up his hands and ran through them into the sanctuary of the light.

The broad, kindly British faces looked at him curiously. "Bless me, a Yank!" the pink-cheeked young sub-lieutenant said. Holman was panting too hard to speak. He heard the mob screech subside. The young officer told his men to stand easy. He led Holman into the matshed. Some Hankow Volunteers were there, in khaki and steel helmets.

"I must hold you until the American patrol stops by," the officer told Holman. "You're lucky to be alive, you know."

"Yes, sir. I know," Holman panted.

He was trembling and sweating heavily. He fumbled open his peacoat, to cool off. Now I'll get a court-martial, he was thinking. Well, it was better for your own side to catch you. Yes, much better. A Volunteer officer walked over.

"This is a friend of mine," he told the British officer. "I'll escort him to patrol headquarters."

It was Graham. His pleasant, homely face looked strange under the round British helmet.

"I shall have to report this," the young officer said doubtfully. "I shall want name and ship and—"

"Joseph Doakes, U.S.S. *Truxtun,*" Graham said easily. "Tell you the rest when I come back, Robert. I'll be responsible." He took Holman's arm. "Come on, Joe," he said.

Holman walked out with him, still panting. It was all very fast and smooth. He began to catch his breath. They turned into Poyang Road.

"Lucky I was on duty," Graham said. "It's my last spell of duty, too."

"Lucky for me, all right." Holman had a sour, copperish taste in his mouth. "You sure done that smooth," he said admiringly.

"Things can always be arranged. I owed you a favor," Graham said. "Glad I had a chance to return it. I'm leaving with the convoy Friday."

They walked along. Street lights gleamed on wet pavement. No one was on the street.

"I'm curious," Graham said. "You could get killed over in the native city. What were you doing there?"

"I'll tell you. Because I want to ask you a really big favor."

He began telling about Maily and Burgoyne. Graham halted.

"Native women are not wives," he said. "I'll bet she's the same woman Bill Collins spoke to me about."

"I expect so. Could you possibly take her, sir?"

"Look, Jake. Come in here out of the rain."

Graham moved into a shadowy doorway. Holman refused a cigarette. Graham lit his own. His face looked sad and thoughtful in the match flare.

"China is a big country, but the American community in China is a lot like a small town. We all know each other," he said. "You can't get away from it, this is a case of a sailor shacked up with a native woman. And nobody can keep secrets in China. My wife's maid is a perfect devil to bring her servants' gossip."

"Why a secret? What's *wrong* with taking her?"

"It's . . . well . . . we live under American law here in China. Not that I think the U.S. Marshal could or would enforce the Mann Act on me. But we have the sentiment of it." He pulled deeply on his cigarette. The glow showed his long, honest face twisted with sadness. "I have business enemies. My wife has social enemies," he said. "They'd make a big thing out of Ed Graham bringing a cabaret girl down to Shanghai."

Holman shivered. He buttoned his peacoat.

"People always believe the lies," Graham said. "They want to believe any lie that hurts someone they envy."

"I guess that's how it is."

"Why doesn't your friend just let her go?" Graham's voice was sad but kindly. "It's that kind of a time in the world. In China, anyway. And she *is* Chinese."

"He won't let her go," Holman said. He could not get angry at Graham. "All right, she's Chinese. Does that mean she ain't got any insides, she's made of paper or something?"

"It shouldn't make any difference, should it? But in our world I'm afraid it does," Graham said. "What I meant, though, was—*mei yuh fah tzu.* The Chinese are fatalists. No matter what, they can bow their heads and go on living."

"Well, thanks for helping me, anyway."

"It wasn't anything. I'm sorry about the other."

"Mei yuh fah tzu," Holman said. "Goodnight, Mr. Graham."

31

Burgoyne was not aboard at reveille. If he came back now, in broad daylight, it would be hard for the officers and chiefs not to see him. If he was not aboard for quarters, it would have to go down on paper.

"I knew it! I knew it!" Farren tugged at his beard. "I logged him in last night."

"We all done it. We're all in the same boat," Perna said.

During breakfast a boat from the flagship delivered Burgoyne under guard to the *San Pablo*. The Sand Pebbles flocked out. Burgoyne stood there quietly while Restorff, who had the watch, logged him in as a prisoner-at-large. He had a purple swelling on the side of his head and blood on his ear.

"What happened, Frenchy?" Wilsey asked him.

"Patrol caught me," Burgoyne said. "I didn't tell them bastards in Flag nothing. You guys ain't in trouble."

He had an animal glare in his mild brown eyes. He turned, with slashing motions, and pushed through them to the engine room hatch.

"Leave him alone, you guys," Holman told the others.

He followed Burgoyne down into the engine room. Burgoyne stood leaning with his hands on the workbench, head bowed. Holman stood quietly behind him.

"Want to talk about it, Frenchy?"

"All I'd tell 'em in Flag was that I got drunk in the Limey canteen and went over to a whorehouse I knew about in the native city," Burgoyne said. "Tell 'em that topside. Tell 'em they ain't none of 'em in trouble account of me."

"I'll tell 'em."

"Reason they caught me." Burgoyne coughed suddenly, deep in his chest. "The block committee threw us out last night. We sat in that alley back of the place all night, wrapped in our *pukow*. I didn't sleep . . . guess I was dopey. Anyway . . ."

"Jesus, Frenchy!"

"I run eight blocks, Jake," Burgoyne said in a stronger voice. "They kept shooting at me but they couldn't hit me. Only in the ear." He touched his ear. "Then I run smack into a second patrol and they clubbed me down with rifle butts. I didn't give up easy."

"Where's Maily now?"

"Settin' in that alley, with her gear."

"You better get in dry clothes, Frenchy. Eat something."

"After while," Burgoyne said. "Jake, I didn't give up easy." He shuddered all over and coughed again. "I'll just set here a spell, first," he said. He sat down on the workbench. "Just leave me be, Jake. I got to think what to do."

After quarters Lt. Collins was called to the flagship. It was about either Burgoyne or Pappy Tung, the crew surmised. They hoped the ship was not in trouble, but they were glad to see the long agony over for Frenchy Burgoyne. They thought his sixteen-year clear record would save him from naval prison.

Mei yuh fah tzu, Holman kept thinking.

A large wupan with two stumpy masts tried to come alongside. Uniformed students and civilian Chinese filled it. Franks drove it back with the fire hose.

"We wish to speak with your captain," a student in the bow hailed.

Three coolies sculled it with a big, rope-anchored *yuloh*. A red-headed woman in the bow was making notes on a pad. She was either a missionary or a Bolshevik.

"Red hair. She's one of them Reds, all right," Bronson said.

"Hey, watch that stuff!" Red Dog said.

The student hailed again. Bordelles came to the bridge wing.

"Tung Chi-fu has confessed that you have opium aboard," the student shouted through cupped hands. "We ask that you surrender it to be destroyed."

"Below, there!" Bordelles shouted. "Hit 'em with that hose!"

The water arched out again, but it would not reach. The Sand Pebbles argued angrily. Someone said they must have tortured poor old Pappy Tung. Someone else recognized Pappy Tung standing in the waist of the wupan. Ping-wen was there too.

"We know exactly where it is aboard," the student shouted. "We ask that you submit to a joint inspection."

"This is a United States ship of war and you can go to hell!"

Bordelles rang it out like bells. The student shrugged.

"We came prepared for that," he shouted.

The people in the wupan stretched a sign between the stumpy masts. In big red letters on white, it read: POISONERS OF CHINA! GIVE UP CONTRABAND! The wupan began a slow circling of the *San Pablo,* just out of firehose range.

It was a damp, gray day. Clouds hung heavy and low. The Sand Pebbles were disturbed at the enormity of the lie. The ship coolies gathered in a knot on the fantail, jabbering excitedly.

"Why the hell they picking on us?" Duckbutt Randall kept asking.

"San Pablo . . . boarding!" Farren shouted.

Lt. Collins fairly leaped aboard. "Send all the chiefs to my cabin, on the double!" he snapped at Farren. "Tell them side arms!" He ran on up the ladder.

The search party went pistoled and grim-faced aft and down to the Chinese quarters. More coolies popped up on deck. In about ten minutes the search party came up. Each man carried three or four wicker-cased packages the size of bowling balls. Lynch caught Holman's eye in the crowd.

"Get below, Jake!" he ordered. "Clear out the coolies!"

The only coolie was the man on watch. Holman sent him up. Lt. Collins and the others brought their packages into the fireroom. Only the center furnace of the port boiler was burning. Holman swung open the fire door and they all pitched their packages in on the bed of coals.

"Leave the door open," Lt. Collins said. "I want to see it burn."

His voice was sharp, his lips white. The wicker casings caught fire. The stuff melted and fried out, spreading and bubbling, almost smothering the fire. The furnace became blue-smoky. The open fire door spoiled the draft. Holman mentioned it to Lynch.

"Slice it!" Lynch said.

Holman worked the long slice bar up through the grates. Coals and clinkers showered down. Pink flames broke through the frothy, smoking surface. They were all stooped looking into the furnace, their faces red and sweating. Bronson came down and shook Franks' arm.

"Chief! The smoke's spreading right above the water!" he said. "They can smell it from here to Shanghai, for God's sake!"

They could smell it in the fireroom, too. Everybody in China knew that heavy, oily, sweetish smell.

"Lynch! Mask it, somehow!" Lt. Collins snapped.

"Rubber, Jake!" Lynch yelled. "Oil and rags!"

Holman ran for the roll of sheet rubber they used in making gaskets. Lynch threw in armloads of oily rags. Then he coaled the fire heavily, slammed the fire door, and gave it maximum draft.

"There, by God!" Lynch said, puffing, hands on hips.

The fire roared. The opium smell in the fireroom thinned out. Holman glanced at the steam gauge.

"Watch steam, Chief!" he warned.

Lynch tapped the gauge. The pointer jumped past the red mark. Lynch's eyes bulged.

"Christ! She's gonna pop!"

"Don't blow safeties!" Lt. Collins said.

"Hit 'er with feed, Jake!" Lynch yelled.

He kicked the ashpan door shut. Holman ran out and twisted open the feed check. The feed pump pounded.

"Start pumps, Frenchy! Kill steam!" Holman shouted at Burgoyne.

It was too late. The safeties popped, with a sustained roar. The mountaining steam flickered its shadow over the engine room skylight. Sweet-stinking black smoke spread like a pall above the ship and its circling wupan satellite. The *San Pablo* was roaring up all the world to come and witness her disgrace.

Through it all Burgoyne sat unmoving on the workbench with his head in his hands. He was sunk in his own trouble. But the Sand Pebbles had forgotten about him in the ship's larger trouble.

At dinner, they were all angry at the mess tables. They hacked their teeth into their food and chomped and glared and wrangled. They could still hardly believe it. It was treachery. They wondered which coolies were involved.

"Every slant-eyed, slopeheaded one of 'em, I bet!" Harris snorted.

They agreed that no one could blame the ship or Lt. Collins for it. The coolies were just aboard working for squeeze and cumshaw. They had no official connection with the ship.

Holman could not get Burgoyne to eat dinner. He would not even speak or look up. Holman went away sadly. He was haunted by the thought that Maily and Burgoyne might have been caught in the backlash of the mob he had stirred up.

Well, *mei yuh fah tzu*. It was not much comfort.

Lt. Collins went back to the flagship. Canteen liberty was stopped for that day. Only Lynch got ashore. He was busy selling his teashop. His wife and her kid cousin would be going to Shanghai in the convoy Friday. In mid-afternoon a motor launch made the gangway and two white civilians tried to come aboard. Crosley had the watch. He stopped them.

"Nobody comes aboard and nobody leaves," he said. "Them's orders."

The men broke out cards to show him. The older one, a thin, gray man, tried to step up on the quarterdeck. Crosley put a hand on his chest.

"Take your hands off me, sailor!" the old man snapped. "I'm a taxpayer and a representative of the press. Any day I can't come aboard an American warship, I want to know about it!"

"This is the day, Joe," Crosley said.

Bordelles came. He looked pale and stern. He backed up Crosley.

"It's splashed all through the native press that your servants have been smuggling opium," the thin man said. "Give us a statement."

"See the Flag Secretary. I can't talk. Orders from way, high up."

The old man argued. He had been to Flag and gotten a runaround and he was angry about it. "Right here's where the story is!" he kept saying. Bordelles could not placate him by saying that he was under orders. The old man began to threaten.

"If an American warship has been smuggling opium, the American people certainly want to know about it!" he said. "My paper can break an admiral like a matchstick, if he tries to dupe the American people!"

"My admiral can break me like a matchstick," Bordelles said.

"Let me, Jason." The chubby, younger man in the tan coat took over. He tried to trap Bordelles. "Give us a little something, like crumbs for the birds," he wheedled. He had a smooth Irish voice. "We won't quote you. How many of the sailors are involved?"

"Sorry."

"Deny it, then. Call it Red propaganda. Where do you think the stuff came aboard?"

He could not charm or trap Bordelles. In the end, he threatened too.

"The American people can make it very hot when they get their moral dander up," he said. "Talk and protect yourself. We'll protect you."

That snapped Bordelles' patience. His face turned red.

"Shove off, or I'll turn the firehose on you!" he commanded.

They chugged off, very angry. Crosley watched them go, hands on hips.

"Them sons of bitches. Them God damned cannibals," he said unbelievingly. "Picking on their own people! What in hell's the *matter* with 'em?"

Even Harris was glum at supper. The men talked in low voices about the power of Stateside newspapers. They knew in a vague way that many Stateside newspapers, like Borah and Kellogg and even Coolidge, seemed to be pro-gearwheel. They blamed all that on the missionaries sending lies home. But now the newspapers had their own reporters in China, and they had seen a sample that afternoon. It gave them a shadowy, cut-off, stabbed-in-the-back feeling. It was a nasty, unpleasant feeling.

"I guess even Coolidge is scared of the papers," Farren said.

"The papers kind of *are* the American people," Wilsey agreed. "Like the guy said."

They only mentioned Burgoyne once.

"You'd think, with all this new trouble, Comyang'd forget about hanging Frenchy," Farren said.

"Once the machine starts grinding, they always hang you," Harris said gloomily.

It was a very subdued supper. They were all afraid the machine was grinding for Lt. Collins and the whole *San Pablo*.

At sunset the mocking wupan went away. It had circled the ship all day like a grinning hyena. When Haythorn announced the captain's return, the men all drifted to the quarterdeck. They just wanted to stand there shoulder to shoulder while Lt. Collins came aboard. It was a kind of closing ranks in the face of trouble.

Lt. Collins did not look at them, but they knew he understood. He went up to his cabin looking worried and angry. A few minutes later Burgoyne came on the quarterdeck. He would not speak or look at anyone. He went up the ladder to the boat deck like a mechanical man.

"He's going to see the skipper," someone whispered.

They waited, wondering, not talking. Franks came to the head of the ladder.

"Holman down there?" Holman pushed forward. "Come up here, Jake, Franks said.

Holman went up. Burgoyne was standing behind Franks.

"Frenchy just told the skipper he won't be a prisoner-at-large," Franks said. "You and your engineers will have to stand watch and guard him."

"Don't put a guard on me, Chief. I might have to kill him," Burgoyne said. He coughed rackingly, bending over. "Hold me with metal, something stronger than muscles," he said. "Shackle me to the rail, or something."

Franks looked at Holman and shook his head pityingly. Holman felt a brief flash of the hell that Burgoyne had been in all day. He understood. Burgoyne had to keep trying while life was in him. Suddenly Holman wished that the patrol that morning had killed Burgoyne. *Mei yuh fah tzu* would not work for an American.

They shackled Frenchy Burgoyne with a leg iron from his ankle to his bunk rail. He lay there, fully dressed and on his back. His face was deep-lined and hard as iron and he would not speak. Only his fierce, animal eyes were alive, turning and shifting. He made it very uncomfortable in the compartment.

The Sand Pebbles stayed out on deck until taps. Then they went in and to bed with none of the usual joking cross-talk. Holman had a hard time going to sleep. He caught himself thinking some very strange thoughts.

32

At reveille Burgoyne was gone. The leg iron was sawed through, half of it still locked on the bunk rail. Perna found the hacksaw blade in the blankets.

"He was here when I come off deck sentry watch at four," Stawski said. "Ellis let him get away."

Ellis was main deck sentry. They called him in.

"It come on a rain squall about five," Ellis said. "I went in the galley."

"That's when he went." Farren kicked Burgoyne's shoes. "He must've swum for it."

Wong brought in the morning coffee. They drank it standing up, uneasily silent, avoiding each other's eyes. They all knew the Yangtze was a fast, treacherous river.

"Anybody know how good Frenchy could swim?" Farren asked finally. "What do you think, Jake?"

"I think Frenchy tried as hard as he could," Holman said.

No one wanted to say it. At last Harris said it.

"Breaking arrest on top of all the other charges, he'd land in Forty-eight for sure," Harris said. "He's better off if he didn't make it."

Forty-eight was the naval prison at Cavite. If a man went in there with a scrap of spirit, the marines would beat it out of him or they would beat him to death.

"You guys stop mooning like a bunch of nutted women!" Harris said brutally. "Frenchy was overdue for it. It was like a mad dog bit him from the first time he ever saw that pig."

That was Frenchy Burgoyne's epitaph. The Sand Pebbles sat down to a troubled breakfast.

It was a troubled day. Despite the cold drizzle, a dozen propaganda sampans came out. They knew the *San Pablo* was wounded in the propaganda war and they were cutting it out for the kill. They sculled round and round the ship shouting slogans like warwhooping Indians circling a wagon train.

Lt. Collins had been up half the night writing a report. He and Bordelles went to the flagship without holding morning quarters. Lynch had to go ashore to close the sale of his teashop.

"Take care of things, Jake," Lynch said. "I won't be back until after I see Liuba and Valentine off on the steamer tomorrow."

The ship's trouble did not bother Lynch. He was too excited. His Hankow lawyer was moving his office to Shanghai too, and Lynch was going to have someone down there he could trust to draw up papers. Things were working out nicely for Lynch.

Lt. Collins was gone all day. The coolies did no work. The ship was in a kind of shock. Holman could not rest. He paced the floor-plates in the engine room. He did not believe that Burgoyne was dead. Sometimes you could glimpse the whole blueprint of a man's life. There was no luck at all in Frenchy Burgoyne's blueprint.

Holman's troubled night thoughts returned to plague him. He absolutely could not share Maily's belief in God's curse. But it did really seem as if some hateful god was torturing Frenchy Burgoyne.

In late afternoon the rain turned to a heavy, wet snow. It was too much for the propaganda sampans. They stopped their circling and went home. It was a blessed relief. Bordelles came back and had the word passed that canteen liberty would be resumed. No one must talk to reporters. Holman rated liberty. When he put on his dress blues, he dug back in his locker and found the Belgian revolver he had taken from the gangster in Changsha. He pouched his undershirt inside his drawers to make a nest for it. The thirteen-button flap of his blue trousers held it securely and invisibly in place.

The *San Pablo* table was all the way aft in the long, smoky room. A big crowd was there that night. Farren and Red Dog sat with Holman. They drank beer glumly and talked about Burgoyne. The other two did not want to believe that Burgoyne was alive.

"He's alive," Holman insisted. "He ain't got that kind of luck."

Up front some British sailors began singing. The other tables were coming in on the choruses. It was a rollicking song.

> *I'll tell you a story of trouble and woe*
> *To make you shake and shiver-r-r,*
> *About a Chinee bumboatman*
> *Who sailed the Yangtze River-r-r.*
> *For he was a heathen of high degree,*
> *As the joss house records show;*
> *His heathen name was Wing Kang Lung,*
> *But sailormen called him Jim Crow.*

The chorus crashed out:

> *Oh muchee come catchee come hai yai-yah!*
> *Chinaman no likee he!*
> *Ai yah!*

On the *ai yah* they all stamped feet and thumped tables. It shook the place. The Sand Pebbles did not join in.

"Know something? We never put the alarm out on Frenchy," Red Dog said. "I just now thought. Things was too fouled up this morning."

"That's right. We never held muster," Farren said.

It jolted Holman. "You sure, Red Dog?" he asked. "Because I think I know where Frenchy is. If I could sneak him back aboard . . ."

"He wouldn't be breaking arrest." Farren nodded. "If it ain't down on paper, it never happened."

They looked at each other. It seemed a cheering upturn in the run of things. But Burgoyne would still be in deep trouble.

"It's a damned shame!" Red Dog said. "You'd think them newspaper guys would get on that, instead of riding the ship about opium."

"They might make Comyang cancel the court-martial," Farren said.

"They can put the fear of Christ into the navy," Red Dog said. "If I didn't know that before, I know it now."

They talked about getting in touch with a newspaperman and getting Burgoyne off the hook altogether. It cheered them. Red Dog began beating his hand in time with the song.

> *. . . he swore a tar-ry-ble oath:*
> *If I cannot marry sweet Wang Koo Fong,*
> *I'll gr-r-rind the gizzards of both!*

"Jesus!" Farren pointed up the room. "Look who come in!"

It was the chubby Irish reporter. The men looked at each other in wonder. It was a sign, their nods agreed.

The reporter stamped snow off his feet and brushed it off his tan overcoat, while he looked around. He stopped at a *Truxtun* table and they pointed aft. He came down the room behind his big Irish grin, directly to the *San Pablo* table. He held up his hands in mock surrender.

"I promise I won't ask you boys one word about you-know-what," he said. "Can I join you on those terms?"

"Sure. Sit down." Farren kicked out a chair.

The man draped his white scarf on the back of the chair and sat down. He unbuttoned his overcoat and put a full bottle of White Horse on the table.

"It's whisky weather tonight, fellers," he said. "I'm Don Fahey. Call me Don. What the hell, I'm South Boston Irish and I belong in this kind of place."

"Arf! Arf!" Red Dog said. "Scollay Square!"

"Revere Beach! You're a Mick yerself!"

"Red Dog Bite-'em-on-the-ass Shanahan, at your service!"

Red Dog introduced Holman and Farren. They poured the whisky into their beer glasses and chased it with beer direct from the bottles. Don had a smooth, infectious charm that made him seem almost at once like an old shipmate. They had to shout at each other above the singing. They all beat time to it.

> *Oh muchee come catchee come hai yai-yah!*
> *Chinaman no likee he!*

"Us kids used to run after Chinks and yell *hiya mucka yi yi,*" Don said. "We thought it was a terrible Chinese cuss word."

> *Ai yah!*

They all hit the table. Don poured more whisky.

"I have a lead on a human interest story from your ship," Don said.

"What's human interest?" Holman asked.

"Makes people feel good, makes 'em laugh or cry," Don said. "Man bites dog, that's news. Boy loses dog, that's human interest. You see?"

"We ain't supposed to talk," Farren said. "I guess that depends on what about, though."

"How many people would read a story you wrote?" Holman asked.

"A story all the papers would run . . . millions of people."

"Must make you draw a lot of water," Red Dog said.

"Oh, I eat tea with the very best people." Don grinned and pantomimed it with his little finger out. "I get in to see the consuls and admirals and bishops. But what the hell, they're officers of church and state and they don't dare to be human. My readers want human interest."

> *Oh itchy go scratchy go hai yai-yah!*

"This story," Don said. "Is there a man missing from your ship who has not been reported missing?"

> *Ai yah!*

"*Is* there!" Farren shouted. "We *want* to talk about that! Don, how in hell did you ever find out about it?"

Don enjoyed their wondering admiration. "I have a nose for news, Boats," he said. "That's what brought me all this way up the line from South Boston." He broke out a notebook and a gold pencil. "When I know the whole story I can ask the right questions and pry an official story out of the admiral," he said. "I won't mention you boys. We always protect our sources. Point of honor."

"Jake, you better tell it," Farren said.

As soon as he began the story, Holman knew something was wrong. The gold pencil stopped scratching. Don's face changed. He held up his hand.

"That's not the story I have the lead on," he said.

"It's a story, ain't it?" Farren said.

"Not one I can use. I know you boys want to help out a buddy and I wish I could give you a hand," Don said seriously. "But here's how it is. My papers just wouldn't run a sob story about a sailor and a native woman."

It jarred them down hard.

"Why wouldn't they?" Holman asked.

"They have to sell papers to stay in business," Don said. "Everybody knows our gallant boys in blue go to bed with native women—what the hell, I have myself, and maybe I will tonight—but the kind hearts and gentle people don't like to be reminded of it in print."

"Prong the kind hearts and gentle people!" Red Dog said.

"They pay the taxes and they run the world," Don said. "Them's the facts of life, fellers."

It broke the happy mood. Don poured more whisky. They drank in glum silence.

> . . . *give the foe another shot!*
> *For if I cannot marry sweet Wang Koo Fong,*
> *Then Wing Kang Lung shall not!*

"Well, Don, chances are a hundred to one that Frenchy's drowned, anyway," Farren said. "We just got to talking and hoping and then you come in and—oh hell!" He took a big gulp of whisky.

In a few minutes Farren and Red Dog had Burgoyne safely dead again and out of his misery. They wanted to believe it.

"I got my lead from a young Britisher at a cocktail party," Don said. "He thought our navy was sitting on the story to keep down war fever, you know, keep cool with Coolidge, that stuff."

It turned out the story he wanted was about Po-han. He was disappointed to learn that it was a coolie and not a sailor, but he said it would still make a story. Holman pushed back his chair.

"Jake! Now Jake!" Farren said.

"I'm only going to the head," Holman told him.

The Sikh watchman did not recognize Holman. "Gel, Johnny?" he asked, flashing white teeth through his beard. The kitchen help had a jury-rig whorehouse going back among the bales.

"Poyang Road, Johnny." Holman gave him a dollar.

"Snow ver-ree cold, Johnny. Gel warm." The Sikh made the girl sign with his thumb and fingers.

> *Oh muchee come catchee come hai yai-yah!*
> *Chinaman no likee he!*

"Poyang Road, Johnny."
"Maskee, Johnny."

> *Ai yah!*

The whole place shook.

Snow fell, muffling, concealing. The air was clean and cold and wet and very silent. In six paces his feet were soaked with slush. He moved in a ghostly bubble of snowlight between buildings half visible. He met no one.

It was the same in the native city. The snow rounded and softened outlines. It masked the filth and stink of narrow, empty streets. He transferred his pistol to his peacoat pocket.

Weak snowlight made the alley a ghostly cave. Long lumps lay around, snow-covered. Maily and Burgoyne were in the far corner, under their *pukow*. One of Burgoyne's bare feet was sticking out. Holman could just see the shape of the tattooed pig on the foot.

Burgoyne had a rooster tattooed on his other foot. That pig and rooster combination was supposed to be a charm to keep a man from drowning.

Holman knelt. The ankle was stone cold. He shook it gently.

"Frenchy," he whispered.

Burgoyne did not awaken. Holman shook him sharply.

"Frenchy!"

"Frenchy is dead." Maily's voice was muffled under the *pukow*. "Go away, please, Jake," she said. "I don't want to have to see you or talk to you."

Then Holman's fingers knew the waxen feel of death and he lifted his hand. He stood up and breathed in once, very deeply. He let the breath out, slowly and silently. He turned and walked out of the alley, with a dumb, bursting hatred of God inside his heart. In the street the snow was a soft white curtain endlessly falling.

33

Lt. Collins' head ached. He looked at the pages before him and the type blurred. He had been up all night writing and revising his statement. Welbeck had spent all night typing and retyping it. It still would not do. He slapped his hand on the paper.

There was just not any good way to set down cleanly on paper the command responsibility for coolies. Officially they were not aboard, except for casual labor. Now the gearwheel was trying to make *San Pablo* into a world scandal. Admirals would read this statement. President Coolidge himself might even read it.

He went out on the boat deck. The cold morning air cleared his head. Several propaganda sampans were already circling the ship. Snow lay whitely on the hills behind Wuchang. On *San Pablo* it was slush grimy with soot and coal dust. He saw Franks and called to him.

"Chief, get this ship cleaned up!" he said angrily.

"Yes, sir!" Franks said. "The coolies been Bolshevik, since Pappy Tung got took. I'll kick 'em into line, sir."

"Persuade them. Don't mistreat them."

He went back and rang for more coffee. He could still see Franks' baffled stare. He went over his statement again, weighing phrases. None of them were right. Some while later Crosley knocked on his door to deliver a signal from the flagship. Lt. Collins felt his face clear as he read it.

"Ask Mr. Bordelles to come in here," he told Crosley.

They had made up their minds in Flag. *San Pablo* would drop out of sight and mind. The wounded tiger seeking its lair. It satisfied a very deep instinct. Bordelles came in, looking apprehensive.

"Make all preparations for getting underway," Lt. Collins said, almost cheerfully. "We will sail for Changsha as soon as steam is raised." Bordelles' face showed his pleasure. "We have a relief for Burgoyne ordered from *Truxtun,*" Lt. Collins said. "Signal them to expedite the transfer."

Bordelles went out with a swing to his shoulders.

Holman did not tell anyone about Burgoyne. It was easier to let them think he drowned. They had forgotten Burgoyne, anyway. The ship was turning frantic.

Duckbutt Randall was making the rounds of the other warships to requisition spuds and onions. Welbeck was ashore buying all the stores he could find and sending them off to the ship. On the fantail Franks and Farren wrangled furiously with the deck coolies about cleaning up the ship. At least fifteen propaganda sampans were circling the ship. The Chinese in them waved placards and whooped like a Pawnee war party. The crew roared curses back at them and began throwing coal and potatoes.

Lynch was still ashore, seeing his wife and cousin off to Shanghai. It took Holman an hour just to round up the bilge coolies. Then they claimed that only Ping-wen knew how to lay a fire and light off a furnace. Even Chiu-pa kept his face blank and his eyes secretive. Holman went up to the compartment. It was messy with unmade bunks and strewn clothing. Perna and Stawski were waiting for shaves.

"Perna, you're senior water monkey, now that Frenchy's gone," Holman said. He told Perna about the coolies. "You lay the fires and light off for 'em," he said. "Then they'll have to take over. They can't claim they don't know how to stoke."

"Well, Jesus Christ. I'm waiting on a shave."

"Better light fires first. The skipper wants steam."

"Don't you snipes do any of their work for 'em!" Bronson warned, from the barber chair. "Don't you cut Farren's throat up on deck!"

Clip Clip went on shaving Bronson, ignoring the argument.

"I'll just tell 'em what to do." Perna rose. "Come help me, Ski."

"I'll kick their slopeheaded asses!" Stawski said.

Holman went out with them. Lynch was just coming aboard. He had Lemon carrying boxes for him, up to the CPO quarters.

"Saw Becky ashore. He give me the word, and I stocked up," Lynch said, winking at Holman. "You got fires lit yet?"

"Perna just went down there."

Holman told Lynch about the coolies. Lynch was not worried.

"We get 'em back to Changsha, they'll toe the line," he said.

Clip Clip was just finishing Holman's shave when the loud voices started on deck. Holman went out. Lynch, with a pistol belted on, was talking to Stawski and Perna. The beefy fireman was knuckling at a small cut above his eye. His face looked outraged.

"He come at me with a slice bar, I tell you!" Stawski said.

Bordelles came from aft. He looked harried.

"Sweet Christ, what is it now, Lynch?" he asked.

"Coolie squabble. I can handle it, Mr. Bordelles," Lynch said. "I'll take personal charge and get steam raised." He turned to Perna. "I bet you ain't even slacked stack guys," he said.

"I told you, we ain't even got fires lit!" Perna said.

"Stawski, get up there and slack them guys," Lynch said. "Come with me, Perna."

"I ain't going back down there without a gun!"

"I got the gun." Lynch slapped his pistol. "Come on, I said!"

Holman stayed topside. It would be several hours before it was time to warm up the engine. He heard shouting and clanging from below. The hydrokineter on the cold boiler began rumbling very loudly. Lynch was going to force steam.

Holman loitered along the main deck. Farren and Haythorn had at last gotten some of the deck coolies working. They had to stand right over them. Beside the galley Ellis and Vincent were throwing potatoes at the circling sampans. Duckbutt Randall was trying to stop them.

"Spuds cost money!" he objected. "Throw coal."

"Coal costs money," Holman said. "Thumb your noses. That's free."

"Throw bullets!" Ellis snorted. "Shoot the sons of bitches!"

Lynch came on deck, sweating and cheerful. "All fires lit and drawing good," he told Holman. "Them coolies will stay squared away, now. How about we go have some coffee?"

"Let's go," Holman said.

In the CPO quarters they drank coffee aromatic with brandy. Lynch was happy about going to Changsha. It was taking the ship off a very bad spot. Things would be all right again, in Changsha.

"I got my business here cleared up just in time," Lynch said.

Renewed shouting started outside. Lynch and Holman carried their coffee cups out to the rail to see what it was. Water was arching and splashing and the same wupan of two days before was trying to come alongside again. Haythorn was keeping it off with the wash-deck hose. A student spokesman was shouting in Chinese. Lop Eye Shing, evil-faced as ever, stood beside the student, balanced on his cane.

"The Boatmen's Union has declared a strike on your ship!" the student called in English. "We demand that you permit us to take off the citizens of the Republic of China whom you are holding against their will!"

Coolies ran and jabbered along the main deck of the *San Pablo*.

"Keep your distance, you Bolshevik sons of bitches!" Bordelles yelled from the bow. "Stop making those threats! We will protect our men!"

A potato hit Lop Eye Shing in the face. He staggered and blinked. Franks came running up to the boat deck.

"Keep your men below! Don't let 'em hear those threats!" he told Lynch. "They're trying to steal our coolies!"

"Guard the hatch, Jake!" Lynch said.

Holman ran down. He stopped Chiu-pa and the coolies at the hatch. They went back below without argument. Lynch joined Holman. He had his pistol belted on again. The *San Pablo* was buzzing like a chopped-open beehive. Men were yelling and running in all directions. Farren and Haythorn were chasing the deck coolies to their quarters. Bronson hustled Big Chew and Jack Dusty aft. Big Chew had on his apron and he was waving a ladle angrily.

"Are your men all safe, Lynch?"

It was Bordelles. Lynch said the men were safe. Holman saw Chiu-pa streak aft along the port side, followed by the other bilge coolies.

"Oh Christ!" he said, pointing. "We forgot the bunker escape hatches!"

Lynch cursed and ran after them. Clip Clip popped out of the compartment and ran aft. Crosley popped out after him, the cloth still around his neck and lather on half his face.

"Clip Clip!" he screamed. "Come back here, you heathen son of a bitch!"

"Crosley! Crosley, lay up to the bridge!" Bordelles barked. "Flag is signaling again!"

They both ran up. It began to seem stupid to Holman. He thought he would go below and tend the deserted fires. Perna charged by and Holman stopped him.

"Get below and take the watch," he told Perna.

About the decks they were all running and screaming. Out in the circling sampans they were all jumping and screaming. The circle was closing in. No one had time to man the fire hoses. A ship's boat came alongside. A man in dress blues came up on the quarterdeck with his seabag and looked around unbelievingly.

"Are you all nuts on here?" he asked Holman. "What the hell's going on?"

"This is how we get underway," Holman said.

"I'm Krebs, watertender. Who logs me in? Who takes my records and stuff?"

He was a lean, dark man with a mustache. He waggled his records and pay accounts accusingly at Holman.

"Pitch 'em anywhere," Holman said. "Better get in dungarees."

"Don't know if I got any. I left half my gear on the *Truxtun,*" Krebs said. "I hate these pop transfers!"

Big Chew came forward across the quarterdeck like a locomotive. He was pushing Ellis and Vincent ahead of him by main strength. They were trying to push Big Chew aft. They were all screaming at each other. Ellis backed into the seabag and fell sprawling. Big Chew hurled Vincent against Krebs and charged up the boat deck ladder. Krebs slapped his records down on the log desk.

"You're all nuts on here!" he shouted at Holman. "I *hate* coal burners! I *hate* this Goddamned floating madhouse already!"

"That's the spirit!" Holman said.

Franks came into the bridge. "They're raising hell, sir," he said. "They want to come up on deck. They want to talk to you."

"Not under this duress," Lt. Collins said. "Later, when we're underway. Keep them below. Don't let them hear those threats."

He rubbed his temples. Pain throb tolled in his head like a bell. He could not stand any more of the roaring and screaming and the whole grotesque business. Crosley, his face scaly with soap, came down from the signal bridge with another message. Lt. Collins read it.

"I'll talk to one man," he told Franks. "Have them choose a spokesman."

Big Chew burst into the bridge, caroming off Franks.

"Cap'n! Cap'n! No moh can stop this side!" he blurted. "S'pose no go shoh side, bad ting happen!" His fat face was agitated.

"They can't touch any of you aboard my ship, no matter what they are saying," Lt. Collins said. "I will protect you. On my word of honor."

"No can, Cap'n! No no no can!"

"We are going to Changsha. You will be safe there."

Big Chew waved muscular arms and spouted pidgin. He seemed to be saying that it would be even worse in Changsha.

"Franks, do you suppose they want me actually to hold them prisoner until we get underway?" Lt. Collins said. "To avoid retaliation and so on?" He rubbed his temples. "Big Chew couldn't tell me that officially, of course. But what do you think?"

Franks thought it was quite possible. Big Chew got the drift of their talk. He howled.

"No, no, Cap'n! I speakee you plopah!" he insisted. "Allo Chinese man wanchee go shoh side! Chinese man no moh tlostah this ship!"

"Don't trust this ship, eh?"

It was like a blow in the face. A bucket of icy water. He turned his back and walked stiffly across the bridge. Below, the clamor was rising to a peak. The sampans were crowding right in to the ship's side, careless of hoses soaking them. They did not trust his ship, he thought. That cut deeply. But perhaps justly. It was simply not down anywhere on paper, what was command responsibility for coolies. Officially, there were not any coolies. It would be so much more simple if that were true in fact. He turned around.

"Let them go, Franks," he said.

They went like rats. They scrambled across the rail with bales and boxes and bundles into the waiting boats. In a few minutes they were all gone. The wupan headed upriver to the native bund. All the propaganda sampans tailed on to make it a triumphal procession. The shouting and the tumult died away.

The Sand Pebbles were stunned. The decks seemed bare, the river empty. The abrupt silence pressed into their ears. They gathered uneasily in the littered compartment. The coffee pitcher was empty. Tullio took it to the galley to fill it. He came back with it and said their dinner was burning on the range. They all looked at Duckbutt

Randall. They were remembering that he was a rated ship's cook. Duckbutt would not meet their eyes.

"Like rats, they went!" Crosley rubbed the unshaven side of his face. "Clip Clip was first one across the rail!"

"They're gone. They're all gone," Restorff kept saying.

He seemed to hope someone would contradict him. They were all looking into each other's outraged faces to find comfort for their own outrage. Lynch came in, red-faced and breathing heavily. He looked at them, hands on hips.

"Stawski! Wilsey! Harris!" he said. "Get below and help Perna raise steam! Holman, start warming up the engine."

"I'm an electrician, Lynch," Harris said. "I got nothing to do with steam."

"I just now give you something to do with it," Lynch said.

"Wait a minute, Lynch!" Crosley jumped up. "We ain't still going to Changsha, for God's sake? We can't steam without coolies! You know that!"

"The skipper don't know it. We're sailing, all right."

They were shocked. They looked at each other. Franks came in. He looked tough and angry also.

"How about it, Franks?" Crosley appealed to him. "The water's too low by now for us to get to Changsha, ain't it?"

"If it is, we'll winter on the first sandbar we get stuck on," Franks said. "On deck, you topside sailors! The skipper wants a scrubdown before we get underway."

They got to their feet, muttering. "Come on, Crosley. You're deck force," Ellis said.

"I ain't either! I'm bridge gang!" Crosley said. "How about it, Chief?"

"You're bridge gang in your spare time, if I decide you can have any," Franks said. "Get out there and man them scrubbers, you dunnigans, before I start banging heads together!"

Duckbutt Randall stood up. His pale blue eyes were wide open and he was pinching his thick lower lip.

"I guess I better go to the galley," he announced, to no one in particular.

It was three o'clock before they could get underway. Holman had the throttle. Harris was oiler. Krebs, Perna, Wilsey and Stawski were stoking. As soon as the engine began turning over, the steam began to drop. Harris went to the fireroom and cursed them. They screamed curses back. It was seeming like the end of the world to them out there with shovels in their hands, Holman knew.

"We got to have more stokers," Harris told Holman. "Get some deck apes down here. They can at least pass coal."

As the *San Pablo* passed each ship in man-o'-war row, she exchanged the customary salutes. They had to give the saluting signal by whistle from the bridge. When they passed the last warship and the stately stone customs house, the bridge rang for ten knots. Holman called on the voice tube.

"I can't even hold the turns I'm making," he told Bronson.

"You got to. Make ten knots. We rang for it."

"Bells don't make steam. Let me talk to Bordelles."

Over the voice tube he told Bordelles about the steam dropping.

"I'll send Vincent and Ellis down," Bordelles said. "Make as near ten knots as you can. We want to leave port in style."

Vincent and Ellis came down in whites, looking mutinously unhappy. The shovel scrape increased. The steam steadied. It began to climb. Harris came to the throttle platform.

"Well, here we go in a cloud of horseshit," he said morosely.

There was a sharp *crack* high above, and a screeching, rending noise, and the roar of escaping steam. It was up on deck. Harris ran. Voices howled in the fireroom and ash doors slammed. The bridge rang stop. Holman closed the throttle and ran to the gratings and secured steam to the whistle and siren. The steam blast halted. The anchor rumbled down.

Holman went up to the boat deck. The top two-thirds of the tall, skinny stack was canted forward at about a twenty-degree angle. They were all standing at a safe distance looking at it, with dismay in their faces. Lynch was almost hysterical. He was shaking both fists above his head and his face was red as fire.

"I'm going to kill that Stawski!" he screamed. "I'm going to *kill* that thick Polack son of a bitch!"

When he had slacked the stack guys, Stawski had skipped the forward guy. When the stack expanded, the unslacked guy had put a one-sided strain on it and made it buckle. It was weakened with rust inside.

"Stop that, Chief!" Lt. Collins said sharply. His face looked frozen with disgust. "Get busy and straighten it up again," he ordered.

"We ain't got the men and the gear, sir," Lynch said. "It's a dock-yard job. We can't go to Changsha, not now, sir."

All the Sand Pebbles nodded thoughtfully.

"Pull it upright with the after guy," Lt. Collins said. "Franks, you take charge of it."

Franks took charge. The ship was still off the outskirts of Hanyang and Chinese crowded the riverbank to watch. Franks tightened the after turnbuckle slowly, levering it around with a crowbar. The guy strained and thrummed. The stack groaned and creaked and showered down rust. The men were all holding their breaths. Then, with a raucous screech, the stack buckled a second time. The top one-third canted aft at a jaunty, rakish angle.

No one cursed. They gave a general sigh. The frozen disgust on Lt. Collins' thin face did not change. Franks threw down his crowbar.

"That does it!" he said. "We're stuck here, now."

He looked at Welbeck and Bordelles. They nodded slowly. The Sand Pebbles looked at each other. They were feeling that they had been saved by the bell.

"Mr. Bordelles, get shores under that forward angle," Lt. Collins said quietly. "Franks, run supporting lines from the masts. Lynch, take out those broken steam lines and blank the flange connections."

He had them all busy. It began to seem not so bad. Red Dog, as the lightest man, scaled the stack to fasten lines for Franks. He barked and yelped when he burnt himself. They could not straighten the stack, but they began to believe that they could hold what they had. When it was done, a weird, webbed rig of shores and supporting lines, they all stood back and looked at it with something like pride. It was almost sunset.

"Prepare to weigh anchor, Mr. Bordelles," Lt. Collins said coldly. "I want to get out of sight up the river, before I anchor for the night."

Bordelles barked orders. The men scattered to their stations with alacrity. They got underway handily. Behind them Hankow faded from sight down the broad river, in the black smoke rolling aft from *San Pablo*'s dogleg stack.

34

The afternoon of the next day Lynch came out of the fireroom shaking his head. "I'll take the throttle the rest of the day," he told Holman. "Give 'em a hand out there. They're bad off."

Holman went out to the fireroom. Wilsey and Perna were stoking. Ellis and Haythorn were passing coal. They were all stripped to the waist and black with coal dust except where sweat made white streaks down their hides. Using his whole body, Wilsey aimed a shovelful of coal into a red-mouthed furnace. The shovel struck the side of the door and spilled and dropped. Wilsey looked down at it.

"Bloody hell," he said, almost in a whisper. "Jake, we got to change shifts again, I just can't close my damned hands."

He looked at his trembling, half-closed hands. They were swathed with wiping rags. There were no gloves aboard and the men's hands were badly blistered. Holman knew what Wilsey was feeling. Your fingers felt thick and lifeless and you had no strength left at all below your elbows. That was where the strength ran out first.

"I'll fire 'em awhile," Holman said. "Go up and rest."

"Thanks, Jake. I'm whipped and I know it."

Wilsey's three fires were in bad shape. The coal was too thick near the front and holes were burnt through in back. All the draft was going through back there and the coal in front was only smoking and coking. Working fast, Holman broke out clinkers with a slice bar, spread the coal evenly with a hoe and then began building up the fires. His hands were already calloused and his muscles hard from working. He enjoyed it all the more because there was need for the work he did.

Coaling had to be done with shoulders, arms and a particular snap of the wrist, to spread a shovelful evenly wherever you wanted it. When a man's wrists gave out and he began flexing his knees and throwing the coal with his whole body, the fire would hole and hump on him. He would have to start spreading with the hoe, working twice as hard to burn the same amount of coal, and it was a vicious circle. All the men were soft as putty and they were all in the vicious circle.

Holman built the fires up smooth and level and red and thick, to where they could burn half an hour without more coaling. Perna was having a hard time on his side. All his cocky, sparrowy air was gone. His mouth hung slack, with coal dust dried on his teeth, and he drooped like a soft candle.

"Let's swap boilers, Perna," Holman said.

Perna nodded gratefully, too weary to speak. Holman cleaned and built up the fires in Perna's boiler. He used almost all the reserve coal on the floorplates. Haythorn and Ellis were both big men, but they were bringing the coal buckets only half filled. They carried a bucket with both hands, bumping it along with their knees, and they looked ready to drop.

"Each of you guys take a boiler. Let Perna show you how to stoke," Holman said. "I'll bring the coal out."

The coolie coal passers had carried two full buckets at once on a short, stiff shoulder yoke. Holman did the same. He was enjoying using his strength to the utmost. After a few trips he learned the knack of maneuvering the buckets in the dark, narrow, dusty wing bunkers. He built up heaps of coal on the floorplates. The other men were recovering. Ellis had gone up for a pitcher of coffee.

"Jake, stop for a cup of joe," Haythorn said. "You bastard, you ain't human!"

Holman stopped and drank coffee with them in the steamy, smoky, sulfurous smell of the place. He rested and felt strength flow quickly back. Then he shouldered the yoked buckets again. "Way hay! Hai lai!" he said, pretending to be a coolie. He got a weak grin from them.

After supper, when they were anchored, he took a shower. Despite rag padding, the yoke had worn the skin off his neck and shoulder. He winced as the hot water hit the raw place. At the trough, Stawski was soaking his hands in a bucket of warm water. He had come out of the fireroom and dropped into an exhausted sleep. The serum from his blisters had dried and stuck the matted rags to his hands and he was trying to soak the rags off.

"Jesus, Mary and Joseph!" Stawski said. He was forcing himself to keep his hands in the water. "God damn!" he said. He kept lifting one foot and then the other.

Holman went to his locker to dress. The compartment had a sour, sweaty stink. Most of the men were too tired and disgusted to take a bath. They had screwed the light bulbs out above their bunks and they were flaked out, still in dungarees stiff with oil and coal dust. They had no razors and they were all sprouting beards. The whole compartment was gritty with ash and coal dust. The pillows were black.

Stawski came out and sat wearily at the mess table. He laid his hands down palm upward and looked at them. Broken blisters the size of silver dollars overlapped on the balls of his thumbs and along the bases of his fingers. Some shreds of skin were left. Coal dust was embedded in the raw. Holman knew the other men were just as badly off. He could not think of any good thing to say to Stawski.

"I got the right stuff for them hands, Ski," Harris said. He had just come in, with a brown quart beer bottle. He set it on the table. "That's turpentine. It hardens skin," he said. "Put some on them hands."

"You just want to hurt me so you can laugh," Stawski said.

"No I don't. It's true! It'll help you!"

"I don't trust you. I never ever seen you do one decent thing, Harris," Stawski said. "To hell with you. They hurt enough when sweat runs down on 'em."

Harris insisted. Stawski would not trust him. Harris was standing oiler watch, and he did not have any blisters to prove it on himself. Some of the other men raised up on their elbows to listen. Harris appealed to them. They would not trust him either.

"I tell you, this is a real old trick. I learned it back when all you punks were still sucking sugartits," Harris said. "Ski, I'll give you a hundred dollars if it hurts you. You got the whole crew for witness I said that."

Silently, Stawski held out his left hand. Harris poured a puddle of turpentine into it. "It don't hurt," Stawski said wonderingly. He spread it delicately with the fingers of his right hand. "It feels cool and good!" he said. "Give me some more!" He held out both hands.

Stiffly, they all climbed out of their bunks and came over to get turpentine for their hands. They went back to sleep with a strong smell of turpentine masking the stink of their sweaty clothing.

The passage was a five-day ordeal. The water was low and still dropping. Twice they nudged mud and spent hours getting through. Bordelles and the chiefs heaved on lines and got dirty. They dropped all pretense of drills and salutes and concentrated on getting the ship through. Whatever the emergency, Lt. Collins was there, clean and cold and calm and ready with the right thing to do. He was being captain of his ship as never before in the Sand Pebbles' memory.

They were being the crew, and they could not endure it. They could not face up to having no coolies. When they were not too exhausted, they snarled and flared at each other. The living spaces became very foul. The men went filthy and bearded. Each meal seemed worse to them than the last, and they cursed Duckbutt Randall every day until he wept. Harris cursed all night in his sleep.

Holman did much of the work in the fireroom. By the time they started up the Siang River, the men were hardening. The new skin on their palms was slick and red and hard and sensitive only in the creases. The hills looked homely and familiar. They began to pick up their spirits with the hope of getting more coolies in Changsha. They knew the cook they would get could not possibly be as good as Big

Chew. But, as they told each other, neither could he possibly be as bad as Duckbutt Randall. By the time they sighted the sacred mountain and the gray shape of Changsha, they practically had their new cook installed in the galley.

They anchored in their usual place. Changsha looked much the same, except for the U.S.S. *Duarte* upriver at a commercial pontoon near the U.S. Consulate. But within minutes demonstrators began gathering on the bund. They waved placards and shouted in unison on signal from uniformed leaders. POISONERS OF CHINA! LEAVE CHANGSHA! one sign screamed.

"What a hell of a welcome home!" Farren said.

They were all weary and disgusted. They stayed on the starboard side, so they could not see it. Bordelles in full dress went off to make the courtesy calls on H.M.S. *Woodcock* and the Japanese gunboat. The *Duarte* was senior ship in port. Taking Welbeck and Red Dog with him, Lt. Collins went to the *Duarte* himself.

They came back after dark with news that flashed through the ship like a bayonet thrust. The worker-peasant council that ran Changsha knew all about the *San Pablo*'s trouble in Hankow. They did not want her in Changsha. That day they had clamped an absolute boycott on all the gunboats and they would not lift it until the *San Pablo* went away. It meant no liberty and no fresh provisions. It meant no coolie help and no stores shipments by rail from Hankow. And the *San Pablo* had brought that on all the other gunboats as well. The Sand Pebbles listened to Red Dog tell about it and they were too crushed even to curse.

"They got us by the balls. We'll have to go back to Hankow."

"Water's already too low."

"Yeah. We're stuck for the winter."

"No coolies. God damn it, no *cook!*"

"Ain't fair. They hit us enough. What the hell they *want?*"

"Skipper's going to talk to us tomorrow."

"He'll tell us to have moral courage," Harris said.

They cursed without spirit. They went dirty to bed with aching bones and without any hope left at all.

೧೨

There was no physical reason, Lt. Collins thought, why *San Pablo* could not winter through. The problem was moral. And morale was a prime command responsibility. And he had, right now, a crisis in morale. He had to act at once.

He sat at his table with lights out so that no one would disturb him. He had to think it out alone.

The new weapon did not yet have a name. *Moral isolation* was as close as one could come to it. In Hankow they had marked *San Pablo* down for the kill. In Changsha they meant to strike the death blow. *San Pablo* was at bay. Wrigley yesterday, in *Duarte,* had scarcely concealed his dismayed resentment that *San Pablo* had come to Changsha. He had warned that his men would probably pick fights with the Sand Pebbles unless the two crews were kept apart. Bordelles had brought back the same impression from *Woodcock* and *Hiro.* No one understood the new weapon yet. *San Pablo* would have to make her fight alone.

Americans had faced hardships, none better. Blizzards and wolves and malaria, searing summers and starvation winters, the raw, wild continent. They had faced men. Treacherous Indians, sneaky Mexicans, proud Rebels, insolent Spaniards, the hateful Hun. All dared, all beaten. But this in China was an assault on the spirit, in an area where simple, forthright people did not have any developed defenses. They did not yet know that in Washington. There was that story one heard in all the clubs. "Oh yes, Shanghai," President Harding had told the man from Shanghai. "I have an aunt who is a missionary out there. Her post office is some little place called Calcutta. Did you ever run into her?"

Lt. Collins chuckled, without mirth. President Coolidge probably thought the Far East was about the size of Vermont. Very likely he had a missionary aunt. No doubt she wrote him long letters about the greedy businessmen and the wicked gunboats.

He checked himself. Presidents had human failings, but one must not think such thoughts about the Office. The American people were the power and the glory and the absolute authority that drew to a blinding focus in that Office, from which it fed down through the ranks to power the last, least man in uniform. To question that Office was to welcome chaos into the world.

He felt chastened. He was himself a small and distant reflection of that blinding focus. That was his solution, grace-given in the night. It was for him simply to be *San Pablo*. To affirm his paramount value in all the symbolic ways open to him. The Sand Pebbles were good men, professionals, all lesser ties long ago severed. *San Pablo* was their collective life. And he looked out the eyes of *San Pablo*. *San Pablo,* despised, rejected, ringed round with enemies, would endure and keep the faith.

He stood up, filled with calm resolution. He would be able to sleep now.

He ate breakfast alone in his day cabin, as he would eat all meals henceforward. He was going to intensify his ritual isolation as commanding officer. After breakfast he sent for Bordelles and told him the plan.

"Tell the chiefs to turn out in their best uniforms," he said. "When I judge the time right, I will have all hands called aft."

"Yes, sir," Bordelles said stiffly.

He was responding to his captain's manner. There was to be no more idle talk. Relations were to be rigidly formal.

Near ten o'clock a student-led hate demonstration began to shape on the bund opposite the ship. Lt. Collins had all hands mustered aft. He gave them time to assemble and then went aft himself, after a last-minute check of his blue uniform. He faced them, as so often before, with the great wheel at his back and the colors above his head. Bordelles and the chiefs were clean and sprucely uniformed. The men were unshaven in dirty dungarees, slouching in two straggling ranks across the fantail. They were acting out a dumb and anguished protest.

"Some of us later in life are going to win medals for less heroic action than the passage we have just made from Hankow," he began dryly. He spoke of the labor and hardship. "I want to say *Well done!* to every man aboard."

It did not touch their sullen faces.

"Now about this boycott," he said. "It cannot defeat us physically." They had enough dry stores aboard to live on, he told them. There was coal ashore already in American hands. "Changsha is our home port," he said. "We have the right by treaty to be here and to buy what we need of food, materials and labor. For reasons I will not go into, we cannot for the present enforce our rights by armed action. But we are not in the slightest degree going to give up our claim to our rights, as they are trying to force us to do."

It deepened their sullen anger. He continued with careful words reviewing what they all knew. He wanted to build their sense of grievance to an intolerable ache.

"Right here months ago I spoke to you of a new kind of war," he said. "We are blooded now, in that war. We know that they can hurt us, if we let them. *If . . . we . . . let . . . them.*" He had all their eyes now. "If we let *them* control how *we* feel and act, *they* will destroy us," he told the men grimly. "Because *they* hate our guts. *They* hate the very linings of our hearts!"

He said it harshly. He wanted to rasp them raw. He emphasized each pronoun with voice and gesture. He made with both hands a fending gesture for *they* and an in-gathering for *we*.

"Who are they? I'll tell you who they are. They are more than the simple, ignorant Chinese whom they are using. They are the clever, seeing ones anywhere in the world who fear and envy America. They make the new kind of war. They have singled out *San Pablo* for destruction, to test and perfect their new weapons. *They* bribed our boatmen to smuggle opium aboard of us. *They* stole away our boatmen. *They* drove us from Hankow."

He was drumming the pronoun into them with voice and gesture. Their whiskered lips were beginning to twitch at each repetition. He had them in hand.

"They are the people who hate America in their hearts," he said harshly. *"They* can even be Americans themselves, and those are most devilish of all. We cannot know them by their faces. But we can know them by their words and actions. And *there they are!"*

He flung his arm and aimed his finger at the demonstrators on the bund. All the heads turned. Hatred twisted the beard-stubbled faces.

"Look at them! We laughed at them once. We know better now. They think they are destroying our pride and our courage, our love for and devotion to America. And maybe they can do that, *if . . . we . . . let . . . them.* Let every man take a moment to remember himself six months ago. *They* have made the difference in us all!"

He dropped his arm and paused. All the eyes were back upon him, wide and wondering. The heads were nodding slowly. It was time to lift them.

"People are still asleep in the States, but we in *San Pablo* are awake now," he said. "We know our ship is under siege here, as truly as Wuchang was under siege. They watch us every minute. They gloat over rust streaks down our sides and Irish pendants along our decks. They point out to each other gleefully every sign of military slackness, every slovenly, unshaven man they see aboard of us. They know it is their handiwork. They know that if they can only keep it up *San Pablo* will fall as Wuchang fell. They expect in the end to haul down Old Glory to shame, disgrace and oblivion."

He saw their eyes lift above his head.

"We will defend that flag," he said soberly. "With our lifeblood, when the time comes for that. And until then, with the cheerful sacrifice of ease and comfort. They expect it to destroy us. But it is only going to make us stronger!"

They were coming to attention, faces eager, ranks unconsciously dressing and covering off.

"We are the same Sand Pebbles we always were," he told them. "We are awake now. We know that we are defending America. We know about the new weapons and what they can do to a man. We know that Wuchang fell only to treachery inside the walls. And *we* know that is not going to happen in *San Pablo!*"

He shook raised fists to emphasize each pronoun. They snatched off their hats and waved them and cheered. Some of the men had tears on their stubbled cheeks. Their gay, defiant cheering surprised the demonstrators on the bund. They fell silent over there. The tables were turned on them.

"That is all I have to say," Lt. Collins resumed, when the cheering ceased. "Take the rest of the morning for a field day in living spaces. This afternoon will be a rope-yarn Sunday."

He turned them over to Bordelles and went forward. He knew he had just won a crucial battle.

Holman, in the engine room, heard the cheering. After a while he went aft to the head, which had been stinking filthy for days. The white tile deck was clean and dry. The water was stopped in the urinal trough, which Crosley was shining. Copper gleamed softly under his busy rag.

"Hi, Jake," Crosley said cheerfully. "Lend a hand."

"Got the watch," Holman said.

Vincent was scrubbing out the showers. In the compartment they were all scrubbing and shining and talking back and forth. The newly-waxed deck had a high red luster. Harris' stiff gray hair flopped as he stroked with the johnson bar. He wore a cheerful grin on his seamed and craggy face.

"I'm getting old, Jake," he said, puffing. "Spell me on this bar."

"Take the watch and I will," Holman said.

Harris went below and Holman finished the polishing. He was glad to see the men cheerful and the place cleaned up. Lt. Collins had worked some kind of miracle with them.

In the afternoon they took their dirty clothes aft to scrub them. The engineers scrubbed theirs between their hands in a bucket of soapy water. The deckforce men laid theirs out on deck and scrubbed them with a hand brush.

"You snipes wear your clothes out faster that way," Haythorn said.

"We get our hands clean too, this way," Wilsey said. "It gets the grease out from around our fingernails."

Farren broke out whiteline and Perna strung extra lengths of it above the boilers. The uptakes were filled with scrubbed clothes.

They all took showers and shaved. Welbeck had been able to get six safety razors and a limited supply of blades and shaving cream from the *Duarte* canteen yeoman. Each blade had to last a man ten days. Restorff had not shaved himself in ten years, and he was clumsy as a boy. When he finished, his blunt face was spotted with the bits of toilet paper he had plastered over nicks. They all laughed at him and he laughed too. There was no malice in it.

In the compartment they made up their bunks with clean linen and put on clean blue uniforms. They shined shoes, with polish Welbeck had gotten from the *Duarte*. They argued happily about the best way to get a real inspection shine. Some held with damp rags and some with spitting on the toes. Restorff was a damp rag man, and he got the best shine of them all.

"That makes up for the face the gunner lost shaving," Red Dog said.

Restorff touched his patches ruefully and grinned.

The clothes dried quickly above the boilers. The men brought them back in great, crinkled armloads. They laid them on their bunks and smoothed and folded them and stowed them neatly in their lockers. Bronson held a folded towel to his fat cheek and sniffed.

"I forgot how good clean clothes smell, when you scrub 'em yourself," he said.

They wandered out on deck in twos and threes. A silent knot of coolies on the bund still watched the ship.

"Them dirty, raggedy-ass, slant-eyed bastards," someone behind Holman said comfortably.

They were all feeling good. They walked around wriggling their toes inside clean socks and flexing their arms and smelling the clean smell of themselves. The compartment was filled with the clean smell of wax and brightwork polish and the cheery smell of the pot of coffee Tullio brought in, setting up for supper.

"I bet this is the first time anybody ever had a rope-yarn Sunday on this old tub," Restorff said. "By God, I *like* it!"

Supper was beans, Vienna sausage and a sticky, lumpy rice pudding. The beans were hard as bullets. It was fodder to keep a man alive, Holman thought, but not much more. For the first time since Hankow, no one griped about it.

"That pudding ain't bad," Harris said. "Hey, Tullio! Can you get seconds on pudding?"

"Sure." Tullio picked up the bowl.

"Tell Duckbutt from me it's a good chow," Harris said.

"Tell him that from all of us," Farren said.

35

Old Ting filled Shirley's can with steaming water and bowed when she gave him a copper. Ting was a wispy, cheerful old man with a few scraggly hairs on his chin. His caldron sat on a clay foundation beside the well. Under it he burnt dried grass and weed stems which he and his wife gleaned from the fields. Against the high red brick wall behind him he had a leanto piled with reserve fuel. Selling hot water to the native staff of China Light had been his living for many years.

Shirley smiled and spoke briefly with Mrs. Chao and Third Wang daughter. The well was a favorite gossip spot. Then she went along to take her bath before her water cooled.

They were all native staff now, with native salaries. She and Gillespie and the Craddocks had clubbed together to rent one of the larger native houses and employ one servant, who did not fetch bath water. But the house was beside the well—it backed flush against the mission wall and old Ting's leanto was in the angle it made—so fetching water was no great task. She did not even have to walk around to the front with her hot water. Under Ting's leanto the house had a small back door through which field coolies carried out slop jars.

They collected them every morning from all the houses. Mrs. Chao thought that back door was one of the distinct advantages of Shirley's house.

It was a good house with walls of whitewashed clay and roof of gray tile. The rooms were on three sides of a courtyard into which all doors and windows opened. There were two trees and some shrubs in the courtyard. Over the front wall she had a view of the long blue bulk of Precious Mountain.

Taking her bath, Shirley thought how good it was to be able to talk with Mrs. Chao and laugh at her argument with old Ting. The big foreign houses were no longer dwellings. One was union headquarters and another the militia armory. The Mills and Armstrong houses had been made annexes of the hospital. But the biggest change at China Light, she thought, was in the feeling between people.

All the old customs governing relations between American and native staff were swept away. The students' infectious enthusiasm spilled over into everyone to mask any scars left behind. There was a different quality to the friendliness.

"It's because they want us here," Gillespie had said, discussing it. "Before, they could not be sure of that themselves, because they were granted no right to reject us. The shadow of the gunboat was always between us. And now it's gone."

"We've made a discovery. We've proven something," Shirley said. "I wish we could tell them at the Alliance Hostel."

Gillespie's face shadowed. "I wish we could tell them in America."

Mrs. Craddock managed the combined household. Shirley and Gillespie called her Tai-tai and for the first time were coming to know and love her. She had real skill in Chinese housekeeping, learned in her youth, and being needed brought her out of herself. Despite the drag of an old illness, she was cheerful and busy all day and she looked years younger.

Mr. Craddock looked years older. He seemed to be graying and stooping more each week. He was becoming oddly gentle. They all worried about Mr. Craddock.

His permission to return was provisional and temporary. He could do pastoral work among converted Christians, but he could not seek new converts. Cho-jen had been very candid about it: what they wanted from Mr. Craddock was his signature to legitimize transfer of land titles and all the other things which had already been done by revolutionary fiat. Mr. Craddock meant to sign; he had returned knowing that he would; but he was trying to negotiate conditions safeguarding the goals of China Light. He was not winning many points.

At the head of the supper table Mr. Craddock asked grace, briefly and with dignity. They all wore Chinese clothing in the evenings. Mr. Craddock looked worn from his day. Gillespie glanced at Shirley across the table. They were to talk about something cheerful.

"I never knew about skin on water before today," she said. She told about Mrs. Chao's quarrel with Ting because the hot water had skin on it. "I was afraid my Chinese was failing me again," she said.

"Oh no," Mrs. Craddock said. "Water has skin."

"It's surface tension. You can see it if you look," Gillespie said. "Mrs. Chao meant the water wasn't hot enough. She wanted it boiling."

They laughed about Mrs. Chao's language.

"I must tell you two young people about old Ting," Craddock said. "I had a bowl of tea with him when we first came back. He has been on my mind ever since."

Twenty years earlier Ting had been a used-up carrier coolie left behind to die by passing soldiers. Some farmers had brought him to China Light, where he had slowly regained his health. He had been very handy and helpful around the clinic.

"I discovered a peculiar simplicity and sweetness of temper in him," Craddock said. "I wanted very much to win him for Christ."

He could not. When Ting was discharged from his hospital, he picked up a scanty living by carrying well water among the houses and selling it where he could, for a few cash. He became the mission's first water coolie.

"Of course after a few weeks it became old custom. It was his rice bowl," Craddock went on. "I had no thought of breaking it. I still hoped to win him."

Ting had started his hot-water business with a five-gallon kerosene tin and two stones. Later he borrowed money to set up his caldron and build his leanto. Not long after, the crisis had arisen.

"Ting was prospering, by his standards. He had been boarding with a Christian family, but now he wanted a wife and a home of his own," Craddock said. "That was a famine summer. We had a refugee feeding station set up outside West Gate. Ting went there and found a woman, one of the homeless, hopeless drifters who pass through at such times. She agreed to be his wife."

The crisis was Ting's request for permission to enlarge his fuel leanto into a small house. It was mission policy that only Christians might have households within the walls. Ting had a Chinese understanding of the danger of setting precedents, but he could not understand why he could not himself become a Christian.

Shirley let her food grow cold, listening. Mr. Craddock was talking of something that was, to her, the very mystery of China.

"He offered to attend church services and to do and say all that I might require of him," Craddock went on. "I had to tell him that would not suffice. Many Chinese have little sense of guilt and sin. But Ting is the only man I ever knew who has absolutely none. He and I searched his heart to the depths, and I had to believe it."

Gillespie had stopped eating. "I'm sure you realize what you are saying, Mr. Craddock," he observed.

"Of course I do." Craddock stroked his beard. "I spent hours in solitary prayer. And here is what I did. I performed a marriage ceremony for them, but I told Ting he would have to build his house outside the walls."

Mrs. Craddock laughed. Shirley looked at her, shocked, and then back to Craddock. Craddock was smiling.

"Tai-tai knows the story," he said. It was the first time they had ever heard him call her that.

Instead of adding his house to the cluster outside West Gate, Ting had built a hut of clay and cornstalks against the outside of the wall precisely opposite his leanto on the inside. And one day when the Craddocks had walked all the way around there to bring red eggs and congratulations on the birth of a son, they discovered that Ting had knocked a hole in the wall between his house and his leanto. That bit of the wall had become part of his premises and, by old custom, his to do with as he pleased. Very stiffly, the Craddocks had walked the long way round to go home again.

"I made him brick it up. I had a stern and narrow sense of duty in those days," Craddock said. "Ting was wiser than I. He did not confuse my sense of duty with the man who was his friend. For years he walked the long way round between his home and his place of business and I'm sure now he never felt the slightest stir of resentment."

"I've come to like him very much," Shirley said.

"When we came back, he asked me to have tea with him," Craddock went on. "He ushered me into his leanto and through that door in the mission wall, opened up again, and gave me the seat of honor in his parlor. After a few minutes, I was certain he was not gloating over me. He was honestly happy, for my sake, that my authority and responsibility were gone. It left me free on my side to be as completely his friend as he had always been mine. And you know, it's true!"

"That's pretty marvelous," Gillespie said. "You say he has a son?"

"One of your students. The boy's name is Tao-min."

"Tao-min!" Shirley was surprised. "I thought he came from . . . oh, away, somewhere."

"Many young people these days are ashamed of their fathers," Craddock said. "But if you can honestly praise Tao-min to Ting, nothing will please the old man more."

"I can," Shirley said. "And tomorrow I will. You have made me love old Ting, Mr. Craddock."

Shirley stood facing the front of the classroom. She, and all of the students standing behind her, bowed gravely three times to the portrait of Sun Yat-sen on the front wall. It was flanked by the new

Kuomintang party and national flags. Then they took their seats. The students had half an hour for review, before they would begin to read aloud.

Heads bent, lips moving silently, they squinted at their wretchedly printed texts. They were younger boys, a whole roomful of them, and they took their learning as a serious revolutionary responsibility. Tao-min, her helper for that day, was studying the assignment as hard as the younger boys.

The U.S. and old Chinese flags, and the portraits of Lincoln and Washington, were gone from the front wall. On Mondays everyone had to gather in the chapel for ritual reverence to the new flags and portrait and to hear the reading of Sun Yat-sen's testament. One of the students—always Cho-jen, if he was at China Light that day—would deliver a patriotic harangue. The resemblance to compulsory attendance of Christian services in the old days was deliberate. Wherever the Kuomintang ruled in China, it was instituting a compulsory cult of patriotism, in Christian chapels and Buddhist temples alike.

"We are doing knowingly what you do without knowing," Cho-jen had told Gillespie. "We are using the James-Lange effect in reverse."

"I only know vaguely what he means by that," Gillespie told Shirley. "How *does* he come up with those flashes of esoteric knowledge?"

"It's his genius."

Gillespie was teaching mathematics and history and enjoying it. The older boys were away from school on political activity, more often than not. Mr. Lin, the new principal, deplored it. Gillespie, at one faculty meeting, had defended it.

"They are in a different sort of school now," he said. "They are learning how to build and govern a nation."

Only in China, with its traditional reverence for learning, she thought, could mere boys take such a part, simply because they were students. Her Chinese was still not good enough to supplement the scanty English of the younger boys she was now teaching. Cho-jen had solved that by assigning her a senior student to help with language crises. It worked well. Quite often, as today, her helper was Tao-min. She suspected that Tao-min did not much relish militia drill and political education work among the peasants.

The student union had torn out of the English textbooks all of the specifically American-patriotic material. For substitute material they had brought in pamphlets of Sun Yat-sen's writings, done very poorly into English. She was teaching the boys quite a bit of grammar and spelling by making a game of finding errors in the pamphlets.

That was what Tao-min was doing, his pencil poised, pudgy face earnest, eyes squinting through his spectacles. As a senior student, he was honor-bound to find more errors than any of the younger boys. Whether he did or not, Shirley knew, she was going to make it seem so.

At the end of the period she dismissed the class and went to the faculty office. Cho-jen was just concluding an argument with Gillespie. No one else was there.

"Good morning, Miss Eckert," Cho-jen said. "Mr. Gillespie has just been telling me that all power corrupts. I think it is lack of power that corrupts. What do you think?"

"I don't know. I don't think power will corrupt you, Cho-jen."

"Present company is always excepted," Gillespie said, smiling.

He was relaxed at his desk. Cho-jen moved restlessly about the room, talking in half sentences and skipping from subject to subject. He had an almost hurtful vibrancy of manner. All by himself, he made the room seem crowded. He looked out the window at a platoon of militia drilling in the street. "I am getting them ten more rifles," he said. "From Pan's old stock." General Pan and his army had been made into a Kuomintang regiment and marched away. The newly-raised militia was the only armed force in the valley. "I may have to go to Changsha soon," Cho-jen said. "I have a thousand things to do here, before I can go." He thought he might head the Paoshan delegation to the provincial worker-peasant congress in Changsha. After a few minutes he excused himself to go and open a student union committee meeting. The room seemed suddenly empty.

Shirley sat down at her desk, in mock collapse. "How can you be so relaxed with him, Walter?" she asked. "He sets me jumping, too. I can't help it."

"I know it's a cliché, but if ever a boy burnt with a gemlike flame, it's Cho-jen these days," Gillespie said.

He unlocked a desk drawer and took out the journal he was keeping of his talks with Cho-jen. He was if possible even more captivated by Cho-jen than was Shirley herself. No one had ever before systematically recorded the life of a teen-age Napoleon, he said quite seriously. They were both certain that Cho-jen was going to become one of the great men of Chinese history.

"He's scarcely eighteen. He knows he's too young," Gillespie said. "He also knows the hour has struck for him and time will not wait."

Gillespie enjoyed keeping Shirley informed of Cho-jen's progress. The power in the valley lay in the worker and peasant unions and their militia. Cho-jen enjoyed the fanatical loyalty of all the senior students. He made them his lieutenants with clerical posts in all the worker-peasant groups, which he visited himself as often as he could. His gift for evoking blind personal loyalty was rapidly binding them all to him.

Legitimacy lay in the Kuomintang power structure, centered in Hankow. Cho-jen held several Kuomintang offices. To please Hankow and Changsha, he had to keep the peasants from going too far and too fast with land seizures. He avoided making enemies as much as he could. Such enemies as he could not help making, he outschemed ruthlessly. He had an instinct for power tactics.

"And as if all that were not enough," Gillespie said, "there's still his father."

It was no longer a secret that Cho-jen's father was the bandit chief on the mountain. He had fiercely refused submission when Kuomintang troops came through to sweep up General Pan. Cho-jen had saved his father then by working out a face-saving arrangement in which his father's armed band became the cadre for the local militia. He still had to make that so in fact.

"He's told me a good bit about his father recently," Gillespie said. "It's fascinating, Shirley!"

All the arts of Chinese soothsaying had predicted greatness for Cho-jen, even before his birth, Gillespie told her. Cho-jen's father had interpreted it as the mandate of heaven for his son to found a new imperial dynasty. He had set out to become a warlord, to serve that single purpose. He had been all ready to defeat Pan and take Paoshan when the Kuomintang forestalled him. He was furious. Cho-jen could not make his father believe that greatness in China was no longer an imperial throne.

"But whatever it's to be, Cho-jen is on his way," Gillespie concluded. "A year from now he'll be a power in Changsha. Before he's twenty-one he'll have the province behind him and be a man to reckon with in Hankow."

"I hope he does. I'm sure he will," Shirley said. "You sound almost as convinced as Cho-jen's father."

"I'll tell you." Gillespie cocked his head. "If someone told me Cho-jen had strangled serpents in his cradle, I think I would believe it."

Only the ghost of a smile belied his utter seriousness.

So the days went. Shirley found them pleasant and stimulating. But often at night she could not sleep for the sound of Mr. Craddock's slow pacing in the courtyard. He had signed all the papers. He held only a native pastorate and one vote on the mission board of control. He was deeply troubled by some of the trends at China Light. But in Hankow he had made his decision to trust in God and the fundamental decency of the Chinese and he would not waver.

Then the new trouble struck. That night when she heard him pacing she could not bear it. She rose and slipped on padded Chinese clothing and joined him in the courtyard.

"Have I been keeping you awake, Shirley?" he asked.

"No. I'm just restless. I want to walk and tire myself."

It would not do to speak of the trouble. Nor of anything. She just wanted to be near him and he would feel her pity and love. But he wanted to talk.

"Are you still happy with our decision?" he asked. "Have you really found it here as you expected?"

"Wonderfully happy. But not quite as I expected."

"It is different and better than I had expected," he said. "I learn. Now in my age, I learn. We don't have to do bold and startling things for them to win their love." He walked a few steps in silence. "I have stopped fretting about the electric light plant," he said. "I am glad now that navy engineer did not come with us. I fear I wanted him only as a bribe to the people here."

"It was for his own sake, too," she said, too quickly. "He was desperately unhappy on his ship. He deserved a better life."

"But he might not have been happy here. For him, the decision would have been irreversible."

He would have been happy, she thought. But in a shamed corner of her heart, when she looked there honestly, she knew that it was of herself she had been thinking, those last days in Hankow. It was the sense of moving into unknown dangers and her wish for a strong man at her side. But there was no danger and her life was filled pleasantly with her work and she had not thought of Jake Holman for a week or longer.

"I think you're right," she agreed sadly. "It's best he didn't come. But I'm glad we came."

"It's like a grace, isn't it?" he said. "Everything I see speaks of it. Even this spirit wall."

They stopped beside it and she put her hand on the new, rough brick. It stood high as their heads, like a baffle before the gate in the front wall. It was to keep devils from entering the courtyard. Devils could travel only in straight lines and they could not turn the corners to get around a spirit screen. In the old days Mr. Craddock had sternly forbidden them as a superstition.

"You know, when the board of control discussed building these, I voted in favor of it," Craddock said. "They have nothing to do with devils any more. They are just part of Chinese architecture." He chuckled gently. "When we built the big house, Tai-tai wanted green shutters," he said. "I had them made and nailed solidly to the side of the house, without hinges, and you could not close them if you wanted to. Why could I not have understood then that a spirit screen is just like those shutters?"

She did not answer. They resumed walking. When she felt tired she said goodnight. He had understood her purpose in coming out.

"Goodnight, Shirley, and thank you," he said.

In her bed again, she still heard his slow footsteps. She had not taken away his trouble. The trouble was a charge of "criminal land-lordism." On a remote and separated bit of mission property there really had been some rent gouging and opium forcibly grown, Gillespie said. Craddock had known nothing of it. Wen, the mission bailiff, was the real criminal. Cho-jen was perfectly frank about it.

"They know he's innocent. It's just orders from Changsha," he said. "They want to take treaty people before our new Chinese courts, to establish our claim to jurisdiction over everyone in China."

Cho-jen was leaving the way open for the Craddocks to go back to Hankow. But he was trying to persuade Craddock to submit voluntarily to Chinese judicial authority. That would be an even more solid blow at the unequal treaties.

"I have always meant to live out my days at China Light," Craddock had said, the one time they had discussed it at supper. "If wrong was done under my delegated authority, that can be determined more surely in Paoshan than by a U.S. court a thousand miles away in Shanghai." Then he had added, "It goes step by step. I fear where the steps may be taking us. I don't know what to do."

In the courtyard, the measured footsteps halted.

He's praying now, she thought. He would stand under the largest tree with his head bowed and his hands clasped on his chest. Shirley always wanted to hold her breath when the footsteps stopped.

She did not know about prayer. Gillespie seldom spoke of religion any more, but once he had told her: "You thin a barrier, a kind of shell around your awareness. You become able to feel directly just a hint of the nearness and love of God, Who is always all around you without your knowing." She did not know about that. But in those silences of the night, she could believe that Mr. Craddock really talked with God.

After a long while the footsteps started again. Firmly and surely they crossed the courtyard and were lost in a door sounding. Shirley went to sleep feeling that Mr. Craddock had reached his decision and that it would be the right one.

36

There were simply not enough men. From the first, the engineers had to work topside to keep the ship looking clean and military. They had no time for cleaning work below decks. The machinery spaces stayed rusty and dirty. Lt. Collins stopped holding lower-deck inspections. He still inspected topside with all the old ritual. He was being very stiff and reserved, but he had a cold, fierce pride in his eye and manner. The Sand Pebbles responded to it. They knew they were holding the fort.

Always, the watchers were on the bund abreast the ship. Usually they were a score or so of loitering coolies. Often enough they were a full-scale hate parade, with massed flags and slogans yelled like football cheers. They were like a shot in the arm to the Sand Pebbles.

"Bear down on them holystones, you Poisoners of China!" Farren would sing out. The men would laugh and scour away all the harder at the teak. They were getting a rough, hard look to their faces and hands.

Every morning they stood colors and ran through their drills. Ship and crew looked smart. The chiefs and officers were always meticulously turned out in pressed blues and shined buttons. That was the work of Hu-bing and Yen-ta, the only two Chinese left aboard. They were not coolies. They were enlisted men in the steward branch. No white man could enlist in that branch. Stewards had special uniforms with "USN" on them but nowhere any eagles or anchors. Hu-bing and Yen-ta did a very good job on the chiefs and officers.

Life was plain and simple. The Sand Pebbles could not go ashore. They could not even visit the *Duarte,* because of the bad feeling over there about the boycott. The *Duarte* took radio guard and Waldhorn moved over there to stand watches. The only news the Sand Pebbles got was the scuttlebutt Red Dog brought back from his guard mail trips. The *Duarte* took most of the military details, but sometimes the *San Pablo* would furnish an armed guard for one of the oil company launches. There was always competition for that among the Sand Pebbles. It was a breathing spell off the ship, and sometimes a man could sneak a good meal.

The food aboard was all dry stores, beans and rice, corned beef and canned salmon. The potatoes had run out. Jennings was rationing each man one slice of raw onion at dinner and four ounces of beer at supper, to guard against scurvy. The men made a small pleasure of it. They sipped their beer with slow relish. They looked at their onion slices against the light, to admire the pattern. They pulled them into rings and nibbled each ring slowly. They argued whether vinegar or salt was best with raw onions.

Holman kept the machinery in good working shape. He did not care about appearances. He became quite friendly with Krebs, the new man. Krebs did not have much ship's spirit, and he seemed to think that Holman did not either. He would talk freely to Holman.

"They're a funny, clannish bunch on here, ain't they?" he asked Holman one day. "They make me feel like I undercut this Burgoyne guy, to steal his job or something."

They were beside the workbench. Holman knew what Krebs meant, but he could not explain it.

"They don't know they're doing it," he said.

"Harris keeps telling me I ought to let my mustache grow out. Did Burgoyne have a long mustache?"

"Yeah. And he chewed snoose." Holman pushed back a strong memory of Burgoyne standing just where Krebs was standing, on that morning the patrol had caught him. "Frenchy had lots of tattoos," he added.

"It's like they want me to *be* Burgoyne!"

"They do. Only they don't know it, not that way."

"Well, I'm Krebs!" He hit the vise handle and spun it. "Krebs wants off this pigiron! Krebs hates coal burners! That's who I am!"

When the thirty days were up, they declared Frenchy Burgoyne a deserter. All hands except Holman knew that he had drowned in the Yangtze, but there was no corpse or witnesses to prove it, so on paper he was a deserter. The word would go out to civilian police all over America. For years to come somewhere in North Carolina police would keep an eye on Burgoyne's kinfolks. They would be hoping that Burgoyne might come visiting and they could nab him and claim the fifty-dollar reward.

By regulations, Burgoyne's clothing had to be sold at auction. Farren stenciled a red D.C. on each piece and piled the clothing on a mess table. Franks, as chief master-at-arms, came down to conduct the auction. It was a break in the monotony. Franks quickly made it exciting. He worked the men up and pitted them against each other.

"Come on, you cheapskates!" he rallied them. "What else you got to spend your money for?"

That was true. They also knew they could not buy any new clothing in Changsha. They crowded around the mess table and bid each garment up far past its worth. They cheered winners and hooted at losers who chickened out. The auction raised almost three hundred dollars. The money would go to the welfare fund, which had once been the coolie fund. But now they could not hire coolies or buy beer or charter a joy junk to come alongside. The excitement ended glumly, with that reminder.

One item remained. It was a framed photograph of Burgoyne and Maily, which had hung inside Burgoyne's locker. Franks held it up and looked at it, cocking his head.

"I guess you'd call this a keepsake," he said. "I ought to send it to his next-of-kin."

"You can't," Bronson said. "Deserters' next of kin ain't supposed to get anything at all."

"Besides, it shows him with a pig," Harris said. "They wouldn't like that in North Carolina."

"All they hate in North Carolina is niggers. California is where they hate the Chinks," Crosley said.

"Who do they hate in New Jersey?" Stawski asked him.

"They hate big dumb Polacks."

"We hate frogfaces up in Michigan," Stawski said.

"All you Polacks can kiss my royal Canadian," Crosley said.

"All right, you guys. Don't get personal," Franks said. He waved the photograph. "Anybody want to bid on this?"

No one did. Franks dropped it over the side into the river.

Chill, damp days passed. Shortages pressed on them. The *Duarte* would not give them anything. The Chinese barber from the *Duarte* came over now and then to give haircuts. He charged two Mex dollars, which was worse than Clip Clip's final prices. The Sand Pebbles hated the *Duarte* crew. The ship's nickname was *Die Hard*.

"I hope them chinchy bastards all die with a hard on!" Red Dog said. The Sand Pebbles repeated the joke with relish.

The paint was gone. Soap ran short. Jennings held out most of the remaining soap for the galley and dishwashing, for health reasons. They used the last of the boiler compound in scrubbing topside paintwork. The alkali in it cut dirt and grease, but it made their hands red and cracked and painful. They could not keep the whole topside clean. They had to let the starboard side go, except for the quarterdeck and a stretch of boat deck outside Lt. Collins' cabin. He restricted his inspections to the port side, which faced the bund. The *San Pablo* did not look any different to the watchers over there.

They were always over there, all day long, watching the ship and throwing the hate. When they built up a real hate storm with bugles and placards and mass shouting, the Sand Pebbles would man the rail and hate back at them. They would jeer and hoot and make obscene gestures. Afterward they would feel dull and listless.

"There's so God damned many of 'em, it uses a man up hating 'em back," Farren said.

Lynch always waited on the quarterdeck for Red Dog to come back with mail. If Red Dog had a letter, he would wave it above his head as the boat neared the gangway.

"Arf! Arf! A letter from Looby!" he would shout at Lynch.

"Her name is *Liuba!*" Lynch would say, taking the letter. *"Mrs. Lynch* to you, you redheaded wonk!"

Lynch had plenty of brandy and he would invite Holman up for coffee and talk about his problems. Liuba always had a different deal lined up in Shanghai, but none of them came off. Lynch wished she would quit horsing around and buy whatever she could. The gearwheel was closing in on Shanghai. He wrote her long letters of advice.

"But I always tell her use her own judgment," he told Holman. "She's plenty smart. She's looking for a really good deal. She'll find one."

Holman sniffed the fragrant coffee and said nothing.

"Find yourself a good woman, Jake," Lynch urged. "Don't wait till you're as old as I was."

"I think about it sometimes," Holman said.

It was Shirley he thought about. He could not take such thoughts seriously. They were only daydreams.

The sardines and Vienna sausage ran out. The onion ration was sliced thinner and Jennings cut the beer to two ounces a day. The food was mostly beans and rice and canned corned beef. The Sand Pebbles remained cheerful about it. "Duckbutt's doing the best he can," they told each other. They became very fond of Duckbutt's rice pudding. He made a lot of it and on Sundays he would put raisins in it.

For their Christmas dinner the *Duarte* gave them three canned hams and some hard candy. Bordelles and the chiefs came down to eat Christmas dinner with the crew. Duckbutt had baked the hams with brown sugar and cloves. With great ceremony Tullio brought in plum puddings flaming with some of Lynch's brandy. The men all cheered. Each man got a small bag of hard candy. It made for a pretty good feeling.

Holman could not share the feeling. He was ashamed because he could not. He was afraid that they would know it about him. The Sand Pebbles seemed to him like kids playing a game. They were make-believing happiness behind a thin, papery screen. By Christmas, even Krebs had joined in. Holman was afraid that just by knowing it was a game he was going to spoil it for them. He had to watch what he said and keep apart. But the ship was too small for a man to keep apart.

On New Year's Eve Lynch sent down three bottles of brandy. The Sand Pebbles got mildly drunk in the compartment and Red Dog started them singing. Holman wanted desperately to join in, but he could not do it. His voice was stiff in his throat and it made a mocking croak in his own ears. When they started on the "Wing Kang Lung" song, he went below to relieve the watch. The song followed him down.

> *Oh muchee come catchee come hai yai-yah!*
> *Chinaman no likee he!*

"I'll relieve you early," Holman told Krebs. "Go up and get some of that brandy before it's all gone."

"Ai yah!" Krebs said, grinning. "You're a shipmate, Jake!"

He ran long-legged up the ladder. Holman checked over the machinery. The song beat through the overhead at him. He tried to listen to the machinery talking, and he had lost the sense of that language. It was just noise. He paced the floorplates, thinking.

What if I were to desert and get across the hills over to China Light? he thought. He knew he would not ever do such a stupid thing. But it was all right to think about it. He began recalling all his visual memories of China Light. He wanted the whole picture of it in his mind.

What crowded into his mind were memories of Shirley. They came fusing and mingling, curve of cheek and chin, sweep of hair, white neck and throat hollows, droop and curve of mouth, her eyes merry and sad and frightened and angry and very tender like soft light. She came like all the facets of a jewel blazing at once. The unsummoned intensity of feeling disturbed him.

He pushed her to a distance and thought about China Light. He wished he could have just once seen the machinery in that sugar mill they couldn't make work right. The daydream lasted him all through the midwatch. He did not even notice when they stopped singing up above.

The Sand Pebbles still wanted to fight. They still talked wistfully about Plan Red. They thought surely someone would be careless somewhere and start a fight. Then it would explode all along the river like a train of powder. They wanted that to happen.

At other times they talked wistfully about getting out when the spring flood came. The word was that Changsha would be completely evacuated then. Only a few paleface civilians were still in Changsha, as custodians of company property. They were not making any money. They were harassed and threatened and were always having trouble with the few coolies they still had. There were supposed to be six or eight white women ashore, mostly missionaries. They were all waiting to get out when the floods came.

One clear, cold day the *Duarte* signaled electrifying news. A mob was attacking the British Concession at Hankow. Lt. Collins went to a conference of commanding officers on the *Duarte*. In his absence the *San Pablo* seethed with excited speculation. All the men crowded on the quarterdeck.

"The Limeys will fight for Hankow like it was London," Farren said. "This is it, guys! Plan Red!"

They named the U.S. ships they knew to be in Hankow: *Truxtun, Isabel, Pope* and *Pigeon.* Blood was thicker than water. Sure as shooting started, those ships would be in it. And so would the ships in Changsha.

"Come over here! Look at them militia lining out on top of the wall!" Ellis called, from the port side.

Holman and some others went over there. Changsha had the word, all right. The junks were battening hatches and there were very few coolies on the bund. Changsha was like a ship clearing decks for action. Lt. Collins came aboard, his face fierce and eager, and sent the Sand Pebbles to their own action stations. They went to their guns spring-legged and alert and ready for anything.

Holman had to go below. They did not get up steam, since they could not go anywhere and they had to save on coal. Lynch came down with the dope and the engineers clustered around him by the workbench to hear it. *Woodcock* and *Duarte* men were guarding the white civilians, Lynch said. The Japs were looking after their own. All the *San Pablo* had to do was to defend herself.

"That's enough, by God! They got it in for us," Krebs said. "They'll hit us first and hardest."

"We'll give it back double!" Perna shook his fists. His eyes gleamed. "How about it, Harris?"

"Ten times, by God!" Harris clashed his teeth and grinned like a shark. "We'll mow 'em like the tall corn!"

As more radio news came to the *Duarte,* they signaled it to the *San Pablo.* Crosley would call it out word by word as he received it and men repeated it all over the ship. The news was perplexing. It was really a coolie mob in Hankow, and not soldiers. It was still attacking. But there was no news about casualties, or ground won or lost. It was very strange. Because with a coolie mob you just chopped into them and they broke. Or else they ran over you. Either way, it was over quickly.

Something's wrong up there, the Sand Pebbles told each other uneasily. We ain't getting all the dope.

All afternoon they stood to their guns. Their nerves grew more tense as time dragged on and the news from Hankow was still the same. The bund was deserted, but worker-peasants swarmed back among the buildings. A noise of bugles and shouting in the city came over the gray walls.

They ate supper at their guns. They could hardly stand the tension. In Hankow the mob was still attacking, with no casualties and no ground won or lost. It was as if time had gotten stuck, up there in Hankow. Across the gray river the sun set flaring red behind the sacred mountain. It made the river look like blood.

Just then it began, in a crackle of small-arms fire downriver by the Japanese gunboat.

"*Stand* ready! *Stand* ready!" Franks roared.

His voice sounded twice as loud as ever before. The Sand Pebbles rose to top pitch. They were trembling eager. The firing moved upriver toward the *San Pablo*. It was a cloud of rapid red winks, like swarming fireflies in the dusk, and a constant scream of voices.

"*Hold* fire! *Hold* fire!" Franks called out.

His voice was savage with disgust. They all saw it at the same time. It was firecrackers. The people were flooding along the bund with torches and paper lanterns and millions of firecrackers.

The news came by blinker from the *Duarte*. The British Concession had fallen to the coolie mob. The landing force had withdrawn to the ships. Not a shot had been fired and no one had been killed. Gearwheel troops had been invited into the concession to protect the white people from the coolies. The news shell-shocked the Sand Pebbles. They could only look at each other.

"Secure from general quarters!" Franks passed the word.

The men gathered in the compartment. They could not say much. They seemed not to want to look at each other now. They were thinking that something beyond human comprehension must have happened up there in Hankow. It was too uncanny even to wonder about.

Holman went back out on deck. He felt guilty about being among them and not feeling as whipped and bewildered as they were feeling. Ashore, the Chinese were going mad with joy. Waves of sound beat against the ship, as if the city screamed with one voice. It was a whole continent mocking and jeering and jubilating, out there in the flaming darkness.

37

Wind and a driving rain howled down off the mountain. There had been no school for several days. The fall of the British Concession in Hankow had stirred the valley deeply, and all the students were away on political work. Cho-jen had been called to Changsha. In the courtyard the bare branches of the trees threshed. The courtyard did not drain well. Water puddled out there, and an unpleasant dampness was seeping into the house.

Shu-ma was being very quiet in the kitchen. In the living room Shirley moved from warming her hands at the brazier to looking out the window and back to the brazier. In the bedroom Mrs. Craddock was at last asleep. But she would wake up soon and ask for news again. If no message came from Paoshan by nightfall, Shirley decided, she would go there herself in the morning.

A gust brought a branch thumping down on the tiled roof. Mrs. Craddock awoke and called out in a weak voice. Shirley crossed once more to the window in forlorn hope.

Her heart leaped. Gillespie had just come into the courtyard. He went to his own room on the other side. He was going to change into dry clothing, but she could not wait for that. She ran splashing across and knocked on his door. He opened it and looked at her in alarm.

"Shirley! What is it? Is Tai-tai . . . ?"

"No worse. Or not much," she said. "Walter, what *news?* Why isn't Mr. Craddock with you?"

Instead of answering her, he drew her inside and closed the door against rain splash. She had never been in his room before. It was small, bare and very neat, except for the mess of papers on his table. He lit the kerosene lamp on his table. His face was pale and drawn in the lamplight.

"The verdict was guilty," he said quietly. "The sentence was death."

She stared at him, afraid to ask. He smiled wearily.

"Mr. Craddock is still alive and well, in the Paoshan prison," he said. "I think it is going to be all right. I will go back in the morning, but I wanted to bring you the news myself."

He told her the story. It was the work of the Chung faction, Cho-jen's chief power rivals. They had a technique of working up mob spirit, which they used for lynch trials of landlords and their agents out in the countryside. They had used it at Mr. Craddock's trial, as a blow at Cho-jen. The delegation from the China Light peasant union, who were there to defend Craddock, had shouted and pleaded in vain. Gillespie had feared for his own life at one point.

"Cho-jen would have outgeneraled them, I think. Or just his personal sway," Gillespie said. "Fu-liang did all he could. But he's not Cho-jen."

The China Light peasants and students had crowded around Mr. Craddock and saved him from summary execution, however. Some were still with him in the prison. They would not leave him until Cho-jen returned to take control. Gillespie had been up all night. They had reached Cho-jen in Changsha by telegraph. He had gotten some sort of emergency stay order from the provincial council. Fu-liang, on guard in the prison, was armed with that. Cho-jen was returning to Paoshan at once.

"So I think it will be all right," Gillespie finished. "But it was a near thing, Shirley." He sat down wearily on his bed.

"How is Mr. Craddock? How did he . . . ?"

"With grace and dignity. He is becoming almost saintly under this stress," Gillespie said. "I do not use that word carelessly."

"I know you don't," she said. "We must tell Tai-tai. But not all of it."

"All the way from Paoshan I've been thinking of how to tell her." He stood up, swaying slightly. "I suppose—"

"Yes. Tell her now. And then you can rest." Shirley became sharply aware of his fatigue and nervous strain. "You'll have to get into dry things and go right to bed," she told him. "I'll have Shu-ma bring you some of the hot chicken broth he's making."

They crossed the courtyard hardly aware that they were hand in hand.

Shirley knew that Cho-jen was acting with his accustomed boldness, and that he would succeed. She worried all day, just the same. She was at the main gate when they came home, marching and singing across the fields from the boat landing. The song told her it was all right, and then she saw Craddock's tall figure. The gateman lit some firecrackers.

She hummed their marching song as she hurried back to tell Mrs. Craddock. Tao-min had written it for the student militia. She thought Tao-min's English version of it had a boyish charm.

> *We are just ready to fight.*
> *To fight the warlords with all our might . . .*

She burst into the sickroom. "Tai-tai, he's safe! He's coming!" she said.

Mrs. Craddock was propped up on pillows. She had unusual color in her wasted cheeks and her eyes were alert.

"I know. I hear the firecrackers," she said. "Would you bring me my comb, please?"

"Oh! Of course!"

Shirley helped her. She pulled the covers straight and tidied the room. When she heard them in the courtyard, she ran out to meet them. She ran to Mr. Craddock and hugged him.

"Go right in. Don't wait to talk," she said.

Craddock went inside. Gillespie smiled.

"We're not needed here just now," he said. "Anyway, Cho-jen wants to see us both right away at union headquarters."

As they walked, he told her how masterfully Cho-jen had handled it. A new link in the Paoshan defenses had been completed, a boom of junks across the river east of the city. Cho-jen had promoted a grand militia review in Paoshan to celebrate it. He had led the China Light contingent himself. They had simply flooded into the prison and carried off Mr. Craddock before the Chung faction had time to react.

"Cho-jen is marvelous," she agreed.

Union headquarters was the old Craddock home. Extra tables and heaps of pamphlets and posters made a sad disarray of the once neat parlor. Fu-liang and several more of Cho-jen's principal lieutenants were there with him. The boys still wore their yellowish militia uniforms. Cho-jen waved everyone to seats and had tea brought in. He did not sit down himself. He paced the room, talking in Chinese and English indifferently.

"I have just designated your house as a prison," he told Gillespie.

That was to make Craddock still technically a prisoner of the state, Cho-jen explained. The house would be under constant armed guard. But it was also a maneuver to make the Chungs lose face in the countryside. Cho-jen was going to swear old Ting, the hot-water seller, into the militia and make him the guard. Ting would be given a rusty old musket. Whenever he left his post by his caldron he would put his skull cap on the musket, and the musket alone would be the sentry. Within the week, all the peasants in the valley would be laughing about it.

"Cho-jen, please don't ever become my enemy," Gillespie said, laughing himself.

He would record that in his journal as soon as he could, Shirley knew. She laughed. The boys were all laughing. Cho-jen sobered them.

"The Chungs are still dangerous enemies!" he said sharply. "More than ever, since what happened in Hankow!"

Striding back and forth, he gave them a lecture on it. The major warlords were all puppets of the treaty powers, he said. Bolshevik

Russia had voluntarily given up the unequal treaties and was aiding the Kuomintang with arms and advisors. But there was reason to believe that the Russians wanted to make the Kuomintang their own puppet in a power struggle with England. Communists within the Kuomintang were behaving correctly. But others, such as the two Chung men in Paoshan, were trying to persuade the worker-peasant groups to seize local power and carry the revolution to unsanctioned extremes.

"The treaty port newspapers are all shouting that Chiang Kai-shek is a Bolshevik because he wants to cancel the treaties," Cho-jen said. "That pleases the Chungs. That is why they want to execute Mr. Craddock. They want the foreign newspapers to shout all the louder."

The Chungs did not want the treaties canceled, Cho-jen went on. They wanted to force war between the Kuomintang and one or more treaty powers, preferably England. If that happened, they thought they could turn the whole revolution Bolshevik. The English probably knew that, and so they refused to shoot at the mob in Hankow. That mob had been the work of other agents like the Chungs. The Kuomintang had had no choice but to take control of the British Concession, once the mob had overrun it.

"I am afraid they will soon control Changsha," Cho-jen said. "That will make it very difficult here in Paoshan."

"I can see how it would," Gillespie agreed.

"Here is how you come into it," Cho-jen said. "My position is that you have all renounced your personal treaty privileges; therefore we must grant you the same rights as ourselves. In Paoshan the Chungs are saying that you are not able to do that, as a private act, and that you are still as much of an insult to Chinese sovereignty as if you were gunboats. They think they are striking at me by saying that."

"If we are really endangering you—" Gillespie began.

"You are not. They would just find something else," Cho-jen assured him. "I want to fight them on that issue, because I know that Chinese hearts are with me on it."

It was dusk and Cho-jen had lamps brought in. He went on pacing tirelessly and talking about his plans. The other boys seldom had a chance to speak. Their awe of Cho-jen was evident. At last Gillespie excused himself and Shirley.

"Remember, do not go to Paoshan," Cho-jen told them in parting. "But you are quite safe here at China Light."

They walked home together in the darkness.

"Hey! You needn't walk so fast!" Gillespie protested.

Shirley laughed. "It's Cho-jen. He's simply *contagious!*" She slowed down. "Hasn't he grown, though!"

"Not noticeably. To my eyes."

"He's taller. He *is!*"

"It's his impression. His presence," Gillespie said. *"That* grows, I grant you!" He whistled, thinking. "To coin a striking phrase, Cho-jen is being tempered in revolutionary fires," he said. "He was born with the proper metal for it. He is a boy meeting his time."

He began whistling softly again. Shirley hummed with him. It was Tao-min's militia song. *To fight the warlords with all our might,* she sang softly. Gillespie joined her.

> *They're big and fat but we'll make them thin.*
> *We're always ready to begin.*

Shirley began laughing. "Isn't it a wonderful song for a revolution?"

"It is for this one. It really is!" Gillespie said.

Lamplight was yellow in the windows. They crossed the courtyard singing Tao-min's song.

38

"That up in Hankow," Farren told Holman. "It was the last straw, kind of. Something's broke in the guys, Jake."

"It sure took the heart out of 'em," Holman agreed

They were on the quarterdeck, where Farren had the watch. Haythorn and two seamen were washing down the portside. Most of the others sat in the compartment unshaven and morose. Half the bunks were unmade in there. It was as if they had been saving back something vital, Holman thought, and in the Hankow alarm they had laid it all on the line and they had lost it. They had nothing left.

"I feel it myself," Farren said. "We been shot at and we ran away too many times. We been rocked and spit on and hated at, more than men can stand." He gripped the log desk with both hands and shook it. "What the hell we doing in Hunan, anyway? There's enough Chinamen in Hunan they could beat us to death with their chopsticks, if they took a mind!"

"We'll get out when the flood comes."

"I wish it was here now." Farren lowered his voice. "It's going bad. The guys are turning ugly inside." He stroked his beard and looked sharply at Holman. "Know what I mean?"

"I think so. Like cattle getting spooky."

When range cattle were spooky, any little thing could set them off. They might stampede. Or if one of the herd got singled out in any way, as by breaking a horn and shedding blood, the others would turn on it and hunt it out of the herd and they would hunt it to death. They had a strange, terrible bellowing they only used at such times. Holman was afraid he was the one the Sand Pebbles might single out.

"It's like a hurt snake, when he starts biting himself." Farren was still looking hard at Holman. "Know what I mean, Jake?"

Holman went below wondering whether Farren had been warning him. Harris and Krebs and Perna were sitting on the workbench. Holman thought they hushed their talk as he came up.

"We ain't going to work on the topside no more," Harris told Holman. "To hell with colors and quarters and all them drills, too."

"Sure," Holman said. "That stuff's all looksee pidgin, anyway."

"Let Franks run us to mast," Perna said. "What the hell can the skipper give us, more'n what we got already?"

They were already restricted to the ship. They couldn't spend money, so fines would not hurt them. There was no brig. Rations could not be reduced more than they already were. Holman wanted to remind them that they could all get general courts-martial when the ship got back to Hankow, and go to a naval prison. They were not able to think that far ahead. They watched Holman narrowly as they talked about it, as if expecting him to disagree. He knew he had better not.

"All I give a damn about is keep her steaming," he said.

"We'll keep her steaming," Harris said.

It was shocking to Holman how fast they fell apart. They just let go. All they had left for bathing and shaving was harsh salt-water soap. Most of them stopped shaving. They had no heart to curse the missionaries who, by being hostages, had kept the British from fighting for Hankow. They cursed each other, instead.

The news did not cheer them. Panic evacuation of palefaces was on in Hankow. America was sending three more cruisers and a regiment of marines to Shanghai. The British were bringing out a whole new army and fleet from home waters. Even Spain and Portugal were sending warships, in case China had to be whipped again. None of it comforted the Sand Pebbles.

"They can scrap this pigiron any old time they want to," Wilsey said bitterly at the mess table. "I'll take a battlewagon in San Pedro."

"God damn the day I ever come aboard!" Restorff said.

That was how they felt. They were striking out at everything. They would not salute colors any more. They wanted to sneer and strike and hurt. Harris spat into the half-eaten plate of beans and salmon in front of him and pushed it away. It struck Restorff's plate and spilled. Restorff and Harris cursed each other. They stood up flailing fists across the mess table. Holman and Farren pulled them down and smoothed it over.

In Changsha, things ashore became much worse. It was decided to send all the white women and a good many civilian men down to Hankow. *Woodcock* sailors would take them down in a convoy of steam launches towing wupans and come back alone. It was a brave thing.

It was drizzling rain the day the convoy pulled away from the *Woodcock*. There were two puffing steam launches, each with a mat-canopied wupan lashed alongside like an outrigger. The *Woodcock* men cheered as it pulled away and the *Duarte* sailors manned the rail and cheered as it passed. The Sand Pebbles manned the rail along the main deck. Holman saw Banger Knox and waved to him. The Sand Pebbles saluted on signal, but they would not cheer.

"All right, sailors! Hip hip—" Franks shouted on the boat deck "—hay—yay—yay!"

Only Bordelles and the chiefs cheered. It sounded pretty feeble. Holman did not cheer. He did not want to single himself out. He wondered what Lt. Collins thought about it. Everyone knew that the skipper was extremely touchy about passing honors. When the convoy passed the *Hiro,* the Japanese sailors gave it three loud, shrill *banzais.*

⌒ↄ

Lt. Collins stopped holding inspections altogether. He never went anywhere about the decks except between his cabin and the quarterdeck, when he came and went from the ship. That was the only part of the topside Farren was still able to keep cleaned up. You could not tell from looking at Lt. Collins that anything was wrong with the *San Pablo,* Holman thought.

Bordelles and the chiefs stayed clean and smart. Welbeck was holding back the last reserves of toilet gear for the boat deck. Holman still shaved every few days, with the harsh salt-water soap. So did Jennings and Bronson. If they stopped, so would he, Holman thought. He felt an increasing danger in being singled out for any little thing.

No one wanted to talk about what had happened. Once, having coffee with Lynch, Holman touched on it.

"Baby 'em along down there," Lynch said. "We just got to give 'em time. They'll come out of their sulks." He seemed not to trust Holman. "The skipper don't want to have to know anything officially," he said. "Neither do I. Just keep her steaming."

"We'll do that," Holman said.

Lynch had his own troubles. He had not heard from Shanghai for several weeks. Three or four men were on the quarterdeck when Red Dog finally brought Lynch a letter. Lynch ripped it open and read it. Then he crumpled it in his hand and ran up the ladder.

"What the hell?" Crosley said. He picked up a clipping Lynch had dropped and read it. "Now, *how* the hell?" he asked.

Several men read it. It was a list of passengers leaving Shanghai on an Italian steamer. The entry *Mr. and Mrs. T. A. Lynch, Havana,* was underlined in ink. Red Dog was the first to understand.

"Arf! Arf!" he yelped. "That kid cousin. He wasn't any cousin! Get it?"

They got it. They whooped with joy and thumped each other's backs.

"They gone to Cuba with all Lynch's money!" Ellis gasped happily.

"Even his name they took with 'em!"

"He's Lynchevitski now," Crosley said. *"Shitevitski!"*

Crosley made a genuine joke about once a year. The rest of the year he just repeated it. Lynch was in for a bad time from Crosley. Holman felt sorry for Lynch. Lynch had rubbed his prosperity in all their faces and he would not have gotten much sympathy at any time. But now the Sand Pebbles were in a mood to laugh at Christ on the cross.

Lt. Collins heard the voices outside his door. One was Lynch.

"I tell you, sir, I got to see him! It's humanitarian!"

"You know he can't help you, Lynch," Bordelles said.

Lynch began shouting. It would not do. Lt. Collins opened his door.

"What's the trouble?" he asked sternly. "Come inside with it."

They were all standing inside. Lt. Collins glanced through the letter, to Lynch from a lawyer in Shanghai. Lynch's woman had bought passports for herself and a Russian man from the Cuban consulate. They had sailed for Havana under Lynch's name.

"Now that they are Cubans, they are under Cuban law," the lawyer wrote. "They could probably defeat any suit we might bring, by bribery in Havana. I could not take such a case on a contingency basis. . . ."

"I'm afraid the lawyer's right," he told Lynch "You can't do anything."

"I want a humanitarian transfer! Right now! To Gitmo, sir!"

"There are no official grounds."

Lynch was red-faced. His eyes bulged.

"God damn it, sir, she's my wife! I'm sorry, sir, but she's my *wife!*" He made a violent clasping motion.

"Watch your language, Lynch!" Bordelles warned. "She was never your wife and you know it. She was technically Chinese when you—"

Lynch whirled on him. "She's Cuban now! Can't I be married to a Cuban woman?" Bordelles looked taken aback. "I knew sailors in Gitmo married to Cuban women," Lynch persisted.

"That's one for the Judge Advocate General," Bordelles said. "I think if you married her again now, you would really be married to her."

"I'm sorry for your misfortune, Chief," Lt. Collins said. "But even if I could get you such orders, which I could not, there's no way for you to get out of Changsha."

Lynch went out. He looked very dejected. Lt. Collins motioned Bordelles to remain.

"How is the feeling among the crew, Mr. Bordelles? Any improvement?"

"It's worse, sir. In my opinion—"

"Very well. Continue as before."

Bordelles' bold young face took on a stubborn look. "If the captain pleases," he said very formally, "I would like to express an opinion and offer a suggestion."

"Yes?"

"My opinion is that we are headed for serious trouble. Since mast discipline is of no use to us, my suggestion is that we exchange a few men with the *Duarte.*" He dropped his formality. "We need a shakeup, sir. This crew is too ingrown, too all tied together somehow. They act too much like one person. I'm sure you know what I mean, sir."

"Sit down."

He motioned toward the table. The two men sat down.

"It is always a blot on a ship's name when the crew has to be shaken up," he said slowly. And on the commanding officer's record, he thought, and knew Bordelles was thinking that too. "When it is done, the men have to be distributed widely, repeat widely," he went on. "Here we have only *Duarte.* And Captain Wrigley would not accept a draft of my men in *Duarte,* and give me some of his men, unless I told him officially that I thought the alternative to be mutiny in *San Pablo.* I do not think that. Do you, Mr. Bordelles?"

"In time, potentially, yes, sir, I do!" Bordelles said defiantly.

"Well, I do not. I have faith in my men."

He had said it all once before to Bordelles, but he explained it again. The men were casualties of the new kind of war. They would come out of it like magic, if fighting started. Or as soon as they reached a port where they could have women and whisky. But for the time being they were not responsible and they had to be protected.

"Keep clear of them yourself," he told Bordelles. "Let the chiefs deal with them."

All officers knew about that. When a man came aboard off liberty wildly drunk, the officers would turn their backs and not see or hear anything, until the man's shipmates could wrestle him below out of sight. Because if a man cursed or struck a commissioned officer, it did not matter how drunk he might be. He would have to pay the penalty.

"I understand, sir." Bordelles did not look convinced. "It's a gamble to save *San Pablo*'s reputation." He narrowed his eyes. "Only . . . what if we lose the gamble, sir?"

"I will deal with that when it happens."

Bordelles cleared his face and nodded. He was resigning the argument. "I was reading some translated abstracts from the native press over in the consulate yesterday," he said. "Did you know old Craddock was back at China Light?"

"Yes, and with several others. They asked Kuomintang permission to go there. They are renouncing their treaty rights again."

"Again?" Bordelles smiled. "They know they can't do that. Anyway, I'll bet Craddock's sorry now. The Bolshevik court in Paoshan has sentenced him to death, for rent gouging."

"They all wish they had the courage to be martyrs. None of them have. Where is Craddock now?"

"Under guard at China Light, I gather. The consul says he can't act just on the basis of a native press report."

"Craddock will appeal before long." Sudden anger shook Lt. Collins. "Damn those people! They are compromising and embarrassing their own government! I wonder how much of it is deliberate?"

"With Craddock I'd say all of it was. That's how he is."

After supper the men played cards at the mess tables and laughed about Lynch. It had brought them back together. Holman sat on his bunk and listened. They had to have something to gang *against,* he thought.

"Old Lynch is settin' up there now, with a bottle."

"Getting a year older every damn minute!" Perna said.

The door beside Holman's bunk crashed open. Lynch came in and stood there, swaying. His coat was open and his tie gone. He looked around and focused on Holman.

"Holman, you sombish, you done thish to me!" he blurted.

He waved an accusing finger. His face was all slubbered loose and sagging. The men at the mess tables stopped talking.

"You jinksh whole Goddamn ship day you come aboard!" Lynch shouted. "Fiddle with engine! Get me married! You're a sombishin Jonah!"

The word struck hard into Holman's secret guilt feeling. He could feel the crowd pick it up. It jolted him.

"Jonah! Sombishin Jonah!" Lynch howled at Holman.

Holman felt real alarm. He felt that they were singling him out. He sat unmoving. Crosley's devotion to his new joke headed them off.

"Valentine Shitevitski!" Crosley yelled. "Three cheers for good old Shitevitski!"

They all yelled it and laughed. Lynch turned and squalled and slobbered at them. They laughed all the harder. Franks and Welbeck came down and took Lynch away. The Sand Pebbles went right on yelling.

"He's all right!"

"Who's all right?"

"SHITEVITSKI!"

They could get carried away like that, unable to stop. They were like schoolgirls in a giggling fit. Holman remembered the first time he had seen them do it. That had been one of Crosley's jokes, too: roundy-go-*thump!* After a few minutes Harris snapped out of it and made them stop. Through it all, Holman sat unmoving. He knew he had had a very close call on being singled out.

The next morning Lynch came down to the engine room red-eyed and roaring. He was wearing a pistol. He found the engineers lounging around the workbench.

"I'm dealin' you birds a new deal down here!" he told them. "Get off your asses and get to work, God damn you!"

Holman felt all the men's eyes on him. He was senior petty officer and they expected him to tell Lynch to go to hell. If he did not, Harris would. Holman slid off the workbench.

"Sure, Chief. We'll clean the place up," he said.

"Damn right you will, or I'll bust you to fireman!" Lynch raked his eyes around the rusty, cluttered engine room. "Clean floorplates!" he ordered.

Holman pried one up with a screwdriver. "We'll all get on it, soon as they hoist ashes," he told Lynch.

Krebs took the cue. "Come on, guys, let's hoist out ashes," he said.

All of them but Harris went with Krebs. Harris sat on the rag barrel with a mocking look on his face, bristly with gray whiskers. Lynch blustered some more at Holman. "I'm coming back to inspect!" he warned, when he went up.

Holman stopped scraping the floorplate. He felt uneasy under Harris' sardonic stare.

"Lynch was drunk," he said defensively. "You got to humor a guy when he's like that."

Harris did not answer. No one did any work. Lynch did not come back down. In the afternoon Franks asked Holman what had happened. Holman told him.

"Becky and me got his brandy locked up now," Franks said. "We won't let him get that drunk again." He looked calculatingly at Holman, as if debating how much to say. "We're worried about Lynch," he went on. "Can you keep something under your hat?" Holman nodded. "I took the powder out of his cartridges and put the slugs back in. I wouldn't want Lynch or anybody else to know that," Franks said. "You might need to know it sometime, down below. But don't talk."

Holman nodded again. His eyes went, despite himself, to the pistol Franks was wearing. Franks smiled grimly.

"No blanks in this one!" he said, patting the holster.

In the days that followed, Holman noticed that Bordelles and Welbeck also went constantly armed. When Lynch came to the engine room, Holman always stood forward to take his abuse and prevent an explosion. That action was separating him from the rest of the black gang, but he did not know what else to do.

Harris was becoming leader of the black gang. Two other gangs formed, one based in the cordage locker and one in the ship's office. They became increasingly jealous and suspicious of each other. They spent less time in the compartment and more in their separate hangouts. The black gang stole corned beef and rice and they would cook it in the fireroom, on a shovel of coals from the furnace. They made coffee in a tin bucket, boiling it on coals and putting salt in it. They had all stopped shaving. Their whiskers made their eyes look glary and white and their teeth seemed whiter than before.

Bordelles and the chiefs made a fourth gang. Jennings was part of it. He had begun living in the sickbay and eating with the chiefs. The boat deck gang stayed shaven and in clean uniforms and they made a kind of screen around Lt. Collins.

The beer was gone. Then the onions ran out. A few days later Restorff smelled onions on Crosley's breath. He consulted with Harris, and their two gangs combined to raid the ship's office. Farren and Holman went along. Farren was not going over the edge, any more than Holman, but they both had to live on the main deck and it was safer to go along. The raiders crowded into the ship's office.

"Where you got 'em hid?" Harris shouted. "Where you thieving bastards got 'em hid?"

He was pulling open desk drawers. The men were all milling and screaming and waving arms except Crosley. He sat quietly on one desk. Stawski batted him off it and pulled open the drawer he had been guarding. The drawer was full of onions.

A great shout went up. A free-for-all fight seemed about to start. Then Ellis snatched one of the onions and began eating it like an apple. That turned the stampede in another direction. They all snatched onions and crawnched them, brown, papery skins and all, while tears streamed down their bearded cheeks. No one spoke a word. Each man was trying to eat faster than all the other men. They ate every last onion, and then they did not feel like fighting.

They never talked about Plan Red any more. They had a new story. No one knew who had started it, but they all believed it. With the spring flood the *San Pablo* would go all the way to Shanghai and there she would be scrapped. As a reward for their winter of suffering, the Sand Pebbles would all get a thirty-day leave in Shanghai. Then they would commission one of the sleek, powerful new gunboats being built there. They talked endlessly about the chow and drinks and girls they would have in Shanghai.

They talked almost desperately about the girls they would have. Their hands would curl with pleasure and their bearded lips roll back. Girls were much more important to a crew's health than beer or onions. Girls helped to keep in its cage a certain Beast that was always trying to get loose in a ship.

The Beast was trying to get loose in the *San Pablo*. There were many little signs. The customary skylarking and horseplay began going a bit too far for comfort. Harris began talking openly about the cruiser U.S.S. *Pittsburgh*. The Beast was notoriously loose in the *Pittsburgh*.

"I'd sooner have a sister in a whorehouse than a brother on the *Pittsburgh*," Farren said one day at dinner. That was the saying in the Fleet, about that ship.

"I wish you had a sister on the *San Pablo*," Harris said. "But I'd settle for your brother."

Holman tensed himself to help Farren, if it came to a fight. But Farren let it go.

The next morning when lights came on there was a small square of canvas, with a handful of damp sand heaped upon it, in Harris' place at the mess table. Harris had the watch in the engine room. Everyone saw the sand and canvas and no one spoke about it. It was an old, old seagoing warning.

When Harris came off watch he stood and looked down at the sand and canvas. Everyone else looked at Harris. His beard was spiky gray, like his hair. Hair thrust out of his nostrils and ears. It was like quills. He grinned his wolf-trap grin around the compartment and he was wearing the very face of the Beast.

He did not see what he was looking for in any of the other faces. Without a word, he picked up the sand and canvas and carried it outside and dropped it into the river. After that there was no more talk about the *Pittsburgh.*

Holman did not believe the Shanghai story. He found comfort in a private dream. He could only dream it when he was alone in the engine room on a night watch.

Without being clear about how he had gotten there, he would be mission engineer at China Light. He would work with vaguely-imaged machinery in various buildings. It would have to do with the food and comfort and convenience of everybody. It was always spring or early summer outside the buildings, with trees and green things. He would have to walk from one job to another, under trees and past flower beds. People would be all around and he would stop and talk a few minutes with some of them.

He would live in a Chinese house and not in one room of it, either, but in the whole house. It would have a courtyard with trees and so many flowering bushes that it would be almost a garden. It was a very pleasant place. But it was just there that the dream became muddied and unclear.

He would have a wife. He could not really get her into the dream. She would be something like Mei-yu and something like Maily and something like all the scores of Japanese and Chinese girls he had been with. She would be very pretty and sweet and happy there with him, but he could not quite see her or believe her.

One night in the engine room he faced very frankly the fact that he loved Shirley Eckert. It was not much like what he had sometimes thought it might be. It could be a giving up just as well as a reaching out. He thought carefully over all his memories of her in Hankow and he believed it would be possible for her to love him. But it could not be.

He kept her deliberately on the edge of his dream. He would get books from her and read them and later they would talk about them. They would be friends, but she would still be just a teacher.

39

After a fashion, they kept things going. When the filth and litter in the living spaces became intolerable, someone would say, "God damn it, we got to do something!" Then a few men would work feverishly for several hours, sweeping and scrubbing without soap, profanely superior to the slothful others. But the next time they would be the slothful ones.

It had to be spontaneous. Farren and Holman, as the leading petty officers, were the only ones who could not initiate one of the fitful work spells. The Sand Pebbles seemed to find pleasure in defiling all their old authority symbols. They did it with foul language and contemptuous behavior and a watchful eye for any of their number who did not go along. They seemed to want a chance to rage at someone who would defend authority. Holman and Farren did not give them a chance.

On one midwatch Farren, who had the quarterdeck, deserted his post to come down and drink coffee with Holman in the engine room. Farren talked about conditions. Holman did not know how frank he dared to be.

"If it was one man acting that way, instead of a whole crew, I might figure he was smokestacking," Holman said.

They discussed the idea. The deckforce called it "gundecking." It was a thing kids did. They came off liberty pretending to be drunker than they really were. Down in their living compartments they would flop and stomp and cry and curse the navy and the officers and all the petty officers they didn't like. They could get away with it because they were drunk. After a reasonable time, long enough for the kid to get most of it out of his system, one of the seasoned older men would slap him and tell him to knock it off. The kid would quiet right down.

"They ain't drunk and they ain't kids," Farren objected.

"I mean, some of it's put on."

"No it ain't. They really lost their military fear." Farren slurped coffee. "So've I. I hate to think it, sitting here now. But if Bordelles and the chiefs came down to the main deck to kick us into line, I'm scared I'd go hermentile right along with the rest of 'em."

Holman pondered that. He was afraid to ask questions.

"It's a hellish bad kind of being scared," Farren said. "The guys figure you ain't with 'em. Not that way."

"I hope it never comes to anything like that."

Farren brightened. "I don't think it will," he said. "I think the skipper's got something up his sleeve. He knows what he's doing."

That might be true. The men seldom sneered about Lt. Collins. They saw him very seldom, but when they did they still saluted. They kept the quarterdeck fairly clean. They were not letting go altogether.

"We just got to hang on till high water," Farren said, leaving.

Hell or high water, Holman thought. He wondered whether Farren had been sounding him out, and on which side. It was just that continuing respect for Lt. Collins that made him hope the crew was only smokestacking. On a destroyer the kids waited until they were across the quarterdeck and aft of number four stack before they let themselves go. That was why it was called smokestacking.

Harris was clearly leader of the black gang. He would have them hoist out ashes when they got knee deep, and that was about all. The machinery was foul with rust and dust and grease. The bilges were usu-

ally awash with stinking black water. Lynch came down every day
or so to bluster. Holman let himself be Lynch's target. It was almost
like a game, he thought. Lynch had a grudge at the world and he
was smokestacking it off on Holman, because he knew it was safe.
Then one day that turned out not to be so.

The men were all sitting on or around the workbench. Lynch came
down, bag-eyed and bloat-bellied and fruit-smelling of brandy. He
squinted angrily around the engine room and began, as usual, on
Holman. "God damn you, Holman—" Then he shifted his gaze to
Harris, who was seated between Perna and Stawski on the workbench. "Harris, get that look off your face!" Lynch ordered.

Harris curled his lips back to show two rows of big white false
teeth.

"I'm telling you, Harris!" Lynch's voice rose. "That's silent contempt! I'll run you up for it!"

He turned to face Harris directly. Only a commissioned officer
could run a man up for silent contempt. Harris continued to look at
Lynch with silent contempt. Lynch snapped his own teeth.

"All right, by God, we'll clean bilges!" he said. "Harris, get in
the bilges. Right now!"

Holman saw it coming. "I'll pump the water out first," he said.
"Come over to the bilge pump, Chief. I want to check with you about
the valve action." He wanted to draw Lynch off.

"Go start the pump. I'll be right over," Lynch said.

Holman went around to the pump. Through the engine he saw
Lynch still facing Harris, shoulders hunched and head thrust forward like a bull.

"Harris, I give you a military order," he said. "Now jump, damn
you!"

"Prong you and all your relations, Shitevitski," Harris said. "All
the way back to Peter the Great."

"What? What?" Lynch's voice was like a bird squawk. "This is
mutiny!" he squawked, slapping his pistol. "We been waiting for
this!"

"Get out of here, you drunk fool. Don't come back," Harris said.

"By the sweet loving Jesus, I'll kill you for that!" Lynch screamed.

He drew his pistol. The men scattered off the workbench. "Stop that!" Holman yelled, racing around the engine. Lynch's pistol went *pop*. He cursed and worked the slide by hand and it went *pop* again. Harris was coming with an axe and a face like hell with gray whiskers. Holman grabbed the pistol from Lynch and started him moving. Lynch ran, Holman after him. Holman felt the wind of the axe on the back of his neck.

Lynch ran all the way into the CPO quarters. "It's come, Becky! Warn the captain!" he yelled.

Welbeck aimed a pistol at Holman. Holman stopped in the doorway. Lynch was fumbling in the CPO arms locker.

"Stand fast, Holman! Drop that gun!" Welbeck snapped.

Holman dropped it and half raised his hands. "Don't let Lynch get a gun that'll shoot, Welbeck," he said urgently. "He's gone crazy!"

"Blast him down, Becky!" Lynch yelled. "Drop grenades down the skylight!"

He was loading a riot gun. Franks pushed past Holman and over to Lynch. "Let me have it, Lynch-boy," he said. He turned, holding the riot gun at waist level. "Now tell me what's the score, Jake," he said suspiciously.

Holman told Franks all he knew about it. He stepped inside. Somehow Bordelles had gotten in there too, with a drawn pistol. They were all on a wire edge.

"Who had a weapon, besides Harris?" Bordelles asked.

"Only him I saw. It was all too fast to see much."

"Where are they now?"

Holman shrugged. "Still down there." He lowered his voice. "Lynch better not go back down."

Their eyes turned to Lynch. He was seated at the table, his face in his hands, and trembling so hard he shook the whole table.

"Becky and me been seeing it coming," Franks whispered. "We'll lock him in the pilot's room."

The pilot's room was a cubbyhole next to the CPO head. They kept no pilot aboard, in port. Welbeck helped Lynch drink some brandy without spilling it and then led him around there.

"You going to report this to the skipper, Mr. Bordelles?" Franks asked.

"No." Bordelles' lips were pinched together.

They talked it over with Holman present, as if they took it for granted that he was now one of the boat deck gang. He gathered that the captain did not want to know officially about things like that. He saw clearly how they were being a screen around Lt. Collins. As long as Lt. Collins did not have to lay his authority on the line, he would still have it. As long as he was untouched, none of what happened would have to go down officially on paper. When the ship reached Hankow the crew would be all right again and everybody would forget everything.

"Three weeks, about, till she floods," Franks said. He shook crossed fingers. "How about you, Jake? You going to be safe now, on the main deck?"

"Better move into the sickbay, with Doc," Welbeck urged.

"I better stay on the main deck, like nothing happened," Holman said. "That way I can still keep an eye on the machinery."

Holman knew they had him singled out after the Lynch episode. Hardly anyone talked to him. They lowered their voices and turned away when he came near. It was unpleasant. When the chance came to spend a day as armed guard on an oil company tug, Holman was glad to go.

The day was warm but Holman wore blues, to save washing a white uniform. When the tug came alongside, he was delighted to see Scharf in the tiny pilot house. They headed upriver, to Siangtan. Scharf looked fit in fresh khaki and as happy as was possible for his long, mournful face. His pale blue eyes twinkled as he greeted Holman. Except for the old Chinese quartermaster at the wheel, they were alone in the pilot house.

"I thought you was long gone out of Changsha," Holman said.

"None of the Germans or their families have gone from Changsha. Nor from Hankow," Scharf said. "There is no reason."

They had not suffered any hostility, he said. Having no unequal treaty rights, they could only be in China with Chinese consent. They were accountable to Chinese law for what they did and they could be sent home if the Chinese found them undesirable. The Germans in China would benefit from a strong, stable Chinese government. With mildly vindictive relish, Scharf recalled how America had pressed China to join the Allies and strip Germany of treaty rights.

"You did us a favor," Scharf said. "Now you need someone to do you the same favor."

Scharf was in a merry mood, for him. He had been hired to be resident agent for several British and American companies, after the treaty people left in April. Everything would be in godowns under consular seal, but they wanted a token white man to keep custody.

"I am to stand before those sealed godowns like Arnold von Winkelried and gather the bayonets into my breast," Scharf said, with a wide gesture. "Ach, yes. So nobly will I die for liberty."

Holman noticed with a slight shock how clean and green and new with spring the country was, along the river banks. The water swirled clear above white sand and scoured boulders. On the *San Pablo* they only had eyes for their own dirt and misery. Holman took the green countryside into his eyes. The day began feeling like a picnic.

Scharf told him about Changsha. The worker-peasants had full control. The gearwheel officials in the city were only figureheads. Victor Shu had bribed his way out of prison and into some minor post with the worker-peasants, Scharf said.

"That Shu. He is a smart one."

At Siangtan Scharf was busy getting the barge loaded and secured alongside. They were taking tinned kerosene down to be sealed in the main godown at Changsha. Holman left his rifle in the pilot house and strolled along the river bank. He dug his feet into the dirt. He plucked a spear of new grass and looked at it. He ate it. It tasted pleasantly green. He ate quite a bit of grass. Scharf called him back to the tug.

A tiffin for two was spread in the small cabin. It was only pork fried rice with slightly cooked green onions cut up in it, but it tasted very good to Holman. He ate slowly with his chopsticks, to make it last.

"This is good, George," he said. "I don't know how to tell you."

"The cook was afraid he would be punished for breaking the boycott if he made food for you."

"Jesus! I hope not!"

"I told him you were really a German spying on the Americans," Scharf said. "I swore it to him on the German flag."

Holman laughed. "Okay, George. I owe you one military secret," he said. "What'll it be?"

Scharf pulled at his nose. "I will ask you when our nations are at war again," he said, eyes twinkling. "We Germans are methodical. We prepare long in advance."

"Damned if I can see you in a spiked helmet, George. You think we'll ever have another war?"

Scharf shrugged. "I think I am becoming Chinese at last," he said. He clicked his chopsticks expertly above his bowl. "Look, how my hand has become Chinese. My stomach is Chinese."

"They say you renew your body every seven years," Holman said. "Hell, I'm all Chinese by now. I never thought of that."

"We do not renew our hearts," Scharf said sadly. "The Chinese will permit one to become Chinese. They think it perfectly natural. The barrier is in our own hearts."

The joking mood was broken. They finished the meal in silence.

The Siangtan coolies rode down to Changsha atop the loaded barge. They wore company armbands. The Changsha coolies were on strike, Scharf said, and the Siangtan coolies had been promised military protection. He did not expect any trouble.

"But you must prance and look martial, Jake," he said. "You are their paper tiger, to frighten away devils."

The thought struck sharply into Holman's vague feeling that it was all a game. It was all a vast make-believe that had been going on so long people thought it was real, in the way machinery was real. They were trapped in it and they did not know it. They did not know they could refuse to play. They did not know they could change the rules without making the real world come to an end. He tried to tell Scharf what he thought.

"We are guardian symbols," Scharf said. "You and me and the consul's seal on my godowns."

"We're a couple of scarecrows!"

"Ach, yes! *Vogelscheuchen!*"

Scharf chuckled and pulled his long nose. It was a trick he had, when he was joking. The sky was a washed blue. The air was clean and fresh-smelling and the land was green along both banks. It felt to Holman like a holiday. He told Scharf that.

"Everyone knows something is wrong on your ship," Scharf said. "If we do not talk about it, then it is not so. *Nicht wahr?*"

"I'm on the inside and I got to know it," Holman said. "I want to ask you about something, George. You're educated." He wanted to know if it could be the effect of the constant watchers and the frequent hate parades on the bund. "Like with so many people hating them, they got thinking they might really be pretty hateful," he explained. "Someone was forced to start *being* hateful."

"Do you feel hateful?"

"No." Holman was surprised. "I never felt like they was aiming any of it right at me," he said.

"Then they can't hurt you." Scharf smiled. "The Chinese have a legend of a prince who was so beautiful the people stared him to death," he said. "It is a fascinating thought. But I think the people ashore are only practicing being national. They are learning to love each other by hating you. They had a better way in the olden time of China."

Holman leaned out across the rail, breathing in the air. "After that chow you give me, I can't hate anybody," he said. "Them green onions in it." He rocked on his heels, breathing in the fresh air. "Something else I felt, in Hankow."

He told Scharf about the strange, sad, left-out feeling he sometimes had, walking the streets. Scharf's manner changed. He looked concerned.

"I withdraw what I said, that they cannot hurt you," he told Holman. "What you feel is the revolutionary love the people bear each other. For those able to feel it, it can be dangerously seductive." He was clearly not joking. "It is their revolution, not yours. They are making it against you," he said. "You will have to give up your treaties and pull your gunboats back to your other colonies."

"Hell, I know that. I don't care."

"I say this for your protection!"

Scharf was very serious. He explained what he meant by revolutionary love. People together in a revolution felt that they were all friends. They turned that face to each other. When they knew someone well enough personally, they might find out that he was not a friend. While the revolutionary spirit lasted, each person had a small circle toward whom he was hostile or indifferent, and everyone else was his friend. Of course it could not last long.

"But it is dangerously seductive while it does last," Scharf warned. "Remember that it is not your revolution."

"All that stuff. Well, it's just weird," Holman said. "The hate parades. What's happened to the guys. It's just *weird!*" He struck the rail.

"Tomorrow is International Women's Day," Scharf said. "You must be prepared for something very weird tomorrow."

He would not say what it was. He was back in his joking mood. "You must wait and see," he said. They were just passing a farmers' market on the right-hand bank, a few miles upriver from Changsha. Farmers' sampans clustered at the foot of the stone steps that led down to the river. People were all around. Up on the bank were booths of matting and baskets overflowing with green stuff.

"Jesus! Look at all that good fresh chow over there!" Holman said. "What do you eat on the ship?"

"Beans and rice and corned beef. Say—" Holman looked from the market back to Scharf. "You suppose that might be what's broke 'em down? No vitamins and stuff like that?"

Scharf didn't think so. "I think you may all have scurvy of the spirit," he said. He would not be serious about it.

It was after dark when Scharf came alongside to put Holman aboard the *San Pablo*. The web of stays and braces around the dogleg stack made a tracery against the night sky. The men were all aft on the fantail, probably watching a fight. Holman went in and undressed to go to bed, because he was going to have the midwatch.

The men trooped in. Crosley had blood on his bearded cheek. Only Farren took any notice of Holman. He came over and sat on Holman's bunk. Holman told him about Scharf and the Changsha Germans.

"They can afford to be neutral," Farren said. "What the hell they got to lose by it?"

"What the hell have you and me got? That we ain't lost already?"

"That ain't for us to ask. We're under orders."

The fight had been between Crosley and Red Dog, Farren said. Crosley had fought like a devil. Red Dog had taken a terrible beating before he went down to stay.

"Where's Red Dog now?"

"Sitting back there on the grating. He won't let anybody talk to him or touch him."

Farren left and Holman stretched out to try to sleep. Footsteps sounded on deck outside the door.

"Arf! Arf!" Red Dog said through the door. "Come out, Crosley! The Red Dog is ready!"

Crosley cursed and jumped up and charged for the door. About half of the men went back to the fantail to watch it. After a while they came back in. Crosley was dabbing at his face with a dirty undershirt.

Holman dozed. The compartment smelled foul with dirty clothes and unwashed feet. The men talked in low voices. Some were going to bed. The footsteps came again, draggingly.

"Arf! Arf! The Red Dog is ready!"

"Crosley's always ready!" Crosley yelled, jumping up. "This time you get the works, God damn you!"

Only a few men went back with Crosley. Farren turned out the lights. The men came back and went to bed, except for Bronson and Crosley. They sat at the starboard mess table talking in voices too low for Holman to hear. He could not go all the way to sleep, for thinking about Red Dog. Holman knew he dared not interfere. He listened for footsteps and did not hear any.

"Arf! Arf!" came weakly through the door. "The Red Dog is ready."

"*This* time I'll kill the son of a bitch!" Crosley whispered fiercely.

Only he and Bronson went back. When they returned, they went to bed. Holman slept fitfully until Perna called him at midnight. He dressed and went to the washroom and splashed water on his face and then he went on through to the fantail. He saw Red Dog still lying there. Sudden, sick anger welled in Holman. Red Dog's wrist was warm and his pulse was beating. Holman went up and tried the door to the sickbay. It was locked. He rapped on it.

"Who is it?" Jennings asked.

"Holman. Red Dog's beat up. You got to take care of him."

"In the morning."

"Now, Doc. I'll kick your door down."

Jennings came out. Red Dog tried to fight them off. When they got him to the sickbay, into the light, his head was like a bloody pumpkin. He could not see at all. He could just balance himself on a chair.

"Oh my!" Jennings kept saying. "Oh my!"

He drew a basin of warm water and began laying out gauze and cotton.

"Okay, Doc. I got to go on watch," Holman said.

As had become his custom on night watches, he began thinking about China Light. It took him away from the chill, nasty feeling of the ship, as the armed guard duty had taken him away from the sight and sound of it. He paced the floorplates, without seeing the rusting machinery all around him, and pondered his talk with Scharf in terms of China Light.

China Light was a collection of people. They grew stuff and made stuff and they ate it and they used it. They grew up and got married and had children and became old and died and they were buried at China Light. It was not as make-believe a thing as a ship. The rules of the game at China Light had been American, but now they were Chinese. And the Chinese were having a revolution. In a revolution they threw out all the rules. As Scharf said, they would soon make new ones. But for a little while everything could be real.

The thought excited Holman. He stopped on the threshold of it and went out and coaled the fire. He came back and swabbed pump rods, hearing the splutter and sniffing the sharp fumes of hot grease. He dipped wicks in the oil box of the throbbing, purring, sparking dynamo. Things between people could be real the way machinery was real, he kept thinking. He was afraid of where that thought would lead him.

He followed it anyway. At China Light there were not now any rules to sort people out and make them be separate. People had their labels torn off. What they brought to a meeting with each other was just what they had inside their skins. At China Light there were no game rules to stop him and Shirley Eckert from loving each other and being married, if they wanted each other that way inside their own skins.

That was where the thought led. It shook him deeply. It threw a new light on his Hankow memories. She did want him that way, he realized. She had known, as he had not. At their last meeting, when she had hinted that he might desert and come to China Light with them, she was giving him the big, one, only chance of his whole life. He had lacked courage to take it.

Not courage, he thought. I was still trapped in the game. They kill you if you won't play, and dying is still real. Well, maybe courage after all.

Well, it was not too late, he thought. He had been drawing his pay in Hankow bills and he had a wad of them in his locker. He could just stuff them in his pocket and get ashore and go, across the hills.

He was pacing excitedly. All right, when? Before the flood, before we sail for Hankow, he thought. A week or two yet. First chance I have to get ashore, I'll keep going. I'll walk fifty miles a day till I get there.

He was conscious of the sleeping ship above his head. To hell with them and their make-believe and their smokestacking, he thought. I know what's real. For the rest of his watch he paced the floorplates in a joyful storm of excitement, as if he were already striding down the miles between himself and China Light.

40

It rained heavily during the night and in the morning it was misty and warm. Only one or two men were on deck to watch the hate parade. It came into sight with gongs and bugles and massed flags from between a yellow brick building and a tin godown, the usual route.

What was different was that all the marchers were female. Grandmothers pegged along on bound feet. Little girls came clutching paper flags. Many of the women and girls had babies slung on their backs. Fresh young girl activists in green almost danced along. They carried the placards. Whole sized-off classes of schoolgirls came marching by. They wore neat blue skirts and jumpers and white shirtwaists and they sang shrilly as they marched. They all went eyes left as they passed the *San Pablo*. They spat and screamed and shook their fists and their placards.

TO HELL WITH CHRIST AND COOLIDGE! one sign read. The girl kept twirling it above her head. The other side read: HANG GEORGE FIVE! Many of the signs mentioned women: FREE ALL WOMEN! HUMAN RIGHTS FOR WIVES!

There was something uncanny about so many women streaming

by, and the clamor of female voices. It was hypnotic. To Holman they were beginning all to have the same face. It was screaming hatred at the *San Pablo.*

In a group approaching he saw with sudden shock that some were naked. His flesh surged powerfully. Twenty, thirty shapely girls in the little beehive bonnets, with red lips and bobbed black hair. Most had something about their hips, but five or six walked bare as daylight between their little bonnets and their blue cloth slippers. They came stepping gingerly in pairs, as if they were trying not to sway their hips.

Their hips swayed anyway. The ship exploded.

The Sand Pebbles boiled out on deck, shock-haired, scrag-bearded, stinking and ragged in dungarees. They manned the rail and pranced and pawed and set up a gobbling howl.

Goddlemightychrist! Look! Look! they roared. *Them shafts! Them knockers! Them round little bellies!*

The women shook their placards and screamed. The Sand Pebbles outroared them. They clutched and struck each other's shoulders. They danced and pranced and snorted and pawed with their feet. They shouted hoarsely and all at once and so fast that it was not words at all. It was a great, collective animal howl of pain.

Holman stood fast. His flesh strained blindly toward that sway-curving grace unbearably multiple in rose and ivory and shadow. Time froze.

Right opposite two women held a ribbon placard. Red letters on white cried out: FREE OF CHRISTIAN SHAME! STRIKE DOWN CHRISTIAN POWER!

Harris howled like a wolf. "Me for you, Sugarboxes! I ain't no Christian!" He put one leg over the bulwark. Someone pulled him back.

Holman saw their faces. Smooth, fresh, pretty girl faces, contorted with hatred, eyes squinted almost closed. Faces terrible with pain and loathing of what they did. One face. A mask of a face. He looked directly into it.

An uprush of deep something carried away his lust. It was disgust and anger and shame and sorrow. *I wish they didn't have to do a thing like that,* he said aloud, unheard in the roaring all around him.

They were moving on. Holman felt deeply shaken. He felt that he had escaped some unnameable danger. The proud, angry naked bodies were dwindling with distance up the bund. The Sand Pebbles stampeded up to the bridge to fight over the long glass and binoculars.

The Sand Pebbles could not get over it. At dinner they gabbled like geese. They described what they had seen to each other, jointly recreating it in the air above the mess tables.

"They was trying to walk just from the knees down."

"They didn't want to bounce their knockers."

"One there, I caught her eye. She shook it right at me."

"It was me she shook it at!"

They could not understand it, but they hoped the women would do it again. They marveled why the women had done it.

"Spiting the missionaries, you suppose?"

"Spiting us, cause we can't have any."

"We get to Shanghai, we'll have us some."

"How about that look on their faces?" Holman asked Farren. "They could hardly stand what they were doing."

"I could stand it all day," Farren said. "I didn't waste time looking at their faces."

Holman saw the faces along the mess table. He saw whiskers and scaly necks and grimed hands and black fingernails. He saw the glitter in all the eyes. He stood up and went outside.

Scurvy of the spirit, he thought. Scharf was not joking. Scars and chancres and obscene tattoos on the spirit! Whatever the spirit might be. He walked around the ship. Wherever he went, he saw all the dirt and smelled all the stink.

His eyes fled away from the ship. The sand on the island was a tawny white. The river, brownish from the rain, was creeping up the sand. Trees and willows were budding out over there, in grayish-yellow and green. They had yellow-green misty shapes and birds dipped above them. Far beyond them, beyond the blue line of hills, a few hundred miles as a bird might fly, was China Light.

Under his feet the teak was gray and stained. At his elbow grimy white paint scaled and cracked. Above his head ripped and sooty awnings sagged. He went back inside, to his locker, and stuffed his wad of bills into his dungarees pocket. He took only about a dozen of the silver Mex dollars. They were still gesturing and gabbling at the mess tables.

On deck again, he tried to think of an excuse to get ashore. He could not just hail a sampan. They were boycotting the ship too. And Bronson, who had the quarterdeck watch, would be nosy about it.

Half an hour later, like the answer to a prayer, the *Woodcock* motor sampan came alongside. Holman went to the quarterdeck. Banger Knox, clean and pink in a faded boiler suit, came aboard. He had a round British canteen slung over his shoulder.

"Hi, Banger!" Holman said warmly.

"Hello, Jake." Banger seemed ill at ease. "I've come to barter, if you've a three-inch valve to spare," he said. "By some wild chance."

"Got a three-inch gate, undrilled flanges, in the storeroom," Holman said. "You're welcome to it."

They had to cross the engine room gratings to reach the storeroom. Banger did not look down through the gratings, but he could not escape the stink of foul bilges that rose up. He measured the flanges and the valve was just right.

"Well, now. This is what I brought to barter," he said. He sloshed the canteen. "Rum. A quart of His Majesty's finest."

"I'll settle for a ride in your motor pan," Holman said. "You put me ashore over behind the island, and we're square."

Banger agreed, with a quizzical look. Holman told Bronson he was going to the *Woodcock* to borrow some packing. One of Banger's stokers was running the boat. Banger told him to go around the island into the back channel.

"Anywhere over there," Holman said, when they rounded the island. "I'll wade ashore."

"Jake, I'm fair curious," Banger said. "Tell me it's no business of mine, if you like."

"I'm going to run away, Banger. Desert."

"Hold up!" Banger jerked erect. "Back all engines!" The stoker cut the motor and they were drifting. "You don't mean that," Banger said.

"I do mean it. I got a place to run to."

"Jake, you're daft! I'll not be a party to it!" Banger's face was turning red.

"You don't have to give a damn about the rules in my navy."

"I give a damn about you. Friendship cuts across rules."

"Not in my navy."

Banger shook his head. He told the stoker to run the boat in among the willows on the island. It smelled cool and green and barky in there. They could not see Changsha or any of the gunboats. Banger sent his stoker up the bank out of earshot. He unslung the canteen.

"Best have a nip, a big one," he said. "Then tell me about it."

Holman tried, and he could not tell about it. Banger's plain common sense made all of Holman's ideas sound silly. They passed the canteen back and forth. The rum was aromatic and fiery. Holman knew Banger was defeating him. He began attacking the British sailor.

"What could your lousy gunboat do against forty million Hunanese, now or ever?" he asked. "You're a scarecrow and they know it. Stick around long enough and they'll make you know it."

Banger raised an eyebrow. They were both feeling the rum.

"You're a paper tiger to scare devils, and the devils are wise to you," Holman pursued his attack. "It's all paper. All make-believe. Set ways of doing things. Treaties. Regulations. Uniforms. Flags. Drills. Guards of honor. Salutes. Visits to warlords. The whole damned business of show-the-flag. All paper, and now the Chinese are tearing up the paper. Banger, you're a paper man!"

"Now just you wait a bit! Wait a bit, there!" Banger waved a finger. "I don't believe I'm a paper man!"

"You are! You ain't real! The Chinese don't believe in you any more. So how the hell can you go on believing in yourself?"

"*I* believe in me!"

Banger was red-faced and very upset. He slapped his knee and squeezed it.

"How can you prove it? How can you prove you're real, even to yourself?"

"I just know it." Banger was regaining his temper. "Is that what's wrong on your ship, thinking and saying things like that?"

"No. Just acting 'em out, I think. But it's why I want to run away, Banger. So I can know I'm real. You savvy now?"

"Can't you bloody Yanks believe in yourselves, by yourselves?" Banger was as dead set as ever against helping Holman to desert. "Find some other way to prove you're real, if you need proof," he said.

They finished the rum, talking about that. Holman thought about the farmers' market on the riverbank above the city. He proposed they go there and buy baskets of food to take back to their ships. The boycott was only against paper men, scarecrows in uniform, he insisted. He did not believe the Chinese hated real men.

"We'll leave our hats. We'll be in dungarees, without insignia," he explained. "We'll just be two-legged hungry men with money in our pockets. And see what happens." He slapped Banger on the shoulder. They were both pretty drunk. "What do you say?"

"I say let's have a go at it!"

They went up the back channel. It was quite wide. The river was clearly rising. Banger unshipped the motor pan's flag and they hid it under a thwart, with their hats. They landed at the stone steps and Banger told the stoker to lie off and wait for them.

They went boldly up the stone steps. The Chinese thronging the lanes of booths looked at them curiously. Holman felt drunkenly reckless. In beggar sign language he patted his stomach and darted his fingers at his gaping mouth. "No mama, no papa, no chow chow," he kept saying. Banger, beside him, grinned and clinked silver Mex dollars from hand to hand. An invisible balance seemed to tip. Suddenly the Chinese were all laughing and nodding and pointing. It was all right.

They could buy anything they wanted. The market was like a little town of bamboo and rush-mat booths loaded with fresh food. Ducks quacked in wicker cages, fish flopped in wooden tubs, young pigs squealed in tight bamboo baskets. Holman bought green onions and husked them with his thumbnails and ate them several at a time. He felt enormously happy.

All the faces smiled back at him, enjoying his enjoyment. They were men and women, young and old, faces out of green fields, under conical bamboo hats, above ragged blue cotton clothing. They were telling him that he was not paper. He bought a basket of eggs from a farmer's daughter. She had a chubby, fresh young face and she smiled shyly and dropped her eyes. She was telling him that what the women had been saying that morning on the bund did not apply to Jake Holman. He loved her for it.

Banger was feeling it too. He was eating green onions and grinning all the way across his broad, honest face. They went from stall to stall, filling their baskets. Holman bought pork strips and four live chickens. It was so simple, he kept thinking. All you had to do was do it. When their baskets were filled and it was time to leave, he could not face going back to that ship. He wanted to start right off for China Light. He lagged behind, wondering how to tell Banger. Banger set down his baskets and looked back and called to Holman.

"Jake! Come have a look here!" His voice was angry.

Holman came and looked. It was a black pig lying on his back on a wheelbarrow deck. He was strangely quiet, except for feebly waving legs. Then Holman saw the cords threaded through the pig's eyelids and tied each way to the barrow deck like guy wires.

"Jesus!" Holman set down his baskets.

The pig was smart enough to know that if he moved he would tear off his eyelids. He did not move. His little red eyes hunted back and forth, back and forth.

"Lord love me, Jake, it ain't right!"

"Let it go. It's how they do it here," Holman said.

Banger took out his jackknife and opened it.

"No, Banger! *Don't!*" Holman cried.

Before Holman could stop him, Banger slashed the cords. Squealing, in one long, fluid motion, the pig was off the barrow and gone like a loosed tornado. He tumbled people and knocked over booths. Men ran and shouted. The mood changed instantly. A line of men formed and moved slowly toward the two sailors. Holman felt sick with regret. He had seen faces like that before, one night in a Hankow street.

"My fault. I'll hold them for a bit," Banger said tensely. "Run for the boat, Jake."

"No. We're together."

They came slowly, like a moving wall. Victor Shu was in the center. He wore farmer's clothes and he was thinner, but he still had a belly.

"*Run,* Jake!"

Holman shook his head. Banger stepped forward, solid and unafraid. He sank his left to the wrist in Shu's belly and slammed a right to the jaw with a sound like a maul on teakwood. Shu dropped. The wall stopped moving.

"*Now* run for it!"

Banger dragged Holman along. Holman's legs unlocked and he ran. They just made it clear in the motor sampan. Stones splashed water around them and the stone steps were crowded with people shrieking curses.

When they were safe out in mid-channel, Banger sadly shipped his flag again and they put on their hats. All the glow of the rum was gone. Holman felt sickly sober. They chugged downriver in silence.

"You meant to go right on, to leave from there, didn't you?" Banger said finally.

Holman nodded.

"I know what you mean now. You're right about it," Banger said slowly. "But it's still no good, what you've a mind to do."

"Yeah."

"That was a stupid thing I did," Banger said. "It was a bloody, stupid, paper thing to do. I spoiled it all proper, didn't I?"

"It's all right, Banger," Holman said. "We got what went before. We know we ain't paper."

They did not talk any more on the way back to the *San Pablo.*

Holman was remembering the farm girl in the market, and how she had smiled at him. He had left his baskets of food behind, but he had brought away that memory. He began feeling that the memory was a better thing to bring away than six baskets of food. Food you ate once and it was gone. Memories you could keep.

41

Holman said nothing about his adventure. He still meant to desert. The resolution made it easier to bear the nasty feeling in the ship.

That was worse than ever. The men had a new, edgy restlessness. They would flop down and shift positions and get back up again. They prowled the main deck. They talked incessantly about the parade of naked women and prayed obscenely for another.

They talked about other things also. News and rumors came aboard. The gearwheel was nearing Shanghai and the big showdown. The U.S. Marines were in Shanghai, still aboard the transport *Chaumont*. Missionary influence kept them from coming ashore. The three new cruisers ordered to China were being held at Pearl Harbor by missionary influence. Once things such as that would have sent the Sand Pebbles into a fury of cursing, Holman thought. Now they did not care.

They did not want to fight. They just wanted to get safely down to Shanghai. They talked most about the scare rumors. A Chinese secret society was supposed to be offering a thousand dollars for every white man's head delivered to them. The gearwheel was supposed to be mounting ten-inch guns at the Chenglin narrows, which the *San*

Pablo would have to pass to get to Hankow. Offsetting those rumors was the slow, steady rise of the river, brownish from early rains. The flood was not far off. The *San Pablo* did not draw as much water as the *Duarte,* and she could probably get out before the full flood stage.

"Why the hell we got to wait for them Die Hards, anyway?" Ellis asked. "Let's shag ass out of here soon as there's water enough for just us."

"Every ship for itself!" Crosley agreed.

The long winter siege was almost over. They could hardly wait the last few days. In their talk, they were practically ashore in Shanghai already.

They all manned the rail for the hate parades. They were afraid they might miss something good. Several days after the market incident the San Pebbles were all on deck and a batch of new signs showed up on the bund.

EQUAL JUSTICE FOR ALL! one said. Behind came two more: MURDERER KNOX TO PEOPLE'S JUSTICE! and GIVE UP MURDERER HOLMAN!

It struck them dumb, at first. It struck Holman dumbest of them all. He knew what it had to be. He felt all their eyes on him. They gathered around him in silence, staring accusingly.

"How come, Jake? What about it?" Farren asked.

Holman told them the bare outline. He said he had been trying to get fresh food for the ship and he had gotten it, before the trouble over the pig came up. All their faces remained hostile.

"Maybe Shu died," Holman finished. "That's all I can figure."

"If it was Banger hit him, then you're clear," Farren said.

"Oh no he ain't!" Perna yelled. "He's still some kind of excessery!"

"We want the ship clear, you stupid wop!" Harris told Perna.

"Well, then, I guess he's clear," Perna said grudgingly.

Lt. Collins and Bordelles had both been called to the consulate. The men assumed it was about the pig fight, as they at once began calling it. They argued furiously about it, as if Holman were not present. They were afraid it would interfere somehow with the ship's getting down to Shanghai. They would not stand for that.

The full, terrible meaning of it begin to hit Holman. He could not desert now. He would have to go with the ship, down to Shanghai or wherever. It tore him inside to think that. He could not accept it. He went down into the stink of the engine room to get away from the hateful sound of their voices.

He heard Lt. Collins announced on the quarterdeck. Shortly after, Franks called down the skylight.

"Yeah! What do you want?" Holman yelled back.

"Lay up here, on the double!"

Holman went up. "Skipper wants to see you," Franks said curtly. He took Holman into the cabin. Lt. Collins and Bordelles were seated at the green table with papers in front of them. Holman stood at attention. Franks stood to one side. It was like being at mast. All their faces were stern and angry.

"Holman, did you and a British sailor go ashore at that market upriver a few days ago?" Lt. Collins asked.

"Yes, sir."

"Tell me about it."

Holman told him the bare facts. He made it clear that going there was his own idea and not Banger's. They seemed to want him to say more.

"Victor Shu was a gangster and squeeze merchant, the same like they been killing themselves," he said. "Why can't they just call it good riddance?"

Lt. Collins' lip curled. "Shu is not dead. He is their witness to identify you," he said. "They have invented a farmer whom you killed."

"We didn't hurt any farmers!"

"Tomorrow they will hold a funeral procession for the murdered farmer," Lt. Collins went on. "They are inflaming the people and making this into a major incident. They are demanding that you and Knox be turned over to their People's Court."

Holman stood there. He felt sick with dismay.

"Of course they have no jurisdiction over any American. That is the so-called grievance they are trying to dramatize, with this new lie."

Lt. Collins' contemptuous anger seemed to include both Holman and the worker-peasants. "You need not worry, of course. We won't give you over to them," Lt. Collins said. "Even the Japanese agree on that. If we have to fight our way out of Changsha, it will be as an allied flotilla."

"I don't . . . will it come to a fight, sir?"

"Rather than give you and Knox over, we will die to the last man!"

His voice rang. It was all too fast for Holman to take in. He did not know how to say what he felt.

"I don't want anybody to die to the last man on my account," he said. "I don't think Banger would, either."

"Neither of you is worth it personally," Lt. Collins agreed, with clear distaste. "Not even to the Chinese. You are only worth it as symbols of your countries."

Scarecrows! Holman wanted to shout. He knew his face was red. He clamped his teeth and kept silent. Bordelles took over the talk.

"This has to be reported to Comyang," he said. "Tell me your story again, in detail."

Holman told it. Bordelles made notes. Holman did not know how detailed to be. He told about the Chinese girl smiling at him.

"Was it the demonstration that morning that made you go there?" Bordelles asked. "Were you looking for a woman?"

"I don't think in the way you mean, sir."

"It's a plausible motive. I want your motive. *Why* did you go there?"

Holman knew he could not explain that. It struck him suddenly that a man *could* feel real for a few minutes on top of a woman. That was probably why American sailors in China seemed to need women so much more than the other foreign sailors did. He was tempted to tell Bordelles that he was looking for *duhai* after all and let it go at that. But instead he made up a theory about lack of vitamins affecting the crew's mind. He stressed that he had bought eggs and onions and would have gotten them back to the ship, except for the trouble about the pig.

All their lips tightened when he mentioned the pig.

"Has your own mind been feeling strange?" Bordelles asked.

"Just how everybody's been feeling, sir. Banger and me got to talking about it."

Bordelles pursued with questions. He pinned Holman down. He wanted word-for-word all Holman and Banger had said to each other. In the end, he pried quite a bit of it out of Holman. Lt. Collins listened closely.

"After Hankow fell, it seemed like all the water ran out from under our keels," Holman said. "I told Banger the *Woodcock* was a paper ship with a paper flag and we were both scarecrows in uniform. So we went to the market to prove we wasn't paper."

"Stop that talk!" Lt. Collins slapped the table. "Our flag is *not* paper, as long as we keep our own faith in it!" His eyes glowed and his voice turned low and bitter. "Let the Chinese sneer at our flag. They'll find out it's a sleeping tiger, not a paper one. They feared it once and they'll fear it again." His voice became a hoarse whisper. "Only *we* can make our flag a paper tiger. And if we do, we do not deserve to live!"

He was pale and trembling. He frightened them all. Bordelles stood up and motioned Franks to take Holman out of there.

"Wait." Lt. Collins held up his hand. He was struggling to control himself. "Holman, God alone knows what consequences your insane action is going to have. It has already seriously embarrassed the United States Government," he said coldly. "In my report to Comyang I am going to recommend you for a general court-martial. That is all."

His eyes were like gun muzzles and his lips were two white lines. Franks pulled Holman outside. Franks seemed more hurt than angry.

"You knew the ship was hanging by a thread. We thought you was one guy we could count on," he told Holman. "Jake, why the *hell* did you have to go do that?"

"I don't know. I can't explain," Holman said miserably.

Franks looked at Holman, shaking his head. His manner was changing. He drew away slightly.

"Well, you're a GCM prisoner now. I suppose you're willing to be prisoner-at-large?"

"Yeah. Where the hell would I run to now?"

Franks had the special manner that sailors always put on when they were around a general court-martial prisoner. It was something like being in the presence of the dead.

All next day the ship had the same tense feeling as during the opium crisis in Hankow. Lt. Collins and Bordelles were ashore again. Farren and Ellis and Vincent took a ship's boat downriver to take soundings across the shoal stretch north of the city. The river was still damping and nibbling slowly higher on the sand flats. The hate parade that morning stopped for a full hour opposite the *San Pablo*. They had a dozen signs about the murderers Knox and Holman. They had a Chinese coffin and a band of mourners shrieking and flinging around in white robes. They made quite a show of it.

The men all kept apart from Holman. Not even Duckbutt Randall would talk to him. But they watched him obliquely and talked about him and sometimes meant him to overhear. What seemed to throw them was the pig. He heard many bitter remarks about somebody being sorry for a pig.

"A pig, God damn it! But who the hell's sorry for us?"

After dinner Welbeck came aboard with more disturbing news. The Hunan Commissioner of Foreign Affairs had declared the treaties null and void in Hunan Province. The worker-peasants were saying no gunboat could leave Changsha until the murderers were given up. It set off a storm of talk. The Sand Pebbles glared and gestured and grimaced through their beards.

"They can't do that, on the treaty. We got to agree."

"So do they got to agree. What do we do if they don't?"

"Get the hell down to Shanghai, that's what!"

"Yeah, Shanghai! Let 'em have this stinking place!"

"But they won't let us go."

"How can they stop us? We'll just go."

"How about them ten-inchers at Chenglin?"

"Jesus, yes! They'd stop a cruiser!"

They talked about the rumored ten-inch guns at Chenglin and still older rumors about an electric minefield at that place. They recalled the old story of how the gearwheel had turned Wu's gunboats back at Chenglin by floating massed fire rafts at them. By the time Farren came back with his boat party, they had themselves convinced that no gunboat could get past Chenglin without gearwheel permission.

"Another foot and we can get across the shoals," Farren said cheerfully. "The blokes can get across now. Crosley, Bordelles wants you on the bridge. He wants to signal that to the *Woodcock*."

"The blokes won't get past Chenglin," Crosley said.

"That's crap about guns at Chenglin," Farren said.

"No, it ain't either crap!"

They all jumped on Farren. He had not had the buildup.

"Well, maybe there's something to it," he said at last, unhappily. "I thought I was bringing good news."

Holman stayed clear of them as much as he could. At supper he ate the lumpy corned beef with his eyes on his plate. The thing began coming to a head. The remarks became more pointed and direct.

"I hear Ho-mang's a short timer."

"He's got his seabag packed."

"He wants to stay here. He's a Chink lover, anyway."

"Pig lover!"

"He's gonna be guest of honor at a neck-chopping party."

Holman raised his head and looked directly at each one in turn. None of them except Harris could quite look back at him. Holman stood up to leave.

"Hold on, Ho-mang," Harris said. "Was you ever right close up to a head chopping?"

"I don't go for that stuff, Harris."

Harris grinned. "The knife goes cr-r-*runch!*" He rabbit chopped his own neck. "The blood spouts in two streams." He moved his forefingers in twin parabolas past his bearded chin. "The head hollers, but it can't make noise come out."

For ten seconds Harris screamed silently at Holman. His mouth gaped and his eyes squinted. His gray hairs bristled. He was a mask of all the hellful hatred and cruelty in the world since time began.

"That's what it's like to die, Ho-mang," he said.

Holman leaned across and slapped the gray-bristled chops once and backhand.

"Don't get your gun quite yet, you son of a bitch," he said. "I ain't dead yet."

Harris bared the teeth in his slash mouth. The compartment hushed.

"If I fight you, Ho-mang, I won't come alone," Harris said.

Chairs scraped. All the men were quiet and tense. Holman backed up against his locker.

"Bring all your friends and relations," he told Harris. "Here. Now. And come to kill. Because I'll kill you."

He wanted them to come. He felt in himself the true and crazy strength to break their bones and snap their necks like cornstalks. He wanted to do that.

"Come on!" he said. "Come on, Harris!"

Harris looked around. Nobody was getting up. But every eye was on Jake Holman and not one was friendly.

"I'll get you, Ho-mang," Harris said. "You got to sleep."

Holman waited a moment longer. Then he rolled up his mattress and bedding and carried it outside. He took it to the engineers' storeroom, above the gratings on the starboard side, and laid it out on deck. He closed the steel door and worked out a way to wedge it closed from inside. He lay down, very weary. The fire was going out of him. But for a little while in there, he was thinking, he had felt very real indeed.

42

Holman did not eat at the mess table again. He ate out of a pie plate in the galley, helping himself from the pan on the range while Duck-butt Randall pretended not to see him. He sat in the storeroom most of the day. He felt better there, cased in steel.

He was sitting there in late afternoon when Lt. Collins was called to the *Duarte*. He was still there when the startling news came by blinker from the *Duarte*. Through his porthole Holman heard them talking about it on the quarterdeck. Gearwheel troops had taken Nanking and they were looting and raping and killing the treaty people. British and American warships had been shelling the city since three o'clock. The lid was off at last.

Several . . . hundred . . . white . . . civilian . . . men . . . and women . . . still . . . trapped . . . in . . . city, they relayed the message about the decks as fast as Crosley received it on the flying bridge. *Until . . . further . . . notice . . . consider . . . Plan . . . Red . . . now . . . in . . . effect. . . .*

Plan Red! Plan Red!

To Holman's ear, their voices put small joy into the words. Some of the men tried to get angry.

"Looted our consulate! Ripped down our flag!"

"We can get the Fleet at the bastards, in Nanking!"

"How about the Japs? Why ain't they in it?"

"Yeah! Their consul got *killed!*"

"The Japs are still trying to outchrist us Christians," Harris said.

"Well, how about us now? We're like rats in a trap."

"Here comes the gig. The skipper'll have all the dope."

"*San Pablo* . . . boarding!" Franks shouted.

"All hands aft," Lt. Collins' crisp voice said a few moments later. "I have important news to announce."

Franks passed the word. Holman decided to go back there and hear it. The men did not form ranks. They stood in a mob and Lt. Collins stood on the grating and talked to them. He was clean and crisp in whites. His thin face was joyful with excitement.

"I can't promise you men it's really Plan Red yet," he said. "That has to come from Washington. But I can tell you our marines are going ashore at last in Shanghai. Our three extra cruisers are starting a speed run out from Pearl. It looks like a fight, men!"

He was trying to lift them with his voice and manner. They shuffled their feet and Holman could feel them wanting to respond. Lt. Collins told them what he knew about Nanking.

The U.S. destroyers *Noa* and *Preston* and the British cruiser *Emerald* had done the shelling. *Noa* had the honor of firing the first shot. The U.S. consul and the naval landing force and a few civilian refugees were safely out of the city. They had swarmed down over the city wall. Both the British and Japanese consuls were thought killed. Most of the Americans still in the city were missionaries. The Japanese warships at Nanking could not get permission to shoot, but the Japanese sailors had massed on deck and cheered the British and Americans. Lt. Collins' voice crackled as he told them about it.

"Now for what it means to us in *San Pablo*," he said.

The few local civilians were sheltering in the large gunboats. The ships would not start anything in Changsha. The plan was to wait quietly until there was water enough for the large gunboats. They would go out as a flotilla with the first few feet of the flood, day or night. The most they had to fear from the local militia was small-arms fire. If the worker-peasants wanted to start something, the gunboats would oblige them. They would wreck the city.

"In a few minutes I will call all hands to battle stations," Lt. Collins said. "Let's show them over on the bund that *San Pablo* is *ready as ever!*"

He smashed fist in palm and smiled a fierce, urging confidence at them. Holman felt the thrill run through their sluggishness. Lt. Collins went forward, followed by Bordelles and Welbeck. Franks stopped to squeeze Holman's arm and draw him aside.

"We're gonna fight 'em, Jake!" he whispered, grinning. "You're off the hook, boy! Now it won't matter if you really did kill a dozen of the slopeheaded bastards!"

A few minutes later Franks was calling all hands to battle stations, with the old, familiar power in his voice. No feet pounded. They shuffled. In the engine room Holman was alone at the throttle. The others went with Harris out to the fireroom. The drill was secured after half an hour, because the men had not had supper yet.

Holman did not eat supper. He used the time to take a shower with the scrap of salt-water soap he had left, while they were eating. He wanted to avoid them. But when he went back to his locker, Bronson, Harris and Restorff confronted him.

"We want to talk to you, Holman," Bronson said.

They were the leaders of the three gangs the crew had split into. The men at the mess tables were all listening.

"What do you want?" Holman asked Bronson.

"We want you to volunteer to go ashore and stand trial for what you did," Bronson said. "So the ship can get out past Chenglin."

"No," Holman said. "Why should I?"

Bronson had not shaved his fat cheeks for several days, but Holman could see the white dimples form at his mouth corners.

"It's only fair. You got us into this jam and only you can get us out," Bronson said. "You been our Jonah from the day you come aboard. Now's the time you can make up for it."

He was trying to hold his temper. He was trying to be dignified and important. There had always been something very paperish about Bronson.

"I never liked you, Bronson, and I don't now," Holman said evenly. "I don't want to get you out of a jam." Since they were all listening, he decided to be reasonable. "The skipper wouldn't let me," he said. "He already told me I'm a symbol of the United States in this business."

"Well, you could offer to go," Bronson said. "Or you could just go."

Harris and Restorff nodded. Harris was not talking, because they hoped to persuade him, Holman thought. He had far more respect for Harris than for Bronson, if they only knew it.

"No smoke, sailors," he said. "I won't go."

"Now listen, Jake—" Restorff began. Perna broke in. "Why the hell won't you go, Ho-mang?" he shouted. He jumped up, shaking his fist. "It ain't *fair,* we all got to get killed, because you felt sorry for a pig!"

The word ignited them. *A pig! A damned pig!* they all said. They were all getting to their feet at the mess tables. *A pig, for the love cf bleeding Jesus! We got to die for a pig!* Harris pushed Bronson aside and thrust his face at Holman.

Oink! he said, grimacing horribly.

Oink! they all took it up.

It became one of those things that swept them away. They could not stop. They began drawing it out. *Aw-ee-ee-eenk!* they were screaming at Holman. Their whiskered lips skinned back to show their teeth. Their noses wrinkled and the cords in their scaly necks stood out. *Aw-ee-ee-eenk!*

Holman stood there a moment loathing them. He wished he could tell them he had more respect for that black pig than for the whole damned lot of them. But they were making too much noise and he knew they would not stop it until he went away. He went out and around and into the storeroom. He wedged the door and lay down weary and disgusted on his bedding. A few minutes later they stopped the racket.

Some while later he heard footsteps and low voices outside. He sat up in the darkness and found the steel crowbar he kept handy. He heard the hasp clank on the outer side, and the click of a padlock. They were only locking him in. He thought about it a while and then shrugged. He lay down again and went to sleep.

It was not Bordelles' knock on his door, so Lt. Collins did not answer it. There were several of them out there. They knocked again and Bordelles heard it and came around through the bridge.

"What do you men want?" he asked sharply. "Come into the bridge!"

Lt. Collins could still hear them, through his door to the bridge. They had a written petition they wanted to present to him. Bordelles read it and told them they could not.

"I can keep this off the record, if you men will drop it right now," he told them. "If you gave this to the captain, it would be open mutiny."

Bordelles did not address the men by name, but Lt. Collins recognized Bronson's prim, stuffy voice and the scrannel growl of Harris. From their talk he learned that they wanted Holman turned over to the worker-peasants to purchase the ship a safe passage to Hankow.

"He's been our Jonah all along. This ship will never be right till we get rid of him," Bronson said persuasively. "Ain't it better for him to go than for all of us to die, him included?"

"Absolutely no!" Bordelles said angrily.

A sick feeling smote Lt. Collins. The long-delayed call to arms, now that it had come, had not fired up their hearts as he had expected. They were more demoralized than he had been willing to believe possible.

"It wouldn't have to be official," Bronson went smoothly on. "You could send him ashore with a letter to somewhere and tip off the worker-peasants to grab him. We wouldn't have to find out he was gone, officially, until after we sailed."

"In my personal opinion, Bronson, you are a scurvy son of a bitch," Bordelles said, with quiet, cold fury.

"I am only speaking for the crew. We are willing to do anything to get the ship to Shanghai. We'll fight to get the ship through. But we won't fight to save Holman. Nobody wants to die to save Holman."

"If necessary, you will die to save the honor of the United States!" Bordelles said. "Even if I have to kill you myself."

Good man, Lt. Collins thought. He could hardly believe what he was hearing. He wondered if Bordelles had chosen to talk to them in the bridge so that he would hear it, unofficially.

"If Holman was dead, that would fix it up," Harris said. "We can just deep-six the bastard, if you make us do that."

"Murder, do you mean?"

"It ain't murder when everybody does it," Harris said. "But what we got in mind is just throw him over the side and make him swim ashore. If you force us to it."

Harris' harsh, ugly voice seemed to take it from the sphere of discussion into that of action. Bordelles' manner changed. He tried, to no avail, to convince the men that there were no guns at Chenglin. Finally he promised to present their petition to the captain himself, unofficially. He promised them a decision on it in the morning, if they would promise to do nothing until then. Harris did not want to promise but Bronson and someone else, probably Restorff, agreed.

"Fair enough, Mr. Bordelles. We'll wait till morning," Bronson said.

Shortly after, Bordelles knocked and Lt. Collins told him to come in. Bordelles came in without speaking and handed him a paper. Lt. Collins glanced at it long enough to see that it was a round robin, the names signed like the spokes in a wheel. Then he crumpled it into the ashtray in front of him and lit a match to it. He did not ask Bordelles to sit down.

"When the shooting actually starts they will rally to their duty, Mr. Bordelles, depend on it," he said. "They have just been disappointed and frustrated too many times and they are not able to believe that we are free to fight, at last."

Bordelles did not answer. They were both watching the paper burn. Lt. Collins poked at it with a pencil, to spread the flame.

"You had best move Holman to the CPO quarters," he said, eyes on the flame. "Give him a pistol to defend himself."

"Yes, sir. And in the morning—"

"I am not ready to discuss that now."

"Yes, sir."

Bordelles went out quietly. Lt. Collins was too heartsick with what he had just heard to talk to anyone. He could hardly believe it. He would not believe it. They were like sick men, raving in delirium. But when *San Pablo* came under attack and he called them to their guns to defend her, that would save them. Only that could save them, now.

The paper was a shell of black ash with glowing red spots. He broke up the shape of it with his pencil, stirring and mixing. Soon they would fight, he thought. Then all that went before could be forgotten.

Holman heard them at the door. He stood up, fully awake and fully dressed, and grasped his crowbar. He moved softly to the door and unwedged it and stood there waiting. He heard them sawing the brass shackle of the padlock. When the door opened, they were Franks and Bordelles.

"Come with us, Jake," Franks whispered.

They both had drawn pistols. He followed them topside. No one was on deck. Bordelles went forward. In the CPO quarters, by the dim night light, Holman saw Welbeck stretched out in a bunk, fully dressed and wearing a pistol. Franks took a holster, belt and pistol from the arms locker and laid them on the table.

"Put 'em on, Jake," he said.

Holman hefted his crowbar. "I could do more damage with this."

"Put on the gun."

While Holman buckled on the pistol, Franks told him about the crew's plan to give him to the worker-peasants.

"The skipper don't know about it officially, but it's mutiny just the same," Franks said. "I'm worried about the skipper. I wonder if he ain't worked himself around to where what he don't know officially ain't true at all."

"You mean he's crazy?"

"Well . . . you can't say that about a skipper. But the crew's crazy. We'll be lucky to get out of this now without some of us killing each other."

Franks was a very worried man. He told Holman that Farren was still loyal, but he wanted to go on lying low on the main deck. Holman was to stay strictly inside the CPO quarters and not let any of the crew come inside.

"Shoot, if you have to. It's them or you now," Franks said.

Franks went forward to confer with Bordelles. Holman stretched out on Lynch's bunk and dozed without sleeping. At daylight, the world through the windows did not look any different. Breakfast was cold rice and corned beef and weak coffee.

Welbeck brought Lynch in from the pilot's room for breakfast. Lynch wore a dirty white shirt and his face was white and flabby and whiskered. He was harmless, Welbeck had said, but he thought nobody had names any more. He did not recognize anybody. He could eat and look after himself well enough.

"We got to shoot every third one," he kept saying, between bites.

"Come on, Lynch-boy, let's go home," Welbeck said, when breakfast was over.

"The first one we got to shoot is Holman," Lynch said.

Welbeck led Lynch out. Holman scraped the dishes.

"At least I can messcook," he told Franks.

"Stay inside. Keep that pistol on you," Franks said. "I'm going to catch me some shuteye."

He lay down. He looked worn and tired. He had been up all night. Holman was careful not to make any noise.

Lt. Collins' breakfast was a mound of rice, with two anchovies nested in it, and a silver pot of coffee. He poured a second cup of coffee and studied the sheaf of despatches and press reports the *Duarte* had sent over.

They were very encouraging. Shanghai expected another Boxer massacre. They were putting into each news broadcast the prearranged code message directing all treaty people to flee to the coast for their lives: *William is sick . . . William is sick. . . .* He smiled wryly at their choice of code word.

More warships had reached Nanking. The treaty people were still trapped in the city. The Kuomintang general had been given until midafternoon to bring them all out safely. If he did not, the allied flotilla would shell the city to rubble. The die would be cast before the day ended. Almost certainly it would turn up war.

He was thinking about calling the crew aft and telling them the news when Bordelles knocked sharply and spoke through the door.

"Trouble, sir. Better come on deck."

He went into the bridge. A wupan flying the gearwheel flag was nearing the ship. Armed militiamen crowded its waist.

"Repel boarders," he told Bordelles.

The men went sluggishly again to their stations. Bronson and Crosley, beside Lt. Collins in the bridge wing, took the canvas housings off their machine guns with insolent slowness. Their faces were sullen and they would not look at him. The wupan stopped and lay to, well clear of the ship. The spokesman was shouting something about the just and equal law of nations. He demanded Holman.

"By the just law of nations, you people are pirates!" Lt. Collins made his voice loud and clear. "I'll not parley with you!"

"We will! Come and get him!" someone yelled on the main deck. "Ho-mang, come down!" someone else yelled.

"Silence on the main deck!" Lt. Collins shouted. "Mr. Bordelles, *silence* those men!" He saw Bordelles running for the quarterdeck ladder. "In the wupan! Shove off or I'll fire into you!" Lt. Collins shouted.

Ho-mang, come down, the main deck chanted. They were making it another of their mass shouting fits. A wild and fearful anger filled Lt. Collins. He had to stop them.

"Bronson! Fire a burst into the water!" Bronson seemed not to hear. "Bronson, God damn you, fire a burst!" Lt. Collins roared at him.

"Gun's jammed, sir."

Bronson clacked the pan, pretending to clear a jam. Bordelles was guarding the quarterdeck ladder with a drawn pistol. *Ho-mang, come down!* they were roaring all along the main deck. He had to stop it.

"Crosley! Fire a burst!"

"It's jammed, sir."

"GIVE ME THAT GUN!"

Lt. Collins shouldered Bronson aside and took the gun. The mount was set too high for him. The gun bore right on the wupan. For a wild, angry moment he thought: *Command decision. Fire into them. Start it now and get it over.* But instead he stood on tiptoes and fired a burst into the water near the wupan.

That was all it took. Very quickly, the wupan got out of there. The shouting stopped on the main deck. Bordelles came to the bridge, pale and angry, still holding his pistol.

"Secure from repel boarders, Mr. Bordelles," Lt. Collins said.

He went back to his cabin. He did not want them to see him trembling. He was afraid that if he stayed on the bridge he might kill Bronson himself.

Holman was taking it as it came, without thinking about it. It was a fine, clear day. The people were thinning out on the bund. By dinnertime Changsha was quieter than he had ever seen it. After dinner it became so quiet that it was ominous. The bund was deserted. All the thronging sampans had gone away. Junks were standing down-river without any of the usual noise and fuss. Franks did not like it.

"I better get some sleep while I can," he said. "I'll die if I don't get some sleep."

Ten minutes later the shots started. It was rifle fire from the top of the city wall. They were shooting just at the *San Pablo* and the *Woodcock.* It was only one or two shots a minute. Cursing and rubbing his eyes, Franks came out to call the Sand Pebbles to their battle stations.

They would not man their battle stations. They were all down on the starboard side of the main deck, sheltered from the fire, and they would not leave. Franks stood at the head of the ladder and cursed them on the quarterdeck. They cursed him back. Lt. Collins called from the bridge wing.

"Franks! Belay general quarters! Come here!"

Franks, Holman, Welbeck and Bordelles gathered in the bridge. Lt. Collins looked very grim. He said they would have to get permission from the *Duarte* before they could return the fire. When they had it, they would open fire with the bridge machine guns, and then they would call the crew to battle stations.

"Once *San Pablo* is in battle, they will be themselves again," he said.

No one dared argue with him. Franks and Bordelles had to do the signaling. All the gunboats were exchanging signals. The Japanese did not want to fight because they were not being fired upon. Lt. Collins paced the bridge feverishly. Holman and Welbeck went into the chart room, to keep out of his way. Finally the *Duarte* and *Woodcock* agreed on a plan. The *Duarte* signaled it to the *San Pablo*.

"Oh, Christ! Wouldn't you know it?" Franks said.

They would not return the fire. Instead, the *San Pablo* and *Woodcock* would get underway. The *Woodcock* would go through to Hankow. The *San Pablo,* if she could get across the shoal stretch, would go on down to the lake. There she would anchor out of gun range and wait for the *Duarte* to come out.

Lt. Collins did not comment. "Preparations for getting underway," he told Bordelles, without opening his teeth.

Bordelles called the engine room on the voice tube and was lucky enough to get Krebs. Krebs said they could have steam up on one boiler in about an hour. One boiler would be enough, going with the current. All they would need would be steerage way.

"Oh hell. Come on back to the quarters," Franks said.

They went back there. It was very uncomfortable being near Lt. Collins. They sat without talking. Once in a while a glancing bullet would screech off metal.

"Oink!" someone cried once on the main deck, when that happened.

They all took it up in unison, crying it each time a bullet hit the ship. *Aw-ee-ee-eenk!* Franks shook his head and grinned wearily.

"I know how they feel, Becky," he said. "Here we are getting shot at, and all we can do is run again. I do know how they feel."

Welbeck stood and looked out the window. "Hey!" he said. "Here comes the *Woodcock!*"

"That's fast!" Franks said admiringly.

They all stood up to watch. As she neared the *San Pablo,* all the rifle fire shifted to the *Woodcock* and the rate picked up. She came along bravely, low and white and trim in the water, with a bone in her teeth, and bullets were splashing white water all around her. Half a dozen British sailors in neat white uniforms came out and manned the rail, on the side exposed to fire.

"They're going to make us passing honors! Under fire, by God!" Franks said. "That's the Limey way, ain't it, Becky? By God, I love them people!"

"All hands! Man the rail!" Bordelles shouted from the bridge.

Franks ran out and repeated it. Holman and Welbeck joined him at the boat deck rail. A whistle shrilled as the *Woodcock* started coming abreast and they all saluted.

On the main deck, the Sand Pebbles did not salute. They thumbed noses and ears and *oinked,* in a dozen cracked and shrieking voices. Pale as paper, Lt. Collins ran aft and down to the quarterdeck, Bordelles following.

"Come on!"

Franks ran, drawing his pistol. They all stopped at the head of the ladder. Lt. Collins stood at the foot of it.

"Hand salute, you mangy sons of bitches!" he screamed at the men on the quarterdeck. *"Hand salute,* God damn your souls!"

They gave him a volley of *oinks* from bearded faces. Harris pushed his bristly gray face almost into Lt. Collins' face.

"Oink you, Collins, you little fart!" he screamed.

Holman saw the square white shoulders wilt. The stern of the *Woodcock,* with its gallant White Ensign, was sliding past. The public shame was already history.

Lt. Collins turned and came up the ladder. He did not seem to see the men clustered there. They drew aside. He went into his cabin and closed the door.

Holman went back and sat in the CPO quarters. Somehow, Franks and Farren got the anchor up. Somehow, they and Bordelles got the *San Pablo* underway. Somehow, they worked the ship across the shoal stretch and as far down the reach as they could get while daylight lasted. They anchored in the last bit of twilight.

Holman came out on deck. The night was cool and quiet and peaceful. Changsha was out of sight. It was green countryside all around. No lights showed, except a few glimmers from farm huts. Frogs croaked along the bank and fish jumped out in the river. Holman looked at the sky. The stars were just coming out clearly.

Franks came aft and Holman followed him inside. Franks collapsed in a chair. He looked exhausted.

"I don't know. I guess we're out of the woods," he said. "Bronson just come up and told Bordelles he was sorry. He said he was speaking for all hands. Now that we're on the way at last, they want to do all they can to get the ship to Shanghai." He flexed his arms and sighed deeply. "Bronson said they won't make any more trouble about you."

"How's the skipper taking it?"

"We don't know. He's locked in and he won't answer when Bordelles talks through the door." Franks shook his head wearily. "Bordelles says we'll break the door down in the morning, if he won't answer then. But I'm scared we'll hear a pistol shot in that cabin before morning comes."

43

For hours he had been sitting motionless at his table, hands flat on the green baize. Between his hands lay a flat black pistol and a pair of Chinese baby shoes with crude U.S. flags embroidered on their toes. He stared at them.

There was a clean, simple animal level where you knew things without thinking and looking. Children and dogs lived there truly. Once you left it, you could never return. On that level the crew knew Holman to be a Jonah.

The gearwheel had destroyed *San Pablo*. Doubt had breached the walls and he had held an inner citadel and now that was fallen. Just so the missionaries spread doubt in China and America. Their clamor for meekness could sicken the spirit beyond recovery. Well, the missionaries were wallowing in blood for that, now. They would recant. They would clamor for blood in return. America would not sicken. The world was not ended because *San Pablo* was destroyed.

He put his right hand on the pistol. It was flat and hard and cold. He thought of a snake's head.

There were people to grieve: his parents, a few others. But he had put them all away when he swore his oath. His oath forsworn now, faith betrayed, honor lost and everything in ruins. Lt. William Collins was now going to live in naval archives as captain of the first U.S. Navy ship ever to mutiny. You did not die just because your heart ceased pumping.

But something would stop hurting. He picked up the pistol. He fondled and hefted it. It was clean and heavy and sure of itself and it loved its purpose. His hand was warming it.

You did not die all at once. The residual life in *San Pablo* would crawl back to Hankow, to Shanghai, to Manila, like floating cancer cells to taint the Fleet. Command responsibility ended with death only when death came naturally in bed or gloriously in battle.

He put the pistol down. His eyes rested on the baby shoes.

Gloriously in battle, he thought.

The way out came to him. The bits crowded pell-mell into his mind. They fitted themselves together in successive illuminations.

Waldhorn was still in *Duarte,* so *San Pablo* could not use her radio. That left his command power unhampered from above. *Nelson's blind eye,* he thought. He would go to China Light and take out those missionaries. In the aftermath of Nanking, they would be frantic for rescue.

He would tell only the trusted men. He would turn *San Pablo* west in the lake. If the men renewed their mutiny, he would put them down in blood. *Bronson! Harris!* He would bunker with wood at Ta An. Intelligence reports said the Chien River was boomed with junks linked with bamboo cable and defended by militia. He would break that boom. He would take a party on to China Light. He would make a last, savage thrust deep into China, dropping his dead as he went, and *San Pablo* would die clean.

His heart fired up. He examined the plan critically for flaws and found it perfect. If America was at war with the gearwheel, as was almost certain now, it would be all right. If the wild rumors were true, and the gearwheel was going to bow to the treaties, then they would have no grounds to complain about *San Pablo* lawfully putting down pirates in defense of American lives. There had been other U.S. Navy mutinies which had not gone down on paper. *Pittsburgh* in

Brazil, he thought. It was not history, unless it went down on paper. What went down on paper for the end of *San Pablo* was going to be pretty glorious after all.

He put the baby shoes away. He holstered his pistol. He stood up, cold and hard and sure again, and it was just four o'clock. He went to call Bordelles.

They were a grim, tense group in the cabin, just before dawn. They understood the plan. They knew they might very likely all die. Holman knew it would be an hour or so yet before that part really soaked into him.

"They might not make trouble," Bordelles said. "I gathered from Bronson they're shocked and ashamed for what they did."

"That's true. But they think they're going to Shanghai," Farren said.

Holman had not thought the missionaries were in danger at China Light. By their own act they were not treaty people any more. They were like the Germans in Changsha.

"Do we know for sure the missionaries are in danger?" he asked.

"Of course, after Nanking!" Lt. Collins snapped.

"Old Craddock is a prisoner at China Light, under a death sentence from a Bolshevik court," Bordelles told Holman. "It's the same kind of propaganda stunt they wanted to work with you and Knox in Changsha."

"I didn't know that," Holman said.

When there were no more questions, Lt. Collins dismissed them. His manner was cold and hard as iron. They went out quietly, into the faint, new daylight.

Lt. Collins, Bordelles and Franks wore pistols. The other men on the bridge were Bronson, Restorff, Crosley and Haythorn. Restorff and Bronson had shaved and Bronson had put on whites. Ellis and Vincent called up soundings from the bow. Franks listened and scanned the water and gave orders to Haythorn, at the helm. Bronson took bearings. They were all being quick and handy. The ship throbbed smoothly with engine power and made its moving pattern in the water. The men made their own familiar pattern of speech and motion about the bridge.

They did not know that death was all about them in the warm sunshine. The ship would turn west in a few more minutes. Lt. Collins kept his eye on Bronson.

Bronson was being very dutiful and military. He kept reporting bearings and other small matters to Bordelles and Franks in the most proper form. They responded with grunts. They would not give Bronson the assurance he sought.

Restorff, with Crosley's help, was cleaning a machine gun. His blunt face, intent on the work, had been nicked here and there by a dull razor. He cleaned and oiled the machine-gun parts with his familiar, loving care. That was Restorff's way of asking forgiveness.

But there could be no forgiving. Franks caught Lt. Collins' eye and raised an eyebrow. Bordelles stepped back to the port wing, hand on holster. Franks spoke to Haythorn, who spun the helm. *San Pablo* turned. The sun wheeled around aft and left the bridge in shadow.

"Steady as you go," Franks told Haythorn.

Bronson realized it first. His eyes widened, but he did not change his behavior. Then Haythorn began fidgeting and finally he called Crosley. Crosley tried to pull Bronson aside and whisper. Bronson would not be whispered to.

"God damn it, then I'll ask 'em!" Crosley said. He turned to Franks. "Where the hell you think you're taking this ship?" he demanded.

"I'll tell you, Crosley."

In cold, clipped words Lt. Collins told them. Crosley's whiskered face expressed incredulous dismay. He had been in a fight and his bruised upper lip made him look even more froggish than usual. He was an ugly little man.

"We will probably have to board and take one of the junks with pistol and cutlass," Lt. Collins said. "We may have to make an assault at China Light."

Crosley's eyes bulged. His mouth worked without sound, like a frog gulping flies. He muttered something about Shanghai. Then he found his voice.

"Christ sake, we'll all get *kilt!*" he screamed in outrage.

Restorff chuckled. "It can't only happen to you once, Crosley," he said. "After that, you're immune."

It was just the right response. The mixed feelings on Haythorn's face gave way to a contemptuous smile at Crosley. Bronson, his fat face white and determined, stepped forward.

"Captain, sir, if there's a boarding party, I want to volunteer for it," he said shakily.

"Granted," Lt. Collins said coldly.

Crosley whirled and ran out of the bridge. Bordelles followed him. Haythorn adjusted the helm.

"Steady as she goes, Chief," he said cheerfully.

The engine room was full of smooth, powerful motion and the good smell of steam, hot oil and packing. Oil made a dull sheen on the rusted engine parts, moving augustly now, light and shadow playing through them. From the fireroom came the ring and scrape of shovels. The main plant was alive again.

Holman stood at the throttle. Welbeck lounged against the log desk. Farren was up on the gratings. They all wore pistols. Welbeck's coming down was the signal that the turn west was soon to be made. Harris came from the shaft alley and went into the fireroom. He gave them through the engine a sardonic glance in passing.

Holman did not expect trouble. Everything he knew was against it, but he was feeling happier than he had in many days. He could not believe that he or anyone was going to be killed. When they got to Paoshan they would find out that there was not any trouble because the missionaries were not treaty people any more. The Bolsheviks had control at Changsha, and even they did not bother the Germans. The boy Cho-jen was running China Light, and Shirley had said that he was definitely not a Bolshevik.

He whistled under his breath. He was happy because the engine room was alive again. And because the ship was going to Paoshan. He might, just possibly, be able to stay at China Light after all. His dream was alive again, too.

The steering engine above the gratings aft began a sustained rattling. Holman felt the ship heel slightly. They were making the turn. Welbeck unsnapped his holster flap and moved up beside Holman.

Nothing happened for quite a while. Then Crosley clattered across the gratings and down the ladder and into the fireroom. He flashed a snarling glance at the throttle station. Bordelles was right behind him. Holman and Welbeck followed Bordelles into the fireroom. Bordelles stopped, still in the passageway between the boilers, and they looked over his shoulders.

"Down shovels! Down shovels, I tell you!" Crosley was shouting. "They're doublecrossing us, guys! They're trying to get us all killed!"

The men stood listening, shirtless and sweating, between coal and ash heaps: Krebs, Perna, Wilsey, Stawski and Harris. Crosley waved his arms and shouted. Harris turned to Bordelles.

"What's this all about?" he asked harshly.

Bordelles told him, in flat, hard words. Harris' eyes stayed rock-steady and his manner did not give an inch. He was thinking about it. Slowly, his sharkish grin began to split his whiskers.

"We're gonna fight? For certain sure?"

"For certain sure."

"You heard him!" Crosley yelled. "Down shovels, guys!"

Stawski flung his shovel clattering. "Mine's down!" he said. Sullenly, Perna and Wilsey laid down their shovels. Krebs held his. He looked very undecided.

"Ski, pick up your shovel," Harris said.

"Oink you!" Stawski said. *"Aw-ee-ee-eenk!"*

With his flat nose and his little blue eyes, he looked like a pig. Perna and Wilsey and Crosley took up the *oinking.* They were trying to carry the ship away again. Harris picked up a slice bar, holding it in the middle. All his stringy muscles stood out. Without warning, he speared one end of it into Stawski's stomach. The big fireman sat down on the ash heap, gasping.

"Shovels!" Harris told Perna and Wilsey, showing all his teeth. They stopped *oinking* and picked up their shovels.

"Krebs, give Crosley your shovel," Harris ordered. "Since he's being so kind as to come down here and want to help us."

Crosley opened his mouth, but it was Stawski who screamed. He jumped howling to his feet, dancing and slapping his buttocks. A live ember bedded in the ash heap had burned through to him. They all began laughing. Even Crosley laughed.

That was how the big Sand Pebble mutiny was ending, Holman thought. With Stawski rubbing his blistered behind and looking around for sympathy with a face like a bearded baby about to cry, while they all laughed at him. They had not known it themselves, but they had been smokestacking all the time.

44

That year spring came early to China Light. Flowers tinted the far slopes of the mountain and the dark, moist smell of turned earth blew off the fields. The farmers expected a fair and fruitful summer. Within the walls trees leafed out, early flowers colored beds and borders and the climbing roses around the small cemetery were forming a host of buds.

Since Mrs. Craddock's death, Mr. Craddock had not liked to stay indoors. They had placed a bench for him against the whitewashed outer wall of his house, beside Ting's caldron, and he would sit there on sunny days. He had turned wholly gray during the winter and the old, dark fire was burned out in him. The serenity that replaced it was curiously Chinese, Shirley thought. He would sit there in his dark Chinese gown and skull cap and make small, pleasant talk with old Ting and the people who came to buy hot water. He knew the domestic affairs of all the China Light households and he had become something like a beloved old grandfather whom they all had in common.

Shirley sat there with him one sunny day late in March, talking idly with several of the Chinese people, when Gillespie came up and broke in. He spoke English rather than Chinese. That, and his troubled manner, seemed abruptly to draw a separating line.

"We'd best go inside," he said. "There's something we must talk about, at once."

They sat in the small parlor and it seemed damp and chill and dark. Gillespie read the news from the flimsy news sheet he said Cho-jen had just brought from Paoshan. The Kuomintang had taken Nanking and British and American warships had shelled the city. Forty thousand were claimed killed. He looked up at their shocked exclamations.

"Cho-jen is certain that's the wildest kind of exaggeration," he assured them.

The rest of the sheet was a violent exhortation to stand to arms and prepare to resist treaty power aggression. The Nanking shelling was taken to be the first step toward open intervention on behalf of the northern warlords.

"Surely the ships had provocation?" Shirley said.

"Of course they did. The troops at Nanking are Hunanese, Pan's regiment among them," Gillespie said. "Cho-jen is inclined to think the provocation was deliberate."

Gillespie wanted to put off discussing what it meant to them personally, Shirley could see. Through Cho-jen he had become intensely interested in the revolution, particularly its development in the Chien Valley. He explained the Nanking episode in terms of the rear-area movement to capture the revolution for Bolshevism. That had gone a long way in Hunan; only Cho-jen and his China Light group were keeping the Bolshevik Chung faction from control of the Chien Valley. The provincial worker-peasant council in Changsha had decreed the treaties canceled in Hunan.

"Cho-jen has heard that they are trying to provoke trouble with the gunboats at Changsha," Gillespie said grimly. "The trouble at Nanking is no doubt more of the same."

The reason for it was the recurrent rumor that Chiang Kai-shek was about to lead the conservative wing of the Kuomintang in a counter-revolution against the entire worker-peasant movement, Gillespie went on. To do so successfully, he would have to bow to the unequal treaties in order to get treaty power support, and the revolution would be lost. But if the radical wing could force a war with one or more of the treaty powers first, they would prevent that. They would make the revolution Bolshevik instead, because then all the support would have to come from Russia.

"We have it right here in miniature," Gillespie said. "The Chung faction is already making this a very severe test for Cho-jen."

He had come to their part in it. As he spoke, he kept folding and unfolding the flimsy news sheet and smoothing it on his knee. Mr. Craddock listened placidly. Chung street orators in Paoshan were clamoring for execution of Craddock's death sentence. They were calling Cho-jen a running dog. By now Cho-jen had a stay of execution from the highest Kuomintang levels in Hankow. But the Chungs were saying that the Kuomintang itself would be a pack of running dogs if it did not take up the challenge of Nanking. They had called up the Chung-dominated part of the local militia and they were making threats of marching on China Light.

"Cho-jen is starting back to Paoshan within the hour, to forestall that by counter-intrigue," Gillespie said. "He knows this is the first major crisis of his career."

Gillespie paused. He and Shirley looked at Mr. Craddock. The old man looked sorrowful but unafraid.

"You two must do as your own hearts bid you," he said.

"It may be war between America and the Kuomintang," Gillespie said. He had almost worn the news sheet out by repeated foldings. "I wondered . . . have you thought . . ."

"Yes. Months ago," Mr. Craddock said gravely. "I believe it is God's will that China be freed of the unequal treaties. If my country makes war on China to reimpose the treaties, that will not change my belief. I no longer hold my God and my country to be identical."

A hush fell. It did not really sound so monstrous, Shirley thought.

"I am an old man and my life is here," Mr. Craddock resumed. "Yet that decision was not easy for me. I do not wish you two young people to be influenced by it."

"I made it too. I am bound." Gillespie stood up. "Only now—" he broke off and paced the length of the small room. "Why should it seem so *different,* just because the killing has begun?" he asked in anguish.

"Because it is not just words any more."

"Mr. Craddock, it is *not* that I fear for my life! I have the utmost faith in Cho-jen. I know we are all safe here."

Shirley wanted to comfort him. "It is because you are a man, Walter, and this is war and weapons," she said. She stood up, suddenly angry. "Why should anyone feel *forced* to choose, in that way? Why can't we just be citizens of the human race?"

"Legally, no such human category is permissible," Gillespie said.

"But it exists. The war brought it into existence," Mr. Craddock said. "I mean the people with League of Nations passports. The stateless persons."

"The White Russians?" Shirley's hand went to her lips.

"Yes. Anyone eligible for a Nansen passport."

Gillespie stopped his pacing. "Does any nation grant the valid existence of a Nansen passport?" he asked. "I'm pretty sure the U.S. does not. We hold the White Russians in China to be Chinese."

"All I wish is to live out my days peaceably in China," Mr. Craddock said mildly.

Gillespie snapped his fingers. "Let's talk about that!" he said.

They talked quite a while. They decided to declare themselves stateless persons, in the event of war and for the duration of it. Gillespie said he would draft their statement and ask Mr. Lin to draft one in correct Chinese. They would mail a copy to the consul in Changsha and deposit another with the officials in Paoshan. The decision cleared away all their anxiety.

"Insofar as the state demands an absolute and unquestioning loyalty, those who put God ahead of country are all in a sense stateless persons," Mr. Craddock said.

"Those who can still conceive of such a possibility," Gillespie agreed. "This will be a great help to Cho-jen, too," he added. "Now the Chungs can't make our status here such an embarrassment to Cho-jen."

"We belong here," Shirley said. "Now let's go back out in the sunshine, with the others."

They signed their declaration just in time. The next day Tao-min took copies in to Paoshan and in late evening both he and Cho-jen returned with disturbing news. There had been fighting in Changsha. Telegraphic warning had reached Paoshan that the gunboat *San Pablo* was crossing Tungting Lake. At once the Chungs had tried to link it with the Americans at China Light. The declaration of statelessness had come just in time to counter that. The river boom was being closed and all the militia groups were being called to defend it. Cho-jen had come to muster the China Light militia.

Shouts and ragged bugling came through the open windows of the faculty office. Shirley watched the militia trying to form up on the street. Nearest the gate were the students, with their skimpy yellow-green uniforms and rifles. Behind them the farmers had only arm-bands and many were armed only with hand-forged spears, tridents and halberds. The weapons gleamed brightly, bobbing and jostling above the massed heads. On the lawns to either side the women and children and old people were standing. Mr. Craddock was sitting on the veranda of what had once been the Armstrong house.

"That's it," Gillespie said. He rattled the sheet out of his type-writer. "You might as well sign it too, Shirley," he said.

Cho-jen waited for it, while they signed. It was an amplification of their statement and a plea for the gunboat to turn back. Cho-jen wrapped all the papers in a piece of oiled silk and put them into the leather pouch at his waist.

"I will go on hoping that there will be a chance to parley," he said. "But I am afraid that the Chungs will make sure that there is not."

He was quiet, almost somber, his tremendous energy more nearly in leash than Shirley had ever seen it. He *had* grown, her eyes insisted; he was tall as Gillespie, although slender and unformed with youth. But his face was as formed as Gillespie's, almost graven, under the pressure of his time.

"I must go. It is a long march," he said.

He shook hands with them and said good-bye. He smiled, and for that moment was a boy again. Then, abruptly, he was gone.

"Good luck!" Gillespie called after him.

"Be careful! Oh, Cho-jen, be *careful!*" Shirley cried.

She crossed to the window, to hide the tears that had started to her eyes. Gillespie came and stood behind her.

"You know he can't be careful. The China Light boys will have to be in the forefront of it, to refute the lies the Chungs have spread."

"Because of us."

"We can at least be glad now that sailor did not come with us."

"If he had, he'd be down there marching with them!"

"Do you mean you feel I should be?" Gillespie asked quietly.

"No. No, Walter." She tried to control herself. "Cho-jen and all my boys are enough," she said.

She could not stop the tears on her cheeks. *And Jake Holman will be on the other side,* she thought. *Isn't that enough for the Lord God of Battles?*

"I want to take arms and march with them. I do, Shirley!"

"You mustn't. Not even think it," she said. "I'm just being a foolish, instinctive woman. But don't you be foolish."

He moved up beside her. "It's a mad game," he said. "A wicked, hateful game." His voice was bitter.

They stood in silence. Jake had used to call it a game, she was remembering. *You choose up sides and kill each other,* he had said once. As she had often before, she wished again that she could have helped him to escape from it. But it was too late now.

Cho-jen came in sight, striding along. As he passed, a wave of form and order seemed to pass with him along the chaotic ranks. The gleaming weapons steadied and aligned themselves. The students struck up their marching song.

> *We are just ready to fight;*
> *To fight the warlords with all our might.*

They were pushing open the great wooden gates. Bugles sounded raggedly and the weapons bobbed and tossed once more as the ranks began to move. New tears started to her eyes and she wanted to rest her head on Gillespie's shoulder, but she would not. From outside the gates she could still hear her students singing.

Don't give up, comrades, just fight!
We'll overcome them, all right!
We'll think we're too small. We'll get them all!
For we're soldiers of China Light!

45

While the light lasted, the *San Pablo* groped her way westward between green marshy islands from which white flurries of water birds rose screaming like lost souls. All the men came down and took their turns at stoking. When they anchored at sunset and banked fires, they had hardly more than bunker scrapings left to burn. They knew there was a timber raft stranded at Ta An from which they would get wood the next day.

Half the sky was red with sunset. Farren had gotten the topside swept and washed down. Bone-weary as they were, the men squared away the living spaces as well as they could. Welbeck shared out the last of the soap and shaving cream. They all bathed and shaved and cleaned up. They were quiet and methodical about it.

It was a cool, crisp evening, sprinkled with stars. The Sand Pebbles were making up all their old feuds. A man would say something friendly and get a friendly response and drift along and repeat it with another man. They did not make apologies. They were all agreeing together without words that nothing had ever happened for which apologies were necessary. It was a matter of grins exchanged, small jokes and friendly slaps and nudges. One by one, they all made peace with Holman that way. He saw Crosley and Red Dog, each still bearing marks of their fight, standing at the rail with their arms across each other's shoulders.

They had the armor flaps down and the windows open. Cool lake air and the croaking of frogs blew through the compartment. It smelled clean and fresh when they turned in at taps.

The strange peacefulness on the ship, the renewed friendliness, Holman thought, were because they believed they were going to fight and probably all be killed. Their belief was so strong that it was hard for him not to share it. He was still hoping that there would be no fight and it would work out somehow that he could break free of the ship and stay at China Light. By the time he went to sleep, it was a pretty slim hope. *However it goes, I hope I at least see her one more time,* he thought. He went to sleep on that.

They reached the timber raft about noon, and just in time. They were burning bunker sweepings so fine that half of it went sparking up the stack with the draft. They moored port side to the raft and it rounded away from the bulwark like a low brown hill. Bordelles, with Yen-ta to interpret, went to the cluster of matsheds on top of the raft to bargain. If the raftmen refused to sell, the sailors would just take the wood.

The raftmen were willing to sell wood. They pulled out the slender pine logs very deftly. The raft was bound with bamboo cables. They were made of long, flexible strips of bamboo braided and then the braids braided to make cables of any size wanted. The raftmen slacked the cables and pulled out logs and slid them down to the fantail of the ship.

On the fantail the Sand Pebbles sawed them into four-foot billets. They split the big ones into quarters with mauls and wedges. Other men carried the billets forward to the bunkers. Holman swung a maul. The men worked quietly and steadily. The maul rang on wedges and the saws rasped and snored through wood. The fresh, resinous smell of sawdust was all about the fantail.

Three raft children, a boy and two girls, watched the Sand Pebbles from far back on the raft. The sailors worked stripped to the waist and sawdust powdered their hair and arms and chests, sweating under the warm sun. Sawdust was heaped on deck and slippery under their feet. In hesitant fascination the children came down log by log for a closer look at the hairy, tattooed men.

Harris dropped his saw. His gray-thatched chest was heaving. "Hard work!" he said, panting. He kicked his foot in the sawdust. "This smells good," he said. "Like way back home in them hills."

He picked up a double handful of the sawdust and sniffed it. He saw the children watching him, wide-eyed. He grinned and held the sawdust out to them. They shrank back and huddled together, ready to flee.

"Makee chow chow!" Harris told them. He pretended to eat the sawdust, gobbling into his hands. He raised his head and smacked his lips. *"Ding hao!"* he said.

They stared doubtfully. Harris puffed his cheeks with air and chewed and raised his hands to his ears. He let sawdust trickle down his arms, seeming to come from his ears. The children stared and moved right down to the rail. They knew Harris was making a show for them.

"Oh boy! Oh boy!" Harris said. "Number one chow chow!"

He took out his false teeth and held them with thumb and knuckles and made them chomp. The children were absolutely fascinated. Harris squatted and let the teeth chomp through a pile of sawdust. The teeth clicked and snapped at it. The children climbed down on the fantail to see better. *"Ding hao!"* Harris said, grinning cavernously at the children. The teeth sidled over and bit Harris on the ankle. The children shrieked.

"Hey! Stop that!" Harris told the teeth. *"Bu hao!"*

The teeth laughed at Harris. The children giggled. They wanted to see the teeth chomp sawdust. Whenever the teeth would try to sneak up on Harris' ankle, the children would shriek a warning. They wanted to touch the teeth. The teeth made little snaps at them and they pulled their hands away with cries of fearful delight. Harris looked over his shoulder at the other sailors, who were still working.

"Any of you guys got a piece of that Christmas candy left?" he asked.

No one had. Harris shook a finger at the teeth and told them to behave themselves. They bowed meekly and indicated that they would. He left the teeth in the sawdust and went forward.

"Who's got any of that Christmas pogeybait left in his locker?" Harris was yelling, somewhere forward. "Where's Duckbutt?"

The children squatted and pushed the teeth around gingerly. They were a bit afraid of the teeth. They kept looking forward. It was no fun without Harris.

Harris came back with a saucer of something. It was a paste of sugar and condensed milk and a pinch of cocoa. Harris squatted and made signs that the teeth were not to know. He and the children heaped sawdust on the teeth. Then Harris dipped his finger in the paste and licked it off.

"Ding hao!" he said, licking and smacking his lips.

He offered the saucer. The little boy tried it first, very solemnly. Then all four were dipping their fingers and licking them off.

"What you got there, Harris? Some one-finger poi?" Tullio asked.

"Shut up, Tullio," Holman said.

Harris and the children worked on the confection until the saucer was clean. Then Harris eased his hand under the pile of sawdust and the teeth burst free again. They went sniffing and casting about, while the children held their breaths, until they found the saucer. They snapped and clashed at the empty saucer and chattered with rage because they had missed out. When Harris laughed and taunted them, they leaped viciously at his ankle. They would not let go until he wrestled them into a handkerchief and stuffed them struggling into his pocket.

The children shrieked delighted applause. Harris stood up with both hands on the small of his back, working out a crick. Then he lifted each child gently in turn across the bulwark to the raft. They moved off a little way and sat down in a row on a log. They still stared at Harris. He turned back to his shipmates and picked up his saw and flexed it in both hands.

"I'm an old man. I need to rest," he told them. "Besides, I was bringing us luck. Kids can give you luck."

The ship stayed moored to the raft all night. They had a very good supper. Welbeck had bought fresh vegetables and pork and shrimp from the raft people. The raft cook had come aboard to prepare it. As at Christmas, Bordelles and the chiefs came down to eat with the crew.

Lt. Collins ate alone in his cabin. He was still being very cold and remote. The Sand Pebbles knew he had not forgiven them.

They had almost forgotten how wonderfully good Chinese food could be. They made a lingering feast of it. No one spoke of what would happen the next day except that Bordelles, at Bronson's table, mentioned that the raft headman had agreed to mail any letters left with him when the raft reached Hankow. Lynch sat at Holman's table. He was shaved and cleaned up. He had sense in his eyes and he could talk and eat all right, but he did not know anyone by name. He made up names for them all. Wilsey was *Moonhead*. Farren was *Redbeard*. Harris was *Jackfrost*. Holman was *Flangeface*. Lynch made the only reference to the next day at Holman's table.

"We're going to fight tomorrow," he said. "We're going to make 'em give us back our real names."

After the meal a few men went to the ship's office to write letters. Franks talked privately to Holman.

"I hate to leave Lynch locked up alone during the fight," he said. "He thinks now he's going to be in the engine room. You suppose it might be all right?"

"Sure," Holman said. "Let him come down."

46

San Pablo got underway at dawn, in misty rain. The eastern sky gleamed rose and pearl. The air was fragrant with woodsmoke. The raft people came out of their huts to see *San Pablo* pull away.

Lt. Collins stayed on the bridge. He spoke to no one and they all kept clear of him. They were all in clean whites and they spoke to each other in low voices.

The rain became mist and the climbing sun burned the mist away. Beyond Ta An the lake broadened out. Green islands and mountains blue to the south rose softly into a picture without a frame. *San Pablo* steamed along smoothly and quietly under a plume of blue woodsmoke.

Westward a far green line grew into a reed marsh wilderness screaming with birds. The mist dried away. The sun rode high and hot in a blue sky. *San Pablo* entered the main channel of the Chien River.

There was almost no traffic on the river. Lt. Collins knew they must have had the telegraphic warning at Paoshan, before now. He did not know how far up the river the boom lay. When the marsh began giving way to green-diked rice fields with buffaloes and blue-clad farmers busy in them, he had the crew piped to dinner. He did not eat anything himself.

After dinner Lynch came down to the engine room. He walked around and looked at the machinery with sense in his eyes. The things he said made sense. He was all right with the machinery.

"Want the throttle for a while?" Holman asked him.

"I'd like to take the throttle," Lynch said.

"Harris is your oiler," Holman said.

He watched Lynch handle the throttle and tend water. Lynch was doing just fine at it. When Holman was sure it would be all right, he went out to the fireroom to lend a hand there.

It was after four o'clock when they sighted the boom. Lt. Collins saw it midway down a long westward reach and it looked like a string of beads across a brown neck. He rang half speed, just matching the current, and *San Pablo* hung there while he studied the boom through the long glass. Bordelles was getting up the armor flaps and posting the men at their revised battle stations. There were twenty-odd junks spaced about a hundred feet apart and the line was bowed downriver by the current. Men moved tinily on their decks. Steel glinted. He could not see well, into the sun.

"Battle stations manned and ready, sir," Bordelles said quietly.

"Very well. Hoist the battle flag."

The junks rode stern on, with thick festoons of bamboo cable linking their bows. The center junk was the largest. A gearwheel flag drooped and flapped at its masthead. It was the command junk. It was the precious pendant of that necklace on the brown neck, and he was going to rip it off.

"Standard speed," he ordered. "Steer for the center junk."

San Pablo moved. A momentary light breeze ruffled the brown water and flashed a thousand sun glints. Crosley was hoisting the big battle flag in jerks up the mainmast. The breeze caught and streamed it. It was very beautiful.

"Prepare to concentrate fire on the center junk, Mr. Bordelles."

"Aye aye, sir!"

Krebs and Stawski had one boiler, Wilsey and Perna the other. The red, roaring furnaces were devouring wood. It made a light, fluffy ash. They had to keep hauling ashes and sogging them with a hose. Ash slushed and charcoal crunched beneath their unceasing feet. Melted pine pitch smeared their bare arms and torsos. Patches of white ash sticking to it made them look like lepers.

Holman carried wood for them from the bunkers. He built the wood head high all along the forward bulkhead. Distant thuds sounded, and the pop of distant rifles. Then their own guns cut loose in a rattling roar.

"I better get back out with Lynch," Holman told Krebs.

Lynch, at the throttle, was doing all right. The engine rolled massively, silently and powerfully.

San Pablo closed range steadily. The two center armor flaps were still down, for better seeing. Lt. Collins took station there alone. On either side of him three men stood to their machine guns, mounted in armored embrasures. Below in the bow Haythorn and Shanahan sheltered behind the small shield of the three-pounder. All the faces were tense and eager.

They would have to wait. The Chinese would have to fire first. Then, with the source of fire plainly visible, *San Pablo* would be authorized to return a fitting answer.

The Chinese began firing at about fifteen hundred yards. It was rifle fire, pale winks along the line of junks, quick splashes in brown water. Then buzzing whines. Spangs and thuds and screeches of hits. Bullets came into the bridge. Lt. Collins held his binoculars to his eyes with a steady hand and kept his face expressionless. Red-shot smoke blossomed on the center junk. A cannonball skipped angling across *San Pablo*'s bow. After it came a *thud!*

"Two-thirds speed," Lt. Collins said quietly to Franks. Then, his voice a sudden whiplash, *"Commence* firing! *Commence* firing!"

The six machine guns blurted a racketing roar. The three-pounder barked sharply. Smoke rose and splinters flew from the center junk. Sampans shuttled like waterbugs between the junks and out from the south bank, where there seemed to be a militia camp. He sniffed the sharp powder smoke with hungry nostrils. Spent cartridges tinkled brightly on deck like a thousand fairy bells. The bow gun fired in steady rhythm: breech slam . . . *bark!* . . . shell clatter on deck. *Thud . . . thud . . . thud,* the Chinese guns responded. It was a joyous litany.

San Pablo closed range slowly. The guns never stopped. The pale winks merged to a steady flickering. Bullets flogged *San Pablo*. Bullets screamed into the bridge, but they would not hit him. Black smoke blossomed redly from junk to junk and thunderclouded above them. Cannonballs ripped the air like silk and furrowed the brown water. One struck the bow and shook the ship. *Slam . . . bark! . . . clatter,* the bow gun went. *Thud! . . . thud! . . . thud!* the old brass cannons responded. A cannonball caromed off the side amidships. Metal shrieked. *San Pablo* shuddered. Steam hissed. He jumped to look out aft. Steam was billowing from the engine-room skylight.

The lights were out. Hot steam was choking. Holman followed a hunch through wet, roaring darkness. He skirted invisibly flying machinery and his hand went surely in the darkness to the root steam valve for the fire and bilge pump. He closed it and the roaring stopped. He ran to the generator. It had tripped from shock. He reset it and jumped it up to speed. Harris was there.

"I'll get it back on the line," Harris said.

The guns still clamored, shaking the ship. The engine rolled on powerfully. A great new bulge in the side had sprung a steam flange and blown the gasket. Holman ran for wrenches. The lights came up. Harris joined him and began hacking out a new gasket. The bolts were stretched and the threads jammed. Holman twisted them in two by main strength. Franks' great voice came down the skylight.

"*Fire!* Main deck aft! *Fire!* Main deck aft!"

They raced the job, careless of their hands. The firing stopped.

Bells jangled. Lynch slowed the engine. Feet thudded on the boat deck. Bordelles ran in on the gratings.

"Below there!" he shouted. "For God's sake give us more pressure on the fire main!"

"Aye aye! Any minute!" Holman shouted back.

They used two spare bolts and two C-clamps and wrapped Harris' shirt around the flange to hold the hiss and drip. Holman started the pump clanking and built the fire main pressure as high as he could. Krebs had come out to see what was wrong. Slow speed meant a breather for them in the fireroom. Harris stared at his trembling, blistered hands. He was an old man for a job like that.

"I'd give my God damned soul for a cup of coffee!" Harris said.

"Hand it over," Krebs said. "Stawski's right this minute brewing a bucketful. I come out to tell you."

A stinkpot had shattered on the port side of the crew's compartment. The sticky black stuff splashed all along the deck and side and bit fire into the wood. When they got pressure on the fire main, the water only spread the flames. Lt. Collins sent all the men down to fight the fire. Only Bronson was left, at the wheel. *San Pablo* was drifting back with the current, nearly out of range already.

The junks stopped firing. Lt. Collins studied them through the long glass. The command junk was splintered and smoking but obstinately afloat. You could not sink a junk with gunfire. On the junks Chinese were dancing all over the topsides. They thought they had won. A few wore yellowish uniforms, but most of them were plain coolies. They were all dancing in joy at their great victory.

Lt. Collins smiled coldly. One of the sacred sayings came into his mind: *No captain can do very wrong if he lay his ship alongside that of his enemy.* He kept repeating it in his mind. Vincent came into the bridge, panting and blackened and hatless. He saluted anyway.

"Mr. Bordelles sends respects and the fire is under control, sir."

"Very well. Go back down." Lt. Collins turned to Bronson. "I'm going down there too. Hold the ship in mid-channel." It was the first word he had spoken to Bronson all day.

"Aye aye, sir!" Bronson said eagerly.

The fire was not yet out. Lt. Collins stood by the galley and watched them fight it with hoses and axes. They chopped burning wood away and pitched it over the side. The whole portside aft was gone, above the steel hull. The boat deck sagged there, burnt through in places. Franks and Farren were shoring it.

Jennings came up to report formally that he had moved the sickbay to the old Chinese quarters in the steel hull. The only battle casualty so far was Tullio, with a bullet in his leg he had not known about. Some men were burnt and some choked with fumes. None were disabled. Jennings was very precise and formal with his report.

"Very well," Lt. Collins said. "Carry on, Jennings."

It took a long time to put the fire all the way out. The crew's compartment was gutted. The low sun turned the long reach of river a dull red. Bordelles came over, black and weary and grinning. The men crowded behind him. They were expecting praise. Lt. Collins was not yet ready to praise them.

"Can we serve out food, sir, some rest and water, before we try again?" Bordelles asked.

"There's not enough daylight left. Serve out cutlasses and pistols," Lt. Collins said. "I'm going to grapple and board."

They all knew the plan, but he reviewed it rapidly. They would keep two machine guns and the bow gun manned, to hold down fire from the flanking junks. They would keep a minimum crew in the engine spaces. Everyone else would board. As he talked, he could see the men nerving themselves to the prospect. They stood proudly. They would not falter. He was proud of them, but he would not let his manner show it.

"I want Harris and Holman from the engineers," Lt. Collins said. "Have them standing by here in the passageway."

"Aye aye, sir!" Bordelles said.

Holman waited with his axe in the midship passageway. The boarding party would come down the port ladder and he would tail on. He would board the junk and cut the bamboo cable.

Harris was there too, with a pistol and cutlass. The smell of burning was all around. The two men did not speak. Both were pink from a light steam burn and Harris had bandaged hands. He kept hefting and balancing his cutlass and sighting along it.

Holman kept drying his palms on his hips so that he would have a good grip on the axe when the time came.

The sun was low behind the boom. The junks darted long shadows. *San Pablo* closed the range fast this time. *San Pablo* was plunging in fast for the kill. On either side of Lt. Collins his machine guns hammered with berserk fury. From the enemy line of battle the pale winks and the black, rose-shot bloomings grew and grew in crackling thunder. They made the air sing around *San Pablo*. They made the air alive with hurtling death.

Slam; bark; clatter! Thud; thud; thud! Faster and faster past endurance the rhythmic litany built onward and upward. Lt. Collins thrilled with a mounting exaltation. The men at the guns felt it. They showed it in eyes ablaze and lips writhed back, shoulders shaking and hips weaving as they drove their bucking guns. The coolies up ahead felt it, leaping and waving steel and voicing a thin, high devil screech through their billowing powder smoke. The mast with the gearwheel flag toppled. The Sand Pebbles set up a wolfish cheering.

Lt. Collins was a spring wound tight to snapping. It was new and terrible in pure intensity. It was uncontainable in flesh. *San Pablo* was very near.

"Half speed! *Cease* firing! *Cease* firing!" Lt. Collins shouted. "Boarding party, take arms!"

They scrambled for them. Lt. Collins threw off cap and tunic.

"Take her now!" he told the smudged and grimy Bordelles. "Lay her alongside!"

He flourished his gleaming cutlass and glanced down at his white undershirt and trousers. He was the only clean white one left aboard. The men formed up behind him. Bells jangled and the engine beat changed. The ruined junk stern, all smoke and yellow splinters, slid by close aboard. Lt. Collins made his voice ring like bell metal.

"Awa-a-a-a-ay . . . the boarding party!"

He led them all in a roaring rush, forward and up and over the wooden bulwark to the junk's foredeck. He slashed and fired and darted through and leaped to the deckhouse. He raced along the top of it to meet them bursting out of the ruined poop, a hedge of steel and screaming faces. Cutlass high, he leaped down to the short after deck and turned his ankle on a dead man's arm. He went to his knees. The gleaming halberd blade slashed down at him and he slugged a bullet to the bare belly and someone from behind thrust in to take the blow. They all went down in a heap and feet trampled them. A storm of shots and clashing steel and screaming human voices raged over their heads.

He struggled to rise and could not. Warm blood pumped rhythmically into his face and blinded his eyes. He struggled and blinked his eyes and saw through rosy mist the bristling white hair on the almost-severed head. He knew in a final, flooding weakness that his savior was Harris.

Steel rang. Shots blasted. Men screamed. Feet thumped and scrambled. Holman, running to the great cable across the junk bow, slipped in blood.

Grunting with full arm swings, he hacked the cable. It was a great, beautiful, complexly interwoven pale-green-and-yellow snake thick as his own body. Bullets keened over. The axe turned and glanced off the resilient bamboo. *Arf! Arf!* somewhere the Red Dog went and *bark . . . bark . . .* the bow gun went and the muzzle blast came in hot pats to Holman's sweaty face. He swung the axe harder, in a driven fury of haste.

Strand by chip by chunk it broke apart, under the splintering axe. Aft on the junk coolies leaped overboard. Men carried one, helped other white-clad, red-splashed shipmates back aboard *San Pablo*. The cable raveled and creaked and stretched. The axe never stopped. Men crossed with metal cans, and kerosene splashed the junk's splintered wood. Flame in a crackling roar warmed Holman's back. He drove the axe with savage desperation. The cable remnant parted with a squeal and a pop and the flaming junk lurched free.

Instantly, the current had it. Holman climbed to the bulwark and made a great leap across to the bow of *San Pablo*. He landed sprawling on knees and elbows, knowing he had skinned them badly, and he saw stupidly that he still had the axe. He stayed down, for the shelter of the steel bulwark.

On the bridge they were cheering and clasping hands above their heads. The firing had stopped. Holman's ears rang with silence.

"Yump, Yake, yump!" Farren shouted down to him. "If you can't make it in one yump, yump twice!"

Grinning self-consciously, Holman stood up. The brown current was sweeping the sundered halves of the boom apart each way like gates opening. Fire doors clanged below. The engine throb gained power. With sparks from her dogleg stack fountaining triumphantly into the twilight, *San Pablo* steamed through.

47

The three men ate cold corned beef and hardtack by the light of a candle stuck in an ashtray. *San Pablo* was anchored in midstream below Paoshan, with all topside lights out because of snipers on the south bank. Bordelles was pleading that he might lead the rescue party to China Light. Lynch seconded him. Lt. Collins prepared to say concisely one more time what he had already told them in detail.

"That rescue is our primary mission and so I must lead it myself," he said. *"San Pablo* and every man of us in her are secondary to that." He spoke with sharp finality. "They will try to repair the boom. You haven't the strength to break it a second time," he told Bordelles. "If I am not back by full daylight, you must consider the primary mission has failed and sail without me. That is all and that is an order."

He stood up. The others rose also. Candlelight showed feeling struggling in their faces. Lynch was about to say something sentimental.

"As you were. Finish your meal," Lt. Collins said, to forestall that. "I expect it will be dark enough to leave in a few more minutes. I don't want you to come out."

He stopped outside by the boat deck rail. An occasional bullet was still striking the ship or whining over. He would have to wait until his eyes adjusted before he could judge whether it was dark enough for a small boat to risk those snipers. He heard Lynch speak inside.

"I'm scared he don't figure to come back, Mr. Bordelles."

Lt. Collins moved aft along the rail. He did not want to hear. Below him on the quarterdeck Farren was assembling the boat party. The motor sampan was already waiting at the gangway. Lt. Collins stood there in darkness and thought about the day with mixed feelings.

San Pablo was purged of guilt and shame. The men were sound and whole again. Not counting engineers, hardly a man but bore his wound. Shanahan and Ellis lay gravely hurt. Franks and three others were immobilized. Harris lay dead at the side of the quarterdeck. He was covered with the day's battle flag. Tomorrow out in the lake they would bury Harris with full honors. Perhaps Shanahan too, by then.

Yet somehow he still could not forgive them. He himself had a sprained ankle, well taped now. He bounced his weight on his right foot. The ankle twinged sharply. He held up his hand at arm's length and he could barely make out the separate fingers. It was almost dark enough. The men on the quarterdeck were just hushed voices down there in blackness.

"Well, guys, I guess we showed them worker-pissants who's boss on the river," someone said comfortably.

"We did! We sure as hell did!"

"Old Harris. I guess he's in them happy hunting grounds."

"Harris was all right."

"He was a good shipmate."

"He saved the skipper's life. I saw him do it."

"They'll name a tin can after him."

"They don't name destroyers after enlisted men."

"Sure they do! How about the *Edsall,* two-nineteen?"

"Who the hell was Edsall?"

"A seaman. He got killed fighting kanakas down in Samoa."

"Quarterdeck, there!" Lt. Collins said crisply. "Man the boat!"

They were burning bean oil with a wick in a saucer, to save kerosene. It made a very dim light and an acrid smell in the small parlor. Mr. Craddock sat with hands folded and lips moving silently. Shirley could not think of anything to say. For hours they had been saying the same things over. Gillespie stood up.

"Please don't pace, Walter," she said. "It makes the light flicker so. I'm getting a headache."

He sat down. "Even if nothing more happened, Cho-jen should have sent another messenger by now!" he said, for the tenth time.

One of the youngest boys had come home, sent with news of a great victory. The gunboat had been hurled back downriver in flames. But midway in his journey the boy had heard more cannonading, and they still did not know.

"Someone will come soon," Mr. Craddock said.

Shirley spoke one of the thoughts that had been haunting them all evening. No one had yet ventured to say it.

"What if the gunboat breaks through? What will they do then?"

"Come here, no doubt. But that one is too old and weak to break through, God grant." Gillespie stood up again. "I can't just sit here," he said. "I'm going back out to the gate and talk to old Wang. Maybe he's heard something."

Wang was the gateman. All rumors from outside seemed to reach him first. Gillespie went out, striding nervously. The wind of his motion set the naked lamp flame jumping. Shadows danced wildly all around the small parlor and Shirley closed her eyes.

Gillespie was feeling the burden of his vigorous manhood, she knew. What he loved was threatened and boys had gone out to fight and defend it. Cho-jen, whom they both loved, had gone out. All that she had tried to say in comfort to Gillespie had only made it harder on him.

The dancing lamp flame steadied. Shirley opened her eyes.

"Poor Walter," she said aloud.

Craddock looked up. "You've become very fond of him, haven't you?" he asked. "Tai-tai saw it beginning. It pleased her."

"Do you think so? I respect Walter immensely," Shirley said.

She did not feel as shocked as she thought she should at Craddock's observation. For some reason, it brought Jake Holman to her mind. She saw with sudden clarity that Walter Gillespie was already the man

Jake Holman might have become, under a more kindly star. In the first period at China Light she had seen little of Gillespie and she had thought of him as conventionally sexless, the way women felt toward preachers. But now, thrown with him as a fellow teacher, living with him like brother and sister in the Craddock household, sharing the grief for Tai-tai and the love for Cho-jen, she knew that Walter Gillespie was a very good man indeed. She had been leaning on him more than she realized.

"Walter is fighting a feeling that he should have gone with Cho-jen to the battle," she said. "That sailor, Mr. Holman, was in the battle, and I know he didn't want to be." She sighed. "I used to think it was hardest being a woman. But it can be hard being a man, too."

"It is just hard being young," Craddock said.

They went straight up the center of the river. Farren held the tiller and Holman sat beside him with the motor popping along and making a gasoline smell in the damp night air. Farren kept his wounded leg stuck straight out. Several times other boats hailed them in Chinese and they ignored it, but no one shot at them. Lt. Collins, in fresh whites, stood like a silent ghost in the bow. Bronson sat as near Lt. Collins as he could. In the waist, muttering curses, Crosley was trying to sleep. Crosley had a painful spear slash along his ribs.

"The skipper's bringing us luck. He's got a charmed life," Farren whispered. "We'll nip in there and grab them people and get out again, while the slopeheads are still down for the count."

Holman did not answer. He was thinking that he would see Shirley, and the thought warmed his blood. He did not think the missionaries would come away. It was against common sense and all that he could imagine, but he felt excited and hopeful. The fire had taken his bunk and locker, including all his money. All he owned was the dungarees he was wearing. It made everything seem free and possible.

Above Paoshan Farren slowed to half speed and eased the boat into the creek. Weeping willows overhung the stone banks and he had to steer chancily by patches of star glimmer on the black water. The bow wave washed against the banks like a steady whisper following them. Here and there dogs barked and one time ducks quacked loudly. All the houses were dark. Farren kept shifting his leg.

"Damn thing keeps itching under the bandage," he said.

At the China Light jetty Lt. Collins waited while Holman and Bronson jumped out to moor the boat. Then he gave Farren his wristwatch and instructed him very sternly.

"If I am not back within two hours, return to the ship," he said. "Tell Mr. Bordelles the primary mission has failed."

"Aye aye, sir," Farren said unhappily.

He would obey, all right. This was war. Crosley begged to go along. He insisted his rib wound was well bandaged and did not hamper him. Crosley had very good spirit.

"Crosley's our best BAR man, sir," Bronson put in.

Bronson was inclined to be officious. He was also right. Lt. Collins climbed up on the jetty, favoring his right ankle.

"Very well, Crosley," he said. "Fall in behind me, the three of you."

He led the way in silence. Ahead across the fields China Light crouched squatly black, like a fortress against the starred sky. He had to watch his step on the narrow dike. The fields were deep mud. Night birds swooped for insects above his head. They made a low bullroar of unseen wings.

Time's winged chariot, he thought, and wondered why.

He tried to hurry and trod heavily on a pebble and felt his weakened ankle turn sharply inside the bandages. It stabbed. He went on without breaking stride, trying not to limp, damning in his mind the successive jolts of pain. The great mission gates were closed, but dim light glowed in the gatehouse. A man came out of the small door to meet them. When he spoke, Lt. Collins realized that he was one of the missionaries in Chinese clothing. Gillespie, his name was.

"Lt. Collins? You should never have come here," Gillespie said. "It will be best for all of us if you will go away at once."

His low voice was angry. It roused Lt. Collins' old angers.

"You must get out of here, without delay," he said. "Have you heard yet what happened at Nanking?"

"Yes. But we are safe here. Only you endanger us."

Lt. Collins heard the disgusted murmur from the men behind him. That was comment enough. Crisply, his voice edged with the pain of his ankle, he told Gillespie about the general evacuation order and about the boom fight.

"No matter what you thought before, this changes it," he said. "We killed them. We took their face. They'll be wild for revenge."

Gillespie was shaking his head. He seemed unable to speak.

"Are there any armed guards here? Where are the others of you? Speak up, man!"

"All our militia went to the battle. I was hoping to see them come back here victorious instead of you," Gillespie said flatly. "I can speak for the others. They will not go with you."

"They must tell me that themselves. Take me to where they are."

"Listen. You've done enough harm." Gillespie gestured savagely. "Go on. Get out of here. You have no business here."

"If you force me, I will break down doors until I find them. It is my duty."

"It is *not* your duty! Listen!" Controlling his anger, Gillespie told an absurd story. They had declared themselves stateless persons, like the White Russians. They had sent their names to Geneva, requesting Nansen passports. "We mailed a copy to the consul," Gillespie finished.

"I know nothing of that."

"You do now."

"No, I do not!" Lt. Collins' patience broke. "Come along, men," he said over his shoulder.

Gillespie went grudgingly ahead of them. Bronson came up to Lt. Collins' right elbow.

"Is your ankle worse, sir? I see you limping," he said solicitously. "Will you lean on my arm, sir?"

"No. Fall back," Lt. Collins said shortly.

He had not yet forgiven Bronson. He began letting himself limp openly. The pain in his ankle was atrocious. Gillespie led them through the school quadrangle and into the Chinese section. No lights showed.

"This is the place," he said. "At least leave your men outside."

It was a Chinese house flush against the much higher compound wall. In a clear space to one side was what looked like the frame and coping of a well. The house made three sides of a courtyard and a head-high mud wall made the front of it. They had to turn sharply just inside the gate to go around a brick spirit screen.

"Detail, halt!" Lt. Collins ordered. "Wait here in the courtyard."

Dim light rosed one half-open window. Lt. Collins followed Gillespie through a door on that side. It was a small parlor with American furniture. The dim light was from a wick burning in a saucer of oil on the table. It threw leaping shadows and made the room smell scorched. Two people in Chinese clothing stood up. One was old Craddock. The woman was young. Eckert, her name was.

"He won't take my word for it. Tell him you're not leaving," Gillespie said. "I'll get him a copy of our declaration."

He went on into the next room. Lt. Collins set his rifle butt down and clasped the muzzle with both hands. That way he could take some weight off his throbbing ankle. He stared grimly at the girl and the old man.

"Well," he said. "Tell me."

Holman wandered about the courtyard. He had a feeling he had been there before. There were two trees leafy above. The surface was packed earth with flat stones to take rain drip from the overhanging eaves. Holman was wishing he could have a chance to ask Gillespie about that paper they had all signed. He had not understood about that.

Crosley was crouching at the half-open window. He motioned Holman and Bronson to join him. They all crouched there, leaning on their rifles. Lt. Collins was talking in a flat, hard voice.

"I know you people do not wish to be the instruments of shame to your country," he said. "If you have no care for yourselves, I appeal to your loyalty."

"We are serving a higher loyalty," Craddock said.

"There *is* no higher loyalty!"

They faced each other in there, frozen. She was wearing pale-blue

Chinese jacket and trousers. She looked soft and shadowy and very beautiful, in the dim light. She made a fire in his stomach and a hurt in his throat and a tingle along the backs of his hands.

Jesus! She's even prettier than I remembered, he thought.

"I suppose you will tell me next that God has told you to stay here," Lt. Collins said finally. "Every padded cell in America is filled with people who talk to God. How are you people any different?"

"Hah!" Crosley said under his breath.

"Read this paper," Gillespie said, holding it out. "By this signed declaration we have temporarily renounced nationality in itself. Are you not able to *understand* that?"

"I understand it to be impossible. No sane person would try."

"Your uniform now gives you no authority over us and no responsibility for us," Gillespie said tightly. "Here. Are you afraid to read it?" He thrust the paper out again and Lt. Collins took it. "If you like, we'll sign it again in your presence," Gillespie said.

Holman stood slowly upright. He felt dizzy. *I can sign that paper myself,* he thought. *However it works, it will work on me too. That's how I'll stay here!* He wanted to walk out his leaping excitement, but he was afraid that he would miss something.

"Hah!" Crosley breathed.

Stronger light flared at the window. Holman knelt again. Lt. Collins was burning the paper in the flame of the little oil lamp on the table.

They were strong men clashing and she was afraid. In the light of the burning paper, Gillespie's face looked savage. Shirley knew she had to intervene.

"Lt. Collins, will you excuse us to talk privately for a moment?" she asked.

He nodded. He dropped the paper flaming into the oil but made no move to leave. Instead, he resumed his curiously still, pitched-forward leaning stance on his rifle. From the first, his face had been white and thin-lipped, like a mask of leashed anger.

"In Mr. Craddock's study, then," she said. "Come, Walter."

She took his arm, trying to smile away his frown, and they followed

Craddock into the study. She closed the door. It was too dark to see each other. They whispered their words.

"Of course we will refuse to go," Craddock said.

"Of course. If we go, we make all that the Chungs have been saying true," Gillespie said. "We make all that we and Cho-jen have been saying into a lie. We would betray Cho-jen."

"We have to make that officer understand," Shirley said.

"His kind would rather die than understand."

"Please, Walter. You've been antagonizing him," she said. "If you will just let Mr. Craddock reason with him."

"Let's just go through the back rooms and outside through Ting's house," Gillespie said. "The people outside West Gate will hide us. Leave him standing in there with his teeth in his mouth."

"No. We must persuade him to go away," Craddock said. "The boys might come back. There would be bloodshed."

"You're right, of course." Gillespie sighed. "One thing, though. Suppose he will not be persuaded? He has three armed men with him." Gillespie's arm trembled under her hand. "What if he threatens to take us forcibly? Let's decide that."

"He wouldn't dare!"

"He would dare. And if he does, I'm afraid I'll fight," Gillespie said somberly.

"If we must, we can simply come in here to confer again," Craddock said. "Then we can escape through Ting's house."

Gillespie agreed doubtfully. They began discussing how they would reason with Lt. Collins.

"Don't mention God. It will only infuriate him," Gillespie warned.

The damned paper was black ash flecks on the oil. Lt. Collins leaned on his rifle. He wanted to sit down, but they had not invited him to do so. He knew he should soak his ankle and rebandage it. Most of the pain was because the bandage was too tight for the new swelling. He would not ask them for hospitality. Besides, there was no time.

Time! *Damn* the ankle and *damn* the loose pebble on the dike!

Damn the farmer who pitched it up there and *damn* whatever it was that made pebbles! *Damn* the luck!

No, the luck is good, he thought. At least they are unguarded. I have been too harsh, because my ankle hurts. I will reason with them. But *San Pablo* had fought the great fight of her history that day and these missionaries were not, repeat not, going to rob that fight of its meaning, his thoughts insisted. He was going to give them the benefit of the doubt and consider that they were religious maniacs. Somewhere behind their careful words they had to be hiding a crazy God.

They were taking forever in that room. There was no time. *Come out, damn you!* he willed at the closed door.

First Crosley and then Bronson had risen and gone away, bored by the talk. Holman still crouched there. Craddock was doing the talking. Shirley was standing back in the shallows, close to Gillespie. She kept putting her hand on his arm and half-smiling up at him, as if she were afraid of something.

Lt. Collins was being very polite now. So was Craddock. The old man looked gray and shrunken and his voice was gentle. Holman could not understand all that they were saying. Some Bolshevik outfit in Paoshan, the Chungs, was claiming that the missionaries could not legally give up their personal treaty privileges. So they had temporarily given up nationality itself, the way you took off a coat when it was too warm.

Nations are paper. People are real, Holman thought. *That's what the old man's trying to get across.*

"We are still Americans in our hearts, but not in the absolutely exclusive way the nation demands of us," Shirley said.

"Surprisingly many Chinese are able to understand instantly what we have done," Craddock said. "I hope you will understand, Lt. Collins. I hope you will go back to your ship and leave us here in the peace and safety our act has made for us."

"I understand what you honestly *think* you have done," Lt. Collins said. "However, neither I nor any of you are competent to rule on that. Suppose you come with me to Hankow, make your renunciation legally, if that turns out to be possible, and then you can come back here. Fair enough?"

"No. We have really done it. To go away now, willingly, would be to deny that."

"Go in flight from Chinese mob violence."

"Such danger as we may face is of your making, by coming here," Craddock said. "Go away again, and the danger will be gone."

"It will not. I know about the death sentence you are under."

"It is appealed. Chinese law protects me also."

"What if it is confirmed?"

"I would consider it unjust. But I would submit."

"And call it holy martyrdom, no doubt!"

Lt. Collins' voice turned harsh. Holman was watching Shirley's face. She stood close to Gillespie and she kept looking up at him. Gillespie was looking very angry. That was what she was afraid of, Holman thought. He kept his eyes on her.

There was no time left, Lt. Collins thought. These people were in a crazed dream. He had to shock and frighten them out of it.

"You are an old man without much life left, Craddock, but you have no right to dispose of yourself in that way," he said coldly. "There is no time for more talk. Delay endangers us all. Now you people listen to me!"

In harsh, vivid words, leaning with clenched hands on his rifle muzzle, rocking it for emphasis, he told them about Nanking and the boom fight. It was another Boxer Rebellion, he insisted. The ugly words took his mind off the pain in his ankle. He turned his fire on the weakest link in their chain.

"You, Miss Eckert. They will strip you and rape you," he said. He deliberately eyed all the curves of her body. "They will subject you to indecency and agony and death," he said. "Is that God's will?"

Her face showed shocked disgust. She shrank against Gillespie, who frowned blackly.

"We are at war. You know how American men, the real men,

avenge their women," Lt. Collins went on. "This whole valley will have to pay in fire and blood. Is that God's will?"

"You don't know them. They wouldn't hurt me," she protested.

"I do know them. I've seen Chinese troops take a city. Many times."

"You've seen warlord troops. The thing you know is your own nature," Gillespie said tautly. "Miss Eckert is just a symbol of national prestige to you, isn't she? When have you ever cared about *Chinese* women raped and butchered? Raped by the warlord troops you favor, because they obey your treaties?"

The girl was recovering from her shock. She stood close against Gillespie and loathing contorted her pretty face.

"You rape them yourselves, with your power to buy their starving flesh!" she cried at him.

"Silence!"

It was his command voice. Bronson and Crosley hurried back to kneel beside Holman. Holman stood up. He closed his eyes and he could still see her twisted face and hear her cry. Her face was the face of those women on the Changsha bund.

Other faces crowded into his memory, scores of Chinese girl-faces crying, and naked, slender girl bodies shrinking and wincing and trembling under him. From seven years and a hundred pigshacks along the China Coast they came all to him at once. Like most American sailors, he had always taken the young and tender ones, and he had paid the extra money that cost. He had always been gentle with them. Afterward he would hold them and stroke them, while they cried and trembled, until they would relax and nestle in to him and cling to him, and he could feel that they had forgiven him. But now he knew that he could never forgive himself.

"That's telling 'em, ain't it?" Bronson whispered admiringly.

He tugged at Holman's trouser leg. Holman crouched. He was afraid to look at Shirley. Craddock was flapping his hands.

"Please. Please restrain yourselves," he said. "Lt. Collins, we will withdraw to confer again."

"No, you will not. There is no time," Lt. Collins said. "Agree now, repeat *right* now, or I will assume you are all deranged and take you along by force."

"You can always shoot us," Gillespie said, turning. "Come on, Shirley."

"Walter! Please, Walter!" She was holding his arm.

"Bronson! Come in here!" Lt. Collins snapped.

Bronson went flying. Holman stood up. He moved slowly toward the door, which Bronson had left open. Now was the time to take their side and fight for them. To strike down Bronson and Crosley and Lt. Collins all three, if he had to. Now was the time.

But he could not look into her face and eyes. He was not clean. Nothing in the world could ever make him clean enough. He lingered. Then Crosley was beside him.

"Jake! Somebody's coming!" Crosley whispered. "Hear it?"

Holman heard running footsteps, not fast but heavy, someone weary. The man burst through the gate and thudded across the courtyard to the open door. He was shiny and stinking with mud. He stumbled and almost fell across the threshold. Holman and Crosley closed in to see what it might mean.

The mud-caked intruder gasped for breath. He pressed his side and gaped around at them like a fish. Shirley knew him first, without his glasses.

"Tao-min!" she said. "What happened?"

He spoke then, in breathless Chinese, and she would not let herself understand the half-voiced phrases. But Gillespie understood. In hard, sharp Chinese he pressed for details and certainties and all the while that she would not understand the knowledge was soaking into her unbearably as death.

They had killed Cho-jen in the battle.

"Oh," she said.

There were no words. She turned unseeing and might have fallen, but then Gillespie was holding her. Her head was on his shoulder. Mr. Craddock was close and both their arms seemed around her.

"Cho-jen is dead," she told them. "He's dead."

"He is with God, Shirley."

They were speaking Chinese. She was struggling to grasp the greatness of it. It could not be true. She felt Gillespie's voice vibration through his chest but she scarcely heard his words. Tao-min was still speaking, in his shrill boy's voice.

"The Chung militia is coming," he panted. "They are coming to execute Mr. Craddock. You must all run away!"

"Everything's lost, if Cho-jen is dead," Gillespie said. "The Chungs will take over the whole valley. We have no choice but to go now, Mr. Craddock."

"The Chungs will kill all the sea devils. I will kill the sea devils myself," Tao-min said. "You must all run away. Let me run away with you."

The officer and sailor were listening intently, heads thrust forward, as if in that way they might understand the Chinese. The officer limped over, thudding his rifle along like a blind man's cane, and shook Gillespie's arm.

"What's this boy saying?" he demanded. "What news have you?"

Gillespie looked at him. "You have killed that boy Mr. Craddock told you about," he said curtly in English. "A boy worth more to humanity than you and your crew twice over."

"Ten times over!" Shirley cried, her voice breaking.

Her tears were starting. Gillespie's arm tightened around her, holding and protecting her. Numbers could no more express it than words. It was as if she could not give way to her grief until she could know how great it was. The officer's lips quirked painfully.

"The boy was—"

"Chinese. Therefore worthless, to you," Gillespie broke in.

"—in arms against me."

"Well, you have won your game," Gillespie said. "You have destroyed everything, and we will have to go with you."

The officer's white grimace did not change. Only his lips moved.

"Very well. Take five minutes to collect personal papers."

"Tao-min, how near are they?" Gillespie asked.

"They are coming like the skin on my heels."

"Hey! Hey in the house!" a hoarse voice cried from the courtyard. "Somebody's coming! A whole mob!"

"Douse that light, Bronson!"

It was all noise and wild motion in darkness.

"Craddock! Old man, come back here!"

Two shapes plunged through the door. Many guns roared all at once in the courtyard, and men's wild shouts. The sailor was crouching and firing through the window. Gillespie threw her roughly to the floor.

"Stay *down,* Shirley!" he said tensely, and left her.

Guns at the spirit screen roared red-mouthed and screeching shadows came around both ends of the screen into the courtyard. Guns answered from the house and Crosley's automatic rifle outroared them all. Holman clubbed his rifle and went for the shadows in a confused, fighting tangle under a tree. Feet stamped and men screamed and the darkness was all *whang . . . whang . . . spock!* with bullets.

Then they streamed out again, dragging wounded and leaving behind dark, blotchy shapes on the packed earth. Crosley was howling curses and firing around one corner of the spirit screen.

"Man that other corner!" Lt. Collins' voice shouted. "Watch the top of the wall!"

Holman knelt at the corner opposite Crosley. He began firing his rifle blindly out the gate. They were yelling and shooting outside, but the bullets went high because of the wall. The bullets that came through the gate *thugged* and *splatted* on the spirit screen.

"Jake! Hold it!" Crosley shouted. "Don't waste ammunition!"

Holman stopped firing. He put his rifle butt-down and leaned on it.

"Just loose off a round now and then to let 'em know we're still alive and kicking in here," Crosley said.

Holman's thoughts went back to how her head had gone so naturally to Gillespie's shoulder and the natural way Gillespie's arm came round and held her. The feeling reminded him of an earlier feeling, and he groped in his memory for it.

"Watch it, Jake!"

Holman turned. One of the bodies near them was twitching and trying to crawl. Crosley rose and smashed his heavy rifle butt down on the middle of its back. Both legs flexed and kicked out wildly, and then it lay still.

"The only good ones are dead ones," Crosley grunted.

At the deep bottom of the seabag of his memory, Holman found it. On winter days after school let out in Wellco, Nevada, he would linger on his way home to look in the bakery window. People would go in and out the door and warm, cinnamon-smelling air would come out. He was just a little boy then. The grown-up feeling was harder to take, he thought. Yes, a hell of a lot harder to take.

"You hurt, Jake? You hit anywhere?" Crosley asked.

"No," Holman said.

"Me neither," Crosley said. "Farren's right. The skipper brings us luck." He felt along his left side with the backs of his fingers. "I started bleeding again, though," he said. "I'm all soggy."

Craddock was dead. Bronson had reported no one else hurt. Lt. Collins sat on the low threshold and tried to follow what Gillespie was saying. He had twisted his ankle yet once again in his lunge after Craddock, and it was hopeless now. He fought his mind clear of the frosting pain and nodded decisively.

"Stand by back there with the girl," he told Gillespie. "The party will leave in two minutes." Gillespie went away. "Bronson!" Lt. Collins snapped.

"Right here, sir." Bronson was kneeling at his elbow.

"Help me out to the spirit screen."

They went sagging and lurching across the courtyard, his arm feeling squeamish over Bronson's fat shoulders. At the screen, Lt. Collins knelt on his right knee. He told the men about the back door through the compound wall into the fields. The attackers were from Paoshan and did not know about it.

"They think they have us trapped," he said. "Bronson, I want you to take charge and get all hands down to the boat as fast as you can. I will stay here and shoot and yell things in English, to make them think we are all still in here."

They crouched in shocked silence, except for the shouting outside and scattered bullets whining over.

"How about you, sir?" Crosley asked.

"Never mind about me. That's none of your business."

"Sir, it is our business," Bronson said. "The primary mission still needs you. It ain't accomplished yet."

"I can't walk. I would only slow you and imperil the primary mission."

"One of us can get on each side of you and hop you along as fast as a man can run," Bronson said. "Somebody else can stay here, to give the party a start, and then catch up."

Crosley swung around and fired a short burst. *"How wow wow!"* he bellowed. "Come and get it, you bastards! It's hot and waiting for you!" He swung around again. "Sounds like it's only one guy yelling out there now," he said. "Maybe he's lining them out for an attack. We better hurry."

"You have your orders, Bronson," Lt. Collins said. "Obey them!"

"Sir, I can't!" Bronson protested. "I couldn't face Mr. Bordelles. He wouldn't dare face Comyang. Maybe the pain is affecting how you think, sir."

The pain was doing that, but not the pain and not in the way that Bronson meant. Yet Bronson, God damn him for it, did have the right of it. It would look very strange in the report. Bronson was right about the primary mission.

"Bronson, damn you, carry out your orders!" he said.

"Sir, I *can't!*" Bronson's voice was agonized. *"Please* don't make us just take you anyway, Captain!"

"I'll stay here," Holman said. "I know what to do."

Bitterly, with the other pain masking the throb from his ankle, Lt. Collins bowed to it.

"Very well," he said. "You will have to fire and shout from different positions, to keep fooling them. Before they attack, they will set up a lot of shouting and firing to mask it. Be sure you escape when that starts, if not before."

"Yes, sir," Holman said. "I got it."

Bronson tugged Lt. Collins to his feet and Crosley took his other arm. Each of them pulled one of Lt. Collins' arms around his neck. They hopped him back across the courtyard so fast that his good foot barely touched the ground.

Well, he had it. They were gone. He fired a shot over the wall. He had to yell something.

"Fire in the hole!" he yelled.

It did not matter what he yelled, because all they spoke out there was Chinese. He could not understand what the guy out there was yelling, either. He was pacing back and forth in the shelter of the wall and counting the laps he made. That helped him guess how far away the party had gotten. The Chinese had a story about a girl who did that in her courtyard, and she sent her spirit to a temple far away. He walked very fast, as if that would help speed them on their way to the boat.

It was stupid. He was just making night noises with his gun and his mouth. He was a scarecrow trying to keep the crows scared for a few more minutes. No it's not stupid, it's serious, he thought. It had become serious just as soon as the others were gone. He missed Crosley, especially. It was time to fire again.

Crack! and the jar to the shoulder.

"How we doing, Crosley, old frog, old shipmate?" he shouted across the courtyard.

After that when he fired he always yelled something to Crosley. A bullet clipped off a twig and dropped it at his feet. He sniffed the green, barky smell of it and stuffed it into his shirt pocket. They had gotten onto the low roofs of the houses across the way and were firing down. It shortened the bullet shadow of the front wall. It was about time for him to leave.

"Ten more laps and we'll shove off!" he yelled to the imaginary Crosley.

All he had wanted was to live among them and do the things he knew how to do best. Now, out there, they had not so much as seen his face, and they wanted to kill him. I should have listened to Scharf, he thought. It ain't my revolution. It sure never was my revolution.

The bullets were forcing him closer to the front wall. The scarecrow is getting very scared, he thought. Three bodies lay strung out in a line parallel to the spirit screen. Crosley would have stepped on arms and legs. Holman curved in and out around the bodies as he paced. From deep in the seabag of his memory he recalled a game they made the kids play in first grade back in Wellco, Nevada. You held hands and you wove in and out like that and you sang a song about go in and out the window. The little boys thought it was sissy, but the teachers made them play. When you grew up they had different games, but you still had to play. Everybody plays and everybody loses, he thought.

He pressed a new clip into the magazine. The cartridges made oily, slithering clicks. Well, all he really ever had to lose was a hope. Well, he did not grudge her to Gillespie. Ten more laps and then I will really go, he told himself.

He was no more ready to face them than he had been when he volunteered to stay behind. He still had to figure how to act toward them. Just natural, he thought. They won't know. But I know. What's natural, anyway? Well, he could not put it off. The rate of firing increased suddenly and a bullet brushed his hair. He jumped closer to the spirit screen.

"Hit him again, he's Irish!" he roared, in fear and defiance.

Something bit him behind the left knee. He tried to jump and his leg buckled and he went down. He rocked back up on his rump and swiveled and smashed his rifle butt against the lifted head. The head fell. It was the same body Crosley had smashed and a knife lay beside the outflung hand.

"You son of a bitch!" Holman told it. "Now you done it!"

He stood up and he could tell that he was hamstrung. He had to lean his back against the spirit screen to stay up on both legs. There was only a stinging back of his knee, but the muscles in that leg were wanting to charleyhorse.

She's got a brother named Charley, he remembered. Charley and Gillespie will take care of her.

The firing was very heavy now and many voices were screaming out there in the dark. Bullets blizzarded all over the courtyard, except in the shadow of the wall. It was to mask the noises they made getting ready to scale both sides of the house. But his ears sought out the very littlest noises and he knew what they were doing. From both ridgepoles they would fire down into the courtyard and then the spirit screen would no longer cast a bullet shadow.

Well, at least there won't be a long time you have to think about it, he told himself. He was having to stand very still to keep the leg from charleyhorsing.

He would not think about it. They were to the boat by now, he thought. Sure they were. Sitting in the waist, the two of them close together. It was a kind of wedding present. If they escaped, they would be beating the game, in a way of figuring. And so, in a very small way, would Jake Holman be beating the game.

It was a very twisted way of figuring, but it made him feel better. He strained his ears through the tumult and he thought he heard the far-away popping of the boat engine. He knew it was his imagination, but he believed it anyway.

The yelling and the heavy firing stopped abruptly. It was only then that the real fear began to grip him. One Chinese voice was shouting orders. They sounded like cat squalls. He tried to shout back, *Go to hell, you bastards!* and the words would not form. His mouth was too dry. He was very frightened and trembling. He could not help it.

They were on the roofs. From both sides he could hear clanks and scrabblings on the roofs. Suddenly he knew he had only seconds left.

He roared wordlessly and began firing at the roofline. Answering shapes rose all along both ridgelines and guns answered in a blazing roar. The flailing storm of lead crumpled and threw Jake Holman like a giant hand wadding wastepaper.

ABOUT THE AUTHOR

Richard McKenna was born, grew up and went to school in the small desert town of Mountain Home, Idaho. In 1931, at the age of eighteen, he enlisted in the Navy and served for ten years in the Far East, two of them on a Yangtze River gunboat. During this time he heard many first-hand accounts of the 1925–1927 Chinese revolution which he has put to use in *The Sand Pebbles*.

Mr. McKenna, a machinist's mate, served in World War II in a large troop transport operating in all oceans, and stayed on through the Korean War in a destroyer. In 1953 he retired from the Navy after twenty-two years of service and entered the University of North Carolina. He received his degree in English in 1956, promptly married one of the university librarians, and settled down in Chapel Hill to become a writer. He has written short stories for the *Saturday Evening Post, Argosy* and other magazines. *The Sand Pebbles* is his first novel.

ABOUT THE EDITOR

Robert Shenk, Commander, U.S. Naval Reserve, is a member of the Department of English at the U.S. Naval Academy. Born in Lawrence, Kansas, he graduated from the University of Kansas in 1965, then served as a communications officer in the USS *Harry E. Hubbard* (DD 748) and as a patrol officer in river boats during the Vietnam War. He returned to the University of Kansas and received his Ph.D. in 1976. In 1979 he was recalled to active duty as a naval exchange officer at the U.S. Air Force Academy; he transferred to the U.S. Naval Academy in 1982. Author of *The Sinner's Progress: A Study of Madness in English Renaissance Drama* and coeditor of *Literature in the Education of the Military Professional*, Mr. Shenk has also written numerous reviews and articles on a variety of subjects in English and American literature.